THE REVEN
ELI MONP

THE REVENGE OF
ELI
MONPRESS

Rachel Aaron

This omnibus edition includes
The Spirit War
The Spirit's End

www.orbitbooks.net

ORBIT

First published in Great Britain in 2012 by Orbit

5 7 9 10 8 6 4

A CIP catalogue record for this book
is available from the British Library.

ISBN 978-0-356-50184-0

Printed and bound in Great Britain by
CPI Group (UK) Ltd, Croydon, CR0 4YY

Papers used by Orbit are from well-managed forests
and other responsible sources.

Orbit
An imprint of
Little, Brown Book Group
Carmelite House
50 Victoria Embankment
London EC4Y 0DZ

An Hachette UK Company
www.hachette.co.uk

www.orbitbooks.net

*For Peggy, without whom this book
would not have been.*

THE SPIRIT WAR

PROLOGUE

The old swordsman was kneeling in the dirt, blowing on the embers of last night's fire when he saw the boy approaching. He paused, keeping low to the dusty ground as he watched the boy start up the hill toward his campsite. The boy was a tall one, skinny and fair but with the large shoulders and wide ribs that spoke of the man he'd become once he finished growing into them. The swordsman pegged him at seventeen, maybe a little younger, but he wore the two short swords at his hips like he knew how to use them.

The swordsman sat back with a long sigh and glanced at the great black sword stabbed in the sand beside him.

"They never give up, do they?"

"No," the sword answered. "Thank the Powers. I think we'd both die of boredom if they stopped coming."

The swordsman sighed. "Speak for yourself."

The sword didn't answer, but the ground creaked as it settled itself deeper. The old swordsman shook his head and sat back to wait.

It took the boy the better part of an hour to climb to the top of the old swordsman's hill. At last, he pulled himself over the final boulders and stepped panting into the circle of dusty brush outside the cave where the swordsman made his home. He caught his breath and straightened up, fixing his eyes on the swordsman with a challenging glare.

"I'm looking for Milo Burch," he announced. "You him?"

The old swordsman frowned. "Why would a boy like you be looking for an old has-been like Burch?"

The boy stepped forward, planting his feet in first position. "I've heard he's the greatest swordsman in the world, wielder of the legendary Heart of War. I've come to challenge him."

"Really?" The old man rubbed his graying beard. "How did you get here?"

The boy paused, thrown for a second. "I walked."

The swordsman looked at him, and then looked out over the scrubby, flat desert that stretched as far as he could see in all directions. "You walked?" he said. "Alone?"

"Yes, alone." The boy's voice was growing frustrated. "Are you Milo Burch or not? I was told he lived out here. If you're not him, then I'll be going."

"Let's say I am," the swordsman said. "Who would be asking?"

The boy straightened up. "I am Josef Liechten, and I demand a duel for the title of greatest swordsman."

The swordsman started to laugh. "You demand it, do you?" he choked out at last, wiping his eyes. "I'm afraid you'll be a little disappointed. 'Greatest swordsman' isn't a hat you can pass around, and it's not like there's anyone out here to see your victory over an old man." The wind blew as he spoke, its lonely whistle a sharp reminder of the vast emptiness around them.

The boy set his jaw stubbornly. "Doesn't matter," he said. "Are you going to fight or not? I didn't walk all the way out here to stand around talking."

The old swordsman stood with a deep sigh and walked over to the scrabbly tree that grew just beside the little space he used as his fire pit. "You certainly sound determined, Josef Liechten," he said, reaching up to break off a dry branch. "I'm too old to go tumbling around with kids, but I can see that trying to talk you out of this duel nonsense would be nothing but a waste of breath."

The boy, Josef, nodded.

The swordsman turned, holding up the branch he'd just taken from the tree. "How about we make a deal? If you can break this, I'll fight you."

Josef stared at the stick in the man's hand. It was a sad thing, knobby and dead, its ends already cracking under the force of the old man's grip.

2

"I think it would be a greater challenge not to break it," he said, his voice turning cautious. "Is this some kind of trick?"

"If it was, I certainly wouldn't tell you," the old man said, his tanned, leathery face breaking into a grin. "Then again, the greatest swordsman in the world would hardly have to resort to tricks, don't you think?"

Josef glowered and shifted his feet. "All I have to do is break the stick," he said slowly. "Just break it, and you'll fight me for real?"

The old swordsman nodded. "That's it."

Josef scowled, and then he drew his swords. They were good work, the old man noticed. Well balanced and a good size for Josef's reach. It seemed the boy knew something. That was good. He was too old to waste energy on idiots.

"Come at me whenever you're ready," he said, lifting his stick.

With one final, annoyed look, Josef charged.

It was a good assault, a straight-on rush and then, three steps in, a feint to the left. Milo Burch stayed still just long enough to let the boy think he'd fallen for it and then quietly ducked out of the way. The boy charged past him and stopped, boots skidding on the loose dirt. He turned around, panting. Milo smiled at him, resting the stick on his shoulder.

"That was good," he said. "Perhaps you should try—"

Josef was running before he could finish, cutting around to Milo's left. Again, Milo let him get just close enough to commit to the blow before ducking down. Josef's sword whistled over his head, and the boy stumbled past him. Josef cursed loudly, and Milo stepped right to avoid the second sword that thrust from below. He spun around as Josef carried the thrust through, bopping the boy on the head with the stick as he passed.

Josef yelped in surprise and stumbled, falling to the ground. Milo sighed.

"If I'd taken your duel, that would have been the end, you know," he said, swinging his stick. "I won't think less of you if you want to give up."

He'd barely finished when Josef dropped the sword in his

left hand. The knife came a second later. Milo opened his hand, letting the stick drop in his grip just before the knife sliced through the air where it had been. As soon as the knife was past, he sidestepped again as Josef followed through with a lunge at his legs.

"Again, not bad," Milo said, grinning. "Why don't you—"

"Shut up!" Josef shouted, grabbing for the stick with his now-empty left hand.

Milo stepped neatly out of his reach, making Josef stumble as he overbalanced. The boy was panting now, his face red from the sun and slick with sweat.

"You're not a bad fighter, you know," Milo said gently. "Surely you're good enough to see the difference between us. You know you can't win. There's no point in pushing yourself."

Josef scowled at him, breathing hard, and then flicked another knife right at Milo's hand.

This went on all afternoon. Josef would attack and Milo would step out of the way. Josef never attacked the same way twice, but the end result never changed. As day wore into evening, Josef's lunges grew slower, but he did not stop until finally, as the sun sank below the horizon, he tripped and fell and did not get up again.

Milo leaned on his stick. "Are we done?"

Josef didn't answer. He just lay in the dirt, panting. Milo sighed and set the stick on the ground beside the fire. He walked over, shoved his hands under Josef's arms, and began dragging him toward the cave.

"What are you doing?" Josef gasped.

"Keeping you from dying of dehydration," Milo said. "I also imagine you would like some food."

Josef stared at him. "But I'm your enemy," he said, the words wheezing.

"You're the only one who said that," Milo said. "I was sitting here minding my own business." He dumped Josef unceremoniously on the floor of the cave. "Do you want some water or not?"

4

"Yes, please," Josef said, lying flat on his back. "Thank you."

"Polite," Milo said, handing him the water skin. "I like that."

Josef was too focused on drinking to answer.

He drank the entire water skin and half of another, and then ate the five loaves of bread that were meant to keep Milo the next week. He was still chewing when he fell asleep. When he was sure the boy was out, Milo tossed his blanket over the boy and walked out to sit beside the great black sword that was still staked beside the fire.

"What do you think?"

"He's stubborn as a rock," the sword said. "He's slow, his movements lack subtlety, and he has no grace."

Milo arched a white eyebrow. "Since when do you care about grace?"

"A minimum is required," the sword grumbled. "Still, he lasted five hours. That's the best yet."

"It is, isn't it," Milo said, rubbing his aching arms. Dodging all day was harder than it used to be. "He's spirit deaf, you know."

He felt the sword's ambivalence brush over him like a shrug. "I've had many deaf wielders. Hearing isn't what matters. It's everything else."

"Well, you'll have to stop being so picky," Milo said quietly. "We don't have much time left."

"I have all the time in the world," the sword answered. "Still, we'll see. Tomorrow, maybe."

"Tomorrow," Milo said, lying back to watch the moon rising over the desert.

Josef woke with the sun in his eyes and the old man standing over him, poking him in the shoulder with the hated stick.

"Morning," Milo said, grinning.

Josef smiled back, and then, fast as he could, rolled to grab the stick. For a second it was in his grasp before the old man snatched it away.

5

"Nice try." He sounded genuinely impressed. "Shall we begin?"

Josef pushed himself up, wincing as every muscle in his body protested, and reached for his swords.

"Ready."

They fought all morning with nothing to show. Everything Josef tried, the old man countered. The desert sun was brutal, burning Josef's skin through his shirt. Sweat soaked everything he owned, but he did not let himself stop. The old man had yet to admit it, but there was no more question in Josef's mind. He was fighting Milo Burch, the greatest swordsman in the world, famous across all the Council Kingdoms. It had to be him; no one else could be this fast. This was the reason he'd traveled all the way to the desert, why he'd walked through the heat and the burning sand for two days. It didn't matter if Burch was toying with him; he could not lose now. Not when he was this close.

Noon came and Josef kept going. His movements were jerky, and he could scarcely see through the burning sweat in his eyes. His limbs were so tired he actually dropped his sword a few times, but he pushed on until, at last, there was simply nothing left to push.

He didn't realize he'd fallen until he saw Milo standing over him, pressing a water skin to his cracked, dry lips.

"You know," he said softly, "there's a fine line between being determined and being an idiot. If you keep this up, I won't have to lift a sword to kill you. You'll kill yourself."

Josef choked on the water. He tried to sit up, but he had no strength left in his back. In the end, he settled for lying back and letting the water trickle down his throat.

"Josef," Milo said. "Give up, would you? When you're as old as I am, you've seen enough of the world to recognize its patterns. You think you're unique, but I've seen you dozens of times. Let me guess: You were the best swordsman in your village, or wherever you came from. Sword work came as easy to you as breathing, and soon there was no one who could give you a challenge. You took to wandering, fighting whoever

6

was strong enough to teach you something. You've probably defeated a hundred men, haven't you?"

"More," Josef croaked.

Milo shrugged. "Your problem is you're young. Impatient. You think that by beating me you can somehow jump to the top, but you can't. You can't beat me, and you can't jump ahead. The sword must be earned, Josef. Strength that comes easily is no strength at all."

Josef opened his eyes, squinting in the bright light. "I know that," he whispered. "But I'm not fighting for strength."

The old man's face was too far away for him to focus on, but Josef felt him frown. "What are you fighting for?"

"I hurt a lot of people when I decided to be a swordsman," Josef wheezed. "Let a lot of people down. That's why I have to be the strongest."

"Do these people care if you're the strongest?" Milo said quietly.

Josef shook his head. "But they will," he said. "I have to show them—"

His words broke into coughs as he choked on the water again. It didn't matter, though. Milo finished for him.

"You have to be the strongest to give meaning to their suffering," he said, tilting his head.

Josef nodded, breathing deeply as the coughing subsided. "I was the one who left. If I'm not the best, then I hurt her for no reason."

"That's a dangerous way to think," Milo said quietly. "There's a good chance you will never be the best. That you will die alone and forgotten, remembered only as a disappointment."

"I don't believe in chance," Josef whispered. He looked at Milo and raised his sword. His hand shook as he lifted it, the sword sliding in his weakening grip. Josef forced himself to be calm, to be strong one last moment. The shaking slowed, and then, for one breath, stopped. That was when Josef moved.

He tossed his sword into the air, over Milo's head. The old man's eye went wide, but Josef grabbed the old man's wrist where he was holding the water bottle, pinning him in place. Trapped, the old swordsman could only watch as Josef's short sword flew through the air, spinning in wobbly arcs, and landed behind him, on top of the stick he'd laid aside when he knelt to help Josef. The blade landed sideways, bouncing away the moment it stuck, but the branch was old and brittle, and it was enough. The stick cracked with a soft pop, breaking into two ragged halves.

For a moment, all Milo could do was sit there, watching the broken remains of his stick rocking in the hot desert wind. Then he turned and looked at Josef with a strange, bemused expression on his weatherworn face. Josef grinned back.

"I never stop fighting," he said. "I'm holding you to your word, Milo Burch."

"And I never go back on my word," Milo said with a sigh. "Tomorrow, then. At dawn."

Josef nodded and released the old man's hand. He grabbed the water skin and drank until he drained it. When he was finished, he crawled across the baked ground and collapsed on a blanket just inside the cave, falling asleep instantly.

Milo picked up the broken pieces of his stick. When he had them both, he sat down with his back against the broad slab of scarred black metal that stood rooted in the sand and began feeding the pieces into the fire.

When Josef woke the next morning, the cave was empty. He took a long drink from the water barrel and helped himself to a breakfast of bread and dried apples from the swordsman's supplies. When he finished, he grabbed his sword from where he'd dropped it and walked out onto the hilltop.

Milo Burch was already there, sitting beside the now cold fire pit with his back against the massive, black metal shape that dominated the open space. As Josef stepped into the sandy ring around the fire, Milo held out the sword Josef had thrown to break the stick. Josef took it, sheathing it opposite its brother on his hip. When they were both ready, he took his stance and waited for Milo to begin.

8

The old swordsman stood with a sigh, rubbing the small of his back as he straightened. But his hands were empty as he turned to face Josef.

"Wait," Josef said. "Where's your sword? I'm here to fight the master of the Heart of War. Let's see it."

Milo shook his head and laid his hand on the wrapped handle of the great metal monster in the ground beside him. Josef's eyes widened. The black slab was enormous. He couldn't even think of what it must weigh. A man Milo's size shouldn't even have had the muscle to lift something that heavy, and yet the old swordsman pulled it up as easy as a farmer pulling a weed out of new-tilled dirt.

"I thought we agreed, no more games," Josef said. "What is that thing? Where's your sword? Where's the Heart of War?"

"This is the Heart of War," Milo said, swinging the black blade in front of him.

Josef almost laughed out loud. "*That* is the Heart of War? That . . . that *iron post* is the greatest awakened blade ever made? You're kidding. It doesn't even have a sharp edge. It couldn't cut paper."

Milo smiled. "A sword cuts whatever its swordsman wants it to cut. The Heart is no different."

Josef scowled. "We'll see."

They took their positions on either side of the dead fire. Josef readied his blades, keeping the man's movements from their earlier fights clear in his mind. He almost thought the old man should have stuck to the stick. There was no way he could move fast enough carrying that enormous weight. There had to be a trick or something. Maybe the sword was hollow? Something that large couldn't be solid metal, not if a human was meant to lift it. Still, the few awakened blades he'd beaten had all had their own oddities. He'd just have to push and see what happened.

"You know," Milo said. "You don't have to go through with this. I meant it when I said you were a good swordsman. Give you a few years and you could very well become the best, but not yet. The Heart won't let me hold back. You should stop now, while you still can."

"I told you before," Josef said. "I never stop. I can't stop." He raised his sword. "Guard yourself."

The words had barely left his mouth when he lunged. He pushed forward, slamming his feet down faster than he ever had before. He would get only once chance. He'd learned the first day that he couldn't beat the old man in speed, but yesterday he'd proven he could still trick him. He'd seen the strain in Milo as he stood up. The days of fighting had taken their toll on his old body. Now, weighed down with that enormous sword, especially after so long fighting with a stick that weighed nothing, there would be a hesitation in his first swing as his body got used to the weight difference. That was when Josef had to strike.

He rushed forward, boots pounding on the sand, watching the old man's arm for the moment he lifted the sword to parry. He had to parry. What else could you do with a sword that big? But the old man didn't move. He just stood there, watching as Josef came closer and closer. When he was one step away, Josef realized he might have been wrong. The old man might be too slow to catch him. There might be no need to wait for the hesitation in the parry. Already his swords were racing for the man's torso, one high, one low, and for one shining moment, Josef thought he might actually land the blow before Milo could move.

One moment, that's all it was. And in that moment, Milo Burch attacked.

It happened so fast Josef couldn't see the blows, but he felt them. There were three in the space of a second. The first shattered his left sword, the second broke his right, and the third hit him dead across the chest. That last blow knocked the breath from his lungs and sent him flying backward. He hit the side of the hill like a stone hurled from a catapult. For a moment, all he could feel was the rough ground on his back and the strange sensation of air against his chest through his

10

sundered shirt, and then pain like he'd never felt before slammed down and he hit the ground with a sound that would have been a scream had he still had breath.

He floundered in the dirt, his whole body convulsing. Somehow, he ended up on his back again. That was when he saw it, though it took him several moments to realize that the bloody mess he was looking at was his own chest.

A deep, perfect cut ran from his left shoulder to his right hip. It was perfectly straight, as though he'd been cut by a razor, but so deep he had to look away. When he turned his head, he saw Milo crouching beside him, leaning on the Heart of War as he bent down to whisper in Josef's ear.

"Worst pain you've ever felt, isn't it?"

Gasping, Josef could only nod.

"This is the pain of defeat," the old swordsman said. "You are dying. I have defeated you utterly. Even if I were to bind your wound right now, there's no saving your life. This is the end. So now I'll ask you: Was it worth it?"

Josef looked at him and wheezed, "Yes."

Milo paused. "And if you'd known this was how it ended, would you still have broken the stick?"

"Yes," Josef said, his voice little more than a grating of breath. "I would rather die trying than ever give up."

"Is that so?" Milo said. "Then prove it. Take another breath."

Josef grimaced and looked down at his sundered chest. He tried to talk, but he had no air for the words.

"I can't," he mouthed.

"If you can't, then all your struggles to this point, all the pain you've caused, it's all for nothing," Milo said, his voice taut. "Take another breath, Josef Liechten."

Josef closed his eyes and focused on his lungs. For an eternity, nothing happened. His body was going stiff. Nothing would obey him. He concentrated, pouring every speck of his consciousness into that one action. The pain was so intense now he could barely think, but he felt his chest rise and fall, and suddenly he had air again.

His eyes popped open just in time to see Milo's face break into a grand smile. The old man held out his hand, offering something. Josef blinked, it was dark and heavy and, he could see now, larger than it looked.

"If you walk the path of the swordsman, you will feel this pain hundreds of times," Milo said. "You will never know a moment's peace, even if you move to a hill in the middle of the desert. Your life will be brutish, violent, and most likely short but it will also be glorious. This is what it means to live your life on the sword. You said you would rather die trying than give up. Now you must try living, or die. If you want to live, Josef Liechten, then reach out as far as you can and take your sword. Rise a swordsman, the master of the Heart of War, or do not rise at all."

His words fluttered against Josef's ears. The world felt very far away now. Even the pain was going, but Josef could still see the black shape of the sword hovering high above him. With the last of his will, he lifted his arm. He saw his hand moving above him, his fingers stretching up to clutch the wrapped handle. The moment his fingers made contact, a voice deeper and broader than any voice he'd ever heard spoke through him.

Welcome to your rebirth, swordsman. The words were more vibration than sound, but they were clear as carvings in his mind. *As you gave your life to become a swordsman, so did I give my life to become a sword. We are the same, you and I. Will you fight with me?*

Josef could not speak, but the answer echoed in his mind. I will.

It is done, the voice said. *Welcome to your mountain, master of the Heart of War.*

As the voice faded from his mind, so did the pain. Strength like Josef had never felt flowed into his body. All at once he could breathe again. His eyes were clear and open to the world. His arms moved without pain, and he was able to stand enough to let Milo guide him back to the cave and wrap him in the blankets, all the while dragging the massive black blade behind him.

12

He fell asleep the moment Milo lay him flat, the Heart of War clutched to his chest. How long he slept, Josef never knew, but when he woke it was night and Milo Burch was gone. The cave was empty except for the bloody blankets Josef lay on, the water barrel, and a large supply of food. A loaf of bread and a water skin lay on the ground beside his head, and Josef ate greedily before falling asleep again. When he woke next, it was evening. This time he was strong enough to stand. He went looking for Milo, but the old swordsman was gone. There was, however, a message scratched in soot on the cave wall.

After fifty years as a swordsman, it read, *I think I've earned the right to live my last few as just a man. Remember why you fight, Josef Liechten, and the Heart of War will never forsake you.*

That was it. No name, no date, no direction. Josef smiled. Nothing else was needed. He read the note twice and then rubbed it out with his palm. He gathered the food and as much water as he could carry. Then, tying the great black blade across his back with strips torn from the blood-ruined blankets, Josef Liechten, master of the Heart of War, set off into the desert to become the world's greatest swordsman.

CHAPTER
1

Den the Warlord, unknowing owner of the highest bounty the Council of Thrones had ever issued, was bashing his way through a jungle. He ripped out the waxy green plants in wet handfuls, kicking the rotten ground whenever it tried to trip him. Insects whizzed by in the humid air above his head, flying at his eyes whenever they dared, biting and stinging and all the while buzzing, "Go away! Go away!"

Den smacked them out of the air and kept going.

He knew by this point that the jungle was another dead end, but he had nowhere else to go but through it. So through it he went, smashing the undergrowth with mechanical efficiency until he spotted something white through the trees. Den slowed at once, sliding into a stance as he pushed the last of the broad leaves back. There, hanging directly in his path between two large trees, was a hole in the world. The hole was rectangular, an inch taller than himself, which was to say very tall indeed, and easily wide enough for him to walk through. Its edges were smooth and white, and they shone brighter than the noon sun reflected off water, which explained the flash he'd seen earlier. But strangest of all was that the jungle he saw through the opening was not the one he stood in. It was as thick as his jungle, just as green and overgrown, but the wind that drifted through the white-edged hole was hotter than the humid air around him. The soil on the other side was sandier, the trees denser and older. Though he'd been following a ridge in this jungle, the new jungle was flat, the land unremarkable save for a knot of trees directly ahead, their roots tangled around the entrance of what looked to be a small dirt cave.

Den frowned and took a moment to consider. He'd seen such a portal once before, the only time he'd ever managed to corner a League man. His face broke into a grin at the memory. That had been a good fight.

If he hadn't already decided his jungle was a dead end, that thought alone was enough to decide for him. Smiling in anticipation, Den stepped forward, ducking through the portal. When his feet hit the ground on the other side, he took up a defensive position, looking for his opponent. But the new jungle was as empty as the old one had been, its trees tossing in the lonely wind. Feeling cheated, Den turned back only to find that the portal was gone, leaving nothing but a fading white line in the baking air.

Den snarled. It wasn't that he was angry to leave the first jungle. When you were searching blindly as he was, one place

14

was as good as the next. But he didn't like unknowns, and he certainly didn't like having fights taken from him. He closed his eyes and listened, ears straining, just on the off chance the League man was waiting for an opening, but it was no use. If the League had been here, they were long gone. Den was working himself into a foul mood over this when he caught a faint sound on the wind, almost like a sob.

All at once, Den's smile returned. Seemed this jungle wasn't so empty after all.

He turned on his heel until he was facing the dirt cave below the tree roots. It was a wretched thing, a black hole in the mud held together by tree roots. The entrance crumbled a little as Den pushed his way in. The inside of the cave was dim and low, forcing Den to stoop almost double until he'd climbed down to the bed of mud and leaves that served as the cave floor. When he reached the bottom, he straightened as best he could and gazed through the dark at the woman hunched against the cave's far wall. Den's smile split into a toothy grin. Not a League man, true, but a better prize, the one he'd been walking through jungles for almost ten years now in search of.

Despite his noisy entrance, the woman didn't appear to notice Den for several seconds. Finally, she shifted against the mud, glancing at him through slitted eyes.

"Oh," she said, looking away again. "It's you."

Den crossed his arms. "It's me."

The woman didn't answer, and Den, tired of crouching, sat down. Normally, he would have just knocked the roof out, but he'd been looking for her a long time and, much as it irked him, a little tolerance was a small thing compared to the hassle it would take to find her again if she ran, miraculous portals notwithstanding.

When it was clear Den wasn't leaving, the woman pressed her face against the cool dirt as though she could somehow ignore him. It was a futile effort, for the cave was very small and Den was a large, large man.

"What do you want?" she grumbled at last.

"What you promised me," Den said.

The woman laughed, a harsh, joyless bark. "Is your life so dull you'd search all across the Empire to collect a bad debt?"

"You promised me a war," Den answered calmly. "I crossed half the world for that promise. Does it really surprise you that I would cross the other half to hold you to it?"

She glanced sideways at him, her dark eyes sharp and almost as he remembered them. "I suppose it doesn't," she said. "My apologies, Bloody Den, but you'll have to find someone else to stage your fights." She turned away, pulling herself against the wall again. "I have no more care to rule."

"No!" Den's shout rattled the earthen walls. The woman jumped, flinching as Den leaned in, towering over her despite his seated position.

"You promised me," he whispered, low and deadly. "Twenty-six years ago you promised me a war. Twenty-six years I've waited, fought your warriors, and prepared your troops. I've held up my end of the deal tenfold, and you owe me. If you want to lie in the mud and feel sorry for yourself, do it on your own time, but right now you need to finish what you started. You will honor your pledge, or I will test your famous immortality for myself, Nara." The name rolled off his tongue like a curse.

The woman leaped up from the mud and turned to face him, staring him down like he was a cockroach. "You will not speak so informally to me, barbarian."

Den leaned back against the cool mud. "I'll treat you like an empress when you start acting like one."

For a moment, the rage burned in her eyes, and she was nearly herself again. Her authority radiated through her mud-stained rags, dismissing her long, matted hair and wretched surroundings until he could almost see the Empress he remembered, tall and dark and terrible in her rage. But then, between one second and the next, it crumbled, and she sank to the mud floor in a broken heap.

"What does it matter?" she whispered, letting the dirty mass of her dark hair fall over her face. "The Shepherdess has

16

abandoned me. Everything I did, my entire life, it was all for her. I gave her everything—my soul, my love, my service—but she doesn't even look at me anymore. All she cares about is that *boy*."

The ragged, naked hatred that trembled through her voice when she said the word *boy* shocked even Den, and he seized his chance. "Of course she doesn't want to look at you," he said. "I can hardly stand to see what you've let yourself become."

The woman hissed and turned on him, lashing out with her fist. Den caught the blow with one hand. "Who could love such a self-pitying, wretched hag?" he said, letting his disgust ring clear through the words. "You were the favorite of creation. The unquestioned ruler of half the world for twelve generations. Now look at you, a rat hiding in a cave, and all because your White Lady found a new pet."

She snarled and the ground began to rumble, but Den held on, pulling her forward until they were eye to eye. "If you want your Shepherdess to love you again, become something worth loving. Even if her boy died tomorrow, she'd never look at you while you're like this. Who would? No one loves a failure, Nara."

Her eyes went wide and she wrenched herself free. Den let her go, watching her with a sneer as she stumbled back to her rut in the mud. She stayed there for a long time, not speaking, not moving. Den matched her silence, waiting to see if his gambit played true. If it didn't, he was in for another long walk. But it seemed he was in luck, for at last she sat up.

"You are a horrible man, Den," she whispered, pushing the filthy hair out of her face. "But you are also a keen one. Fine. My years of begging have earned me nothing. Perhaps it is time to see what action can do. We shall see who is called favorite when I rule all the world. After all..."

She closed her eyes, and the air in the cave rippled like water. Den flinched as her spirit opened over him. It rolled out of her, a roaring wave of power, and everywhere it touched, the world began to change. The cave walls shook like leaves, the spirits crying in obedient awe as they reshaped themselves to please her.

The roof of the cave vanished, replaced by clear, blue sky. The mud Den sat on flattened, drying and hardening and spreading until he sat in the middle of a court pressed with spiraling patterns of impossible beauty. At the edge of the clay circle, the jungle trees lifted their roots and began retangling them into walls of beautifully knotted shapes. Then, as quickly as it had started, the changes stopped, and Den found himself sitting in a beautiful open court as grand as any he'd ever seen. At its center, seated on a raised throne of living wood, was the Immortal Empress. The dirt had fallen from her skin and hair, leaving her radiant, her body almost glowing beneath a sheath of beautifully patterned silk, the ends of which were just finishing weaving themselves from the remnants of her rags. Her glossy black hair was piled on her head, each hair holding itself of its own accord in an impossible arrangement that seemed to float over her ageless face, now as stern and as proud as he remembered it.

"After all," she said again, leaning back on her throne, "I am the Immortal Empress still, a star of the Shepherdess, and I will be victorious."

She held out her hand, and a white line appeared in the air. Den blinked in recognition as it sank silently through the empty space, glowing like the full moon. Through it, Den could see the interior of the throne room at Istalirin, her war palace, and the chaos of the panicking staff as they realized what that glowing line meant.

A wide grin broke over Den's face and he hopped to his feet. "So it was you then," he said. "Suits me. Let's go."

"I have no idea what you're babbling about," the Empress said. "But this is for me. You're walking."

"What?" Den roared.

"You were very disrespectful toward your Empress," she said with a cutting look. "Your punishment is that you must walk back to Istalirin. Your commission will be ready when you arrive."

18

Den frowned. "And you will honor your promise at last?"

The Empress gave him a cruel smile. "Beyond your wildest dreams, Bloody Den."

And with that, she was gone. The white line shimmered and faded, leaving Den alone in the beautiful court under the sky. He stood a moment, grinding his teeth until he could feel the pain shooting down his neck. Finally, he turned and stomped out. That had been petty, even for her, but he should have expected it. The Empress was a woman, and women were always petty, especially when their pride was bruised. Still, it didn't matter. He'd just spent almost fifteen years walking the breadth and width of her cursed land, what was another few weeks? What mattered was that he'd done it. He'd found her, and better, he'd won. He would have his war.

A great smile broke over Den's scarred face, and he began to walk faster, jumping into the jungle at the clearing's edge. This time the trees parted for him, whispering apologies. Now that he was in the Empress's favor again, the world was bending over to make his life easy. His walk became a run as the forest opened for him, and Den began to laugh. A war at last. Finally, after so long, he would reclaim his paradise.

Still laughing, Den fell into a mile-eating jog, running through the now-genteel forest. He didn't know where he was still, but it didn't matter. The spirits had their mistress again, and they would make sure he got where she wanted him to be. Grinning at the thought, Den picked up his pace, running full out along the path the trees made him, following the setting sun west toward the war palace of the Immortal Empress.

Two Months Later

"Are you sure?" Queen Theresa of Osera leaned forward, frail fingers tightening to white-knuckled claws on the velvet arms of her chair. "Absolutely sure?"

The fisherman looked almost insulted. "I can tell you only what I saw with my own eyes, your queenship," he said, lifting his head to look at her for the first time. "For years now, my crew has sailed the roughest ocean in the world to be your eyes on the Unseen Coast, and I'm telling you the shipyards are active again."

"But why now?" The queen shook, though with fear or rage even she could not tell. "She built like mad for twelve years after the war, and then fifteen years ago, everything stopped. Now you're telling me she's building again? Why? Why ships? Why now?"

The fisherman flinched and gave no answer.

None was expected. The queen had already hauled herself to her feet and was now pacing the length of the small stage at the end of her private-audience chamber, muttering under her breath.

"What changed?" Her whisper was tight and raspy. "Did we show some weakness? Or perhaps I was the fool to think she had given up." Her jeweled heels clicked faster on the glossy wood floor. "How many ships?"

The fisherman jumped. "Too many to count. I took the time to spy on only one of the yards before coming to you. Was I wrong?"

"No," the queen said, shaking her head so sharply that she knocked loose one of the carefully pinned curls of her once famous golden hair, now mostly white. "Without your information we wouldn't have a candle's chance in a storm. Tell me, though, in your hurry, did you see what kind of ships was she building?"

"I did," the fisherman said, licking his chapped lips. "They was palace ships, lady. Every single one."

The queen stopped walking and pressed a bony hand to her forehead. "Lenette?"

A strikingly beautiful woman in an elegant dress of stiff black silk appeared from a side door. "Yes, my queen?"

"Pay him. Double."

Lenette nodded and walked across the room to the strongbox. She took a fist-sized bag from the bound chest and walked to the fisherman, holding it out for him with both hands. He took

20

it with a blush and opened the bag at once, eyes bulging when he saw the pile of gold it contained. But the smile slipped from his face when the queen looked at him with a glare that could have cut iron.

"Spend it quickly."

The captain swallowed loudly, but the queen's attention was already back on her pacing. Lenette took the man's arm and led him back to the doors, gently pushing him into the hall. Thus dismissed, the fisherman bowed several times before the guards shut the doors in his face. The moment they closed, the queen collapsed into her chair with a pained sigh.

"And there's the other shoe," she muttered. "Twenty-six years after her first invasion, the immortal sow finally rousts herself to finish the job."

"The man was a fisherman, my lady," Lenette said gently, walking over to kneel beside the queen's chair. "Not a trained spy. He could have been mistaken."

The queen gave an unladylike snort. "I'm not sending the fleet into the Unseen Sea to check his story. The deep trawlers are the only ones who dare that crossing. Fortunately for us, the same reckless greed that sends them chasing leviathan spawn in the deep current spurs them to take my money to spy for their country. Anyway, without that 'fisherman,' the old harpy would have caught us naked as a cheating lover." She nodded at the closed door. "The captain is Oseran born and old enough to remember the war. If he says they're palace ships, they're palace ships. It's not something you forget."

"But we only know that she's started building again," Lenette countered. "Those ships might not even be for us. She could have a new target."

"Where?" the queen said with an exasperated huff. "The woman rules half the world. There's nowhere left for her to conquer save the Council Kingdoms, and our little island is dead in her way. Her army will roll over us without even a pause. When I think of all—"

A racking cough stopped her midsentence. The queen doubled

21

over, pressing a lace handkerchief to her mouth as her body convulsed. Lenette was with her in an instant, rubbing the queen's back with her small, delicate hands until the attack subsided.

"You shouldn't think about such things, lady," Lenette whispered. "You'll only worsen your condition. Remember, Osera and the Council have pushed the Empress back before."

"Yes," the queen wheezed. "Two and a half decades ago, when I was young." She looked at her blood-streaked handkerchief with disgust. "When I wasn't sick. When I could stand to look at myself in the mirror. Back when I was truly queen."

She raised her gaunt face and gazed across the chamber at the portrait that took up most of the wall. It was enormous, large as life and set in a gilt frame that touched both floor and ceiling. On it, a steel-gray sea pounded the rocky eastern shore of Osera. The stony beach below the cliffs was filled with soldiers raising their swords in salute, or perhaps taunting, for the choppy sea was scattered with the Immortal Empress's warships, some crashing on the reefs, some ablaze, all fleeing defeated back across the Unseen Sea. In the painting's foreground, a young woman dressed in the heavy black armor of the Eisenlowe stood with her feet in the sea. She faced the fleeing ships with her head held high, hair flying behind her like a pale gold banner. Her hand was stretched out toward the ocean, the gloved fingers tangled in the long, black hair of the enemy general's severed head.

Queen Theresa smiled. That was not how it had ended, but it was the way she wanted the war to be remembered—bloody, glorious, an absolute victory. The way it should have been and, she closed her eyes, the way it could never be again.

"Osera has always been ruled by the strong, Lenette," the queen said quietly. "We've grown wealthy and civilized thanks to the Council, but it will take more than these few generations to tear us away from our bloody past. Were we a softer kingdom, more deeply rooted in law and nobility, perhaps I could re-create the miracle I stumbled onto all those years ago. But we are not. The Empress is coming, and an old, sick woman cannot lead Osera to war."

Lenette stiffened, her face, still so lovely despite her advancing years, falling. "Will you abdicate, then? Give the country to your cousin?"

"Finley?" The queen made a disgusted sound. "He'll get his soon enough, much as I hate to think of it. But he's no Eisenlowe. Much as he hated to, father entrusted our line to me after my brothers died. I've spent the last thirty years fighting to stay on my throne. I do not intend to meekly hand it over now."

Lenette shook her head. "But what will you do, lady?"

"Crisis demands stability, Lenette," the queen said grimly. "I'd thought I could give him a little more time, but circumstance has left us little choice. The Throne of Iron Lions must follow the proper succession, whatever the cost." She settled back into her chair with a pained sigh. "Wake up the Council wizard and have him bring me the Relay point. We must warn the Council tonight. I'll need to speak with Whitefall personally, and then I'll need that cousin of his, the one who runs the bounties."

"Phillipe Whitefall?" Lenette said.

The queen waved her hand dismissively. "Whoever. I never could keep all the Whitefalls straight. Just get me the head of the bounty office. Also, get Adela in here. Your daughter is a sensible girl, and she has a larger stake in this business than most."

Lenette pursed her lips. "It's time then, is it?"

"Long past," the queen said, patting her friend's hand. "If the Immortal Empress is on her way, then we have no time left for patience. That boy is out there somewhere, and I don't care if I have to hand over every scrap of gold in Osera, he will come home and do his duty."

Lenette nodded and bent to kiss the queen's hand. "I will bring Adela to you, lady," she said, rising to her feet. "And send someone to fetch the Relay keeper. Meanwhile, I'll have the maid bring up your medicine."

The queen smiled. "Thank you, Lenette. What would I do without you?"

23

Lenette smiled and stepped off the little stage. She walked to the door, her heels clicking delicately across the polished floor, and vanished into the hall with a curtsy.

When she was gone, Queen Theresa lay back in her padded chair, staring at the picture of what she had been. As her eyes struggled to focus on the familiar brushstrokes, she remembered not the gory glory of the artist's rendition, but the real morning, twenty-six years ago, standing on the windy beach, too large for her armor at nine months' pregnant, weeping in relief at the retreating ships while her guard made a square around her so that no one could say they'd seen the Lioness of Osera cry.

When the maid arrived a few minutes later with the medicine tray, the queen dabbed her eyes with her handkerchief and took the cup that the girl offered, drinking the bitter concoction without so much as a grimace.

CHAPTER
2

The Perod bounty office was packed with the usual riffraff. Dozens of men and a few scowling women lounged on long benches stolen from the tavern across the street, boredly polishing a startling variety of weaponry and trying to look like they weren't waiting. It was a farce, of course. It was criminally early on a Monday morning, and the only reason bounty hunters ever came into a regional office before noon was to get their hands on the weekly bounty update from Zarin.

The only person who didn't try to hide his anticipation was a young man toward the back of the crowd. He stood on his bench, hopping from foot to foot and ignoring his dour-faced companion's constant attempts to pull him back down, an anxious scowl marring the boyish face that everyone should have recognized, but no one did.

"Honestly," Eli huffed when Josef finally managed to drag him down. "Are they walking from Zarin?"

"It's not even eight," Josef said, his voice low and annoyed as he nudged the wrapped Heart of War farther under the bench with his foot. "The post isn't due until eight fifteen. And can you at least pretend to be discreet? I love a good fight, but we walked all night to get here. I'd like some breakfast and a few hours of shut-eye before I have to put down an entire room of bounty hunters, if it's all the same to you."

Eli made a disgusted sound. "Go ahead. I could wear a name tag on my forehead and these idiots still wouldn't notice. No bounty hunter worth his sword goes to a regional office for leads. There's not a soul here who's good enough to see what they don't expect." He slouched on the bench. "Sometimes I think there's no pride in the profession anymore. You were the last of the bounty hunters worth the name, and even you got so bored you took up with the enemy."

"Not bored," Josef said. "I just learned that working with you got me better fights than trying to catch you. Anyway, Coriano was perfectly decent, and what about that man who attacked you at the hotel? Gave you quite a scramble for a dying profession, didn't he?"

Beside him, Nico did her best to stifle a laugh, but her coat gave her away, moving in long, midnight waves as her shoulders shook. Eli rolled his eyes at both of them.

"Well, too bad you killed them, then," he said with a sniff. "Knocking over the best of a dying breed without even leaving a calling card—it's such a waste. No wonder your bounty's only ten thousand."

Josef shrugged. "Unlike some people, I see no need to define myself by an arbitrary number."

Eli bristled. "Arbitrary? I earned every bit of that bounty! You should know; you were there for most of it. My bounty is a reflection of our immense skill. You should take some

25

pride in it. After all," he said, grinning painfully wide, "I'm now the most wanted man in the Council Kingdoms. Two hundred and forty-eight thousand gold standards! That even beats Nico's number. My head is worth more than a kingdom— no, two kingdoms! And to think, just last year I was struggling to break thirty thousand. This is an achievement no one else in the world can touch, my friends. You are sitting beside a *national power*. Tell you what. When they hand out my new posters, I'll sign them for you. How's that?"

Josef looked decidedly unimpressed and made no comment.

"It *is* a large number," Nico said when the uncomfortable silence had gone on long enough. "But you're not the highest. There's still Den the Warlord with five hundred thousand."

"Den doesn't count," Eli snapped. "He was the first bounty, made right after the war. The Council hadn't even decided on a valuation for its currency yet. If they'd made the bounty properly with pledges from offended kingdoms rather than just letting old Council Daddy Whitefall pull some grossly large number out of his feathered helmet, Den would never have gotten that high. Anyway, it doesn't matter. I'll be passing him soon enough, just you watch. This time next year I'll be at a million, and see if I offer to autograph your poster then."

"I'll take my chances," Josef grumbled, eyeing the crowd. "Look lively. I think the post is here."

Eli was on his feet in an instant, elbowing his way through the crowd that was no longer even pretending to look bored. The hunters thronged around the door as a sleepy-eyed bounty officer and two harried men in Council uniforms with piles of paper under their arms attempted to push their way in.

"No shoving!" the officer shouted. "Stand back! Individual posters can be purchased after the official notices are hung!"

The crowd took a grudging step back as the Council postmen began tacking up the latest posters under the bounty officer's direction. First they hung up the small-fry, lists of names with tiny descriptions and even tinier numbers beside them. Next came the ranking bounties, criminals with a thousand or more

26

on their heads whose notoriety had earned them a sketch and a small poster of their own. These were all pinned between the floor and waist level. The top of the wall was reserved for the big money. Here, the Council men hung up the famous names.

Izo was gone. The men stripped his old poster down with minimal fanfare, moving those bounties below him up a notch. The old, yellowed poster offering two hundred thousand for the Daughter of the Dead Mountain was left untouched, as was Den's large poster at the top of the board. Between these, however, the men tacked up a fresh, large sheet featuring a familiar face grinning above a rather astonishingly large number.

Eli stopped shoving the men in front of him and gazed up at his poster, his eyes glowing with pride. "It's even more beautiful than I imagined," he whispered. "Two hundred and forty-eight thousand gold standards."

Josef pressed his palm to his forehead as Eli resumed shoving his way forward. Thankfully, no one else seemed to have heard the thief's remark. The bounty hunters were all loudly clamoring for copies, shouting over each other while the bounty officer tried to shout over everyone that no one was getting posters until the official copies were up.

Eli vanished into the fray only to reappear moments later with a scroll tucked under his arm. Josef raised his eyebrows and began easing the knives out of his sleeves, just in case, but the bounty officer was too busy screaming at the bounty hunters to get in line to notice that one of his carefully protected posters was already missing.

"They get better with every likeness," Eli said, proudly unrolling his poster. "If it wasn't black and white, I'd say I was looking in a mirror."

Nico nodded appreciatively, but Josef wasn't even looking. Eli turned to berate his swordsman for his shocking lack of attentiveness, but Josef was just standing there, staring at the bounty board like he'd seen a ghost. Eli followed his gaze, glancing over his shoulder at the bounty wall where the Council men were hanging one last poster, just below Den's and just ahead of Eli's. As the Council men tacked the poster's corners up, a familiar, stern face glared down at the room, and below it, in tall block letters, was the following:

JOSEF LIECHTEN THERESON ESINLOWE.
WANTED ALIVE, 250,000 GOLD STANDARDS.

"Josef," Eli said, very quietly. "Why is your bounty larger than mine?"

Josef didn't answer. He just stood there, staring. Then, without a word, he turned, pushed his way through the crowd to their bench, grabbed his bag and his wrapped sword, and stomped out the back door.

Eli and Nico exchanged a look and ran after him.

"Josef," Eli said, running to keep up with the swordsman's ground-eating strides. "Josef! Stop! What's this about? Where are you going?"

Josef kept walking.

"Look," Eli said, jogging beside him. "If you're worried I'm upset that you have a higher bounty than I do, you shouldn't be. I mean, I am upset, but you shouldn't be worried. I'm sure it's just a mistake. If you'll stop walking for a second, I can go nick your poster and we'll take a closer look. Maybe they added an extra zero by accident or—"

"I don't need a closer look."

Eli stumbled a little. Josef's voice was quivering with rage. Quick as he'd taken off, Josef stopped and turned to face them. Eli shrank back at the cold, white anger on his face, nearly falling into Nico.

"It's no mistake," Josef said. "That bounty is her last card. I can't let her do this."

"Her who?" Eli said.

"Queen Theresa."

"I see," Eli said, though he didn't. "Well, if it's not a mistake, then I'm stumped. What did you do to this queen to earn a number like that?"

28

The side of Josef's mouth twitched. "I lived."

Eli arched an eyebrow. "Could you try being a little less cryptic?"

"No." Josef pulled his bag off his shoulder and tossed it to Nico. "I have to go away for a while. There's food enough for the next day in there. Nico, I'm counting on you to keep Eli from doing anything stupid. I realize it's a tall order, but do your best."

Nico scowled at him and tossed the bag back. "I'm going with you."

"And I'm with her," Eli said, straightening up. "You can't just walk out on us now."

Josef crossed his arms. "And I suppose my opinion in this doesn't matter?"

"Not in the least," Eli said. "Where are we going?"

For a moment, Josef almost smiled. "The port at Sanche. We can catch a ferry from there to Osera."

"Osera?" Eli made a face. "You mean the island with the carnivorous yaks, endless rain, and zero-tolerance policy toward thieves? Why?"

"Because," Josef said, setting off down the road. "I've been called home."

Nico fell in behind him, her feet kicking up little clouds of yellow dust as she hurried to catch up. Eli stared at their backs a moment longer, and then, cursing under his breath, he shoved his new poster into his bag and ran down the road after them.

Alber Whitefall, Merchant Prince of Zarin and Head of the Council of Thrones, was having a terrible morning. Actually, considering he hadn't slept since yesterday, morning was a misnomer. What he was having was a terrible night that refused to end.

There were two others sitting in his office on this terrible morning. Sara was there, of course, and Myron Whitefall, his cousin and director of Military Affairs for the Council. As usual, Sara looked equal parts miffed at being called away from her work downstairs and intrigued by their new problem. Myron, however, looked like a man who'd just learned he's dying from plague.

"Is there a chance she's overreacting?" Myron said, pulling at his stiff military collar. "The queen is getting older."

"Theresa is younger than I am, Myron," Merchant Prince Whitefall said flatly. "She's hardly to the age of senility."

"And this is Osera we're talking about," Sara added with a sniff. "They're not people who'd ask for help unless things were desperate. *Especially* Theresa. Shouldn't you know that?"

Myron gave the wizard a disapproving look. Sara stared right back, daring him.

"Be that as it may," Alber said, bringing the conversation back to himself before things could get any worse. "Osera's borne the brunt of the Empress before, and they've never forgotten. If Theresa says the Empress has reactivated her shipyards, then I believe her. The only real question is, how much time do we have left to prepare?"

Sara looked away from Myron with a dismissive huff. "A decent amount, I'd wager," she said. "Unless she's spent the last twenty years making upgrades, palace ships are slow and the Unseen Sea is wide and treacherous. Even if she set sail tonight, we wouldn't see her fleet for two months. Maybe three, if she's bringing a larger army this time, which I assume she would."

"Three months is hardly a 'decent amount,'" Myron snapped. "Even if we called in conscripts today, I can't raise an army on such short notice."

Alber scratched his short beard thoughtfully. "It doesn't make sense," he said. "Why is she moving now? Her initial attack was the disaster that birthed the Council. She was the only thing scary enough to finally convince the kingdoms to stop fighting each other and stand together. And stand together we did, but anyone in the know understands that the only reason we survived was because we had the Relay and the Empress didn't. That, and the fact that her fleet was too far from home to maintain a supply line. Still, it was hardly what I would call a decisive victory. Were I the Empress, I would have renewed my attack the very next year while the Council was still unstable. Even five years later we couldn't have turned back any sort of invasion force, but now? We're stronger than ever. She has to know that. So why did she wait?"

"Maybe she was rebuilding?" Myron said. "The combined Council forces sunk nearly a hundred ships before her fleet retreated. Maybe even the Empress can't pull that kind of firepower out from under her skirt."

"This is the Empress, Myron," Sara said, exasperated. "If our reports are anywhere close to right, she has enough people and resources to bury us in boats without batting an eye."

"So why hasn't she, then?" Myron said. "How do we know this resurgence is even aimed at us? There's been no declaration of war. All we have is some fisherman's tale about palace ships."

"Where else is she going to go?" Sara said. "There are three continents in the world: hers, ours, and the icy wastes in the north sea. You don't build a fleet of palace ships to go ghosthound hunting, so I think we can safely say she's coming for us."

Myron's face went scarlet, but Sara seemed to have forgotten him entirely. She leaned back in her deep-cushioned chair, thin arms crossed over her chest as she met Alber eye to eye. "It's a bad position any way you look at it. Forgetting the issue of whether or not the Empress is actually immortal, her empire has been a stable ruling power for as long as we've known there was another continent across the Unseen Sea. We know she has wealth, resources, and a troop capacity we can't even quantify. Considering this, the force we sent running twenty-six years ago was likely little more than a small excursion."

"*Small excursion?*" Myron cried.

"Yes," Sara said calmly. "I wrote as much in my report at the time, which, by the way, you should read."

Myron looked away with a sniff. Sara ignored him, focusing on the Merchant Prince.

"I believe it was a test," she said. "An opening strike to

reveal the strength of the opponent. That said, I don't know why she's waited so long to strike again. Maybe she truly is immortal and twenty-six years is nothing. Even so, now that she knows what we're capable of, her course is simple. If our strength is our ability to communicate instantly through the Relay and move our troops to counter her attacks with our full strength at a moment's notice, all the Empress needs to do is send enough soldiers that it doesn't matter. Move, counter move. This time she will overwhelm us, plain and simple."

"So what would you have us do?" Myron growled. "Roll over? *Surrender?*"

"I'm only being realistic," Sara said. "The Relay was our trump last time, but that card's been played."

"So make us another," Alber said, leaning back in his chair. "If she knows how to counter our advantage, make us a new one. That's why you're here."

Sara clenched her jaw. "I'm working on it."

"Well, it's not going to be enough," Myron said. "We can't beat the Immortal Empire with wizard tricks. The Relay was fine and dandy, but it was our soldiers who fought and won. Talking tables and carts that roll themselves don't sink ships."

"Yes, Myron, thank you," Alber said before Sara could snap back and make things even worse. "Your opinion is noted. Now, if you're done antagonizing my wizard, what have you got for me?"

With one final, dirty look at Sara, Myron reached into his jacket and pulled out a packet of folded papers.

"We have five thousand soldiers on active duty across the Council," he said, spreading out the stack of figure-covered papers on the table. He pulled a map from the satchel beside him and laid that out as well. "I think we can safely assume that any attack will begin as before, at Osera." His finger tapped a long island just off the Council's eastern coast. "As well as being geographically in the way for an invasion from across the Unseen Sea, Osera is the Council's greatest naval power. Ignore them, and the Empress will have Oseran ships at her back while she's fighting us on the mainland. Go far enough to get around them, and she lands in the mountains." His finger traveled north, tapping the wild mountain country that formed the Council's northern border. "Or the jungle." His finger went south to the lush, tropical nightmare that covered the Council's lower tip. "There's no way around it. She has to take Osera first. Now, I can have our current forces to the coast in a month. With reserves, country-by-country conscripts, and heavy recruitment, we can probably field another ten thousand in the next two months. Training will take another four."

"That's six months," Sara said. "We don't have—"

"I can't pull soldiers out of the air!" Myron roared, standing up so fast that his chair toppled behind him. "I'm talking about men, wizardess, not spirits! Men take time. I have to move them, equip them, train—"

"Myron."

The general stopped. Alber Whitefall was sitting at his desk as before, calm as ever, but his eyes were narrow and his mouth was a thin, clamped line.

"Myron," he said again in a soft, measured voice. "Do your best. Don't worry about Sara. Just get me as many soldiers as you can. Understood?"

"Yes, Merchant Prince," Myron grumbled.

"Excellent." Alber gave him a smile. "You'd better go get started. Time is wasting."

Myron Whitefall did not look pleased by the dismissal, but he gathered his papers and stomped into the hall without comment.

"Why is he in charge of our army again?" Sara said the moment the page closed the door.

"Because his mother was very insistent," Alber answered, standing up with a sigh. "And because he's not a bad general. He did secure the northlands, if you'll recall. You're seeing him at his worst. He was never one for politics, but he's quite good with the soldiers."

Sara glanced at the door and gave a dismissive snort. "*I* could have told you the Empress would go for Osera."

"Yes, well, you have the benefit of experience, don't you?" the Merchant Prince said, pouring himself a finger of brandy from the bottle on the table behind him. "And the day you feel like marshaling our army, I will be more than happy to let you. Until then, Myron will have to do." He paused. "It would also help if you didn't treat him like some idiot child."

"I treat him as he shows me he deserves to be treated," Sara said, pulling her pipe out of her coat pocket. She lit it with a spark from a tiny ruby, one of nearly a dozen she kept on a chain in her pocket, and took a deep drag, pointedly ignoring Alber's glare.

"He's right, though," she said softly.

Alber sipped his drink. "About what?"

"I don't have a trick to beat the Immortal Empress."

Alber lowered his glass. "Then why am I paying for your little playground downstairs?"

Sara grew very still. "The Relay was the idea that started my career, Alber. If I could have flashes of genius on call, I wouldn't be working for you. But brilliant as the Relay was, we were fighting the Empress's army, not the Empress herself."

"Come now," Alber said. "You don't actually believe all that malarkey about the Empress being an unkillable, magical queen, do you? Everything we know came from captured soldiers who knew they were going to die. Of course they'd tell us the Empress is our doom incarnate."

"There's something going on with her," Sara said. "Maybe she's just a powerful wizard who's good at selling herself, but one thing's certain, Alber. I have a dozen different projects going right now, all with good potential, but I don't have a miracle. Not this time, and not like we're going to need."

"Sara," Alber said, swirling his drink. "I am an old man who has been up for nearly thirty hours. If you have a point, get to it."

Sara took an angry puff from her pipe. "My point is that no matter how many poor farmers Myron shoves into Council uniforms, it's not going to be enough. The Empress's army

34

isn't just men. In the last war, the Empress's forces used spirits on a scale I've never seen before. She had amalgam spirits, blends of fire and metal better than even Shaper work, specifically created for war and directed by trained teams of wizards."

"How could I forget?" Alber said dryly. "And I suppose you're going to say we can't field something similar?"

Sara nearly choked on her smoke. "Powers, no. Even forgetting the combination of spirits for war, I would have written wizards working in teams off as impossible if I hadn't seen it with my own eyes. I've tried for years to duplicate it, but individual wizards' wills are simply too different to..." She trailed off when she saw Alber's bored look. "Never mind. The point I'm trying to make is that we caught a very lucky break last time. We can't count on that kind of lightning striking twice. If we're to have any real hope of keeping our lands, we're going to need a different sort of army than Myron's putting together. A wizard army."

"You have wizards," Alber said.

"A hundred, maybe," Sara answered. "And that's counting the idiots I give Council kingdoms to mind their Relay points. A hundred's not an army. I'm talking about a large-scale, organized, combat-ready force."

The Merchant Prince's eyebrows shot up. "You can't seriously be suggesting what I think you are."

"I am always serious," Sara said. "The Spirit Court accounts for almost every wizard born in Council lands. We cannot do this without them."

Alber sighed heavily, shaking his head slowly from side to side. "Banage is going to be a problem."

"Who's talking about Banage?" Sara said. "Banage hates the Council. Has for years. The only reason he goes along with us is because we're too powerful for him to openly antagonize if he wants his Court to have any say on the continent. The second you go to him hat in hand asking for help, he's going to try and shove his doctrine down our throats."

"I am well aware of Banage's low opinion," Whitefall said.

"He's never bothered to hide it, after all. But the years have made you too jaded, Sara. Even Banage can't stand around on his principles doing nothing while the Immortal Empress destroys everything he's built."

"Banage will stand on his principles until they gnaw his legs off," Sara said with a puff of smoke. "But we don't need Banage to get the Court. There are several Spiritualists, especially among the Tower Keepers, who would have no problem working with the Council."

"Sara!" Whitefall said, shocked. "We are on the verge of a perhaps unwinnable war. I will not cause a schism in what might be our only salvation just because you don't want to work with your former husband."

"The Spirit Court's already broken," Sara countered. "Banage's constant hard line has driven many of the more moderate members away. He almost tore the Court apart last year when they put his apprentice on trial. If Hern hadn't gotten himself tangled up in that Gaol nonsense, the Court would already be ours."

"Put it out of your mind," Whitefall said. "You don't win wars by ripping up your allies. Not if there is any other hope." He turned away, looking out over the city. "I'll send Banage an invitation to talk. Compromise is always possible, and who knows? Maybe this Empress thing will make him see we're not actually that bad."

Sara chuckled. "Want to wager on that?"

"I already am," Whitefall said, looking at her over his shoulder. "I'm wagering our survival on the hope that Etmon Banage likes being Rector Spiritualis more than he dislikes working with you. After all, if we can't find some way to work together, the Empress will crush us both, and you can't be Rector when there's no more Spirit Court."

Sara bit her pipe between her teeth. "I wish you wouldn't group the rest of us in on your impossible wagers."

Whitefall set his empty glass on his desk. "We're all going to have to do the impossible before this mess is done. Now,

36

get downstairs and start working on that miracle. I'll take care of Banage."

Sara stood and walked out without a word. When she was gone, Alber called his pages in. One he sent to the Spirit Court, and the rest he set to opening windows. When his office no longer reeked of smoke, he poured himself another glass of brandy and lay down on his silk couch to contemplate the wreck his carefully cultured plans had become.

CHAPTER
3

"So," Miranda said. "One more time. The demon under the Dead Mountain is sealed, but he can sneak out shards of himself, called seeds, that bury themselves into host bodies, who become demonseeds."

"Correct," Slorn said. "Demonseeds are tiny slivers of the demon itself. Each seed has the potential to grow into a new demon, given enough time and food. The stronger the host and the longer the seed is able to incubate, the stronger the resulting demon is at awakening."

Miranda shuddered, blinking her eyes against the memory that refused to vanish—the hideous black shape standing over the woods outside Izo's bandit city, its black wings blotting out the sky as it ate the screaming world.

"How do we stop it?" she said quietly. "Stop the seeds from coming out?"

"I don't know," Slorn said. "Unawakened demonseeds constantly travel through the shadows in and out of the mountain, bringing their master new vessels. There is a human cult that serves there, presenting wizards to the demon in hopes of becoming demonseeds themselves. The League has cleared out the mountain several times—killing the human followers, setting up a perimeter, but the seeds always get through. All demonseeds can hear the demon's voice in their heads, and he moves them like pieces on a board that only he can see the whole of. This makes them very hard to block completely, especially as the League can find them only when they cause a panic. Alric gave up trying to blockade the mountain years ago. Staying on the mountain for any length of time is dangerous, even for the Lord of Storms, and the reward wasn't worth the risk. They now focus on the eradication of seeds that cause problems."

"Well," Miranda said with a huff, "it doesn't seem to be working."

"It works," Slorn said, looking at her with his black, calm, bear eyes. "We are still alive."

Rebuked, Miranda shut her mouth and focused on the path ahead. Seeing that the lesson was at an end, Slorn leaned back on the roof of his walking cart to stare thoughtfully at the wispy clouds flowing like silk across the pale blue sky.

They were high in the mountains, riding north. It was slow going, even for Gin. The constant wind kept the ground clear from snow, but the stone itself was icy and treacherous. The ghosthound kept his eyes on his feet, delicately picking his way across the steep slopes, his dappled silver coat shifting with the wind. Still, they could have gone faster if not for Slorn's wagon. The wooden cart climbed at a snail's pace, rattling and scraping as its carved wooden legs scrabbled on the ice despite the metal hooks Slorn had attached. Sometimes they barely made ten miles in a day, but the pace didn't bother Miranda. She'd learned more from Slorn in the two weeks since they'd left Izo's camp than from all three years she'd spent training to begin her apprenticeship with the Spiritualists. Gin, however, didn't seem to be enjoying himself.

"I don't like him," the ghosthound growled when they stopped for lunch.

"You don't like anyone," Miranda said, smearing a sliver

38

of cold butter across her hard baked bread as best she could. "And keep your voice down."

"He asks too many questions," Gin said, loud as ever. "And he looks at the sky too much."

Miranda glanced at Slorn. He was standing beside his cart, talking to it softly as he checked the wooden legs. "What does that have to do with anything?"

Gin made a *harrumphing* sound. "He shouldn't be doing it, is all. Or talking about the Dead Mountain like he does. I've never understood you humans and your constant need to know things. You're the nosiest spirits in creation."

"And you're the biggest curmudgeon in creation," Miranda said, smacking him across the haunches. "You saw that thing at Izo's the same as all of us. I'm a Spiritualist, but that thing, demon or demonseed or whatever, makes the usual Spirit Court worries look like children's games. It's not something I can just ignore, and until I find out what I can do to stop what happened at Izo's from happening again, even if that turns out to be nothing, I can't go back to Zarin. Not while still calling myself a Spiritualist."

Gin flattened his ears. "Not everything's a crusade, Miranda. The bear man's leading you places you shouldn't go, and you're going to get hurt if you keep following."

"I'm a big girl," she said, reaching out to scratch his nose. "I won't get in over my head."

Gin moved away from her hand and shook himself, sending dirt and ice everywhere. "Just watch yourself," he said, trotting away.

Miranda frowned. "Where are you going?"

"Hunting," Gin growled, stalking off down the frozen path.

Miranda started to remind him that there was dried meat in Slorn's cart, but the ghosthound had already vanished into the frosty landscape, his shifting fur blending into the white mist rolling down from the peaks.

"I'm starting to understand why they call them ghosthounds."

Miranda turned with a start. Slorn was standing behind her,

smiling in a way that was probably meant to be reassuring but never quite made it, thanks to his sharp teeth.

"Sorry about that," she said. "Gin doesn't have a lot of tact."

"Don't worry about it," Slorn said, sitting down on the large, flat rock that sheltered their little fire from the wind. "It's a ghosthound's nature to be protective and wary of outsiders, and I never fault a spirit for following its nature. Besides, he's not exactly wrong. Spirits have learned over countless centuries that some things are better left alone."

Miranda frowned. "You mean the demon?"

Slorn shrugged. "The League, the Dead Mountain, demonseeds, these are all things that spirits, even Great Spirits, have learned to ignore. Must learn to ignore. You can't have a life worth living when you're constantly worrying about things you cannot fight or change. All they can do is trust the system that has worked for thousands of years and go on with their lives."

Miranda's frown turned into a scowl. "And where does the thing we saw at Izo's fit into that system?"

"It doesn't," Slorn said. "That's why we're going to the Shaper Mountain. If the League will not listen, then I must make my case to an outside party. If I can find even one voice to speak for me that the Shepherdess will heed, Nivel's death won't have been in vain."

Miranda bit her tongue. Slorn spoke his wife's name with such sadness that words felt pointless. But there was so much of what he said that she still didn't understand and she could not keep quiet.

"The Shepherdess," she said. "I've heard of her, of course, but never in any detail. Most Spiritualists are lucky if they ever get to talk to a Great Spirit." Mellinor found that amusing, but Miranda ignored his bubbling laughter and pressed on. "She's the greatest spirit, isn't she? The one at the top of the spirit world."

"Assuming she's a spirit at all," Slorn said. "Which I don't think she is. The Shepherdess is the force that guides the world and commands the spirits. She also controls the League and keeps

40

the demon locked beneath the mountain, among other things."

"How can she not be a spirit?" Miranda said. "Everything has a spirit."

"I don't know the answer precisely," Slorn answered. "But I do know her control is nothing a spirit could manage. No spirit except a human's can control another, and humans can't touch the spirits of other humans. But, so far as I understand it, the Shepherdess can command everything. Therefore, she's not a spirit. Or, at least, not a spirit like we are familiar with."

Miranda slumped down. "I feel so ignorant," she muttered. "You'd think I'd have at least heard more than a passing mention of something so important." A tremor of reproach went through her before she could stop it, and deep in her mind she felt her rings twinge.

"Don't blame your spirits," Slorn said. "Nothing talks about the Shepherdess unless they have to. It took me decades to piece what little I have together, and even I don't know for certain. All I have are theories. Suppositions based on years of asking too many questions, as your dog would say. It may be that the Shaper Mountain can do nothing and this journey is little more than a waste of time."

"But we have to try," Miranda said.

"Yes," Slorn said quietly. "We have to try." He leaned back, looking up at the snow-covered slope they'd been following all day. "If we keep this pace we'll make Knife's Pass by sunset. From there it's a straight shot to the Shaper Mountain. We'll reach the gate by noon tomorrow, weather permitting. After that, there's no turning back."

Miranda laughed. "There's been no turning back for a while now. Remember, I was the one who asked to come along."

"I have not forgotten," Slorn said, standing up. "Let's go. We have more miles to cover than we can make if we dawdle."

Miranda took his offered hand, and he helped her to her feet. They had almost everything together by the time Gin returned with a scrawny mountain goat in his jaws.

* * *

41

It was late when they reached Knife's Pass and Miranda was too tried to look at anything besides her bedroll. When she woke at dawn, Gin was still sleeping, his body curved to shelter her from the icy winds. She smiled and packed her blankets, and then, stepping softly so she wouldn't wake the ghosthound, she tiptoed to Slorn's wagon. As always, Slorn was already awake. He was sitting on the fold-out steps, staring up at the clear morning sky. There were two steaming mugs of tea on the step beside him, one half empty, the other full. Miranda took the full one.

"How much farther?" she said, blowing on the steaming liquid.

Slorn looked at her with an incredulous expression and pointed north. Miranda's eyes followed his gesture and she nearly dropped her tea. The sheltered pass they were camped in wasn't a pass at all, or at least not a natural one. It was a road cut between the mountains, running due north in a perfectly straight line between two sheer cliffs, and at the end of that road stood the largest mountain Miranda had ever seen. It was impossibly tall, soaring above the surrounding mountains like a spire. Its steep sides were snowbound and blinding white in the morning sunlight, but the mountain's peak was too sheer and tall even for snow. It loomed far, far overhead, naked and gray-white, a porcelain knife set against the pale sky.

"That's the Shaper Mountain?" Miranda said when she could speak again. "How does anyone live on a slope like that?"

"Not on," Slorn answered. "In."

Miranda frowned and looked again, squinting against the glare. Sure enough, the tiny dark spaces beneath snowy overhangs that she had first taken to be shadows were now clearly windows. There were balconies as well, each placed so elegantly along the mountain's natural cliffs that Miranda would never have spotted them if not for the faint glimmer of the icy railings. Panes of glass flashed between the snow banks, and at the end of the pass she could just make out the unnaturally straight edge of what looked like a door set deep in the mountain's base.

"The upper body of the mountain is given over to the Shapers for their work," Slorn said. "In return for its protection, leadership, and instruction, the Shapers serve the mountain and work in its name."

Miranda shivered. "And what kind of work does a mountain need done?"

"All kinds," Slorn said with a toothy smile. "Though only the Great Teacher understands how it all fits together."

"Great Teacher?"

"You'll see soon enough," Slorn said, standing up. "Let's get moving. We have far to go."

Miranda looked back at the mountain. It didn't seem that far away. But she obeyed and walked back across the camp to wake up Gin. The hound was already up and waiting when she reached him, his orange eyes narrow and guarded as he watched Slorn's wagon pack itself. He answered her "good morning" with a gruff snort, and though Miranda tried several times as they packed their camp, that was all the comment the hound would make.

Though the mountain looked like it was only a few miles away, the distance was deceptive. Knife's Pass was an endless corridor between the lesser peaks, a straight, flat slab of rock large enough to march a legion down walled in by two featureless stone walls. Ahead, the Shaper Mountain rose over everything else, filling the end of the pass, but no matter how fast they ran along the smooth road, it never seemed to come any closer.

The sun was high overhead when the end of the road finally came into sight. Gin was panting hard, his feet swollen after running full out for miles on the hard stone. Slorn slowed the pace, and Miranda started to thank him on Gin's behalf when she realized that Slorn had not slowed for them.

Just before the towering spire of the Shaper Mountain took over everything, the mountains fell away. The ground simply stopped, leaving an enormous gap of empty air between them and the Shaper Mountain. As they got closer, Miranda saw that it was a canyon. The divide cut between the rest of the mountains and the Shaper's peak like a sword stroke. At the very bottom, a deep blue, freezing cold river glittered in the noon sun, but it was so far away that Miranda couldn't even hear the sound of the water, only the endless wind howling between the cliffs.

The road, however, did not stop. A bridge of arching stone just wide enough for two carts running side by side spanned the enormous divide, linking Knife's Pass to the mountain on the other side. The bridge was all one piece, a great length of curved rock that sprouted like a branch at one end from the stone under their feet and on the other from the roots of the Shaper Mountain itself. There were no railings, nothing to save a careless traveler from plummeting into the ravine, but the bridge itself was free of ice, and Slorn's wagon stepped onto it without hesitation.

With a nervous swallow, Miranda followed, leaning with Gin into the wind that threatened to toss them both into the canyon below. She was so focused on not falling that she didn't notice Slorn had stopped until she was past him. She turned around, nudging Gin back until they were pressed against the wagon.

"What's wrong?" she shouted over the wind.

Slorn looked down at her from his seated position on the wagon's roof, his small bear ears blown flat by the wind. "Things might get a little tense in the mountain," he said. "No matter what happens, I need you to stay calm and follow my lead."

Gin began to growl. "What do you mean 'tense'?"

"You'll see soon enough," Slorn said, starting his wagon forward again. "Just stay with me and everything will be fine."

Gin snorted, sending a poof of white vapor into the air that was instantly snatched by the wind. "If he thinks we're just going to roll over—"

"Gin!" Miranda said sharply.

The hound shut his mouth, and Miranda pushed him forward. She didn't like this any more than he did, but they'd come too far to stop now. All she could do was press herself flat against the ghosthound's back and follow Slorn's wagon across the final half of the ravine.

The bridge ended at a sheer wall in the mountain's side, the smooth stone road butting up against an unnaturally straight, unnaturally square cliff. The wind here was stronger than ever, buffeting them against the cliff face. Miranda kept low on Gin's back, her eyes darting up the mountain for another path, but there was nothing, just the bridge and cliff. She was about to ask Slorn where to go next when a loud crack sounded over the wind. More cracks followed until the ravine sounded like a breaking glacier, and then, all at once, the cliff opened.

An enormous slab of stone twice as wide as Gin was long swung into the mountain with a long scrape, revealing a cavern larger than anything Miranda had seen before, including the Relay chamber below the Council. For a moment, she just stood, gawking at the sheer size of it, the perfect smoothness of stone so white it seemed to glow as it arched up to the domed ceiling. It was only when Gin began to growl that she realized they were not alone.

Just inside the stone door, a sternly handsome older man with a long, white beard stood with his arms crossed, as though he'd been waiting. Two younger men flanked him on either side. They were all strangely dressed. The two younger men wore what looked like work shirts and simple trousers, but the cloth was nice enough to take the front window in the best Zarin shops. The old man, however, was dressed in a padded silk robe finer than any Miranda had ever seen.

It was the old man who broke the silence. He lifted his chin, eyes narrowing as he looked Slorn over from boots to ears. "Heinricht."

"Guildmaster," Slorn answered, his deep voice strangely flat.

The old man's expression wavered, and for a moment he looked almost heartbroken. Then the stern frown was back, and he flicked his fingers. At the signal, the two men stepped forward, each carrying a pair of iron cuffs. Slorn held out his hands as the men lay the cuffs on his arms, one at the wrists, one farther up at his elbows. They held the cuffs in place as the iron rings fastened themselves with a dull clank.

"Wait just a moment," Miranda said, sliding off Gin's back. Forget staying calm, this was ridiculous. "What's going on? What are you doing?"

"They're arresting me," Slorn said, lowering his bound arms.

"As you knew we would," the old man said, his voice as deep and solid as the mountain beneath their feet. "You knew the punishment for leaving, Heinricht. Why did you return?"

"Nivel is dead," Slorn answered. "I've come back to honor my duty as a Shaper and return our knowledge to the Teacher."

One of the men who'd cuffed him looked at Slorn with a sneer. "What knowledge could a deserter have for the Teacher?"

"Knowledge has no faction, Krevich," the Guildmaster said.

The young man blushed and bowed his head, but the Guildmaster didn't look at him. His eyes never left Slorn. "You may bring your knowledge to the Teacher. As for the outsider you've brought"—his eyes flicked to Miranda—"leave. This is no place for Spiritualists."

"Spiritualist Lyonette brings knowledge as well," Slorn said before Gin's growling could get any louder. "My story would be incomplete without hers."

The Guildmaster's face darkened, but he turned and walked away without another word, his beautiful silk robe moving with him. The men grabbed Slorn and marched him inside, the sound from their boots echoing through the beautiful cavern. After a moment of hesitation, Miranda followed, guiding Gin into the Shaper Mountain as the enormous door swung closed behind them.

"And there they go."

Sparrow slid down the icy rock and tossed the spyglass to Tesset. "I told you this was going to end in tears."

Tesset caught the spyglass and stowed it carefully in his belt pouch. "No one's crying yet."

"Sara will when she hears that her sea on a leash and pet

bear are gone for good," Sparrow said. "Assuming she could do something so human as cry."

Tesset didn't reply. Sparrow shook his head and pulled his now-ratty coat closer. It didn't help. The wind on the cliffs above Knife's Pass was cold enough to freeze his bones. "No point in dragging it out," he said, fishing the Relay link out of his pocket. "Let's face the music."

He twirled the Relay link until it turned bright blue. Since Sparrow didn't have enough spiritual presence to wake up an awakened sword, Sara had created his link to activate when it was shaken. She'd given him a huge lecture about this when she'd handed it over. Fortunately, Sparrow hadn't wasted his time listening.

It took Sara an uncommonly long time to answer the Relay. When her scratchy voice finally did speak, she sounded harried and annoyed.

"Well?"

"No luck," Sparrow said. "Papa bear and Banage's darling were swallowed by the mountain. We couldn't catch them, which should come as no surprise, seeing how you failed to provide us with either a walking cart or a ghosthound."

Sara's voice grew thoughtful. "So they *were* going to the Shapers."

"Of course they were," Sparrow snapped. "Where else would they be going up here?"

"With Slorn, you never know," she said. "Anything else to report?"

"Yes," Sparrow said. "We're coming home. I'm sick of being poorly dressed and freezing. And since there's nothing left for us to—"

"Don't be stupid," Sara said with a puff from her pipe so vivid Sparrow could almost smell the smoke. "The job's not done. This Empress situation is getting out of control. I need Slorn and the Spiritualist girl's sea more than ever. Actually, Tesset, are you there?"

"Yes, Sara," Tesset said, straightening up.

47

"I want you to come back to Zarin. I'm headed down to the desert for a few days and I need someone here whom I can trust to deal with Myron."

Tesset arched an eyebrow. "Myron?"

"The Whitefall in charge of the army," Sara said, yawning. "He seems to think I'm made of Relay points."

"Isn't there someone else?" Tesset said, scratching his stubbly chin. "It's a long walk back to Zarin just to run interference on a Whitefall."

"No one he'll like," Sara said. "He's a military man. He'll like you. And that's an order, so stop questioning it."

Tesset furrowed his brows, giving the matter careful consideration. "It will take me a few days," he said at last. "I'm not as young as I used to be."

Sara sighed loudly. "Just do your best."

"And what am *I* supposed to do?" Sparrow said. "Surely you have more members of the Whitefall family who need corralling."

"I do," Sara said. "But you've got your orders."

"Sara!" Sparrow cried. "The bear man I get, but Miranda? I understand she has fantastic powers or whatever, but you and I both know you only pulled her into this to make Banage steam. Why should I have to risk my neck just so you can stick it to your—"

"Sparrow."

Sparrow snapped his mouth shut. He knew that tone in her voice.

"That's better," Sara said. "Tesset, report to Zarin. Sparrow, your orders stand. Secure the Spiritualist and the Shaper and bring them to me."

"And how am I supposed to do that without Tesset?" Sparrow said. "In case you forgot, Miss Lyonette doesn't feel too kindly toward our office at the moment. Even if I get to her, she's not going to just come back. What do you want me to do, arm wrestle the ghosthound?"

"You're charming," Sara said. "Figure it out."

Sparrow flopped back against the icy rock in disgust, but the

48

link's light was already fading. Sara had severed the connection.

He shoved the orb into his pocket with an exasperated huff. "Can you believe this?"

"That Sara is being unreasonable?" Tesset said, buttoning his coat. "Of course. What Sara have you been working for that this behavior comes as a surprise?"

"And you're just going to abandon me?" Sparrow said, his voice pathetic.

Tesset didn't even have the decency to look hurt. "I'm going to do my job, as are you. I couldn't help you in the Shaper Mountain anyway. It can see me, remember? Just make sure you get a good look around or Sara will never forgive you."

"Right, right," Sparrow said, rubbing his eyes. "She must be distracted not to mention that angle. This Empress thing really has her on edge."

"If the Immortal Empress doesn't put you on edge, you're a fool," Tesset said, lacing his boots tight. "Good luck."

Sparrow nodded, but when he looked up, the older man was already gone, jogging down the path and picking up speed with every tireless step. With a frustrated groan, Sparrow pushed himself up from the rock. He shrugged off what was left of his brocaded coat and tossed it on the ground. Then, dressed only in his drab pants and shirtsleeves, he began to walk along the ledge toward the Shaper Mountain, fading instantly into the gray landscape.

CHAPTER
4

Eli sat on the prow of the schooner, sulking at the blue ocean that spread out in all directions. Ahead of him, the shadowy peaks of the islands of Osera dominated the horizon.

Eli sulked at them too. They'd made record time to the coast, thanks to him. Not an hour after Josef had announced they were suddenly and inexplicably going to Osera, Eli had found an express carriage. After a little excessive bribery, the driver somehow found time in his schedule to take them from just south of Zarin to the port at Sanche in a little over a day and a half. At the port, Eli had found a private fishing schooner willing to take them to Osera the very next morning, well before the commercial ferries. It was nothing short of a miracle that they were on the ocean at all right now, but Eli might as well have saved his miracle making for all the thanks he got.

Josef had been in high dudgeon since they'd left the bounty office. He hadn't said more than a syllable at a time the whole trip. This wasn't remarkable in and of itself, but considering that Eli was bending over backward to get them to Osera for as yet unknown reasons, the swordsman's silence irked him more than usual.

Eli sighed and fought the urge to scratch under his wig. They were deep in civilized lands now, where people actually read bounty posters, and he didn't have the luxury of running around like he usually did. The golden wig wasn't enough to fool anyone who was actually looking for him, but it was fine at throwing off the casual glances. It was also unbearably hot. Even sitting on the prow with the sea wind in his face and the slightly fishy shade provided by the lofted nets, Eli could feel the sweat crawling down his scalp. But no matter how bad it got, he kept his hands on the railing. The ship wasn't big, and the sailors had enough to talk about with Josef's swords. The last thing they needed was for bored, curious fishermen to start wondering why the blade-covered man's business partner was wearing a wig.

He was just starting to work himself into a really foul mood when something soft touched his arm. Eli jumped and nearly fell off the boat. He grabbed the railing and turned to see Nico standing beside him.

"Don't do that!"

"I said hello," Nico said, sounding a little hurt.

Eli took a deep breath. "Sorry. What can I do for you?"

Nico shrugged and sat down beside him. Eli shifted uncomfortably. They'd never really talked about what had happened in the valley, but he liked to think that he and Nico were square these days. Still, it was hard to tell where you stood when the other party in the relationship never said more than five words together under the best of circumstances. After several awkward moments, he tried again. "I don't suppose Josef has told you why we're rushing to Osera?"

"No," Nico said, looking down at the water. "He hasn't said anything."

Eli was immediately sorry he'd asked. The girl looked heartbroken. He glanced over his shoulder toward the back of the boat where Josef was standing with the Heart in his hands, practicing his stances. He looked so calm as he brought the enormous sword around (narrowly missing a tied-off line, much to the crew's displeasure) that Eli wanted to strangle him.

"Who does he think he is?" Eli growled, turning back around. "We're supposed to have a plan when we enter a new country. We *would* have had a plan three days ago if I'd had my way, but *no*. I don't know what he expects us to do when we land in Osera. Powers forbid he actually tell us anything."

Nico shifted uncomfortably. "I'm sure he has his reasons."

"Oh, I'm sure he does," Eli said. "I just wish he'd share them. We're *supposed* to be a team."

For the first time in days, Nico smiled a little. "Well, we were the ones who decided to come along. I suppose we can't complain if he doesn't share plans that he didn't want us along for in the first place."

"I can complain about anything," Eli said, straightening up. "And if you ever quote that back at me, I'm never speaking to you again."

Grinning at her arched eyebrows, Eli spun on his heel and walked off to find the captain to ask, yet again, how much longer this unbearably long boat ride was going to take.

* * *

Nico listened to Eli's light footsteps until they were lost in the crashing waves. Fifteen steps, she noted to herself. Fifteen steps from a famously light-footed thief on a rocking ship in the middle of the sea. She gripped the railing until her already-white fingers were the color of bleached bone. It wasn't her imagination. Her hearing was getting better.

And it wasn't just her hearing. Ever since she'd taken back her body from the demon, her strength had grown as well. Her night vision was now better than her normal sight, and she could smell the tiniest traces of scents lingering days after whatever had made them was gone. She could hear the turning of the sleeping spirits and the laughter of the winds as they rushed overhead. But all this she could accept. It was reasonable that her senses would get better now that she was her own master. What didn't make sense, what she couldn't accept, was that she wasn't just seeing the world more clearly. She was seeing things she'd never seen before, things that were not there.

Nico tilted her head back, squinting up at the clear sky overhead. At first, she saw nothing but the sky, deep blue and cloudless. Then her eyes adjusted, and she saw them. High overhead, great *things*—she had no other name for them—streaked through the air. They were as faint as shadows, but they were always there, swimming through the sky in great colorless coils, turning and flashing so quickly it made her nauseous.

The snakes in the sky weren't all she saw, the strange things were everywhere: in the boat, in the sails, in the nets. Unlike the things in the sky, these were stationary, twitching only slightly, mostly when Eli walked by. The sea, however, was roiling with half-seen shapes. They flowed with the waves, thousands of millions of little sparks swimming in and out of each other.

The first time she'd seen the shapes was the day after she'd beaten the demon. They were so dim then, barely more than shadows, that she'd dismissed them as a trick of the light. But the trick never went away. Day and night she saw them like a second world over the real one. As the days passed and it was clear the things weren't going away, she'd finally decided to talk to Eli. Other than Slorn, he was the only person who might know what they were. But just when she'd finally worked up the courage to ask him, Josef had declared they were going to Osera. Nico decided to keep her mouth shut after that. Whatever Josef needed to do in Osera, he had enough to worry about without her adding more.

Nico closed her eyes. When she woke up on the valley floor, it hadn't occurred to her that she might be different. How stupid. You couldn't be torn apart and rebuilt and expect to still be what you were. What had happened in Izo's valley had changed her. Was still changing her. But whatever was different, whatever changed, she was still the master of herself. The demon was still buried. She could feel the rock in her mind keeping him down as clearly as she felt her own arms. The shadows weren't his doing, but that almost made things worse. The demon she could deal with, but these new visions were alien and frightening. Every time she saw them, which was all the time now, she couldn't help thinking that maybe she hadn't been truly rebuilt that day. Maybe something was still missing, something important.

Maybe she really had gone mad.

Against her better judgment, Nico opened her eyes and looked up again, past the coiling snake creatures that streaked through the air and up to the sky itself. It was hard to make out under all the movement, but if she stood very still and focused on one spot, there was no mistaking it. There, at the very top of the world, something was moving. Something enormous, something sharp, dragging across the other side of the sky's dome.

Fear closed over her like ice, and she slammed her eyes shut. It made little difference. From the moment she'd first seen the things clawing the sky, she could not unsee them. The dread followed her waking and sleeping, eyes open or closed, and through it all a thought went round and round and round her head, like a marble rolling around the inside of a bowl.

Only mad people saw shapes against the sky.

She stayed like that for several minutes, eyes shut, forcing her breath to remain calm. Finally, when she'd worked up the courage to open her eyes again, Nico looked over her shoulder at Josef. He was standing at the back of the boat with the Heart in his hands, moving through his stances. His face was blank, eyes half closed. To an outsider, he probably looked bored, a man going through a routine, but Nico had been watching him all her life that she cared to remember. She could tell he was upset as well as if he'd screamed it. It was written all over him: in the tenseness of his footing, the way his hands folded white-knuckled around the Heart's hilt, the clench of his jaw. Something about this trip to Osera bothered him deeply, and until she found out what, and why, she could not add her fears to that burden, no matter how desperate she got. Whatever had changed in her that day in the valley, nothing could change the fact that Josef was the center of her life. He was her partner, her savior, the one person who had never done her wrong, who had always believed in her even when there was nothing to believe in. Whatever he needed out here in the middle of the sea, she would help him reach it, and no madness, no bizarre other world that crept across the real one would keep her from being whatever he needed her to be.

That thought alone drove the fear back, and Nico gripped it like a lifeline as she turned again to face the islands rising like swords from the sea.

Seen on a map, the kingdom of Osera looked like a wall separating the Council's eastern seaboard from the wild waters of the Unseen Sea. Though even those who lived there called their land "the island," the kingdom of Osera was not one island, but dozens, a long line of mountaintops rising vertically from the ocean along the Council coast. Most of these islands were uninhabitable, their sloping sides too steep for anything other than sea birds, but at the center of the chain the islands grew wider, and there was room for people, especially on the island of Osera itself.

Even on its largest island, Osera was like a wall. Over fifty miles long, the main island Osera measured barely twenty miles at its widest point. Dominated by the peak at its center, the island was constantly sloping. This slope was long and gentle on the Council side, but steep and short on the side facing the Unseen Sea. Because of this quirk in geography, and the fact that the face the island turned to the open ocean had borne the brunt of the Empress's attack, the eastern side of the island had been left to ruin. After the war, Osera had turned its back on the sea and the Empress, embracing the Council's new prosperity by covering its gentle western slope in city.

"Covering" was the right word. Buildings on the island's western slope crowded every inch of land that was flat enough to lay a foundation. Tiny streets ran seemingly at random, following the flattest paths upward or sideways along the mountain and sometimes changing into stairs without notice when the island's geography took a sudden turn for the vertical. The farther up the mountain the buildings climbed, the shorter and narrower they became, clinging to the mountain's rising cliff like barnacles. But down by the water, the buildings were tall and broad, a busy tangle of workshops, warehouses, and shipyards spilling out onto Osera's pride and greatest source of wealth: the marina.

The marina ran nearly unbroken for thirty miles along the island's western edge. Docks jutted far into the calm water of the protected channel that ran between Osera and the Council coast. Endless lines of moored ships waited their turn to be unloaded and reloaded by the armies of barefoot dockworkers while captains did business on the large, permanently moored barges that served as mobile offices for the hundreds of trading companies that called Osera home.

Eli's ship tied in at one of the long sloops jutting from the floating tangle of deepwater docks at the center of the marina. Josef hopped off the moment they stopped moving, and by the time Eli had worked out a payment for the schooner captain that was large enough to make sure the old man didn't remember them should anyone ask, but not enough to send him bragging in the taverns and drawing unwanted attention, the swordsman was halfway to the island. Nico trailed behind him, a black blot in the bright sun.

With a final, frustrated sigh, Eli pressed the gold coins into the captain's hand and jogged down the planks after his companions.

"Well," he said, raising his voice over the squawk of the sea birds. "Here we are. Do you have further directions to find your queen, Mr. Cryptic, or shall we just turn ourselves in at the local bounty office?"

Josef didn't even honor that comment with a sneer. "We're going to the palace," he said, boots clattering on the wooden boards.

"The palace?" Eli fell in step beside him. "Of course. Brilliant. Where else do you find queens? Out of idle curiosity, what's your plan for getting into said palace?"

"We're going to walk up to the front gate and ask the guard."

Eli nearly tripped. "Are you out of your bleeding mind?"

He would have said more, but Nico elbowed him hard in the back. He grunted and gave her a hurt look over his shoulder. She didn't even have the good grace to look apologetic, just pressed her finger to her lips and glanced pointedly at the sailors crowded on the dock beside theirs, most of whom were now unloading their cargo suspiciously slowly with their ears turned toward Eli.

Eli shoved his hands in his pockets. "The question still stands," he said, albeit more quietly. "All you had to do was say, 'Eli, I need to get into a castle' and I could have done it in a heartbeat, but *no*. You've apparently taken too many hits to the head to remember that you're traveling with a master thief. And since you never thought to share any of your *magnificent* plans, I don't have anything ready. No false papers, no aliases, no nothing. That kind of throws a kink in the whole front door plan."

"Really," Josef grumbled.

"*Really*," Eli grumbled back. "I never saw a palace that just let random people in off the street, especially not when one of them was carrying enough blades to open his own armory, but maybe I'm just being negative."

56

Josef stopped and turned to face the thief. "Are you done?"

Eli opened his mouth and then snapped it shut and threw out his arms for Josef to lead the way. Shaking his head, Josef resumed his march down the wooden dock and into the packed, tangled streets of the city itself.

Put out as he was, Eli enjoyed the walk. For a country burned to the ground by the Immortal Empress, Osera looked remarkably well. Narrow streets merged into large courtyards strung with vines that shaded merchant stalls of every sort. The buildings were brightly painted and cheery, and though their upper stories loomed over the streets, the vertical nature of the island made it impossible to feel claustrophobic. Every corner came with a grand view of the port below, and, narrow as they were, the streets were impeccably clean, probably because of the constant wind tunneling down them from the mountain above.

Nothing in the city looked old or dilapidated. Everywhere Eli looked he saw new construction, most bearing the clean architecture and ornate accents that had come into style with the Council's rise. Every building had glass windows, tiled roofs, and iron window grates that grew only more ornate as they climbed away from the docks. Storefronts showcased impressive displays behind large picture windows. In the space of two blocks, Eli saw clothes, fabrics, cheeses, pastries, and metal goods as fine as any in Zarin. Tastefully painted signs advertised restaurants that, this close to noon, were full of well-dressed men and a few women. Eli could almost smell the money in the air, and he was beginning to wonder why he'd never come to Osera before.

Josef led the way, forging a path upward through the busy streets and toward the top of the island. He kept his eyes ahead and said nothing, and Eli, thoughtful friend that he was, took the opportunity to do a little digging.

"So," he said, pushing through the crowd until he was walking beside Josef. "You're from here, right?"

"Yes," Josef said without looking at him.

"Not what I expected," Eli said, smiling as they passed

57

through another of the vine-shadowed merchant squares, this one with a large, ornate, bronze fountain done in a fanciful representation of a whale gushing water from its enormous mouth. "I'd always heard Osera was an island of barely reformed pirates, terrible weather, and fish smokehouses. This place rivals Zarin."

Josef stopped to let a cart go past. "Being burned to the ground leaves a lot of room for improvement."

"But all this?" Eli said. "In twenty-six years?"

Josef shrugged, picking up the pace again. "Osera bore the brunt of the war so the inner kingdoms didn't have to. In return, the Council waived most of our sea-trade tariffs. That's the kind of thing that can make a small country rich enough to build just about anything."

Eli grinned. "So I see. My only question now is what to steal first."

"Nothing," Josef said.

Eli's smile faded. "Why not?"

"Because we're not going to be here long enough for you to steal anything," Josef snapped. "We're going to the palace, hearing what the queen has to say, and then we're leaving."

"What?" Eli cried. "Wait, wait, wait. That's it? That's why you dragged us all the way out here? Powers, Josef, if we're just going to tell this queen to shove off, why did we even come?"

"Because even I feel guilty sometimes," he said. "Now come on. And shut up. The last thing we need is more attention."

Eli stopped, affronted. The street was packed with people on their own business. No one so much as glanced their way. Still, when Josef was this prickly it never did any good to push him further. So with great difficulty, Eli kept further opinions to himself as he stomped up the hill after Josef and Nico.

The sun was high and hot overhead when Josef finally stopped them. Eli fell against a building, panting. "Please tell me we're there," he said, fanning himself. "We've been walking for years."

Josef rested his hands on the swords at his sides, infuriatingly untouched by the heat or the long climb. "Almost," he said, nodding across the street. "There's the palace."

Eli looked up. The road ahead opened into a large square. It was the most open space he'd seen since arriving in Osera, and the flattest. They were on the mountain's shoulder, a long stretch of relatively flat land before the final assent to the peak. The buildings surrounding the square were as rich as any Eli had seen in any country, but the square itself looked old and almost shabby. There were no shady vines, fountains, or merchant carts, just open stone baking in the noon sun. The crowds were thinner here as well, mostly men in formal dress carrying leather cases and looking very important.

They were very high now. To the west, Eli could see the whole of the city stretching down the mountain like a mushroom forest made of red-and-yellow-tiled roofs, but looking east, the view was entirely different. At the edge of the square, the mountain's sharp peak rose dramatically, and wrapped around it was a building unlike any Eli had seen in Osera. The palace of Osera was a hulking mass of rough-cut, weatherworn stone wrapped around the mountain like an ugly scarf. What windows it had were narrow as arrow slits, and its roof was tiled with stone shingles worn white by time and rain. There was no proper gate or guardhouse. Instead, the palace's face fronted directly onto the square, its tiny windows glaring down on the lovely modern buildings below like the squinty eyes of a disapproving old man.

Staring up at the old, ugly, ungainly mess, Eli felt crushingly disappointed. If the brightly colored city below had been modern and inviting, the building in front of them was gloomy and aggressive, more like a lonely fortress on an embattled front than the royal palace of a prosperous, modern nation. Just the sight of it was enough to kill any joy left lingering from the beautiful climb up, not to mention Eli's fledgling dreams of a glorious heist.

"Lovely," he said at last, fiddling with his wig.

Nico shot him a nasty look, but Josef didn't even seem to

hear. The swordsman wiped a spare bandage across his face to clean off some of the day's grime, and then, tying the bandage tight around his wrist, started across the square like a man beginning his death march. Eli and Nico exchanged a final, worried glance before falling in behind him.

The front entrance to the palace was protected from the main square by a guard box, a wooden structure slightly larger than a shed, attached to the castle wall beside the narrow main gate. There were two guards on duty that Eli could see, and they came out to stand at attention only when Josef had cleared the center of the square and was obviously headed their way. The guards wore minimal equipment, just a simple chain jerkin under their uniform jackets and a short sword like the ones at Josef's hips, but they carried their swords like they knew how to use them, which was more than Eli usually expected of gate guards. The men kept their faces blank as Josef approached, but their hands were on their sword hilts when he stopped in front of them.

The older guard gave them a long, disdainful glance. "Business?"

Josef pulled himself straight. "I am Josef Liechten Thereson Eisenlowe, here to answer the queen's bounty."

Eli gritted his teeth. Trust Josef to find the baldest way to say anything. He eased his feet carefully, ready to jump if the soldiers made a move to arrest his idiot swordsman. But, to his surprise, the guards didn't budge.

"Josef, you say?" The older guard looked at his companion, who seemed to be smothering a laugh. "And do you have proof?"

"What proof do I need?" Josef was starting to sound annoyed. "Show me to the queen and that should be proof enough."

This time the younger guard did laugh. "If I had a silver for every time I'd heard that one..."

"We wouldn't be working here," the older guard finished. He grinned and turned back to Josef. "Listen, idiot, the queen doesn't have time to go over every two-bit con who says he's

60

Josef Liechten. If you're going to try and impersonate a long-lost prince—"

"Prince?" Eli said before he could stop himself.

The guard gave him a funny look. "Aye, prince. As I was saying, if you're going to try and impersonate a prince, at least have the decency to clean up a bit. Look at you—knives head to foot, scars, worn boots, you look like a highway bandit." The guard snorted. "At least the last fool who claimed to be Josef Liechten had a crown. That was a nice touch. 'Course, it got all bent when we sent him packing, but you can't complain when you're scamming, can you?"

"But I *am* Josef Liechten," Josef said, his voice tight with anger. He pointed inside the guard box, where his wanted poster was prominently displayed. "Look at the picture."

The guard didn't turn around. "I seen the picture," he said, crossing his arms. "Drawn by some Council hack off the account of some witness who probably didn't witness anything. I've been working at the palace for close to twenty years. I saw the prince plenty of times when he was a boy. He was a handsome lad. I find it frankly insulting, you coming up here saying Queen Theresa's son'd grow into something like you."

Josef took a deep breath. "You won't take me to the queen?"

"No," the guard said. "Now shove off before I do it for you." And with that the guard spat on the ground by Josef's foot.

Josef didn't move. He just stood there with his hands clenched so tight on his swords that his arms were beginning to shake. Beside him, Nico was easing into a fighting stance, preparing to back Josef the second the swordsman moved. It was clear things were about to get bloody, and bloody was not how Eli liked to start his jobs, planned or not. Clearly, it was time to step in.

"Well," he said cheerfully. "I guess that's that."

Nico, Josef, and the two guards all turned to look at him.

Eli gave them a large smile. "Can't fault a fellow for trying, can you, gentlemen?" he said, his voice bright as the noon sun.

"I don't suppose you'd believe I was Eli Monpress, would you?"

The guards stared at him for a moment more, and then they burst into laughter.

"Powers," the older one said, wiping his eyes. "No offense, friend, but you three look like beggars. Monpress is stinking rich. Wasn't even six months ago he robbed Gaol blind, so I hear. You do look like him, though. I'll give you that. 'Cept for the hair, of course." He eyed Eli's blond wig. "Tell you what." The guard reached into his pocket, pulling out a silver coin and tossing it at Eli. "Take this and get out of here. Go get a haircut and some better clothes, and then you come back and try that line again next shift. I'd love to see Wallace handle Eli Monpress at his door, the old stuffed shirt."

"Next shift," Eli said, catching the coin neatly. "I may just do that. What time?"

"Eight o'clock even," the guard said.

"Much obliged," Eli said. With a final, farewell grin, he grabbed Josef's arm and began to steer the swordsman back across the square. "Thank you, gentlemen. You've been exceedingly kind."

The guard waved. "Shove off. And if Wallace guts you later, you got none to blame but yourself."

"I'll bear that in mind," Eli called. "Good afternoon."

The guards started laughing again and walked back into the guard box. Eli kept grinning the whole way across the square. When they were safely out of sight around a building, he dropped the smile and slammed Josef against the wall.

"*Prince?*" he shouted. "You're a prince and you *never told me?*"

Though he could have broken Eli's hold easily, Josef let it stay, leaning in to the wall at his back. "Not anymore."

"Well, your mother's a queen," Eli said. "That sounds like a prince to me."

"Eli." Nico's hand closed on his shoulder. "Stop it. Now. I'm sure Josef had his reasons." She looked at Josef. "Didn't you?"

Josef glowered at them. "Do I need reasons?"

"Oh *come on!*" Eli cried. "What kind of a question is that? I thought we were partners. I thought we were *friends.* How do you just go hiding something like that? Never mind all the times before, how do you justify hiding it when you're bringing us back to your own country to turn yourself in?"

"Because I'm not a prince anymore," Josef growled. "I told you before. And I am your friend. That's why I let you come along."

Eli let his look say exactly what he thought of that logic, and Josef lay back with a deep sigh. "You know what? Never mind. This is all wrong."

Despite his anger, despite how hurt he was, Eli couldn't help laughing at that.

"Of course it's all wrong, idiot," he said, letting Josef go. "You didn't have a plan. You just expected to walk right in and then walk right out. This is what you get for not clueing us in, you know. If you'd just told me what you wanted to do, I could have made a plan that would have had us in your mother's throne room enjoying your embarrassing childhood stories at this very moment."

Josef shook his head. "All right then, Mr. Greatest-Thief-in-the-World, I give up. How would you do it?"

Eli straightened up and casually tossed the silver coin the guard had given him in the air, catching it in his palm. "I thought you'd never ask."

He gave Josef a final I-told-you-so sniff and started down the alley, tossing the coin as he went. Josef pushed himself off the wall with an enormous sigh. "Now I've done it."

"You should have done it days ago," Nico said, crossing her arms.

"Right as usual," Josef said. "Shall we?" He nodded down the alley.

Nico gave him an exasperated look and they started after Eli, walking side by side down the clean-swept alley.

CHAPTER
5

In the stinking swamp that would one day become the richest soil in the Empire, a girl ran through the muck. She ran wildly, arms flailing as she scrambled over clumps of grass and sticky clay. Behind her, men with lanterns were giving chase, the lights bobbing in the dark. The girl was quick and desperate, but the men knew this swamp better than she did. By the time she realized she'd gone the wrong way, they had surrounded her.

She cowered in the mud as their circle tightened. When the men were an arm's length away, the largest held up his lantern to get a good look at her face.

"This is the one," he said. "Gutted the captain proper, she did."

"'Swhat the old coot gets," said another. "Messing around with trash." He grabbed the girl's hair, yanking her up. "Mountain monkeys are for working, not sleeping with."

He spat in her face, and they all began to laugh. The girl hung by her hair, kicking wildly. And then, from nowhere, silver flashed in the lamplight. The man dropped her with a scream to clutch his arm. The girl landed hard and rolled to her feet, brandishing her small knife, its tip bright red.

"Filthy animal!" the man shouted, clutching his bloody arm. "We'll string your carcass up for the birds! Get her!"

The men charged her. The girl lashed out, swinging her knife, but the men were too many, too large. They grabbed her hand and pinched the nerve until her fingers went slack. The knife fell to the ground and was quickly trampled into the mud. She gasped for breath as their hands gripped her throat. The long, cold blades of their machetes pressed against her chest, and the girl realized that she was going to die. She was going to die in this swamp miles from her home. Die under the boots of the slavers with nothing to show for her suffering but an old, dead captain who would probably be replaced with someone even worse. But as despair swallowed her mind, something even deeper suddenly snapped, and her spirit ripped itself open.

Years ago, before the invaders had come, she'd learned spirit talking from the village elder. The old woman always said that spirit talkers may only ask, never demand. To demand was to lose the world's respect, and thus lose everything. But now, with the machetes pressing into her ribs and the fingers crushing her throat, what did she have left to lose?

She reached out with the roar of her open spirit and stabbed her will into the mud. The dirt screamed as she touched it, but her will was absolute, and it had no choice. The blades vanished from her chest as the men were yanked off her. Their laughter turned to terrified screams as the ground beneath their feet turned against them. They flailed as they started to sink, screaming in panic, but the girl dug her now-freed hands into the mud and tightened her grip, snarling as she slammed her will down. The moment it landed, the men vanished into the swamp, the sticky mud closing over their heads without a trace.

The swamp fell suddenly silent, empty except for the droning of distant insects. The girl crouched in the mud, her dark eyes bright in the flickering light of the toppled lanterns until the mud took those, too, and everything fell dark. Sensing its chance, the mud began to buck against her Enslavement. She let it go, staring dumbstruck at the bloody knife in her hand. What had she done? Killing the captain had been bad enough, but now she'd killed the foremen as well. They would slaughter the camp for this. They would find her and kill her, kill her brothers, kill her people, all to make an example for the other camps. They would all die and it would be her fault.

Bleak despair filled her mind, drowning out even her panic, and she began to weep. The sobs shook her until her bones ached, but the more she cried, the worse she felt. There was no escape, no hope. Nothing.

Finally, her crying subsided, and she realized something was different. The swamp was silent. Not just night silence, true silence. There was no rustle of water, no insects chirping. Even the gentle wind had stopped. Her body went tense, and the girl edged her head up, peeking cautiously through her tangled hair. The dark swamp was bright as noon, but that was impossible. Dawn was still hours away, and in any case, this was no golden daylight. The light was white, stark, and cold as fresh snow. She would have called it moonlight, but no moon had ever shone this bright. She raised her head to stare, and that was when she caught sight of a woman's white foot resting delicately on the surface of the swamp.

The girl jumped and scrambled back. The woman stood less than a foot away. She was naked, her skin flawless and alabaster white. White hair fell in a cascade across her white shoulders, and her white eyes were sparkling as she looked down at the muddy girl at her feet.

Hello—the woman's voice was like cold silk—*Nara*.

"How do you know my name?"

The question was out before the girl could stop it. Nara was her tribe name. Ever since the invaders took them to the camps, she'd shared it with no one. She should be furious that this woman, this obvious outsider, knew it, but she could not be angry with her. The woman was simply too beautiful.

The White Lady knelt, and Nara couldn't help noticing that the mud did not smudge her perfect skin. The woman extended her hand, cupping Nara's dirty cheek in a burning grip.

I know everything about you, the woman said. *I am your Shepherdess. I have been watching you since you were born. You are a brave girl, Nara. Brave and beautiful.* The white fingers stroked her cheek, leaving burning trails that made Nara tremble. *So beautiful. More beautiful than anything else I've created.*

"Created?" Nara whispered, the word little more than a feathered breath.

Well, the Lady spoke and smirked, as though this were some long-standing joke, *not fully. I am not the Creator. But I shaped you, you and all humans, in my image.* Her beautiful face fell. *For all that, you always were ugly, ridiculous creatures, fitting*

66

for the ugly job I made you to do. Even so, every now and then I catch a glimmer of something more. The fingers slid down to brush Nara's lips. *Like you. You are beautiful, Nara. From the moment I saw you, I knew I had to have you. Knew that you and you alone of all the ugly, blind humans were worthy of being my star.*

Nara's eyes widened as the White Lady leaned down and pressed a burning kiss to her lips. It was the briefest touch, but the proximity alone was enough to send her reeling. Still, Nara had never been quick to trust, and, though it went against every instinct she had, she pulled away, putting space between her and the woman who called herself Shepherdess.

"Your star?" she said with as much strength as she could muster. "And what is that?"

The White Lady looked at her with a smirk. *My servant.*

Nara scowled. "I'm done being a servant."

I am not like your human masters. The Lady laughed. *Those deaf sacks of meat. I am Benehime, a Power of creation. I am the Shepherdess, all spirits serve me. But my stars are different. They are raised above all others, and answer only to me. As my star, there will be no want you can think of that I cannot provide. No wish I cannot grant.*

"Any wish?" Nara said, her throat dry.

Anything at all, the Shepherdess answered, spreading her arms. *All you have to do is worship me. Fear me. Obey me. Love me more than any other. Become my star, beautiful girl, and whatever you desire will be yours.*

She must have seen the hunger in Nara's eyes, for the White Lady smiled. *You have a wish, don't you? Speak it.*

Nara had never told her wish to anyone, but it came tumbling from her lips before she could think of denying the White Lady.

"I've been a slave for ten years," she whispered. "I and my people and all the peoples I met when I was a child, we all were made slaves when the invaders came because we could not fight back. They crushed the spirits of the forest and forced the stone to vomit its riches into the mines. The Enslavers

67

turned our lakes into swamps and our mountains into open pits that we were forced to work. But that's how the world is. The strong step on the weak, and the weak can do nothing but weep. I want to change that. You said you could give me anything I wish—that's it. I want to stop the cycle of war and Enslavement. Can you give me that?"

The White Lady's face broke into a brilliant smile. *So noble,* she said, running her white fingers through Nara's dark, tangled hair. *So determined. I like you even better now, little darling. You might even become my favorite if you keep it up.*

"So you can grant my wish?" Nara said.

The Shepherdess leaned back a bit, her lovely white mouth pursed as she made a show of thinking about it.

I won't just give it to you, she said at last. *That would be no fun. But I will give you the power to take it for yourself.* She leaned in until her lips were a breath away from Nara's own. *I will give you power unlike anything you have ever seen. You will bear my mark, speak in my name. I will give you dominion over all spirits great and small and the life span to see your wish come true.*

Nara's stomach clenched. She still wasn't sure if this was a dream or not, but the Shepherdess was there in front of her, white and cold and more beautiful than anything her mind could make up. And in that realization, she knew her answer.

"If you give me the power to make the world what it should be," she said, trembling at the beautiful woman's closeness, "I will love you above all others until the day I die."

Though the shameful truth was, Nara already did. The woman was so beautiful, so powerful, Nara was already lost. But the Lady expected a wish, and Nara would give it to her. She would give her anything, Nara realized with a sinking feeling, and from the look on the Lady's face, the Shepherdess knew it.

The White Lady smiled and leaned in to kiss Nara gently on the lips. It was a bare brush, but the connection that opened between them nearly made Nara faint. Power burned through her, pouring into the well of her soul until she feared she would burst. Light seared her body from the inside out, burning her away until Nara was sure that she had died and her spirit simply hadn't realized it yet. And then it was over. The Shepherdess pulled away, catching Nara's falling body in her arms.

It is done, she whispered, cuddling the girl to her chest like a kitten. *You bear my mark forever, now. You are mine, mine alone.*

"Yours alone," Nara said, looking up into the Lady's white eyes. Eyes she now knew as well as her own. The white fire was still burning through her as tears rolled down her cheeks. "I will love you forever," she swore, leaning into the Lady's embrace. "Forever and ever, beautiful, beloved Benehime."

The Shepherdess laughed in delight as Nara said her name. She stood, taking the girl up with her. As they rose, the dirt fell reverently away, leaving Nara clean and perfect in the Shepherdess's glory. A white slit opened in the air in front of them, and Benehime carried her through, away from the swamp, away from the mud and the pain of slavery, into a perfect, white world.

When the sun rose the next morning on the slave camp, an unknown woman in golden armor carrying a gleaming sword strode into the master's tent and began killing the officers. She killed them quickly and efficiently, leaving only one alive to bring the word of what had happened to the other camps. After she'd sent him running, the woman turned to the buildings that held the cowering slaves. The stones barring the doors rolled away at the barest touch of her will, desperate to do what she ordered, for the mark of the Shepherdess was plain on her soul. The people cried in fear as the doors opened, but the woman held up her hand for silence. When the silence came, she told them they were free. Some of the people fainted, some ran in terror, but others raised their arms in praise, swearing their lives to the woman who'd won their freedom.

This was the Immortal Empress's first conquest.

Eight hundred years later, the Immortal Empress treasured this memory. By the time she'd conquered her first kingdom,

Benehime had named her favorite, the soul beloved by the Shepherdess above all others. Many joys had followed in the centuries after, but that first night was still dearest in Nara's heart. Even now, the smell of mud brought a dreamy smile to her face.

"Empress?"

Nara opened her eyes and turned to face her commander. The old man winced, but he did not shrink back. He had been her general for many years before she'd vanished, and he knew her well. Now, however, he looked as though he had something to say, and so, regretfully, she let the memory go and returned to the bitter present.

"Report."

"Empress," the man said again, bowing. "Your return could not have come at a better time. The storm has been blowing for weeks now without weakening. Tidal waves have devastated your southern coast. Those who survived the initial flood escaped to higher ground, but they are now stranded and running low on food. I ordered your army to aid in the evacuation, but the storm is too dangerous. Now that you are with us again, however, I am sure—"

He fell silent as the Empress stepped up to the edge of the balcony. They were standing on the observation tower of her southern-most fortress, the one she'd left to remind the desert tribes who had conquered them. That was two hundred years ago now, but the fort was still one of her largest. From its tower, she could see clear across the sandy desert to the coast, miles away, but even if she'd been on the ground, she couldn't have missed the storm. It loomed off the edge of her continent's southern coast, a wall of black clouds and forked lightning stretching as far as she could see in any direction. Great winds blew in the smell of rain and sodden mud, and though the smell triggered her memories again, Nara did not smile. The storm chewed at the edge of her lands, destroying everything in its path beneath a rain of lightning and the endless booming thunder she knew too well.

The Empress shook her head. "I cannot banish this storm."

The general's eyes widened. "But surely," he began. "You are queen of everything. The spirits would not dare—"

"You question me?" the Empress said coldly.

The general froze. "No, Empress," he said, bowing so low that his helmet slipped off. "Forgive me, Empress. Your voice is the only law."

She nodded and held out her hand, letting the storm-tossed winds sweep over her fingers. When she felt a particularly strong one, she closed her fist. The wind squealed at first but grew still when it realized what will had caught it.

"Hail, Empress," it whispered.

Nara glanced pointedly at the enormous storm. "What is *he* doing here?"

"The Lord of Storm is in disgrace," the wind said, wiggling in her hand.

"I can see that," the Empress snapped. "He's been in disgrace for weeks, apparently, and wrecking my shore in the process. What did he do that Benehime would impose such a harsh punishment?"

The wind jerked. Lesser spirits were so obedient that even the mention of the Lady's name was enough to send them into a fit of reverential terror.

"He raised his blade against the favorite," it whispered at last. "The Shepherdess's wrath was swift."

White-hot fury roared through Nara's mind and, for a moment, she forgot everything. Forgot the storm, the general standing beside her, even the wind in her hand. Time seemed to flow backward, carrying her back to that hated day when everything in her life had fallen apart. The day the Shepherdess brought that boy into her white world.

She could see him clearly in her mind even now, a skinny, dark-haired thing sitting smugly on Benehime's beautiful lap as the Lady doted on him. The memory made Nara tremble with rage. That spoiled brat had stolen the Shepherdess's love from her, and with it everything Nara cared for. All the things that had given her pride—her victories, her legions, her unified

71

country, the fairness and efficiency of the government she had built, the peace she had brought to her people, her loyal spirits, even her great wish of a fair and peaceful world—none of it meant *anything* when Benehime, her beautiful, beloved Shepherdess, was ignoring her in favor of that hateful, conniving, selfish child.

Nara bared her teeth at the enormous waves washing over the ruins of her sea towns. How could the Shepherdess love that brat enough to punish the Lord of Storms this severely just for raising his blade? He'd raised his sword to Nara several times, and the Lady had never done anything like this. Was she finally sick of his disobedience? Or was it because she loved the boy more than—

The Empress stopped that line of thought dead. She could not believe it. The Lady's love was for Nara alone. The boy was nothing more than an infatuation. He'd beguiled the Shepherdess. What else would explain Benehime's abandoning her Empress after eight centuries of Nara's ceaseless devotion? Her undying love? Nara clenched her fists. Den had been right. For eleven years she'd lived in her misery, waiting for the Shepherdess to remember who truly loved her, and all she had to show for it was the suffering of her own lands. She was through hiding, through crying. If the Lady loved her as an Empress, then Empress she would be. She would rebuild her army as never before. An army fit to conquer the rest of the world. And when all the lands of creation were united under her good rule, her wish would be fulfilled. She alone would rule a world without war, without unfairness, a world that was guided by her wisdom alone. And then Nara would take this perfect world and throw it at the Lady's feet. There, she would say, who is your favorite now?

Just the thought of it brought the smile back to Nara's lips. With such a grand offering, the Shepherdess would have no choice. She would cast the thief aside and return to her true favorite. Benehime would take Nara in her beautiful embrace once again, and together they would laugh at the memory of the boy called Eli, when they thought of him at all.

She was still savoring that thought when a high-pitched squeal brought her back to the present. The wind was writhing in her clenched hand. The Empress eased her grip, letting the wind slide gratefully through her fingers.

"Go to my war palace at Istalirin," she said. "See if Den has arrived yet."

"Yes, Empress," the wind panted, flitting gladly away.

Nara nodded and turned to deal with the mess the Lord of Storms had made. Without a word of warning to her general, she walked to the edge of the balcony and jumped off. The desert winds caught her fall, setting her down gently on the fortress's stone yard. The soldiers dropped to their knees when they saw her, pressing their heads to the ground in reverence. She ignored them, focusing instead on the stone beneath her golden boots.

"You," she said, stomping on the ground. "Wake up."

The stone rumbled as it woke, and then lowered itself in obedience.

"Yes, Empress?"

"Form a wall along the coast. This storm is no concern of ours. We will protect our borders and wait it out."

"Yes, Empress," the stone said again.

The Empress nodded and slammed her foot on the ground a second time. The stone obeyed instantly, and a pillar of rock shot up beneath her feet, lifting her back to the edge of the watchtower balcony. Her general ran forward to help her over the railing. When her footing was solid again, she turned to watch as the bedrock spirit followed her orders.

All along her coast, a great wall of stone exploded out of the sandy beach, forming a barrier between the water and the land. The stone wall ran as far as she could see, following the snaking coastline until her continent's entire southern tip was cut off, safe from the storm surge behind a fifty-foot barrier.

Nodding in approval, the Empress turned back to the waiting wind, who had just returned from the north.

"Den has arrived," the wind said. "He's demanding to see you."

"He would," the Empress sneered. "Well done. You are released."

The wind bowed and fled, vanishing into the clear, desert sky.

"General," Nara said, turning to face the old man who was still bowing in reverence. "You will leave five hundred men here to resettle those misplaced by the storm. The rest of your army will march to my war palace at Istalirin. I want everything: support, supplies, siege troops, the full panalopy. March them hard, I want my armies gathered by dark tomorrow."

The old man paled. Istalirin was miles away. Such a deadline, even on the Empire's awakened roads, would be nigh impossible. But the Immortal Empress expected the impossible from all her subjects as a matter of course, and her general knew better than to complain.

"Yes, Empress," he said, bowing lower than ever. "Is it war then?"

"War indeed," the Empress said. "It is time at last to bring the entire world into the light of my Empire." And to show Benehime who was truly worthy of her love.

The general eyed her nervously. "Permission to speak, Empress."

"Granted," the Empress said.

"Your army marches wherever you command," he said. "But the man Den is not to be trusted. While you were gone, he did nothing but wander your Empire, terrorizing your towns and challenging every strong fighter he could find. We lost several of your best to him. He has no discipline or loyalty, and he does not follow orders. You are the chosen of the land, Empress, and I would never question your judgment, but can such a man truly be a servant of the Empire?"

"No," the Empress said. "Den is a traitor. He betrayed his homeland to join our invasion as soon as the tide turned. He is a monster who thrives on conflict with no loyalty to anything but his own lust for battle. I know full well that he will never be my soldier, but I do not need another soldier, general." She looked

74

west. "Soldiers I have in plenty, but the other half of this world is a barbarous, uncivilized, lawless place. If I am to bring such lands into my enlightened peace, soldiers won't be enough. If my control is to be complete, I must conquer swiftly, completely. We must devour their land before they realize they have lost it, and for that, I need a monster." She turned and smiled at her general. "Have no fear, this is the last war. When we are done, the whole world will be under my law, and there will be no more need for monsters. If Den is still alive when we reach that glorious end, I will see that he meets a monster's death."

The general bowed, his eyes shining. "As you command, Empress. Your soldiers march for Istalirin and the endless glory of your Empire."

"As they should," she said. "I will expect you there."

With that, she waved her hand, and a white line appeared in the air, twisting open to reveal the ornate map room of her war palace. Her officers stopped what they were doing and stood at attention as she stepped through the hole in the world. They murmured praises in her name, but the Empress paid them no mind. She marched straight past the table to the great window and looked out over the bay.

All she saw was ships. Her fleet spread to the horizon, her palace ships filled the great bay of Istalirin until no glimpse of water was visible between the hulls. Pride welled up in her chest. Twenty-six years ago, when she was the favorite and the world was as it should be, she'd sent a handful of ships to test the strength of the other half of the world. They'd returned defeated, but that was to be expected. She'd conquered close to a hundred countries since becoming Empress, and she'd learned early to use a small force to sound out the enemy's strengths before attacking in earnest. What had surprised her were her generals' reports of the enemy's ability to talk across distance. That had caught her for a moment, but the counter proved easy. If they could gossip about her movements and pile all their troops to meet her at full strength wherever she hit, then she would simply build so many ships that such a small advantage wouldn't matter.

The Empress enjoyed such simple, effective plans, but even for her, it took time to raise that large a force. But again, she was the Immortal Empress; time wasn't an issue. As soon as she'd heard her defeated generals' report, she'd put her ship-yards to work and sat back to wait. For eleven years, everything went as planned. But then, just as her army was nearing completion, the boy had appeared and ruined everything.

Nara took a deep, shamed breath. When the boy first took Benehime away from her, she'd gone a little mad. She'd abandoned her lands, abandoned her nearly finished fleet, abandoned her people, abandoned her wish to hide in a cave like an animal. Fifteen years she'd lost to worthless misery, and then to be rescued by Den, of all people. It was her greatest shame. One she meant to undo with the fleet that lay before her.

Satisfied, the Empress turned away from the window and took her place at the head of the table as her generals began to arrange the battle maps for her inspection. As the papers were laid in place, she spotted Den himself entering the war room. Her officers stiffened visibly as he stepped up to the table, but Nara motioned for him to stand beside her. Mindless of the great honor, Den walked up and sat on the table by her elbow, his hard face sullen and bored.

"I'm here," he said. "Can we go?"

"Soon," Nara promised, nodding for her generals to begin their presentations.

Den sneered and walked over to the window overlooking the bay. As the generals began to speak, Den paid them no attention. His eyes never left the ships, and he stared at them with the ardor of someone witnessing the birth of his heart's desire. That look alone set Nara's mind at ease. Confident that her monster would be loyal for now, she turned to hear the greatest military minds of her Empire outline their plans to crush all who stood in her way.

Just beyond the bay at Istalirin, at the outskirts of the Empress's control, an enormous wind flew over the growing fleet. It blew through every ship, taking note not only of the mountainous hulls and cavernous crew quarters but of the great war spirits that slept deep in the ships' bellies. The wind looked as long as it dared, skirting the edge of the Empress's awareness. When it had seen enough, the wind turned west, flying as fast as it could back to its lord who waited on the far western edge of the world.

Far across the Unseen Sea, Tesset sat on the plush window seat in the Merchant Prince of Zarin's office, watching his employer pace a rut into the fine silk rug.

"Whitefall's an idiot if he thinks this is going to work," Sara muttered around the pipe she clenched between her teeth. "Compromises don't work with men like Banage."

"It's my impression that he doesn't have much choice," Tesset said. "Council and Court must stand together or face mutual destruction."

"Which is exactly why it won't work," Sara said, walking faster. "Mutual destruction loses its teeth when one party is willing to die for his beliefs."

Tesset leaned against the window. "If the Merchant Prince is showing any lack of judgment, Sara, it's not trying to compromise with Banage, but inviting you to attend."

Sara shot him a look that would have frozen the Whitefall River. Tesset settled his shoulders against the cool glass and stared back.

"There's no point in leaving me out of things," she said, resuming her pacing. "Whitefall may fancy himself the shadow king of the world, but this is as much my Council as it is his. He can't make a decision involving wizard matters without my say-so, and Banage knows it. Etmon won't agree to anything without me there for him to gloat over." She puffed on her pipe, adding more smoke to the haze that already filled the room. "This is ridiculous. I got back from the desert not an hour ago. I don't have time for this farce. Not if Alber wants his miracle, anyway."

Tesset started to comment, but a soft sound outside the door caught his attention. "Well," he said, "here's your chance to tell him so yourself."

The words were scarcely out of his mouth when the door opened and Alber Whitefall swept into the room. He was dressed in full regalia, with the white suit and golden medals of the Merchant Prince of Zarin as well as the maroon sash of the Council of Thrones, which the prince's valet was still attempting to tie as he followed his harried master through the doorway.

Tesset smiled approvingly. A clever move, playing to Banage's pride by greeting him with full honors as an equal. But Whitefall was a subtle, clever man, and Tesset never got tired of watching him maneuver. Pity he was spirit deaf. With the right training, he could have made a dangerous fighter.

"Banage is on his way," Whitefall said, holding out his arm so the valet could fasten his cufflinks. "Remember, let me do the talking. If you antagonize him, he'll just leave."

"It's what he's going to do anyway," Sara said, blowing an enormous puff of smoke at the ceiling.

Whitefall smiled. "We'll see. Our dear Rector is about to run out of options."

Sara eyed him curiously, but the Merchant Prince's face was all politeness as he glanced at the enormous clock on the wall. "Time to take our places."

He turned and walked out of the room, valet trailing in his wake. Sara followed, handing her pipe to Tesset, who tamped it out and placed it carefully in his pocket.

They walked through the citadel and into the large room at its heart, the Council Hearing Chamber. The chamber was empty this late in the evening, and Tesset got the feeling Whitefall had planned it that way. Another clever move. He was robbing Banage of his audience, hoping that the lack of witnesses would help the Rector compromise his principles. Tesset wasn't sure if that hope would pan out, but Whitefall was wise to seize whatever advantage he could.

They took their places, Whitefall at the head table, Sara beside him with Tesset standing at her back. Moments after the valet had finished pinning the final length of gold braid to Whitefall's shoulder, the doors at the opposite end of the chamber opened and Banage swept in. The Rector was in full regalia as well, the red robes of his order smothered beneath the heavy chain of his office. The enormous rings on his fingers glowed brighter than the lamps on the walls as he strode proudly across the polished marble to the table that had been prepared for him, but he did not sit. Instead, he stood, hands crossed at his waist, and waited.

Tesset bit back a smile. Banage had come ready to fight. This might prove more interesting than he'd hoped. For a moment, the two parties simply stared at each other, and then Whitefall made an almost imperceptible gesture with his fingers. The servants took their cue, closing the chamber door with a soft crack, leaving the three most powerful people in Zarin alone.

"So," Whitefall began politely. "Would it be a waste of my breath to ask you to sit?"

"It would," Banage answered, his blue eyes flicking from Sara to the Merchant Prince. "Let's not dance about, Whitefall. What do you want?"

"It's less what *I* want and more what *we* need, Banage," Whitefall said, lacing his fingers together. "I'm sure you've heard by now, but I'll tell you formally: War is coming. Twenty-six years after we drove her fleet back to the ocean, the Immortal Empress is on the move again, and we have precious little time. If our continent is to survive this assault, we must stand together. All of us. Even you."

Banage's eyes narrowed. "The Spirit Court is a peaceful organization dedicated to the protection of the spirit world. We do not go to war."

"And I am head of a trade coalition dedicated to beneficial coexistence and mutual profit," Whitefall said with a shrug. "These are times of extraordinary threat. We must all reach outside our normal parameters."

"And you're demanding my help?" Banage sneered.

"I'm asking for it, yes," Whitefall said. "I'm *asking* for everyone's help." He leaned forward, cool affection gone. He was staring earnestly at the Rector Spiritualis, and when he spoke again, his voice was full of real emotion. "I shouldn't have to explain this to you, Etmon. You fought with us in the last war against the Empress, you know how bad things could get. We may never have seen eye to eye on everything, but I know you care about what we've built. This war could destroy all of that—the Council, the Spirit Court, everything. The Empress isn't coming to expand her borders or seek a treaty. She's coming to conquer. If we're going to stop her, we must find a way to work together."

He ended with his hands on the table, eyes locked on Banage. On his side of the room, the Rector Spiritualis sighed.

"I understand what you're saying, Alber," he said quietly. "But the Spirit Court is not a political organization. We have worked together with the Council many times to our mutual benefit, but war is different. We serve the spirits, the land itself, and the land does not care who rules it. I cannot ask my Spiritualists to violate their oaths and put their spirits in danger to defend your borders."

"This isn't about borders," Whitefall said, his voice growing heated. "Do you think the Immortal Empress is going to let the Spirit Court continue to operate? You were with Sara and me on the beach at Osera when her wizards dropped their flaming war spirits on our heads. Do you think a woman who uses that kind of force is going to sit back and let you keep running your towers as you see fit?"

Banage lifted his chin. "Perhaps."

"*Perhaps?*" Whitefall repeated sharply. "That wasn't how you felt last time."

"It is because I fought then that I cannot ask my wizards to fight now," Banage said. "How many times must I say it? Our duty is to our spirits, not your Council. Our oaths are built on a trust deeper than anything your spirit-deaf mind can imagine. I lost two spirits in the war with the Empress. I will not make my Spiritualists go through that pain as well."

"We all lost friends in the war," Whitefall said. "I lost an entire legion in one night alone when Den the Traitor turned against us. Every single one of those men had a soul, had a mother, had a family. Are you saying your spirits' lives were worth more than theirs?"

"Men fight for countries," Banage said. "They choose to risk death in the name of their cause. But spirits have no countries or causes. This is their world, we are the interlopers. We have no right to drag them from their sleep into our petty conflicts. You are a leader of men, Alber. It is right for you to be concerned with their struggles. But I am a custodian of the Spirit World. If I compromised that position for human interests, I would be unworthy of the name Spiritualist."

Whitefall heaved an enormous sigh and collapsed back into his chair. "What will it take, Etmon? What can I do to bring you over?"

Banage tilted his head, and his eyes took on a gleam that Tesset knew well. He'd seen it on every fighter: the look that came just before the finishing blow.

"The Spirit Court exists to ensure the greatest good for all spirits," Banage said. "I was very young when we first fought the Empress, and I thought, as young people do, that the enemy was evil because she was our enemy. That we were right and she was wrong. But I am no longer young or naive, and I'm no longer sure that I am on the right side."

"That is very close to treason," Sara said, but she fell silent when Whitefall put out his hand.

"We are the right side, Banage," Whitefall said earnestly.

"Are you?" Banage said, his eyes flicking to Sara. "Then why does the Council hide its business with spirits down in its bowels? Why is its head wizard allowed to do as she pleases without Spirit Court oversight?"

Sara shot up from her seat. "I knew it!" she shouted. "I knew this was all just a ploy to—"

"Sara!" Whitefall's voice echoed through the chamber.

Sara flinched and shut her mouth. Across the room, Banage looked positively triumphant. Whitefall, on the other hand, looked dogged.

"Sara's achievements support the Council," the Merchant Prince said, picking his words carefully. "The Relay is what keeps the countries tied together. It's what makes them *need* us. Therefore, we need her, and she needs the freedom to innovate."

"Then it's time to weigh which need is greater," Banage said, crossing his arms. "Sara's secrecy or my Court. I know you are a man who plays with words, Alber, so I will say this as plain as possible. If you want our help, you must change your ways. I will lead the Court toward whatever end supports its purpose. Black as you paint the Empress, her crimes against the spirits are as yet only possibilities. Sara's crimes are far closer to home. You need my Court? Prove you are worthy of it. Tear down the wall of secrecy Sara has built. Allow my people to inspect the Relay and all other works of Council wizardry, and swear to fix whatever abuses we find. Show the Spirit Court that you deserve our loyalty, and we will follow the Council wherever you need us."

Sara's face was scarlet with rage as Banage finished, yet she said nothing. Tesset could see why. Whitefall's hand was at her wrist, his long fingers pressed into the pressure point. The Merchant Prince was calm, his eyes half lidded as they regarded Banage. Tesset leaned back, watching the old man with interest. When Whitefall had nearly lost his temper earlier, Tesset had been worried he'd misjudged the man. Now he saw with satisfaction that the earlier bluster had been a feint, a ruse to draw out Banage's real objective just as a swordsman feigns injury to trick his enemy into revealing his finishing strike. But now that he knew what Banage really wanted, Whitefall didn't seem quite sure what to do with it. Tesset watched him carefully, waiting to see how he would counter. However, when the Merchant Prince finally did answer, even Tesset didn't see the blow coming.

"I'm afraid you leave me no choice," Whitefall said, drawing a folded piece of paper out of his pocket. "Give this to him."

Tesset stepped forward and took the paper. He walked across the chamber to Banage, who accepted the note with a suspicious glare before dropping his eyes to read.

"What is this?" he asked as Tesset returned to his position behind Sara.

"It's a conscription notice," Whitefall answered.

"*Conscription?*" Banage roared. "What is the meaning of this?"

"You've put me in a bind," Whitefall said, his voice growing cold and sharp. "I would like nothing more than to throw open the Council and let the Spirit Court scour every inch of it, but I don't even need to ask to know Sara's response. You know as well as I do that her word is final when it comes to Council wizardry, and yet you bring me this impossible request. If I didn't know better, I'd think you wanted this to fail."

Banage stiffened. "I want only what I have always wanted," he said. "Humane treatment for all spirits. If you will not let my Spiritualists inspect the Council's practices, then I no longer have suspicions. I now *know* that the Council of Thrones is abusing spirits, and you can't possibly think I would ally my Court with such a shameful organization."

"Be that as it may," Whitefall said. "Take a closer look at that paper in your hand. Like it or not, every member of your order is also a citizen of this 'shameful organization,' and it is my right, as written under section three of the Council edict, to order citizens of the Council to war for our mutual defense. If you and your wizards do not comply in full, then, by Council law, I have no choice but to declare you traitors."

Banage's face grew very pale, and Whitefall leaned forward. "Don't be a fool, Etmon," he hissed. "It doesn't have to be like this. Join me willingly and I will do everything I can to keep your spirits from harm. I swear it."

Banage looked the Merchant Prince directly in the eye, but he did not speak. Instead, he raised the conscription notice in the air between them and ripped it cleanly in two.

Whitefall watched tight lipped as the torn paper fluttered to the polished floor. "You realize you've just committed treason."

"One cannot commit treason against an authority he is not part of," Banage answered. "The Spirit Court was doing its duty centuries before you even imagined the Council of Thrones. We do not answer to you."

Whitefall let out a tight sigh. "As you like," he said. "Tesset, arrest the traitor."

Tesset stepped out onto the smooth marble, watching Banage warily as the attack played out in his head. The tall Rector had reach on him, but the man was not a hand-to-hand fighter. The hardest part would be taking him down before he could call his spirits. Quick jab to the stomach should be enough. Decision made, Tesset dropped and began to run. But fast as he was, Banage was faster. Just before his fist landed, a wall of wind sent Tesset flying.

He turned in the air and landed on the Merchant Prince's table, catching an ink pot just before it blew into Sara's face. Across the room, Banage stood in the center of a small tornado, his robes flying like flags.

"Keril," the Rector said, and the pale blue stone on his index finger flashed like a small sun. The wind intensified, forcing Tesset to a crouch as he shielded Whitefall and Sara.

Tesset squinted against the wind. Banage was moving his other hand now, bringing a green cabochon of glowing jade to his lips.

"Duesset," he said, his deep voice clear over the roar of the wind.

The entire hearing chamber rang like a bell, and then, with a roar that cracked the windows, an enormous creature exploded through the stone floor. Tesset's eyes widened. It looked like a warhorse carved from jade, but it was larger than any horse Tesset had ever seen. The creature lowered its head, and its stone mane fell into easy steps for the Rector to climb onto its back.

Banage looked down on Sara, Tesset, and Whitefall from the creature's back, his face a stone mask.

"I am the voice of the Spirit Court," he announced, his words booming through the room. "I speak for us all, and I say this: The Spirit Court exists for the spirits. Just as we will never allow them to be coerced, so shall we never allow ourselves to be ordered to war by an outside authority. Fight the Empress with your own blood, Alber, for you shall have none of ours."

With that, the wind gave one final howl, shattering the large glass windows that looked out over the city. As the glass fell, the stone horse leaped, carrying Banage through the broken window. It landed with a crash in the courtyard below, but when Tesset ran forward, all he saw was a crater in the paving stones and the flick of the jade horse's tail as it charged the citadel gate. The iron bars crumpled like paper as the creature galloped through them, its stone feet striking the cobbles like smithy hammers on new iron as it vanished down the street and into the city below.

"Well," Whitefall said, pulling himself up. "That could have gone better."

"Could it?" Sara said, reaching out her hands for Tesset to help her up. "How many times have I told you? You can't speak sense to Banage. The nerve of that man, forcing his morals on the whole world. Spiritualists poking their noses into my workshop, can you imagine?" She shook her head. "You were right to turn him down, Alber. If they discovered the truth of the Relay, we'd have a full-out rebellion on our hands."

"I'm not sure we won't as it is," Whitefall said, his voice tired. "But I had hoped to avoid breaking the Court."

"It was already broken," Sara said with a sniff. "Banage is a fanatic. There's no place for him in an order as old and vested in its power as the Spirit Court. Forcing him to reject conscription was the best thing you could have done. Some of the old guard will stick to Banage's banner of high morality, but the majority of Spiritualists won't risk treason just to keep their hands clean, especially not when they can say they were only fighting for their country."

Tesset had to agree. In one move, Whitefall had taken Banage's ultimatum and turned it around, forcing the Rector Spiritualis into the weakest position possible. If the Merchant Prince had simply let him leave the first time he refused, or worse, threatened him with force, Banage could have stood on his principles, turning himself and his supporters into moralistic objectors. But with the conscription notice, Whitefall had backed Banage up against his own ultimatum. He could no longer stay aloof. It was give in and go with the Council as a conscript or be declared a traitor. Of course, Banage had still refused, but in refusing he'd doomed his own chances at keeping the lion's share of the Court. After all, while there were plenty of Spiritualists who would have jumped at the chance to avoid the war by siding with their Rector, only the true fanatics would be willing to be branded traitor for him. Tesset grinned. He loved a good turn-about.

"Get the message out to your contacts among the Tower Keepers, Sara," Whitefall said. "The Council will welcome any Spiritualists who wish to fight for their homes. Those who join Banage will be declared traitors, and their property and lands will be seized."

"Consider it done," Sara said. "But what are you going to do about Etmon? He'll only muck things up if you leave him to run loose."

"I don't think you'll have to worry about that," Tesset said, glancing out the crashed window. "Look."

Across the city, the Spirit Court's tower was moving. The white stone walls, clearly visible even at this distance, rippled like water. Windows vanished beneath a wave of stone, and the great red doors of the Tower fell like trees as they watched, crashing to the ground as the entrances they guarded vanished beneath a wall of stone. One by one, every escape to the outside world vanished beneath the rippling white stone until the Tower was completely sealed, an impenetrable, unblemished spire of pure white.

"Well," Sara said softly. "I suppose that takes care of that."

"What was that?" Whitefall said.

Sara held out her hand and Tesset handed her her pipe. "Banage's sealed the Tower," she said, tapping a measure of fresh tobacco into the bowl. "Took his toys and went home. Typical." She made a scornful face as she lit her pipe and took a long draw. "If you're done with me, Alber, I'm going to get those messages out before Banage can convince the Spiritualists they're being persecuted. The last thing we need is a bunch of self-righteous wizards fighting us instead of the Empress."

Whitefall nodded, still staring. Sara turned on her heel and marched out of the room. Tesset fell into step behind her, still smiling. Whitefall watched the sealed Tower a moment longer, and then, shaking his head, he walked to the door and called the servants in to start cleaning up the mess Banage had made of his hearing chamber.

CHAPTER
6

Five hours after their failed frontal assault, Eli had everything he needed to get them into the castle. Business finished, they were now sitting at a tucked away table in one of the large inns overlooking the palace square, washed, dressed, fed, and killing the last hour before the guard change with a few hands of Daggerback. Josef was winning, which might have been the only reason he was still at the table.

"I don't understand why you wasted your money," Josef grumbled, picking up his cards as fast as Eli dealt them. "There's no point. I told you, we're just going to leave."

Eli pursed his lips as he turned over his bid card, a knight. "It wasn't a waste," he said. "We have to look at you, too, you know. And the guard was right. You were starting to come off a bit terrifying."

Josef made a *harrumphing* noise, and Eli grinned. Despite the swordsman's scowl, he was looking very well. They'd found a barber to cut his hair and give him a proper shave, and while nothing could be done about his scars, Josef had looked almost civilized when he got out of the chair. Eli had also bought him a new shirt, a white one, with no bloodstains or suspicious holes, as well as some nonpatched trousers. Small changes, really, but the overall effect was a wonder. With a pressed shirt, blond hair cut short and neat, and his chin shaved clean, Eli could almost believe that the man sitting across the table really was a prince. Provided, of course, he looked past the belts of blades Josef refused to take off.

"Five to open," Eli said, tossing his coins on the table. "Stop complaining, you look lovely. Nico thinks so, too. Don't you, Nico?"

Nico jumped and peeked over her cards. "He looks nice," she said, placing her ante next to Eli's. "But he looked nice before, too."

Josef gave Eli a "there, you see" smirk as he dropped his money onto the pile.

"There's nice that's fit for gutting people and nice that's fit for palaces," Eli said pointedly. "Besides, boys shouldn't visit their mothers in shirts that have stab holes, or with hair that looks like he cuts it with a throwing knife."

"Skinning knife," Josef corrected. "I use my skinning knife."

"Moving on," Eli said. "We are all agreed that you look quite well now. Looking well is universally useful, so the money wasn't wasted. I bet two."

Josef slapped two coins on the table without looking up. "Match."

Nico glanced at Josef, then at Eli. "Fold."

"One down," Eli said, grinning as Nico lay her cards on the table. "Two again."

Josef matched his bet with a nasty look. They went back and forth for another minute, trading coins until the pile was quite impressive. Finally, Eli called it, and they showed their hands. Josef won with a pair of kings. He scooped up the money with a satisfied smile while Eli watched glumly. When it was all gone, the thief stood with a resigned sigh.

"I think I've lost enough for one day," he said. "Josef, since you have all our gold at the moment, would you settle the tab?"

"Since it's your money, sure."

Josef set the Heart in the corner and made his way to the bar. When he was gone, Nico turned to Eli.

"Why did you keep betting?" she asked quietly. "You knew he had a better hand."

"That I did," Eli said. "But there's more to the game than gold, and Josef's always in a better mood when he wins."

He gave Nico a brilliant smile as he grabbed his bag and made his way toward the back door. Nico watched him with a puzzled expression until Josef returned.

The swordsman paused. "What?"

"Nothing," she said, rubbing her eyes.

Josef shrugged and motioned for Nico to lead the way to the alley where Eli was waiting.

At eight o'clock precisely, the guard changed as scheduled. Five minutes later, a carriage pulled into the palace square. The carriage was a fine one, with a matched pair of bays and a liveried footman who jumped down the moment the wheels stopped. The footman opened the door and flipped the folding stair out with a clack. From the shadows inside the shuttered carriage, a gloved hand reached out, and the footman hurried to help the gentleman down.

The passenger was a genteel figure in an old-fashioned long coat, fitted pants, and short boots cut from two shades of black leather. His face was obscured by a full, gray beard trimmed to a neat point, but his blue eyes were magnified by the silver spectacles that sat on the bridge of his nose. The old man moved slowly, leaning on the footman. He looked so fragile as he climbed down that the junior guard started forward to help him, but the senior guard stopped him with a shake of his head, and they held their position as the footman helped the old man down to the street.

As soon as the gentleman cleared the carriage door, another man exited almost on his heels. The second man was dressed similarly to the first, same old-fashioned coat and two-tone boots, but he was younger, much larger, and armed with two swords at his side as well as a long, sword-shaped-wrapped bundle on his back. He had a silver-tipped cane and a leather-wrapped satchel tucked under his arm, both of which he handed to the first man as soon as he reached the ground. The older man took the cane and the satchel gratefully, leaning on the first while he undid the straps on the second.

The younger man paid the footman without comment. From the way the footman began to bow and scrape, it must have been an impressive amount. After much groveling, the footman climbed back onto his perch and the carriage pulled away, leaving the two men alone with the guards.

The senior guard eyed the way the armed man rested his hands on his sword hilts and stepped forward, putting himself between the new arrivals and the palace gate.

"May I help you?"

"One moment, if you please," the older man said, still digging through his satchel.

The guard relaxed just a fraction. The expensive clothes had been a good hint, but now he was sure these were men of import. No one with an accent that refined could be up to trouble.

After much digging, the old man pulled a small book out of his bag and began thumbing through it. "Here we are," he said, stopping somewhere in the middle. "I'm looking for a Mr. Wallace." He glanced over his spectacles at the older guard. "That would be you?"

"Yes, sir." The senior guard, Wallace, stood at attention. "Are you expected?"

The old man sighed and adjusted his spectacles. "I shouldn't think so, Mr. Wallace. My name is Velsimon Whitefall and this is my bodyguard, Officer Fuller. We're with the National Obligation Audit Division of the Council Tax Bureau."

The man with the swords nodded, but Wallace didn't see him, the gate guard was too busy turning a pasty shade of grayish pink. He didn't know much about the inner working of the Council of Thrones, but he knew the name Whitefall, and he knew that anyone from an office with "Audit" in the title was no one you wanted at your gate.

"I apologize for our late arrival," the old man continued. "We were delayed leaving the mainland, but our business here is of the most pressing urgency. There was a bit of a miscalculation on Osera's last payment and I need to speak with your treasury officer, Mr..."

"Lord Obermal?" Wallace suggested.

"Ah yes, Obermal." The old man closed his little book with a sigh. "There are so many countries now, they all start to"— he waved his hands in a circle—"roll together." He finished with a shrug. "Would you be so kind as to take us to him?"

"I'm afraid Lord Obermal is at dinner," Wallace said carefully.

"Then I think you should fetch him," the old man said. "As I said, this is a matter of some urgency. I wouldn't be wasting my evening begging at gates were it otherwise, would I, Mr. Wallace?"

If possible, Wallace went paler still. "I—"

"Perhaps you could show us to his office and we could wait for him there?" the old man suggested helpfully. "So Lord Obermal doesn't have to come all the way to the gate?"

He punctuated this last bit with pointed lean on his cane. Wallace took the hint. "Of course, Lord Whitefall, of course." He looked over his shoulder. "Higgins!"

The younger guard snapped to attention.

"Take our guests to the treasury office. I'll go and fetch Lord Obermal."

The younger guard saluted and ran to open the gate for the Council Auditor and his guard. "This way, please, Lord Whitefall."

The old man smiled his thanks and hobbled into the palace, his cane clicking on the cobbles. His bodyguard went next, followed by Wallace, who walked with them just long enough to make sure Higgins was taking them the right way. When he saw the younger guard leading them up the stairs toward the treasury office, he grabbed a pair of guards from hall patrol and sent them to watch the gate. His duty satisfied, he ran to find Lord Obermal before things got any worse.

Fifteen minutes later, Lord Obermal, Keeper of the Treasury of Osera, excused himself from dinner with the Crown Secretary and the Officer of the Queen's Horse and set off for his office at a dead run.

"You're *sure* they said the National Obligation Audit Division?" he said, panting at Wallace, who was jogging beside him.

"Positive, my lord," Wallace said.

The treasury keeper made a noise like a mouse getting stepped on. "Audit officers, and a Whitefall no less, here at eight in the evening! Oh, there must have been some terrible mistake. I don't know how. I reviewed all the numbers myself. Did he say what payment he was here to inspect?"

"No, my lord," Wallace said. "But he made it seem deadly urgent."

"It's always urgent when it comes to the Council and money," Lord Obermal said, voice trembling. "The queen will have my head if we get audited now, what with everything going on."

Wallace jogged ahead to open the door to the treasury office. "I had Higgins put them in the receiving room," he said as Lord Obermal rushed past him. "Anything else I can do for you, my lord?"

"Yes," Obermal said, grabbing a stack of ledgers from his assistant's desk. "Don't tell anyone about this until I've had a chance to talk to the queen. We can't afford a panic."

"Understood, sir," Wallace said, stepping back into the hallway. "Good luck, sir."

Obermal nodded and took a deep breath. Then, hugging the ledgers to his chest, he walked through his office and into the receiving room.

"Lord Whitefall," he said, trying his best to sound like he wasn't panicking. "I'm sorry to have kept you waiting. I have all of Osera's payment records right—"

He stopped, the account books slipping as his fingers went slack.

The receiving room was empty. Obermal stood frozen for a moment as his brain switched from one panic to another. When he could move again, he turned and ran for the hall as fast as his old legs could go, shouting for Wallace.

"There," Eli said, peeling the fake beard off his face as they walked briskly through the back halls of the palace. "What did I tell you? Not even ten minutes."

"Fine, you were right," Josef said, unbuttoning the stuffy longcoat. "How did you know it would work?"

"Have you ever been through a Council audit?" Eli said, taking off his spectacles. "Nasty, expensive business, and the auditors are the last people you want to be out of sorts. That's actually the third time I've pulled that scam. Works every time."

Josef rolled his eyes. "Uh-huh, and why do I always have to be your bodyguard when we do these things?"

"Because, my dear Josef, you are a fighter, not an actor," Eli said with a smile. "The only expressions your face can produce are surly and murderous, so I have to cast you in rolls that highlight those particular aspects. Also, since I have about as much chance getting you to leave your swords behind as you have of convincing me you're lead soprano at the Zarin Opera, it seemed the most prudent course of action."

Josef shook his head. "Why do I even bother?"

"I haven't any idea," Eli said, grinning wider. "Where's Nico?"

Josef glowered at the convenient subject change, but let it slide. He was wondering the same thing. "She should be somewhere around—"

A brush on his shoulder stopped him, and he turned to see Nico stepping out of a deep-shadowed corner.

Eli bundled his somber coat together with Josef's and put them, along with his false beard and spectacles, into the leather satchel, which he then stashed in the nearest closet. He made a mental note of the door just in case they ever got a chance to come back. The Council Audit scam was a sure bet, but it was horrendously expensive to set up. He didn't want to abandon the coats unless he had to.

When he was satisfied he could find the closet again in a hurry, he turned to Josef. "Well, my lord prince, where now?"

"Don't call me that," Josef snapped, setting off down the hall. "And this way. We're going to see the queen."

"Just like that?" Eli said, frowning.

Josef nodded. "Just like that. Nico, you're on scout. I've got point. We're headed for the north wing. Keep the guards away."

"Right," Nico said, vanishing into the shadows like smoke.

Eli whistled, impressed. "Nice to see she's got it back."

Josef stomped off down the hall without comment. Eli sighed and fell into step behind him.

They took a convoluted path through the servant passages, though any route would have been twisty, considering how the old palace wrapped around the mountain peak. Eli had been disappointed to see that the palace's outward shabbiness continued on the inside. The whole place seemed to be nothing but oppressive stone walls and wooden floors hollowed by centuries of feet. The narrow halls would have made avoiding people difficult, but, fortunately, most of the palace seemed occupied with after-dinner entertainment. Eli heard voices through doors and around corners, but they never encountered another person, servant or guard, even when they entered what was obviously a private wing. He was just starting to feel a little unsettled by this when Josef turned a corner and stopped.

They were standing in a long gallery. One wall had sets of narrow windows paned with leaded glass; the other was lined with portraits of stern, fair-haired men. At the end of the gallery, directly across from where they stood, two guards were slumped on the floor. Nico stood beside them, rubbing her hand.

Eli sighed. Of course.

"Nice work," he said flatly as Josef went to help Nico roll the soldiers aside.

"They'll be fine," Josef said. "I taught her how to do it. Right, Nico?"

Nico nodded. "Clean strike to the neck from behind," she said, looking at Eli. "What? It's never bothered you before when we knocked out guards."

"But these are his *mother's* guards," Eli said, pointing at Josef. "It feels rude."

Josef's lip curled into a dark smile. "They're guards in Osera. If they can't take a little hit to the head, they shouldn't be here." He turned away from Eli's grimace to face the closed door at the end of the gallery. "Let's get this over with."

He strode down the hall and opened the door with a shove. The first thing Eli noticed about the royal chamber was that, for the home of the monarch of a wealthy nation, it was remarkably cramped. The room was as narrow as the gallery, and the dark tapestries depicting battles and hunts that covered most of the stone walls made it feel only smaller. Same for dim light coming from the half-lit candelabra that hung from the high, but not impressively high, ceiling. There was a raised, wooden dais at the far end of the room, obviously meant for receiving guests in royal fashion, but the ornate chair at its center was empty and the gold-plated lamps were dark. For several seconds, Eli thought they'd come all this way for nothing, but then his eyes drifted to the small fireplace in the corner. There, a low couch was pulled up to the feeble fire, and on it, lying buried under a large blanket, was an old woman.

The firelight dug deep shadows below her eyes, painting her wrinkles in long black gouges. There was a stack of papers on her lap, but she wasn't looking at them. Instead, she lay back on the pillows with her eyes shut and her thin mouth pressed in a tight line, as though she were biting her teeth against some long-running pain. Her hair, a thin, brittle mix of pale gold and white, lay spread out on the pillows behind her, freshly washed and combed, though Eli saw no one who could have combed it. The three of them hung at the door, hesitant. The room was so dark, the scene of the old woman sleeping by the fire so private,

95

Eli felt almost guilty stepping inside. Even Josef seemed to have lost his urgency. He stood hovering beside Eli, his scarred face strangely blank as he watched the old woman sleeping.

It was the woman herself who broke the silence. One second Eli would have bet his bounty she was deep asleep, the next her voice rang clear and cold through the room.

"I gave strict orders I was not to be disturbed," she said, pale eyes cracking open under her narrow, furrowed brows. "If this is not a matter of national emergency, I..." Her voice trailed off when she spotted Josef, and her whole, skeletal body went white as chalk.

Josef stiffened, and Eli leaned back to watch. He loved family reunions. He rather hoped the old woman would cry, if for no other reason than to see how Josef's stony swordsman routine would hold up under a mother's tears. But when the queen spoke again, her voice was even colder than before.

"Home at last," she said. "Why am I not surprised to find you sneaking in like a thief in the night, Thereson?"

"You put the bounty on my head," Josef said. "How else did you expect me to arrive when you made me a criminal, mother?"

The anger in Josef's voice made Eli wince, but the woman, whom Eli now knew was Queen Theresa, seemed unmoved.

"You left me little other recourse," she said. "It is a sad lot for Osera when her prince requires such drastic measures to bring him back to his duty."

Josef crossed his arms over his chest. "I'm not here to relive old fights," he growled. "I came only because you made it clear that you were willing to bankrupt Osera to get me home. So here I am. Now tell me what you want so I can tell you no and we can be done with this idea that I'm still yours to command."

Theresa's pale lips curled in a long, slow smile. "But you are, child. You've proved it, just now. You came back. It is but a tiny shred of the responsibility my son should hold, but it is a shred more than many thought you had."

Josef gritted his teeth. "Get on with it."

Slowly, with great effort, Queen Theresa sat up. She pulled

her thin, bony hand from beneath the blanket and held it out, pointing out the tiny window east, toward the Unseen Sea. "The Immortal Empress has returned."

Josef's shoulders tensed, but his voice remained insultingly casual. "So? What do you want me to do about it?"

Theresa's eyes narrowed. "Your duty," she spat. "After fifteen years of silence, the Empress's shipyards are active again. My spies report a fleet of palace ships nearly finished. You are Oseran; you know what that means." Her voice began to quiver. "She is coming, Thereson. If we are to stand against her, Osera must be strong."

"Osera is strong," Josef said.

"But I am not," Theresa said, her bony hand clenching into a shaking fist.

Josef sighed. "You don't look that bad."

"Really?" the queen snapped. "Look at me again." She raised her hand to her face, pressing her thin fingers into the deep hollows of her cheeks. "Look."

Josef looked, jaw clenched. "Fine, you look terrible. Is that what you want me to say? I'm sorry you're sick, but—"

The queen's gray eyes grew stony, shutting Josef's mouth with a single look. "Sick?" she said softly. "*Sick* is what I've been for the last five years, not that you would know. But I'm no longer sick, Thereson. I am dying. Even my doctors have stopped pretending I will see another year."

Eli could hear Josef's teeth grinding, but the queen didn't flinch. For the first time, Eli could see the family resemblance. The queen looked like Josef did right before he threw his sword away and grabbed the Heart.

"Disappointment that you are," she said, "you are my only child, the only full-blooded heir remaining to the Throne of Iron Lions. If our line is to continue, you must—"

"Must what?" Josef said with a bitterness Eli had never heard in his voice before. "Maybe you've forgotten in your old age, Mother, but you were the one who told me I would never be king. That you would disown me if I continued my 'swordsman nonsense.'" He laid his hand on the Heart of War's wrapped hilt. "My sword has stood me better than your throne. I won't abandon it just because you've changed your mind."

"My mind remains as it ever has," the queen said through clenched teeth. "So does your stubborn ability to hear what you want instead of what I say. Listen closely, boy. I'm not asking you to be king."

Josef froze. "You're not?"

"Of course not." Theresa lay back on her lounge with a huff. "Do you have any idea how hard I fought to inherit when my father died? How hard I fought to stay queen when my own cousins said a woman could never lead Osera? Do you think I'd leave that hard-won legacy to a selfish, violent, shift-less brat who doesn't have the presence of mind to be a prince, much less a king?"

She tilted her head, waiting for an answer. When none came, she continued. "Your cousin, Finley, will become king when I pass."

"Finley?" Josef roared. "Powers, woman! If you had an heir, why did you drag me all the way out here?"

"Because Osera has no heir!" the queen roared back. "Finley's not an Eisenlowe. He's blood enough to take the throne in an emergency, but not to pass it on to his son. Honestly," she huffed, "after all I spent on your tutors, I'd have hoped you'd remember something of Oseran law."

Josef shook his head, but Theresa held up her hand, cutting him off before he could get a word in. "I'm not asking you to be king, Thereson," she said coldly. "But I am asking you to do your duty to the family. There is only one royal blood line in Osera, and, tragically, that line runs through you. We have no other options. You must give Osera an heir."

Josef recoiled in horror. "An heir? You mean—"

"A baby, yes," his mother said. "I'm sure even you can manage that much. I know the princess can."

This was enough to make Eli break his uncharacteristic silence. "Wait, princess?"

"Yes," the queen said, raising her voice. "Adela!"

Josef pressed his hand to his forehead as the door to the queen's chamber burst open and a squad of guards marched into the room. There were a dozen of them at least, but Eli's attention was on the woman who led them. She was shockingly lovely. As tall as Josef and clad in shining silver armor with an ornate short sword at her hip. Her hair was deep brown, almost black, and braided tight against her head. Her skin was the warm, healthy tan of someone who spent most of her time outdoors, but her brown eyes were narrowed in the cold stare of an absolute professional as she marched toward them.

Eli raised his hands without prompting, but the woman brushed past him, going straight for Josef. Eli felt Nico stiffen, and he put a warning hand on her arm. The other guards were fanning out around them, cutting off the exits. Nico glanced at him, then at Josef, and then at the door, but Eli shook his head. Josef hadn't moved yet.

Now that the door was open, another woman, older but also shockingly lovely despite her simple black dress, walked briskly into the queen's chamber and hurried to Theresa's side. Eli tilted his head, watching as the woman began to fuss over the queen. But Theresa shook her head and gently pushed the woman's hands away.

"I'm fine," she said. "Thank you, Lenette."

The woman in black nodded and fell back, surrendering her place beside the queen to the young, armored woman. The circle of guards tightened, and Eli glanced at Josef, but the swordsman still hadn't moved. He simply stood there, staring at the queen. For her part, Theresa was leaning back on her pillows, enjoying the turned tables.

"Thereson," she said, placing her hand on the lovely young woman's arm. "You remember Adela, don't you?"

"How could I forget?" Josef grumbled. His mother arched an eyebrow, and he adjusted his tone. "Good evening, Princess Adela."

"Prince Thereson," the woman said with a nod.

Eli looked from the lovely woman to Josef and back again. There wasn't much resemblance, but...

"Your sister?" he guessed.

"No," Josef said. "That's my wife."

Utter silence descended. Even Eli was speechless. But it wasn't Eli who recovered first. The voice that broke the silence was Nico's.

"Wife?"

Eli groaned inwardly. Nico was staring at Josef, eyes wide with a look of complete betrayal.

"Wife?"

"It's not what it looks like!" Josef shouted, stabbing his finger at the queen. "*She* married me in absentia last year. I didn't even know about it until a few months ago."

Eli took a deep breath. He *knew* he shouldn't rise to it, that now was not the time, but for once his tongue was faster than his good sense. "*Months ago?*" he cried. "And when exactly were you planning on sharing this bit of important social news?"

"Never," Josef said. "Because it's *not* important. It wasn't like I had a say. I can't control what my mother does without my knowledge."

Nico took a step back. She was still staring at Josef, her eyes so wide Eli could see the whites all the way around.

"Nico," Josef said, his voice warning.

She took another step.

Josef looked at her, his face as close to panic as Eli had ever seen it. "Nico, listen—"

Before he could say anything else, Nico vanished. There was no sound, no flash. She simply snuffed out like a candle.

After that, everything happened at once.

Josef roared curses as the startled guards rushed forward, swords drawn. Eli put up his hands as a blade pressed into his back, but when a guard tried the same to Josef, the swordsman whirled around, grabbed the sword out of the guard's hand, and threw him to the ground so hard the man bounced. The guard's sword followed a second later as Josef, still cursing, threw it hilt first at the man's head.

With that, Josef straightened up, rolled his shoulders, and started for the door. Started, and then stopped cold. Eli blinked in surprise. He hadn't seen her move, hadn't heard her, but the princess was suddenly right behind Josef, the tip of her short sword pressed into his right shoulder.

"That's enough, Prince Thereson," she said quietly. "One more step and I sever the ligament that moves your sword arm. Hands where I can see them, please."

Josef put his hands out slowly, and the princess turned him around to face the queen again.

"What was that?" the queen said in a low, angry voice. "What have you gotten yourself involved with, Thereson?"

Eli gritted his teeth. Things were rapidly falling apart. It wasn't so much the sword at his own back. He could duck out of that easily enough. But he could see Josef's hands shaking as the queen questioned him. The swordsman was pale with rage, the kind that took some good old-fashioned violence to pull him out of, and the queen wasn't letting up. It was up to Eli to act fast before Josef did something they'd regret.

"Your majesty," he said, stepping past Josef and the princess with a florid bow, much to his guard's surprise. Josef whipped around, but Eli stomped on his toes before the swordsman could say anything and smiled his best smile at the queen. "I believe we've started this on the wrong foot."

The queen looked down her nose at him, quite a feat, considering he was standing and she was sitting. "And who are you? What makes you think you have the right to speak in my presence?"

Eli's smile grew even more charming. "Because I am the son of one of your oldest allies." He reached into his coat pocket and drew out a creased slip of paper, which he handed to the queen with a flourish. "Eliton Banage."

"Banage?" The queen frowned, confused. "You are Etmon's son?"

"The very same," Eli said as she took the paper from his fingers. "And every bit as much of a disappointment to him as our dear Josef is to you."

The queen glanced at the paper. "This is a Council identity paper for a child," she said. "And it's almost two decades out of date."

"I don't get home much," Eli said, his voice deepening to a tragic note. "My father and I don't get along, as you can see. But he always spoke very highly of you and his time fighting for Osera against the Empress."

Queen Theresa arched an eyebrow. "I sincerely doubt that," she said, handing the slip of paper to the lovely lady in black. "You won't object if I ask Lenette to check the validity of your statement? I will admit there is a family resemblance, but I must be sure. Still"—her eyes narrowed—"you are the right age."

Eli gave her his best innocent look. The queen didn't seem to buy it.

"Well," Theresa said, sitting back. "If you are indeed Etmon's son, then I welcome you, but this is a family matter. You'd do best to stay out of it."

Eli's face clouded with a look of deep pain. "I understand your reticence, your grace," he said gently. "But your son and I have been thick as thieves for a while now. I know him as I know myself, and, if I may be so bold, I don't think you have things quite by the right end." He clasped his hands, and his voice shook with earnest emotion. "Whatever terms he may have left you on, your majesty, Josef dropped everything to come here when he saw those posters. Even I was inspired. He's trying to do the right thing, but it's not easy. He's been living his life moment to moment as a mercenary for years, and now, to suddenly hear that he's expected to father a child with a wife he's known about for only a few months, that's a bone for any man to swallow. As you saw, the mere mention was too much for our other companion."

"Yes," the queen said, leaning forward. "What about your companion?"

102

"Oh, Nico does that all the time," Eli said, waving her words away. "She's quite the escape artist. Some people swear she disappears into thin air, but I'm sure your majesty is not one to be fooled by such cheap tricks."

The queen glared at him. "I don't care for your quick tongue, Mr. Banage. Get to the point."

Eli's smile faltered just a hair. "My point, majesty, is that we've been traveling for a week solid to come into your presence, and we're tired. Surely you would not begrudge your son a night to think things over before he's forced into the marriage bed?" He turned his smile to the princess, who still had her sword pressed into Josef's back. "Lovely as this young lady is, it's a big change for our Josef, and he takes to change about as well as a rock takes to floating. I'm sure that in the morning, once he's had time to think about what he owes his family, he'll be much more tractable."

The queen tilted her head, considering. "The young Banage makes a good point," she said. "Adela, release him."

The sword vanished from Josef's back, and the princess stepped aside to stand next to the queen once again. The other soldiers stood down as well, and Eli breathed a sigh of relief.

Josef lowered his arms and turned around, glaring daggers at his mother. The queen met him in kind, glaring so hard Eli was afraid the air between them would start to boil.

"Your friend has bought you a night of reprieve," she said at last. "You will stay in the palace tonight. The guards will take you to your rooms, but before that, I want you to look at me."

Josef's jaw clenched, but the queen cut him off before he could get a word out.

"No," she said quietly. "Do not speak. Look."

And with that, the queen tossed aside her blanket with a bony hand. Lenette and Adela both moved to help her, but the queen pushed them away. Slowly, painfully, Theresa pulled herself to her feet, standing by her own power before the fire.

It was a sad sight. The silk nightgown hung from the queen's bony shoulders. Her arms were so thin, Eli could have wrapped his hand all the way around her bicep. If her back were straight, she might have been as tall as Josef, but the queen was bent with age, her spine curved in an unnatural arc that forced her to lean forward. Even so, she straightened as well as she could before holding out her arms.

"Look at me, Prince Thereson," she said, her voice as hard as the stone around them. "Look at what is left of Osera's queen. The Empress's hammer falls on our shores, and this weak, dying body is all that stands to face her. You've been stubborn as a pig all your life, but if I ever did my duty as your mother, as your queen—if I ever instilled even a stirring of love for you homeland in that bitter, guarded heart of yours, then, just this once, listen to my command. Do your duty. Be Osera's prince, if only to pass on the blood of our ancestors, and I will never bother you again."

She stood a moment longer, and then fell back onto her couch. Lenette was at her side immediately, fussing and pressing the queen's blanket back across her legs. The queen paid the lady no mind. Her eyes never left Josef's, daring him to defy her again. Josef didn't say a word. When the guards moved to lead them away, Josef let them, but he never stopped watching his mother until the guards closed her doors behind them.

In Eli's experience, "room" was a royal euphemism for prison cell, and his suspicions proved correct. The guards led them up a flight of stairs to a nondescript hall lined with heavy wooden doors, not barred but not exactly inviting either. They stopped at two doors right next to each other. Josef went through the first, Eli the second, stumbling in as the guards locked the iron bolt from the outside with a solid click.

Eli sighed at the barred door and then took a moment to consider his situation. He'd been in nicer cells, but not many. There was a feather bed, a porcelain washstand, an ornate wooden table with books, cards, and a lamp turned low. The wooden floor was carpeted, and the bars on the narrow window were tastefully obscured behind thick curtains. It was all very well done and, for a lesser man, very secure. Eli, however, was the greatest thief in the world. Five minutes after the guards left, he was hanging off the palace's outer wall, banging on Josef's shuttered window.

The swordsman opened the shutters on the third knock, and Eli wiggled through the bars to land in a heap on Josef's rug.

"Well," he said, brushing himself off. "That was exciting. Ready to go?"

Josef sat down on his bed and didn't answer. Eli stood up, casing the room as he did. It was identical to his own, but Josef had pushed the writing table into the corner and was using the chair to prop up his weaponry with the Heart leaning against the wall. Eli grimaced, glancing from swords to swordsman. Josef bladeless was always a bad sign. Nico was also still conspicuously absent, despite the dozens of shadows available. Very bad indeed. He would have to tread lightly.

He walked over and took a seat on the bed, sinking down beside Josef.

"Listen," he said. "Remember the plan? We made it. We talked to your mother. She told you what you were going to do, and then you told her what you were going to do. So that's it. We're done."

Josef stared straight ahead and said nothing.

"I've been thinking about finding a nice job down south," Eli continued. "Big money, exotic locals, lots of good fights. If we leave tonight we can probably catch the pirate king's fleet before he goes back to sea. He's supposed to employ some of the nastiest swordsmen on the continent. What do you say?"

He turned to Josef with a bright smile, but the swordsman didn't even look his way, and Eli's smile fell into a scowl.

"*Powers*, Josef," he said, kicking the bed. "Snap out of it. We're thieves, remember? No one expects anything from us. The queen makes a nice speech, but no country teeters on the presence of one man. You already have a cause, remember? You swore to become the greatest swordsman in the world, the worthy wielder of the Heart of War. That's a noble goal, and you can't achieve it here." He stood up, tugging Josef's sleeve. "Come on, get your things. I'll call for Nico and we'll all get out of here together, tonight, just like we planned."

He walked to the window and was getting ready to climb out when Josef finally spoke.

"I can't."

Eli closed his eyes and cursed silently. When that was done, he turned, keeping his face cheerfully neutral. "Why not?"

Josef made a frustrated sound and ran his scarred hands through his newly trimmed hair. "Do you know why I became a swordsman?"

"Because you're good at it?" Eli guessed.

"Because it's the *only* thing I'm good at," Josef said. "I was a miserable failure at everything else, being a prince, being a son, being a politician. I hated it, all of it. Swordsmanship was the only thing that made life livable. The only thing I wanted to do."

He stopped, and Eli shifted awkwardly. This was the most Josef had ever told him about his past, and he wasn't sure what the swordsman expected him to say. Finally, he settled for putting a comforting hand on Josef's shoulder. Josef didn't seem to notice.

"I made my choice when I was fifteen," he said, his voice low. "In Osera, everything's about the queen. You live for the queen, fight for the queen, die for the queen. I didn't want to live for her, didn't want to live for anyone. I wanted to be a swordsman, to fight for the sake of getting better, not because I was ordered to. So I took my swords and I left. Just walked out. I swore that I would return only when I had become the greatest swordsman in the world." He clutched his fists together with an intensity that made Eli flinch. "The *best*," he said again. "Don't you see? If I falter, if I take even one step back, then all the problems I caused by leaving—my mother's suffering, the messed-up succession, Osera's shame at having a runaway prince—it will be for *nothing*."

"Josef," Eli said. "It's not—"

"That's why I never came home before when she tried to

106

make me," Josef rolled right over him. "But as soon as I saw the poster, I knew this time was different."

He looked up, and Eli saw with a shock that his eyes were red.

"She's dying, Eli." Josef's voice was so soft Eli could barely make out the words. "My mother is dying. Believe me, I want to dive out that window with you, but I can't. Not now." He took a deep breath and leaned back, staring up at the ceiling. "Her telling me she didn't want me to be king was the final straw, you know. If she'd been unreasonable and demanded that I give up swordsmanship and take the throne, I could have told her to shove off. But all she wants is an heir, a child of the blood to preserve the family. How can I deny her such a small request?"

Eli didn't think a child was a small request, but he said nothing. They sat for a long while, letting the silence hang like a dead thing in the air between them. Finally, Eli heaved an enormous sigh.

"Bugger all," he grumbled, pushing himself off the bed. "You picked a really bad time to have a fit of responsibility. Nico's back on her game, we finally have the chance to pull some real heists, and you have to get all prodigal son on me, *Thereson*."

"Don't start, *Eliton*," Josef snapped. "You must be feeling suicidal, posing as the Rector Spiritualis's son. What made you think of that?"

"It was the best trick I had," Eli said, keeping his voice casual. "Queen Theresa's debt to Banage is well known. The name gave her cause to think twice at the very least, and if I hadn't given her a compelling reason not to throw me out, you'd be spending tonight with the lovely Adela. Of course," he said, glaring down at Josef, "if I'd known you were going to get all noble prince on me, I wouldn't have bothered."

Josef let the barb roll off with a shrug. "You're being thicker than usual if you think it isn't going to come back around," he said. "This isn't some idiot guard you're bluffing. You know the queen is going to check. I'd bet money the Spirit Court is here tomorrow morning, hunting for your hide."

"Really?" Eli said. "How much money?"

Josef arched an eyebrow. "You have a good reason why they wouldn't be?"

Eli folded his arms behind his back. "Let me come at this from another angle for you. Anyone who pays attention to bounties knows that Josef Liechten pals around with Eli Monpress, right? So think, what happens when you show up out of nowhere with a handsome young man who looks even a little like the posters? Queen Theresa hasn't hung onto her throne as long as she has by being an idiot. She'd figure things out real quick. By giving her another trail to sniff, I bought us time to escape. Which, of course, is wasted now."

Josef rolled his eyes. "Yeah, yeah. Still doesn't explain why you chose Banage. Seems needlessly reckless to me."

Eli smiled grimly. "I wasn't lying when I said the Rector Spiritualis was ashamed of his son. Let's just say that Banage has more on the line than most in making sure that any Eliton appearances stay uninvestigated. Your mother can send messages all she likes, but if we see so much as an apprentice come down to investigate, I'll eat your sword."

"Now that I'd pay to see," Josef said, tugging off his boots. "Get out of here, I'm going to bed. If I have to be home, I'm not doing it on no sleep."

"Bridegrooms do need their sleep," Eli said sagely.

The look Josef gave him wiped the smile clear off Eli's face, and the thief wisely decided it was time to leave his friend alone. He stood up and wiggled out the window as easily as he'd wiggled in. He had time for one last wave before Josef slammed the shutter behind him. Duly rebuked, Eli hung on the stone ledge momentarily, searching the shadows for Nico. He knew she was there. He could almost feel her watching. He called her name softly, but there was no answer, nothing but the wind blowing up the mountain and the sound of the city below.

Feeling defeated and more than a little angry, Eli pulled himself along the ledge and through the bars into his room. He landed on the carpet and picked himself up, snuffing out the lamp with a wave of his hand. He crossed the dark room and collapsed facedown on his bed. He rolled around awhile, wiggling out of his clothes and tossing his wig over the bedpost. Finally undressed, he flopped onto the pile of pillows, turning his head from side to side in a futile attempt to cut off the massive headache he could already feel forming. Fifteen minutes later he was still awake, his head throbbing full force. Eli sighed in a drawn-out curse, grinding the heels of his palms deep into his eye sockets.

It was going to be a long night.

CHAPTER
7

Miranda stomped five steps across her cell, hit the stone bars, turned on her heel, and stomped five steps back to the wall. She slapped her hand against the smooth, feature-less stone before turning around to start all over again. Five steps, slap. Five steps, slap. Miranda gritted her teeth. The endless stomping was stupid, a waste of time and energy, and yet she could not stop. If she didn't do something with all the rage inside her, she would explode.

Across the hall, Gin shoved his nose through the stone bars of his cell, orange eyes narrowed to slits against the constant white glow that seeped from the mountain's stone. "Do it," he snarled. "It's past time for patience."

Miranda shook her head and glanced at Slorn. He was sitting as he had been since they'd arrived, cross-legged at the center of his cell. His dark bear eyes were closed against the white-ness, his breathing was deep, and his face was slack, as though he were asleep. It was his ears that gave him away. They stood taut on his head, shifting to follow every sound Miranda made.

He'd been like this since the Guildmaster had locked them

in here two days ago, completely silent, no matter how many questions she asked. It was his silence that made her angrier than anything else. She'd followed him here like a little dog, licking up every bit of information he'd thrown her, but now that he'd landed her in prison, he wouldn't even talk to her. Just thinking about it made her shake with fury, but as much as she wanted to follow Gin's urging, Miranda held back. It wasn't the bars that kept her in. Gin could have broken them, she was sure, or any of her spirits could have, for the Shapers had not taken her rings. Once she was free, she was pretty sure that she could find her way out of the mountain if it came to that, but she didn't try to leave. She couldn't. Angry as she was, she'd followed Slorn to this mountain to help right whatever was going wrong with the world. Now that they were finally here, she wasn't about to give up and leave just because things weren't going like she wanted. Of course, that didn't mean she was going to forgive Slorn for clamming up on her when she needed him most.

Across the hall, Gin pressed his nose against the stone bars, his tail lashing across the wall behind him. Miranda shook her head again, more firmly this time. Gin snorted and looked away, grumbling to himself. Miranda just took a deep breath and went back to her stomping. It might not help anything, but at least it gave her something to do. So she walked, watching her worn boots slap against the glowing white stone, five steps forward and five steps back.

She was still going two hours later when Slorn finally spoke.

"He's coming," Slorn said.

Miranda nearly tripped over her own feet. "What?"

On the other side of the stone lattice, Slorn was getting up. Gin was on his feet as well, his quivering nose pressed against the stone bars. Miranda ran to the edge of her own cell. They'd gotten their food an hour ago, so it couldn't be time yet for the guard to return. But if she strained she could hear the distant sound of footsteps. One person, coming this way.

Miranda pushed away from the bars and started waking her rings, stirring each spirit. Mellinor was already awake when she touched him. He waited at the bottom of her consciousness, a deep, quiet pool, ready if needed. Gin was pacing in his long cell, his patterns shifting in tight swirls. He kept his head down and his teeth bared, ready to jump the second Miranda gave the signal. Only Slorn was calm. He stood at the door to his cell, arms folded behind him, waiting patiently as the steps came closer.

By the time the footsteps reached them, Miranda was ready. She clung to the barred door, rings flashing, but when the person came around the corner, she blinked in surprise. She'd expected another guard, but it was the Guildmaster himself who walked into view.

He wore a silk robe even finer than the one he'd worn the first time Miranda saw him. He did not look Slorn in the eye when he stopped in front of the bear-headed man's cell, but his voice was the essence of calm as he addressed them, opening the cells with a wave of his hand.

"The Teacher will see you now."

And with that, the Guildmaster turned on his heel and marched back the way he'd come. Slorn stepped out of his cell, falling into pace behind the old man. A moment later, Miranda did the same. Gin brought up the rear, stalking along with his head down and his ears flat, growling deep in his throat.

When they'd first entered the mountain, the Guildmaster had taken them down to their cells through a maze of white glowing tunnels. This time, he led them up, following a wide, inclined tunnel that seemed to curve in on itself in a tightening spiral. He did not speak. Neither did Slorn. Miranda had several things she would have liked to say, but she kept her mouth shut as well. After all, it wasn't like she was going to get an answer.

After ten minutes of climbing, the curving tunnel ended at a wide, circular platform. Miranda looked around, confused. It looked like a dead end, but even as she started to bring this point to the Guildmaster's attention, the high ceiling slid away with a soft scrape, revealing a long tunnel up through the mountain. Forgetting her dignity for a moment, Miranda gaped openly at the enormous hole that had suddenly appeared above her. It seemed to go up forever, a curved tunnel of pure, glowing white stretching as far as she could see.

She was still gawking when she heard Gin take a hissing breath. A second later, the floor began to vibrate under her boots, and then it started to lift. Miranda gasped and flung out her arms for balance, but it was Slorn who caught her hand and kept her from falling. The bear-headed man held her eyes just long enough for a small, subtle wink before letting her go as the stone platform under their feet rose smoothly into the glowing tunnel. The platform picked up speed as they went, moving faster and faster until Miranda could feel gravity pulling on her bones. Then, as quietly as it had started, the platform slowed. A new, stronger light flashed overhead as a door opened in the side of the tunnel as their platform slid to a gentle stop before the largest, most beautiful hall Miranda had ever seen.

The sheer size of it took her breath away. The hall stretched out forever, larger than the Spirit Court's hearing chamber, larger than the throne room at Mellinor, larger than the cave below the Council, larger, in fact, than any room she'd ever seen. The stone was the same glowing white as the lower levels, but where it had been smooth down below, here the rock was carved in subtle patterns that played with the stone's light. Fat pillars dozens of feet across sprouted like trees from the polished floor at regular intervals, rising up to meet the arc of the carved ceiling high, high overhead. The walls curved as well, following the natural slope of the mountain. There were several large doors leading to smaller halls that branched into unseen rooms, but the largest of all was at the other end of the hall, directly across from where they stood. There, a great door pierced the wall of the mountain itself, opening out onto a large, circular balcony that looked down on the sleeping mountains, their snow-covered peaks glittering in the light of the full moon.

Miranda caught her breath. Locked in the mountain, she hadn't even realized it was night. She also hadn't realized that the moving platform had taken them so high. They must be close to the mountain's peak.

The Guildmaster stepped off the platform and into the hall, walking briskly across the carved, glowing stone. Miranda pulled her coat tight around her shoulders and followed. The hall was nearly empty, but those few Shapers who were milling between the great stone pillars stopped to stare as the Guildmaster led his prisoners past them and through the middle of the great, white hall.

Miranda stole glances at Slorn as they walked, but the bear-headed Shaper's face was carefully neutral. Still, the Guildmaster was far ahead, and she decided to risk it.

"What is this place?" she whispered, careful not to look at him.

"The Hall of the Shapers," Slorn answered, just as quietly. His muffled voice sounded almost wistful.

Before Miranda could ask what that was, the Guildmaster stopped. They were standing directly in the center of the hall, between the moving platform that had brought them up here and the balcony door. The hall's center was marked with a circle of raised stone carved in looping patterns that made Miranda's head swim. The Guildmaster stepped into the circle and motioned for them to do the same. When they were all inside, the Guildmaster stepped out again.

"I don't know why the Teacher bothers," he said. "I only hope you do not disappoint him, Heinricht."

Though he hid it well, Miranda could hear the lingering resentment in the Guildmaster's voice, and she got the feeling he wasn't used to being excluded from whatever was about to happen. Slorn, however, looked almost relieved.

"I am already outcast and imprisoned," he said. "What more can he do?"

The Guildmaster's face darkened. "Do not take these things lightly. The Teacher's decision is final, but even he is not without mercy." The old man leaned in, dropping his voice. "For once in your life, Heinricht, bow your stubborn head and ask the Teacher's forgiveness. Let me welcome my son home once again."

Slorn met the Guildmaster's gaze. "I will do what I have to, Father. Just as I always have."

Miranda's eyebrows shot up, but before she could comment, the Guildmaster made a sharp gesture and the floor below their feet began to move. She scrambled for balance as the entire circle of stone began to rise upward, taking them with it. She caught one last glimpse of the Guildmaster as the old man's face fell, collapsing from anger to a look of deep sadness. Then he was gone, hidden by the rim of the rising stone pillar.

She turned to Slorn. "Father?"

"Yes," Slorn said.

She gave him a look of disbelief. "Your own father locked you up?"

"He is Guildmaster first," Slorn said. "There will be those among the Shapers who will say he is being too lenient with me, letting me see the Teacher. I am an oath breaker, after all. Shapers are sworn to the Mountain for life, but we ran when Nivel became a demonseed. It doesn't matter that they would have killed her if we stayed; we both broke our oath as Shapers."

Miranda folded her arms across her chest. "You could have told me."

"I could have," Slorn said. "I could have told you a lot of things, but anything I told you in the cell I would also have told the Teacher."

"What do you mean?" Miranda said. "There was no one there but us."

"This is the Shaper Mountain," Slorn said. "It is always listening."

Miranda frowned. "Who is the Teacher, then?"

"You'll know when you see him," Slorn said.

Miranda bit her lip. She was getting pretty sick of these half answers, but Slorn would say nothing more. In the end, all she could do was watch in silence as the stone above them lifted away, and the rising pillar vanished into the hall's ceiling with a soft scrape.

They were in another vertical tunnel. Glowing stone

114

surrounded them on all sides, filling the air with cold, white light. The pillar of stone under their feet seemed to have no end. It rose slowly, pushing them farther and farther up into the mountain. Miranda arched her neck, trying to see where they were going, but she saw nothing except the endless white. Still, things were changing. The air was growing colder and thinner, the light brighter.

Just as Miranda was starting to feel light-headed, the platform began to slow. Stone scraped overhead and the white walls of the tunnel fell away, leaving them standing in a brilliant white glare. Miranda covered her face, blinking furiously. Slowly, her eyes adjusted to the brilliance, and she saw that they were standing in another enormous, white chamber.

It was smaller than the Hall of the Shapers below, but there were no pillars here, no supports of any kind. Just a perfect circle of stone, white and brilliant as the morning sun on fresh snow, and nothing else.

"There's no one here," Miranda whispered. "I thought you said we were going to see the Teacher."

"Just wait," Slorn said. "He likes to make an entrance."

Miranda didn't see how. The white chamber had no doors save for the stone platform they were standing on. But as she opened her mouth to ask Slorn what he meant, the light went out.

She gasped and nearly fell into Gin. For a heartbeat, the chamber was pitch black. And then, as suddenly as it had vanished, light returned, and everything changed.

Color flooded the walls, a wave of brilliant green, brown, and blue that washed over the stone, leaving mountains, forests, and sky in its wake. The floor underfoot came alive with pinks and yellows, blues, whites, and soft greens, all flowing together in a wash before separating out into thousands of flowers. Suddenly, they were standing in a high mountain field. A stream sprung to life a few feet from Gin's tail, bouncing merrily down a bed of smooth white stones. Mountains loomed in the distance, their peaks taller than any Miranda had ever seen. Clouds drifted across the perfectly blue sky overhead, and the bright sunlight turned her hair fiery red, but when she held her hands up to the light, there was no warmth in it. The rushing stream threw off no spray and, despite the waving flowers under her feet, she could still feel the cold stone through the soles of her boots.

She looked at Slorn for some explanation, but he was staring across the valley at the mountains beyond. Or, rather, at the one mountain that rose above all others. Almost half again as tall as the next tallest peak, the Shaper Mountain stood before them in all its majesty. Its summit scraped the clear blue sky like a white knife. Its snowy slope was the same as Miranda had seen from Knife's Pass, but there was no sign of the windows and balconies of the Shapers, nor was there any sign of Knife's Pass itself. The road should have been directly below them, but it wasn't. The ravine and the bridge were also missing, leaving the smaller mountains whole and uncut all the way to the Shaper Mountain's feet. The little mountains were dotted with high mountain meadows just like the one they stood in, little verdant patches, peaceful and blooming in the golden sunlight.

Miranda blinked and turned to Slorn, waiting for some sort of explanation, but Slorn said nothing. He just stood there, staring at the sky, his brown bear eyes open as wide as they could go. Frowning, she turned to Gin, but the ghosthound wasn't any better. He was crouched at her feet as close to her as he could get, his orange eyes wide as dinner plates.

"Gin?" she whispered.

The dog didn't even look at her. "Can't you see it, Miranda?"

She frowned. "What?"

Next to her, Slorn took a shuddering breath. "I thought… I mean, I always suspected, but I never imagined it would be so large. So…endless."

"*What?*" Miranda asked again, growing supremely annoyed.

"The world," a deep voice rumbled. "Or what it was."

Miranda jumped before she could stop herself. The voice came from under her feet, vibrating up through her legs from the stone below the fluttering illusion of flowers. Beside her, Gin lowered his head with a soft whine.

116

"Tell me your names." The words buzzed through Miranda's body, more vibration than sound, but they carried an authority she could feel in her bones.

"Teacher," Slorn said. "I am Heinricht Slorn."

"I know who you are," the mountain said, for Miranda knew it could be no other. "I remember all my children, even the ones who desert me. I am eager to hear what excuses you've thought up to convince me to take you back, but for now, tell me, who is this woman?"

Miranda stepped forward. "I am Miranda Lyonette, a Spiritualist of the Spirit Court. This is Gin, my—"

"I do not need the lesser spirits' names," the mountain rumbled dismissively. "They know their place. But I am curious as to how the core of a great water spirit came to live inside a human. Mellinor, can you still speak?"

"I can."

Miranda steeled herself as Mellinor's spirit surged forward, rising in a plume of deep blue water from her fingers, which she held out for him.

"I see you have escaped your prison," the mountain said.

The water dipped in a bow. "With Miranda's assistance, great mountain."

"A strange arrangement, to be sure," the mountain said. "But then, you water spirits always did flow down the easiest route."

"I did what I had to," Mellinor said.

The meadow flickered as the mountain laughed. "As do we all, inland sea, as do we all. I am satisfied. You may return to your human shore."

The water retreated, and Mellinor flowed back into Miranda, who lowered her arm cautiously. Something odd was going on, besides the obvious. Mellinor was being surprisingly deferential. Her sea spirit wasn't rude, but he was a Great Spirit and he didn't tend to let others forget that. This meekness was very out of character. Perhaps it was because the mountain was so much bigger than Mellinor's diminished form? But he'd shown no such deference to the West Wind.

"Now," the mountain said. "To business. Why have you come home, Heinricht? Or do I call you Heinricht anymore? You are as much bear as man, now."

"I am still myself," Slorn said. "And I came home because I had no more reason to run. Nivel is dead. Her seed has been taken by the League."

"I am sorry," the mountain said.

As the stone spoke, the flowering grass began to dance in an unfelt wind. All over the valley, the sunlight faded, and Miranda looked up to see dark clouds rolling in from the south. Within moments, the meadow was covered in a thin, misty rain. But though she could see the rain falling, hear it hitting her shoulders, she was not wet.

"What's happening?" she whispered.

"The Teacher is grieving," Slorn answered.

"Of course I grieve," the mountain said. "Nivel was my student before she was your wife."

"Then you should know she continued to abide by your teachings," Slorn said bitterly. "Even after you would have murdered her."

The soft rain became a downpour as Slorn finished, and the ground shook with the mountain's anger.

"It was the demon who murdered your wife," the mountain said. "Not I. Nivel died the moment the spirit eater took her. All you achieved by running was to delay the inevitable, putting all of us at risk in the process."

Slorn bared his sharp teeth. "The end might have been inevitable, but our work was not in vain. Nivel lived for ten years with that seed inside her, and even then it was not the demon who killed her. She was murdered by a rogue League member who took her seed for his own. Had he not appeared, she would still be alive, doing your work."

"And what work of mine could a demonseed do?" the mountain said. "Demon-panicked spirits cannot be Shaped."

"The first affirmation of all Shapers is the collection of knowledge," Slorn answered. "That's the pledge you have us make, and Nivel and I never forsook it. We spent those ten years researching demonseeds. Through our work, Nivel lived eight years longer than any seed on record." He reached into his coat, taking out a small, leather-bound book. "I have here detailed observations," he said, holding the book up in the phantom rain. "Mine and hers, from the day we left the mountain to the day I surrendered her seed to the League. I believe our research contains more information about the demon than any spirits have ever collected before, including the League, and I am prepared to give all of this knowledge to you. With the Shapers' help, we could save countless lives, maybe even one day reverse the demon infestation."

The rain began to slack as he spoke, and the clouds rolled away, leaving the mountain gleaming white in the freshly washed sunshine. Its stone slope had not changed, and yet, somehow, Miranda got the feeling the mountain was sneering at them.

"You would give me knowledge of how to prolong a demon-seed's life?" the Teacher said.

"Yes," Slorn answered. "I can already make manacles that retard the seed's growth and cloth that hides the demon's presence, allowing it to walk among spirits without terrifying them. But these are only crutches, stopgaps. With your help, I hope to find a way to reverse the seed's conquest of the host, perhaps even remove the seed without—"

"Enough."

Slorn stiffened. "What do you—"

"You wasted your freedom studying the wrong thing," the mountain said. "Extending the seed's life? Hiding it? Why would we want to do that? If you'd found a way to pinpoint seeds before they wake, that I could perhaps condone, but demonseeds are a menace, Heinricht, not something to be coddled and hidden."

"Menace?" Slorn growled. "A feral dog is a *menace*. Demon-seeds are the greatest disaster we've ever known waiting to happen. Each seed has the potential to become a demon every bit as dangerous as the one imprisoned under the Dead

119

Mountain. I don't know if you were paying attention, but it nearly happened a few weeks ago not far from your own slopes. To ignore such a danger, to refuse to learn as much as we can about its nature, to remain willfully ignorant of the greatest threat to the spirits that form this world, *that* is the menace, Teacher. And that is why Nivel and my research is so important.

"Think what could happen if we could safely remove seeds from their hosts without killing them. Demonseeds would come forward willingly to be cured instead of running. The League would no longer have to hunt the seeds down or risk fighting them. Who knows? Each seed is an identical shard of the demon of the Dead Mountain itself. If we learn more about them, we might find a way to stop the Dead Mountain from sending them out, maybe even a way to get rid of the demon altogether. This knowledge, Nivel's knowledge, could be the beginning of the research that saves us from the demon forever."

The mountain rumbled as Slorn finished, a long, grinding slide of stone on stone that rattled Miranda's teeth. She barely noticed. This was it. This was why they'd come all this way. If the mountain got behind Slorn's plan, then this could well be the birth of an age of safety and freedom greater than anything the Spirit World had ever known. Not just freedom from the crippling fear she'd felt at Izo's and in the throne room at Mellinor, but also freedom for the seeds themselves. Unbidden, her mind flicked to Nico. Despite the company she kept and the wound she'd given Gin, Nico didn't deserve to be eaten by the demon. Neither had Slorn's wife. No spirit deserved it, and today she would make sure that, if the first steps toward ending the demon's infection of the world were not taken, it would not be because she did not try.

All around them, the scenery was changing. The flowering meadow withered and turned brown. Deep snow appeared on the mountain's slopes, and the sky grew dark as raw iron. Though the air had not changed, Miranda felt colder than ever. Still, she did not move until, at last, the mountain spoke.

"I am very sorry, Heinricht," it said, "but you have wasted

your time. I don't know why you even thought to start this line of questioning, other than sentimentality. You should know better than any that demons are the sole realm of the Shepherdess and her League."

"But there's no reason we can't help." The words burst out of Miranda before she could stop them. "I've seen the League in action, and they are marvelous, but they would have lost at Izo's if not for Slorn and Mellinor's help."

"Who gave you leave to speak, human?" the mountain thundered, sending snow tumbling down its slopes. "Slorn is in disgrace, but he is still a Shaper. You are nothing to me. Why do you think you can raise your voice here?"

"Miranda!" Gin hissed, pressing his paw on her foot.

"No," Miranda said hotly, shaking her leg free of Gin's grip. "I've had enough of this. I may not be a Shaper, but I am a spirit. It's my world too. Why shouldn't I do whatever I can to help it?"

"It is not your place," the mountain rumbled.

"It is my place!" Miranda shouted back. "I am a Spiritualist! I am sworn on my life and my soul to protect the spirits from harm, and that's what I intend to do. You say this is League business, but I think it is reckless and ridiculous to leave the entirety of our well-being in the hands of a League we cannot call or control."

"The League is the only reason our world still exists, wizard," the mountain said.

"And I am grateful!" Miranda cried, shaking off Slorn's warning hand. "But if they, if *you* truly wanted to save the world rather than just preserve the status quo, you'd accept our help. If Slorn's knowledge truly can change the way we deal with demonseeds, if there's even a chance that this could prevent what happened in the mountains outside Izo's camp from happening again, then how can anyone say it is not worth trying?"

Miranda stopped, panting. She hadn't meant to say it that way, but the tirade had burst out of her. Gin was whimpering at her feet, his muscles tensed to grab her and run, even though there was nowhere to run to. Overhead, snow drifted silently from the gray sky, filling the valley in soft drifts until it was up to Miranda's knees. The snow hid the mountain like a veil, but nothing could dim the mountain's white, terrible presence. When the stone voice spoke again, its words were even colder than its icy slope.

"And what would you have me do, *Spiritualist*? Bring seeds here, into my stone, among my people, so that Heinricht can have his little experiments?" It gave a rumbling huff. "*You* are the one who is being ridiculous. Understand this, if you can: Letting a seed grow, even under controlled circumstances, is the most dangerous, reckless undertaking possible. Even if all of your postulations are correct, and some miraculous cure was found for the demonseeds, it would still not be worth the risk to my stone, my spirits, my people, or my standing with the Powers to pursue it. We have a system ordained by the Shepherdess for the protection of her flock. The Lord of Storms and his League have held back the demon since it was imprisoned. That is enough. Let it alone."

Miranda flushed and took a step forward, her mouth already open to challenge the mountain again, but Slorn's hand on her shoulder stopped her cold. She looked back to see the bear-headed Shaper staring up at the mountain, his yellow teeth bared.

"Were you just a Great Spirit, I would accept that logic," he growled. "But I am not the man I was ten years ago." He raised his hand and placed his longer fingers across his muzzle, the tips pointed at his large, brown, bear eyes. "I have seen many things since I merged with the bear. Learned many things that spirits have been taught never to speak of. But I am not a simple spirit. I am human. A human who *sees* as we were never meant to see, and I see you now, Durain, Lord of the Mountains."

"Stop," the mountain said.

But Slorn did not stop. "I thought the spirits deferred to you because of your great age and size. Now I see I was only half right. I see her mark on your soul. You are a star, a chosen spirit of the Shepherdess, elevated above all others. You are right. It would be intolerably risky for the Shapers to work on this problem alone, but we don't have to, do we? You can bring my knowledge to the Shepherdess herself—"

"*Enough!*" The mountain quaked, nearly knocking Miranda off her feet. Slorn stumbled too, but caught himself at the last moment. His eyes, however, never left the mountain.

"I begin to understand at last why the Shepherdess made your kind blind," the mountain said, its voice deep and annoyed. "Even though you see, you do not understand." The stone's shaking fell off to a slight vibration, almost like a sigh.

"What don't we understand?" Slorn said.

"Anything," the mountain grumbled, lowering its voice. "To start, you're right. I am a star of the Shepherdess, but the meaning of that title has changed over the long years." Its voice grew wistful. "We old souls were the greatest spirits left at the beginning. When the Shepherdess came into being and was given charge of the sphere, we worked together. She gave us her mark, her authority, which she herself had been given by the Creator, and made us her overseers. We were her hands in the world, keeping order among those spirits of our own kind. My twin brother and I were tasked with watching the mountains, and it took us both, for in those days all the mountains were awake. But then the world changed. The demon appeared."

The snow around the mountain began to swirl angrily. "Such a thing was supposed to be impossible. We gave up our freedom and entered the shell specifically to keep their kind out, and yet here was a demon, right among us. To this day, no one knows how it got in, but it destroyed half the world before the Shepherdess and her weapon, the Lord of Storms, cornered it. By that time the demon was so large the Shepherdess could not destroy it without breaking the world itself in the process. In the end, there was only one solution. It was my brother who made the sacrifice. He gave up his stone and his name to trap the demon so that we might live in peace. The Shepherdess took his body and buried the demon beneath it, fixing the prison in place with her seal. The moment the seal was in place, my brother's verdant slopes were abandoned, and his corpse became what we now call the Dead Mountain."

"Your twin brother," Miranda said, her face pale and her eyes wide. "You mean a mountain as large as you died to trap the demon?"

"Not died," the Shaper Mountain said. "Not entirely, though you would not recognize him if you saw him now."

The snow swirled, and Miranda shuddered as the weight of the mountain's full attention landed on them. "I tell you this, Heinricht, so that you may understand what those ill-gotten eyes of yours see. I may be her star, but it is the Shepherdess who rules this sphere, not us. Star or no, I am as much a slave to the Lady's will as any broken pebble."

"But you are no pebble," Slorn said. "You are the greatest spirit left in the world. And if you will do nothing—"

"You are a Shaper, Heinricht," the mountain said. "It is your nature to see a broken thing and wish to fix it. But this is our world, not a broken sword. We cannot simply reshape it into something better. We must live as the Shepherdess commands and hope things change before we all grow too sleepy and stupid to care."

Slorn frowned. "Too sleepy?"

"This world you know is a sad, diminished shadow," the mountain said. "Every year, more spirits fall asleep and do not wake. Of all my mountains, only a handful still answer when I call. The spirits grow small and stupid. They forget what lies beyond, what came before. But those of us who were Shaped by the Creator himself, we remember. We know the truth..."

As the mountain's voice faded, the landscape began to change. The snow slowed, and then stopped. The light shifted from slate gray to golden yellow as the icy clouds evaporated. Sunlight burst down onto the field, and the snowdrifts began to melt before Miranda's eyes. As they melted, flowers pushed their heads through the ice, opening in tiny bursts of color as the shrinking snowbanks gave way to bright green grass. But the flowers died almost as quickly as they had bloomed, their petals dropping to the grass, which was now fading to dead brown. The mountains vanished beneath a blanket of snow yet again as the meadow withered. But no sooner was the snow on the ground than it began to vanish, and the cycle began again.

Each time it was faster. The meadow and the mountains flashed between snow and life, blooming flowers, withered grass, and crusted snow trading places in breathless transition. Miranda shrank back against Gin, clutching his fur, but the ghosthound offered no comfort. His orange eyes were shut tight, and he was whining deep in his throat as the landscape around them melted, greened, bloomed, withered, and froze over and over again until Miranda was nearly sick from change.

Unlike Gin, Slorn's eyes were wide open. He was standing with his head tilted back, staring open-mouthed at the sky. Miranda swallowed and, against her better judgment, followed his gaze up. She was immediately sorry. The sky was changing just as fast as the world around them, flashing between day and night so rapidly it almost made her retch. But before she could look away, the cycle of dawn, day, dusk, and dark began to slow. At last, it stopped altogether, leaving her staring up at a night sky unlike anything she had ever seen.

She never knew how long they stared in silence. It felt like a lifetime. When she finally found her voice, the words came out more air than sound.

"What are they?"

"I don't know," Slorn answered just as quietly.

High overhead, cast around the crescent moon like scattered sand, points of light shone against the black velvet curve of the night sky. There were thousands of them, millions, more than Miranda could count if she spent the rest of her life doing nothing else. The twinkling lights seemed to gather at the middle of the sky, forming a road of light so beautiful and enormous, it brought tears to her eyes.

"This is my memory," the mountain said, its voice drifting on the gentle wind. "Here at my center, I am free of what the

Shepherdess would have us forget. Here I remember the world as it was before, when time moved forward, when there were seasons and lights in the sky beside the sun and the moon. Back when there was no need for a Shepherdess. Back when every spirit woke and slept as it chose, when there were no humans, no wizards, and we hunted our own demons."

As the mountain spoke, the beautiful night sky full of lights faded. The valley faded, too, so did the mountains, and Miranda found herself standing beside Slorn and Gin in the plain white room.

"But that world is gone," the mountain said, his disembodied voice echoing through the empty chamber. "Broken, eaten, lost forever. We live in the Shepherdess's world now. If I question her methods, even to bring a new idea, even I could end up like Gredit."

"Gredit?" Slorn said, stepping forward. "You know what happened to the Great Bear?"

"We all know," the mountain said. "Before, stars were named so because they were the greatest, the only spirits large enough to watch over their own. But the Shepherdess picks her own stars now. Small spirits, creatures not even worthy of the name, elevated only because the Shepherdess found them beautiful. Even now she ignores the world to play her favorites against each other for no reason other than she likes to be fought over. Gredit, stubborn, noble old bear, thought he could make her see sense. To that end, he made the mistake of threatening her current favorite darling, and she killed him for it."

Slorn made a keening sound deep in his throat. Miranda flinched. It was the most animal sound she'd ever heard him make.

"With my twin dead, I am the last of the great mountains," the Teacher said. "I cannot leave my sleeping brothers without guidance. I cannot risk sharing Gredit's fate, no matter how noble the cause. I do not know if the Shepherdess is mad or simply foolish, but she has shown that she will kill an ancient spirit if the fancy strikes her, and we do not have so many

126

stars that we can throw them away on your theories, Heinricht. Do you understand?"

"I understand, Teacher," Slorn said. "But I do not agree. I cannot accept that a Shepherdess who kills her flock when they question her is worthy of such worship."

"Then you should keep that opinion to yourself," the mountain rumbled. "I have heard your knowledge, Shaper. This hearing is adjourned. Go and make peace with your father. I cannot help you."

"Wait!" Miranda cried, but it was too late. The mountain's voice vanished without even an echo. A second later, the platform under their feet shook, and they began to descend. Miranda turned to Slorn, burning with questions, but one look at his face was enough to kill them on her tongue. She'd never seen him so angry. Behind her, Gin was still on the ground with his eyes closed, breathing the deep, measured breaths he used to keep himself calm when he was injured. Even Mellinor would not speak.

They emerged from the ceiling of the Hall of the Shapers to find the Guildmaster waiting for them with half a dozen Shapers spread out in a circle around the descending pillar.

"Heinricht Slorn," the Guildmaster said. "The Teacher has declared you a threat to the safety of the mountain. You will be taken back to your cell, there to live out the rest of your natural life."

"What?" Miranda said. "The mountain just said he couldn't do anything. How is Slorn a threat?"

"Do not speak!" one of the Shapers shouted, but he stopped when the Guildmaster raised his hand.

"Outsiders do not have a voice within the mountain," the Guildmaster said. Miranda glowered, but the old man wasn't talking to her. He was talking to Slorn. "The Teacher did not like your knowledge, it seems."

"Knowledge worth having is rarely pleasant," Slorn answered. "But I am not convinced the Teacher has truly made his decision."

The Guildmaster stiffened. "Was the Teacher not clear?"

"He was very clear," Slorn answered. "But he showed us much before throwing us out. The Mountain has and will always be our teacher, and a teacher does not show his students the truth if he does not wish them to learn. If he truly had no use for Nivel's and my work, or Miranda's presence, he would never have called us up in the first place."

"A wise observation," the Guildmaster said. "Though you may spend the rest of your life waiting to learn the Teacher's true intentions."

"I am prepared," Slorn said.

"But what about your companion?" the Guildmaster said, turning to face Miranda. "Is she ready? Or have you not told her yet?"

Slorn's jaw clenched, and a tremor of fear ran up Miranda's spine. "Told me what?"

"I'm afraid my son has done you a great disservice," the Guildmaster said. "You see, no outsider who has seen the secrets of the Shaper Mountain is ever allowed to leave."

"*What?*" Miranda shouted, turning to stare at Slorn. "What does he—"

The stone beneath their feet erupted, cutting her off. Great hands of white rock burst from the ground and clutched her body, crushing the air from her lungs. She fought the hold on instinct, but all she managed was to hurt her neck, the only part of her body she could still move. Slorn and Gin were caught as well, but when she snapped her head around to look at the Guildmaster, his old face was truly pitying.

"I am sorry," he said. "But Shaper secrets must be maintained. Out of respect for the great good your order has done for the world, I promise that your life with us will not be uncomfortable." He gave her a sad smile. "Good-bye, Spiritualist."

Miranda opened her mouth to tell him exactly what she thought of that, but the stone closed over her head before the words could form, yanking her down into the mountain.

CHAPTER
8

Dawn had barely broken when Eli woke to the feeling of something cold tracing a burning line across his cheek. He gasped before he could stop himself, his body going rigid. Slowly, deliberately, he forced himself to take deep, calm breaths. Only when he was sure his voice was neutral did he dare to speak.

"I asked you not to do that," he said, opening his eyes.

Beautiful, hated laughter floated through the glowing air as the too-white hand left his face and moved to linger on his chest. Eli swallowed against the bile that rose in his throat. Not now. He couldn't lose it now.

Benehime lay stretched out in the bed beside him, her white body pressed against his. Eli could feel every spirit in the room watching, their souls bowed in reverence to the White Lady, but the Shepherdess didn't seem to notice. Her attention was entirely on Eli as she buried her face in the hollow of his throat.

Remember when we used to spend every morning this way? she whispered, nipping at his windpipe with a little burst of the painless fire he'd learned to loathe. *You were so happy then.*

"I was very young then," Eli said, shifting away from her as much as he dared. "Why are you here, Benehime?"

Do I need a reason? she said, pushing up so that she was looking at him.

Eli said nothing, and Benehime relaxed against him with a long sigh. *If you must know, I've brought you some news. You always did love a bit of gossip.* She smiled, her hand tracing Karon's burn. Deep in his chest, Eli felt the lava spirit roll over in fear. Benehime felt it, too, and she laughed, leaning forward so her white hair fell across them both.

Nara's embraced her power again, she said, moving her hands up to play with his tousled hair. *She's putting together quite the little show. I have to say I'm impressed. She hasn't been this Empress-like in centuries. I'm beginning to remember why I loved her.*

She paused, watching his face for jealousy, but Eli flashed her a genuine smile.

"What a marvelous turn for everyone if she should manage it," he said. "The Empress always did adore you more than I ever could with my black heart."

Benehime's smile faded, and her fingers tangled painfully in his hair. *Don't be cold, Eliton*, she whispered, dragging his head back. *You need to remember that my love is something to be coveted, not taken for granted. I've played your game for many years now, watching you run free, chasing your ridiculous dream of that absurd bounty. It's been an adorable show, but the time for play is over, and I grow tired of waiting.*

"Why are you waiting for me?" Eli said. "Surely there's someone else who can keep you company. The whole world loves you."

What do I care about the world? Benehime said, her beautiful face falling into a sullen frown. *You're the only soul that matters to me, love. That's why I came to warn you.* She released her grip on his hair, pulling her hands down to cup his face instead. *Nara is coming to take me from you*, she whispered. *She's marshaled an army like none I've ever seen. There's no way you can beat her alone.*

Eli had to grit his teeth to keep from flinching as she stroked his cheeks. "With all due respect, Shepherdess, there have been a lot of things you've said I couldn't do, and I've done most of them."

Benehime stiffened, her hands tightening on his face, and for a moment Eli was afraid she was going to rip his head clean off. But then she smiled and leaned in, pressing a soft, burning kiss against his lips. *So arrogant*, she whispered, moving up to kiss the tip of his nose. *So self-assured. That's*

130

why I love you. She kissed him one last time and pulled back. *Really, though, Eliton, you've never been an idiot. For all your puffed-up talk, you must know you'll lose in the end. Nara commands half the world, and now that she's got her spine back, she means to control the whole thing.*

Benehime began to laugh. *Poor thing still hasn't realized that ruling the world doesn't solve all its problems. I should know; I've tried.* She sighed against him, patting his cheeks with her fingers. *She's a lost cause, darling, but she's one you can't possibly hope to beat. Better come home now while things are easy. If you make me save you, I won't be so gentle.*

"But that's the game, isn't it?" Eli said, lying still as a board beneath her. "If I ask you for help, you win."

The Shepherdess's fingers froze against his skin. *You're not still on about that old thing, are you?*

"I most certainly am," Eli said. "And so are you, which is why you haven't just yanked me back yet. You want to win, but so do I, and I'm not one to just roll over." He broke into a wide grin. "You'll have to find something scarier than the Immortal Empress if you want me to come crying back to you, Benehime."

The Shepherdess's face closed like a slamming door. She sat back on top of him, suddenly cold and distant. *I was trying to let you keep your dignity,* she said with a sneer. *I should have known better. You always did enjoy throwing my kindness back in my face. But mark me, favorite, the Empress is coming and she has no love for you. I am your only hope. Try to keep that in mind the next time you decide to be rude.*

Eli didn't answer. He just lay there, his body perfectly still against hers. The Shepherdess watched him a moment longer, and then she leaned down. *I'll be waiting,* she murmured against his mouth, kissing him one last time.

She kept her white eyes open the whole time, staring at him as her mouth crushed his. Eli stared back, not moving so much as a fraction as the burning feel of her lips grew from ticklish to nearly unbearable. Finally, with a slight smile, Benehime vanished. There was no white line, no change. She was just gone, leaving behind nothing, not even a warm spot on the bed. Eli didn't dare move a muscle. He lay perfectly still as the seconds ticked by with painful slowness, counting them one after another until he reached a full minute. Then, like a dam breaking, he collapsed into the bed, gasping as the lingering feel of her presence faded from his body.

Powers, he thought, rolling over as he curled into a ball, clutching his knees against his chest as he fought to get the burning feel of her off his skin. Powers, did he hate her.

"She's getting pushier," Karon whispered, his rumbling voice vibrating up from Eli's chest. "You better watch yourself. You might be the favorite, but it's unwise to push the Lady too far."

Eli squeezed his eyes tighter as he tried to find the words to tell his lava spirit that not pushing wasn't an option. Whatever she said, whatever she threatened, he couldn't go back. Not ever. Not to her. It wasn't just giving up his freedom, or the way she touched him whether he wanted to be touched or not. It wasn't even the fear, or the constant feeling of walking on eggshells whenever she was around for fear of sparking her terrible temper. No, what he hated most was the feeling of being owned.

The moment she'd decided he was her favorite, his life had stopped being his own, and from the time he'd been old enough to understand what that loss meant, what she really was, he'd been fighting to get away from her. He'd lied and conned and traded everything he had, his entire future, for the limited freedom he enjoyed now. But the slack she'd released into his leash depended on his continued ability to make it on his own. That was their wager; *that* was the game. The moment he admitted he couldn't make it on his own, the moment he reached out to her for help, Benehime won, and he went back to being her plaything forever.

"Do you think she's serious about the Empress?" Karon said. "Osera has no hope at all if Nara's coming this time, not unless you mean to take her yourself."

"I'm doing no such thing," Eli said, opening his eyes at

132

last. "Nara won't come. The only thing that could get that woman to move is Benehime herself, and there's no way the Shepherdess would start a continental war just to squeeze me into asking for help. She's nuts, but not *that* nuts."

Karon rumbled deep in Eli's ribs. "I don't know what the Shepherdess is capable of anymore. She has changed very much from when I was young."

"And how long ago was that?" Eli asked.

"Not as long as it should be to account for so great a change," Karon said. "Be careful, Eli. Benehime was always a dangerous Power, but she seems to lose all sense when it comes to her love for you."

"No argument there," Eli muttered. There had been times when the Shepherdess was so angry that Eli had been sure she'd kill him. Sometimes, the dark times, he'd almost hoped she would. At least then he'd be free of her. But the older he got, the more he realized that even death wasn't an escape from Benehime. If he died, she would just catch his soul and put him back together. There was no escape from the Shepherdess's love.

"It has to be a bluff," Eli muttered. "The Empire has been planning to invade Osera for decades. Now that they are, Benehime is just using the timing to try and scare me. But I'm not a stupid kid anymore, and she's going to have to push a lot harder than that to break me." He forced himself to smile. "It's just another of her games, Karon. And I'm the best when it comes to playing games."

Karon grumbled, unconvinced, and Eli patted his chest with a confident thump, though he wasn't really sure whom he was trying hardest to convince with such bravado, the lava spirit or himself.

Outside, the sun was creeping over the castle walls, and Eli decided he'd better get up. He sat and stretched, running his fingers through his hair in a vain effort to remove the feeling of the Shepherdess's hands. He was just reaching for his blond wig when he heard the soft click of the door lock. Eli moved in a flash, grabbing the wig and tossing it on his head. He fell back into his bed just in time to see a young manservant carrying a shaving tray slip through the heavy door.

"Can I help you?" Eli said, his voice drawling in exaggerated sleepiness.

The servant, who obviously thought he was being stealthy, jumped a foot in the air. "Good morning, sir," he said when he'd recovered. "I am here to assist with your morning toilet."

"Splendid," Eli said, sitting up. "What's your name?"

The servant shuffled. "Stefan, sir."

Eli stood with a groan and walked across the room. He took the young man by the shoulder with a firm hand and turned him back toward the hall. "Stefan," he said. "Excellent. Now, when I need assistance with my morning toilet, I'll know exactly whom to call."

"But, Mr. Banage," the servant said, digging his heels into the rich carpet. "The queen ordered that we were to dress the prince and his guests for court."

"How lovely," Eli said, pushing harder. "Did she also order that we were to be starved to death?"

"No, sir!" the servant said, horrified.

Eli flashed him a winning smile. "Well, then, since I am perfectly capable of dressing myself, why don't you go above and beyond the call of duty and find me some breakfast before I eat one of your fancy end tables? Could you do that for me?"

The young man frowned. "I suppose I could, sir, but—"

"You are a prince among men, Stefan," Eli said, giving him a final push out the door. "Of course, considering the princes I've met, that might not be a compliment, but it was meant in good faith."

The servant stumbled into the hallway. "Are you sure you do not wish my help, sir?" he said one last time. "I could ask one of the others to fetch your breakfast."

"I trust no one but you," Eli said, slamming the door behind him. "Don't let me down!" he shouted through the wood.

If Stefan answered, Eli didn't hear. He was already across the room, digging through his bag. He pulled the wig off his

134

head and brushed it out with his fingers before placing it on the washstand. Using hot water from the shaving tray, he washed his face and then wet his real hair, combing it back slick before pressing it dry with one of the hot towels. Next, he picked his shirt and breeches from last night up off the floor and, as they were far and away the nicest clothes he had, put them back on. When he was dressed and his hair was mostly dry, he pinned his wig back in place. He was adjusting the fall of the blond hair across his shoulders when he heard the lock turn again.

Eli glanced up, expecting the servant, or at least a breakfast tray. Instead, Josef marched into the room. The swordsman was also dressed in the same clothes from yesterday, but the fine shirt and trousers were wrinkled as though he'd slept in them. His knives, all of them, were belted on and the Heart was across his back, ready to go. For one soaring moment, Eli thought Josef had changed his mind about staying, but then he saw the pair of guards hot on Josef's heels and a servant hovering with lather bowl and razor in hand, and his spirits dropped.

"Have you seen Nico?" Josef said.

"Good morning to you, too," Eli said. "And no."

Josef grimaced. "I was sure she would come back, but she never did. I waited all night." He scrubbed his hands through his short blond hair. "Something's wrong, Eli. It's not like her to be gone this long without a reason."

Eli turned back to the mirror to contemplate his position. His swordsman could be unusually insightful about some things, but he was thick as a wagon of bricks about others. There was no easy way of explaining to him that, underneath the semisentient coat, monstrous strength, and shadowy past, Nico was a girl as well as a demonseed. Her relationship with Josef might be a nebulous, nameless sort of thing, but hearing that the man she trusted more than anything in the world, the man she followed with unquestioning loyalty, was *married*, had been married for a year, and never even thought to mention it...well, that had to sting, and Nico didn't exactly talk about her problems.

135

"I'm sure she's fine," Eli said, glancing at Josef and then pointedly flicking his eyes to the guards and the servant hovering behind him.

That, at least, Josef got. "Get out," he growled.

"But, my lord," said the guard at his left. "Your lady mother was very specific—"

"Where do you think I'm going to run?" Josef said. "This cell is the same as the one you just let me out of. I need to talk to my friend in private, so shove off. Now."

The guards backed off as one, bowing their way out the door. The servant, however, stayed, heated towel ready. Josef stared at him a moment, and then grabbed the man's shoulder. The servant made a sort of squeaking sound as Josef shoved him into the hall, closing the heavy door in his face.

"I can see why you had problems being a prince," Eli said, leaning on the washstand. "Not exactly the genteel epitome of magnanimity and tact, are you?"

"Shut up," Josef said, but there was no venom in it. He walked across the room and sat down on Eli's bed, putting his head in his hands with a deep breath. "I can't believe she'd leave without telling me."

"She didn't leave, Josef," Eli said with a long sigh. "She probably just needs some time to work things through. It's been a pretty dramatic week."

"But she's never done that before," Josef said. "Vanished like that, in front of everyone." He glanced up. "You're the wizard. You would have heard if something happened to her, right? With the demon?"

Eli watched the swordsman with new interest. This wasn't just bullheaded tactlessness. Josef was really worried. It was rather touching, actually.

"The whole castle would have heard if something had happened between Nico and her demon," he said gently. "The fact that we were able to sleep last night is proof that she's fine. She's probably hiding somewhere, waiting for us to follow the plan and get out. My biggest worry is how we're going to

136

let her know the plan's toast. Assuming, of course, you haven't changed your mind since last night."

"No," Josef said, shaking his head. "I can't leave. I told you that."

"So you did," Eli said, exasperated. "But you couldn't have picked a worse place to have this fit of conscience. We're wanted criminals, remember? The longer we stay, the more likely it is that someone's going to put the pieces together and come after us, if they haven't already. Staying doesn't help anyone—not us, not Nico, and not your mother. You did your duty by showing up, so let's cut our losses, find Nico, and get out of here before things get worse."

Eli finished with a sinking feeling. Josef's head was down, his hands clasped behind his neck. When he spoke at last, his voice was very calm and very, very serious.

"Eli," he said. "I'm only going to say this once." He looked up, and his eyes were the eyes of a swordsman who has bet his life on his next stroke. "I may be in disgrace, but Queen Theresa is still my queen, and she's still my mother. I let her down before, and if staying here long enough to give her an heir is all she wants from me to make things right, then that's what I'm going to do. End of discussion."

Eli loomed over him, his mouth pressed in a tight, flat line. Josef glared right back, hands on his swords. Finally, Eli's shoulders slumped, and he flopped back against the washstand with an enormous huff.

"All right, all right," he said. "You win. When are you going to tell the queen your decision?"

"Right now," Josef said, standing up. "And you're coming with me."

"Wait," Eli said, holding up his hands. "Wait, wait, wait. Unless you're planning to steal that lovely set of antique tapestries she has above her fireplace, I don't have anything to do with this. For the next few weeks at least, you're the crown prince of Osera. I'm still the most wanted criminal in the Council. I don't care how forgiving your dear mother is, it's not exactly a winning match. Actually, it would probably be better for all involved if I lit out for a while. Go steal something and get my mind off things until you're done being a good husband."

Josef shook his head. "You have to be here."

"Why?" Eli said, truly mystified.

Josef looked away. Eli pursed his lips thoughtfully. If he didn't know better, he'd have said the swordsman looked sheepish.

"Being prince means I have to go to court," Josef said at last. "Court means politics and a lot of talking to people who can't be insulted. I'm not really—" He stopped and took a deep breath. "You're the one who's good with that kind of thing, all right? You have to stay."

"Josef," Eli said with a growing smile. "Could it be? Are you asking me for help?"

Josef glowered at him. "Not if you're going to say it like that."

"No, no, no," Eli said, placing his hands on his chest. "I'm flattered. I would be delighted to be your adviser."

"Good," Josef said, nodding. "That's settled, then."

"Of course," Eli added, raising one long finger. "You'd have to say what I told you to say, exactly as I told you to say it."

Josef grimaced, and Eli shook his head. "That's the only way it works. You can tell me to stay all you want, but if you're not going to listen to my advice, I'm not going to waste my breath giving it."

"Fine," Josef grumbled. "Just don't get carried away."

Eli flipped the edges of his golden wig. "When have I ever gotten carried away?"

Josef rolled his eyes and didn't answer.

"Now," Eli said. "Let's get started. Normally, I'd say we should put off seeing the queen. Let her sweat a bit. However, seeing as she's your mother, sweating would probably only make her more stubborn, so we're going to go see her immediately. When we arrive, you're going to tell her that you're staying and doing your part as a dutiful prince, but only if you get to keep your friends with you, and as soon as a pregnancy is confirmed, you're leaving. Also, you want full freedom of movement and all royal privileges for you and your entourage, meaning myself and Nico." He shot Josef a smile. "No reason we can't have a little fun while we're stuck here. Does that sound fair?"

Josef rubbed his chin. "I guess it does."

"Excellent," Eli said. "I'll need a full rundown on Osera's political situation before we do any more politicking than that, but hopefully we won't have to. If war's truly coming, Osera has bigger problems than us. All we need to do is keep our noses down, keep you in bed with your wife, and we'll be out of here in two months. Tops."

Josef winced. "I'm not a stud bull, you know."

"You are now," Eli said cheerfully, walking to the door. He opened it to find Josef's guards, his overzealous manservant, and Eli's own Stefan (now with a breakfast trolley instead of the shaving tray) standing in the hallway, whispering together. They all jumped when they saw Eli, but came when he beckoned, tiptoeing into the room as meekly as they could.

"So sorry about earlier," Eli said, clapping Josef's servant on the shoulders. "The prince had a bit of a bad night, but food will set everything to rights. Now," he said, pushing the man toward Josef, "if you would be so kind as to make your prince presentable, we'll see the queen as soon as she's ready."

Both servants cheered up immensely once they were free to do their jobs. Eli stepped aside to let Josef sit down at the washstand as both servants moved in and began cleaning him up. The swordsman sat glumly, letting them lather his chin and comb his hair. Meanwhile, Eli helped himself to a cup of tea, a plate of ham, and several scones from the breakfast tray before flopping down on the bed to watch the show. When Stefan asked if he would like a shave as well, Eli politely declined.

"It took me weeks to grow what I have," he said, rubbing his fingers over the sparse beard on his chin. "I'm not quite ready to sacrifice it yet. Besides," he nodded at Josef, who

139

was gripping his swords as the manservant deftly ran the razor over his taut neck. "I wouldn't miss this for the world."

Josef shot Eli a murderous look. Eli answered with a wide smile as he shoved another slice of ham into his mouth.

When he was shaved and clean, Josef sent the servants running with a growl before joining Eli at the breakfast tray. He ate five slabs of ham in rapid succession and then stepped away.

"Let's go," he said, wiping his hands on the shaving towels.

"Not so fast," Eli said. "You can't go see the queen like that."

Josef looked down at his shirt. "Like what?"

Eli sighed and walked over to the mirror on the washstand, tilting it until Josef could see his whole body. Blades were strapped everywhere they could go. Hilts were visible at his sleeves, neck, waist, and boots. Bandoleers of throwing knives were crushing his dress shirt and his short swords were wearing a matched set of grooves into his new belt. Finally, there was the Heart of War itself, the wrapped hilt poking up high over his shoulder, just in case anyone wasn't intimidated enough by the rest of it.

Josef crossed his arms over his chest. "No."

"Josef," Eli pleaded. "You asked me to stay and help you be a prince. This is step one: not looking like a murderer."

"I'm not going unarmed," Josef said.

"No one's going to challenge you to a duel in the palace."

Josef snorted. "You obviously don't know Osera."

"Fine, fine," Eli said, throwing up his hands. "One sword, but you're leaving the rest."

Josef planted his feet, daring him. Eli glared right back, and then he started to push.

In the end, they compromised on one short sword, all the hidden knives, and the Heart, which Josef absolutely refused to leave behind. Eli would have kept going, but it was nearing midmorning and his plan of not making the queen wait was already an hour off schedule. He tapped his foot impatiently as Josef slowly divested himself of the knives he'd agreed to leave, and then he pushed the swordsman into the hall.

The soldiers were more than happy to escort the prince and his friend to the queen's chamber. The castle was bustling with morning activity. Servants, their arms full with trays, linens, and other vitals of a noble household, ran up and down the narrow halls, pressing themselves into the wall to make way when Josef and Eli passed. Eli watched the comings and goings with a keen eye. The queen ran a tight ship. Every servant was well groomed and well dressed in simple livery of good quality materials right down to their polished boots. It was little details like this, far more than any ostentation, that confirmed Osera's wealth in Eli's mind. He also noticed that everyone, even the servants, was armed with at least a dagger. He filed that tidbit away for questioning later. At the moment, though, he had more important blanks to fill in.

"Josef," he whispered, leaning toward the swordsman as they walked down the hall. "If I'm going to help you be a prince, there are a few things I need from you."

"Like what?" Josef said, visibly annoyed by the slow pace the guards set.

"Let's start with the princess," Eli said. "I'm guessing you two knew each other before all this?"

Josef nodded. "She's Lenette's girl."

"Lenette?" Eli said. "The queen's maid?"

"Lady-in-waiting," Josef corrected him. "Lenette is my mother's confidant and best friend. Has been for years. Adela's her daughter. We grew up together."

"I see," Eli said. "Your mother married you to your childhood sweetheart in the hopes you wouldn't complain as much."

"We weren't sweethearts," Josef snapped. "But otherwise you're right."

"Well, at least she tried to make you happy," Eli said, scratching his chin. "That's more than most royal mothers."

Josef didn't say anything to that, and they walked the rest of the way to the queen's chamber in silence. But when they

141

got there, the queen was nowhere to be seen. Instead, her lady-in-waiting, the lovely woman in black from before, greeted them in the queen's entry chamber.

"Lenette," Josef said with a stiff nod as the soldiers left. "Where's the queen?"

"Your mother is unwell this morning, Prince Thereson," Lenette said, returning to the little table where she'd been sitting when they'd arrived.

"Let me see her," Josef said, crossing his arms.

Lenette took her time, focusing her attention on the leaves in the little stone grinder in front of her. "The queen's health is a delicate thing," she said at last, pushing the grinding wheel until the leaves were crushed into a fine powder. "Her rest is not to be disturbed."

"I'm sure she'll want to hear this," Eli said, cutting in before Josef could say anything he'd regret. "Can't you take us to see her?"

"No," Lenette said without looking up as she emptied the freshly ground leaves into the glass jar at her elbow. "Since you're here, I assume you mean to tell her that the prince has decided to stay in Osera and do his duty?"

Eli and Josef exchanged a look.

"More or less," Eli said.

"Good," Lenette said with a nod. "I'll tell her when she wakes up."

"Listen," Josef growled. "I don't care how far you've crawled into the queen's ear since I left—probably more than you should have, considering you convinced her to marry your daughter into the royal line of Osera. But you're not so important that you can keep me from seeing my own mother."

Josef's anger was usually enough to turn people into jelly, but Lenette remained calm and collected.

"I'm not the one keeping you from your mother," she said. "These are her doctor's orders. If she is to be fit enough to appear at court today, she must be allowed to rest undisturbed. If you have an issue with that, the doctor keeps his office on

142

the third floor. Take it up with him. Now, if you still feel the need to brag about your sudden decision to return to your duties, I suggest you find Adela. As your wife, it's her job to take an interest in whatever you have to say. She's at the guard keep, overseeing drill." Lenette gave him a slow smile. "My daughter is a fine guard captain and a dutiful child, which is more than I can say for some."

Josef's hand moved toward the blade at his hip in a way that would make anyone who knew him at all dive for cover, but Lenette just smiled and stood up, carrying her pot of ground herbs to the tea service against the far wall.

"I must take the queen her medicine," she said, tapping a spoonful of the ground leaves onto a silver mesh strainer before pouring a measure of hot water through the leaves into the cup below. "Is there anything else I can help you with, Prince Thereson?"

Josef turned on his heel and walked out of the room. Eli followed, glancing over his shoulder just in time to see the queen's lady-in-waiting smile as she blew on the steaming water. She was placing the cup on a serving tray when the door closed and Eli saw no more.

"Charming lady," he said, running to catch up with Josef as the guards fell in beside them. "Has she always been like that?"

"Long as I've known her," Josef answered with a growl.

"So, is she noble?" Eli said. "A cousin or something?"

"This is Osera, not Zarin," Josef sneered. "We don't marry our cousins. Lenette's not even Oseran. She married into money, turned that into a court invitation, and then wormed her way into the queen's favor. She's been glued to Mother's side for as long as I can remember. People used to complain about a foreigner having so much power, but she's been here so long now, I don't think people even remember she's not from the island."

"Time changes many things," Eli said. "Are you going to see your wife, then?"

"And prove Lenette right?" Josef said with a snort. "Not a

chance. We're going to use our time before court to look for Nico. I'd rather see her than Adela any day."

Eli smiled. "I'm sure Nico would be delighted to hear that."

"Why?"

"No reason," Eli said, rubbing his forehead with a long, deep sigh. "Lead on."

Josef shrugged and started walking faster. They ditched the guards on the next turn and went out on the rooftops to start their search.

After two hours of looking and nothing to show for it, Josef suddenly announced it was time to go to court. Tempting as it was, Eli resisted the urge to point out that they still had plenty of time before the ceremony began. For one, it might very well be time in Josef's mind. He was famously insistent about showing up early. Two, Eli had lived with the swordsman long enough to know that you didn't try reasoning with him when his face was set in that particular expression of cold rage.

As it turned out, it was good that they went down when they did. Despite being nearly an hour before court was scheduled to start, the throne room of Osera was already packed.

"I see you come by your predilection for early arrivals naturally," Eli said, poking his head through a side door to survey the scene. "I think we're the last ones here."

Josef didn't answer. He was standing by the door with his hands on his knives, looking suspiciously pale.

Eli poked him in the shoulder. "What's wrong?"

"Nothing's wrong," Josef said, taking a deep breath. "It's just been a while since I had to deal with this idiocy."

Eli gaped at him. "Josef, you're the wielder of the Heart of War. You've fought Berek Sted *and* the Lord of Storms. How can you be nervous about facing some nobles?"

"I'm not nervous," Josef snapped. "I just need a moment."

"It's a room full of rich, soft, old men!" Eli cried. "It's not an army."

"I'd prefer an army," Josef said. "You don't know what

those people are like. If they would fight me openly, everything would be fine. But they don't. They just *talk*."

Eli smiled and held up a finger. "Just relax and remember the first rule of thievery: Shown weakness is your only weakness. Go in there with your head held high and leave the talking to me. That's why I'm here, remember?"

Josef released the death grip on his sword long enough to wipe the sweat from his brow with the back of his sleeve. "Just promise me you won't turn this into one of your over-complicated Eli things," he muttered. "Please."

"I have no idea what you're talking about," Eli said, taking Josef by the arm and steering him toward the door. "Chin up. Try to look princely."

Josef nodded and set his features in the steely expression of a man bravely facing his own death. Eli grimaced, but didn't comment. Bad as it was, it was better than the cold rage from earlier. He gave Josef a firm push, and the two of them walked into the hall.

The Oseran throne room had what Eli thought of as a paranoid setup, usually found in kingdoms with a violent history. It was all one large room with a row of narrow support columns forming a corridor up the middle, but rather than placing the throne on a free-standing platform as in Mellinor or other, more peaceable kingdoms, Osera's throne was flush with the back wall, leaving no space for attack from the rear.

The throne room had no wings, but there was a gallery running around the upper level that was already full. Above the gallery, a line of thin windows carved the bright island sunlight into slices that struck the crowd at regular intervals, painting the hall in stripes of light. Down on the floor, the people were better dressed than in the gallery, but Eli saw none of the sort of ostentation normally found in the court of such a wealthy country. There was little jewelry to be seen, even on the older women. Dresses were muted colors, dark reds, greens, or navy. The men wore black almost exclusively, and everyone, even the women, was armed.

"I'm sorry I gave you a hard time about the knives, now," Eli whispered.

"What did you expect?" Josef said, pushing his way toward the throne. "This is Osera. They didn't call my grandfather Bloody Liechten because of his contributions to the arts."

Eli grimaced. Parts of Josef's personality were becoming more understandable by the second.

"I'm surprised no one's come up to you yet," he said, looking around. People were certainly staring but, oddly, no one had made a move to approach their long-lost prince. In Eli's experience, a prince, even an outcast runaway like Josef, was still someone who garnered favor-currying by social climbers. These people seemed almost afraid.

Josef just shrugged. "They probably don't recognize me. I'm a lot bigger than I was when I left."

Eli kept his mouth shut about the likelihood of that explanation and focused on following the path Josef opened through the crowd.

As it happened, they made it all the way to the railing that separated the dais from the rest of the room without being approached. This close, Eli could see the throne easily. Like everything in the castle, the throne of Osera radiated age and deep-rooted authority. It was enormous, a naked stone bench wide enough to seat two men of Josef's size with room to spare. The stone was the smooth, dove-gray rock of the mountain the castle sat on. It was carved with undulating patterns that mimicked the crashing sea so that whoever sat on the throne looked to be floating on a stone wave. A nice trick, all told, but the thing that really caught Eli's attention wasn't the throne itself, but the statues flanking it. Two enormous lions cast from midnight-black iron were anchored on either side of the throne. The lions stood rampant on their hind legs with their backs to the wall and their front paws reaching out to claw whoever defied Osera's ruler.

"Throne of iron lions, indeed," Eli whispered, leaning in to admire the delicate metalwork of their curling manes.

"What?" Josef said, looking up from his spot leaning against a support pillar.

Eli shook his head and set about studying the court instead. He scanned the people around them, trying to pick out Josef's relatives from the crush. It proved harder than he'd thought it would be. Tall, blond, and grumpy seemed to be the motif among Oseran nobility. He'd never seen a sourer-faced crowd in his life.

"Josef," Eli whispered. "Wasn't Osera founded on piracy?"

"Among other things," Josef said dryly.

Eli waved at the scowling crowd. "I thought pirates were supposed to be jolly."

Josef made a sound in the back of his throat that reminded Eli of a ghosthound's growl. "Maybe you haven't been paying attention, but Osera doesn't have a lot to be jolly about at the moment."

"I don't see that you were ever jolly," Eli said, glancing again at the lions.

Josef followed his gaze. "Not much room for it," he said quietly. "Osera has always been ruled by the strong. Has to be. The sea eats the soft and the weak. The lions are there to remind people of that."

"Point taken," Eli said. He was about to ask another question when Josef suddenly pushed off the pillar.

"Eyes front," Josef said, pulling his jacket straight. "The queen's coming."

"But there's still half an hour before court!" Eli protested.

"Why do you think everyone gets here early?"

Eli's answer was drowned out by a peel of trumpets as a six squad of guards in full armor marched into the throne room. People scooted out of their way, clearing a wide swath down the middle. The guards walked the full length of the hall, peeling off in pairs to stand at attention before each pillar until they had formed an armed corridor from the door to the throne. When they were in position, the trumpets sounded again, and the room filled with the sweep of cloth and the creak of leather as everyone, nobles and servants, bowed in reverence as Queen Theresa herself entered the throne room.

The queen looked very different from the night before. Her white hair was pulled up beneath a plain, masculine crown of heavy gold. She was clothed in black, a widow's mourning dress of stiff, raw silk. Her lined face looked pale and pinched, but she stood straight, walking on her own with one hand resting on the arm of the tall, lovely woman in armor walking beside her—Princess Adela, Josef's wife.

The princess made an impressive sight. With her dark, glossy hair and bright silver armor, she shone like a beacon beside the queen's dour black, an effect that was not lost on the crowd. People glanced up from their bows as the princess passed. Their faces were a mix of envy and adoration. More adoration than Eli had expected. With great care, Adela helped the queen up the dais stairs to the wide throne. Beside him, Eli felt Josef stiffen, but the swordsman said nothing as his wife helped his mother down to the hard stone bench. When she was settled, Adela stepped aside, leaving Theresa to survey her court.

Eli swallowed. The queen of Osera on her throne was an impressive sight indeed. The black of her dress shone from the gray stone like a rock among the waves. Above her, the lions' extended paws framed her head like a second crown, a reminder of the power her position held, an ancient, bloody, visceral power that had nothing to do with the Council or Osera's newfound wealth. Theresa's pale eyes moved over the crowd, noting and dismissing each face until she found Josef's.

"You," she said, her voice echoing through the silent chamber. "Up here."

Josef and Eli exchanged a final look, and then Josef pushed off the pillar, stepped over the railing, and climbed the stone steps to stand beside his mother.

"My son," Theresa announced in a voice so harsh it made Eli wince. "Prince Josef Liechten Thereson Esinlowe, has returned from his travels to grace us with his presence once again."

A murmur rose up from the crowd, and Josef shifted uncomfortably. Eli bit his lip, half expecting Josef to walk out, but he stayed rooted to the step beside the throne, glaring at the crowded room like he was daring them to do something about it.

"Last year," the queen continued, "I declared the marriage of my son to Adela Theresa Reiniger, daughter of Lord Reiniger and his wife, the Lady Lenette, my dearest friend and lady of the chamber. Today, I reaffirm that bond."

She beckoned, and Adela stepped forward, her hard-soled boots clacking against the stone until she was standing directly at the queen's right. Theresa motioned again, and Josef reluctantly moved closer. Theresa took Adela's hand and pressed it to Josef, who took it hesitantly. The queen smiled as the connection was made and gave them both a push.

"People of Osera," she announced as Josef and Adela turned to face the room. "I give you your prince and princess. Through this union, the blood of the House of Eisenlowe shall flow to a new generation. May the strength of the Iron Lions breed true, and may the House of Eisenlowe never fall."

Applause erupted throughout the court, but the noise rang hollow in Eli's ears. No one looked particularly happy. Not the couple, and certainly not the party of large, blond gentlemen in rich suits standing across the aisle.

The room fell silent again as the queen raised a skeletal hand. "The royal couple will now perform the Proving," she announced. "Clear the hall."

"Clear the hall!" The cry went up as the guards began directing people to the edges of the room.

Eli glanced around in alarm. Up by the throne, the prince and princess separated without so much as a glance, Adela down the stairs toward the back of the room, Josef back toward Eli with a glum look.

"What's the Proving?" Eli hissed when Josef reached him. "You didn't say anything about any Proving." He looked sideways at the large, clear space that had formed at the center of the room. "Is this like the first dance, or something? Is her father going to give her away?"

"Adela's father is dead," Josef said, plucking knives out of his clothes and handing them to Eli. "And the Proving is an old Oseran tradition."

"Right," Eli said, taking the knives with trepidation. "So like a dance with quaint folk music?"

"It's not a dance," Josef said, lifting the Heart from his back and setting it gently against the pillar. "It's a duel."

"*A duel?*" Eli said, more loudly than he would have liked. The comment drew several nasty looks from the people around them. Eli gritted his teeth and dropped his voice. "I thought you just got married?"

"We did," Josef said, checking the short sword at his hip. "This is the next part of the ceremony. It's the duty of all members of the royal family to protect Osera. So whenever someone in the family gets married, both husband and wife have to fight a demonstration duel to prove they are capable of holding the throne."

"Holding the throne?" Eli said. "What century do you think this is? Are you going to drag her to the marriage chamber by her hair next?"

"Osera is an old country," Josef said. "My grandfather nearly killed the woman who was to be his first wife. Stabbed her twice before sending her away for being too weak."

"That's *horrible*," Eli cried.

Josef shrugged. "That's how things are here. But don't worry, I won't hurt Adela. I'm just going scare her into an honorable surrender." He grinned, patting the sword at his hip. "Shouldn't take long."

In anyone else, Eli would have called that remark arrogant, but this being Josef, Eli had to spot him that one. "Try not to embarrass her too badly," he said. "Remember, our getting out of here depends on your mother getting her grandchild, and that'll be a little difficult if your princess is making you sleep on the floor."

"I'll do what I can," Josef said, walking through the parted crowd.

Eli bit his lip and followed, clutching Josef's cast-off blades

150

to his chest. Adela was waiting for Josef at the center of the makeshift dueling arena. She was flanked by two armored men, one young, one gray haired. Both looked unhappy, but the princess was smiling. She turned to her escorts and whispered something that made them smile as well before they stepped back, leaving her alone at her end of the cleared hall. The princess turned to face Josef as he moved to take his place opposite her, drawing her heavy short sword with a metal hiss as she took up her position. Josef drew his sword as well and stopped in a stance Eli recognized: first position, the root of swordsmanship.

The queen looked down on the combatants from her throne, her wrinkled face like a crumpled paper mask. Only her hands betrayed her true feelings. They were knotted in her lap, the heavy rings biting into the taut skin of her fingers as she lifted her chin.

"Begin."

The word was scarcely out of her mouth before Josef sprang forward. The crowd gasped, and even Eli stepped back. Josef charged like an avalanche, enormous and unstoppable with his sword flipped in his grip, the flat of the blade already whistling down to strike Adela's sword hand.

If Eli had not spent years watching Josef fight, he would have missed what happened next. As it was, he still wasn't sure how it came about. One second, Josef was perfectly on target, the next, Adela was behind him, her feet turning neatly as she slid around his blade.

Josef turned as the lunge carried him past where her hand had been, throwing his weight to bring his sword up in time to catch hers before it landed in his back. Their blades crashed in a shower of sparks, and Josef stumbled at the impact. Eli caught his breath. They were fighting with infantry short swords, so they were very close. That left little time to react to a strike and less to dodge. Adela had done both *and* come around with a counter. He could see the same thoughts on Josef's surprised face as he fell back, catching himself at the last moment with his free hand. The second his fingers touched the floor, he pushed up, forcing Adela back with his superior height and breaking their lock. The princess retreated neatly, letting her sword follow the force sideways and down for a blow at Josef's side. But surprise attacks work only once. This time, Josef was ready. He parried her blow with a dip of his blade and stepped in, slamming his shoulder into her chest. Adela grunted and fell, landing hard on her back with a clatter of metal. Josef followed her as she went down, planting his feet on either side of her body and placing his sword's point on her exposed neck.

Adela held up her hands immediately, and the crowd began to applaud. The duel was over. Josef had won. Josef stared at the downed princess a moment longer before swinging his sword away and offering his hand. Adela took it, and he pulled her up. The applause died down as they walked through the throne room and up the dais stairs to stand again before the queen.

"The proof has been made plain," Queen Theresa announced, smiling widely as prince and princess took their places at her side. "Both have shown before all they can wield a sword in Osera's name. The bond begun a year ago is now complete. Bow before your prince and princess."

The room filled with the rustle of silk as the crowd obeyed. Eli bowed as well, but he kept his eyes on Josef. The swordsman had that look on his face, the one he got when he was extremely angry and trying to hide it.

As people began to raise their heads, the queen said something to Adela that Eli couldn't hear. The princess nodded and motioned to someone down the steps. At once, Lenette appeared from the crowd and hurried to the queen's side. Theresa reached for Lenette, and the lady-in-waiting pulled her up, supporting the queen by her shoulders. The princess and Josef turned to help, but the queen shook her head and firmly pointed for them to turn back and face the people. They obeyed, Adela more swiftly than Josef, as Lenette helped the queen hobble slowly down the dais steps and out a side door.

With the queen gone, court was over, and people began coming up to the royal couple to offer their congratulations. Josef shot Eli a look that would have been panic on anyone

152

else's face, and Eli, recognizing his cue, sprang into action, sliding deftly around the guards and up the dais stairs.

"Princess," he said, dropping another, shallower bow as he fell in beside Josef. "Congratulations on your nuptials. I don't think I've ever seen a more succinct royal wedding."

Adela gave him a skeptical look. "With war on the horizon, the queen saw no purpose in needless expense," she said. "Osera is a practical country, Mr. Banage."

Eli flinched in surprise before remembering the identity he'd chosen for this foray. Fortunately, the princess was too distracted to notice. She was already turning to greet the thin man with graying blond hair, a hawkish nose, and a stern expression very similar to Josef's, who was the first to climb the stairs.

"Duke Finley," Adela said, bobbing her head.

The man didn't even look at her. His eyes were on Josef, looking the prince up and down with his hands on his hips.

"The wayward prince, back at last," the duke said. "I suppose that means Osera is now mortgaged to whatever bounty hunter dragged you in?"

Josef stiffened. "There's no hunter involved. I came back on my own."

"Really?" the duke said. "Prince Thereson, doing his duty? That would be a first."

He said this last bit over his shoulder to the well-dressed group standing behind him, many of whom laughed out loud at the duke's daring. Josef clenched his fists and took a menacing step forward before Eli jabbed him hard in the small of the back.

"Do you think it is wise for you to speak so of the prince in the queen's hall, Finley?"

Josef and Eli both blinked. The words had come from Adela, who was glaring at the duke like he was a pebble she'd found in her boot.

The duke sneered back. "No wiser than addressing the next king of Osera without his title, *Adela*."

The princess's scowl deepened, but Duke Finley wasn't

looking at her anymore. He leaned in to Josef, a smug smile on his face. "You've been gone awhile, cousin," he said in a low voice. "One man to another, let me give you a little advice. Theresa thinks she can cling to her father's throne even in death by marrying her failure of a son to the daughter of her favorite gold-digging maid, but you won't last a day past the queen's funeral. I am the named heir, but even if I weren't, the people of Osera would never stand to have a common murderer as their king. The only reason they tolerate one as their prince is because of your mother. In any case, I wouldn't get too comfortable, were I in your position."

Eli winced. Though the duke's voice was soft, the room around them had gone deathly still, and Eli had no illusions that the insult had somehow gone unheard. But before he could say anything to diffuse the situation, Josef opened his mouth and made it worse.

"I have no intention of being king," he said. "Never have. As for me being a murderer..." Josef lifted his chin, and his hands drifted to the sword at his side. "You're right. I've killed people. But I'm a swordsman, and so was every man I defeated. Death is something you learn to expect when you choose the life of the sword."

"You're quick to draw such a fine line," the duke said, leaning back. "Must help you sleep at night." He flashed the couple a final, thin smile and turned to walk back down the dais steps. "Congratulations on your marriage. I can't think of two people who deserve each other more."

Eli arched an eyebrow at the duke's retreating back. "What a lovely individual."

Josef grunted in reply, but Adela cast a cold eye at her husband. "Finley's not the only one who thinks that way," she said softly. "I wouldn't speak so freely of the men you've killed, Prince Thereson."

"I am not ashamed of what I am," Josef said hotly.

"But others are," Adela said. "You'd do well to remember that."

Josef stared at her, but Adela was the picture of serenity as she turned and took the hand of the elderly lady who was next in line to wish the royal couple well.

It took almost two hours to greet all the nobility. They were arranged by rank, but Josef glowered at everyone equally, so it was quite fortunate that Adela was there to give the proper greeting to each noble before any offense could be taken.

After all the Oseran noble families had their say, the royal couple was shuffled down to the front gate to be announced before the crowd that had gathered in the square. The people cheered when Adela appeared, and she smiled and waved at them like a perfect princess. Beside her vibrant happiness, Josef looked like a looming vulture, hunched and dour, glaring at everything.

Eli watched the whole thing from the back, blithely ignoring the servant who was trying to convince him that he would be more comfortable waiting in his room. He tried sending Josef cues to lighten up, but Josef was too far gone in his dudgeon to notice, and Eli soon gave up in favor of watching Adela.

It was quite the show. The princess was the perfect mix of sweet shyness and hard Oseran duty with her long, glossy hair, pretty smiles, and shining armor. The crowd was mad for her. They cheered wildly, pressing against the guards. Adela smiled and waved back, looking down with becoming modesty whenever the people grew too wild. This, of course, only made the crowd cheer louder. It was a perfectly played performance. So perfect that Eli was beginning to wonder how long she'd practiced.

Finally, the presentation ended, and the royal couple was escorted back to the throne room. Josef looked like a ten-year veteran returning from the front as he walked over to the pillar to retrieve the Heart of War and the rest of his weaponry. Adela, on the other hand, was prettier than ever, with her cheeks glowing from the warmth of the crowd. She stopped a moment to greet the knot of royal guardsmen who were waiting at the throne room entrance, and then she excused herself and walked over to her husband. Josef stopped strapping swords to himself long enough to give her a questioning look.

"The queen asked that I give you a tour of the barracks," she said, her voice almost shy. "In case you wanted to resume your duty as head of the Queen's Guard."

Josef wrinkled his nose. "Who's head now?"

"I am," Adela said.

"Impossible," Josef said, getting back to the business of reattaching his weapons. "That's a royal position, inherited by blood. Your father wasn't even titled. How'd you end up with it?"

"Because your mother was too sick to do it herself and she didn't trust Finley with her guards," Adela said, putting her hands on her hips. "It should be the prince's duty, but it's not like you were here, was it?"

Josef stopped midstrap. "I get it, all right? I wasn't here. I let people down. I'm a terrible prince. Message received, so you can all drop the guilt routine."

"You know, it doesn't have to be like this," Adela said, crossing her arms. "You could *try* being a prince, at least in public."

"I have tried," Josef said, buckling his second sword back onto his hip. "Didn't do me any good then, won't do me any good now. I just want to get this over with and get on with my life."

Adela gave him a scornful look. "Then I'll see you tonight," she said, turning on her heel. "And we can get on with getting this over with. Good afternoon, prince."

Josef sighed. "Adela..."

But the princess was already walking away. Josef watched her go and then he turned and grabbed the Heart of War, slinging it on his back with so much force that Eli winced.

"You know," Eli said as gently as he could, "she does have a point."

"Shut. Up," Josef said.

"It could be worse," Eli went on. "At least you're not stuck with some insipid court flower. I mean, despite the hobble of being married to you, she seems to be a popular princess.

156

She's certainly not bad to look at, not stupid, and we've all seen she's a decent fighter."

"That's the thing," Josef said, dropping his voice. "I can't shake the feeling something was wrong with that duel."

"Josef." Eli *tsk*ed. "Calling foul just because she gave you a harder time than you expected isn't very princely."

"I'm not calling foul," he said softly. "Adela and I were kids together, remember? We had the same sword instructor, and we dueled a lot. I knew she would be good. I just didn't expect her to be that good."

"That fast, you mean," Eli said, lowering his voice to match Josef's.

"It's not even that," Josef said, shaking his head. "She could have dodged that blow to the chest. I saw her feet start to move, but then she stopped. She let me win."

Eli fought the urge to smile. "Maybe she didn't want to embarrass you?"

"She's not *that* good," Josef grumbled, marching toward the door. "Come on. I need a drink."

"But you don't drink," Eli said, running after him.

Josef started walking faster. "I do now."

Eli left it at that and focused on keeping up with his swordsman. This was going to be some wedding night.

Two hours later, Josef had almost finished his one drink when a servant entered and told him his room was ready.

"I have a room," Josef said, scowling up from where he sat on the floor with the Heart of War propped on his shoulder. "What do you think you just walked into?"

The servant flinched, and Eli gave him a sympathetic look from his spot on the bed, but he didn't do anything to save the poor boy. In the five years he'd known Josef, he'd never seen him in such a foul mood. He was happy to let someone else take the heat for a bit.

"Forgive me, my lord," the servant said at last, eying Josef's knives, all of which had found their way back to their places on Josef's body. "This secure chamber is for noble guests. I've been ordered to escort you to the rooms you will be sharing with your wife."

Josef set his glass on the floor with a bitter sigh and stood up. The servant stepped aside as Josef walked out the door, but when Eli tried to follow, the man cut him off.

"I am sorry, sir," he said. "The queen's orders were that the prince was to go alone. Respect for his wedding night, you must understand."

"Well, I would never disrespect a wedding night," Eli said, glancing over the man's shoulder. He caught Josef's eyes and gave him the look they'd shared a thousand times: *Do you want to get out?* Josef shook his head, and Eli stayed put, watching from the doorway as the servant escorted Josef down the hall. When they disappeared around the corner, Eli stepped back into the room.

He picked up Josef's half-empty glass from the floor and finished it in one long drink. He set the empty glass on the table and grabbed the bottle of spirits instead. He corked it tight and slid the bottle into his belt. When it was secure, he walked over to the window and hoisted himself up, sliding between the bars with practiced ease into the city night.

CHAPTER
9

"Did you see his face?" Henry was laughing so hard he could barely get the words out. "You'd think he was standing for execution, not affirming his marriage."

Adela smiled and refilled Henry's cup from the fat bottle of dark wine. They were sitting in the officers' lounge of the castle guard, a little hallway of a room at the very top of the palace just below the tower where the Council wizards kept the queen's Relay point. There were three of them seated around the polished table: Adela; old Beechum, her sergeant; and Henry Finley, Duke Finley's eldest son and Adela's vice captain.

Henry took the refilled glass and downed its contents in one swallow. Adela leaned on the table, watching him with a wary eye. "Maybe you should stop, Henry," she said. "You're on duty tonight."

"Why?" he said, tossing his empty cup on the table. "If the prince of Osera is a murderer, why can't I be a drunk?" He lurched forward, bumping the table so hard he set the other glasses rocking. "It's a tragedy, that's what it is, you having to go to bed with that bloodthirsty—"

"Finley." Sergeant Beechum's voice was heavy with warning. "Like him or not, Thereson is our prince. You will be civil."

"Civil." Henry snorted. "There's a word that has no place in the same breath with Thereson. When my father's king, he'll turn that failure prince out on his glowering face. Just see if he doesn't. Then you'll be free, Dela."

"I'm sure your father will toss Josef into the sea the moment the crown's on his head," Adela said with a smile. "Just as I'm equally sure my mother and I will be tossed right behind him. The dear Duke Finley doesn't care much for us."

"My father doesn't like competition," Henry said bitterly, and then his face broke into a smile. "He doesn't know you like I do, princess. He's angry that the Queen's Guard loves and follows you with a devotion not seen since Theresa was young, or that the people cheer you louder than they cheer him. He doesn't understand that those things don't have to stand in his way. I keep trying to tell him that an alliance—"

"Is impossible now," Adela finished. "My husband's come home, Henry. I'm no longer a wife in name only. I'm afraid I now truly am the competition your father always accused me of being."

"More's the bad luck," Beechum said blackly. "Thereson is

159

the shame of the Eisenlowe name. It's a disgrace for a prince of the Iron Lions to be a murderer and a thief and who knows what else. We'd have all been better off if he'd never come home."

"I don't doubt it," Adela said. "But he's here now, and we must make the best of it."

Henry sat back in his chair with a huff. "I still can't believe you let him beat you in the Proving. It would have done the country well to see that traitor get the beating he deserved."

"Who says I let him win?" Adela said, reaching for her own cup. "He *is* a renowned swordsman."

"Come off it, Dela," Henry said with a sly smile. "We all know you're the best fighter in the guard. There's no way that wastrel prince could beat you. What *I* want to know is how much the old battle-ax leaned on you to take the fall and make her brat of a son look good."

"Henry!" Beechum cried, eyes wide. "Mind your tongue!"

Henry shrugged and poured himself another drink. Adela sat back, swirling her own half-full cup thoughtfully. She was about to take a sip when a soft knock sounded at the door. A servant in royal livery poked his head in when she called, looking sheepishly at the princess. Adela took the hint with a sigh, setting her cup on the table.

"Excuse me, gentlemen," she said, standing. "It seems it's time for me to do my wifely duty."

"Good luck, Captain," Sergeant Beechum said, saluting her as she followed the servant out into the hall. Henry said nothing, just stared into his wine as Adela closed the door behind her.

She was scarcely down the stairs when she heard it open again. Adela stopped with a deep breath, catching the servant's sleeve.

"I know the way," she said. "Go on."

The servant looked at her, and she could see the conflicting orders warring in his mind, the queen's command that the royal couple be escorted to the chamber versus the princess's trusted word. But the princess was here and the queen was not, so the man excused himself, hurrying down the hall as Henry caught up with Adela.

"Don't go," he whispered, catching her hand.

"I don't have much choice, Henry," she said, deftly dodging as his face closed in for a wine-soaked kiss. "I'm married, remember?"

"Doesn't matter," Henry whispered. "The only reason anyone still cares about that runaway is because Theresa's still alive. When she's dead and my father's king, I'll be the prince, not him. But that doesn't mean you have to stop being a princess." His hands circled her waist, emphasizing his point. "Or don't you love me anymore, Dela?"

"Henry," Adela whispered, stopping him with a finger pressed against his lips. "Josef coming home changes nothing. You know that. But so long as he's here, we can't be seen like this. If the queen finds out, things could get very sticky."

"No, they wouldn't," Henry whispered, kissing her fingertip. "Theresa could never be mad at her perfect princess. Even if she was, your mother would smooth things over. Everyone knows the queen would never do anything to hurt her beloved Lenette."

"I'm glad you're so confident," Adela said, gently extricating herself from his arms. "But for the moment there are appearances to keep up."

Henry's face screwed into a pout, and Adela leaned in, lowering her voice to a purr. "Don't worry, love," she whispered. "This will all be over soon."

"I hope so," Henry said, crossing his arms with a scowl. "The thought of you with that highwayman they have the nerve to call a prince makes me ill. If I could, I'd call him out tonight and finish him. Then you'd be mine for good."

"That's sweet, Henry," Adela said, smiling. "But don't go challenging Josef. You're a decent swordsman, but I wasn't entirely faking today, and I prefer you whole."

Henry beamed at that, and Adela kissed him quickly on the cheek before turning away. "I'll see you tomorrow, Henry."

Henry stood in the hall, gazing after her. "Tomorrow, Dela," he whispered.

She waved one last time and vanished around the corner, leaving the young Finley alone with his longing.

Once she was away, she picked up the pace, walking briskly. Servants bowed as she passed, smiling knowingly. Adela smiled back, but her mind was only half on the princess act. She'd taken the long way to the royal quarters without thinking, walking along the castle's eastern face, the face that looked out over the Unseen Sea. The sun was behind her now, and the ocean lay glittering beneath the light of the last sliver of the waning moon. She watched it as she walked, gazing at the long, flat line of the horizon. Somewhere out there, the Empress's fleet was preparing. Ever since the queen had declared that the Empress was on the move, Adela had been watching the sea day and night, waiting for the first glimpse of the ships that would change her life forever. Her hand sank unbidden to the heavy, ornate short sword at her hip. When the Empress came, she would be ready.

The servant led Josef to a suite in the oldest part of the palace. There were five rooms in total: a sitting room with a single, narrow window overlooking the castle's front courtyard, a dressing chamber, a washroom with a tiny fireplace and an iron tub, a small library, and, of course, the bedchamber with its massive bed cut from the wood of the last of Osera's oaks before the entire island had been deforested to make way for the growing city. The servant insisted on giving Josef the full tour, and Josef let him, despite the fact that he knew the suite with his eyes closed. After all, for the first half of his life, these had been his rooms.

Very little had changed. The rooms had been cleaned and divested of the clothes and toys he'd left behind the night he ran away to become a swordsman, but the suffocating feel of the place hadn't changed at all. If anything, the dark rooms seemed even smaller than before, though Josef supposed that was because he'd grown several inches since he was fifteen.

Josef let the servant finish his tour before ordering him to get out. When the man finally left, Josef sat down on the silk couch in the sitting room. The sky was dark outside the tiny slit window. Torches flickered down in the courtyard below, making it feel far later than it was. Sitting on the creaking couch, the same couch he'd sat on with his mother while she lectured him on being a prince, he felt strangely outside of time. He could still see his mother as she had been, tall and golden and unapproachable. A queen in every sense, not that bent, old woman sleeping in the room above him. Josef looked up, glaring at the wood-beam ceiling. Hot, childish anger welled up in his chest, surprising him with its vigor. The anger had been building since he'd set foot in Osera, since he'd first seen his increased bounty and realized what it meant. Being back here, in this palace, and now in these rooms, he felt like he was fifteen again—still trapped by duty he hadn't asked for and expectations he could never meet, still desperate to get out, to get away.

Josef frowned and took a breath, a swordsman's breath, as his old sword master had taught him, and let the anger drift away. The Heart's weight pressed on his back, reminding him of how far he'd come. He reached up with a reverent motion, drawing the black blade from its wrapping and laying it across his knees. He was not trapped, he told himself as his fingers traced the Heart's scarred surface. He was here by choice, a son doing a good turn for his mother, to whom he owed his life. When he was done, he would leave by choice. He would turn and walk away from the court and the crown and everything else that had no claim over him anymore.

Feeling slightly better, Josef leaned over and set the Heart against the stone fireplace. Realizing it could be a while before Adela arrived, Josef flicked a dagger out of his sleeve. He fetched his whetstone from his pocket and, sitting up on the pillows, began to sharpen his knives, killing the time with long, slow strokes as he waited for his wife.

He didn't have long to wait. He'd scarcely finished his

daggers when the door creaked and Adela stepped into the room. Her armor was gone, replaced by a close-tailored jacket that showed off her figure and long leather trousers tucked into short boots. Her sword, however, was still at her side, and that comforted Josef. Princesses baffled him, but an opponent he could understand, and Adela had always been up for a fight when they were kids.

She stopped when she saw him, and he got the feeling she didn't expect him to just be sitting there, waiting. But, as always with Adela, she adapted, stepping into the room like this was how she ended every evening.

"Have you eaten?" she said, her voice bright and cheery.

Josef shook his head.

"I'll ring the bell, then," she said, stepping over the blades he'd laid out on the carpet.

Josef just nodded and began putting his knives back into their sheaths.

Dinner arrived a few moments later, a series of trays carried in by servants who gave Josef knowing smiles until he reached for his sword. After that, dinner was laid on the table with great efficiency and the servants vanished out the door as silently as they had come in.

Adela walked over to a cabinet and pulled out a bottle of dark wine, carefully pouring two glasses and setting them on the table.

"Sit," she said, sitting down.

Josef walked to the table. "Is that an order, captain?"

"No," she said. "You can starve if you like."

Josef arched an eyebrow, but he pulled out the chair and sat down. She pushed a plate of roast meat across the table at him. "Eat."

"Why the sudden concern for my well-being?" Josef said, taking the fork and helping himself.

"I want this over as much as you do," Adela said, spooning a pile of roasted vegetables onto her own plate. "And it's kind of hard to get a baby from a dead man."

Josef stabbed his fork down so hard the tines bent. "I can't

164

believe you agreed to this," he muttered. "Marriage to an absent husband is one thing, but a baby?"

"You think too much of yourself, Josef," Adela said between neat bites of her food. "All you are at this point is an impediment to the progression of the bloodline, same as I'm little more than a useful vessel. The only thing anyone in this kingdom wants or expects from us is a child to carry on the line of Iron Lions. My life has always depended on being what was expected of me, and when you look at it that way, being a mother isn't so different from being guard captain."

Josef winced. "When you put it like that it kind of removes the nobility from the whole affair."

"There wasn't much to begin with," Adela said, drinking her wine. "We'll be done pretending one day. Until then, it doesn't have to be all bad, does it? I mean, we used to be friends."

"We did," Josef said quietly. "A lot can change in fifteen years, Dela."

"Nothing that matters, Josef," Adela said, putting down her cup and tossing her napkin on the table. "I'm going to bed," she announced, standing up and starting toward the bedroom. "Finish your damn wine and let's get this done."

Josef looked after her. "But I don't dri—"

The slam of the bedroom door cut him off. Josef sat at the table fuming for several minutes, and then he let the battle calm fall over him. He grabbed the small glass of wine and drained it in one gulp. When it was gone, he stood up, threw the empty glass on the table, and turned toward the bedroom. He marched across the room and opened the door with an angry tug, slamming it behind him as he vanished into the candle-lit bedchamber.

Nico crouched on the edge of the kitchen chimney, staring through the tiny strip of Josef's window at the closed bedroom door. She stared for a long time, digging her fingers into the sleeves of her coat until the fabric growled.

She was such an idiot. What had she been thinking, vanishing right in front of the queen? Hiding from Josef when he'd come looking for her? It was stupid, dangerous, and, worse, childish.

Nico put her head down, burying her burning face into the folds of her coat. Josef would be so disappointed in her. He'd always said she was a survivor, a fighter. He didn't know she was a coward, hiding away on the rooftop because she couldn't stand to see him with... with...

Nico sighed and jumped down, sprawling herself out on the steep slope of the palace roof to stare up at the long, snakelike creatures that were just barely visible against the flat black of the night sky. The worst part was she didn't even have a right to be this angry. After all, what was Josef to her? A partner in crime. A friend. A trusted companion. But all those things could be said about Eli, and she wouldn't be up here if Eli was the one who was married, would she?

Nico rolled over and punched the palace roof, breaking the tiles with a hard crunch. If she were honest with herself, she could trace her love for Josef back to the moment he picked her up off the shattered slope of that mountain. Maybe even earlier. She might have loved him from the moment she first saw his shadow, but whenever it had started, her love was her problem, not his. He hadn't asked her to love him, didn't return her love. And even if he miraculously did, she wouldn't let him. Though she was her own master now and the demon was sealed away, the seed was still inside her. She was still a demonseed, still a monster. If it wasn't for the coat, the world would turn on her the instant it recognized what she was.

And who could love a monster?

Nico closed her eyes. At once, the world faded away. She was standing in a dry, sun-drenched field, staring at the boulder that was sitting on the pit that held the demon. It was still secure, and Nico breathed a sigh of relief followed by a rush of profound self-pity. She might be her own master, but her control was still unstable. Even now she could feel the demon patiently pressing on the weight of the will that kept him trapped. He was always there, waiting for her guard to go down, for her determination to falter. Nothing she did could ever banish him for good. If she was ever weak, he would win, and she would become the monster the world thought she was. How could she ask Josef to love something so dangerous? She had no right.

She was still in her sunny field staring at the boulder when something cool, smooth, and hard touched her cheek. Nico jumped backward, returning to the dark rooftop with a jolt as she landed with her fists up to see Eli leaning against the chimney. It actually took her a few seconds to recognize him, on account of the light. Where everything else on the roof was dark and still, Eli was strangely bright, his skin almost luminous, like he was lit up from the inside. She'd never seen anything like it, and yet, almost as soon as she noticed it, the light vanished and Eli stood before her, same as always. He had a bottle in his hand, the cool thing she'd felt against her cheek. When he caught her eyes, he sat down and held out the bottle in obvious invitation.

Nico stayed back, suddenly embarrassed. She had almost certainly put him on the spot last night, vanishing like she had, but he didn't look angry. He just sat there, bottle out, his black hair standing up in all directions in celebration at being freed from the ridiculous blond wig.

Finally, she crept along the roof and sat next to him, taking the offered bottle gingerly, as though it might explode.

"It's brandy," he said before she could ask. "Drink."

She put the bottle to her lips and gagged almost instantly.

"It burns." She coughed, nearly throwing the bottle back at him.

"That it does," Eli said sagely, taking a sip himself before recorking the bottle. "But a little fire can be good at knocking people out of their self-pity."

She flinched and cursed herself for a fool. Of course Eli would know.

"I admit Josef's been an idiot about handling all this," Eli said, his smile fading. "But you can't hide up here forever, you know."

"I know," Nico said slowly.

167

Eli scowled. "Not that he doesn't deserve the cold shoulder after what he pulled. Honestly, married for months and didn't even—"

"No," Nico said, shaking her head. "It's not our business what he does with his private life. It wasn't like it was a problem until now."

"And now it's a very big problem," Eli said. "One that's going to get even worse if my instincts are right, and they usually are." He glanced at her. "I'm going to need you with me, Nico. Josef's in way over his head. He needs us, both of us. So, are we a team? Just like always?"

Nico sighed. "Yes," she said. And it felt good. It was time to stop sulking. But... "I reserve the right to get out if I need to, though." Just in case she couldn't take looking at his perfect, beautiful, demon-free princess.

"Fair enough," Eli said, grabbing her hand and shaking it before she could snatch it back. "Now that that's settled, there's something else I was meaning to ask you."

Nico froze. She'd been with Eli long enough to know that overly casual tone meant trouble, but he was just leaning back on the roof, completely relaxed. However, the moment their eyes met, the strange glow flashed again, brighter than before. Nico jerked back, covering her eyes. It did no good. The light shone through.

"Thought so."

Nico dropped her arms to find Eli was sitting up, looking at her like a cat who'd just cornered a mouse. "You can see, can't you?"

"See what?" Nico said, cringing.

"Spirits," Eli said. "You can see them, like Slorn."

Nico stared at him, dumbstruck. Of course. That's what they were.

"This is amazing!" Eli said, scooting so close he was practically sitting in her lap. "How long?"

Nico leaned away. "Since the valley," she said softly. "How did you know?"

168

Eli grinned. "I first suspected it on the boat. You were staring at the scenery a little too much, and that got me wondering. After all," he said, dropping his voice, "demons can see like spirits, and you're as close to demon as humans get. It makes sense that you should pick up a bit of sight along with your other gifts."

"They're not gifts," Nico said sharply.

Eli waved his hand dismissively. "But you *can* see, right?"

"I think so," Nico said. "I mean, it didn't exactly come with instructions. And I've never seen spirits, so it's not like I have something to compare it to." She left out the part where she'd thought it was another trick of the demon's. No reason to give Eli any more reasons to think she was unstable. But if she'd had any fears of Eli's rejecting her over this new development, they died right then. The thief was almost trembling with delight.

"Tell me about it!" he cried. "Slorn never tells me anything. He's so stingy. I think it's the bear in him. But you'll tell me, right?"

Nico frowned, confused. "Tell you what?"

"Everything!" Eli said. "Look, I've been wondering my whole life: What do spirits see that we don't? What does the world look like to them? What's hidden from us? I have so many questions, and you can see my answers."

Nico looked up at the long, weaving, transparent shapes that coursed across the night sky. Winds, she now realized. She was seeing the winds. "They're kind of hard to describe."

Eli rolled his eyes enormously. "Try me."

Nico bit her lip. At least he didn't think she was crazy. Honestly, the fact that the things she'd been seeing were spirits made her feel enormously better. Spirits she could deal with.

"Well," she said, pointing up. "There are hundreds of winds above us. Earlier, they were blowing in from the sea. In the daylight they looked like long, clear snakes, only without heads or tails. Just long, um, tubes."

"Tubes?" Eli said, arching an eyebrow.

169

"Shut up," she muttered. "I'm trying. So earlier they were all blowing in from the sea, but now they're turning around."

"Ah, the night wind from the land," Eli nodded. "Do they look different?"

"Yes," Nico said, squinting. "They're clearer. During the day they're kind of opaque, like frosted glass. But at night they're clear, and it's easier to see the stuff on the dome of the sky."

The catch in Eli's breath made her jump, and she turned to find him staring at her, pale as death. "Dome of the sky?"

Nico nodded. "It's hard to see because of the winds, but sometimes I can see movement in the sky. It looks almost like the dome of the sky is a cloth, and something's pressing on the other side. It's very faint most of the time, but if I look for it, I can always find it somewhere. Sometimes I see it on several parts of the sky at once." She looked up again. "They're always there somewhere. I can probably find you one if—"

A sharp pressure on her wrist cut her off, and she looked down to see Eli's hand gripping her arm. The thief was still smiling, his face still calm, but the look in his eyes was the closest to true fear she'd ever seen on him.

"Nico," he said, his voice quiet. "You can't look at the sky."

"Why not?" Nico said, tugging her hand away.

"It's the one of the rules all spirits must obey," he whispered. "The first rule the Shepherdess spoke."

"Rule?" Nico said. She didn't understand what he was talking about.

Eli nodded. "There are a lot of rules, actually. Humans don't know them because we're blind and we don't need to. But if you're going to keep looking, Nico, you have to stay away from the sky. If you keep staring at it, bad things will happen."

"What do you mean 'bad things'?" Nico said. "How do you know all this?"

Eli leaned back. "A long time ago I made a childish decision that led to a very strange period in my life," he said slowly. "I learned a lot of things that people aren't supposed to know."

"Are you talking about the other Monpress?" Nico said.

Eli smirked. "No, not that. Giuseppe might be an old fox, but this isn't exactly his area. This happened before my apprenticeship, and it has nothing to do with thievery." The smile fell off his face, and Eli suddenly grew very serious. "I don't actually know what you are now, Nico. You're a demonseed who beat the demon. I've never even heard of something like that, and so I don't know if the rules even apply to you. But, just in case, now that you can see, you should at least know the rules before something comes down on you hard for breaking them. Make sense?"

Nico nodded.

"Good," Eli said, raising one finger. "Rule one: Don't look at the sky. Even the winds don't look at the sky."

Nico scowled. "But why? What's wrong with—"

Eli put his hand over her mouth. Nico almost bit it, but she stopped and contented herself with glaring at him until he took it away.

"Rule two," he said. "Never ask about the sky. Ever. Ever, ever. Now, there are other rules, like don't tell humans about stars and obey Great Spirits and so forth, but those are the two really important ones. The ones you really can't break."

"Why not?" Nico whispered. "And what are stars?"

"Can't tell you," Eli said. "That's a rule. Weren't you listening?"

Nico crossed her arms with a scowl. "Who made these rules, anyway?"

The laughter vanished from Eli's eyes, and he looked back and forth, even though the roof was empty as ever. "The Shepherdess," he whispered at last, his voice so low she could barely hear him. "She makes the only rules that matter in this world. She's the power around here, and all spirits want to please her, which means any spirit who catches you looking at the sky or talking about it will try to stop you whether they know what you are or not, and if they peek under your coat, the jig is up. They could report you to the League, or worse, the Shepherdess

171

herself." He took a deep breath. "Anyway, just don't do it. There's a rule against looking at the sky for a reason."

Nico tilted her head, still not fully convinced. "And do you know that reason?"

"I have a theory," Eli said. "But I'm going to leave it at that. Let's just say that's a mess even I won't touch. Now"— he clapped his hands together, making her jump—"let's move on to the good stuff. I have so many questions."

Nico stared at him, still trying to catch up with the subject change after all the puzzles he'd dumped on her, but Eli was already on his feet, reaching for her hands to pull her up as well.

"Come on, come on," he said. "Night is burning, and we have so much to look at."

She shook her head and let him pull her to her feet. He led her along the stone gutters all the way to his window. Eli swung in first. He was calling for the servants before he landed, demanding food and a whole list of other things that made no sense at all. Nico shook her head and jumped after him, closing the window firmly behind her against the evening chill.

High overhead, ignored and unseen, the outlines of the enormous claws scraped harder than ever on the black dome of the sky.

CHAPTER
10

Heinricht Slorn sat cross-legged on the floor of his cell, staring at the mountain. Looking with that sight that his human mind could still barely comprehend, even after so many years, he could see the pulsing core of the mountain's strength beneath the cell walls. The power of the spirit flowed like a glacier from its peak to its roots buried in the very foundation of the world. The Shaper Mountain surrounded him, cutting him off from the outside, and yet the more he looked, the closer he came to understanding the world he had seen in the mountain's memory.

But as he studied the spirit, a tiny sound drew his eyes away from the mountain to the much humbler shape of the vent above his door. Strong as it was, the Shaper Mountain had no dominion over the winds. This deep in the mountain, the Teacher had been forced to create ventilation shafts so his human followers would not suffocate. The vent in Slorn's chamber was far too small for a man of Slorn's size, but not all men were Slorn's size. His ears flicked as the tiny noise sounded again, the light, small sound of leather on stone. Slorn turned his head, bear eyes slowly moving back and forth across his tiny cell, but he saw nothing. In fact, he saw less than nothing, a blank emptiness that was itself telling. He smiled and focused his large brown eyes to see not as spirits saw, but the mundane shape of the physical world, and as he did, the man slowly appeared.

"Hello, Heinricht," Sparrow said, flashing a superior smile as he straightened up from where he'd landed below the air vent. "Been a while."

"Not long enough," Slorn said.

Sparrow shrugged and leaned against the door, his shape flickering. Slorn blinked in annoyance, struggling to keep his eyes focused only on the physical world, the only place where Sara's little weapon was visible.

Sparrow's smile widened at his frustration. "Aren't you going to ask what I want?"

"Why should I ask such an obvious question?" Slorn said. "You're here to offer me freedom in exchange for joining Sara's menagerie, correct?"

Sparrow shrugged. "Good guess."

"It was no guess," Slorn said. "You don't have to know Sara long to know she would never let a situation like this slip by without playing her hand."

"Way I see it, Sara has all the cards now," Sparrow said,

looking around at the small cell. "You've gotten yourself into quite the mess, haven't you? Whatever you came to tell your former masters, they must not have liked it since you're in a cell rather than at the head of a workshop where you belong. Sara can change that."

"I'm sure she could," Slorn said. "But Sara's price is always too high."

"All she asks is that you share your knowledge," Sparrow said. "Is that so much?"

Slorn's calm expression turned into a snarl. "I've seen how she treats her people, Sparrow. I'm already a bear. I have no interest in becoming a dog. Besides"—Slorn looked down at the floor, toward the mountain's roots—"I have unfinished business here."

"What business can you finish here?" Sparrow said, laughing. "The Shapers are so bound in by law they've locked away their greatest asset for a minor transgression from a decade ago. Such people don't deserve access to talent like yours." He pushed off the wall, walking across the tiny cell until he was barely a foot from Slorn's muzzle. "Sara's different," he whispered. "She doesn't care about pasts or traditions, only results. Come with me to Zarin and nothing will ever stand in your way again."

Slorn looked him in the eyes. "And that is exactly why I'm not coming with you. I cannot work with someone who values only the ends and never the means."

Sparrow's face fell. "You're not exactly in a position to judge, bear man," he said in a low, sharp voice. "You were the one who led that poor, ignorant Spiritualist girl straight into the Shaper Mountain, knowing full well she'd never be allowed to leave. Tell me, Slorn, is that something a moral man would do?"

"No," Slorn said. "But I had no choice. I knew when I decided to return to the Shapers that I would never leave this mountain again. That's why I needed another wizard, someone I could trust, who could hear my argument and the mountain's reply and take that knowledge where I no longer could."

"And where was she supposed to take it?" Sparrow said. "Into her cell? Because that's where she is, you know. Alone, suffering, without even her puppy for comfort, and it's all because of you."

"I am fully aware of my fault in this," Slorn said. "But Miranda has a much bigger role in things to come than she knows. A role I forced her into by bringing her here, and a role I will force her to continue by hiring you to free her on my behalf."

Sparrow snorted. "I don't think you can afford me."

"Ah, but I won't be paying you," Slorn said, taking something from his jacket pocket. It was a fat, leather-bound notebook tied with a loop of string.

"What's that?" Sparrow said, leaning in for a better look. "Your diary?"

"My research notes," Slorn said, holding the book like a precious relic. "This book contains the complete record of Nivel's and my work for the last ten years. I may not be able to afford your services, but this book should be plenty to buy the services of the woman who owns you. Every answer to every question Sara has asked me about demons over the last decade is in his book. I'm giving it to her in exchange for Miranda's freedom, plus freedom for all her spirits."

A sly smile spread over Sparrow's face. "*All* her spirits?" he said, scratching his chin. "A clever touch, bear man." He eyed the book, and Slorn could almost see the scales weighing the danger of freeing Miranda versus the danger of angering Sara. Sara must have won out in the end, for a moment later, Sparrow's hand swooped in and snatched the book from Slorn's fingers.

"The Council accepts your offer," he said, hefting the book in his hands. "But I must say, you've become a very trusting bear in your old age, Heinricht. How do you know I won't just take this and leave poor little Miranda to the mess you made for her? I mean, it's not like you can go for a stroll to see if I kept my word."

Slorn smiled. "It was because I knew you were following us that I risked bringing Miranda to the Shaper Mountain in the first place. Sara's too good a judge of opportunity to abandon a spirit like Mellinor. My guess is that you have orders to take us both back to Zarin. However, breaking someone out of the Shaper Mountain is no easy feat, and since I'm not going, you might be tempted to cut your losses and just leave. With this in mind, think of that book as collateral. You'll find a letter to Sara on the inside cover explaining that Miranda is supposed to be with you."

Sparrow's smile faltered, and he flipped the book open, glaring at the note scrawled across the inside cover, impossible to rip out without ruining the first half of the notes.

"You can be a very conniving bear, Heinricht," he said, snapping the book shut with a deep sigh. "You know, of course, that this little payment is between you and Sara and won't spare the Spiritualist the enormous debt she'll owe the Council for her escape."

Slorn shrugged. "Miranda is a competent woman. I trust her to handle her own obligations."

"I'll be sure to tell her you said so," Sparrow said, tucking the notebook into his pocket as he walked back to the wall. "Lovely chatting with you, Heinricht."

"You take care of Miranda, Sparrow," Slorn said, his voice heavy with warning. "She knows things now that could save us all."

"What, haven't you heard?" Sparrow said, glancing over his shoulder. "The Empress is on the move. Nothing can save us now." He pressed himself against the wall and jumped, catching the edge of the vent with one hand. "Good-bye, old bear," he said, pulling himself expertly into the opening. "Maybe we'll meet again someday."

"Likely not," Slorn said.

Sparrow laughed and folded his thin body, slipping out of the cell like smoke. Slorn watched the place where he had been for several minutes, blinking his eyes every time his focus drifted from the physical world toward the spirit. Someday, he told himself, someday he would ask Sara where she'd found Sparrow and how his spirit invisibility actually worked. It was a lie, of course. In all likelihood he would never leave this cell again. Still...

Letting the spirit sight take over again, Slorn looked down through the heart of the mountain, down to its base, the enormous shelf of rock that supported all the mountains around the Shaper peak, and then down farther still to where its roots ended at the very bottom of world. There, the stone suddenly stopped in a smooth, curved base, as smooth as the arc of the sky, but upside down. Slorn swallowed. He'd never looked so deep underground before, and it was only because the mountain was one single spirit that he could do it now.

He almost wished he hadn't.

Slorn pressed his broad hands to the stone floor. Tiny tremors, too small for anyone who wasn't feeling for them to notice, ran through the Shaper Mountain. They came in long, jagged scrapes, as though something far away was rubbing against the stone. Every time the stone shook, he saw a flicker of movement far, far below, a flicker of movement in the horrible, familiar shape of an enormous, clawed hand.

Slorn lifted his hands from the stone and folded them in his lap. If the hands were above as well as below, then Gredit was right. There was something terribly wrong with the world, something the Shepherdess didn't want the spirits to see. The Shaper Mountain knew this, but it could not act because of the Shepherdess. However, Slorn was certain that, while the Teacher made all the motions of an obedient servant, not even the Shepherdess could cow such an old, stubborn spirit forever. All he had to do was wait.

With that, the problem of how to spend his imprisonment was decided. Slorn looked away from the bottom of the world and leaned back, settling against the cold stone of the mountain. When he was comfortable, he opened his mouth and, in a quiet voice, began to ask questions. He asked about the demonseeds, about the Dead Mountain, about the clawing hands. He asked about spirits, about humans, where they'd come from, why the Shepherdess had made them, why they were blind. Everything he wanted to know, he asked. No answers came, but Slorn did not stop. He would never stop until the stone replied. Nivel had told him once that he was as stubborn as a mountain. To honor her memory, to give meaning to her death, he was going to prove her right. And so he kept asking questions in the white silence until, far sooner than he expected, the cell door opened.

Miranda lay facedown on the stone floor, her eyes closed against the constant light of the mountain. It did no good. The light bled through her eyelids until even her dreams were suffused in white. She pushed herself up with a groan and stared glumly at the room that had become her world: a white box, ten feet by ten feet by ten feet, no door, no windows, nothing even to mark which wall was which. Twice a day, the wall opened and a Shaper appeared with food, but otherwise she had no outside contact, no company at all. After the stone swallowed her, she'd lost consciousness and woken up here, alone. She hadn't seen Slorn since the meeting, but worse than that, Gin was missing. His absence bothered her more than her own imprisonment, and since he wasn't a bound spirit, she couldn't even feel if he was alive or dead.

After she woke up, Miranda had spent the first dozen hours of her confinement trying to break out. Normally, this wouldn't be a problem. Again, the Shapers had left her rings, and though the walls of her cell were part of the mountain, they were still stone. Mellinor's water had broken down larger walls than these, so had Durn's boulders. But the problem wasn't the walls; it was her spirits. No matter how she harangued them, they refused to act against the mountain, and every time she asked why, every one of them gave the same answer: They could not raise their strength against a star.

Miranda pressed her cheek against the cold stone. A week

178

ago, she wouldn't have bought that excuse for a second. Now, after her meeting with the mountain, she understood a little better. Stars were spirits even greater than Great Spirits, chosen and backed by the greatest spirit of them all, the one called the Shepherdess. Spiritualist oath or no, so long as the Shaper Mountain was her jailer, her spirits could do nothing to help her. Not unless she forced them. Revulsion flooded her mind at the thought. She would die here before she Enslaved any spirit, much less her own.

Of course, dying here was looking more and more like her fate. She didn't even know how long she'd been in her cell. Two days at least, but without a window she couldn't be sure, and the guard never answered her questions. All she had was the endless, unchanging light and the slow feeling of time crawling over her skin.

Abandoning sleep, Miranda pushed herself up with a frustrated sigh. She walked to the white wall across from where she'd been lying and began running her fingers over the smooth stone. It was a futile effort. She'd already checked the walls hundreds of times. There were no cracks, no weaknesses. Still, she kept looking. She had to keep looking, keep trying for an escape, or she would go mad.

She was standing on tiptoe, running her fingers along the corner where the ceiling met the wall, when she heard the familiar soft grinding of stone. Miranda fell back on her heels and turned just in time to see the stone of the far wall fold in on itself to create a small door. It happened instantly, the flawless stone she'd run her fingers over just a minute before curling away to reveal the stern face and tall, heavy frame of the Shaper who served as her jailer. He was glowering, as usual, and Miranda glowered right back.

She was about to make her traditional demand to be set free when she noticed something was wrong. The man's scowling face was off, somehow, his dark eyes unfocused and glossy. That was all she saw before he fell forward.

Miranda danced back with an undignified squeal. The

Shaper landed face-first on the floor with a hollow thump, his arms flopping beside him in a way that made her stomach twist. She stared at him for several seconds before an infuriating, familiar voice brought her eyes back up.

"Well, well. Still alive?"

Sparrow was leaning on the door to her cell, a smug smile on his thin lips.

Miranda took a step back. "You!"

"Your gallant hero," he said, spreading his arms with a flourish.

Miranda took another step back, keeping her distance as Sparrow stepped into the cell. He was dressed in the same dull brown he'd worn to chase Eli, and though the color should have stood out like a stain against the pure white walls, she was having a hard time focusing on him. Slowly, subtly, she hid her hands in her pockets and began to wake her spirits, just in case.

"Why are you here?"

"To rescue you, of course," Sparrow said, his voice all sincerity.

Miranda didn't buy it for a moment. "If you think I believe that you snuck in here and killed a man to rescue me out of the goodness of your heart—"

"Perish the thought," Sparrow said. "I'm here because Sara wants you alive and useable, which means not locked up. And I didn't kill anyone, for your information." He kicked the downed man with his boot. "It's a paralytic poison. He'll wake up in an hour with pins and needles like he's never felt, but otherwise unharmed. Not to crush your ego, but Sara doesn't care enough about your rescue to risk angering the mountain by killing a Shaper."

"But freeing a prisoner is fine?"

Sparrow gave her a withering look. "My patience is very thin today, Spiritualist. If you would rather not be rescued, I can leave you here."

"No, no," Miranda said quickly, her shoulders slumping. "I'm in your debt, Sparrow."

"You don't know the half of it, dear," he said, walking farther into the cell. "Shall we be off?"

"No," Miranda said, shaking her head. "Gin and Slorn are still prisoners. I can't leave without them."

"Way ahead of you," Sparrow said. "I knew you wouldn't turn down an offer of escape, so I took the liberty of freeing the dog first. As for Slorn, he's decided to remain in the mountain, so we'll just have to make do without his sterling company."

Miranda gave an incredulous snort. "You actually think I believe that?"

"I don't much care what you believe," Sparrow said. "But understand that Slorn is worth a lot more to Sara than you are. I would gladly trade you for him if I could, but the bear man said he had unfinished business with the mountain."

"So you left him?" Miranda said, horrified. "Just like that?"

"Just. Like. That," Sparrow answered. "I have many jobs, Miss Lyonette. Bear wrestler isn't one of them. We came to an arrangement of mutual benefit to the reasonable satisfaction of both parties. Let's leave it at that. Now, we should be going before the Shapers miss our friend here." He tapped the prone man with his boot again. "Or before your overprotective dog gets nervous and decides to come find you himself."

Miranda paled. She wouldn't put it past Gin. "Fine," she said. "How are we getting out?"

Sparrow smiled and slipped his hand into his pocket. "The Shapers must not think too much of you," he said, pulling out something small, flat, and dark. "This cell is right up against the mountain's outer wall, so that's the way we're going to go."

"What?" Miranda said. "Through the wall?"

"A bit flashy, I'll grant you," Sparrow said, tossing the small, black object with one hand and catching it in the other. "But thanks to your overly inquisitive and suspicious nature, we don't exactly have the luxury of time."

Miranda's eyes darted to the thing he was tossing between his hands. It was shaped like a teardrop, smooth, dark, and slightly wrinkled, like a peach pit. "What's that?"

"One of Sara's experiments," Sparrow said, bending over and tucking the thing into the crook where the wall met the floor. "You may want to step back."

Miranda's eyes widened, but she obeyed, stepping back to the door to her cell while carefully avoiding the paralyzed guard. Sparrow followed a moment later. In the hall was the small cart that the guard had been pushing before Sparrow had interrupted him. It was loaded with plates of cold prison rations, which Miranda recognized far too well, and a stone pitcher of water, which Sparrow grabbed.

"This should do," he said, hefting the full pitcher with both hands.

Before Miranda could ask what he meant by that, Sparrow turned and threw the pitcher's contents across the room. The water flew in an arc, glittering in the mountain's white light for a moment before splashing down on the peach pit Sparrow had left against the wall.

The moment the water hit, the thing exploded. Miranda jumped back as a sound like a breaking tree cracked her eardrums. She slammed her hands over her ears, but it did no good. The sound was as much spiritual as physical, throwing her spirits into an uproar. Looking up, she saw why.

The peach pit was now a tangle of roots and branches. The wood seethed like a nest of snakes, coiling and shooting in all directions. Roots dug into the white stone of the mountain, crumbling the rock as they pushed their way down. The cell wall came apart in chunks as the growing limbs, now covered with the first growth of new leaves, shot out in search of sunlight. The cluster of wood doubled in seconds. Whole chunks of stone were breaking off the cell walls, falling away as the newborn tree fought to reach the open air. The mountain began to shake under Miranda's feet, but it was too late. With a final snapping crash, the tree broke through the last layer of stone and golden sunlight streamed into Miranda's prison.

She stood there gaping for a split second before Sparrow grabbed her hand and yanked her off her feet. They jumped over the paralyzed guard, now dangling from the branches like a caught kite, and ran up the trunk of the newborn tree. Branches were still exploding from the trunk under their feet as great clusters of green raced to catch the newly won sunlight. Sparrow dodged them deftly, pulling Miranda up through the hole in the mountain and into the sun.

"You've still got that sea in you, right?" he shouted over the roar of the growing wood.

"What did Sara do to this poor spirit?" Miranda shouted back, nearly slipping when a branch suddenly sprouted under her foot. "This violates—"

"Shut up and answer the question!" Sparrow snapped. "Sea, yes or no?"

"Yes," Miranda yelled. "Why?"

The tree bucked beneath them as the mountain wind tossed the branches. They were outside, but Miranda could see nothing but the backs of leaves. Sparrow grabbed her hand and pointed it down. "Make a chute of water here."

Miranda tried to rip her hand away. "What do you—"

A horrible sound of snapping wood cut her off, and she whirled around to see the white stone of the Shaper Mountain chomp down on the hole the tree had broken. The trunk squealed as the rock clamped down, shaking violently as the mountain began to chew through the wood. Miranda grabbed for a branch to steady herself, but Sparrow still had her hand. He yanked her forward until she looked at him. The minute he had her eyes, he made a good luck gesture with his free hand and pushed her off the tree.

For a breathless moment, Miranda felt almost weightless as her feet left the pitching trunk. Then gravity kicked in, and she began to fall. She plummeted through the branches, grabbing for them desperately as she passed, but every one broke in her hand, too new and thin to stop her fall. Sunlight blinded her as she burst through the canopy into the icy air. The mountain towered above her, enormous and blindingly white against the pale morning sky. The freezing wind tossed her as she plummeted

183

in free fall, unable even to turn and see what waited below. It was at this point, hurtling through the air, that her mind finally caught up with her falling body and she began to scream.

The sound was scarcely made before Mellinor answered. Water poured out of her. It flowed through the air, catching her fall in a series of pools. She splashed through each one only to drop to the next, but every pool slowed her fall until, at last, she landed safely in the snow on the mountain's slope. Sparrow landed beside her and rolled just in time to dodge Mellinor's water as it hit the ground.

As soon as the water landed, Sparrow was on his feet. "Keep going!" he shouted, pushing her.

Miranda ignored him and looked up. High overhead the enormous tree still clung to the side of the Shaper Mountain. Its branches were still straining toward the sun, but its trunk was a gnawed mess of broken wood where the mountain was clamping down harder and harder as it fought to break through the tree and close the wound. The branches shook one last time before the mountain closed up entirely, cutting the core of the trunk with a final, echoing snap.

"Mellinor," Miranda said softly as the enormous tree began to fall, the wide green crown flying like a broad arrow straight at their heads. "Get us out of here."

Water exploded out of her, shooting down the mountain in a torrent. Sparrow jumped in first, and the water swept him away like a twig. Miranda went next, throwing herself into the fast-moving water just before the broken tree crashed into the ledge. The tree screamed as it hit, sending a wave of snow crashing down the mountain, but Miranda was already far away, racing down the icy slope on Mellinor's water.

It should have been a horrible ride. The mountain was almost vertical below the shelf where they had landed, and the slope was strewn with sharp outcroppings and sudden crags. But Mellinor was adept at keeping her afloat, and the inland sea's water buoyed her over the roughest bits. Ahead of her, Sparrow seemed to be having a much harder time of things, but she had no time to see why. Less than thirty seconds after picking them up, Mellinor washed them out onto the bridge spanning the ravine between the Shaper Mountain and Knife's Pass.

Miranda fell coughing and gasping on the cold stone, but before she'd pulled herself together enough to handle more than a simple breath, Mellinor's voice roared in her ears.

"Keep moving," he thundered as he drew his water back into her. "The mountain is furious."

As soon as he said it, Miranda heard it too. A deep roar vibrated through the air, and the whole world began to shake with fury.

"Sparrow!" she shouted, jumping to her feet.

Sparrow was lying on his stomach a dozen feet from her. He rolled over with a groan when she reached him, coughing and clutching his ribs. "Powers," he muttered. "How do you do that all the time?"

"We have to go," Miranda said, yanking him up. "The mountain's destroying the bridge."

Even as she said it, the stone beneath them started to rock violently back and forth. She pulled Sparrow to his feet and they began to run. The rumbling grew worse with every step, and a new sound began inside the mountain's furious scream, the sound of stone cracking.

"It's trying to cut us off," Sparrow wheezed.

"I know, I know," Miranda cried, dragging him faster up the arch of the bridge. Cracks spidered under their feet as they ran, spreading like lightning across the smooth stone. Miranda cursed and pushed them faster.

"Come on!" she shouted, dragging Sparrow until she was nearly ripping his arm out of its socket. "*Run!*"

They ran. They ran as fast as they could, but they could not escape the mountain's anger. Huge chunks of rock were breaking free all around them, plummeting into the ravine below with small, terrified screams. The cracks under their feet grew larger as the shaking grew more violent until, with a final, echoing crack, the bridge itself broke free.

They weren't going to make it. The realization hit Miranda

like a blow to the face. Already the world was tilting crazily as the bridge, shaken free of its ancient supports, lurched sickeningly sideways. Even so, Miranda kept running. She didn't know what else to do.

Suddenly, something white landed on the falling bridge in front of them. At first, Miranda thought it was a pile of snow, but it was too gray for snow, almost silver, and moving in swirls. Then the pile stretched out and began to run. Miranda's eyes went wide, and she felt the scream leave her throat before she realized she'd made a sound.

"Gin!"

Gin tore down the falling bridge faster than the wind itself, barreling straight at them. Miranda held out her hand and jerked for Sparrow to do the same. Gin reached them a second later, and as he passed, she dug her fingers into his thick, coarse fur. The moment her fist clenched on his coat, she was ripped off her feet by the ghosthound's momentum. He turned on a pin, claws digging into the crumbling stone, and then he kicked off again, running even faster back toward the pass.

Miranda clung to his side, her legs tangled with Sparrow's as they fought to hold on. This close, she could feel Gin's lungs thundering, his legs pumping faster than ever before. But in the seconds since Gin had appeared, they'd already fallen a frightening distance. The wall of the ravine rose above them, sheer and white and impossibly tall, the edge completely out of reach. She felt Gin's muscles tense as his back legs folded beneath him, and then he sprung, kicking the broken bridge off behind them as he launched into the air.

For a breathless moment, they were flying, soaring up out of the ravine. The jagged edge of the bridge's broken end hung just above them, ten feet, five feet, nearly in reach. And then, just as quickly, it began to move away. Gin's legs kicked frantically, and Miranda realized they were falling. It was too far. Gin had missed.

From this point, everything happened both painfully slow and blindingly fast.

Miranda's hand shot out, Durn's cloudy emerald already flashing with light. The rock spirit tore himself from the ring, grabbing the bridge's broken edge with one enormous boulder of a fist. At the same time, his other hand swung down to grab Gin's middle. The stone wrapped around them in a vise and then released, flipping them up. Miranda's fingers were torn from Gin's coat as they tumbled through the air and landed sprawling on the smooth stone paving of Knife's Pass. She grabbed the ground and lay still, pressing herself into the stone to make sure it was real and, more important, not falling. When she was sure she really was grounded, Miranda lifted her head to check on the others. Gin, of course, had already rolled to his feet. Sparrow, on the other hand, was still flat on his stomach, staring at the ground like he'd never seen it before.

With a long, shaky breath, Miranda sat up and held out her hand for Durn. The stone spirit was still hanging from the remains of the broken bridge. When he saw her reaching, he pulled himself up and rolled to her.

"Thank you," Miranda said, patting the stone with a smile.

"My pleasure, mistress," Durn said, his gravelly voice smug with pride.

Miranda grinned. It wasn't often the stone got to play hero. Gin would never hear the end of it. She held her hand steady as Durn broke down and returned to her ring. When he was finished, Miranda let her eyes drift back across the ravine. The Shaper Mountain rose above her, as cold and enormous as ever. Its slopes were smooth and snowy with no trace of the hole Sparrow had punched or the tree he'd used to punch it. Two jagged edges at either side of the ravine, the remains of the broken bridge, were the only signs of the mountain's anger or their narrow escape from it. The ground, however, was still rumbling.

"Come on," she said, standing up. "Let's get out of here."

"What a wonderful idea," Sparrow said. "Little help, please?"

Miranda walked over and grabbed his hands, pulling him to his feet. He grimaced as he stood, bending slowly, like his ribs hurt him, but he didn't say anything when Miranda finally got him to his feet.

She left him to get his balance on his own and hurried to catch up with Gin, who was already making his way down the pass.

"Don't ask," the ghosthound growled, moving to walk so close Miranda couldn't take a step without bumping into him. "He'll hear."

Miranda nodded and kept her mouth shut.

"He showed up about two hours ago," Gin continued. "They had me chained in the front hall with the carriages. I would have eaten him, but I didn't know where you were. He kept saying he was going to get you next. I didn't believe him, but it's better to be out than in, so I let him spring me. If you hadn't shown by noon, I would have hunted him down."

"Thank you for the sentiment," Miranda said, glancing back at Sparrow, who was limping to catch up with them. "How did he get you out?"

"Picked the lock," Gin said. "Impressive bit of work, actually. He's almost as good as Eli."

"That's saying something," Miranda grumbled, looking back again. Sparrow was falling behind. His face was set in a smug smile, but his body was moving in jerks, and Miranda realized that he must be really injured.

"Stop," she said, turning around. She caught Sparrow's eye before climbing onto Gin's back. "Get on. We'll be walking forever if we wait for you."

"How kind," Sparrow said, walking over to the ghosthound.

"Kind nothing," Miranda said. "Practical. We may owe you our freedom, but that doesn't mean I want to take a hiking holiday together. I just want to get to Sara and discharge my debt as soon as possible. And don't think I've forgotten about that horrible abuse of a tree spirit. I will be making a full report to the Court about that."

"I'm sure you will," Sparrow said, pulling himself slowly onto Gin's back.

Miranda glared, suspicious. "How did you get so injured, anyway?"

"Bit too much excitement for me," Sparrow answered, finally sliding into place behind her on Gin's back. "I don't usually get out this much."

Gin snorted. "Lies. He's a born sneak. I saw your crazy ride down the mountain. Mellinor cushioned you, but bird boy was bouncing all over, probably because Mellinor couldn't see him."

"See who?" Mellinor said, sloshing in Miranda's head.

Miranda tightened her grip on Gin's fur. "Don't do that," she whispered. "It makes me dizzy."

"Well, I don't know what you're talking about," the sea grumbled.

"Don't blame the water," Gin said. "I can't see him unless I look with my eyes. He doesn't even have much of a smell. You can't trust a man with no smell, but at least he's not flickering so much anymore."

"Would you care to explain any of that?" Miranda said, poking Gin in the back.

"I've already told you," Gin said. "Weren't you listening all those times I said he flickered?"

"You didn't explain then either!" Miranda cried.

"It's not something that can be explained to a human," Gin said, lashing his tail. "Right now, for instance, I can't see him at all unless I look with my actual eyes. Otherwise, he's like a nothing, a blank. I would say I've never seen anything like it, but I wouldn't know if I had, so forget it. You've thrown our lot in with his already. Just watch yourself."

"I still don't know what you're talking about," Mellinor said. "Who's a blank?"

Miranda shook her head with a frustrated sigh. Behind her, she felt Sparrow lean back. "Is everything all right? Your dog is growling more than usual, which I didn't think was possible."

For a moment, Miranda considered just asking Sparrow about the flickering, but quickly decided it would be a waste of time. Sparrow wasn't a wizard. He probably had even less of a clue than she did about whatever it was about him the spirits didn't like. Even if he did know, this was Sparrow. Getting a trustworthy answer out of his mouth was like a flood in the desert—not impossible, but very unlikely, and cause for alarm if it did actually happen. So Miranda dropped the subject and moved on to questions she might actually be able to get a straight answer for.

"Everything's fine," she said. "Where to?"

"Zarin, where else?" Sparrow said. "I've had all I care to see of mountains."

"There at least we agree," Miranda said. "Did you hear that, Gin?"

"No," Gin growled, more annoyed than ever. "I can't even hear him unless I concentrate. What is wrong with that man?"

"I don't know," Miranda said. "But I'm going to find out. Zarin, fast as you can."

"Got it," Gin said, laying his ears back. "Hold on tight."

Miranda didn't have time to relay the warning before Gin launched himself down the pass, nearly knocking Sparrow off. By the time Sparrow had regained his seat, they were well away from the Shaper Mountain. Miranda leaned forward over Gin's neck, getting as far away from Sparrow as she could, which wasn't very far. She had a lot to think about, but her mind kept drifting back to the mountain looming behind her and the man it still held prisoner somewhere deep beneath its stone. The image of the Shaper Mountain's memories still stood clear in her mind, and she gripped Gin's fur even tighter. Lock her up, would it? Well, she would tell everyone. She would tell Banage, she would tell Sara, she would tell anyone who would listen. That was her promise to Slorn, and she made it over and over again as they ran through the icy pass back toward civilization.

* * *

At the very, very top of the Shaper Mountain, perched on the crusted snow at the tip of the mountain's peak, a man stood with his arms crossed. Pure white hair covered his body like a coat except for the white hands stroking the long white beard that covered his front as he watched the three specks of the wizard girl, the ghosthound, and the man who looked like nothing flee down the path through the mountains.

You play a risky game, Durain.

"Nonsense," the mountain rumbled under his feet. "I am ever a loyal servant to the Shepherdess. And to you, Weaver."

The white man smiled. *I wouldn't say that too loudly. The Shepherdess doesn't like to share.*

"All the Powers are equal," the Shaper Mountain said. "Though she seems to have forgotten."

My sister forgets many things, the Weaver said bitterly. *And what she remembers, she ignores. But that is no call for you to risk our plans by openly defying her. Showing your memories to that group of children and then letting all but one free, what were you thinking?*

"They saw nothing that was not true," the mountain said. "I cannot help if I remember the truth. Anyway, I tried to keep her from escaping, but I am an old spirit. Too old to be looking after young idiots and too busy to spend my limited energy catching them when they run away."

Of course. The Weaver chuckled. *Very old. But do be careful, Durain. This is the Shepherdess's domain. I cannot protect you here. If she suspects, she will not hesitate to act, and we have lost too many irreplaceable spirits to risk another.*

"I have not forgotten Gredit," the mountain said, his great voice heavy with anger. "And I am not the only one. When the Hunter returns, we will be ready. I have already started the process. Heinricht is being briefed by his father as we speak."

The bear man? The Weaver frowned. *You put a great deal of faith in him.*

"I must," the mountain said. "He is the only one who can finish Fenzetti's work."

Is that so? The Weaver pursed his lips. *How fortuitous that he should appear now.*

"Fortune has nothing to do with it," the mountain rumbled. "The Creator is still with us. We will be free again."

You still believe that? the Weaver said.

"Yes," the mountain said. "You forget. We old ones, we were the first. I am older than you or your siblings, Shaped by the Creator's own hand. I remember the world as it was, as it was meant to be, and I know that world will return. It *must* return, or why are we still living?"

Why, indeed, the Weaver said, looking up at the sky. *I must go. I leave it to you.*

"We will not fail," the mountain said, but the Weaver was already gone, vanishing through a white cut in the thin air as though he had never been. The mountain rumbled at the Power's sudden absence and shifted its focus away from the outside world and the distant feel of the fleeing figures. Instead, it tilted its attention inward, down toward the long hall at the very heart of its roots. There, two humans, the current Guildmaster and the wizard who shared his spirit with a bear, walked the mountain's deepest path toward the vault where Durain, the Shaper Mountain, kept its greatest hope, the small, white kernel of a desperate plan many, many years in the making.

CHAPTER
11

Josef woke with a gasp. He froze, hands knotted in the sheets, body braced to kick or leap away, whichever was needed. That was when he realized he was in his old bedroom. He collapsed back into bed with a silent curse and took stock of his situation. He was naked, his knives stacked carefully on the bench against the wall beside him. But he had no memory of removing his knives or his clothes. He had no memory of going to bed.

Josef frowned. To wake that violently, he must have been sleeping very soundly. Even now, his head was still groggy, and that made him nervous. He'd shaken the sound-sleeping habit the first year he'd left home. Maybe being back in his old room had brought back old habits, but Josef didn't think so. He glanced at the bed. The space beside him was rumpled. Someone had slept there, but the sheets were cold when he slid his hand over them. His frown deepened. Whatever bad-sleep habits his old room could have lured him into, he'd *never* sleep that soundly next to a stranger, married or not. Something was going on, and he meant to find out what.

Josef slid silently out of bed and looked around for his clothes, but they were gone. He cursed under his breath and quietly took a knife from the pile. The door to the sitting room was closed, but he could hear movement on the other side of door that led to his dressing room. He put the knife in his teeth and pressed himself against the wall, easing his bare feet along the carpet until he was directly beside the dressing room door. Then, in one lightning-fast movement, he stepped in, opening the door with one hand while grabbing his knife with the other. He swung forward and grabbed the man on the other side, pressing the blade against his jugular.

The man screamed and began to thrash, nearly slitting his own throat in the process. Josef grabbed his shoulders and whirled him around, lowering the knife before slamming the man face-first against the wall.

"What are you doing here?" Josef growled, pressing the knife into the man's back.

"Please, my lord," the man whimpered. "I am here to help you dress."

Josef glanced down, noticing for the first time that the man was dressed in the well-cut, somber suit of Osera's high-ranking servants. With a horrible, sinking feeling, Josef released his grip and stepped back. The man fell to the floor, gasping and grabbing his throat.

The servant looked up with horrified eyes, and Josef felt his stomach sink even further. This wasn't going to help his reputation.

"Sorry," he muttered, reaching out to help. The man shied away from Josef's hands, using the shelves to pull himself up instead.

"Forgive me, your highness," he whispered, averting his eyes from Josef's nakedness. "I did not mean to startle you."

"Forget it," Josef said. "Where are my clothes?"

The man's eyes bulged like Josef had just asked for a carcass. "I gave them to the laundry, sir. I have fresh clothes for you, straight from the tailors." He nodded toward the chest against the wall where several starched shirts, jackets, and breeches lay neatly folded. "I can fetch your old clothes back, if you would like," he added cautiously.

"Those are fine," Josef said. He grabbed a shirt, jacket, drawers, and pants at random, pulling them on carelessly. He could still see the servant out of the corner of his eye, but the man made no move to help Josef dress. He seemed to be glued to the wall, eyes wide as a fish's. Josef grit his teeth and dressed faster, ticking the facts over in his head. It had been this man who'd taken his clothes, not Adela. Sleeping through Adela he could maybe understand; she was a fighter and knew how to move, but he would never sleep through this idiot entering his room, collecting his clothes, and leaving. There was simply no way two nights in Osera could have dulled his senses to the point where a servant could sneak past him.

By the time Josef had finished dressing, the man had collected himself enough to fetch Josef's boots, freshly polished and resoled, from the boot stand. He held them out with a shaking hand, keeping his eyes on the floor as Josef took them.

"Thanks," Josef said, sitting down to tug his boots on over his new socks. "Where's Adela?"

The man had already returned to his corner. "I'm not sure

of the princess's whereabouts, sir," he said, wringing his hands. "I can send someone to find her, if you desire."

"No," Josef said, standing up. Best not to let Adela know he was looking for her before he knew what role she played in this. First, he had to find Eli. If the thief was good for anything, it was rooting out trouble.

He went back to the bedroom and grabbed the rest of his knives, slinging them into place as he walked into the sitting room. His frown tightened into a solid grimace at the bright, midday sunlight streaming through the narrow window. Not only had he slept soundly, he'd slept late.

"Worse and worse," he muttered, grabbing the Heart of War from the fireplace where he'd left it the night before. He slid the enormous sword over his shoulders and onto its spot on his back. When the blade was secure, he stomped toward the door that led to the rest of the castle. He stopped when he reached it, looking over his shoulder at the servant who was still clutching the dressing room door, trembling like a kicked dog.

"Sorry, again," Josef said, struggling to think of the appropriate action for cases like this. "You can, um, have the rest of the day off."

The servant just stared at him blankly as Josef slipped out of the prince's chamber and started jogging through the halls toward Eli's room.

Eli's door was partially open when he reached it. Josef stopped, eyeing it suspiciously. He couldn't see any outward signs of trouble, but he checked his blades anyway, easing the knives down in his sleeves in case he needed them. When he was satisfied he could get any weapon he needed in a moment's notice, he stepped inside.

He stopped again almost immediately. The room was a disaster. There were piles of junk everywhere—furniture, produce, paper goods, candles, silverware, weapons, tapestries, building tools, a pile of locks, and the other things he couldn't see enough of to name. It was all piled around the room as though it had been thrown there, and sitting in the middle, perched on the rubbish like the king and queen of trash, were Eli and Nico. Judging by the dark circles under their eyes, they'd been up all night, but doing what he couldn't even begin to say. Neither of them seemed to have heard him enter. Instead, they were both staring at what looked to be the carved wooden end of the banister from the grand staircase in the castle's front hall.

"All right," Eli said, hefting the carved wooden hunk in his hands. "Closer to the door or the chess piece?"

"Neither," Nico said, scowling. "It looks almost fuzzy."

"Fuzzy," Eli muttered, scribbling on a piece of paper so covered with similar scribbles it was almost entirely black. "Interesting. Fuzzy like the fork or fuzzy like—"

"*What is going on?*" Josef roared.

They both jumped and looked at Josef, eyes wide with surprise.

"Good morning," Eli said.

"Don't 'good morning' me," Josef said, kicking the junk aside until he'd made enough space to close the door. "Did you rob a dump? What is all this garbage?"

"Not garbage," Eli said. "Experiments." When Josef gave him a skeptical look, he clarified. "Wizard stuff, as you would say."

"You know what?" Josef said. "I don't even want to know. All I care about is where you've been."

This last bit was leveled at Nico, and she flinched appropriately.

"Doesn't matter," she said quietly. "I'm here now."

"Doesn't matter?" Josef was surprised at his own anger. "*Doesn't matter?* Of course it matters! Do you even know how...how..."

"Worried?" Eli supplied.

"You keep out of this," Josef snapped. Eli held up his hands, and Josef locked his eyes back on Nico. "I didn't even know where you were! How can we be a team when you're not here?"

"I'm sorry," Nico said, fiddling with her coat. "It's done now, anyway. Won't happen again."

196

Josef clenched his fists. She wasn't giving him an answer, but he didn't know if he was ready to press for one. He was fighting battles on all fronts right now, and forcing Nico to tell him the truth would open up another. A close, dangerous fight that he wasn't sure he could win. Worse, he was still mad, furiously mad, though he couldn't say exactly what he was mad at. But he couldn't deal with this now. He needed his wits about him, so he took a deep swordsman's breath and made himself let it go.

"So long as we're all on the same front going forward, everything is well enough for now," he said. "We've got other problems. Something happened last night."

Eli leaned back with an infuriating smile. "Things tend to happen on wedding knights, Josef."

"Shut up and listen," Josef said, ignoring the murderous look that Nico shot at the thief. "I just woke up with no memory of the night before. I don't remember Adela getting up or the servant coming in. I don't even remember going to bed."

"Well," Eli said, standing up. "It isn't unheard of for humans to lose consciousness for six, sometimes eight hours a night. I know this may come as a surprise—"

"Can you stop being a smart-ass for five seconds and listen?" Josef snapped. "This is serious. I think I was drugged."

"Nonsense," Eli said. "Who would drug you?"

"I don't know," Josef said. "That's why I have you. Figure it out."

Eli scratched his chin. "Someone who doesn't want an heir for Osera?" he guessed.

"The duke," Josef said. "An heir by me would keep Finley's children from inheriting."

"Seems a little shortsighted," Eli said. "He can't expect to drug you every night. And how did he do it without drugging the princess as well? I can only assume that the drug was in your food, unless you were cut in the night?" He paused until Josef shook his head. "Food or drink then, for certain. But you ate with Adela, right? So unless you had something she didn't,

197

she'd be down too. But she was up bright and early this morning. I saw her ride out myself."

"We ate from the same plates," Josef said. "Whatever I had, she had. Poison isn't the Oseran way, though. If the duke wanted me dead, he could challenge me to a duel at any time."

"Well, we still haven't established it was him," Eli said. "And you were drugged to sleep, not to death. Anyway, no one in their right mind is going to challenge you to a duel, especially not after your performance yesterday. You're the greatest swordsman in the world, remember?"

"Not yet," Josef said. "We need to find out what happened last night and why. We also need a who. Eli, I want you to go to my room and see what you can find. Nico, I'll need you to stake out the duke. I want to know what he's planning. Meanwhile, I'm going to go down to the kitchen and get the truth out of whoever cooked my food last night."

"Josef," Eli said cautiously, taking off his wig so he could look at the swordsman without hair getting in his eyes. "I know you don't generally listen to these, but the first rule of thievery is never jump without knowing where you're going to land. You're making a lot of assumptions here. We're not even sure you were poisoned."

"Of course I'm sure," Josef said. "I can tell when I've been poisoned."

"I don't doubt that," Eli said. "But try to consider this objectively. So far, all we have is that you slept until noon without waking and missed some people entering and leaving your room. Now, I can't remember you ever sleeping late, but it's not exactly enough proof to justify going down to the kitchens and scaring the daylights out of the servants. Especially considering the rumors going around."

Josef glowered. "What rumors?"

"That you're a killer, a bounty hunter gone bad, and a thief," Eli said with a shrug. "Of course, since all of that is true, they're less rumors and more facts-in-a-bad-light."

"How did they get to you?" Josef said.

"You hear things when you spend all night bribing servants to fill your room with junk," Eli said, flashing him a grin. "Seriously, though, is it really so unexpected that people think poorly of you? You haven't exactly been the storybook icon of the long-lost prince."

"Good thing I gave up being a prince, then."

"But you *are*," Eli said, rubbing his temples. "So long as you insist on staying here and playing along, you are a prince, like it or not, and people are going to judge you as one."

"Then they'll just have to get over it," Josef said, crossing his arms. "I'm here only to help my mother."

"Well," Eli said, crossing his arms as well. "You're not helping her by acting like a thug. You can't have it both ways, Josef. I'm not asking you to embroil yourself in politics. I'm not even saying we shouldn't investigate what happened last night, but if we're going to stay here, you're going to have to learn some *tact*."

Josef tilted his head back, bumping it soundly against the door. Leave it to the thief to make everything more complicated. "Fine," he said at last. "What do you suggest I do?"

"Leave it to me," Eli said, standing up. "We'll go to your room and see what we can find. Since no one knew in advance that you were coming back, whoever poisoned you had to set things up fairly quickly. Haste leaves clues." He paused. "I don't actually think that's a rule of thievery. I should make it one."

"Whatever," Josef said, pushing himself off the door. "Let's get this done. It's nearly noon already, and I want to be able to go to sleep tonight knowing I'll wake up."

"Fair enough," Eli said, setting the wig on his head again. "After you, Prince Thereson."

Josef rolled his eyes and tugged the door open, stepping into the hall with Nico right behind him and Eli on her heels.

His room was empty when they reached it. Josef let them in before entering himself. He closed the ancient door carefully, and then took the Heart of War from his back and leaned it against the door. The blade leaned heavy against the wood, blocking it from opening inward.

Eli's eyes widened in horror. "You're using the greatest awakened blade in existence as a door stop?"

"Why not?" Josef said. "I don't want servants disturbing your work, and it's not like anyone besides me can move it."

Eli sighed loudly and turned back to the task at hand. "I suggest you get comfortable. This may take a while."

Nico and Josef exchanged a look and sat down together on the couch. As soon as they were settled, Eli got down on his knees and started waking up the room.

"There," Eli said, straightening up. "That should do it."

Josef folded his arms and gave the thief a skeptical look. So far as he could tell, Eli had just spent the last hour crawling around on his hands and knees and muttering to himself. The thief had always been a little odd when he was doing his wizard nonsense, but this had been downright strange and a little embarrassing. He was doubly glad he'd thought to put the Heart in front of the door now. Forget keeping their investigation secret, he was more concerned that no one would barge in and see Eli acting like a lunatic.

"All right," Eli said, clapping his hands together as he looked around the room like a mayor about to give a speech. "Listen up! There's a lot at stake here. Someone has been poisoning the prince." He pointed at Josef. "We need to know how."

Eli looked over his shoulder and motioned for Josef to stand. After a moment of hesitation, Josef got off the couch and stood beside Eli, feeling uncomfortably stupid. But, as soon as he was in place, the room began to rattle like it was the epicenter of a tiny earthquake.

"One at a time," Eli said, holding up his hands.

The rattling stopped except for the fireplace. Eli turned and knelt down, nodding as the stone mantel began to creak. Occasionally, another piece of furniture would rattle. When that happened, the stone mantel would rock violently until every other sound stopped. Eli listened patiently, nodding the whole time. Back on the couch, Nico kept very still, her eyes as wide as saucers.

When the mantel's movements finally stilled, Eli stood up with a long sigh. "How many wizards have been in your family?"

"Are you talking to me?" Josef said.

Eli rolled his eyes. "Who else?"

Josef gestured at the rattling room. Eli just gave him a sharp look.

"I don't think we've ever had a wizard," Josef said. "Maybe a cousin or something, but no one I can think of."

Eli frowned. "And how long has this room been like this? With this furniture?"

"Like this?" Josef said. "Forever. This has always been the prince's room, or princess's, in mother's case. Everything in here's a family heirloom."

"Well," Eli said. "At least that explains it."

"Explains what?" Josef said.

"Them." Eli pointed at the room. "They seem to have you confused with another prince. Several other princes, actually. Which one started a fire?"

"That would be my great-grandfather," Josef said. "Knocked over a lamp twice when he was ten, starting fires both times. Earned him the name Wallace the Clumsy for a while, until he became Wallace the Black Scourge."

Eli winced. "That hardly sounds like an improvement."

"It was fitting," Josef said. "He sank a lot of ships. Don't forget, Osera was a nation of pirates before the war made us part of the Council."

"How fascinating," Eli said. "But if we can leave the history lesson aside for a moment, I'm afraid we're in a bit of a bind. I don't think a wizard other than myself has entered this room in a century. The whole place was dead asleep before I came in, which was why this took so long. If they had been awake, it would still have been tricky since you, Adela, and the servants all seem to be spirit deaf, but I could have found out *something*. As it stands, they just want to tell me stories of grievous abuse at the hands of your violent ancestry."

"So," Josef said. "No wizard solution?"

"No wizard solution," Eli said, shaking his head. "But while I was waking things up, I did find this."

He held up a plain porcelain medicine bowl filled with a dull yellow powder that smelled vaguely bitter, like walnut shells. Josef looked at Eli skeptically. "Is that poison?"

"No," Eli said, pulling his hand back. "It's called orobin, and it's a perfectly normal stimulant. I've taken it myself on long jobs where I couldn't afford to be dozing off."

"If it's perfectly normal, why are you showing it to me?"

"Because this is a very large amount of orobin," Eli said, hefting the bowl pointedly. "A pinch dissolved in tea is plenty for any normal person. This is enough to stock a reasonably sized shop."

"So?" Josef said, crossing his arms.

"*So*," Eli said. "I found it tucked away in a cabinet full of lady's supplies, which means, unless you've taken to washing your hair with essence of rose water, that this bowl belongs to your lovely wife. Who, I might add, eats and drinks the same as you, but does not seem to suffer from involuntary deep sleep."

"Wait," Josef said. "You think Adela's behind this? That she's drugging both of us but is taking the stimulant to counteract the effect?"

"That would be where I'm going," Eli said, placing the bowl on the table.

"But why would she drug me?" Josef said. "That doesn't make any sense."

"Maybe your pillow talk needs some work," Eli said with a smug smile.

"Shut up and listen," Josef growled. "I'm not saying I trust Adela, but she owes the queen everything. Even if she didn't, why would she knock me out? She needs this baby to secure her position or Finley's going to send her and her mother packing the second the crown is on his head."

202

"I don't know the whats and whys," Eli said. "I'm not even saying for sure that she's the one drugging you, but I think we can safely assume she knows what's happening and how to counteract it. That alone is proof enough that things aren't what they seem. If Adela was pregnant, this would be more damning. But with you being, well, you, and totally uninterested in the throne, a baby's her only shot at keeping her position. That leaves us with circumstantial evidence but no motive, which isn't much better than where we started."

"Well, I intend to find out," Josef said, crossing his arms. "Next time I see Adela, she's not leaving until I have an answer."

Eli frowned. "I'm not sure direct threats are going to—"

He was interrupted by the soft clatter of someone trying to open the door. Nico, Eli, and Josef froze as the door's handle turned down. But the person on the other side didn't get much farther. The moment the door hit the Heart of War, it stopped cold. The person cursed and tried again, harder this time. The sword didn't even wobble.

Silence fell again as the person stepped back, and then there was a soft, almost embarrassed knock.

Josef walked over and pulled the Heart out of the way, opening the door to reveal an elderly man in a somber suit. He looked shocked and a little bewildered by the sudden opening, but his face quickly arranged itself into an expression of bored politeness the second he recognized Josef.

"My lord prince," he said with a perfunctory bow. "I was sent to find you."

"So I gathered," Josef said, sliding the Heart back into place on his back. "Get on with it."

The man's eyes widened, but he gathered himself again. "My master, the excellent Duke Finley, requests your presence this afternoon."

"Oh yeah?" Josef said. "What's Finley want?"

"Only your company, my lord," the man said.

Josef looked back at Eli, who shrugged. "Company, huh? When?"

"At your earliest convenience, sire," the servant said. "Though I have been led to believe it is a matter of some urgency."

Josef glared at the servant, who just smiled politely. Shaking his head, Josef looked over his shoulder. "I'm going to see what this is about," he said. "You two stay here and keep working on what we were working on."

"Sure thing, boss," Eli said with a salute. But Nico met Josef's eyes as she nodded. Josef smiled. She at least could be trusted to stay on target. That would be enough. He checked his blades one last time before he followed the servant into the hall, closing the door solidly behind him.

CHAPTER
12

As many times as she'd seen the white walls of Zarin rising in the distance, Miranda had never been so glad to be home. Gin's time chained in the mountain seemed to have left him ready to run. Even with two passengers, he'd raced down the mountains in record time, though Miranda wasn't sure if that was because of the urgency of the situation or if he just wanted Sparrow off his back. For his part, Sparrow hadn't changed a bit. He still took up every bit of breathable air.

"Finally," he cried as Zarin came into view. "Civilization. Powers, it's been too long. I can't wait to eat something that hasn't had dog slobber all over it."

Miranda sniffed indignantly. "You're free to catch your own food, you know."

"Hardly matters now," Sparrow said. "We'll be at the gates in an hour if your little puppy keeps up the pace."

Miranda winced and glanced down at Gin. He'd threatened to eat Sparrow if the man called him a puppy one more time, but the ghosthound kept running as though nothing had happened. She sighed. Sparrow had no idea how lucky he was that spirits had a hard time hearing him. Of course, Miranda could hear him just fine, and that was enough to make her consider letting Gin eat him anyway.

As their road joined the main highway connecting Zarin to the northern Council Kingdoms, Miranda was astonished by the volume of traffic. Loaded carts filled the paved highway, forcing people on foot and horseback to spill over onto the fields beside the road. Since a ghosthound isn't the sort of thing you want in the middle of a crowd of horses and ox-drawn carts, Gin had to turn out farther still, beyond the hard-beaten grass that lined the road and into the mud of the freshly plowed fields.

"Lovely," Sparrow said, lifting his boots as high as he could.

Miranda ignored him. "What's all this?" she said, nodding at the packed roar. "It's months too early for the new year's market, unless I am drastically wrong about how long we were under that mountain."

"Those aren't farm carts, either," Gin added. "I smell steel."

"You're right," Miranda said, straightening her knees so that she was almost standing on his back. "And they're marked, look."

Every cart was marked with a flag or seal. The traffic went on farther than she could see in both directions. Hundreds of carts from more countries than she could name hauling what had to be thousands of tons' worth of goods into Zarin. But for what?

"They're supply wagons," Sparrow said, yawning. "You know, for the war."

Miranda stopped Gin right there, nearly throwing Sparrow off. "*War?*" she yelled, whirling around. "*What war?*"

"The upcoming war with the Immortal Empress," Sparrow said, resettling himself.

Miranda was staring at him like he'd just grown a second head. "The Immortal Empress?"

"Yes," Sparrow said. "You know, terrible lady? Comes from across the sea with thousands of ships to kill us all? Don't they teach you any history in that little social club of yours?"

"*I know who the Immortal Empress is!*" Miranda shouted. "What I want to know is what is she doing *back*? I thought she was defeated at Osera two decades ago?"

"Defeated?" Sparrow snorted. "She lost a few ships and a little pride, but women who own half the world don't roll over just because you beat up their forward fleet. She retreated is all. Your real question should be, what took her so long to come back and finish the job?"

Miranda stared at him. "Well?"

"Well what?" Sparrow said, leaning back tiredly.

"What took her so long?" Miranda said, gritting her teeth on each word.

"How in the world should I know?" Sparrow said. "But she's back now, and word is she's got a fleet large enough to crush us flat five times over. Of course, that's probably an exaggeration, but there must be some truth to it if Whitefall's worked up enough to squeeze the Council Kingdoms this hard. There must be carts from here to Gaol."

"I can see that," Miranda snapped. "What I want to know is, if you knew all this, why you didn't see fit to *tell me*."

Sparrow arched his thin shoulders in a nonchalant shrug. "What good would it have done you to know? You were already running your darling dog into the ground to get to Zarin, so it's not like the knowledge would have spurred you any faster."

Miranda's jaw clenched. "And did it never occur to you that a continent-scale war is something I should be informed of?"

"It did," Sparrow said. "But quite frankly, Miranda dear, you have a bad habit of getting bent out of shape over things that have nothing to do with you. Remember who sprung you out of your charming little cold cellar under the mountain. You're working for Sara now. She, not I, decides what you need to know and when, and she said nothing about telling you anything about the war."

Miranda's eyes went wide. "*Said?*" she hissed. "When did you—"

Before she could finish, Sparrow flicked his hand and a blue ball the size of a marble attached to a leather cord rolled out into his palm. Miranda snapped her mouth shut. Of course. She'd forgotten he had a Relay point. How stupid could she be?

"You still should have told me," she grumbled.

"Think that all you like," Sparrow said, rolling the Relay point in his hand. "I'm not sticking my neck out for your desperate need to meddle." He flicked his hand again, and the blue orb disappeared. "Remember, little Spiritualist," he said, smiling at her startled jerk. "Sara owns you now. I suggest you do as I do and do just what she says, no more and no less. In the meanwhile, get moving. You're wasting our time."

Gin snarled and craned his head back, enormous teeth bared, but Miranda shook her head.

"Ride," she said.

Gin snapped his teeth. "Let me teach this—"

She dug her fingers into his fur. "Go."

Gin snarled one last time, but then he turned and dashed toward the northern gate as fast as he could go, his fur bristling in wild gray swirls. Miranda hunkered down on his back, grateful that the rushing wind made further conversation impossible.

Zarin's gates were thrown wide open to accommodate the massive influx of people. The northern gate was staffed with a squad in Whitefall's white and silver directing traffic. They waved Gin forward without question, and Miranda immediately turned them down a side street, dodging the crowds as best she could. When they were clear of the gate's confusion, Miranda nudged Gin west, toward Whitefall Citadel. It felt strange to enter Zarin and not go directly to the Spirit Court, but she had the feeling that if she didn't see Sara first, things would get ugly. Still, she couldn't help craning her neck as they rode, watching for any flash of the Spirit Court's white walls between the buildings as Gin began the run up the hill to the citadel.

The approach to the Council's stronghold was even more crowded than the road into Zarin. The city was packed to bursting. Troops in a rainbow of country colors clogged the streets and side alleys in noisy, suspicious packs. Everyone made room for Gin, even bravado-filled soldiers weren't stupid enough to stand in a ghosthound's way, but it was still infuriatingly slow going. Finally, after almost an hour of climbing, they made it to the citadel gate.

The guards stepped aside the moment they saw Sparrow, and Gin trotted into the citadel's paved yard. Even here, the traffic was heavy. Ornate, official carriages clogged every inch of the Council's entry, and servants, footmen, and guards stood in every available space, waiting for their masters with sullen, suspicious looks. Gin turned immediately, sticking to the fence until he found a space under the ornamental trees wide enough for his passengers to dismount.

"Wait here," Miranda said, eyeing the other carriages nervously. "And try not to startle the horses. I'm going to see what's going on."

Gin nodded and sat down with a huff, growling deep in his throat. He was still biting mad, but he'd been with Miranda long enough to know that acting out wouldn't get him anywhere but into her bad graces. Still, swallowing anger graciously was not a ghosthound virtue, and so Miranda had to content herself with leaving him growling in the shady corner of the packed citadel yard. This should have made her nervous, but today she was too angry herself to care. And so, filthy, bedraggled, and furious, Miranda marched past the carriages and up the stairs of the Council of Thrones. Sparrow drifted along behind her, thoroughly amused by the whole affair.

A page separated himself from the flock in the entry hall the moment they entered to inform Miranda and Sparrow that Sara was expecting them.

"Of course she is," Miranda muttered, waving for the page to lead the way.

But rather than leading them down to the dark cavernous room where Miranda had met Sara before, the boy led them up a grand staircase and into a series of richly appointed halls.

The outside commotion was here as well. Servants in a rainbow of liveries were constantly running by with papers tucked under their arms. Here and there, doors were guarded by solemn-faced soldiers who watched them suspiciously as they passed. These crowded hallways lasted only two floors, however. After climbing another set of stairs, they entered a quieter hall of elegant offices with important-looking brass nameplates on the doors, all of which were closed. After climbing yet another set of stairs, they entered an elegant waiting room full of serious-faced men in excessively expensive jackets talking in hushed, urgent voices. The men fell silent the moment Miranda stepped into view, and she paused at the top of the stairs, watching to see where the page wanted her. But the page walked right past the waiting men to the closed door at the far end of the room, which, unlike all the others, bore no nameplate at all.

The page stopped at the door and motioned for Miranda to step forward. The waiting men were openly glaring at her now, and Miranda glanced back at Sparrow only to find that she was alone. She turned in a full circle, eyes wide, but Sparrow was nowhere to be seen. Miranda cursed under her breath. She was less annoyed at Sparrow for vanishing than at herself for being surprised. For a moment, she considered turning around and walking out, obligation or no, but even as she thought about it, she knew she couldn't. Sparrow and, through him, Sara had saved her from the mountain. The least she could do was show up and see what Sara wanted. After that, she would go straight to Master Banage and tell him everything.

Decision made, Miranda lifted her head and smoothed her dirty hair and travel-stained clothes with quick fingers. When she was as presentable as she could make herself, she walked past the glaring men and through the heavy wooden door the page opened for her.

A roomful of people turned to look at her. A few she recognized at once. Sara stood beside the large wooden desk at one end of the lavish office, a pencil in her mouth and a stack of papers dangling from her hands. Opposite her was Tower Keeper Blint, one of Hern's old cronies. He was leaning over the desk as well, tapping the map that covered its surface with his jeweled fingers and looking just as displeased to see Miranda as she was to see him. Seated at the desk between them was a man Miranda had never seen personally, but whose face she knew by heart. Though he'd gone a little grayer since the parade days of her youth, no Zarin native could fail to recognize the current head of the family who had ruled Zarin since there was a Zarin: Alber Whitefall, the Merchant Prince himself.

Left alone, Miranda might have stood gawking in the doorway forever. Fortunately, Sara didn't have that kind of patience.

"Finally," she said, snapping her fingers and motioning for Miranda to come stand beside her. "What took you? I was beginning to think Sparrow was lying."

Miranda started to answer, but Blint cut her off.

"What's this, Sara?" the Tower Keeper said, his voice dripping with insult. "The Lyonette girl? This is your plan? She's cut from the same cloth as Banage. What good do you hope to accomplish, bringing in another traitor?"

"More than I can accomplish waiting on you to do more than complain," Sara said, crossing her arms with what felt like a long-standing huff.

"Enough," Prince Whitefall said, glaring at both of them. "If you must bicker like children, you can do it outside. I've got representatives from every kingdom in the Council waiting for audiences today, and that's enough childishness for any man. Now," he said, glancing at Miranda, "who are you, young lady?"

Miranda straightened up, self-consciously hiding the worst of her stained clothes by clutching her arms in front of her. "Miranda Lyonette, your majesty," she said with a deep bow. "Spiritualist of the Court and former apprentice of the Rector Spiritualis Etmon Banage."

She said this last bit with a pointed scowl at Blint, but it was the Merchant Prince who spoke next.

"Ah yes," he said with a wry smile. "The one who keeps losing Eli Monpress."

Miranda felt her face go red.

"You see?" Blint snorted. "Incompetent as well as treacherous, just like her master."

"Now see here!" Miranda said, her voice quivering with rising anger. "Master Banage has never betrayed anyone. If anyone is a traitor here, it's you, Blint. How dare a Tower Keeper speak ill of the Rector Spiritualis to outsiders?"

Blint arched a gray eyebrow at her. "Incompetent, treacherous, and ignorant," he said, glancing at Sara. "You certainly can pick your champions."

Sara's jaw clenched, pressing her lips into a thin line.

"What is he talking about?" Miranda demanded.

Merchant Prince Whitefall looked pointedly at Sara. She tossed down her papers with a sigh and walked over to Miranda, grabbing her arm and steering her toward the large bay window that took up most of the office's right wall.

Miranda tried to yank her arm away. "What are you—"

"Just look," Sara said, pushing her toward the window.

Miranda stumbled forward and landed on her knees on the padded window seat, her face inches from the clear glass that separated her from all of Zarin. The city lay spread out before her, every street alive with activity and packed to bursting. But that much she had already seen, and her eyes moved up, following the city east, down the slope of the river, and then up again to the other colossal building that dominated Zarin's skyline, the Spirit Court's white tower.

Even from this distance, Miranda knew something was wrong. The Tower looked strange. Its sides were stripped of the usual red banners and the great red doors had vanished. The spiraling windows were gone as well, leaving the Tower smooth and solemn, an impenetrable spire of cold, white stone.

"The Tower is sealed?" she said at last, her voice shaking

211

as the truth dawned on her. Every apprentice in the Court knew the Tower could be sealed, though Miranda had never seen it happen. But...she looked over her shoulder at Merchant Prince Whitefall. "Why?"

"As you no doubt know, our lands are soon to be under siege by a foreign power," Whitefall said calmly as Sara returned to his side. "Any hope of survival rests on our ability to stand together. To that end, I asked Banage for his help in the fight against the Empress. He refused. The rest you can see."

So that was it. Miranda swallowed.

"With all due respect, Merchant Prince," she said, turning away from the window, "the Spirit Court exists to protect spirits from human abuse. We do not go to war."

Whitefall's eyes narrowed. "And whose land do you dig your heels into to make that statement? When the Council falls and the Empress makes slaves out of every man, woman, and child, do you think she will spare the Spiritualists?"

Miranda stiffened. "Every Spiritualist swears an oath to protect their spirits, to use them only in self-defense. They are not weapons."

Whitefall sighed. "So that's a 'no' for you as well, then?"

"I am a Spiritualist of the Spirit Court," Miranda said. "I follow the will of my Rector."

Whitefall leaned back in his chair. "And I suppose that appealing to your sense of duty to your country would be a waste of time? No point in reminding you how many of your countrymen will die when the Empress rolls us over because we cannot stand up to her wizards."

"Or how she owes the Council her life, at the moment," Sara added, resting her hands on her narrow hips.

Miranda swallowed against her suddenly dry throat. "I owe you my life and my freedom," she said, picking her words carefully. "But you should know by now, Sara, I choose my oaths over my life every time. But even if helping you didn't violate my pledge to guard my spirits, I would still say no. I am sworn

212

to follow the will of the Rector. If Master Banage has already refused as you said, then his refusal is the Court's refusal. Though," she glared accusingly at Tower Keeper Blint, "apparently some Spiritualists understand their obligations differently."

Blint rolled his eyes in disgust. "Spare me," he said. "I've followed Banage longer than you've worn your rings, little girl. Long enough to see the cliff his absolute refusal to compromise is leading us toward. This is the real world, Miss Lyonette, not some morality play. Standing firm on the letter of our oaths may sound noble, but the reality is that the Empress is coming, and her wizards have no qualms over using spirits in the fight. We will all perish if we do not meet her in kind."

"So because our enemy abuses her spirits, we must abuse ours?" Miranda cried. "Is that what you're saying?"

"I'm merely stating fact," Blint said. "The army with spirits defeats the army without. The Spirit Court represents nearly all of the wizards within the Council Kingdoms. If we all follow Banage and bury our heads in the sand, the Council will be defenseless. The Empress will conquer everything, and if you think she will let an organization like the Spirit Court remain when these lands are hers, then you are delusional."

Miranda clenched her fists, her rings glowing like torches on her fingers. "I will not abandon my oaths," she said fiercely. "And I will not abandon Master Banage."

Sara and Blint both started to speak, but the Merchant Prince cut them off with a wave of his hand. He turned in his chair to look at Miranda directly, and when he spoke, his voice was kind and genteel. "I understand you've been through a lot lately, and this may all be a bit much. Please know that I admire your loyalty. I wish I had someone on my staff half as willing to stand up for me as you do for Banage, but a lot has changed since you last left Zarin."

He stood up and walked around his desk, taking Miranda gently by the arm as he turned her back to the window. "Look there," he said softly, pointing down, toward the streets. "Do you see those soldiers?"

Miranda nodded. She could hardly miss them. The streets of Zarin were full.

"Three days ago I called in the pledges for the first time in Council history," Whitefall said. "Three days, Spiritualist, and already we have so many men ready to defend their homes. Every country in the Council is sending its army to help defend the whole against the Empress. Several of those men down there are conscripts, boys taken from their mothers' skirts. Most have never even seen the coast they are going to defend." He looked down at her, his eyes sad. "Banage told me he would not force the spirits to fight a war that has nothing to do with them, but those young men are here to fight a war that ostensibly has nothing to do with them either. Even so, here they are. They have come to fight because their countries have spent the last two and a half decades benefiting from the Council, and the time has come to pay."

Miranda stiffened. "The Spirit Court is not part of the Council of Thrones."

"No," Whitefall said. "But the Rector has had a place at our meetings since the beginning. The Court has benefited from the peace and prosperity of the Council as much as any country. Maybe more. But even if the Court was as fully aloof as you claim, you and Banage and every Spiritualist who serves the Court were born on what is now Council land. Spiritualists you may be, but that membership doesn't change the fact that you are all citizens of the Council, and you are beholden to the same rules that govern everyone else."

Miranda stepped away. Though the Merchant Prince had not said it, she could read his meaning plainly. "You mean to conscript us too?" she said softly.

"Not 'mean to,'" Whitefall said. "I have. I delivered the order to Banage himself, and then he tore it up, threw it in my face, and sealed his Tower. Do you know what we call that, Spiritualist Lyonette?"

Miranda began to tremble. "Treason?"

"Treason." Whitefall nodded. "It is a mistake to think that

your duty to the Court outweighs all others, my dear. Tower Keeper Blint here understands that. So do the other Spiritualists who have chosen to fight for their homes and way of life. They understand that if we continue to divide ourselves, the only person who will triumph is the Empress."

"Merchant Prince," Miranda said. "I understand what you're saying, but if Master Banage refused, I'm sure he had good reason."

"Really?" Whitefall said, his voice low. "How sure?"

"Absolutely," Miranda said, drawing herself up. "You may call it treason, but we must follow our oaths to the Court and our spirits above all other obligations. Master Banage understands this better than any Spiritualist I've ever known."

"I'm sure he does," Whitefall said. "That's why I'm sending you back to him with a compromise."

Miranda blinked. "What?"

"A compromise," Whitefall said, his stern face breaking into a smile. "I realize you Spiritualists don't have much knowledge of the concept, but they can be very useful."

"But you just said Master Banage was a traitor," Miranda said, staring at him.

"He is," Whitefall said. "But he doesn't have to remain one. Listen, child, no one wanted things this way less than myself. Banage is a hard man. I thought if I laid things out in hard terms he would see reason, but all I managed was to divide the Court, which was the last thing I wanted." He tightened his hand on her arm. "I don't want Spiritualist defectors. I want the Spirit Court—the *whole* Court—fighting with us against a common enemy."

He turned Miranda around to face him, looking down at her with a sad, serious expression. "I am not a proud man," he said quietly. "I am not afraid to eat my own words if that's what's best for the Council. If the Spirit Court will agree to help us in this war, I swear that they will be kept in a purely supportive roll—no fighting, no risk to your spirits, no danger to your oaths. In addition, I am prepared to give Banage

215

something he's been angling at for a long time: a Council law making Enslavement illegal."

"Illegal?" Miranda said.

Whitefall nodded. "Think of the possibilities. The Court will no longer have to deal with rogue wizards alone. You'll be able to call on Council law to demand backup from local officials. The Court will have authority like it's never had before. Plus, you will save your Spiritualists from a division that could doom your entire organization without compromising your ideals, *and* you'll help me keep our necks out from under the Empress's boot. Now"—he smiled—"is that a compromise that could interest you?"

Miranda bit her lip. It was a good offer, a potentially fantastic offer, but... "I'm not the person who can make that decision."

"I know," Whitefall said. "Sara says you owe us a debt. I'm calling it in. Take my compromise to Banage. I've tried sending him messages, but he won't open his Tower for anything. That said, I'm betting he'll open it for you. Make my case to your master and I'll wipe your obligation to Sara and the Council clean. There is no downside for you in this, Spiritualist Lyonette. Even if Banage refuses, you'll still be with him, and your debt to us will still be forgiven. What do you say?"

Miranda thought the words through carefully. "Just support?"

"Just support," Whitefall said, nodding.

"All right," Miranda said at last. "But I want everything in writing first."

Whitefall smiled. "Very shrewd, but I expected no less." He walked back over to his desk and drew out a thick stack of papers. "I had the clerks draw it up the moment Sara told me you were on your way."

Miranda took the papers. The offer was all there, just as he'd said. Copied in triplicate, she noticed with a sigh, but what else could you expect from the Council?

"I'll take this to Banage at once," she said, tucking the papers under her arm. "But I wouldn't get your hopes up."

"With Etmon, I never do," Whitefall said, sitting down at his desk. "Nice meeting you, Spiritualist."

Miranda bowed from the waist, turned on her heel, and left. The men in the waiting room sneered at her as she pushed past them, but Miranda didn't even notice. Her head was reeling with everything that had happened. This morning she'd been preparing for the potential pitfalls of telling the story of the Shaper Mountain to Sara, now she was bringing the Council's compromise to Master Banage with war looming over them, and there was still the issue of the demons, the stars, and the Shepherdess. She didn't even know what crisis to focus on anymore but, pressing the papers hard against her chest, she knew where to begin. First she had to find Master Banage and explain everything. Once all the cards were on the table, he would know what to do.

That thought alone was enough to calm her mind as she marched down the stairs toward the citadel yard where Gin was waiting to take her home to the Tower.

Tower Keeper Blint turned to face the Merchant Prince, brandishing his rings as he did. "You do realize you just gave Banage back his greatest weapon?"

"A calculated risk," Whitefall said, leaning back in his chair. "And the best choice, given our options. She certainly wasn't going to turn against Banage, and you can't force a Spiritualist to work. That left locking her up, which I don't have the resources for at the moment, or sending her running home to sulk with her master. At least this way I can get an offer through that stone wall of his, and who knows, the old zealot just might take it."

"He won't," Blint said. "Banage would die before he compromised his integrity."

"We also thought he would die before he split his precious Court," Sara said. "But he laid down the line and shed you Tower Keepers without so much as a look back, didn't he? But you saw the girl's eyes light up when Alber offered to outlaw Enslavement. The Court's been after that apple for *years*. It might just be enough to convince Miranda that the Council's position is in the right, and she can be very persuasive when she thinks she's on the moral side of things."

"It will take more than an apple and an earnest girl to talk Banage out of that Tower," Blint said, his voice dripping with superiority. "The Rector Spiritualis is a slave to his pride. I don't even know why you want him along. He'll just get in our way."

"With all due respect to you and your Tower Keepers, Blint," Whitefall said in a tired voice, "you'd better hope Sara's right. It's no secret that Lyonette and Banage are the two strongest wizards in the Court. They are weapons we cannot afford to lay by, however much trouble they may be. If sending the girl doesn't work, we'll just have to try something else. Now, if you'll excuse me, I have other people to mollify today."

Blint opened his mouth, but he closed it again as Sara swept by to open the door. Duly dismissed, Blint stomped out. Sara followed right behind him, stepping out of the way as the pages showed in the royal ambassador from some country she couldn't be bothered to remember.

As ordered, Sparrow was waiting in the hall for her. He was freshly washed and dressed, and his hair was pulled back in a long, blond snake of a braid over the shoulder of his impressively garish orange coat. He stood aside for Blint with a flourish as the Tower Keeper stomped down the stairs and then turned to Sara, smiling as he handed her a lit pipe.

"Thank the Powers," she muttered, snatching the pipe from his hand and putting it to her mouth with a deep draw that she held for nearly half a minute. "At least something's going right," she said, letting the breath go at last. "Do you have it?"

"Of course." Sparrow pulled a worn leather book from his sleeve. "Just as I told you."

Sara snatched the book with greedy fingers, her eyes widening with delight as she flipped through the pages. "Not as good as the man himself," she said. "But I'll take what I can get."

"You're welcome," Sparrow said pointedly as they started down the stairs.

Sara blew a line of smoke at him. "Did you manage to plant the point?"

"Not an hour ago," Sparrow said. "Just before we entered the city."

"And she didn't notice?" Sara asked, taking in a fresh lungful of smoke.

Sparrow looked affronted. "Who do you think you're dealing with?"

"Just checking," Sara said. "I've been far too much in the company of idiots lately."

"That's the risk you take working with the Council," Sparrow said cheerfully. "Are you sure about this Miranda thing? I mean, I went through all that trouble to get her in debt to us, I'd hate to think we let her off the hook too easily."

"I'm sure," Sara said, flipping through Slorn's book. "I got back from the desert this morning, but Alber's weapon isn't ready yet, and at this rate I don't know when it will be. I need more wizards, and fast. Myron's already drawn up plans for more spirit defense points than I can man, even with Blint's deserters. That militaristic idiot doesn't seem to understand that wizards are not interchangeable. There's a huge power difference between a man like Blint and our Miranda. I'd hoped that by making Banage a traitor we could squeeze the Court enough to get what we needed, but it looks like all the true talent has stayed loyal so far." She blew an angry line of smoke. "They're worse than burned sugar, the way they stick together."

"If you're holding out for Miranda to turn, it'll be a long wait," Sparrow said. "Banage could say the sky was green and she would still back him."

"It's her loyalty I'm counting on," Sara said with a sad sigh. "Blint was right, you know. Banage will never back down now that Whitefall's forced him to make his stand. He won't budge an inch from that tower until I roll over. We've been playing this game for twenty years now, he and I, but not for much longer. I didn't want it to be like this, but the Empress is the trump that forces all hands, even mine."

"Well, that's the problem with games," Sparrow said. "Sooner or later, someone has to lose."

Sara sighed again and tapped out her pipe. Sparrow just smiled and held the door for her as they started down the dark stairs toward her office in the Relay chamber.

Outside, at the edges of Zarin, another hundred soldiers arrived at the gates.

CHAPTER
13

Josef stomped after Duke Finley's servant as they wound down through the ancient warren of Osera's royal offices. But rather than stopping at one of the venerable old doors, the servant led Josef out past the stables to the little paved yard at the rear of the palace. A black carriage was waiting there for them, and the servant hurried forward to open the door.

Josef paused. This was all getting a little too suspicious— the sudden invitation, the backdoor exit, the unmarked carriage. Though, Josef reminded himself, suspicious as it was, he wasn't exactly a soft target. If Finley wanted to try something, let him. At least it would be a straightforward fight. Grinning at the thought, Josef climbed into the carriage. It rocked under his weight as he pulled himself inside. The servant followed, shutting the door behind them. The moment the door closed, the carriage shot forward, clattering through the yard and out the iron gate.

The back gate of the palace faced east, toward the Unseen Sea. Here, on the side of the island farthest from the Council and the wealth it brought, the scars of the war with the Empress were still evident. The houses were still built in the old way, stone shacks never more than a single story tall, most without windows, only a chimney and a door covered with oil cloth to keep the weather out. The houses clustered together, leaning on each other for comfort, but between the clusters, breaking up the flow of buildings like rocks in a stream, were the craters.

Josef wasn't born when the Empress's fleet first attacked, but he knew those craters same as any Oseran. They were the legacy of the Empress's war spirits, great monsters of stone and fire that came from the sky, striking the ground in enormous eruptions of burning rock. Even now, decades later, the ground was still black at the crater's base, the bedrock itself scorched and broken where the Empress's wizards had struck.

As they drove down the island's eastern slope, the houses grew smaller and the craters more numerous. The road they followed was narrow and winding, changing from smoothly paved stone to gravel and finally to rutted, sandy dirt as it snaked down the mountain. Ahead of them, Josef could see the glitter of the Unseen Sea. He knew where they were headed now. Osera, steep and rocky as it was, was not without beaches. This road led to the only sheltered bay on the island's eastern side, a protected curve of sand called the Rebuke, for it was here that the Council forces, led by his mother, had finally turned the Empress away.

The carriage bounced down the rutted road and came at last to a halt. Josef was out before the wheels stopped moving. Finley's servant hurried after him only to find Josef standing at the bottom step of the carriage, staring at the water with a strange look on his face.

The Rebuke was a curving oval bay ringed in by steep cliffs to form a narrow mouth leading out to sea. This much at least was still as Josef remembered it, but everything else had changed. When he'd come here as a boy to swim, the Rebuke had been little more than a grassy hill leading down to a narrow strip of rocky sand wedged between a cleft in the sea cliffs.

Now that scrubby hill was gone, replaced by a smoothly paved walkway wide enough to march ten men abreast circling the inside of the bay all the way to the cliffs. Squinting against the salty wind, Josef ignored the servant's insistent tugging and walked out onto the stone. The paved area wasn't just a flattening of the old hill; it wasn't even just a walkway. It was a rampart, the flat top of a great wall that ran all the way along the bay's inner curve, forming a third, manmade cliff to join the natural barriers on the bay's north and south. Below the flat walkway he stood on was a steep, unclimbable slope of enormous, sharp, piled stone held together with sandy cement.

Josef looked over his shoulder. "When did they build this?"

The servant, not at all pleased by this delay, answered in a clipped voice. "Construction on the storm wall was finished five years ago, sir. It is the duke's greatest project."

Josef looked down at the solid stone beneath his feet. Not bad. Considering the gentle hill that had been here before, the wall of sharp rock and the wide rampart running along its top were certainly defensive improvements. Leaning into the wind, he looked over the wall's edge. Down below, the narrow beach had been widened as well, the sand combed and relayed to create a wide space between the surf and the wall. A tiny stair, steep as a ladder and barely wide enough for one man, cut down between the sharp rocks at the wall's midway mark, the only access Josef could see to the wide wooden docks that crowded the new beach. The docks themselves were large and freshly built, the tar still gleaming on the jutting joints that pushed out into the bay's blue water, but they were nothing compared to the ships.

Oseran runners filled the blue bay in long, precise lines, the fresh-cut wood of their narrow, high-running hulls gleaming white in the afternoon sun. Josef whistled appreciatively. Runners were the pride of Oseran shipbuilding and notoriously hard to make. It was no easy task getting hardwood long and straight enough to bear the carving needed to make a runner's long, curving keel, but that difficult shape was what let a runner weave through shallows and move faster on open water than any other ship on the sea. Back when Oserans had been pirates, the runners had been the reason they were feared. There had to be near a hundred of them bobbing in the water below, more than Josef had ever seen in one place, and every one of them new.

"Finley had this built?" he said, trying not to sound as impressed as he felt.

"Yes, your majesty," the servant said with barely disguised disgust. "*Some* members of the royal family cherish their position and strive to serve Osera's interests."

"I bet," Josef said. "All right, take me to him."

The servant bowed and turned toward the large tower that dominated the storm wall's northern half. Josef followed him, squinting up against the bright sunlight. The tower was square and solid, four stories tall with foot-thick walls and made of imported granite twice as strong as Osera's native stone. The door was solid iron, as were the stairs that wound up the tower's core. They passed an armory filled with racks of crossbows and crates of bolts, a small but well-equipped mess and sleeping barracks, and a nicely appointed officer's lounge. There were soldiers everywhere, navy officers mostly in their distinctive tight coats, but there were palace guards as well, standing watch in their chain and quilted surcoats with their short swords ready on their hips.

The top floor of the tower was separated from the others by a heavy door. Finley's servant stopped and knocked, a rapid double tap. The response was instant.

"Enter!" The heavy door did little to muffle Duke Finely's booming voice.

The servant opened the door and stepped aside with a sweep of his arm. Josef looked back down the winding stair, checking for emergency exits, just in case. There was only one, the way they'd come, but he was certain he could overpower the soldiers if it came to that, so he set his face in a scowl and marched into the room.

The top of the tower was unlike the other floors. Instead of smaller partitions, it was one open room, a great loft with a high ceiling going all the way up to the tower's pointed peak. There were tables here, including a large desk at the tower's center, all done in the same style as the rest of the tower's furnishings. But where the other floors were dark and sheltered by the tower's thick walls, this room was bright with sunlight streaming in through enormous, panoramic windows that ringed the room on all sides. The windows were set with thick glass, high-quality stuff, showing the view without so much as a single distorting wobble. And what a view it was. Josef could see the entire sweep of the bay below, the wide ocean spread out in front of him, the tops of the high cliffs to his right and left, and the eastern slums behind him running almost all the way to the weathered walls of the palace at the peak of the mountain.

Finley was standing beside the window that looked due east, talking into his palm while an older man in somber civilian clothes stood beside him, watching intently. He glanced at Josef as the prince entered, and then turned away, continuing his low speech into his palm where Josef couldn't see him. Josef glowered at that, but before he could say anything, Finley finished speaking and held out his hand to the man beside him. The older man moved forward, taking what looked like a small, blue marble from Finley and placing it carefully into a padded box.

The man bowed slightly to the duke and, holding the box in both hands, walked to the door. He did not bow to Josef, just slid by him and started down the stairs. Josef ignored the insult, focusing instead on his cousin and, so far as Josef could tell, greatest enemy in Osera.

"Ah," Finley said, turning at last to Josef. "The prince graces me with his presence."

Josef hooked his thumbs into his sword belt. "What do you want?"

Finley blithely ignored him. "I was just reporting our latest bit of bad luck to the Whitefall running the Council's forces, Lord Myron." He crossed the room as he spoke, stopping in front of a small wooden cabinet set between the windows. He unlocked the door with a key from his pocket. Inside was a cut-glass bottle filled with amber liquid. Finley took it out with loving hands, smiling at Josef over the glass stopper. "Would you like a drink?"

"No," Josef said. "What are you doing out here with the Relay point? It's supposed to be kept in the palace for the queen's use only."

"The first one is," Finley said, reaching back into the cabinet for a crystal tumbler. "That was our second point, provided for this watchtower."

"Osera has two Relay points?" Josef scoffed. "Since when? I thought they were incredibly rare."

"They are," Finley said, filling his glass halfway. "But considering how this tower will be the first to spot the Empress's fleet, I convinced the Council to give us another."

Josef narrowed his eyes. "So what were you relaying just now?"

"That," the duke said, tipping his glass toward the southern window.

Josef turned skeptically. He couldn't see much because of the cliffs, but he could see what looked like a plume of black smoke billowing up from somewhere down the coast.

Josef glanced back at the duke. "What's that?"

"Our clingfire depot," the duke said. "Or, rather, it *was*."

Josef swallowed. Clingfire was an old Oseran secret, a blend of pitch and sticky oil that clung to wood and burned even when wet. It had been invented so that Oseran pirates on their fast, narrow ships could take down larger freighters. It was also the only way the Oseran navy had been able to fight the Empress's palace ships.

"What happened?"

"We're not sure," Finley said, his voice grave. "The whole depot went up sometime early this morning. It's been burning for nearly twelve hours already, and since we had almost five tons of clingfire ready for the Empress's assault, it will likely burn another twelve."

"Five tons?" Josef took a step back. He'd never heard of so much clingfire in one place.

"At least," Finley said. "Osera's not the little fishing village you left, Thereson. My factories have been producing clingfire day and night on the queen's order since word came that the Empress was on the move. I'd ordered it stored on one of the uninhabited southern islands for safety purposes, and good thing too. If we'd kept it in the city, the whole island would be burning by now."

Josef glanced again at the column of smoke. "You think it was arson?"

"Arson or carelessness," the duke said, sipping his drink. "Your wife's investigating as we speak, so I suppose we'll know soon enough. I may not like Adela, but even I can admit she's good at what she does." He left the words hanging, watching Josef over the rim of his glass.

Josef got the point well enough. "Better than me," he finished.

"Well," the duke said. "You ran away, so I guess we'll never know what could have been."

Josef barely stopped himself from rolling his eyes. "I've got better things to do today than listen to you gripe, Finley," he said. "If you've got something to say, say it. Otherwise, I'll be on my way."

"You haven't changed a bit, have you, Josef Liechten?" Finley said, setting his drink down on the window ledge with a clink. "Still unable to even play at manners."

"I don't play at anything," Josef said. "Get on with it."

The corner of the duke's mouth twitched. "Very well," he said. "I called you out here because I would like to propose an arrangement. These last two days have been very hard on you, haven't they, prince? You've never bothered to hide how much you hate being in your own country. Frankly, I'm surprised you're still around."

Josef's glower deepened, and the duke began to grin. "I can see I'm taxing your minuscule patience, so I'll get straight to the point. I want you to leave."

226

"I know that," Josef growled.

"No," the duke said. "I mean I want you to vanish. Go. Crawl back to whatever miserable, violent life you enjoyed before Theresa got this fool idea of grandchildren."

Josef bared his teeth. "If this is about the damn succession—"

"The succession does not concern me," the duke said. "Whatever hopes your mother holds, the truth is that my line will inherit the Throne of Iron Lions. Ancient as the blood of the Eisenlowe is, Osera is a land ruled by the strong, not by unborn children."

"And you would be that strength?"

"Of course," the duke answered. "I've been leading Osera since your mother first fell ill years ago. It was my money and my sway that fortified this bay. My pull with the Council that got us two Relay points, my shipyards that built a fleet of runners, and my factories that produced the five tons of clingfire it's going to take to sink an armada of palace ships."

Josef cocked his head toward the plume of smoke. "You mean the five tons that's burning right now?"

"A minor setback," the duke snapped. "The Empress won't be here for another month and a half. That's more than enough time to rebuild our supplies and secure my rule."

"*Your* rule?" Josef said, scowling. "I hate to disappoint you, Finley, but last I checked, my mother was still alive."

"Not for much longer," the duke said, smiling. "For all your faults, Thereson, you're a loving son, but you're kidding yourself if you actually believe our dear queen will be alive to lead Osera to another victory over the Empress."

"Shut your mouth, Finley," Josef said, taking a menacing step forward. "Or I will shut it for you."

Finley rolled his eyes. "Spare me the bravado. Believe it or not, my boy, I'm actually on your side. You don't want to be here, and I don't want you here either, so why shouldn't we work together to get you out?"

"Because I'm not going," Josef said. "I made a promise to my mother, and I mean to keep it."

"How novel of you," Duke Finley said, grabbing his drink again. He downed the rest of the glass in one swallow, keeping his eyes on Josef the whole time. "Tell me, Thereson," he said when he'd finished. "Are you trying to be as difficult as possible, or it is your natural state?"

"What do you care, anyway?" Josef yelled. "You just said you're not worried about the succession. Shouldn't you be off giving orders and being kingly? Why are you wasting time with me?"

"Because *you* are in my way," Finley yelled back, slamming his glass on the stone so hard it cracked. "You are a millstone around this country's neck, Josef Liechten. You always were, what with your moods and your stubbornness. But just when the people were learning to love you for your mother's sake, you run away to become a traveling swordsman and a thief." The duke let go of his cracked glass with a scowl. "We all breathed a sigh of relief when you left. The selfish boy was gone, and good riddance. But your selfishness knows no end, does it? For here you are again, back to weigh down your country one last time at the hour of her greatest need."

Josef took a deep, shaking breath. "You think I don't know that I let this country down?" he said. "No one was more aware of how great a failure I was than myself."

"Good," the duke said. "So prove it. *Leave.* Your presence in Osera is a disruption. The people are confused. They fear that this wandering swordsman, this no-account murderer who abandoned them has returned to be king. This fear causes division and distraction at the time when we must be the most focused and united. If you love your mother, Thereson, if you want to preserve the country she fought so hard for all her life, then do us all a favor and remove yourself from it. I swear I will take good care of our people. I will defeat the Empress and lead Osera into an even brighter age of wealth and prosperity. I will be the king you never could be, and I will even make sure your legacy of failure is forgotten. All you have to do is go."

Finley reached into his pocket and pulled out a heavy bag. He swung his arm, tossing the bag on the floor between them. It landed with a bright, metal *chink*, spilling open in a shower of gold coins.

"That's a hundred gold standards," the duke said. "There's also a pledge that can be used in Zarin for five hundred more. If you ever loved Osera, take it and leave before you do irreparable harm."

Josef stared at the bag of coins, and then, without a word, he swung his boot back and kicked it as hard as he could. The kick sent the gold flying, the coins tinkling like golden bells as they scattered across the heavy wooden planks.

The duke stepped back in surprise as coins bounced across his boots. When he raised his head, his face was pale with rage. "That was very foolish."

"Then you should have expected it," Josef said. "Given your opinion of me."

Finley began to shake, but before he could open his mouth, Josef moved in. He closed the distance between them in one long step, pointing his finger right in the duke's face.

"There's only one understanding we need between us, cousin," he whispered, his voice sharp as his blades. "Whether my mother is alive to see it or not, I will honor her wish and continue the blood of our house. That wish is the only thing keeping me in this country, and the moment it is fulfilled, I will vanish so quickly not even you will be able to find fault. But until that time, nothing, not gold, not threats, not even poison in the night, *nothing* is going to make me abandon the one duty my mother has ever asked of me that I could actually deliver. Everything else, the throne, the people, I gladly leave to you, but I will not betray my promise now that I've made it, and I'm not going anywhere."

With a final glare, Josef turned on his heel and walked toward the door. Behind him, he heard the duke's boots scrape as the old man recovered.

"Thereson!"

229

Josef stopped and looked over his shoulder. The duke had pulled himself up to his full height, his face scarlet with barely leashed fury. "I have given you every chance to do right by your country, but if you will not leave on your own, I will not hesitate to do what is best for Osera."

Josef's hands went back to rest on the swords at his hip. "You're welcome to try, old man." With that, he flashed the duke a long, bloodthirsty smile and walked out the door.

The servant was waiting just outside. Josef pushed past him, sweeping down the stairs. When he reached the bottom of the tower, he kept going, walking past the waiting carriage to the rutted road leading back to the city. The moment he hit the dirt, he started jogging, his legs eating the distance in long steps as he pushed up the slope into the poor, crater-pocked neighborhoods covering Osera's eastern side. People came out to gawk at him as he passed, the tall man with his fine clothes hidden under blades. Josef ignored the stares and kept running, his hands clenched in white-knuckled fists.

The sun was going down by the time he reached the palace at the top of the mountain. Servants threw themselves out of his way as he stomped through the rear gate. He heard them whispering his name as he crossed the yard, as well as other things—thief, deserter, murderer, disappointment, failure—before he shut his ears and set himself on a single-minded path back to his room.

When he arrived, he opened his door to find Nico and Eli sitting at his table eating his dinner.

"Welcome back," Eli said around an enormous mouthful of food, glancing over his shoulder just long enough to give Josef a stuff-cheeked smile. "How was the meeting?"

Josef ignored the question. "What are you doing?" he said, shutting the door.

"Dinner," Eli said, turning back to the table. "We started without you. Hope you don't mind."

"Wouldn't matter if I did," Josef said, looking at the decimated plates. "There's not enough left to get mad over."

"You should be grateful," Eli said, shoving another forkful of potatoes in his mouth. "A man came by about a half hour ago with a message from your wife. Something about a fire? Anyway, he said that she said to tell you that she's going to be late tonight and you should eat without her, so *I* took the liberty of telling him to go ahead and bring up your dinner. After all"—Eli swallowed loudly—"we'll never get a better chance to test it for poison without having to worry about the sweet princess."

Josef's eyebrows shot up. "So you decided to test the food for poison by eating it all? That's the stupidest idea I've ever heard."

"You have no vision," Eli said. "I'll have you know I have a very sophisticated palate for this sort of thing. The old Monpress fed me every poison under the sun during my thief training days. Ah," he said, licking his fingers. "Memories."

Josef shook his head. "So what have you found?"

"Nothing," Eli said, snatching the last delicately folded roll from the basket at the center of the table. "Your food seems perfectly safe, so either your poisoner decided to take the night off, or it's not coming through the food."

"Or it's something you don't recognize," Josef added.

"Impossible," Eli said. "If it's used in the Council Kingdoms, I've tasted it. Poisoning's a subtle art, but it's very set in its ways."

"I'll keep that in mind," Josef muttered. He walked over to the table and picked up a plate of beef scraps, all that was left of what must have been a lovely roast. "Meanwhile, you can get out. I'm going to wait up for Adela. I have some questions to ask her."

Eli shrugged and stood, taking his wineglass with him. "I'm going to poke my nose down around the castle," he said, refilling his glass to the rim from the bottle on the mantel. "Do a little goodwill work with the spirits, just in case we have to make a quick getaway."

Josef ignored the stab of bitterness that came with that. "What makes you think we'll be leaving?"

"First rule of thievery: Never be without a quick exit," Eli said, sipping the top of his now very full glass. "Of course, there's also the fact that you just walked in from a meeting with a powerful man who doesn't like you very much looking like you're ready to kill something. Even without the rules, that's reason enough for me."

Josef couldn't argue that point, so he let Eli go. But when Nico got up to follow, he reached out.

"Stay," he said, grabbing her shoulder gently. "Please. I want you to help keep an eye on things, in case I fall asleep again."

"You want me to stay here," she said, slowly. "With you and your wife?"

"Yes," Josef said. "In case I—"

"Fall asleep again," she finished, turning away. "I heard you the first time."

She vanished into the long shadows of the dressing room before he could add anything else, and Josef bit back a curse. He was trying to think of something to say when the door creaked, and he snapped his head around to see Eli hovering.

"Josef," he said, very quietly. "Do you want to talk about—"

"No," Josef said.

Eli bit his lip and, for a long, tense moment, Josef worried that the thief would push. But then Eli nodded and vanished into the hall, closing the door silently behind him. Once he was sure Eli was gone, Josef sat down on the couch and stared at the destroyed remains of his dinner, mechanically shoving the last scraps of the roast into his mouth as he waited for his wife to appear.

CHAPTER
14

The Empress stood on the balcony at the top of her war palace, looking over her fleet. It was an impressive sight.

Even Nara, who had fielded countless armies in her conquest of the continent that was now her Empire, had never seen its like.

Palace ships filled the bay, packed so close that the sailors could step from one ship to the next without stretching their legs. Overhead, wind spirits kept a smooth inland wind blowing at her command, filling the enormous sails and keeping the ships together against the ocean's tide. Each palace ship was large enough to fill three blocks in one of her well-ordered cities and as tall as the war palace at Istalirin would be were it perched on the sea instead of a mountain. Square sails as large as wheat fields hung from the tower masts, and each enormous, tar-black, iron-girded wood hull was packed to capacity with men ready to die at her command.

For the first time in many centuries, Nara felt a quickening of the excitement that came before a conquest. She had emptied her garrisons for this day, marched her troops to the bay at Istalirin from all corners of her Empire. Before her lay the largest fleet ever assembled, carrying the largest army she'd ever fielded, the largest army the world had ever seen.

"It's beautiful," said a deep voice beside her.

Nara caught herself seconds before she jumped. Excitement turned to cold rage as she turned to face the man who had impertinently joined her on her balcony.

Den wasn't even looking at her. His eyes were locked on the fleet, his face pulled into a wide, white-toothed grin that was more snarl than smile. "I think that's the most beautiful thing I've ever see."

"I'm glad you're pleased," Nara said sharply. "But I didn't build it for you."

"Pity," Den said with a sigh. "It would be a real challenge to take that army."

Nara sighed. "That's an absurd joke, Warlord."

"I don't make jokes," Den said, reaching in his pocket. "Look here, I made you something."

He pulled out a folded paper and jabbed it at her like a

spear. Nara took it gingerly, eyebrows going up in surprise as she shook the paper open. It was a map. A hand-drawn, surprisingly detailed map of lands she did not recognize.

"The western continent," Den said. "Your maps were a bit sketchy. I filled in the details."

"My maps were taken from description given by the winds," Nara said crossly.

"What do winds know of war?" Den said, shrugging. "War is a human enterprise, woman. See here." He snatched the map back and laid a calloused finger on the long chain of islands just off the continent's eastern seaboard.

"Osera," Den said. "We have to take them first or you'll have their runners on your back the whole campaign. Now, your maps showed only the coastline, but look here." He moved his finger to the cross-hatching that surrounded the islands. "These are the shallows, the rocks and reefs that guard Osera's eastern shore. Your big ships run deep. They'll ground themselves if they get too close."

"I am well aware of that," Nara snapped. "You presume too much. Remember, my generals have fought at Osera before."

"And they let Whitefall and his cronies lure them into the handful of deepwater approaches like idiots," Den countered. "That one act of stupidity narrowed their fleet, lowered the effectiveness of superior numbers, and lost them the war. If I hadn't switched sides and taken out Whitefall's army on the cliffs, your ships would never have made it back here to report their own defeat."

Nara glared at Den's weathered finger on the cross-hatched shading marking the dangerous water. "You never did tell me why you turned that day. You were the greatest threat to our soldiers, greater than the wizards or the ships with their clingfire." She glanced up at his dark eyes. "Tell me, why did you do it?"

Den looked genuinely puzzled. "Why do you ask?"

"As your new master, I think it is wise to know what triggers your betrayal."

Den threw back his head and laughed. He laughed long and

loudly, frightening the servants who hovered just out of sight. Nara stayed still, growing angrier with every passing second. Finally, Den's laughter died away, leaving him grinning at her like a wolf.

"You don't get it, do you?" he said. "That war was the happiest time of my life. For the first time ever, I could fight as much as I wanted. Strong men literally jumped out of the sea at me. No more wandering looking for a challenge, no more wasting my time. Truly, I'd found paradise. So when your fleet started to lose, it was the natural choice to switch sides and keep my paradise going. It worked for a bit, but then your coward of a general ran home. I considered slaughtering him and what was left of his crew, but I wanted to meet the woman who could start a war without even going to the front herself. I thought if you could start one war, maybe there were others." His grin widened. "But you should know, Nara, it wasn't betrayal. Betrayal requires loyalty. I had no loyalty to Whitefall, and I have no loyalty to you. You can call yourself my Empress all you like, but I have no king by myself."

With that, he started to laugh again, and for a moment, Nara seriously considered killing him. She turned the idea over, toying with how to do it. She could order the air around him to stop moving and suffocate him where he stood. She could open the floor below him and let the fall break him on the rocks. But she did none of these things. Instead, she turned back to her fleet.

"You know I could kill you before you lifted a hand."

"But you won't," Den said. "A woman who's spent ten lifetimes conquering knows better than to throw away her best weapon."

Nara stiffened. "And if we start to lose now, will you kill five thousand of my men and join the other side?"

"Five thousand of your men wouldn't even be a dent," Den said, grinning down at the endless ships. "But what a fight that would be, eh?"

The Empress shook her head. "Go and take your place,

Bloody Den. Take your map to the fleet head and tell him I said to put you on the first-wave flagship."

Den took his map back, folding it neatly. "Just so long as you promise I won't die of old age waiting for you to get moving. We're not all immortal here, Nara."

"I'll throw you into war soon enough," the Empress said. "When this is done, even you might have had your fill of fighting."

"Impossible," Den said, laughing as he vanished through the curtained door.

Nara did not watch him go. She watched her fleet, standing still as a gold-plated statue on her balcony until, hours later, the last of her army had finally marched up the plank from the dock to the waiting ships. As the captain called for the plank to be raised, a shiver went through her. Almost, she breathed to herself. Soon, sooner than Den could dream, her fleet would be landing on the far-western shore. Soon she would carve a swath across the world large enough that even Benehime would notice. She would force the Lady to look up from her spoiled boy, and when she did, she would see Nara standing triumphant with the world in her hands, ready at last to shape it to the perfection she'd dreamed of that night in the swamp so many years ago.

Will you, darling girl?

The voice broke over her like a shower of ice water. Nara froze, unable to breathe, unable to think as the thrill of that beloved, beloved voice tore through her. When she could move again, she turned and fell to her knees before the pure white light.

Benehime sat on the balcony railing like a great white bird, a smile on her perfect, white face. She was glorious, beautiful, and so beloved Nara could barely look at her. Instead, the Empress kept her face down, biting her lip against the overwhelming tide of emotion threatening to capsize her.

Are you crying? Benehime's voice was cool and soft as her white fingers lay their burning touch against the crown of Nara's head. *Did you think I had forgotten you, Nara?*

"No, Lady," Nara lied, raising her tear-streaked face to kiss the Lady's fingers.

I could never forget my dashing Empress. Benehime's voice floated over her mind. *Just because you are no longer first in my heart does not mean I do not care for you.*

Nara shook with rage. Second. Second. How could she be *second*? Above her, the Shepherdess put on a hurt face.

Why are you mad, darling?

"How can I not be?" Nara cried. "You love that boy more than me!"

The Shepherdess smiled, stroking Nara's face with her fingertips. *Jealousy becomes you. You were so dull while you were sulking.*

Nara flinched, cheeks coloring with shame. "I am through with that," she said bitterly. "I love you, Lady. More than he ever could."

Do you? Benehime's voice was close to laughter.

Nara looked away. Her words sounded so needy, so desperate, even to her. But she could not stop. The Lady's presence was intoxicating after so long without.

Benehime's sigh floated over her, and when Nara looked up, the Lady was gone. Panic shot through her, but before she could move, white arms encircled her from behind. Relief so strong it was almost painful hammered her chest, and Nara fell back, letting Benehime's white beauty engulf her.

There, there, my love, Benehime whispered, pulling Nara into her lap. She kissed the Empress's forehead, cradling her armored body to her breast. Nara gave herself over, burying her face in the impossibly soft cascade of Benehime's white hair as she began to weep in earnest, surrendering completely to the burning, beloved feel of her Lady's touch.

"You forgot me." Her words were broken to pieces by sobs.

Benehime made a soothing noise. *I did not forget you. I simply had others more worthy of my attention. How could I visit you when you had cast yourself into that stinking cave?*

"What else was there for me?" Nara whispered. "I was lost

237

without you." She raised her head, looking into the Lady's white eyes. "I love you," she whispered. "I live for you, Lady. I always have, ever since that first night. I will never hide again. I swear it, so please, please come back to me."

Come back? Benehime's voice was soft as new snow. *How could I come back to you now? What have you done to deserve me?*

"I'll do anything," Nara whispered, digging her fingers into the white flesh of Benehime's lovely shoulders.

Benehime bent down, cupping Nara's chin in her burning fingers as she laid a kiss on Nara's lips. Nara shuddered, her eyes slamming closed to shut out everything but the feel of the Shepherdess. It was a brief touch, barely more than a flash of heat, but it was enough to bring centuries of memories flooding back. Nara reached out desperately, clinging to the lost time when Benehime loved her best of all. But no matter how tightly she held them, the memories were flat. That time was gone, leaving her alone and forgotten, empty but for one burning desire.

When Nara opened her eyes again, she was no longer crying.

"Lady," she promised. "I will be your favorite again, or I will die trying."

Such talk, Nara, Benehime said, stroking her hair. *Second in my heart is still beloved. Is that not enough?*

"No," Nara said, sitting up straight. "I know now, life without your attention is no better than death." She reached out, seizing the Lady's hand between her own. "Tell me what to do," she whispered. "How can I make you love me best again?"

Benehime smiled and stood, taking Nara with her as though the Empress weighed nothing. She turned slightly, facing them toward the fleet that spread out across the sea. *I always loved you best as a conqueror*, she said. *Do you remember when I first found you? The wish you made?*

"To bring all the world under righteous rule," Nara said.

Benehime smiled. *It was those words that made me love*

you then. So audacious, so determined. If you want me to love you now as I did then, use the power I gave you to fulfill that wish. Give me the world, Nara. Be the conqueror, the righteous, perfect Empress I saw in you so long ago. Crush all who stand in your way, and maybe I will have reason to love you best again.

Nara leaned back, her hand going to the beautiful sword at her hip. "Watch me, Shepherdess," she said, her voice firm as stone. "You will see your conqueror in all her glory and terror. I will give you a world made perfect, a world without unfairness or disobedience. A world deserving of you."

Benehime laughed, a beautiful chime, and leaned in to drop a kiss on the Empress's forehead.

I'll be watching. Her whisper thrilled against Nara's skin. *Do not disappoint me, darling star.*

And then she was gone, her beautiful whiteness vanishing into the air, leaving only the blinding afterimage of a white line. Nara fell to her knees as the overwhelming feel of the Lady's presence vanished. She knelt for several moments, clutching herself and trying not to sob at the loss. When she was sure of herself again, she stood and walked to the balcony's edge, reaching out with her spirit as she did. The war palace answered at once.

"Hail, Empress," the stones rattled.

"Are the ships loaded?"

"Yes, Empress," the stone said. "The docks report that the last of your legions and the man called Den are boarded."

Nara nodded. "Time to go."

The stone gave a final, sobbing shudder before bowing to her will. "Yes, Empress. As you command."

As the words faded, the war palace began to shake. The bay rocked as the tremors shot through the ground. She could dimly hear the cries of her men on the ships, but Nara brushed them aside, focusing her attention on the palace around her. She stretched out her spirit, wrapping it through the stone and down to the very roots of the mountain she'd used to form the

239

fortress hundreds of years ago, and then, one by one, she ripped those roots out. The stone screamed every time she pulled one free, yammering in pain as she severed its connection to the world's foundations.

Nara scowled. *Quiet.*

The command left her with a stab of her will, and the screaming stopped. After that, the mountain bore the pain in silence as she tore the last of its roots free.

Move, she said, pouring her will into the command.

The stone obeyed. With a great crash, the war palace Istalirin, and the mountain it was attached to, fell into the sea. The stone docks crumbled with a cut-off cry as the mountain fell on top of them, and the ocean rose up in a great wave from the impact, tossing her palace ships like toy boats. Her winds moved the moment she brushed them, tearing down from the sky and forcing themselves between the ships to cushion them as they bumped against each other. Other winds pressed on the water itself, flattening the bay until the sea was as smooth as glass and the war palace floated among the fleet, a true palace ship riding atop a great stone island.

"Empress," the mountain's voice was pleading. "I cannot hold, Empress. I will sink."

"You will not," the Empress said. She flung out her will, reaching over the bay, over her ships, and out into the ocean. The moment she hit open water, her spirit dove. She plunged into the water, ignoring the mad rush of the water spirits and sinking deep into the black abyss until she found what she wanted. At the bottom of the trench that ran along her continent was a current, one of the great highways of the sea. This current was not a spirit in itself, but a union of the tattered remains of shredded water spirits torn apart by the ocean's pull. These spirits, no longer large enough to have minds of their own, banded together to flow as one in one direction, operating with a herd mind that had only one purpose: to flow. And that was the purpose Nara took.

She grabbed the current with her will. The water screamed

240

and fought as she pulled it up, too mindless to care that she was a star. But Nara fought harder, crushing the spirits until the water cried out in surrender. When it was pliant in her grip, Nara pulled the current up from the seafloor and into her bay. The deep, cold water flooded into the warm shallows with a scream, lifting her fleet in a great swell before slamming into the gap between her war palace and the seafloor. The palace shook in relief as the current lifted the uprooted mountain, floating it like a cork under Nara's iron command.

Nara smiled as her palace bobbed and shifted her focus westward. Screaming, the current had no choice but to follow. The blast of water caught the palace ships at once, and her fleet shot out, riding the great wave of water westward toward the unconquered half of the world.

Panting, Nara fell to her knees, clutching the balcony rails to keep herself upright. Even as a star, moving such enormous spirits was exhausting. But it was done. Her fleet and her war palace were racing out of the bay, carried into the sea by the great current that flowed at her command. There was nothing that could stop her now.

Slowly, she stood and drew her sword, raising its gleaming blade to the fading sunlight. "Are you watching, lady?" she cried, holding her sword to the sky. "With this, I begin your war."

As she spoke, words appeared on the sword's blade, a single sentence etched in gleaming steel.

Sleepers wake, I am coming.

Nara held her breath. The rushing wind filled her ears, but if she strained, she could hear the Shepherdess's beautiful laugh at the very edge of her hearing. That was enough. Smiling, Nara sheathed her sword and walked into her palace.

High overhead, those winds who were not yet loyal turned and rushed west to bring word to their master of the star's coming.

* * *

Duke Finley arrived at his town house shortly after sunset. His servants ran out to greet him as the coach pulled to a stop. Finley stepped down, letting the valets take his overcoat while his footmen ran to close the elegant iron gate that separated the mansion from the street. Henry was waiting for him at the door, a glass of wine ready in his hand.

"Welcome home, father," he said. "How was your day?"

"What are you doing here?" Finley said, snatching the glass with enough force to spill half its contents on the marble entry. "You're supposed to be heading the palace watch tonight."

"The captain gave me the night off," Henry said. "She heard about your meeting with our beloved prince and thought you could use the company."

"Did she?" Finley downed the wine in one gulp and tossed the glass at his manservant, who caught it expertly. "How thoughtful of our dear princess."

Henry's smile wavered as he followed his father into the house. Like all high-ranking Oseran nobility, Duke Finley's mansion was located in the tangle of fine houses just down the mountain from the palace. But though his house was less than a block from the castle, it was worlds away in style. Where the royal palace was a stalwart relic of a lost era, the duke's home was impeccably modern. The smooth, austere facade presented a clean face to the street while delicate flourishes of carved waves lapped tastefully at the cornerstones. Inside, wide halls paneled with carved slats of imported wood led to rooms filled with windows. Elegant lamps enhanced with crystals hung from the ceilings, and fine rugs covered the floor with rich colors. The furniture was ornate, painted gold and upholstered in silk in the Zarin style.

But for all this modernity, Finley was still the heir to the throne, and he was guarded accordingly. Because of this, the delicate ambiance of his brightly lit stone foyer was marred by a pair of guards in full armor standing at attention. A second pair of guards, scarred veterans, stood at the top of the grand stair where they perpetually got in the way of the servants. A third pair of guards watched the door to the duke's small garden, their great armored shapes ridiculous against the outline of the delicate fruit trees. Each post saluted the duke as he passed, and the duke saluted back, muttering to himself the whole way up to his study.

"Honestly," he growled as Henry closed the leather padded study door. "You'd think we were still an island of savage barbarians murdering each other in our beds."

"The queen cares deeply for your safety, father," Henry said. "As do we all."

"Nonsense," the duke said, sinking into his cushioned chair by the fire. "Theresa may set the guard, but I'm the one who has to pay for it. And you can stop trying to butter me up with that 'as do we all' rot, Henry. You're not going to be king."

The dutiful look fell off Henry's face. "What?" he cried.

"He didn't take the bait," the duke said, shrugging. "Josef Liechten is determined to stay and get his mother her grandchild whether she's alive to enjoy the brat or not. You'd think after abandoning every other shred of duty, this would be easy, but *no*."

"What are we going to do?" Henry said, sinking into the chair beside his father's.

"Nothing," the duke said and snorted, staring into the fire. "We're going to sit and we're going to wait. Even if he got her with child last night, the queen won't live long enough to confirm the pregnancy. Once the old cow is dead and I'm on the throne, no one will care what's in the princess's belly."

"Father," Henry said delicately, sitting on the edge of his chair. "Aren't you dismissing Adela too quickly? She's very popular with the people. We could use that. I—"

"I am well aware of your shameless infatuation with the princess, Henry," the duke said dryly. "Now, and I'm not going to tell you this again, forget her. She's nothing but trash who knows how to play a crowd, just like her mother. If you speak of her again, I'll pull you off the guard and put you on a deep-water patrol boat for the rest of the year. Do you understand?"

243

Henry bit his lip. "Yes, father."

"Good," the duke said, sitting back. "Powers, the way my luck's been going, you'll be the one to get the princess pregnant and lose your throne to your own son."

"Father!" Henry cried.

"You can't hide things from me, boy," Finley said, glaring. "Not that you've tried. Honestly, I don't know why I'm working so hard to secure your place in the succession when you seem intent on ruining your reputation, cornering the princess in hallways in sight of anyone who walks by."

Henry looked away, cheeks scarlet. "Doesn't matter, anyway," he grumbled. "Everyone's saying we're done for now that the clingfire's up in flames."

Finley sat up. "Who's saying that?"

"All the guards, for one," Henry said. "It's common talk on the docks, and why not? You could see the smoke from the mainland. Everyone knows that we can't down the palace ships without clingfire, and if the palace ships don't go down, the Empress wins."

"A minor setback," the duke said dismissively. "I'll have the crown make a statement tomorrow that we have a backup clingfire stock hidden."

"But we *don't*," Henry said.

"Well, no one needs to know that, do they?" Finley said. "The last thing we need is a panic. If we are to stand before the Empress, we must be united, and we can't do that if people are scared."

"You can't just lie about things like that," Henry said.

"I can and I have," Finley said. "How do you think this island's been functioning for the last month? We've been plagued by setbacks since we heard the Empress was on the move. First there was the queen's dramatic turn for the worse that put everything in uproar and brought back the idiot prince, and then we had that horrid mess with the tar eating through the wood in the new ships. We had to scrap half a fleet of runners thanks to that one. And there was the dry rot in the

244

corn vault." The duke shook his head. "Trust me, Henry, this fire was nothing. Just another headache in a long line of bad, bad luck."

Henry stared at his father. "I didn't hear about any of that."

"Of course you didn't," Finley said. "That's what it means to keep things *secret*. Fortunately, we've still got time to make up the shortfalls before the Empress arrives. Assuming, of course, nothing else goes wrong."

Henry paled. "What else *can* go wrong?"

"Never ask, my boy," Finley said quietly. "Never ask."

They sat in silence for several minutes, both lost in their own dark thoughts as they watched the fire burn lower and lower. And then suddenly and without warning, Henry sat bolt upright.

"What was that?" he said. "Did you hear that?"

"No," the duke grumbled, sinking lower in his chair. "Probably our idiot porter getting into the—"

The sound cut him off before he could finish. It was a soft, rolling thump, followed by a clatter. Finley looked at his son, all tiredness gone, and they stood up together. The duke's hand dropped down to the old sword at his side as he crept toward the library door.

Just before his hand touched the handle, the door flew open, and a white-faced servant burst into the room.

"My lord!" he whispered, his voice cracking with panic. "You have to get out!"

"Why?" the duke said. "What's happened?"

The servant looked over his shoulder at the dark hall. "An intruder, sir."

"Intruder?" the duke said. "Nonsense, let the guards have him. That's what I pay them for."

The servant shook his head, grabbing the duke's arms. "The back, quick—"

The word ended in a tight gasp. The servant's mouth was still moving, but no sound came out. His eyes were wide as he crumpled, the back of his neck cut wide open. He was dead before he hit the ground.

The duke jumped back before he realized what was happening, drawing his sword on instinct alone. Now that the servant was out of the way, he could see the guards at the end of the hall. Both men were down, lying in dark pools with the back of their necks cut, spines severed cleanly, just like the servant's.

Finley grew very still, eyes searching the shadows while his fingers tightened on his sword. But the house was still, silent except for his own ragged breaths and those of his son behind him.

Without taking his eyes from the door, he motioned Henry back to the fireplace. Other than the windows, the room had only one entrance. Finley kept his sword up, watching the shadows for any trace of movement. On the floor, the servant's blood was seeping into the thick carpet. It was so quiet the duke could hear the liquid spreading through the fibers. Panic began to rise in his stomach, but Finley fought it down. He took a deep breath, ignoring the taste of blood in the air and forcing himself to be calm, to look.

That was when he saw the killer.

The man stood at the corner where the stairs met the hall, less than five steps from the fallen guards. He was so still that the duke's eyes had a hard time picking his dark clothes out of the shadows. Finley blinked several times, still not sure if his eyes were telling the truth. If the man was standing at the other end of house, there was no way he could have killed the servant, not from that distance. Perhaps there were two intruders? As Finley's mind scrambled to reconcile the facts, the man began to move. He rushed forward, racing down the hall in a handful of seconds, his padded feet completely silent on the hardwood floor.

Finley gritted his teeth and cursed himself for a fool. He'd just wasted his only chance to escape. Now the man stood in the study door, blocking the only exit with his body.

"What do you want?" Finley said, surprised at how stern and clear his voice was.

The man didn't answer. Now that he was standing in the well-lit library, the duke could see the intruder was slender and tall. He was wrapped head to toe in dark cloth, and even his eyes were hidden beneath black netting. He had a sword at his hip, the sheath wrapped in black as well, but Finley could tell it was a short blade. The duke hefted his own sword. There was still a chance. He had reach on the assassin, so did Henry. The killer had lost his chance at surprise by running forward, and it was two on one now.

At once, Finley felt his confidence returning. He inched his feet forward, stepping into position. Behind him, he heard Henry follow his lead. Finley licked his lips, getting ready to shout for Henry to begin the attack. But the words died on his lips, for at that moment, the assassin drew his sword.

The sword appeared with a flash of silver. Its blade was heavy, short, and gleaming with its own silver light. Finley sucked in a breath. A man in Osera didn't go through a lifetime of sword training without learning to recognize an awakened blade. The duke was no wizard, but even he could see the sword's surface trembling in anticipation as the assassin stepped over the servant's body.

The blow came before the duke could think to raise his sword. One moment the assassin was facing them, short sword in hand, the next the sword was *through* him. Finley gasped more in surprise than pain, looking down at the blade through his chest, and then up again at the man still standing in the doorway holding a sword that was no longer short, but long as a spear with its point jutting out Finley's back.

On the other side of the room, the assassin flicked his hand. The sword flashed like a wave, the steel sliding out of Finley's body, and Henry began to scream. The duke jerked in surprise and turned to help his son, but his body wasn't moving anymore. He toppled, falling to the carpet. He turned as he fell, looking back just in time to see the glowing blade snap like a whip as it finished slitting his son's throat.

The duke could only stare as Henry fell, hitting the carpet

with that now-familiar soft thump. Behind him, he heard the hiss of steel on steel, and he rolled his eyes to see the swordsman's blade shrinking back to its original size, the glowing metal folding into itself until the assassin held a short sword once again. The killer lifted his gleaming weapon and walked to the window, using the duke's velvet curtains to wipe Henry's blood from the blade. Finley's breath was growing scarce now, but he hardly noticed. Rage filled his body in a way life no longer could, and he lunged across the carpet, grabbing the man by the ankle.

"You dare!" he hissed. "Who are you?"

The swordsman turned to face him and slowly raised his hand to the cloth over his face. He unhooked something behind his ear, and the covering fell away. The duke's hand went limp with surprise, and he collapsed back to the carpet.

"You," he whispered in disbelief. And then, with his last breath: "Why?"

The question was barely past his lips when the sword swept down, giving Duke Finley the last and only answer he would ever receive.

CHAPTER
15

It was full dark when Gin pushed through the last crowd of soldiers and under the gate that separated the Spirit Court's district from the rest of Zarin. Miranda clung to his back, staring bleakly at the wide, suddenly empty streets. The colored lamps were lit and swinging gently in the night air, but no one was around to enjoy the light. From the moment they entered the Spirit Court's district until Miranda slid off Gin at the foot of the Tower, they didn't see a single soul.

Stomach sinking, Miranda started up the stairs. She'd always known that the Rector Spiritualis controlled the Tower, but it was an academic, abstract sort of knowledge. She'd seen it in action only once, at her trial. Even so, she never would have imagined something like this.

The Tower was completely sealed. Its enormous red doors lay abandoned on the ground, shed like outgrown scales. In their place, a wall of white stone rose smooth as river rock from the ground. It was as though the entire Tower had become a solid stone pillar, and though she walked all the way around the base, Miranda could find no way in.

"Try knocking?" Gin suggested.

Feeling more than a little foolish, Miranda reached out and rapped her knuckles on the stone. Nothing happened. She pulled her hand back, frowning, and then she reached out again, with her left hand this time, knocking with the heavy gold band on her ring finger, the one set with the Spirit Court's perfect circle. The gold made a lovely ringing sound when it touched the Tower, and the stone began to twist. The Tower wall rumbled softly, opening like a flower to reveal a tunnel just large enough for Gin to squeeze through.

With one final glance at the empty street, Miranda stepped inside. Gin followed on her heels. The moment his tail was clear, the Tower closed behind them.

They came out in the Spirit Court's grand entry hall, which looked exactly as it always had except that the grand doors were now grown over with stone and the center of the room was full of huddled people. Spiritualists sat in circles on furniture pilfered from other parts of the Tower. Several had their fire spirits out, and the warm, flickering light filled the void left by the missing windows, giving the room a primal, cave-like feel.

She was scarcely inside when someone shouted, "Miranda!"

She looked up to see a young man break away from the main group and run toward her, waving.

"Jason!" she cried, recognizing him at once.

He stopped in front of her, grinning wide in the light of the will-o'-the-wisp that floated in his wake. Miranda smiled back. She and Jason had been in the academy together and taken their oaths on the same day. He'd gone on to apprentice for some distant Tower Keeper after that, and they saw each other only rarely. Still, they'd always been friends.

"I'm happy to see you," she said.

"Not as happy as we are to see you," he said. "Hello, Gin."

Gin blinked slowly, which was as nice a greeting as one could expect from a ghosthound.

"The Rector said you'd entered the city this morning," Jason said. "I have to admit, when you didn't show up at once, some people worried you'd gone over to the Council. I knew better, though. That bunch of traitors are as bad as Hern."

"No one's as bad as Hern," Miranda said. "Where's Master Banage?"

"Upstairs," Jason said, nodding toward the grand staircase. "Powers, I'm glad you're here. The Rector has been looking grimmer than usual." Jason lowered his voice. "I don't think he expected quite so many of the old guard to turn on him."

Miranda frowned. "How many are here?"

"A little over a hundred," Jason said. "We're mostly Journeymen Spiritualists down here. The Tower Keepers are upstairs in the private rooms for the most part, or the library." His hands moved as he talked, and the will-o'-the-wisp followed his fingers like an eerie, blue-green firefly. "We've got close to eight hundred Spiritualists still unaccounted for, though I don't know what's taking so long. It's been three days since the Rector called us in. That's enough time for a determined Spiritualist to get to Zarin from anywhere on the continent." Jason bit his lip. "You don't think they've all gone over to the Council?"

"No," Miranda said, shaking her head. "I just came from there. Blint's in charge, and he had only three hundred a few hours ago. Hern's old cronies, mostly, but that's no surprise. They always did prefer politics to spirits."

"Three hundred," Jason said with a dismayed sigh. "Still, where's everyone else?"

Miranda shrugged. "Probably waiting to see how things play out before they cast their lot."

"Cowards," Jason said, sneering.

"Maybe," Miranda said. "But they're still Spiritualists." She turned and started toward the stairs. "Speaking of which, I'm going to see Master Banage."

"Of course," Jason said. "Good to have you back!"

She waved as he jogged back to the main group to share the good news. Miranda started up the shadowy staircase, Gin slinking behind her.

The climb to Banage's office was surprisingly short. It was the Tower's doing, Miranda was sure. Things had always been a little strange inside the stone pillar the Spiritualists called home, but what else could one expect from a tower raised in a day by Shapers? After her unwilling stint in the Shaper Mountain, Miranda was surprised the Tower didn't move more. Even so, despite the shorter-than-expected climb, she was still out of breath when she reached the landing outside of Banage's office where Spiritualist Krigel, Assistant to the Rector Spiritualis, was waiting.

"Took you long enough," he said.

"Sorry," Miranda panted. "I didn't even know there was a war until this morning. Where's Master Banage?"

Krigel jerked his head toward the closed door.

Gin sat down without being asked, stretching out down the long staircase. Krigel gave the dog a nasty look, and Miranda took the opportunity to slip past the old Spiritualist, pushing open the door to Banage's office as quietly as she could.

The office of the Rector Spiritualis had changed dramatically. The first thing she noticed were the windows. The large panes of clear glass were still there, but they looked out into a wall of solid white stone. Still, the office was not dark. White light radiated from a small, unflickering flame burning at the bottom of a large, metal bowl on the floor. Miranda recognized the fire immediately. It was Krinok, a rare type of chemical fire spirit Master Banage had rescued from a rogue Tower Keeper turned Enslaver back when she was still his apprentice. Krinok's harsh, white light threw everything into sharp, monochrome relief, but even that couldn't drown out the light coming from Banage himself.

The Rector Spiritualis was sitting on his desk, which was uncharacteristically empty. For the first time Miranda could remember in many years, he was dressed not in the formal red robes of the Rector's office, but in a plain, somber suit. Over that, around his neck, the regalia of the Rector Spiritualis shone like a collar of light. The heavy necklace with its golden chain of jewels glowed in a rainbow of colors, humming with power. Even standing at the door twenty feet away, Miranda could feel the enormous pressure of the Rector's connection to the Tower and, woven into and through that, the power of Banage himself. She took a deep breath, her own spirits waking to the familiar weight of Banage's soul, and for the first time in a long time, she felt like she was home.

"Miranda," Banage said, opening his eyes. "It is good to see you. I wish the circumstances were better."

"Whatever the circumstances," Miranda said, walking across the room to stand before him, "it is good to be back."

Banage smiled, a slight turn of his thin mouth. "Sit," he said softly, "and tell me what you have seen."

With a deep breath, Miranda sat cross-legged on the stone floor and told him.

She started from the moment she left Zarin, chasing Sara's tip about Eli north with Tesset and Sparrow. She told him about entering Izo's camp and the Council's deal with the Bandit King. She told him about catching Eli and losing him again. She told him about Slorn and the wondrous things the bear-headed Shaper could do. After that, things got harder. She told him about Sted, about the demon and the League. She told him what she had seen in the arena after Josef beat Sted and about working with Alric to defeat the creature Sted

252

became. Then, after a couple of deep breaths, she told him as best she could about the thing she'd seen in the woods beyond Izo's camp, the creature made of shadows and hunger, eating the world. Even as she told him, the afterimage of the hideous shape flickered across her vision, forcing her to turn away. When she had control of herself again, she looked her master in the eye and told him how that vision had cemented her decision to go with Slorn to the Shapers. She told him about their arrival at the mountain, her imprisonment, and what she'd seen in the mountain's memory. She told him about stars, the spirits lifted above all other. She told him all the mountain had told her about the Shepherdess, the sleeping spirits, everything. The world the mountain had shown her was still clear in her mind, the great valley changing between life and death and the endless night sky filled with strange, sparkling lights, but describing it was harder than she imagined. Still, in fits and halts, she told him the whole naked, disjointed truth Slorn had asked her to spread.

She finished in a great rush, panting as the weight of the secrets lifted from her chest. She paused, waiting for the questions that were sure to come, but Banage just sat back and motioned for her to continue.

Miranda nodded and moved on to her cell. She told him about her solo imprisonment, Sparrow's offer and their escape from the Shapers, the journey home, and learning about the war. Finally, she told him about the meeting with Sara, Blint, and Whitefall. She handed him Whitefall's written promise as she told him the details of the Merchant Prince's compromise. Banage took the paper with a strangely closed look on his face, reading it over as Miranda's long story finally came to an end.

When it was done, she leaned back, exhausted. Though in all her years with the Court, all the missions she'd done in its name, none had taken so long or so much to tell. With the windows blocked, it was impossible to tell how long she'd been speaking. It felt like hours. However long it was, Banage had not moved at all. He was still sitting on his desk, his stern face warped into a mask of itself by the strange light of the mantel and the bright white fire on the floor.

"I'm not surprised Slorn stayed," he said at last. "How very like him to pit his stubbornness against a mountain."

Miranda looked up. "You know him?"

"Some," Banage said. "He's hard to avoid when you involve yourself in the politics of spirits to any depth. He's a good wizard, though, and a good man. You made the right choice to go with him."

Miranda let out the breath she didn't realize she'd been holding. "Thank you, Master Banage."

Banage nodded. "So," he said. "The mysterious Shepherdess who commands all spirits. I'd heard snippets, hints, but you can never get a spirit to talk plainly about such things. To hear it from the Shaper Mountain is something indeed, though I suppose demons large enough to make Alric panic can get even Great Spirits talking about things they'd rather not." He started chuckling, like this was some kind of joke, and looked over at Miranda. "You never bring good news, do you?"

"You never send me anywhere easy," Miranda protested.

Banage smiled. "You would be wasted on easy things."

"It seems nothing is easy anymore," Miranda said with a deep sigh. "It feels like the world is falling apart. Enormous demons, the League in panic, spirits growing sleepier, the Shaper Mountain talking about the Shepherdess with her stars and favorites and how this world isn't as it was. Two weeks ago, I didn't even know for sure if the Shepherdess existed. Now I'm terrified that she's not doing whatever it is she's supposed to do. How can we do our job and protect the spirit world when we know so little?"

Banage shook his head. "As my spirits love to remind me, humans are creatures of blindness and ignorance. We must always remember that although we tend to see this world as ours, we are only tiny pieces of the larger whole and there is only so much we can change. The demons, for instance, we must leave to the League. We certainly cannot fight them, not without risking our spirits. Even if we were willing to face them, we would only be defeated. As for the rest, we can only do what we have always done. The Court will stand by its oaths and do what it can to protect the spirit world from whatever threatens it—wizard, star, or Shepherdess."

"Master Banage," Miranda said, her throat going dry. "With all these threats, I have to wonder, perhaps we should take the Merchant Prince's compromise."

The Rector's head snapped to look at her.

"He promised it would only be defense," Miranda said quickly, before she lost her courage. "Look around, we are alone. The Spirit Court is splitting in two. How can we stand firm when we are so divided?"

"We are not divided." Banage's voice cut the heavy air like a bitter, burning knife. "The true Court is here. Those who choose political ambition over their oaths are not Spiritualists."

"But this is the Immortal Empress!" Miranda cried, her voice pleading. "If this were just a war between countries, I would not question your decision, but the Empress is different. Her first attack was terrifying enough to make the warring kingdoms forget their bickering and unite as a Council to face a common foe. But even united, it took everything we had to turn the Empress away. Now she's coming to finish the kill, and everything we have might no longer be enough. I don't like Blint, but I understand where he and every Spiritualist who went to the Council stands. They are fighting to defend their lives as they know them."

"And there they betray their oaths," Banage said. "Spiritualists do not fight for their own comfort, but for what is good and right for the spirit world."

"How do we know the two aren't the same?" Miranda countered. "Every child in the Council learns about the Empress's invasion, and the terror trotted out more than any other are the stories of the Empress's wizards. There are tales of them working together to control enormous spirits of fire

255

and iron, monsters built only for war that fight until they're torn apart. Those spirits *died* fighting for the Empress, and though I don't know for sure what the empire wizards did to whip those poor spirits into such a frenzy, I'd wager Eli's bounty that it wasn't nice. Enslavement, or close to it. That is the enemy we face, and you're saying we should just sit back and let her come? That it is politics to side with the Council and fight her? If anything of that sort went on here, we would mobilize the Court to stop it at once. Is it any different when it comes from across the sea?"

Miranda stopped, terrified she'd said too much. Master Banage's expression was unreadable in the harsh light, but he didn't look angry. When he spoke, his voice sounded tired.

"Your reasoning is sound as always, Miranda," he said. "But no matter what, I can never allow this Court to go to war again beside the Council of Thrones."

"Why not?" Miranda demanded, frustration rising.

Banage looked up, his dark eyes catching hers with a look that killed her anger in one shot.

"May I tell you a story?"

Caught off guard, Miranda nodded.

Banage got up from his desk and walked over to the window, looking out at the lid of solid stone that covered it.

"I fought in the first war against the Empress," he said. "I've told you about it before."

Miranda nodded again, though, since Banage had his back to her, it scarcely mattered.

"I fought with the fledgling Council," Banage said, his voice soft. "With Sara." He looked over his shoulder. "We were younger than you are now, a year out of our apprenticeships, and newly married."

"Married?" Miranda could scarcely form the word. She could scarcely believe what she was hearing. "You were *married*? To *Sara*?"

"Are married," Banage corrected her, turning back to the window. "We never formalized our separation. I think we each

256

believe we'll eventually bring the other around to our way of thinking."

"But...Sara?" Miranda shook her head. "How? *Why?*"

"I was young," Banage said. "Sara is a genius and very charismatic in her own way. I'd like to say she's changed over the years, but she's always been high-handed, single-minded, and cruel. However, she was also ambitious in a way I'd never seen. She wanted to do things with magic I'd never even imagined. When the Empress attacked, the lands we now call the Council were in chaos. No one had ever seen anything like the fleet that was pounding Osera's shore. In her desperation, the young Oseran queen threw away centuries of isolationism and begged for help. Zarin was the first to respond, and Sara went with them."

He took a deep breath. "I'd known for some time that Sara was drifting away from the Spirit Court, doing her own work with money from the Whitefall family. When she said she was following Whitefall to war without even asking permission from the Rector, the Tower Keepers, who did not yet understand the threat of the Empress and had no interest in risking themselves for Oseran pirates, threatened to strip her of her rings and kick her out of the Court. And they would have, but I volunteered to go with her as the Court's eyes on the front. That was how I ended up at her side when the Empress's forces made their second, largest attack on Osera."

"The project she was working on for Whitefall," Miranda said, wide-eyed. "Was that the Relay?"

"It was," Banage said, his voice strangely strained. "The Relay was the only way we kept ahead of the Empress's forces. By this time, rumors of the Empress's army were beginning to catch up with its actual size. More and more countries, seeing that this could well spread to their lands if left unchecked, began sending their armies to the coast. But they were a rabble, a hodgepodge of men who'd spent centuries fighting each other. Only the Relay could coordinate them into

257

a force capable of meeting the Empress's fleet, and Alber Whitefall knew it.

"But that came later," Banage said, waving his hand. "Before the other countries joined in, Queen Theresa's ships with their ever-burning fire were all that held the Empire at bay. The event I want to tell you about happened late at night the second day of the attack. I'd left Sara with Whitefall and gone to help the Oserans repel a charge. The Oseran clingfire were simple spirits, easy to direct. I had made a cliff out over the bay and was using my fire spirit to guide the clingfire throwers and sink the incoming ships. But then my stone spirit was hit by one of the Empress's war spirits, and I fell."

"You fought a war spirit?" Miranda said, breathless.

"Not at first." Banage's voice grew raw. "I fell nearly fifty feet into the sea. My stone spirit shattered beyond repair trying to break my fall. I would have died there, if not for him. As it was, my fire spirit went out when I hit the water. I managed to swim to shore, but I was disoriented. I'd never lost a spirit before, and now I'd just lost two. I did not know what to do with the enormous emptiness that is left when the connection vanishes."

He stopped for a moment and sat very still. Miranda held her breath, afraid to make a sound. At last, Banage continued.

"When I made it to the beach, the Oseran guard was fighting the siege spirit, or trying to. Swords did nothing. The spirit killed a dozen men as I watched, and then it turned to me."

Banage lowered his head. "I was terrified and enraged. I knew I was about to die. That I would be crushed, and all my remaining spirits crushed with me. So I did the only thing I could think of. I opened my soul and took control of the siege spirit."

Miranda's breath caught in her throat. "You Enslaved it?"

"I tried to," Banage said, his voice very low. "Desperation is no excuse. I tried to take control of the spirit to save my life in violation of all my oaths. Tried, and failed."

Miranda looked away, scrambling to get her feelings under

258

control. The thought of Master Banage Enslaving anything nearly made her sick. He was the Spirit Court, the embodiment of everything it stood for, and yet.

"Failed?" she said. "How could you fail? You are the strongest wizard I've ever met."

"Strength has nothing to do with it," Banage said, shaking his head. "The problem was with the spirit itself. No matter how hard I pushed, it would not bend to my will. It did stop, however. I think it was confused. But then it looked at me. Not looked, exactly, for it had no head to speak of, but I knew it was studying me. And then it spoke."

Miranda swallowed. "What did it say?"

" 'Loyalty to the Empress,' " Banage quoted, tilting his head back. " 'Always and forever, I will be loyal.' And then it turned and walked into the ocean, back toward the ships where the Empire wizards waited."

"It left?" Miranda said. "Why?"

"I don't know," Banage admitted. "I have asked myself the same question over and over. But one thing was certain. That spirit was not Enslaved. There was no fear in it, no panic. It was bound through a loyalty so deep, so intense, so *primal* that even with my panicked strength I could not break its will to be faithful to its mistress. A mistress who wasn't even there."

Banage ran his hand through his graying hair. "After that, I knew no peace. I kept wondering what kind of person this Empress was to command such loyalty. As Whitefall's forces grew and the war began to turn around, I saw several of the Empress's war spirits go down. Every one of them fell fighting to the last inch, and every time I saw it happen, I wondered why? But the war was over before I could find out. The Empress's ships retreated as quickly as they'd come, and Whitefall, ever the opportunist, used fear of her return to found the Council of Thrones with himself at the head and Sara's Relay holding it all together."

Banage looked down at his glowing spirits. "It was around that time that Sara quit the Spirit Court of her own volition," he said. "I was furious, of course, but she was within her rights. She'd freed her spirits and received the Rector's approval, done everything properly. I was promoted to Tower Keeper after the war, but Sara was still my wife, and I stayed in Zarin to be with her. But as she spent more and more time in the caverns she'd built beneath the Council Citadel, I began to wonder. Sara gave me Relay points several times during the war, and afterward I went down to the Relay tank rooms often to see her. Even so, she would never let me near the heart of the Relay that lay at the bottom of the large tank she still uses as an office, nor would she ever agree to tell me exactly how the Relay worked. Every time I asked we would fight, and eventually I became suspicious."

Miranda bit her lip. "What did you do?"

"There was nothing I could do," Banage said. "Sara wasn't a Spiritualist, and the Spirit Court had no jurisdiction within Whitefall's rapidly growing Council. I also had no proof she was doing anything wrong, but I knew. Why else would she refuse to show me?"

"There could have been a reason," Miranda said softly.

"Do you honestly believe that?" Banage said, turning to face her. "You've worked with her, you've seen how ruthless she can be. If you were in my position then, would you have come to a different conclusion?"

Miranda shook her head. "What did she say when you confronted her?"

"Nothing," Banage said bitterly. "She said nothing. The Spirit Court would not listen to me and call for an investigation. They were too busy courting the Council. Everyone was then. So I went to her one last time and told her that if she didn't show me how the Relay worked, I was leaving. Again, she refused, so I went. I took our son and went as far away as I could."

"Wait," Miranda said. "Son?"

It might have been her imagination, but Miranda thought she saw Banage wince. "Yes, I have a son."

260

"But where is he?" she cried. "Why have I never heard of him?"

Banage turned back to the stone-blocked window. "He left. Many years ago."

Miranda cringed at the edge in his voice and dutifully dropped the subject.

Banage continued as though nothing had happened. "I came back to Zarin only when they told me I'd been chosen to be the new Rector Spiritualis, and the first thing I did was try to use the Court's sway to finally break open whatever Sara was hiding. But by that time the Council was the greatest power on the continent, and I could make no headway. To this day I don't know what she's got beneath the Council citadel, Relay or otherwise, but I understand Sara well enough now to know it can't be good." Banage shook his head. "As Rector, I have danced to the Council's tune along with everyone else, waiting for my chance to force Sara to open up and accept the Court's standards. When Whitefall asked for my help in the war, I thought I'd finally found it, but I was wrong." He looked up. "Whitefall doesn't want change. He wants warriors. I've been to war, Miranda, and I am poorer for it. I cannot, will not, order my Spiritualists into that suffering, especially not as ally to an organization that may well be worse than the enemy we're fighting."

"How can you say that?" Miranda said, horrified. "I'll grant Sara's pretty suspicious, and I'm positive she's up to no good, but worse than the Empress?"

"Yes," Banage said. "Weren't you listening? I told you. I met one of the Empress's war spirits. I saw firsthand the deep loyalty she commands. It's not so different from the loyalty our spirits give us as Spiritualists. You can't fake loyalty like that. Think about it, Miranda. On the one hand we have the Council of Thrones, an organization of profit and power built by a merchant prince and a ruthless woman on a work of wizardry so suspect Spiritualists aren't allowed near it. On the other, we have an Empress who commands the abject love and loyalty of the spirits. Put that way, it's not a hard choice."

Banage began to pace. "I gave Sara and Whitefall every chance to make good. I flat out told them I would fight if they would only open the Council to Spirit Court inspection, and I was met with nothing but excuses. Sara does not share our respect for the spirits, nor our duty toward them, and I am tired of playing her game. The more I see, the more I'm convinced that the future she and Whitefall are building isn't one I want to live in. It may well be that the Empress's coming is the dawn of a new age for the Spirit Court and the spirits."

Miranda stared at her master, horrified. "What you're saying is treason."

"Is it?" Banage said. "I've sworn no oaths to Zarin. My only oaths are here, with the Court and the spirits, and I see no reason to take either to war for a government that cares nothing for them."

Miranda licked her lips. She knew that calm tone in Master Banage's voice. He'd already made up his mind. Made it up long ago, it seemed. She wasn't happy at all with the idea of sitting back and letting the Empress conquer her homeland, but she wasn't about to go against her master, not after everything he'd done for her and the spirits. Still...

"We must do *something*."

"We will," Banage said. "We'll keep doing what we have done for the last four hundred years—protect the spirits and obey our oaths. Do I make myself clear, Spiritualist Lyonette?"

Miranda swallowed. "Yes, Master Banage."

"Good," he said, standing up. "For now, I want you to write up your experience inside the Shaper Mountain. When you're finished, you have my permission to go through the archives for any information on this Shepherdess and the Great Spirits called stars."

Miranda perked up considerably. "All the archives?"

"Yes," Banage said. "The Shaper Mountain did not show you that vision by accident. Far more important than this war is what is happening at the top levels of the spirit world. I want you to find out whatever you can. The Court will not sit idle."

Miranda couldn't help grinning. The Spiritualist archives were the repository for the collective knowledge of the Spirit Court. Every Spiritualist report ever written was stored there. Previously she'd had access to only the lowest level of common reports. Now she'd get to read the recollections of the secret missions as well. Bad as everything else seemed, that, at least, was something to look forward to.

"Go on," Banage said, waving her off. "But get some sleep and food first. You look dreadful."

Miranda blushed and glanced down at her filthy clothes. "Yes, Master Banage," she mumbled, dropping a deep bow before retreating. Her mind might still be racing with everything that had happened, but her body was more than glad to put it all off in favor of food, a bath, and a bed. Smiling at the prospect, she closed Banage's door softly behind her and went to wake up Gin, who was sleeping on the stairs where she'd left him.

Sara leaned back in the tall armchair, heavy smoke trailing from the corner of her mouth. Alber Whitefall sat across from her, his chin resting on his hands. They were both staring at the blue ball on the table between them as the soft, watery light began to fade.

"Well," Sara said. "I think that should be proof enough."

Whitefall dropped his head into his hands. "Sara," he said, grinding his palms into his eyes. "I'm not going to ask how you got a Relay point into Banage's office. I'm not sure I want to know. The only thing I'm going to ask is *why*."

"I thought that would be clear," Sara said. "You heard it from his own lips, in his own impossibly long-winded style. Etmon Banage is a traitor. He's sided with the Empress against his own people."

Whitefall sighed. "We need him."

"We need the Court," Sara countered. "Banage is the one standing in our way. It's loyalty to him that keeps those idiots in the Tower. Break Banage and the Court will come to us.

Well," she said, putting her pipe stem back in her mouth. "Most of them. Some attrition is unavoidable."

"We'll never get this to stick," Whitefall said, moving his hands down to his mouth as he considered his options. "An overheard confession's not enough on its own, and he's not going to repeat it."

"Of course he will," Sara said. "This is Etmon Banage. The man can't lie to save his life, or anyone else's. Pull him out and ask him openly whom he supports, the Council or the Empress, and then sit back while he digs his own grave."

Whitefall gave her a long-suffering look. "Isn't this a little much, Sara? The man is still your husband."

Sara sniffed. "I loved Banage when I was young and stupid enough to get caught up in his idealism. But that world never existed, Alber. There's no place for men like Banage who refuse to admit that there is no absolute right or wrong, that everything is relative, even morality. Never was. I won't see my life's work stomped under just to keep his hands clean."

She reached out and snatched the Relay point off the table, sliding the blue marble into her pocket as she stood. "We need those wizards if we're going to survive, Alber. I've given you your linchpin. All you have to do is pull it."

Whitefall turned and stared unhappily into the cold, empty fireplace. "Fine," he said quietly. "Send word to Myron."

Sara nodded and marched out of the room. Sparrow fell in silently beside her, giving Whitefall a sickening smile as he closed the door behind his mistress. As their footsteps faded down the long hall, Whitefall stood and walked to the window, opening the glass pane to let the night wind clear out the stinking pipe smoke. As he stared down at his brightly lit city, the streets packed and humming with life, he wondered, not for the first time, who really ran the Council of Thrones.

"That was impressively ruthless," Sparrow said as they walked through the dark, empty halls of the Citadel. "Even for you.

Good to know the enormous risk I took planting that Relay point paid out."

Sara arched an eyebrow. "Enormous risk?"

"Have you *seen* the dog she rides?" Sparrow shuddered. "I could have lost a hand. Or more."

"Your sacrifice wouldn't have been in vain," Sara said as they started down the stairs to her underground workshop. "I couldn't have asked for a better confession. I always knew something changed in him the night he lost his spirits, but I didn't know he'd gone that far."

"Well," Sparrow said, smiling slyly. "He certainly had enough to say about *you*."

Sara shrugged. "No worse than he's said to my face."

"I never could understand what you saw in him."

"He was uncompromising," Sara said. "I felt like a better person when I was around him, like I was one of the good guys. But he had no vision, no reach. He never understood that some of us can't be happy just maintaining the status quo. It didn't matter what miracles I showed him, he always found some fault." She shook her head. "Uncompromising men are easy to admire, but they're impossible to live with."

"I can imagine," Sparrow said as they reached the foot of the stairs. "Still, congratulations. You won!"

"Hardly a glorious victory," Sara said, walking between the suspended Relay tanks toward the brightly lit platform at the center of the enormous cavern. "I'd always hoped that Etmon would see things my way someday, understand the great work I'm doing." She heaved an enormous, smoky sigh. "Considering our history, I suppose it's only fitting that I be the one to deal the breaking blow."

"How *do* you mean to do that, by the way?" Sparrow said. "He's locked himself up quite nicely, and I don't think he's going to come out to talk to you."

"The Spirit Court's Tower is still only stone," Sara said with a smile. "And I've been needing something to test our new weapon on."

265

"It's done, then?" Sparrow said.

"Done enough," Sara said, sticking her pipe into her mouth. "Words won't do it justice, though. You'll just have to wait for tomorrow."

Sparrow smiled a wide, toothy smile. "And see the haughty Spiritualists brought low? I can't wait."

"I'm sure," Sara said distractedly. "Come on, we've got work to do."

Sparrow fell in behind her as she marched out onto the platform around the enormous tank that served as her headquarters and began shouting for her assistants.

CHAPTER
16

Josef woke with a snort, hands going instantly to his blades. He looked around a moment in groggy confusion, grinding his teeth as the world came together. It had happened again. He was still on the couch where he'd sat down to wait for Adela, only now it was morning. But the sunlight streaming through the window was still more white than yellow. Early morning, then. That was better than yesterday.

He looked around for Nico and found her sitting behind the couch, wrapped in her coat with her back resting against his through the wooden frame, sound asleep. Josef smiled. Catching Nico asleep was rare. Then his smile fell. Rare, and a sign of something very wrong.

A knock sounded at the door, and Nico's eyes popped open. She saw him at once and rolled to her feet, a confused and slightly alarmed look on her pale face. Josef put up his hand, motioning her to keep out of sight. She nodded and shrank back behind the couch. The knock sounded again, soft but urgent. Josef pulled his shirt straight and started for the door, but whoever was knocking must have grown impatient. Before Josef had gone two steps, the lock rattled. The door opened with a click and Eli stepped in, palming his lock pick with a hurried glance over his shoulder.

"Good," he said, closing the door behind him. "You're up. We have a problem."

"We have several," Josef said as Nico stood up from behind the couch. "What's going on?"

"I'm not sure," Eli said. "But word is the queen's up and on the warpath. I'm surprised she hasn't—"

A banging on the door cut him off, and the three of them froze. Josef was the first to recover. He caught Nico's eyes and glanced at the corner. She nodded and slid sideways, fading into the small shadow behind the fireplace. When she was gone, Josef walked to the door. He motioned for Eli to get behind him before lifting the latch.

A page stood in the hallway, his hand raised to knock again. He was flanked on both sides by stern, armored guardsmen and looking decidedly unhappy about it.

"My lord prince," the page said, recovering from his aborted knock with impressive speed. "Your royal mother requests your presence."

Josef frowned. "Now?"

"Now would be good," the man said.

Josef shook his head and turned back to the room, leaving the door open. He walked to the corner and grabbed the Heart. When it was securely on his back, he walked back to the door. Eli stepped into place beside him, ready to go.

The servant glanced nervously from Josef to Eli. "My lord," he started. "Your mother specifically asked—"

"My adviser comes with me," Josef said, stalking into the hall.

Eli gave the servant a winning smile as he followed Josef out the door. The guards fell in around them, setting the pace as they walked up the stairs toward the royal suite.

A larger than usual squad of guards lined the gallery leading up to his mother's door, all of them at full attention. Josef pushed his way through, opening his mother's door with a rough jerk.

The queen was waiting for them. She was dressed and sitting on her chair at the center of the raised platform at the far end of the room, Lenette at her side, as always. There were several nobles in the room as well, all of whom Josef knew he should probably recognize. But he'd never been good with remembering court officials, even back when he was actually trying, so he dismissed them and focused on his mother. Queen Theresa looked more tired than ever. Her papery skin was almost gray against the harsh black of her dress and veil, but her eyes were as sharp as knives, and they pinned Josef to the floor.

"Where were you last night?" she asked the second the door closed behind Eli.

"Asleep," Josef said.

The queen arched her eyebrow. "Asleep? All night?"

Josef crossed his arms. "All night. Why?"

For a split second the queen looked relieved, and then the scowl was back. "Finley is dead."

"Dead?" Josef said. "How?"

"Stabbed," the queen answered. "Someone, or several some-ones, broke into his mansion last night. His honor guard is dead, as are most of his servants, his son, and, of course, the duke himself."

Josef frowned. "Was there a fight?"

"Adela is investigating as we speak," the queen said. "In the meantime, why don't you tell me."

The room filled with whispers as the nobles began to talk. Josef ignored them.

"How should I know?" he said.

"You were with the duke a few hours before he died," the queen said. "You had an argument, a loud one, after which you left. What did you talk about?"

"Nothing of consequence," Josef said. "He told me he was going to be king, and I said go ahead."

The queen's eyes narrowed. "Really? That's all?"

"That's all," Josef repeated firmly. "I didn't kill him, if that's what you're implying."

The queen's fingers tightened on the arms of her chair. "The report said the guards died with swords in scabbard, killed by a blow to the back of the neck from a long blade. Finley was heir to the throne of Osera, guarded by the best the country can offer. So either his guards were killed treacherously by someone with enough rank to avoid a challenge, or they were taken out by a master swordsman before they could draw. You are both, so you can see how suspicions could rise."

Josef rolled his eyes and reached over his shoulder. He drew the Heart with a flourish, slamming the point into the wooden floor at his feet. All around the room, people began to shout. The guards drew their swords and encircled the queen. Even Lenette shrank back against her mistress, but Queen Theresa just watched, her eyes hard as iron as she glared at the large chunk that was now missing from her floor.

"Blow to the back of the neck?" Josef said, turning the Heart so everyone could see the size of the blade. "This is the only blade I keep that could be considered long. If I struck someone across the back of the neck with this, I would take their head off."

The queen sniffed. "Are you saying you're not clever enough to hide a murder weapon?"

"I'm saying I had no reason to kill Finley other than he's an ass," Josef answered. "And if I was going to kill him for that, I would have challenged him openly and had the pleasure of thrashing him in front of everyone."

"That, at least, I agree with," the queen said with a long sigh. "You can put away your iron bat, Thereson. I don't think you killed Finley, but the fact remains that the heir to the throne of Osera is murdered, and I have to determine how, by whom, and why."

269

Josef slid the Heart back into place on his back. "Easy enough," he said. "We'll go investigate."

"You will do no such thing," the queen snapped. "I said I don't think you did it, but that does not remove you from these matters. You are still under suspicion, and until my people get to the bottom of this, you will remain in your rooms where I can keep an eye on you."

"What?" Josef shouted.

"I don't see why you're surprised," the queen said, her voice rasping. "You were the one who chose to pursue a life of violence. You cannot now turn and condemn us for judging you by it. Our country is on the brink of war, and the people have just lost the man they thought would be their king. Now more than ever, Osera must be united. Lawful. Its throne without reproach."

"But I didn't do anything!" Josef cried.

"I believe you," the queen said earnestly. "And I have no doubt our inquiry will absolve you of all guilt, but I cannot shield a known murderer from investigation just because he is my son."

"I never murdered anyone," Josef said hotly. "I killed swordsmen in battle. There's a difference."

"A subtle one," the queen said. "Countries on the brink of war that've just seen their duke murdered don't appreciate subtlety."

"I don't care what they appreciate," Josef sneered. "I'm not going to let you lock me up for something I didn't do."

"You don't have a choice," Theresa said. She turned to her guard. "Take his swords. The prince is under arrest."

"Are you out of your mind?" Josef roared. "You're not taking my swords!"

"I am queen!" Theresa roared back. "I take whatever I—"

The queen's words dissolved into a coughing fit as she doubled over, heaving into her handkerchief. Several of the nobles started to run forward, but Lenette was there first, waving the rest away.

270

"The queen's medicine!" she yelled. "Hurry!"

A servant grabbed a kettle, a cup, and a folded paper sachet from the tray in the corner and ran to Lenette, pouring the steaming water into the cup as she went. Lenette grabbed the sachet and the cup. She shook the folded paper open, dumping green powder into the hot water. She stirred it once with the spoon the servant offered and then, grabbing the queen's convulsing shoulders, pushed the cup to her lips.

The queen drank, choked, and drank again with Lenette's help. Her coughing subsided, and she slumped back into the chair. For several minutes she did nothing but sit with her eyes closed, breathing as though taking in air were the hardest task she'd ever attempted. When she did finally open her eyes, they looked immediately at Josef.

"My order is final," she said in a strained, husky whisper.

Josef stared at her, helpless, and then looked plaintively at Eli, but the thief was already a step ahead of him.

"My lady," Eli said gently, stepping forward. "Think a moment. Someone out there is knocking off members of the royal family. Do you really think disarming the prince at such a time is a wise—"

"I will not be disobeyed," Theresa said, closing her eyes again. "This meeting is over. Take the prince to his chambers and make sure he stays there."

The guards bowed and moved to Josef's side. With a final glare at his mother, Josef raised his hands and let the guards guide him toward the door. Eli followed with his own escort. Looking back, Josef caught a final glimpse of his mother slumped between Lenette and the serving girl, and then the door closed and he saw no more.

The palace seemed empty as the guards marched Josef and Eli back to the prince's suite. The usual bustle of nobles and servants rushing on Osera's business had been replaced by grim-faced guards standing in knots wherever corridors connected.

When they reached Josef's rooms, the entire squad circled

round as Josef disarmed to make sure he surrendered every blade. It took a good thirty minutes, partially because Josef was taking his time about it, but mostly because he wore a lot of weapons. It took two men to hold Josef's arsenal of daggers, throwing knives, and short swords, and Josef spent the entire time making it very clear what would happen if every one of those blades didn't return to him.

When he finally announced he'd handed everything over, the guards stepped in to pat him down, just in case. This uncovered another two blades, one at the small of his back below his belt and one tucked into the heel of his shoe, both of which Josef claimed he'd forgotten. The guards gave him a sour look and added the blades to the pile. Then they came to the main bone of contention.

"The sword on your back," the soldier said. "Hand it over."

"This?" Josef lay his hand on the wrapped hilt of the Heart of War. "I don't think so."

The soldier crossed his arms. "The queen said every blade, Prince Thereson."

Josef smiled at him. "Fine," he said. "You want my sword?" He reached up to his shoulder and undid the strap that held the Heart on his back. "Take it."

The Heart fell to the floor with a crash that rattled the windows. The soldier jumped back in surprise, and Josef, still grinning, stepped aside so the guard could retrieve the Heart. The soldier glowered and reached down, grabbing the Heart by the hilt to lift it onto his own back.

Nothing happened.

The soldier's anger turned to confusion. He added another hand to the Heart's hilt and pulled again, harder. The Heart didn't budge. The soldier braced his legs against the wall. His face turned pink, then red. Sweat poured off his brow as he pulled with all his might, and nothing happened.

He let go at last, panting as he stared at Josef. "What is that thing?" he said, too out of sorts to remember the proper address for a prince. "It weighs more than a bloody mountain."

272

"It's my sword," Josef said. "Everything else you can take. This one stays with me."

The soldier shook his head. "Queen's orders," he panted. "I can't leave you with a weapon."

"Forget it," Josef said. "I didn't kill the duke. The queen knows that. Now, you cannot lift this sword. No one can, except me. You've done your job disarming me as best you could. Let it alone."

The soldier glanced at his companions, rubbing his strained shoulders. The other guards eyed the Heart with trepidation and, one by one, shook their heads.

"Right," the guard said at last. "Move out. You," he said, looking Eli up and down. "Coming?"

"I'll stay here, if it's all the same to you," Eli said, flopping into a chair by the hearth.

"Suit yourself," the guard said. "But no one gets out of this room until the queen gives the order."

"That's fine," Eli said. "I think our poor, maligned prince could use the company during his wrongful incarceration. But thank you for your diligence, officer."

The soldier gave Eli a sideways look, like he wasn't sure if that was sincerity or an insult, maybe both. In the end, he let it go, walking out with a shallow bow and locking the door behind him. As the lock clicked, Josef grabbed the Heart and returned it to his back.

"This is a fine mess," he grumbled, walking over to the tiny window.

"Mmm," Eli said, staring absently into the fireplace. "Josef, is your mother-in-law a card player?"

Josef blinked in confusion. "What?"

"Lenette," Eli said. "Is it possible she used to be a cardsharp?"

"No," Josef said, appalled. "Why in the world would you even ask that?"

"Because she pulled the best snake-in-the-sleeve I've ever seen," Eli said. "And I've seen a lot."

If possible, Josef grew even more confused. "Snake-in-the-where?"

"Snake-in-the-sleeve," Eli said slowly. "It's a gambling move. Watch." He held out his empty hand, and then, very subtly, flicked his wrist. Out of nowhere, a Daggerback card appeared between his fingers. "See?" he said, turning the card over. "Looks easy, but it takes years of practice."

"Wait a second," Josef said. "That's a Shepherdess." His eyes widened. "How long have you had a trump up your sleeve?"

"A long time," Eli said, grinning wide.

Josef crossed his arms over his chest. "I want my money back."

"Josef," Eli said, looking hurt as the card disappeared back up his sleeve. "I would never cheat you."

Josef rolled his eyes.

"Anyway," Eli said. "That's hardly the point. What matters is that I saw Lenette do that exact move when the servant handed her the cup."

Suddenly, Josef was paying very close attention. "Are you sure?"

"I wasn't at first," Eli said. "I caught it only by chance. But then I saw her do it a second time, while she was stirring. That time there was no mistaking it."

"Right," Josef said, rubbing his neck. "And what did she take out?"

"I don't know," Eli confessed. "As I said, she was really good. I couldn't even see if she was taking something out of her sleeve or putting something in. But I saw her wrist move, and I've been in enough card games to know that when you see someone flick their hand that way, you either call your bets or start cheating better."

Josef scowled. "What would Lenette be putting in the queen's cup? She owes my mother everything. Her position, her wealth, her daughter's place as princess, everything. The second the queen dies, Lenette goes right out the door. She knows that better than anyone. So why would she take the risk of doing something that could possibly be seen as treasonous?"

"I have no idea," Eli said, standing up. "But the royal family's luck is getting a little too bad for me to buy."

Josef winced. He knew that look on Eli's face. "What are you going to do about it?"

"First," Eli said, walking over to the table beside the door, "I'm going to find out who's been drugging you at night, and how. I'm guessing it happened again?"

"Yes," Josef said. "And it got Nico too."

"Really?" Eli said. "How curious."

Josef frowned. "Why curious?"

"Because it didn't get me," Eli said. "Which rules out the food."

"And you think the sleeping thing is related to the duke's death?"

"I don't know," Eli said, running his hands along the wall. "But as I said, this is too much bad luck, even for you. Now keep your voice down." He glanced pointedly at the door. "Bored soldiers have surprisingly sharp ears."

Josef looked skeptically at the door, but he nodded and moved over to the couch, sitting down with the Heart between his legs.

"Where is Nico, anyway?" he said, trying to keep the annoyance out of his voice.

Eli ducked his head to examine the bookshelf. "Probably making herself useful. She's not locked up, after all. No point in sticking around here."

Josef had to give him that one. Still, it annoyed him that he didn't know where Nico was. But complaining wasn't going to get him anywhere, so he sat and stared at his sword, letting his mind go blank as he traced the Heart's scarred surface. He could feel the battle coming, like a storm on the horizon. Good. Let it come. He would be ready.

Josef took a deep breath, letting the anger and frustration

flow out of his mind. Then, in one smooth motion, he stood up and stepped into first position. Mindful of the small space, he raised the Heart and began to practice his swings. Eli shot him an annoyed look and stepped out of the way, continuing his investigation around Josef's sword work.

Outside, dawn turned to morning as the sun peeked over the mountain.

Josef had just passed his one hundredth swing when Eli shouted, "Got it!"

Josef lowered his sword. Eli was standing in the corner looking unbearably smug and holding a candelabra.

"It's the candles," Eli said, wrenching a candlestick out of its holder. "Here, smell the wax."

"No," Josef said. "You just said it's poison."

"Only if you burn it," Eli said, shoving the candlestick in his face. "Smell."

Josef sniffed, wrinkling his nose. "Smells like bitter greens."

Eli nodded. "That's incenteth. Doctors use it to knock patients out for amputation, usually by making them smoke it. I never even thought of putting it in candles." He sounded deeply impressed. "Kind of brilliant, actually. The candles burn down, slowly filling the room with the drug. Servants and others can enter and leave with no ill effects except a little drowsiness, but anyone staying in the room would get the full dose and fall into a deep sleep until the candles burned out and the drug stopped."

"Well, I'm glad you're impressed," Josef grumbled. "But unless someone signed their name on those candles, we still don't know who did it."

"Up to this point, I'd have said the duke," Eli said, putting the candle back with a long sigh. "I still think it could be, but that's a moot point now, isn't it?"

Josef scowled at that comment, but before he could answer, he heard a familiar step on the carpet behind him. He turned just in time to see Nico step out of the deep shadows by the window.

He smiled, but his smile dropped when he saw the expression on her face. "What?"

"Something's going on down at the storm wall watchtower," she said. "Two guard squads have already been sent in."

Josef caught his breath. That was where he'd had his argument with the duke the day before. "What have they got against me now?"

Nico shook her head. "I don't think that's it," she said, her voice low. "They called in medics as well."

Josef frowned. "How close did you get?"

"Close enough to smell the blood," Nico answered.

Josef nodded and turned toward the door.

"Josef," Eli said. "Hold on just a—"

Josef didn't wait to hear the rest. He grabbed the door handle and turned it sharply, snapping the lock. He pushed the door open in time to see the two door guards turn and scramble to block his way.

Josef glowered. "Move."

"I'm sorry, my lord," the left guard said, shaking his head. "We can't let you—"

Josef reached out with both hands and grabbed each guard by the helmet. Bracing his feet, he slammed their heads together as hard as he could. The helmets hit with a metal crash, and the two guards dropped.

Josef nodded and stepped over their prone bodies.

Eli poked his head out, his mouth forming an O when he saw the moaning guards. "Aren't you Prince Charming?"

"Their fault," Josef said, starting down the hall. "They didn't move."

The palace was surprisingly empty. The guard posts were abandoned, probably in answer to the new threat at the bay. That suited Josef just fine. He jogged through the empty halls, following the twist of the castle toward the kitchens. He trundled down the narrow servant's stair and burst out into the paved yard where he'd met Finley's carriage the day before, scaring the daylights out of a serving boy in the process.

"You," he barked before the boy could bolt. "Two fast horses. Now."

The boy stared at him wide-eyed. "This is the back stable, sire. We only got—"

"I don't care about the quality," Josef said. "If it's fast, bring it. *Now.*"

The boy ran off, returning moments later with two long-legged bays already saddled and bearing the queen's colors.

"Aren't these reserved for messengers?" Eli said, scrambling onto the smaller of the two.

"Royal privilege," Josef said, pulling himself onto the other. He held out his hand for Nico, but she stepped away.

"I'll meet you there," she said, wrinkling her nose. "Horses and I don't get along."

Josef nodded, but she was already gone, her body dissolving into shadows. Behind them, forgotten, the serving boy shrieked.

"He'll get over it," Josef said. "Come on."

He kicked his horse and thundered out through the open gate. Eli shook his head and followed, bouncing in his saddle behind Josef as the prince forged a path through the crowded streets to the sea.

The queen supplied her messengers well. The horses made the trip down the mountain to the Rebuke in record time. Ahead of them, the flat walk of the storm wall was crawling with soldiers.

Eli stood up in his saddle, squinting at the horizon. "I don't see any ships. No invasion yet, at least."

Josef hopped off his horse and started pushing his way through the crowd. The soldiers looked at him sideways and whispered among themselves, but no one tried to stop him as he made his way to the heavy watchtower. Once they were inside, Nico was suddenly there.

"They're at the top," she said. "The light's too good for me to get in and the only door is guarded. Sneaking's not an option."

"Good thing we're not sneaking," Josef said, starting up the stairs. "Come on."

278

They climbed the four flights of stairs without challenge, but the door to the watch room at the top of the tower was blocked by a man in the polished chain of the royal guard. The soldier gripped his short sword when he saw Josef's face and pulled himself as tall as he could.

"Prince Thereson," he said in a voice that failed to be as authoritative as he probably wanted it to be. "You're supposed to be under arrest."

"Change of plans," Josef said. "Step aside."

The guard tightened his grip and held his ground.

Josef reached for the Heart, but Eli's hand on his shoulder stopped him. The thief leaned forward, fixing the guard with his sweetest smile.

"Listen, young man," he said. "The prince has had a really bad morning. So either you step aside and let us take responsibility for what's about to happen, or Thereson here lives up to his murderous reputation. We clear?"

The soldier looked from Josef to Eli and back again before he let go his sword and stepped aside in one shaky motion.

"Good choice," Eli said as Josef slammed the door open and stepped inside. He stopped again almost immediately, eyes going wide. He felt Eli stop as well and then hastily turn away. Josef didn't blame him. The sight was enough to turn even his stomach.

The watch room where he'd met with Finley was now slick with blood. Six dead guards lay on the floor below the windows, their necks slit at the back. Blood pooled on the wooden floor, reflecting the morning sunlight, and the smell of it was thick in the air. Around this gruesome scene stood a ring of royal guards, their faces pale and tight beneath their helmets. Medics waited at the edges, but there was very little for them to do when the patients were already dead. At the center of the room, two men stood over a wide table where a seventh dead man sat slumped over a blood-splattered pile of maps, his fine-tailored gray suit now a sickly reddish black thanks to the gaping wound at the back of his neck. Josef frowned and

279

flicked his eyes to the men standing over the table. The one on the left in the fancy coat he recognized as his mother's admiral, though he couldn't remember the old man's name. The other man also looked familiar, but Josef couldn't place him either.

Eli, however, had a better memory. "Josef!" the thief hissed, grabbing his wrist. "That's Tesset!"

"Who?" Josef said.

"*Tesset!*" Eli whispered again. "Council man from Izo's, works for Sara. Powers, he'll ruin everything."

Josef stared at the man in question. He vaguely remembered that swarthy face and large figure standing outside the hut with Sted, the one who'd gone after Nico. He could already feel Nico fading into the shadows behind him. Eli was still tugging his arm, trying to pull Josef back down the stairs, but Josef shook his head and yanked his arm free. If this Tesset was good enough to subdue Nico, then he'd already seen them, and running would do no good. Besides, Josef had questions to answer.

The admiral looked up when he heard Josef enter, and his face went scarlet.

"Prince Thereson!" he shouted. "You are confined to quarters!"

Josef ignored him, focusing on Tesset as the Council man looked up with a knowing smile.

"Good morning, Josef Liechten," he said. "Or Prince Thereson, I should say. I trust you're well."

"Well enough," Josef growled. "What are you doing here? When did you arrive?"

"Last night," Tesset said. "And I'm here as the Council's forward agent to help Osera prepare for the war. Your mother welcomed me herself just before all this unpleasantness. Condolences, by the way, on the death of your cousin."

"Keep 'em," Josef grumbled, making his way over to the closest body. The guardsman was on his stomach with his arms splayed out in an instinctive attempt to catch himself from a fall he'd never get up from.

"Back of the neck, just like the duke's men," Josef said, kneeling to get a better look at the gash that severed the man's spine. "Quick too. Poor bastard couldn't even get his sword out." He nodded down toward the guard's belt where the short sword was still snugly in its scabbard.

"Prince Thereson," the admiral said again. "Stop this at once! This tower is controlled by her majesty's navy. Prince or not, I won't hesitate to lock you up if you do not return to the palace at once."

"What?" Josef said, straightening up. "You can't blame this one on me. Eli and I were stuck in my rooms since this morning, just like the queen ordered. Look at the blood. These men haven't been dead more than half an hour. I was probably still being disarmed when it happened. And since it's clear that whoever did the duke's house did this as well, I'd say I've been exonerated. Isn't that right, Eli?"

"Beyond a doubt," Eli said.

The admiral stiffened. "When your mother hears—"

"So go tell her," Josef said. "Later. Now, what was security like in this room?"

The old man clenched his teeth, his brow furrowing into a knot as he weighed his outrage against the presence of a prince, even a despicable one. Royalty must have won out, for the admiral's shoulders slumped and he began his report.

"Security is as you see," he said. "Six guards watching, two at the door, four in the room, and the Council's wizard for the Relay so that we could notify Zarin the moment enemy ships were sighted."

"Yet all are dead inside," Eli said, silently counting the bodies. "Including the ones who were supposed to be in the hall. And they all died with their swords in their sheaths, correct?"

"Yes," the admiral said, looking cautiously at Josef. "Sir."

Eli grinned manically at his newfound authority. "I can see from the lack of blood trails that the bodies haven't been moved. Combine that with the sheathed swords and we can safely assume that all the soldiers walked in here of their own volition. That means whoever did this was someone the guards knew, else they would have barred the entrance and died outside. Someone respected, for they escorted this person in and were subsequently too shocked to draw their swords when this known, respected person turned on them."

"Impossible," the admiral said. "Only officers and members of the royal family can enter this room without challenge." He said this last bit with a pointed look at Josef, which Josef ignored.

Eli scratched his chin thoughtfully. "My real question is, why the watchtower? The duke I could understand, but why here?"

"I believe I can answer that one for you," Tesset said.

They all turned to look. Tesset had been standing quietly beside the table. Now, though Josef had not seen or heard him move, he was several feet away, kneeling on the floor. The boards there were scuffed and dusty like any well-used surface, but one spot was darker than the rest. Josef frowned and walked over, kneeling for a closer look. It wasn't blood, though there was certainly enough of that around. It almost looked as though someone had spilled a tiny bit of water and then tried to wipe it up.

"What's that?" Josef said.

Tesset leaned down and pressed his finger delicately against the floor. When he lifted it, something was stuck there, glinting in the light. A tiny, curving splinter of glass.

"Question still stands," Josef said, glancing at Tesset.

"It's the Relay point," Tesset said. "Or what's left of it."

"Powers," the admiral whispered, staring at the wet sliver of glass. "I never knew they could be broken."

"They're quite delicate, actually," Tesset said, standing up and placing the sliver of glass on the table. "Sara will be extremely distraught. Relay points are difficult to make, and we are very short at present."

"I don't understand," Josef said. "Why would someone break a Relay point?"

"To cut Osera off from the Council," Tesset said.

"But, why?" Josef asked again. "Osera has ships going to the mainland all the time. Any disruption in communication wouldn't last past low tide. Six hours at most."

"Six hours is plenty of time for many things," Tesset said, pointedly not looking at Eli. "For example, if a thief were going to pull a heist, six hours would be amply sufficient to grab the goods and get away."

"Nonsense." Eli's voice was equally disinterested. "No thief worth the name would break something as rare and valuable as a Relay point. Not when he can steal it, anyway. Honestly, what kind of idiot thieves do you chase?"

The admiral looked from Eli to Tesset, utterly confused. "Thieves? What are you talking about?"

"Nothing," Tesset said. "An idle comment. Anyway, if the criminal's objective was to isolate us, he failed."

"How's that?" Eli said. "Point looks pretty broken to me."

"That it is," Tesset said. "But Osera has two Relay points. This tower's point was a first alert supplied by the Council specifically for this emergency. Osera's official point is kept in the palace for the queen's use."

Josef set his jaw, glancing from the dead solders to the dead wizard and back again. "Admiral," he said quietly. "Who reported this?"

The admiral blinked. "Excuse me?"

"Who found these men dead?" Josef said, his voice annoyed. "You? A guard?"

"Oh." The admiral wiped his sweating brow. He looked as though this was all getting to be a bit much for him. "It was Princess Adela."

Josef stopped. "Adela?"

"Yes," the admiral said. "She had me take over here so she could go secure the Relay point at the palace."

"Adela went to the palace?" Josef shouted.

"Yes, your highness," the admiral said, baffled by his sudden outburst. "She thought that would be the criminal's next target. But don't worry, sire, I've yet to meet a swordsman who could get the better of your—"

Josef didn't have time to listen, he was already headed for the door. A hundred things were clicking together in his mind: the precision of the sword strokes, the speed with which they must have been laid down, Adela circling him in the throne room, holding back. The deep sleep that he felt and she didn't, the drugged candles and the bowl of stimulant. He glanced out the window at the castle high above them on the mountain. Even with the horse, it would take him five minutes at least to get to the back gate and another three to run to the Relay room at the top. Josef shook his head. He had no time. He had to get there now.

He hit the door to the stairs with his shoulder, slamming the poor guard on the other side into the wall. Josef didn't even notice. He stared into the dark and shouted.

"Nico!"

She appeared before he'd finished saying her name, and Josef took a relieved breath. For a moment he'd been afraid she wouldn't come. "I need your help."

Nico's pale face broke into a thin smile. That was all the answer Josef needed.

"I have to get to the palace," he said. "Can you take me?"

Her eyes widened. "Through the shadows?"

Josef nodded.

Nico bit her lip. "I can try."

"Try is all I need," Josef said. "Take me to the top, if you can. The queen's point will be in the palace watchtower."

Nico nodded and Josef stepped forward, snatching his hand away a second before Eli's fingers grabbed his wrist.

"I'm going," he said before the thief could speak.

"I realize that," Eli whispered. "But think a second, Josef. Just because she's been drugging you to sleep doesn't mean she's guilty of everything else. This could all be a setup."

Josef moved to stand beside Nico. "We'll see soon enough, won't we?" He looked down. "Ready?"

Nico nodded and hesitantly slipped her arms around his waist. She didn't look at him while she did this, keeping her face tilted down so that she was hidden in the deep folds of her hood. That was the last thing he saw before the world twisted and everything went black.

Eli jumped back with a curse as Josef vanished, tripping over the top stair and right into the point of the door guard's sword. He raised his arms on instinct, letting the guard walk him back into the watch room. The admiral was still staring at the space where Josef had been, his wrinkled face as pale as chalk.

"Before you do anything rash," Eli said, arching away from the sword in his back, "I'll have you know that there's a perfectly reasonable explanation for this."

"Hang it all," the admiral muttered. "I don't care anymore. You're all going in irons until we get this mess straightened out."

"All this is a bit much, don't you think?" Eli said. "It's just me at the moment."

"Then we'll start with you," the admiral growled. "Tie him."

Eli heaved an enormous sigh as two guards stepped forward to secure him. They were fastening the rope around his hands when the admiral turned to Tesset.

"I am so sorry you had to see this, Councilman Tesset," he said. "Prince Thereson has always—"

His voice trailed off. Tesset wasn't listening. He was standing at the window, staring out at the smooth sea. The admiral blinked and looked as well, squinting against the morning sun, and then what little blood was left in his face drained away.

"Powers help us," he whispered.

No one answered. Everyone, even Eli, was staring at the line of tiny dots on the eastern horizon. Far below, the water on the beach began to churn against the rocky face of the storm wall. Out in the bay, the lines of docked Oseran runners rocked against their moorings as the sea swelled beneath them, the bay's water pushed aside by the new, enormous current flowing from the east in a perfectly straight line.

CHAPTER
17

Josef gasped as the dark washed over him. This was true dark, not just lightless, but light consuming, and so cold he felt it like a punch all over his body. He couldn't hear anything, but he could *feel* the darkness screaming, vibrating against his skin. Panic like he'd never felt began to close over him like a sheet of ice, and he began to sink. The darkness sucked him down like a hungry mouth, screaming and laughing at the same time. Josef couldn't even move to defend himself, all he could do was sink and wait as the darkness poured down his throat, eating everything it touched.

Just before he was consumed, Nico's arms tightened on his chest, pulling him back. All at once, the sinking stopped, and his limbs were free. The feeling of motion was so beautiful, Josef almost laughed with joy. Instead, he clung to the familiar realness of Nico's wiry body with everything he had.

In less than three heartbeats, the light returned.

Josef fell to the ground, clutching his chest. He felt heavy and weak, like he'd been laid up with fever for weeks, and cold like he would never be warm again. He could feel Nico's hands on him. Her voice was in his ear, asking if he was all right. Josef nodded and reached for the hilt of his sword. The Heart leaped into his hand, and the weakness began to fade. When he was sure he could stand, Josef pushed himself up and looked around.

He recognized the place at once. They were in the hall that ran through the center of the royal guard's headquarters at the top of the palace. They'd come out next to the barracks door, but the barracks were empty. So was the hall. Josef's stomach began to sink. This was the heart of the guard. Given the current crisis, it should be crawling with soldiers as the reserves reported in, but the floor was silent. His face set in a grim line, Josef drew the Heart. He turned the sword in his hand, testing the grip in his palm. An echo of power flowed back like a greeting. Josef held the sword close as he tugged open the door to the stairs leading up to the watchtower. Nico fell in behind him, skipping from shadow to shadow.

The stair was a narrow spiral ending at a heavy door that was usually guarded and locked. But there were no guards now, and the heavy door hung open a crack, as though someone had just stepped inside and forgotten to close it. Pressing his body flat against the wall, Josef reached out with his sword, opening the door with the Heart's blade.

Even though he knew it was coming, the sight of the watchtower stopped him in his tracks. Men lay sprawled on the floor, their white faces still wide with shock above their severed necks. Josef took a quick count. Fifteen bodies, all guardsmen, far too many for the small tower. Josef set his jaw and raised his eyes to the only figure still standing.

Adela stood beside the table where the Council wizard lay slumped in his chair. Her helmet was off, and the dark braid of her hair hung free down her back, which was turned to Josef. For a moment, Josef thought maybe they'd snuck up on her, but before the thought could even finish, Adela turned to face him with a warm smile.

"I told you one day we'd be done pretending."

Josef cursed. No point in hiding now. "Adela," he said, stepping fully into the doorway. "Stand down."

"Little late for that, husband," Adela said. Her hand moved, and Josef raised his sword, but she wasn't drawing a weapon.

287

Instead, she held up something small, round, and blue between her fingers.

"What's that?" Josef said with a sinking feeling.

Adela's smile widened, and she clenched her hand in a fist. There was a sharp crunch, like an eggshell breaking, and then she opened her hand again, letting broken glass and a tiny amount of water fall to the floor.

"It *was* a Relay point," she said, shaking the last drops of water from her fingers. "The last Relay point in Osera."

Josef stared at her, trying to put words to everything that was going through his mind. But he wasn't Eli. Words didn't come easily. In the end, he managed only one.

"Why?"

"Because it is my duty," Adela said calmly. "And because I have waited my entire life for the day when I could leave this miserable dirt scratch of a kingdom."

"*Duty?*" Josef roared. "The queen raised you up from nothing! Defended you and your mother when everyone else wanted you cast out. She made you an Eisenlowe, captain of her guard, and this is how you repay her?" He swung his sword over the dead soldiers. "You have a twisted sense of duty, *princess*."

"And what of that matters to me?" Adela sneered. "I serve a higher power than you could ever imagine." Her voice grew deep and resonant as she spoke, and her eyes lit with a fire Josef had never seen there before. "There is no loyalty except loyalty to the true queen of the world," she said. "No duty except in her service."

Josef was beginning to wonder if she might be truly mad. "What are you talking about?"

Adela reached down and drew her short sword with a metallic hiss. Josef braced himself, but she didn't point the blade at him. Instead, she held the sword in front of her with the flat side facing him. Josef was so busy trying to guess her ploy, he didn't see the words etched into the metal for several seconds.

Sleepers wake. I am coming.

Josef's eyes darted from sword to swordswoman. "Who is coming?"

"Who do you think?" Adela laughed, swinging her sword until the point was leveled at the eastern window.

Josef kept his eyes on her, but she made no other moves. Finally, he risked a glance. He had to glance twice before he realized what he was looking at. There, miles out on the line where the Unseen Sea met the sky, the horizon was peppered with tiny dots running north and south as far as he could see.

"Oh yes," Adela said as the realization broke over his face. "The Immortal Empress is here at last to finish what she started two and a half decades ago." She brought her sword back around, aiming the point at Josef's heart. "We are the sleepers," she said, her voice trembling with emotion. "For years we've worked to weaken this island in her name. Now, your country, divided and hollowed by our hands, shall break like rotten fruit when her boats strike the shore."

"That's impossible," Josef said, forcing himself to ignore the rapturous smile on her face and keep his eyes on her sword. "You weren't even *born* when the Empress invaded."

Adela lifted her chin with a haughty sneer. "Loyalty to the Immortal Empress is not constrained by time. Our duty is passed down from mother to child, for generations if need be. We who sleep are called the ever faithful, all of us waiting generation to generation for the day she calls our blade."

"*Loyalty?*" Josef shouted. "*Faithfulness?* You betrayed your country and your queen! You killed your own men, and for what? Loyalty to an Empress you've never met?"

"Yes," Adela said, holding her short sword steady. "And I will be rewarded in ways you cannot comprehend."

"Not if I can help it," Josef growled. "Nico, go tell the admiral I have our traitor."

Nico didn't even get a chance to respond before Adela started to laugh.

"Go ahead, little girl, it doesn't matter now. Your kingdom is broken, your queen dying and alone. Her duke, the only man who could have rallied Osera, is dead. Your army is terrified and without leadership, your clingfire, the only weapon against the palace ships, destroyed. And since both Relay points are gone, you can't even use what little time remains to warn your allies. Now do you understand, prince? Send your girl, it will do no good. Osera has already fallen."

Josef glowered. "I never picked you for a fool, Adela," he said. "But I guess I was wrong about that too. Only a fool counts a battle won while the defenders are still standing."

Adela smirked at him. "Not for long."

Behind him, Josef felt Nico tense, ready to jump through the shadows and land on Adela's back. He stopped her with one word.

"Go."

Nico snarled at Adela one last time and vanished into the dark. If Adela was surprised by this, her face didn't show it.

"Quite the little monster you've got there, Thereson," she said. "Are you sure it was wise to send her away?"

"Yes," he said. "I'm the prince of Osera. It's my duty to finish you myself."

"Duty? You?" Adela laughed with delight. "The murderer prince who ran away?" She paused. "Actually, you were the only variable. When Theresa gambled the treasury to bring you home, we never thought you'd actually come home. But I'm glad you did, husband. Having the marriage bed for an alibi gave me more freedom to move than I could have hoped for, and your presence made my mother's job easier. The queen gets herself very excited when you're around. Such exertion makes it so much easier to explain her worsening fits."

Josef's eyes widened. "My mother's not sick at all, is she?" he said in a low, dangerous voice. "You've been poisoning her."

Adela shrugged. "Hard to say, at this point. After close to

ten years of drinking my mother's tea, Theresa's condition has become quite real. I doubt she'll last out the week, especially once she hears that her son, her last, ridiculous hope, finally gave in to his violent nature and had to be put down like a mad dog."

"If that's how you see this playing out, you haven't been paying attention," Josef said, raising the Heart as he stepped into position. "I may not be much of a prince, but I am the best and, unless you surrender now, the last swordsman you will ever meet."

"We'll see about that," Adela said, stepping into first position.

Josef looked her over. His instincts during the proving had been right. The stance Adela took now had none of the stiffness from before, and her fingers gripped her sword with a master's assurance. But even so, even if she somehow was a master duelist, there was no way she could hope to beat the Heart of War with an infantry short sword.

He glanced down at the Heart. It was a pity to use it for a fight like this, but he didn't have the luxury of a handicap. He needed to end this quickly and warn his mother. If he moved fast enough, he might even be able to save her. Josef gripped the Heart with both hands, sliding his feet forward across the stone. Finish it fast, he thought. Finish it now.

The Heart hummed in agreement, and they moved as one, bearing down on Adela like an iron wave. The princess's eyes widened at his speed, but she didn't try to dodge or spin away as she had in the Proving. Instead, she lifted her short, stocky blade and braced for the Heart's impact. The short sword looked so pathetic before the Heart's monstrous weight, Josef almost laughed. But Adela didn't break her guard, even as the Heart struck her sword with the force of a mountain.

The two blades met with a scream of metal, and Josef watched in satisfaction as the short sword crumpled. He could feel the impact moving through her blade like the Heart was an extension of his own arm, but as he stepped in for the follow-through that would shatter Adela's ribs, he realized something was wrong.

The short sword was still breaking. The metal was still folding in on itself, still crumpling like ash as it absorbed the Heart's strike. Josef's eyes widened. He could feel the blow spoiling even as he carried it, feel himself slowing as Adela slid backward, letting her sword break and break and break, drinking in the blow. Before the force could fade completely, Josef abandoned the strike. He swung the Heart back and turned midstep, using the last of his spoiled momentum to step out of her range, coming to a stop a few feet away with the Heart between him and Adela as he tried to figure out what had just happened.

Adela straightened with a smile and raised her sword, holding up the crumpled blade for Josef to see. Josef didn't see how there had been enough metal in the sword to crumple as much as it had, let alone enough to absorb the enormous power of the Heart. He was still trying to make sense of it when Adela's sword began to change. The etched words on the blade flashed with blinding light, and the crumpled blade began to straighten. The metal moved like a living thing as it pushed out of the stocky, confined shape of the short sword, growing longer, sharper, and slightly curved. The whole process took no more than a handful of seconds, and then Adela was holding a sword that looked nothing like the one she'd held a moment ago. The new blade glowed with a light of its own. It was delicate and straight now, without a single mark from the crumpled mess it had been moments before. Even the handle had changed, pushing out of the squat single hilt to a two-handed hold with a thick guard chased all around with stylized waves that seemed to dance across the glowing steel.

Josef kept his face neutral, refusing to let her see his surprise. "An awakened blade," he said. "Are you a wizard as well as a traitor and a spy?"

"I could scarcely be a sleeper if I was a wizard," Adela answered, swinging her newly changed sword in a whistling arc. "Wizards attract attention. To serve the Empress, we must be invisible. But this blade is not the crude, half-alert spirit you people call 'awakened.' Like me, it is a servant of the Empress." She held the sword out for him. "What you see before you is one of the Hundred Conquerors, a treasure of the Empire given only to those who serve behind enemy lines."

"Really?" Josef played along. "What's it made of that it crumples like trash when struck? Tin?"

"Steel," Adela said. "A mile of steel compressed into a blade by the Empress's own hand."

This time, Josef couldn't hide his surprise. "A *mile* of steel?" he cried. "How can a mile of steel become a blade?"

"All things bow before the Empress," Adela said. "Metal is no different. It followed her command as everything does, becoming her soldier, just as I am. The Hundred Conquerors have served thousands of soldiers in countless battles, passing from sleeper to sleeper as the Empress conquers the world. Each sword has been trained over hundreds of years to follow pressure commands so that even the spirit deaf can use it to its full potential. This blade cannot be defeated, it cannot be escaped, and, as you just saw, it cannot be broken." Her eyes flashed with a cruel light. "Not even by the Heart of War."

Josef's mouth twitched. After all her revelations, he shouldn't be surprised she knew his sword. But... "If you think a mile of steel will be enough to save you from the Heart, you've got another thing coming."

Adela sneered, but whatever she meant to say, she never got the chance. Josef was already flying toward her. This time, he kept both hands on the Heart's hilt, letting the blade guide him. He could feel the Heart's spirit moving through him, filling him until he could see the mountain behind his eyes, the great peak cutting the clouds, the deep roots holding up the world. An awakened blade was nothing. A mile of steel was nothing. The Heart of War moved with a mountain's rage, and Josef gave himself to it, letting its strength take him over with a furious cry.

Again, Adela raised her blade to parry, but her smug look faded as the blades collided. As before, her glowing sword crumpled, the metal folding over on itself so fast it sparked, but this time, it wasn't enough. Josef's cry became a roar as the Heart's power thundered through him, forcing Adela and her collapsing sword backward. They crashed together into the wall of the watchtower with an explosion that carried them through the stone and out into the air. As the blow finally left him, so did the overwhelming will of the Heart, and Josef realized he was falling. In front of him, almost lost in the enormous cloud of dust and broken stone, Adela was falling as well, her face a mask of shock and horror as the last of the Heart's force ran through her crumpled blade to finally hit her body. As he felt the strike connect at last, Josef got one final glimpse of her face screwing up in pain before the blow sent her flying out of the dust cloud like an arrow.

Josef was still trying to see where she'd gone when he crashed into something hard and brittle. He grunted as he hit and rolled on instinct. The landing hurt far less than it should have. The echo of the Heart's power was still crashing through him, drowning out every other sensation. He'd joined with his sword before, but never like that. The black blade had moved not with him, but *through* him. Its power was his power, its will, his will, and as it began to drain away, Josef felt emptier than ever. But as he lay still and fought to steady himself, the Heart's hilt pressed against his hands, warning him that the fight was not over.

Like a man waking from a deep sleep, Josef shot up and the world returned. He was in a crater on the roof of the palace's western wing. The watchtower, what was left of it, loomed above him. Its entire north face was gone, the stone sundered by the force of the Heart's blow. There were great holes in the tile roofs of the stylish buildings around the castle where the blown-out chunks of the broken tower had landed, but Josef's eyes skipped over them, looking for his target.

Adela lay in the ruins of what had been the top floor of the most prestigious bank in Osera, her body cradled by a great wave of shining steel. The metal moved as he watched, throwing off the rubble, and Josef cursed as it lifted Adela to her feet. When she was steady, the metal retreated, flowing back into the shape of the long, curved sword.

She shook her head, as though trying to clear it, and Josef started to grin. Challenge the Heart, would she? But the weakness lasted less than a second. At once, her head snapped up, her eyes finding him instantly among the wreckage. Josef got to his feet, watching to see what she would do. Even after cutting through a mile of steel and the wall of the watchtower, the Heart's blow had been enough to throw her far. It was a long jump from the wrecked bank where she stood to the palace roof. He planted his feet, easing the Heart in his hands as he waited to see how she would handle it, but Adela made no move to close the distance. Instead, she raised her sword, pointing the tip at Josef's chest in challenge.

Smirking, Josef held up the Heart in answer, his mouth opening to taunt her into a wild charge.

He never got a chance. The moment he moved the Heart, the tip of Adela's silver blade shot out. It flew like an arrow, cutting through the air with a screaming whistle. By the time Josef realized what was happening, it was nearly too late. With no time to duck, he defended the only way he could. He raised his sword and flipped it, holding the Heart's broadside like a shield over his chest. For a split second, it looked like this would work, but then the tip of Adela's blade flickered, and the sliver shot forked left in midair. There was no time to adjust, no time for Josef to do anything but brace himself as the sword point slipped around the Heart's defense and stabbed through his left shoulder.

It happened so quickly, there wasn't even any pain. One

moment he was braced, the next a length of shining steel pierced his shoulder like a spit through a roast. He could feel the metal in his muscle, slick and burning hot from the expansion. He was still staring dumbly at it when the blade began to lift. Across the expanse, Adela was raising her sword, lifting Josef up until his feet were dangling.

Now it hurt. Every centimeter she raised him sent a new bolt of pain sharp enough to make his vision go dark radiating from his shoulder. He struggled because he felt he should, but it was a futile effort. Her sword had skewered him like a speared boar. He couldn't even slide himself off the blade. All he could do was grip the Heart as Adela lifted him farther and farther into the air like he weighed nothing.

Just when Josef was sure his arm was going to rip off, Adela flicked her wrist. The sword snapped in a mirror of the motion, slinging Josef off the end. He was dimly aware of tumbling through the air, but his real attention was on the blinding pain of the sword as it slid out of his body. The agony made him sluggish, too sluggish to do more than tuck his head as Adela's throw sent him through one of the palace chimneys. The bricks crumbled when he hit, falling on him in a rain of broken stone as he tumbled down the slope of the palace roof until, at last, he hit one of the stone gutters and stopped.

For several moments, all he could do was lie still and try to breathe. His body was seizing up around him, his blood grinding to a halt in his veins. His right arm was a bar of pain, but even though he couldn't feel his right hand, or form a coherent thought, Josef clung to the Heart instinctively, knowing without knowing that it was his best chance of survival.

As his mind slowly came back to the present, the first thing he heard was the soft hiss of steel as Adela's sword shrank back to its usual shape. Groaning at the effort, Josef turned his head to see her walk to the edge of the bank's broken roof and hold out her sword again. He sucked in a breath, bracing for another blow, but her sword was pointed down. The blade extended again with a metallic whine, and he heard the stone shatter as the tip hit the street below. Then, using her sword as a pole, Adela stepped out into the open gulf of air between the bank's ruined roof and the palace. The sword began to fall at once, carrying her across the gap until she landed neatly on the edge of the palace roof. Her sword retracted the moment her feet were firm, returning to the long, gently curved blade as Adela advanced on Josef.

He sank to the ground, bringing the Heart up as high as he could. The wound in his shoulder burned like a hot poker, but the Heart's strength was already washing the pain away. He probably could have stood if he'd really tried, but Josef stayed put, watching Adela as she stopped by his feet. Her braid was skewed from the impact earlier, and the wind whipped her long hair across her face as she stood over him, surveying her kill. Her sword shone with harsh light, steam rising off the blade in long tendrils as she planted the point between the tiles and leaned on it like a walking stick.

"Still alive?" she cooed.

That was when Josef struck. He pushed up with his uninjured shoulder, the Heart of War moving in a black flash as he swung straight for Adela's neck. For a split second, he saw true panic in her eyes, and then her fingers tightened on the hilt of her sword.

The blade responded instantly. It flew out like a silver rope, loping up and back with a scream of steel to hook the Heart's blade. Josef grunted as the Heart of War jerked in his hands. Had he been standing, he could have held the blow on course, but striking up from the ground and on one injured shoulder, he simply didn't have the strength. Adela's sword pulled the Heart's trajectory off at the last second, flipping the black blade and Josef with it.

Josef cried out as he slammed into the tiled roof for the third time, rolling as he hit in a desperate effort to save his injured shoulder. He ended up on his stomach, but just as he kicked his legs under to get up, Adela's boot landed on his neck and slammed him down again.

Adela leaned over him, panting wildly as she ground her boot down with all her weight. Josef gritted his teeth and shifted, turning his head so he could see her face. She was glaring down at him with pure, righteous fury. One hand held her sword, its flexible blade still wrapped around the Heart, but her other hand was pressed against her neck, staunching a shallow wound half an inch from her windpipe. Despite the boot grinding into his neck, Josef grinned. She wasn't quite as fast as she liked to think.

"How are you still alive?" Adela whispered, her voice shaking with rage. "You should be bleeding to death." Her dark eyes darted to his hands, still gripping the Heart of War with all their might. "I wonder."

She jerked her fingers along her sword's hilt. The flexible blade followed the motion, slinging down in a flashing arc. Josef's eyes widened, and he dropped the Heart a second before the whipped blade would have sliced off his fingers. Adela laughed above him, but Josef had both hands free now. He reached up with his free arm, fingers closing around her boot before he threw her as hard as he could. Adela's laughter cut off with a strangled cry as she fell, but Josef had already put her out of his mind. Every sense he had was focused on the black blade lying crooked on the tiles. He'd been separated from his sword for only a few seconds, but already the pain was threatening to knock him out. The Heart was all that mattered. If he couldn't reach it, he was down for good. But as his fingers brushed the hilt, a flash of silver cut him off.

Adela's sword whistled over his head, landing on the Heart with a whine of cutting metal. Josef snatched his fingers back with a curse as the flexible blade wrapped itself around the Heart like thread around a spindle, and as it wrapped, the blade began to spin, surrounding the Heart in an impenetrable cocoon of whirling steel. The moment the sword was completely covered, Adela flicked her hand like she was cracking a whip and the blade of her sword snapped off, freeing her from the tangle of whirling metal she'd woven around the Heart.

"There," she said, smiling as the broken length of sword in her hand folded and re-formed until it was a slender, curved blade once again. "Let's see how well you fight now, Thereson."

Josef's eyes flicked back to the Heart. Despite Adela seemingly snapping her blade in two, the cocoon of spinning steel around the Heart was going strong, grinding into the tile below with a whining scream. He crouched on his knees, considering his options. It didn't take long, since there was only one. Blood soaked his arm, back, and chest, and he was starting to feel light-headed even through the pain. If he was going to do anything other than sit here and bleed to death, he needed the Heart, but there was no way through the spinning coil of Adela's blade. Not without losing a hand, or worse.

Josef gritted his teeth with a growl of frustration. "That's a very annoying weapon you have there, Dela. Does your Empress fight all her battles so cheaply, or am I the exception?"

"The Empress fights for victory," Adela said. "Anything else is merely the conceit of prideful swordsmen." She tapped his shoulder with her blade, forcing him to turn and face her. "You are defeated, Prince Thereson," she crowed, beaming down at him. "Your wound is bleeding as it should now that I've separated you from that hunk of iron you call a sword. Give up. As it stands, I can still save your life, but you will be dead for certain if you persist in fighting."

"Why should I give up?" Josef said, sitting back on his heels as he pressed both palms against the hole in his shoulder in a futile attempt to hold in the blood. "You think I believe you'll let me live? After everything you've admitted to me?"

"Of course," Adela said. "With the duke dead and your mother soon to follow, you are next in line for the throne. If you die here, the succession will be broken completely."

"What do you care about the succession?" Josef wheezed.

It was getting hard to sit straight now. "I'm not about to make you queen, if that's what you're after."

Adela's lips peeled up in a sneer. "Why would I want to be queen of this pit? Osera is a savage place, even by the standards of this savage, backward continent. To be honest, I don't think this island is worthy of the Empress's conquest, but my lady is more forgiving than I am."

Adela lowered her sword and leaned down, bringing her head to Josef's level. "The people of Osera are stubborn brutes," she whispered. "Even without a king, they will throw themselves at the Empress's soldiers, breaking like waves on the wall of her palace ships until the sea is red with Oseran blood. But there's no reason the Empress's coming has to be a massacre. Think, Thereson. If you live, you will become king of Osera with the power to make your people surrender. Since you came home when your mother raised the bounty, I can't believe you're as indifferent to your homeland as you pretend. It's true that nothing you do can save Osera now, but there's still a chance you can save your people. Pledge your loyalty to the Empress, and she may be merciful."

Josef stared at her for a moment, and then he started to laugh. Each seize of his chest sent a wave of pain that nearly knocked him out, but he couldn't stop. "You actually think..." He gasped. "You actually believe Osera would listen to *me*?"

Adela scowled. "If you don't like the terms, I can always stand here and watch you die." She straightened up again, flicking her sword until the point was level with Josef's throat. "What will it be, Josef Liechten Thereson Eisenlowe? Life for you and your people at my Empress's mercy, or certain death for every soul on this island? Choose quickly, we're drawing a crowd."

Josef glanced down. Sure enough, the square in front of the castle was packed with people. Some were pointing up at the prince and princess; others were simply staring dumbstruck at the cratered roof and shattered buildings. The crowd was entirely citizens, no guards or military, and Josef turned away to focus on the more important matters of Adela's sword and his bleeding shoulder. But, just before his eyes left the crowd, he caught a pair of familiar faces.

A second later, a cool breeze ruffled Josef's hair.

"Can't we go faster?" Nico said, leaning out the carriage window.

Eli clung to his seat for dear life. He'd been making the most of his first nonthieving-related arrest when Nico had come charging out of the shadows by the door and told everyone Adela was their traitor, that she'd killed her own guards and broken the queen's Relay point, and that Josef was fighting her as they spoke. That was five minutes ago. Now, thanks to a few well-placed scares from Nico and Eli's quick hand with knots, they were in a requisitioned military cart hurtling over the rutted streets of east Osera toward the palace.

"Any faster and we'd end up flat against a building," Tesset answered from his perch on the driver's seat, holding the horses straight as the road veered and dipped. Tesset had come along without being asked, but Eli hadn't complained, as the Council man had offered to drive. He was starting to regret that decision. Tesset made him nervous. Despite the plunging horses, the man's expression never changed from interestedly neutral, as though this was all nothing more than a play he hadn't quite decided he liked yet.

Of course, if this was a play, Eli didn't like the way the plot was going one bit. Clinging to the vibrating carriage, he glanced up at the rapidly approaching palace. It looked fine from this angle, but they'd heard the enormous crash a few minutes ago. From here, Eli couldn't see what had caused it, but whatever it was, it couldn't be good. Nothing good ever came of noises that loud.

"We're turning," Tesset said. "Hold on."

The carriage careened sideways, nearly sending Eli and Nico tumbling into the street. Nico was back in her seat a second later. Eli took significantly longer to pull himself upright.

"What was that about?" Eli groaned, clutching his bruised shoulders as he watched the palace fly by on his left. "Stop! The palace is right there."

"The fight's on the western wing," Tesset said. "We're on the wrong side. If we stop here we'd have to walk through the palace. Better to drive around."

Eli grimaced. "Just don't take us into the front square. That's where every—"

He cut off as Tesset careened the cart again. "Would you stop that?" Eli shouted, holding on for dear life.

If Tesset heard him, he gave no sign. They were darting through the rich neighborhood just below the palace now, weaving in and out of the growing traffic. But as they turned down a street that led to the palace square, Tesset reined the horse to a skidding halt, forcing Nico and Eli to hold on or be thrown.

"Didn't I tell you?" Eli cried. "Not the square!"

Tesset ignored him and hopped down. Shaking and cursing, Eli followed, leaving the cart and the panting horses standing in the middle of the street. As Eli had predicted, the entrance to the palace square was blocked by a mass of people crawling over each other to see what was happening.

"I told you," Eli said again, pointing disgustedly at the wall of backs. "We'll never get through now."

"What's the matter, thief?" Tesset said. "Afraid of a little crowd?"

Eli started to tell him exactly what was wrong with that question, but before he could get a word in, Nico and Tesset stepped up to the edge of the crowd and began pushing people out of the way. Fortunately for all involved, the crowd in the square was too preoccupied to care about a little pushing. They were all staring up at the palace roof. Some were pushing toward it, but more were trying to get away. Eli didn't blame them. The western side of the palace was a wreck. The palace watchtower was half gone, its northern side blown out completely, which explained the *boom* from earlier. Fallen hunks of stone littered the square and the buildings around it, especially the elegant building at the castle's northwest corner, which seemed to have lost a large chunk of its roof. Eli was still wondering what could have caused such massive destruction when Nico grabbed his arm and pointed up at the palace roof.

Of course, Eli sighed. Who else?

Josef was on his back on one of the castle gutters with Adela standing over him. Even at this distance, Eli could see it was bad. The stone beneath Josef was dark with blood, and the Heart was nowhere to be seen. Adela's mouth was moving, but this far away her words were lost in the noise of the crowd and the endless wind.

"It's a bad position."

Eli glanced at Tesset, who had stopped pushing the crowd and was now eyeing the battle with professional interest.

"Liechten should be able to take a girl like that," he continued. "She must have a gimmick, and he must have fallen for it hard if he's on his back, especially considering how he took Sted. Still, won't be long if he keeps bleeding like that."

"Josef will win," Nico hissed.

"I'm with Nico," Eli said. "I would be an old man by now if I let myself panic every time I saw Josef at death's door. He'll win, I'm sure. Our problem is what comes after."

Nico shot Eli a furious look. "What do you mean?"

"Listen," Eli said, dropping his voice.

Nico and Tesset obeyed, falling silent as the noise of the crowd rolled over them.

"Go on, princess!" an old man shouted. "Kill the traitor!"

"Thereson is a murderer!" someone else shouted behind them. "He killed the duke! Avenge Finley!"

"He's no prince of ours!" a woman cried. "Kill him! Kill the traitor!"

And on and on and on.

"I see what you mean," Tesset said at last.

"They're all idiots," Nico said at the same time. "How dare they—"

"Nico," Eli's voice held a sharp warning. Nico glared at him, but shut her mouth. Eli smiled apologetically at Tesset and grabbed Nico's shoulder, turning her around and leaning down so that their heads were together.

"Listen," he whispered. "Josef's going to win this fight, but it's our duty to make it count."

Nico nodded. "What have you got in mind?"

"We're going to clear his name," Eli said. "But first, I need you to find me a wind."

Nico gave him a skeptical look, but she didn't question him. Instead, she looked up, her eyes darting across the sky. "There," she said, pointing up.

Eli followed her finger with his eyes. "You!" he cried, layering just a hint of power into his voice as his finger shot out, pointing at the same spot in the sky as Nico. "Can I ask a favor?"

He felt immensely stupid yelling at the empty air, but he hid it with a confident smile. Thankfully, a few seconds later, a strong breeze ruffled his hair.

"Good guess," the wind whispered in his ear. "I'm impressed enough to hear you out, wizard."

"You're too kind," Eli said. "I have a bit of an odd task for you, but I promise I'll make it worth your while."

His shirt fluttered as the wind turned in a circle. "I'm listening."

Eli glanced at Nico with a wry smile and launched into his plan. Beside him, Tesset listened with growing interest. By the time the wind agreed and blew away, he was grinning as wide as any of them.

"Never boring with you, is it, Monpress?"

Eli flinched at the mention of his name, but he hid it flawlessly, turning on Tesset with a winning smile.

"I should hope not, Mr. Tesset."

He would have said more, but Nico smacked his arm and put her finger to her lips. Eli nodded and turned back to Josef, who was still lying on his back looking at Adela, who wasn't talking anymore. The seconds crawled by, and then, without warning, a great wind picked up around them.

That was his cue. Eli cleared his throat and cupped his hands over his mouth. A small, thin flow of air whistled through his curled fingers. Eli licked his lips as the wind brushed over them and very softly began to speak.

High above the crowd on the palace roof, Josef held Adela's gaze, his lips pursed in exaggerated consideration as he made a show of thinking her offer over. But his attention was on the wind in his ears and the familiar voice it carried.

"Josef," Eli's disembodied voice whispered. "If you can hear me, give a sign."

Josef shifted his knee, nudging a chunk of broken stone so that it clattered down the roof.

"Good enough," Eli said. "I'm guessing Adela has come clean as a traitor by now?"

Josef nodded without thinking, and then froze when Adela's eyes narrowed suspiciously.

"*Powers*, don't do that," Eli hissed in his ear. "Listen, before you roll out whatever you're planning, I need you to follow my instructions to the letter."

It took all his willpower not to roll his eyes, but Josef stayed still, listening to Eli's plan. Adela tilted her head at his silence, obviously growing impatient, but by the time she got mad enough to show it, Josef knew exactly what to do.

"I grow weary of this," Adela said, edging her sword a little closer to Josef's neck. "Which will it be, Thereson? Die here and doom your island, or surrender and spare yourself and your people?"

Josef leaned back. "You tell me."

Adela paused. "What do you mean?"

"This is the day you've been preparing for all your life, right?" He jerked his head to the east. "Your Immortal Empress is finally coming, and you've dutifully done everything you could to pave the way for her. You killed Duke Finley and his son, poisoned the queen, probably burned the clingfire stock too, now that I think about it. Doesn't really matter anymore, I guess."

Adela's hand tightened on her sword. "What are you playing at?"

"I never play, princess," Josef said, his voice deadly serious. "It's no secret I'm a terrible prince to Osera. I don't even know what's going on half the time. Now you're standing there asking me to make decisions about the country's future?" He shrugged as far as he could with his wound. "How should I know? Traitor or spy or whatever your true colors, the sad truth is you've done more as Osera's princess than I ever did as her prince. This is your moment, Dela, not mine. So you tell me, what should Osera do?"

Adela lowered her sword with an exasperated look. "Leaving his country's fate to her betrayer? You truly are a terrible prince, Thereson."

She stabbed her blade point down into the roof and leaned on it, the loose strands of her dark hair blowing wildly in the strong wind. "You want to know the fate I would choose for Osera?" she said, smiling down at him the way she used to when they were kids. "Fine. I want it to burn. All of it. Do you know what it was like, growing up here? You people are barbarians, with your insistence on blood lines and noble houses. My mother grew up in the bosom of the Empire. She told me stories of a perfect land where everyone is judged on merit and loyalty. Where disobedient idiots like you are cast away while people like me become leaders because of our skill, not our birth. People still die of hunger here. Can you believe it? In the Empire there is no war, no famine, no natural disasters. Spirit or a human, everything there is clean, ordered,

306

and perfect, and all the Empress asks in exchange for this perfection is obedience."

She flung out her arm, pointing at the city below. "You can't know what it's like!" she cried in disgust. "To *know* that paradise exists while you are trapped in this pigsty. But my exile is over." She grabbed her sword and swung it back toward him with a mad, enraptured smile. "My mother and I have fulfilled our purpose. We have cleared every obstacle that stands in the Empress's path and offered up this pathetic excuse of a kingdom to her like a peeled grape on a platter. When the Empress arrives, we shall be rewarded beyond anything you can imagine, and when I'm standing at her side, I will look down on the burning shell of Osera, and I will laugh. I will laugh and sing my Empress's praises while her soldiers slaughter every last one of you ignorant, barbaric savages."

"Then you're not sorry," Josef said, leaning away from the quivering point of her sword. "Not about killing the duke and his son? Or about the years you've spent poisoning my mother?"

"Of course not." Adela laughed, her voice echoing in the wind. "I'd kill Finley again if I could, the pompous bore. And Henry. I can't tell you how happy I am that the Empress came quickly and I don't have to waste my life being his queen and bearing his dull-witted children. As for Theresa, she deserves what she got for being so trusting. The only thing I regret is that I had to pretend to lose to you at the Proving, but I intend to remedy that now." Adela smiled, her sword inching forward to press against the naked skin of his throat. "You should have been smarter, Prince Thereson, than to let your enemy choose your fate."

"I don't think so," Josef said, tilting his head into the wind. "Is that enough?"

"More than enough," Eli's voice drifted on the breeze. "We heard the whole thing."

Adela's eyes went wide, and she swung around, searching for the source of the voice, but the roof was empty.

"Who's there?" she shouted. "Show yourself!"

Her only answer was the wind's low moaning as it swept past her, blowing her voice down over the now completely silent crowd.

"Well," Josef said, pushing himself up. "If you've got all you need, we'll finish it from here."

Adela spun back around, bringing her sword right up to the skin beneath Josef's chin. "What do you mean 'we'? You are alone! No one can save you!"

Josef didn't move, not even to flinch away from the blade at his throat. "Wrong, princess. You were the only one who was fighting alone."

Adela bared her teeth with a snarl and flicked her wrist, sending a wave of steel down her sword that would slice Josef's neck in two. But before the wave was halfway down the blade, the Heart of War's spirit exploded open, and the weight of a mountain fell on the palace.

CHAPTER
18

Eli watched in amazement from his place in the equally amazed crowd as the corner of the palace where Josef and Adela's drama had been playing out suddenly fell straight down. There was no warning, no crumbling, no falling stone. One moment Adela was standing with her sword at Josef's throat, unknowingly incriminating herself to all of Osera, and the next the entire western side of the palace had flattened as though stepped on by an enormous, invisible foot.

For three heartbeats, the people simply stared, and then the crowd turned as one and began to stampede out of the square. Tesset calmly retreated to the recessed entry of a nearby building as the tide of people surged past. Eli dove behind him far less calmly, pressing himself flat against the painted door as far from the panic as he could get. He was thinking about picking the lock when a wind's voice giggled in his ear.

"Helping you was more fun than expected," the wind said. "Now, you said you'd make it worth my while?"

"Of course," Eli said, recovering instantly now that there were deals to make. "How about a favor of your choosing from the prince of Osera?"

"A favor from a human?" the wind puffed, considering. "That's a fine turnaround. I'll take it. I'll call him when I think of something."

"Do, please," Eli said.

But the wind was already blowing up into the sky to tell the others about how a *human* owed *him* a favor.

Tesset patted down his collar where the wind had blown it up. "You do realize that when the wind comes to claim that favor, the spirit-deaf Prince Josef won't be able to hear him."

"Winds like having favors more than claiming them, in my experience," Eli said. "But if it does ever come to that, I'm sure the wind will find a way. They're very resourceful."

"I'm sure," Tesset said, eyes darting pointedly to the square. "You should look to your young lady."

Eli followed Tesset's look and saw, without surprise, that Nico was no longer beside them but across the square and pushing her way toward the palace wreckage. With a long-suffering sigh, Eli started after her. Tesset went with him, gently pushing the panicked people out of their way with his long arms.

They caught up with Nico at the edge of the crushed palace. Eli was about to ask why she'd stopped when he felt it. The Heart's spirit was still open, sitting on the wreckage of the palace's western corner like an invisible mountain. Another step and Nico would have been on the ground like everything else.

The Heart had done a very neat job, crushing only the area

around Josef and Adela but leaving the rest of the palace intact. It looked like someone had dropped a brick on this corner of the building, ripping away the walls and the roof but leaving everything else mostly intact. Servants were already peering over the ragged edge from the now-open rooms, their eyes as wide as dinner plates.

Where the Heart's spirit was open, however, nothing moved. Even the dust was pressed indelibly into the ground. The stone wall had been crushed into the palace's foundations by the Heart's weight, bringing the roof down to eye level from the ground, and there, lying on her back and half buried under a cascade of cracked tiles not a foot away, was Adela. She lay completely still. So still that, for a moment, Eli thought she was dead. Then he saw her chest rise in a tight, tiny gasp, and he realized the truth. She was crushed, like everything else. In fact, the only thing not crushed beneath the Heart's enormous weight was Josef.

He sat at Adela's feet, watching her with a disgusted look. When he saw the three of them waiting at the edge of the destruction, Josef stood, walked over to what looked like a tangled ball of steel, and held out his hand. With a squeal of ripping metal, the Heart cut up through the twisted steel like a knife through ribbon and leaped into Josef's grip, its hilt pressing firmly into its swordsman's palm. The second Josef's fingers closed on his sword, the monstrous weight lifted.

There was a whoosh of air as the winds rushed to fill the void. Josef let it blow over him, breathing deeply as the bleeding from his shoulder eased, then stopped altogether. When the wound was staunched, he turned and walked back to Adela. Now that the weight had lifted, the princess was coughing and struggling to roll over. She'd made it to her side by the time Josef reached her, and Eli saw her eyes widen in fear as she brought her hand up with a silver flash.

The Heart was there before she finished, the black blade slamming down just above her fingers. A spirit screamed, and Adela looked down in horror.

Just above the guard that protected her fingers, Adela's sword was now little more than a ripped metal edge. On the ground in front of her, the rest of the bright steel blade twisted like a trapped snake beneath the Heart of War. The metal screamed as it thrashed, but every scream was fainter than the one before it. Finally, the sword fell still, its light fading like a dying ember, leaving the blade motionless, dark, and dead in the rubble.

"No," Adela whispered, her fingers trembling on the hilt of her broken sword. "*No. It's impossible.*"

Josef looked away in disgust. "Nico?"

Nico was behind Adela before Josef finished speaking her name, her hand coming down on the back of the princess's neck. The blow hit with a solid *thwack*, and Adela slumped forward, her eyes fluttering closed.

"That should keep her for a bit," Josef said, leaning on the Heart.

Nico stepped over Adela's body to stand beside him, her eyes locked on his blood-soaked shoulder.

Josef began to fidget under her scrutiny. "I've had worse," he muttered.

Nico's eyes widened, but she let it lie.

"Well," Eli said, stepping onto the rubble as well. "Now that that's over, what next?"

"Get to the queen," Josef said. "Before Lenette hears her daughter failed."

"What about..." Eli tapped Adela's body with his boot.

"They can handle it," Josef said, nodding over Eli's shoulder.

Eli turned to see the admiral and several guards marching toward them across the now-empty square. When he turned back, Josef was already off, trotting into the palace through the sundered wall with Nico hot on his heels. Muttering the usual curses about bullheaded swordsmen, Eli ran after them. Tesset followed a step behind, swift and silent as a shadow.

The wall the Heart had collapsed at this level turned out to be the outer wall of the pantry. Josef ran through the stocks

311

of grain and flour, bursting through the door to the kitchen with a swift kick. The kitchen staff screamed and scrambled to get out of the prince's path. Eli called out apologies as he ran past, but he stayed right on Josef's heels as they cleared the kitchens and started up the servant's stair toward the queen's chambers.

They'd reached the third floor and were rushing toward the royal wing when Josef skidded to a stop, causing Nico and then Eli to run into him.

Eli poked his head around Josef's broad back. "What is it n—"

The question died in his throat. Queen Theresa was at the other end of the hall. She was in a dressing gown, her face sweat soaked and pale as death. Long white hair tumbled loose from her head, the wispy ends nearly brushing her bare feet. Lenette was at her side, and the queen clung to her with skeletal hands. A small knot of worried guards trailed behind them, following the queen and her lady as they made their way slowly down the hall.

It was Lenette who saw Josef first. Adela's mother stopped in her tracks, her face suddenly stricken, as though she'd seen a ghost. Theresa stumbled at the sudden stop and raised her head, her eyes lighting up as she saw her son.

"Josef," she said, her voice relieved. "They said you were fighting Adela."

Josef didn't seem to hear the queen. His eyes were locked on Lenette. "You," he hissed, marching forward. "Get away from my mother."

Nico started to follow, but Eli grabbed her shoulder. Lenette, on the other hand, stepped forward, putting herself between the queen and Josef.

"My queen!" she cried. "This man is a murderer. He killed his cousins and now he comes for you. Look at the blood on him." She clutched her chest with a sob. "Where is my daughter, killer?"

"Step away, Lenette!" Josef shouted, walking faster. "It's

312

over. Adela confessed. We know everything. You're an agent of the Empress left here to destabilize Osera after the war, and you trained your daughter to follow in your footsteps. You've been poisoning the queen for years, but your treachery ends now. *Step away!*"

Theresa looked at her lady-in-waiting. "Lenette?"

But Lenette's face had changed. She glared at Josef with open hatred, and that was when Eli saw her hand flash.

"Josef!" he shouted.

He was too late. Lenette's hand flew from her skirts, the knife flashing silver before it plunged into the queen's chest. Josef and the guards rushed forward, dragging Lenette off the queen, but Lenette twisted free with surprising strength. She staggered, the knife dripping red in her hands.

"Long live the Empress," she said, raising the knife to her own throat.

Eli winced and turned away, but it didn't save him from the unmistakable *thump* as Lenette's body hit the floor. When he looked back, she was lying crumpled on the carpet at the center of a spreading, dark stain. Josef didn't even look at her. He dropped the Heart and ran to his mother, falling to his knees as he dragged the queen into his lap. Theresa's dressing gown was more crimson than white now, and her breath came in ragged little gasps. Her face, however, was calm.

"Josef," she whispered. "Listen."

"Stop talking," he said, pressing one hand against her wound as he slid his free arm under her. "We're going to get you to the surgeon."

"No," she ordered, grabbing his hand with surprising strength. "For once in your life, mind me."

Josef froze, letting his mother guide his hand up to her face.

"Listen," she said again. "You've never made a secret of how much you hated being a prince, and for that I've tried my best to spare you, but now I'm afraid we no longer have a choice." She took a shuddering breath. "The throne of Osera has endured for centuries. Through our history we have lived as outcasts and pirates, shunned by all. I spent my life pulling us out of that pit, turning Osera into a land of prosperity and peace. Now the Empress comes again, and now more than ever we *cannot* fall. Promise me, Josef. Promise, no matter what happens after, no matter your feelings, you will take the crown and lead our people through this crisis."

Josef gripped her hand. "Mother, this isn't—"

"*Promise me*," the queen gasped, pulling herself up until her face was inches from her son's. "One last battle," she whispered, clutching his fingers. "Swear to me you will not let Osera perish."

Josef pressed his lips to her pale forehead. "I swear, mother," he whispered. "I swear it."

The queen fell back with a pained sigh. "You are all witnesses," she said, glancing at her guard. When they nodded, she turned back to Josef, reaching up to touch his cheek with her thin, bloody hand.

"Hail the House of Iron Lions," she whispered, her voice little more than a breath.

"Hail the House of Iron Lions," Josef repeated. "I will not fail you, mother."

For a moment, Eli thought he saw the queen smile. Then her body shuddered one last time, and she lay still.

The guards began to creep forward, but Josef didn't move. He sat on his knees, cradling his mother's skeletal body. He made no sound, no noise at all, but when the light shifted, Eli saw his cheeks were wet, and he realized Josef was crying. He looked away at once, painfully aware that he was seeing something he shouldn't. But the moment was just that, a moment, and by the time he'd turned away, it was over.

"You there," Josef said to the closest guard.

The guard stepped forward with a salute, and Josef stood up, bringing his mother's body with him. "Take the queen," he said, gently passing Theresa's body to the guard. "See that she is laid in state."

"Yes, majesty," the guard said softy, taking the queen as gently as he could.

Josef stepped back, his hands lingering on the dark stain that covered the front of his shirt, though whether it was his blood or his mother's, Eli couldn't tell.

"You." Josef looked at the next guard. "Bring someone to clean that up." He nodded at Lenette's body. "The rest of you, I want whoever's in charge of the military to report to the watchtower at once. Every man who can hold a sword is to report for duty immediately."

"Everyone, sir?" the guard said.

"Yes," Josef answered, scooping up the Heart as he marched down the hall. "The Empress is here. We're going to avenge our queen."

The guards looked at each other, their faces pale with disbelief. Then, in unison, they saluted and began to divide the prince's orders between them.

Eli watched them work for a second, and then he jogged after Josef.

"You're serious about this?"

"I made a promise," Josef said, walking faster. "I intend to see it through."

"All right," Eli said softly. "But if it's war we're talking about, I should point out that we have a problem."

Josef sighed. "What?"

"The Relay," Eli said. "Adela destroyed both of Osera's points. I don't know if you had a chance during all that to actually look at the ocean, but the Empress's fleet fills the horizon. There's no way Osera can stop all that on its own. If we're going to survive, we have to get word to the Council immediately for reinforcements."

"That's not a problem," Nico said.

Eli glanced at her. "Pardon?"

"We've got a Council representative following us."

Everyone stopped and looked at Tesset.

"What a remarkably good point, Nico," Eli said, all smiles.

315

"Don't get your hopes up," Tesset said. "I don't have a Relay point on me."

Eli blinked. "That's a bad joke, sir. You want me to believe that Sara let you loose without an ear in your pocket?"

"Relay points are short these days," Tesset said with a shrug. "And I *was* going to a country that had two points of its own."

"Well, that's just perfect," Josef grumbled, resuming his previous pace. "A Council watchdog with none of the benefits."

"You should be counting your luck," Tesset said, falling into step beside him. "I did just watch a known conspirator of the world's most notorious thief become king of Osera without comment, after all."

"Flattery will get you everywhere," Eli said. "But outing us would have hurt your cause too, so don't pretend you're doing us a favor. If you actually want to be useful, you could think of a way for us to get word to the mainland."

Tesset scratched his chin. "What about the Spirit Court? Osera has a Tower just like anywhere, and Spiritualists are always talking among themselves."

Eli looked at him, genuinely impressed. "That is a surprisingly good suggestion," he said. "To think, the Spirit Court, useful at last!"

By this time they'd reached the back door of the palace. A crowd of guards was waiting in the kitchen yard, whispering nervously as they stared down the mountain at the fleet stretching across the horizon.

"You," Eli said, grabbing the closest solider. "Would you be so kind as to fetch us Osera's Spiritualist?"

The guard stared at him in confusion. "Sir?"

"Do it," Josef snapped.

The guard, obviously not sure if the traitor prince's orders should be obeyed, took one look at Josef's bloody front and enormous sword and decided to save his doubts for later. He bowed and ran down the hall as fast as his legs could carry him, pausing only to salute the admiral as the old man appeared from another door flanked by the queen's guards who'd witnessed her death.

"Prince Thereson," the admiral said, falling to his knees at Josef's feet. "My king, I just heard. Forgive me for insulting you with my suspicions."

"Get up," Josef sighed. "We don't have time for this."

"Yes, my lord," the admiral said, standing.

"What's our situation?"

"Not good," the admiral said. "I've sent fast ships to all the villages and the bells should be ringing any moment now to summon the sailors to their posts. With any luck, the runners will be ready to sail within the hour, but without clingfire, I don't know—"

A great jangling racket of bells drowned out the rest of his report. More bells followed, until the entire city shook with the clanging sound.

"We'll cross that bridge when we get there," Josef shouted as a military carriage pulled up through the palace's eastern gate. "What about the guard?"

The admiral's face paled. "When the princess turned traitor, she killed out the barracks. The sergeant…"

"Beechum, sir," the closest guard put in.

"Beechum," the admiral said. "He's taking the body count as we speak, but it may be a while before we know how many guardsmen are still in service."

"Why so long?" Josef said as he climbed into the carriage.

"If I may, sir," the guard said, holding the carriage door as Eli, Nico, and the admiral climbed in after Josef. "The princess was our captain like Theresa was our queen. She raised most of us up from the city guard, and we were loyal to her like none other. Some of the men still don't believe she betrayed us. If I hadn't seen the queen's death with my own eyes…"

"She was certainly thorough in her treachery," Josef muttered, leaning out the tiny window. "Just tell the sergeant to send whatever guards he can down to the storm wall. Meanwhile, I want the city watch to start moving people toward the

317

western docks. Get them as far from the east coast as you can. I want Osera empty if war spirits start falling."

"Yes, sire," the guard said, saluting.

Josef saluted back, and the carriage pulled away with a lurch, leaving the guard to deliver the king's orders.

"I can't see how she could have put us in a worse position," the admiral said, rubbing a handkerchief across his ashy face as the carriage rattled out into the street. "The queen, the clingfire, and now the guard in shambles. She certainly knew where to hit us."

"Adela always was good at her job," Josef said quietly.

The admiral went paler still and kept any other opinions to himself.

The storm wall was crawling with sailors by the time they arrived. The man made way for the carriage, and the driver pulled them right up to the tower door. The admiral led Josef and his companions up the stairs, calling for his captains as they went. When they reached the top of the watchtower, Eli was pleased to see that the bodies from earlier had been removed. The stains on the wood floor remained, however. A grisly reminder.

"Right," Eli said, surveying the room and the commanding view of the sea. "This will be our headquarters. Can we get a map of the coastline?"

The admiral jerked. "I don't take orders from—"

"Eli's with me," Josef said firmly.

The admiral dropped his eyes. "Yes, majesty."

Eli smiled as the admiral turned and started toward the steps. "And don't forget my Spiritualist!"

The old admiral's shoulders twitched, but he nodded as he disappeared down the stairs.

"I could get used to this," Eli said, but Josef wasn't listening. He was standing at the window, his face pale as he stared at the now clearly visible line of ships on the horizon.

"Surely the master of the Heart of War is not afraid of death," Tesset said, stepping up beside him.

"Not mine," Josef whispered as the admiral returned with soldiers bearing tables and maps, which they set up under Eli's direction.

Thirty minutes later, news of the queen's death had spread throughout the city. Surprisingly, this seemed to calm the panic spurred by Josef's fight with Adela. Whatever his faults, Josef was an Eisenlowe, and with news of the princess's betrayal and the Empress's arrival spreading fast, having a murderer as a king suddenly didn't seem so bad. Riders moved constantly back and forth between the bay and the palace, bringing Josef reports. The royal guard had recovered faster than the admiral had estimated. Adela's betrayal had caught them hardest of all. Of the two hundred men once under the princess's command, half were now dead by her hand. This had galvanized the hundred that remained, however, and they marched to the coast to put themselves under Josef's command.

Men from the city were pouring down the mountain as well, answering the call of the bells to defend their homeland. They gathered on the storm wall, accepting their orders from the captains with stern-faced determination. Eli watched from the tower, impressed. He'd expected a riot, or at least more panic, but the people of Osera seemed to be handling the wave of change that had crashed into their kingdom by focusing on the one thing that was still the same—defending their home against the Empress.

The captains were dividing the crowd into crews when a carriage pulled onto the storm wall. A few minutes later, a guard poked his head into the watchtower and announced that Eli's Spiritualist had arrived.

"Excellent," Eli said. "Show him in."

The guard opened the door for an elderly man whose elegant jacket was cut short at the sleeves to show off his four large, jeweled rings. He stepped into the tower and stopped, casting disdainful looks at the soldiers huddled around the maps, particularly Josef.

319

"Spiritualist," Eli said, shaking his hand. "How nice to meet you."

"It's Tower Keeper," the old man said with a sniff, snatching his hand back. "Who are you? I was told the king wanted me."

"The king doesn't deal with 'wizard things,'" Eli said with a smile. "He leaves those to me."

He glanced pointedly down at Eli's empty fingers. "And again I say, who are you?"

"We have a bit of a crisis on our hands here," Eli said, ignoring the question. "I need you to send a message to Zarin."

"Why?" the Tower Keeper said suspiciously. "What's wrong with the Relay?"

"I've heard that Spiritualists have their own way of communicating with Zarin," Eli said. "*Outside* the Relay."

"Yes," the old man said testily. "They're called letters."

"I'm not talking about *letters*," Eli said. "I'm talking about emergency messages." He stopped and looked around pointedly, lowering his voice to a conspiratorial whisper. "Look, chum, the Relay's down and the Empress is about to fall on us like a hammer. We need to call for reinforcements immediately."

"The Relay, down..." The Tower Keeper's lined face turned ashy. "Powers, man, why didn't you call the Council earlier?"

"If we could have, we would have," Eli said. "If you Spiritualists have something up your sleeves, now's the time to show it."

"And I'm telling you we use letters!" the Tower Keeper cried. "An express courier switching horses can get a letter to Zarin in a day."

Eli stared at him. "You're kidding. The great and mighty Spirit Court uses *couriers*? That's *it*? What about wind spirits?"

"Wind spirits?" the Tower Keeper said, aghast. "Do you know anything about wizardry? There aren't five Spiritualists in the Court who've bound wind spirits. It's not like I'm just keeping one in my pocket."

Eli leaned back with a groan. "Please don't tell me I had it good with Miranda."

"Miranda?" The Tower Keeper jerked as though he'd stepped in something. "Lyonette? How do you know Banage's favorite?"

"I can hardly seem to avoid her," Eli said, ears perking up. "But why so bitter, Mr. Tower Keeper?"

"Bitter?" The man drew himself up to his full height. "Hardly, sir. Say what you like about our letters, but you're the one out of touch if you haven't heard that Banage's turned traitor. He refused to help the Council fight the Empress and shut himself up in the Tower. I imagine Lyonette is in there with him, along with all the other traitors."

Eli paused for a moment. "That is actually very interesting," he said finally. "And not entirely surprising." He sighed loudly. "Well, Mr. Tower Keeper, I'm afraid I've wasted your time. Thank you very much for coming. I'm sure someone will show you out."

The Tower Keeper looked at Eli with utter confusion, but Eli just turned him around by the shoulder and pushed him toward the soldiers. "See he gets home safely!"

The soldiers saluted and began to escort the Tower Keeper down the stairs. The old man recovered his wits about three steps in and began protesting loudly that the prince had sent for him personally. That was all Eli heard before the door slammed shut.

He caught Josef's eye and motioned him over.

Josef nodded to the admiral and stepped away from the map, joining Eli by the window. "Well?"

"No dice," Eli said. "I keep forgetting what a gulf in power there can be between Spiritualists."

"What about a broker?" Josef said. "They talk to each other, right?"

"Actually, that's a phenomenal idea," Eli said. "I never thought of using a broker to *send* information instead of finding it." He thought for a few seconds and then shook his head. "If we had more time I'd try it, but brokers go to ground when trouble comes, and I'm not about to waste the few hours we have trying to root one out now."

"What about Nico?" Josef said. "She can jump there."

"Who'd believe the Daughter of the Dead Mountain?" Eli said, biting his lip. "There's nothing for it. I'm just going to have to send a message myself."

"You?" Josef snorted. "If people won't believe Nico, they'll never believe you."

Eli held up his hands. "I admit, aside from you and Nico, there are very few people who know me well enough to know when I'm being sincere, and of those people, only one has the power to bring the kind of help we need. Fortunately, thanks to our guest, I have a pretty good idea where she is."

Josef gave him a horrified look. "You can't be serious."

"Normally I'd agree," Eli said. "But today is a serious sort of day. You worry about all that king nonsense. I'll take care of this."

Josef shook his head. "Just don't mess it up."

"Do I ever?" Eli said, but Josef was already walking back to his map.

Eli arched an eyebrow at the king's back and went to look for Nico. He found her deep in conversation with Tesset, of all people. He approached silently, hoping to catch a snatch of whatever it was they were talking about, but his efforts were fruitless. Both of them fell silent before he was close enough to hear anything.

She walked over when he beckoned. "Spiritualist didn't work?"

"Not at all," Eli said, glancing over her shoulder at Tesset, who was watching them. "What were you and the Council man talking about?"

"I was thanking him," Nico said. "His advice was very useful."

"Advice?" Eli said curiously. "What kind of advice?"

"Good advice," Nico said in a tone that signaled the end of that part of the conversation.

For once, Eli took the hint. "Glad to hear it. Now, I was hoping you could do a little repeat of our exercise earlier today. I need another wind."

"That's easy," Nico said. "They've been swarming ever since you talked to the first one. I think they want a wizard indebted to them as well."

"Really?" Eli grimaced. He hated owing favors, and winds were impossible to escape, but he had little choice at the moment. "Can you pick me out a fast one?"

Nico stared up at the afternoon sky for a moment before her hand shot out, pointing at something just above the horizon. "There."

Eli popped the latch on the window, opening it just enough to stick his hand out. He opened his spirit a crack as well, sending out a beckoning tendril of power. A few seconds later, a strong breeze rushed over his face.

"My," the wind whispered. "Aren't you a bright one? Are you the wizard making deals?"

"I am," Eli said. "And do I have a deal for you. How fast can you fly to Zarin?"

"Where?" the wind said.

"Large city," Eli said. "West of here on the mainland, white buildings, river through the middle?"

"Oh, there." The wind circled around them. "Fast enough, if I have reason to hurry. Why?"

"I need you to take a message to the Spirit Court."

"That'll cost you," the wind huffed. "Spiritualists can be pompous."

"That they can," Eli said. "But a powerful, clever wind can make them listen, I'm sure."

"Of course," the wind said. "If the price is right."

"Friend," Eli said, leaning into the breeze. "Today's your lucky day."

The wind rushed away from the watchtower feeling extremely pleased with itself. For being a gullible sap, the bright wizard certainly knew how to sweeten a deal. The promise of a personal debt from the human who'd freed Mellinor was a prize indeed, and all for passing on a few words. Plus, he'd been so nice looking, so bright. The wind spun in a circle. It wasn't every day you met a wizard like that.

By this point, the wind had cleared the strip of ocean between the island and the mainland. It dipped on the warm air, readying itself for the straight push overland to the white city with the tall towers. But as the wind turned west, it jerked to a stop, frozen in the air. For five long seconds the wind hovered, completely unable to move, and then it curled in a deep bow.

"All hail the lord of the west."

The air flickered as the West Wind suddenly filled the sky, his breezes reaching as far as the wind could see. "Where are you off to in such a hurry, little wind?"

"Zarin," the wind answered, trembling against the West Wind's hold. "I promised a wizard I would bring a message to Spiritualist Miranda Lyonette."

"I see," Illir said. "And the wizard who gave you this message, he was a bright wizard, was he not?"

"The brightest I have ever seen, my lord," the wind whispered.

"Thought so," Illir said. "Very well, give me the message. I will deliver it."

The wind hesitated. "But," it whispered. "My deal—"

"Nothing *that* wizard promises ever comes out as you would like," Illir said. "I'm taking the message. Give it to me and you will have my high regard."

"Yes, Lord Illir," the wind whispered, trembling as it repeated the bright wizard's words.

"Thank you," Illir said, freeing the little wind with a toss of his gale. "You may go."

"Yes, my lord," the wind whispered, bowing. "Thank you, my lord."

But Illir was already gone, flying across the sky with the impossible speed only the greatest winds could dream of. With a great sigh, the little wind sped away to brag to its brothers about how Illir himself had stopped just for it, the wizard's deal already forgotten.

CHAPTER
19

After ten hours of sleep, a bath, and an enormous breakfast, Miranda was a new woman, and the first thing she'd done with her newfound energy was attack the restricted shelves of the Spirit Court archives. She'd spent all morning reading spectacular stories of Spiritualists doing the impossible—talking down erupting volcanoes, brokering peace between warring rivers, even ending a five-year drought by freeing a wind spirit whose capture by an Enslaver had so angered the wind courts that they'd held off the rain in retaliation. There was even a description of the meeting four hundred years ago between the first Rector of the Spirit Court and the Shaper Mountain that had led to the raising of the Spirit Court's Tower in a single day. The actual deed the Tower was in thanks for had been carefully omitted, but Miranda's frustration was soothed by the dozens of secrets that hadn't been crossed out.

For someone who'd given her life to the Court, it was breathtaking reading. It was also infuriating. All of the restricted reports dealt in one way or another with a star. Of course, they were never *called* stars, but now that Miranda knew what she was looking for, it was easy enough to read through the sometimes excruciatingly vague language and find the truth. The Spirit Court had encountered stars numerous times over centuries of enforcing the good treatment of spirits, but every time the real nature of these greater than Great Spirits had been hushed up and locked away in the archives. It was enough to make Miranda grind her teeth to stubs.

"I don't understand," she said, yet again. "What's the point of hiding this? If we were only taught about stars, told these stories...Look here, the great river Ell that runs through the southern kingdoms is a star. All that time we spent two years ago badgering the Felltris River to flood the fields and not the houses? Wasted. We could have solved the whole thing with one trip down to the southern delta to chat with the river all the others have to listen to."

Gin flattened his ears against his head with a whine. "Can you *please* stop talking about stars? You're going to get us all in trouble."

"*In trouble with whom?*" Miranda said, slamming down the report and spinning around in her chair.

Gin looked away.

"You mean the Shep—"

"Stop," Gin growled, lashing his tail. "Don't say her name. It attracts her attention."

"Fine with me," Miranda said, crossing her arms. "There are several things I want to ask her."

"Get in line," Mellinor rumbled bitterly. "But if the Shepherdess could be appealed to, I wouldn't have spent four centuries locked in a pillar of salt."

"Mellinor," Gin said in a warning tone.

"No," Mellinor said. "I don't care if it's forbidden to speak of the Shepherdess's business with humans. The Shaper Mountain already broke the edicts. Why should we bother keeping them?"

"The Shaper Mountain is one of the oldest spirits in the world," Gin said. "He's also the biggest. He can afford to take risks."

"So can we," Miranda said firmly. "Slorn said the Shaper Mountain showed us the truth for a reason."

Gin snorted. "Yes, because the mountain knows you're ignorant. The old rock pile wants you to take the fall for asking questions spirits shouldn't ask."

"What do you mean?"

The ghosthound sighed. "There are things that it's better not to know, Miranda. And just because some great mountain and his pet bear man are fed up with the Shepherdess's antics doesn't mean you should go putting yourself in danger."

326

"If the Shepherdess isn't doing what she should, then I have to take action, danger or no," Miranda snapped. "I'm sworn to protect the spirits."

"Good," Gin snapped back. "So do that. Kill Enslavers, stop abusive wizards, but don't go poking your nose where it'll get bitten off."

Miranda turned away with a huff. Gin crouched low, his swirling fur moving in quick little patterns, and Mellinor began to rumble.

"Listen," she said, calmly now. "Whatever happens from here out, I'm always going to choose the path that leads to a better, fairer world for all of us. That's my job. That's why I became a Spiritualist. And if that path leads me off a cliff, then so be it, but I will not turn back. If you don't like it, you don't have to follow."

Gin bared his teeth. "Don't even try," he growled. "I go where you go, no matter how reckless or stupid. But that doesn't mean I have to keep my mouth shut about it."

Miranda couldn't help grinning at that. "Nothing could make you keep your mouth shut, mutt."

Gin snorted and put his head on his paws. "Better put away your reading. Someone's coming."

Miranda glanced at the door a split second before the knock sounded. Gin gave her a superior look, and Miranda rolled her eyes. She stood up, carefully marking her place before closing the record book, and walked to the reading room door. A young man in apprentice robes was standing on the other side. His face lit up when he saw her.

"Spiritualist Lyonette? Master Banage wants to see you at the top of the Tower. He says it's urgent."

"The top of the Tower?" Miranda said, wrinkling her nose. "You mean his office?"

"No, ma'am," the apprentice said, shaking his head. "He said the top."

"The top?" Gin said, suddenly behind her. He grinned, showing a wall of teeth. "I've never been to the top."

327

"Neither have I," Miranda said, elbowing her dog. The apprentice was staring at Gin's teeth like he might faint. "Take us there."

"Yes, Spiritualist," the boy said, starting down the hall sideways so he wouldn't have to put his back to Gin. "This way."

Miranda shook her head and followed. Behind her, Gin crawled through the door, slipping his long body through the small opening with practiced ease. They climbed up and up, past floors of meeting rooms, guest rooms, and storerooms, until they reached the landing outside the Rector's office. This was where the stairs usually ended, but now there was a new opening in the wall beside the Rector's office door, a set of stairs Miranda had never seen before, leading up.

"We can make it from here," she said, smiling at the apprentice. "Thank you for your service."

"It is an honor to serve, Spiritualist," the boy said with a halfhearted bow. After a final, terrified glance at Gin, he vanished down the stairs like a frightened rabbit.

"That one knows his place," Gin said, flipping his tail smugly.

"Stop it," Miranda muttered, starting up the new stairwell. "You'd better stay here."

Gin growled and sat, ears turned forward so he wouldn't miss anything.

The new stairs wound up for a dozen feet before stopping at a little stone door barely larger than she was. It opened when Miranda touched it, and a blast of wind nearly blew her back down the stairs. The door let out on the very top of the Tower's spire. Below, she could see all of Zarin and the plains beyond. The white buildings were almost blinding in the afternoon sun, and the Whitefall River was little more than a glittering thread between the dark shapes of the bridges and barges. The wind roared around her, and for a moment Miranda was afraid it would blow her off altogether. Thankfully, the door was set back in the Tower's spire, and the tiny alcove provided just enough shelter to keep the wind from ripping her off the Tower. Master Banage was already here, standing with his back pressed against the stone and his head tilted up toward the sky.

"Miranda," he said in a voice that carried over the wind. "Glad you could join us."

The moment he said it, Miranda felt the truth. The wind howling around them wasn't the usual gusts found this high up. There was a familiar heaviness to it, a great spiritual pressure that made her ears pop, and she didn't need Eril's frantic clamor to know who, or what, she was facing.

"Lord Illir," she said, clutching her wind spirit's shaking pendant against her chest. "It is a pleasure to meet you again."

"Pleasure tainted with crisis, I'm afraid," the wind hummed around her. "Let the little one pay his respects before he bursts."

Miranda let Eril fly at once. The smaller wind tore out of his necklace, spinning in a reverent circle before returning to Miranda's side.

She exchanged a brief look with Master Banage, and then the Rector Spiritualis stepped out a fraction and addressed the wind. "Lord of the West, Miranda Lyonette is here, as you asked. Now, how may we help you?"

"I bring a message," the great wind said. "From Osera."

That threw Miranda. Who in Osera could use one of the four great winds as a messenger?

"The Immortal Empress has arrived," the wind continued. "Her ships will reach Osera by evening, if not sooner. War is here."

Miranda and Banage exchanged a wide-eyed look, and then Miranda looked toward the Council's citadel. It looked the same as ever—no panic, no surge of troops.

"They don't know," the wind said, answering her question before she could ask it. "And they won't, unless you tell them. Osera's Relay points were destroyed by a traitor on the inside. That is why I've come." There was a shift in air pressure as the wind turned to focus on Banage. "I know you have declared that your Court will not enter the human's war, but I am here to ask you, on behalf of all spirits on this continent, not to let the Empress land on this shore."

For the first time in all their years together, Miranda saw Master Banage look completely bewildered.

"How do you know..." he said, and then shook his head. "Never mind. Why do you care what human rules this land? The Court will always look after you no matter who calls themselves Merchant Prince or Empress."

"You don't understand," the wind rumbled. "If the Immortal Empress were only human, I would agree with you. But she is more, far more."

Banage scowled. "What do you mean 'more'?"

"I cannot tell you," the wind said. "It is forbidden, even for me."

Miranda frowned. Forbidden? Even for a spirit as great as the West Wind? But as she tried to puzzle out what Illir meant by that, the wind shifted and grew colder. Suddenly, she could smell cold stone, snow, and thin high air. The smell of the mountain filled her lungs, and everything came together.

"The Empress is a star."

"What?" Banage turned to her. "Impossible. The Empress is human."

"Humans are spirits as well," the wind said. "And the Empress is not called Immortal for show."

The blood drained from the Rector's face. "Then the obedience I saw?" he whispered. "The war spirit's devotion?"

"Any devotion you saw is the result of the obedience stars command," the wind said. "She is no Enslaver, so I doubt you would feel anything wrong, but the truth of her control is almost worse. Enslavers are human. They can be defeated. They can die. But the Empress is immortal, her life held sacred by the White Lady. Her control over the spirit world is complete, eternal, and inescapable. To disobey a star is to disobey the Shepherdess herself."

The West Wind grew cold enough to make Miranda shiver.

"The Empress comes here to bring the whole world under her control, but I am the West Wind. I am freedom itself. The winds have no star; we have no need of one. It is not our nature to serve, but if the Empress comes here, we won't have a choice. Nothing will. So I am asking you as a spirit, as the voice of all spirits on this continent who as yet have no idea of what they are about to lose, fight the Empress."

"How?" Miranda said. "My spirits couldn't go against the Shaper Mountain even to set me free. What can we do against the Empress?"

"Your spirits could not," the wind said. "But you are different. Even a star cannot change the laws of magic. Immortal though she may be, the Empress is still human, and no human spirit can force another. That's why she needs an army to beat her human opponents the old-fashioned way, and that's why you humans are the only ones who can stop her and save us."

Miranda looked at Banage, but he was gripping the Tower wall, his face deathly pale. "How could I have been so mistaken?" he whispered. "All this time I thought spirits obeyed the Empress out of love and respect, as our spirits obey us."

"That is our own fault," the wind said. "We are forbidden from speaking of the stars to humans. It is the Shepherdess's will that you stay ignorant. Really, I shouldn't even be talking to you, but the secret's already out, told by a star, no less."

"Wait," Miranda said. "The Shaper Mountain told you about us?"

"No," the wind said coyly. "But I always find out. The wind is everywhere, Miranda. You should know that by now."

"Our path is clear," Banage said, straightening up. "We must fight. Star or not, the Empress is human. Though she's not technically an Enslaver, I think we can all agree that controlling spirits by force is an abuse the Court cannot tolerate."

"We must warn the Council and get down there as soon as

we can," Miranda said, looking up at Illir. "You said she was landing in Osera?"

"Yes," the wind said. "And precious little stands in her way."

"Then we will ride at once," Banage said.

"Hurry," the wind whispered.

"Wait!" Miranda cried as the wind turned. "Why did you not ask our help earlier?"

"I could not," the wind sighed. "All spirits are forbidden from interfering in a star's affairs by order of the Shepherdess. The Shaper Mountain might have told you about stars, but talking about them and asking for help in fending one off are entirely different matters. Were it not for this message, or, more correctly, for the wizard who sent it, I couldn't have asked your help in this at all."

Banage scowled. "What wizard is powerful enough to command you to break the Shepherdess's law?"

The wind turned, and Miranda got the feeling it was smiling. "I believe you call him Eli Monpress."

The tower fell utterly silent. Miranda and Banage stood stunned, unable to speak, and the wind used this gap to make his exit. As the pressure of the Great Spirit faded, Miranda clenched her hands into angry fists.

"Always," she muttered. "I swear, he's always at the center of everything that goes wrong in the world."

"It doesn't matter," Banage said quietly, running his hands over his face. "We have to get to Osera."

"At least the Council will be with us now," Miranda said. "If we're going to fight the Empress, then we have no more quarrel with Whitefall."

"I fear it's too late for that," Banage said. "Look down."

Confused, Miranda grabbed the wall and leaned out, peeking over the Tower's edge. It was a terrifying view. She'd never really appreciated how tall the Tower was until she was looking straight down it with nothing but her own grip for an anchor. Still, it wasn't the height that made her flinch back.

Directly below, the Spirit Court's district was no longer

empty. Soldiers in Council white circled the Tower on every side. There had to be a quarter legion of infantry down there with another squad of archers on the rooftops to back them up. But worse than the soldiers was the line of wagons set up across the main boulevard and watched over by a small figure standing beside a man wearing a pink coat so vivid Miranda could see it from the Tower's peak.

"Sara," she hissed, leaning back.

Banage nodded. "They've been setting up since shortly after dawn. Apparently, Whitefall has decided he cannot afford to harbor traitors."

"But we haven't done anything except sit here!" Miranda cried.

"We," Banage stopped. "*I* refused to help. Whitefall's played the game of nations long enough to know that those who won't be allies will eventually be enemies. He's taking us out early rather than risk us at his back while he's fighting the Empress."

"What are we going to do?" Miranda said. "We have to get to Osera. *They* have to get to Osera, while there's still an Osera to get to."

"Then we'll have to hope they'll listen to reason," Banage said.

Miranda bit her lip. "I hate to say this, master, but they're never going to believe you've changed your mind."

"They'd also never believe I'd tell a lie to save my skin," Banage said. "Being intractable has its advantages as well as its pitfalls."

Miranda gaped at him in disbelief. "Master Banage," she whispered. "Was that a joke?"

Banage looked almost affronted. "I have been known to tell them on occasion," he said, starting down the stairs. "Come, we don't have time to stand around with our mouths open."

Shaking her head in wonder, Miranda hurried down the stairs after her master as the Rector Spiritualis called for the Tower to spread the word. The Spirit Court was going to war.

* * *

"How much longer does Myron mean to make us wait?" Sara grumbled, trailing smoke as she stalked back and forth in front of her wagon. "He has an entire city full of soldiers. How long can it take to surround one tower?"

"I think the good general is dragging his feet on purpose," Sparrow said, buttoning his garish pink coat against the wind. "He doesn't care much for wizard business, after all."

"And I don't care for standing around," Sara snarled. "We were supposed to crack the Tower at ten. It's nearly noon."

"Well, here's your chance to tell him yourself," Sparrow said, nodding at the knot of armored men riding toward them.

Sara turned and marched toward the riders, biting her pipe as the leader, Myron Whitefall, the Council's general, dismounted.

"Are you done wasting my time?" she cried over the clatter of the horses.

"Only if you're done wasting mine," Myron answered. "I have a war to prepare for, Sara. The Empress could arrive as early as next month. I don't have men to waste on your marital spats."

Sara lifted her chin. "Try fighting the Empress without the wizards that I'm going to get by cracking this Tower and then say that again, Myron."

Myron's reply was predictably nasty, but Sara wasn't listening anymore. Sparrow had touched her arm. She turned, and her eyes widened. "I don't believe it."

"What?" Myron snapped. "That you're a waste of Council resources and—"

His voice sputtered out as Sara hurried away. She ran to the front of her wagons and stopped, watching in amazement as the blank face of the Tower peeled open like a curl of shaved wood and Banage himself stepped out into the sunlight. He was dressed in a dark suit with the great gold and jeweled mantle of the Tower on his shoulders. Bow strings creaked as the Council archers trained their arrows at his chest, but Banage paid them no mind. He just stood there, glaring defiantly at Sara with his arms crossed over his chest.

"I'd never believe it if I wasn't seeing it myself," Sara said, grinning around her pipe. "Have you come to your senses at last, Etmon?"

"I never took leave of them, Sara," Banage answered, glancing at the gathered troops in disdain. "Unlike some."

"That's enough, traitor!" Myron shouted, recovering at last. "You have exactly three seconds to surrender before—"

Sara rolled right over him. "What brings you out of your little spire? I can't believe you're giving up."

Banage straightened. "You can't 'give up' being right, Sara. But the situation is no longer what it was." He reached out his arm, pointing east with one ring-covered finger. "The Empress has arrived. She is about to attack Osera, if she hasn't already."

"Are you mad?" Sara laughed. "We've heard nothing of the sort."

"You wouldn't," Banage said. "Both of Osera's Relay points were broken this morning, just before the ships appeared."

Never taking her eyes off Banage, Sara reached down, sorting through her pouch for the two orbs that controlled Osera's Relays. She brushed each of them with her spirit, probing the connection. But her prod faded off into nothing. There was no echo, no reply.

Her mouth pressed into a thin line against the narrow stem of her pipe. "It seems the Rector is right," she said slowly.

"That's impossible!" Myron shouted, stomping up to stand beside her at last. "We heard the Empress shipyards were reactivated only a week ago. Even if she'd sailed that day, there's no way the Empress could have a fleet here so quickly. It's a bluff!"

"He doesn't bluff," Sara said with a sigh. "But even if you're right, and the Empress *is* about to attack, it doesn't explain what you're doing out, Etmon. The whole reason I'm standing here is because you swore up and down that your Court would never go to war."

Banage stiffened. "We have our reasons, Sara. Unfortunately, I am not at liberty to share them. You will remove your troops and let us pass. There is no time to waste."

"Enough," Myron said. "Do you think just because you've decided to fight that you can do as you please? The Merchant Prince's order is still in effect. The Spirit Court is under the control of the Council. You'll do as we tell you."

"The Spirit Court obeys no laws but its own," Banage said, his voice deepening as the mantle on his shoulders began to glow. "Step aside, General."

As he spoke, the ground began to rumble. All across Zarin, buildings began to shake. Windows rattled against their panes and awnings rippled like water above the merchant stands. Down on the river, barges rocked and bumped together. Even the Whitefall Citadel was shaking, its golden-roofed towers trembling in the sunlight.

Back at the Spirit Court's tower, the Council soldiers gripped their swords, bracing their feet against the shaking ground. Myron grabbed Sara's wagon, his face as pale as cheese. Sara smacked his hand away, blowing out a huff of smoke.

"Enough dramatics, Etmon," she said. "Myron, move your troops and let them through."

Myron gaped at her. "What? You can't be—"

"Do it," Sara said.

The general's face went from pale to scarlet, but Sara cut off his tirade before it could start. "*Now*, Myron. That mantle of his is tied to the great bedrock spirit that runs below Zarin. He can destroy this city in a heartbeat if he wants to. I'm not about to risk that to keep him from doing what we were trying to make him do in the first place."

"But, Sara," Myron's voice was almost pleading. "He could be lying."

"He's not lying," Sara said.

Myron snarled. "How do you know that?"

"Because the world's not ending," Sara said with a sigh. "Move your men, Myron. That's an order."

She smacked her closest wagon, and it began to trundle out of the way. The other wagons followed, each wheeling itself over to the side of the road. Myron sputtered a moment before turning on his heel, waving for his men to follow. As the Council soldiers reluctantly cleared a path, the shaking stopped. Banage stepped back into the Tower, and Sara peered through the hole to see him removing his heavy gold mantle. She arched an eyebrow as he handed the gem-studded chain of his office to old Krigel before stepping out of sight.

When the road was clear, Banage came out again. With a final glare at Sara, he held out his hand. The heavy ring on his middle finger flashed dark green, and his enormous jade horse erupted out of the ground beside him. It knelt so Banage could climb onto its back. The moment he was seated, the Spirit Court rode out. They flashed down the street, Banage first on his jade horse followed by Miranda on her ghosthound. The dog snapped at Sparrow as they passed, but Sparrow looked more amused than frightened as he leaned out of the way. They were gone in an instant, replaced by more Spiritualists, apprentices, Tower Keepers, journeymen, everyone in the stone spire who'd ever sworn an oath. Sara sucked on her pipe, more interested than ever. Whatever caused this change of heart, it was deathly serious if Banage was emptying the Tower.

The Spiritualists thundered down the street and vanished into the city at full speed, riding east as fast as they could. The soldiers watched in awe as the wizards rode by, keeping well out of the way of the sand tigers, stone snakes, and, of course, the ghosthound. When the last Spiritualist was out of sight, Myron turned to Sara.

"What do we do now?" he asked, his voice uncharacteristically bewildered.

"Well," Sara said, tapping out her pipe. "*You* had better get on those Relay points I've been giving you and start ordering the Council fleet to Osera. You should probably also warn Alber that the Empress is running ahead of schedule."

"And what are you going to do?" Myron said, his face pale.

Sara just smiled and walked away. She snapped her fingers as she went, and with each snap, a wagon rolled out. Sparrow jumped onto the driver's seat of the largest and lowered his hand to Sara. She took it, and he pulled her up. The moment her feet left the ground, the wagons tore off down the road, following the trail of dust left by the Spiritualists until they too vanished into the city.

Myron Whitefall stood staring for several moments. Finally, he turned and began shouting for his Relays. Within the hour, the news had spread across the continent. The Empress had arrived. The Council was going to war.

CHAPTER
20

Josef Liechten, king of Osera for nearly two hours, stood at the watchtower window. Eli stood beside him, watching the sea with an uncharacteristically serious expression on his face. He'd finally ditched the ridiculous blond wig, and even his hair looked subdued after so many days of being pinned down.

"Not you too," Josef grumbled, glancing at his friend. "If you're looking gloomy I might start thinking we really are doomed."

"Well," Eli said softly. "That *is* a lot of ships."

Josef looked back at the sea. "That it is."

The Empress's armada stretched from horizon to horizon. Black ships, each the size of a small city, rode deep and heavy in the water. Their sides were like cliffs, rising a hundred feet above the ocean's surface. Their masts were great towers, and their decks swarmed with countless men in black armor. Josef swallowed. He'd seen paintings of the Empress's ships before, but nothing could have prepared him for their true size. For the first time in his life, he understood why they were called palace ships.

"Majesty?"

Josef looked to see the admiral standing in the door. "The fleet is ready, sir."

"Good," Josef said. He turned to go, but stopped again as Eli's hand closed on his wrist.

"Are you sure about this?" Eli whispered.

"Doesn't matter," Josef said. "If even one of those ships makes landfall, we'll be overrun. Our only hope is to sink them before they reach the shore. The real question is, are you sure you can hold up your end of the plan?"

"Not in the least," Eli said with a broad smile. "But we're going to try." As he said this, he laid his hand on his chest, just above the burn that held his lava spirit.

Josef nodded and started for the door. "Tell Nico to meet me on the ships when she gets back. And Eli," he said, glancing over his shoulder. "Good luck."

"You too," Eli said.

Josef waved and stomped down the stairs. When he reached the landing, he saw Eli turn back toward the window, his face strangely determined, almost angry. The light around him seemed wrong, too white for this time of the afternoon. And then, as the door swung, Josef caught a glimpse of what looked like a woman's white arm slide around Eli's chest. Josef froze as the door clicked shut, and then he shook his head. It was way too early in the fight for him to be seeing things. He took a deep breath to clear his mind and hurried down the stairs.

Eli stood perfectly still as the Shepherdess wrapped herself around him from behind.

Why so dour, darling? she whispered in his ear. *I told you this was coming, didn't I?*

Eli closed his eyes. "I was wondering when you'd show up."

Benehime laughed in delight and spun him around. *You were waiting for me?*

"Don't get the wrong idea," Eli said, pulling away. He reached out, pointing to the endless line of ships. "Did you do this?"

Benehime tilted her head. *Do what?*

Eli had to fight to keep the shaking rage out of his voice. "You said that the Empress was coming to kill me in revenge for taking you away. Did she think of that herself, or did you plant the idea in her head?"

What a thing to say. Benehime pulled her arms back with a pained expression. *I'm the Shepherdess. I don't start wars.* She paused, waiting for Eli's expression to soften. When it didn't, she walked to the window with a sigh. *I don't see how this is so difficult for you to grasp, love. Nara is a warrior; war is her nature. What other retaliation can she have but to come and kill the one who stole me from her?*

"She could be mad at you," Eli snapped. "You were the one who left. I was eleven and unconscious when you made me your favorite. That hardly counts as stealing."

She can't be angry with me, Benehime said, her voice ringing with musical laughter. *Nara loves me. Everything does. You said it yourself.*

Eli could feel the anger boiling up his body, and he forced himself to bite his tongue before he said something he'd regret. Beside him, the floor creaked in reverence as Benehime leaned over and laced her arms around him.

Don't be stubborn, darling, she whispered, pulling him close. *I don't want this war any more than you do, but I can't help you unless you ask. Your rule, remember? Not mine. Even so, I tried to warn you. I told you to come home, but you never listen.*

Eli jerked out of her grip. "The moment you say something that isn't self-serving, I will."

Benehime's eyes narrowed, and her fingers tightened, digging into his shoulders like claws. *Must you always be so*

340

stubborn? she hissed, pulling him against her with terrifying strength. *How can you stand there and play that you're still capable of getting by on your own? Give up, darling! It's over. You and I both know your swordsman's pathetic little country has no hope of beating the Empress. All those men down there are going to die if you don't ask for my help, maybe your Josef along with them. Can you bear that much blood on your hands?*

"Blood on *my* hands?"

The words ripped out of him before he could stop them. This was too far.

"What of that is my fault?" he cried. "*You* were the one who abandoned the Empress. *You* were the one who made me your favorite. I had no say in any of it! I was a child. All I wanted was to live my own life. Now the Immortal Empress is here to destroy a kingdom in order to kill me because you don't care for her anymore, and you're saying the blood is on *my* hands?"

Dress it up however you like to make yourself feel better, Benehime said, her white face cold and haughty. *Nothing changes the fact that you could stop this war right now. All you have to do is draw on my power, your rightful power as my star, and you could set everything right, but you won't. People and spirits are going to die today, and it's all because you're a prideful, hateful boy who's too stubborn to know his place and come back home where he belongs.*

"You think I don't want to go back because of *pride?*" Eli shouted. "Do you have any idea what it was like to live with you?"

Benehime's voice grew frigid. *Yes,* she hissed. *It was paradise, but you were too spoiled to know it.*

Eli squeezed his eyes shut. He was going too far. The Shepherdess was very dangerous when she got cold, but he was so sick of this. So sick of walking the line of her favor. So sick of pretending.

"I'm not going to ask for your help, Benehime," he said, his voice as cold as hers when he opened his eyes again. "I'm

341

not going to use any power you gave me. And I'm *never* coming back to you."

The temperature in the room dropped as the Shepherdess studied him. *You shouldn't tell lies, Eliton.*

Eli balled his hands to fists at his sides. "I'm not lying."

The Shepherdess looked at him a moment longer with that cold, terrible expression, and then she turned away. *We'll see how you hold on to that arrogance once the dying starts*, she said, her voice tight. *I will see you soon, beloved, and when I do, it will be on your knees.* She looked over her shoulder one last time. *That I can promise you.*

She pursed her lips in a silent kiss, and then she was gone, vanishing through a white hole in the air.

Eli stood with his fists clenched and his chest straining, holding in all the foul names he desperately wanted to fling after her. Some risks were too great even in his anger, but he didn't hide the look of disgust as he turned away from the empty air where she had vanished and began marching toward the door.

"Eli?" Karon whispered cautiously. "What are you doing?"

"What do you think?" Eli snapped, nearly pulling the door off its hinges. "We're going downstairs, and we're going to help Josef win this bloody war." And he was never going back to her. Never. *Never.*

Karon didn't say another word as Eli took the stairs three at a time down to the storm wall.

Josef's admiral was waiting for him on the vertical stair leading down the storm wall to the bay. Tesset was standing beside him. They both stepped aside to make room as Josef joined them.

"You coming out on the water with us?" Josef said, studying the Council man.

Tesset smiled politely. "Absolutely not. I don't care for boats, and I have a feeling I'll be more useful here."

342

"Have it your way," Josef said. "But it'll be a boring post. Nothing's getting to the shore."

"Consider me as insurance," Tesset said. "On the off chance anything should slip by your blockade."

Josef shook his head and pushed by, slapping Tesset on the shoulder as he passed. Tesset didn't even wobble under the blow. He just stood there, smiling as he watched Josef and the admiral head down to the beach.

"Are the boats supplied like we talked about?" Josef asked, taking the steep, treacherous steps two at a time.

"Yes, majesty," the admiral said. "All our remaining cling-fire has been loaded, though I don't know what good it'll do."

"We only need a little," Josef said. He jumped the last stair and hit the sand running. All the boats but one were already out in the water. The last and largest, the Oseran flagship, was waiting for him at the end of the dock. It was a beautiful runner, twenty feet long and narrow as a barrel with a crew of fifteen strong oarsmen as well as a high, narrow sail. The men saluted as Josef ran up the plank, jumping onto the deck with a force that rocked the ship.

"I've put archers on the cliffs to cover your retreat, my lord," the admiral said from the dock. "Remember, there's only two hours left until the tide. I'll set the signal fire thirty minutes before. You'll have that much time to get in."

"More than enough," said the flagship captain, an enormous sailor who looked like he'd spent his life on the sea. He turned to Josef, and the swordsman saw a flicker of disgust on the sailor's face. Josef tensed. King he might be, but most of Osera still thought he was dirt. But whatever the captain's private feelings, he hid them with the discipline that made the Oseran navy famous.

"On your word, sire," he said with a sharp salute.

"Go," Josef said, moving up to the prow of the ship.

The moment the word was given, the deck jerked under his feet as the oars hit the water, and the narrow ship darted into the bay. The other ships rocked to life as well, falling in behind

343

the king's flagship as the fleet shot out of the sheltered Rebuke and into the blue water of the open sea.

Josef stood on the prow, letting his body adjust to the wind and the pitch of the boat. He'd almost got it when the boat suddenly dipped. Josef turned as the sailors cried in alarm, and his face broke into a smile as he saw Nico stepping out of the shadows beneath the mast.

"We're fine," Josef said. "She's with me."

This didn't seem to reassure the sailors, but they kept rowing, glancing sideways at Nico as she squinted at Josef from beneath her dark hood.

"How'd it go?" Josef said.

"Pretty well," Nico answered. "I went to every one of the outer villages just like you said. They didn't believe me at first, but once I pointed out the Empress's ships, they went along just fine. The catapults are being set up right now. If a palace ship gets within two hundred feet of the outer island shores, it'll be bombarded."

"Good," Josef said. "Won't be enough to sink a palace ship, but a barrage will make landing troops hairy. That'll have to be enough to protect our flank for now." He squeezed Nico's arm and stepped past her, climbing back up on the prow so he could look the rowers in the eye. "Listen up!" he shouted. "The admiral and I explained this earlier, but since we're the flagship and everyone's following our lead, I'm going to say it again. We're not out here to fight the Empress's fleet. Our only objective is to stop her advance long enough for reinforcements to arrive from the mainland."

He threw out his arm and pointed down at the water. This far out, it was beautifully clear. Down below, the shadow of their boat shot across the bright, rocky reef that waited thirty feet below the waves, the natural barrier between their island and the sea. "See that?" Josef said, stabbing his finger at the reef. "That's our weapon. All we have to do is hold them over the shallows and let the tide do our work for us."

The captain gritted his teeth. "Begging your pardon, majesty,

344

but how are we going to hold ships that big with no clingfire? The admiral said you had some kind of secret weapon, but, and I ain't intending to be speaking above my station, I don't see nothing on you but a big metal bar."

Josef grinned wide and reached over his shoulder, drawing the Heart in a smooth arc. "This big metal bar is all we need. Just row where I tell you to go. I'll do the rest."

"Aye, sire," the captain said, though he couldn't hide the tremble in his voice. "Full ahead."

The flagship shot forward, cutting through the water like a knife toward the front line of the palace ships.

The Empress's fleet slowed to meet them, the palace ships halting their unnatural speed as they reached the edge of the reef. Josef fell to a crouch. The other runners had fanned themselves out around the flagship and were keeping pace, just as they were supposed to. Josef was just starting to feel good about this whole crazy operation when he felt Nico tense beside him.

"What?" he said, glancing at her.

Nico was staring straight ahead, eyes wide. "Was there always an island there?"

"What are you talking about?"

Nico pointed at the sky behind the palace ships. Josef squinted against the bright sun, and then his eyes went wide as he saw it too. There, rising like a specter over the enemy fleet, was the shadowy shape of a large, rocky island. But that was impossible. Osera was the last land in these waters. Yet there it was, sturdy and large as any of the Oseran mountain islands. Even this far away, Josef could make out the shape of buildings clinging to the island's rocky slope. Buildings in a style he'd never seen before.

His blood began to run cold, but even as the fear rose, Josef made himself let it go. "Forget it," he said, raising his voice. "Nothing has changed! Full ahead!"

"Aye, sire," the captain said. "Steady!"

The sailors obeyed, and the Oseran fleet flew at the line of

345

palace ships like a tiny bird flying at a wall that spans the world.

Nara stood on the balcony of her war palace, watching the tiny specks of the Oseran fleet approaching her front line. Her ornate sword was out and naked in her hand, a rare sight, and one that made her general extremely uncomfortable.

"Hail, Empress," he said after waiting a solid minute for her to notice he was there.

"One of the Hundred Conquerors has fallen," the Empress said, raising her sword for him to see. "I still don't believe it. I haven't had a sleeper fall since I took the high mountains. What was that, two hundred years ago?"

"Two hundred and fifty-three," the general said. "If my Empress is referring to her war with the Ascetics of the Great Glacier."

"Oh, yes," the Empress said. "That pack of ice builders. A good war, if I remember. I think I ended up commanding their glacier to provide the water that turned the northern plains green."

"For which your people will forever sing your praises, Empress."

The Empress nodded and sheathed her sword. "So long as the sleeper accomplished its task, it matters little, I suppose. I'll just have to make a new Conqueror when this is finished. We have more with us, don't we?"

The general bowed. "Seventy-three of the Hundred ride with your fleet, Empress. They await your command."

"That should be more than enough," the Empress said. "Report."

The general stood at attention. "A hundred ships approaching from the island, all light attack craft, just as in the last war. None have shot the clinging fire yet, but your wizards are standing by to squelch the flames if needed."

The Empress nodded. "And the shallows Den warned us about?"

346

"At our present speed, our front line should cross them in plenty of time to avoid the tide," the general said.

The Empress frowned. "The front line is fifty palace ships?"

"Fifty-five, Empress," the general corrected gently. "More than enough to take such a small island. We'll begin bombardment as soon as the first ships are in range. The land will be yours before nightfall."

"See that it is," the Empress said.

The general bowed and backed into the palace, closing the curtain behind him. The moment he was gone, Nara felt the hair on the back of her neck prickle in a familiar way. A smile of pure joy spread over her face as she turned to find the Shepherdess lounging on her imperial couch.

"My Lady," the Empress whispered, falling into a deep bow.

How goes the invasion?

Nara stiffened. The Lady did not sound happy.

"We're about to crush the Oseran fleet," she said quickly. "Do not worry, Lady. I told you I would give you the world, and I will, starting with this island."

It is a dour little island, the Lady said, twisting her snowy hair between her fingers. *Promise me you'll burn it to the ground.*

"I will crush it into the sea," Nara swore. "Anything to make you smile."

And to her great joy, the Shepherdess did. She held open her arms, and Nara ran to her, falling into the Lady's lap like a lost child.

Darling, loyal Nara, the Shepherdess said, stroking her dark hair. *Would you die for me?*

"In an instant, Lady," Nara said, tears rolling down her cheeks as she pressed her fingers against Benehime's bare, white skin. "I am loyal to you body and soul, life or death. Every breath I take is yours, as it always has been." *Unlike the boy*, she wanted to say, but she did not dare. She would not bring that thief into this precious moment when she had her Shepherdess to herself at last.

347

The Lady pet Nara's head like a cat's. *Remember*, she said. *Crush this island and its defenders. Break them utterly. I want them desperate.*

"It will be done, Lady," Nara said, clinging tighter than ever. "I swear it."

The Lady smiled one last time and vanished, her body slipping through a white line in the air. Nara fell forward, collapsing on the couch where the Lady had been. As always, her absence left Nara reeling, and she lay gasping on the silk cushions, her eyes shut tight against the hateful darkness that remained when Benehime was gone.

When the weakness finally passed, Nara pulled herself onto the couch and opened her soul a fraction. A wind answered at once.

"Tell the front line commanders to fire as soon as they're in range," the Empress said. "I mean to make an example of this island. Tell the wizards to use every war spirit we've got. I want Osera burned to ash."

"Yes, Empress," the wind whispered, spinning away.

Nara smiled. She wasn't sure what the island had done to deserve the Lady's displeasure, but it was a boon to her. An absolute victory here could be enough to make the Lady remember at last who her true servant was. That thought made her sigh in happiness, and Nara sank into the pillows to watch the show as the first of her palace ships hit the Oseran fleet.

The Oseran runners darted between the palace ships, the flagship shooting ahead as arrows rained down on them from the enemy decks.

"Hold steady!" Josef cried, cutting an arrow out of the air just before it landed in the rower behind him. "Are the others in position?"

"Right behind us!" the captain shouted.

Josef looked over his shoulder. Sure enough, the other runners were coasting right on their tail with their clingfire already lit in the throwers. Josef grinned and pointed the Heart at the palace ship on their left. "Bring us up right next to the hull."

The flagship surged forward, cutting through the breakwater until they were an arm's length from the palace ship's cliff-like side. Josef set his feet on the bucking deck and held the Heart in front of him, closing both hands on the wrapped hilt. He closed his eyes with a deep breath and let his thoughts go. His mind cleared like the sky after a storm, leaving only the sword in his hands. He could feel the Heart's presence resonating with his own, and the image of a mountain appeared behind his eyes. An enormous, sharp peak, cutting the clouds. A sword cutting a ship.

The cut would have to be perfect, a niggling voice whispered. Any amount of drag and he would crash his own ship before the enemy's. Josef snarled and pushed the doubt away. He gripped the Heart until his hands ached, letting the sword's weight anchor him as the rest of the world fell away, leaving only the feel of the wind and a profound stillness. As the quiet settled, he could almost feel Milo Burch standing in front of him, his old face smug as ever as he spoke the first truth of swordsmanship.

A sword cuts whatever its swordsman wants it to cut.

Josef gripped the Heart tight, relaxing his body until the Heart was part of it. Part of him.

A sword cuts whatever its swordsman wants it to cut? Josef smiled. Time to test the limits.

Giving himself fully to the weight of the mountain, Josef opened his eyes, and the world rushed in.

The palace ship's hull was right beside him. He could smell the tar on the wood, feel the iron strength of the enormous black beams. His body moved with the buck of the sea as he braced the Heart in his hands and lifted the blade, its scarred face a black hole in the afternoon sunlight. And then, in the emptiness between one wave and the next, between the breath let out and the breath inhaled, he struck.

The Heart flew in his hands, moving like an extension of

349

himself. He did not feel the wood as it passed. Did not feel the nails as he cut them. All he felt was the *will* to cut swelling through his body and into his sword. The Heart sang as it struck, a great iron *gong* vibrating through the sea.

Josef's knees buckled as the blow left him. He fell into the boat as the runner turned midstroke and began to race away from the palace ship. The sailors were rowing with all their might, arms straining as they pushed the runner faster and faster. For a moment, Josef couldn't understand why they were running, and then he looked back at the palace ship, and he saw.

The palace ship was carved open, its great side split just above the water, starting at the ship's middle and running all the way to the stern. The cut was perfectly clean, slicing through the wood without so much as a splinter, and wherever the wood was cut, the ship was bowing. A great creaking sound drowned out the waves as the palace ship's side began to slide, pushed sideways by the ship's own enormous weight. The ship groaned as the sundered boards ground together, and then, with an earsplitting crack, the wooden supports snapped, and the ship's side began to fall open.

Suddenly, Josef could see the inner decks and the sailors running through them, scrambling for cover as the metal skeleton that held the ship together folded under the pressure of the unsupported hull. Already the water was flooding through the crack to fill the lower decks, soaking the sailors who scrambled for the pumps as the entire ship began to tip. But then, just before the hull cracked completely and began to crumble into the sea, the falling wood stopped. For a breathless second, the ship hung frozen, the collapsing side poised in midair. And then, with an ear-splitting crack, the wood shuddered and began to pull itself back together.

"Now, you idiots!" Josef screamed. "Do it now!"

His voice shot across the water, and the crews in the assist ships stopped gawking and began to scramble. The air was filled with the sound of snapping rope as crews hit their clingfire launchers and a rain of ever-burning fire shot out from the Oseran fleet into the palace ship's closing breach. The clingfire exploded when it hit, sending sticky, burning pitch flying in all directions. Everything it touched caught fire, no matter how wet. If it could burn, it did.

The moment they'd launched their fire, the runners peeled away, darting across the water as arrows from the other palace ships chased them. The blobs of clingfire had been small, and only half the runners had shot on this attack, but the damage was done. As the fire spread through its belly, the broken palace ship began to groan. Even Josef heard the agony in the sound as the hole that had been pulling itself together began to slip once again, the great beams falling into the water as the hungry sea rushed in to fill the void.

The palace ship was leaning at a thirty-degree angle now. Sailors slid overboard as the enormous deck tilted, their bodies vanishing into the churning waves as the sea surged through the broken hull. Through the ship's cracked side, Josef could see sailors flinging water at the clingfire, but it did no good. Clingfire could burn for three days underwater so long as it had fuel. The ship would keep burning even after it sank.

When they were safely over the shallows again, the flagship slowed, and the oarsmen turned to survey the destruction.

"It's a miracle. That's what it is," the captain muttered as the palace ship began to sink in earnest. "A bleeding miracle."

"No," Josef said, pointing out to sea. "That's the miracle."

The sailors' eyes followed his gesture. A few hundred feet away, the Empress's fleet had ground to a halt. Several of the palace ships were dropping lifeboats as men jumped from the sinking ship, and the whole fleet seemed to be turning in on itself. In toward its own, and away from Osera.

"And that's how one runner fleet stops the Empress," Josef said, leaning on the Heart as Nico helped him to his feet. "And the longer they stay like that, the closer we get to low tide and the *real* miracle. Now, bring us around. Those ships may be stopped, but they've still got their bows, and we've more palaces to sink."

The captain blinked, eyes wide. "Aye, my king."

Josef just nodded and pushed off Nico to resume his position on the prow as the runner turned to join the others already darting between the stopped fleet.

Den the Warlord hung over the railing of the palace ship, watching with an enormous grin as the ship ahead of his begin to sink. Beside him, the captain was throwing a full-on fit.

"We cannot lose a palace ship before we've even reached land!" the man was screaming. "Get the wizards on deck and take out those blasted fishing boats!"

There was more, but Den ignored it. He was watching the man standing on the prow of the fastest boat, the man who had just sliced open a palace ship. Den breathed deep, savoring the anticipation. Now there was the kind of opponent he'd been waiting for, but how best to go about it? A duel on boats would be no fun. No real footing, not for the kind of power he'd be throwing around. Maybe he could spoil the man's ship and send him running to shore?

Den was still thinking over his options when he felt something brush against his spirit. He froze, taking in the feel of it. It was a wizard's will, a familiar one. He focused on the pressure, trying to place it, and found himself facing the shore. Den leaned out over the railing. A man was standing on the beach. This far, his face wasn't clear, but Den didn't need to see his face. That stance was unmistakable.

Pure joy flooded through him. He'd thought he was lucky to find the swordsman, but here was a fight Den had been waiting on for decades. He glanced back at the Oseran boats. They were coming around again, the swordsman riding the prow of the flagship with his sword out. Shaking his head, Den turned away. The swordsman could wait. If he was good enough to split a palace ship, then these idiots wouldn't be able to touch him. He'd still be around later.

Meanwhile, he was going to deal with some unfinished business.

Den turned to the panicking captain and grabbed him by the shoulder, lifting him clear off the deck and holding him there until he was sure he had the man's undivided attention.

"I need a boat."

The captain's face went pale with terror. "The Empress said—"

"The Empress and I have a deal." Den tightened his grip. "I get to kill whomever I want. Now give me a boat."

"Fine!" the captain cried. "Just put me down!"

Den dropped him, and the captain collapsed in a heap. His officers rushed forward, but the captain waved them away. "Give the Empress's champion a boat," he gasped, clutching his shoulder. "Let him do as he likes."

The officers looked at Den, and then one ran off toward the lifeboats. Den nodded to the captain and turned to follow. He stepped into the boat and sat down, waiting impatiently as a crew lowered him down the long drop from the deck to the sea. The moment he hit the water, Den opened his spirit.

"Take me to the shore," he said, stomping on the boards.

The boat gave a terrified creak and obeyed, shooting across the water as fast as it could go.

"Sire!" one of Josef's rowers shouted. "There's a boat headed for the shore!"

Josef looked over his shoulder. They were circling to avoid the arrows, waiting for their chance to strike the next palace ship. Now was the perfect moment for the enemy to counter.

"I'd hoped we'd have a bit longer," he said. "How big a boat?"

The captain grabbed the glass from his neck and peered through it. "Looks like a lifeboat, sire. I see one man."

Josef held out his hand and the captain handed the glass over. Sure enough, a rowboat with one occupant was rushing toward the shore faster than their runners. Josef scowled. The sailor looked normal enough. Huge, certainly, and a fighter, but he didn't seem to have a weapon. The man's face was in profile, but he looked familiar, somehow. Josef was trying to place him when he heard Nico suck in a breath.

"That's Den the Warlord."

"The traitor?" the captain said, squinting at the tiny boat. "Impossible. He'd be an old man by now if he's still alive at all."

"It has to be Den," Nico said with absolute certainty. "He's the only person whose soul could look like that."

Josef had no idea what she meant, but he was too preoccupied to care. "Captain, turn us around. Den the Warlord killed five thousand men in one night when he defected. We can't let him land."

"No," Nico said.

Josef looked at her in surprise, but Nico just clenched her fists.

"You're the only one who can sink the palace ships," she said. "And that's the only thing keeping the fleet at bay. If you leave now, the fleet will cross the shallows before the tide and this whole mission is for nothing."

"It won't matter if Den's already finished the job," Josef growled. "Turn us around."

"*No*," Nico said again.

Josef jerked at the determination in her voice. "Nico..."

"You're king now," Nico went on. "Your duty is here." She looked back at the shore. "I'll stop Den."

"Nico, no," Josef said. "Den's the highest bounty in Council history and maybe the best fighter in the world. I have to—"

"You can't make it there fast enough," Nico said, her voice firm. "I can. Or don't you think I can win?"

Josef set his mouth in a stubborn line. "It's not that I think you can't win," he said. "It's what I think you'll have to do to get there."

"I already won my hardest fight," she said, lifting her chin.

"Stay and be king, Josef. It's what you promised. Besides, it's my turn to do something for you."

Josef clenched the Heart's hilt. "This isn't some damn give-and-take, Nico. You don't owe me this."

"You're right," Nico said. "I don't. It's my choice to fight for you, and that's what I'm going to do."

Josef turned with a curse. "Fine," he growled, running his free hand through his wet hair. "Just promise me you won't do anything stupid."

"I'll do what I have to," Nico said, sliding into the mast's shadow. "Same as you."

"Nico!" Josef's arm shot out, but his fingers caught nothing but air. He was too late. She was gone.

The boat rocked as he lurched toward the shore, but he couldn't see anything from this angle. He cursed again, louder this time, slamming the Heart's pommel against the boat so hard they nearly tipped.

"Sire?" the captain said nervously when the worst of the boat's rocking had passed. "Are we going back?"

Josef closed his eyes and took a deep breath. Nico was a survivor. If she decided to win, she would win. She would survive and come back to him, no matter what. Josef held that truth in his mind as tight as he held the Heart and he forced himself to let the anger, and the fear at its root, go. Slowly, the battle calm settled over his mind again. When he was sure he could trust himself, Josef straightened up and turned to face the captain.

"Our job hasn't changed," he said. "But we're fighting on two fronts now. Nico will hold the beach, so it's up to us to hold the water. Now bring us around, and let's hit another ship."

"Aye, sire," the captain said. "Full speed!"

The men shouted to the other boats as the Oseran fleet shot forward. Josef stepped back onto the prow, Heart in his hand, but when he tried to clear his mind in preparation for the next strike, all he could see was Nico vanishing into the dark.

The Heart jerked angrily in his hands, and Josef pushed the vision away, pouring himself into the present as the runners raced toward their next target.

CHAPTER
21

Nico stepped out of the shadows and onto the small crescent of sand beneath the storm wall. Tesset was already there, standing with his boots in the surf as he watched the lone boat that was just now entering the bay's mouth.

"You should not have come," he said without looking. "This man is mine."

"And this island is Josef's," Nico said, moving to stand beside him. "I have no interest in interrupting your fight, but I cannot let Den past this beach."

Tesset laughed softly. "What did the swordsman do to deserve such devotion? Save your life?"

"Countless times," Nico said. "But that's not why." She raised her arms, pushing back her hood. "He believed in me, even when there was nothing to believe in."

"You are a strange creature, daughter of the demon," he said, shaking his head. "I am glad I met you."

"And I you," Nico said, walking back up the beach. "Fight well, Tesset."

Tesset nodded, but his eyes never left the man standing in the boat that cut across the bay on its own power.

Nico sat down on the narrow stair that led up the storm wall, keeping herself well out of the way as Den's boat hit the surf and beached itself with a terrified squeal. Twenty-six years later, his face still looked exactly like his wanted poster. Den the Warlord, traitor to the Council, the most wanted man on the continent. He was bigger than Nico had expected, taller than Josef by several inches with shoulders to match. He was dressed in the Empress's black, but he wore no armor, just a long-sleeved sailor's shirt, heavy woven breeches, and tall boots. His dark hair was cut ragged around his face without a trace of gray. He had no weapons, not even a knife. Instead, his hands were open, hovering ready at his sides. Even so, the sight of him was enough to make Nico cower against the rocks.

Unarmed and alone, Den radiated a killing instinct like nothing she'd ever felt, and worse, nothing she'd ever seen. The glimpse she'd caught on the boat with Josef was nothing compared to seeing him up close. She'd always thought of Tesset as a man who'd made himself iron, but Den was a man who had made himself a fortress. Now that she saw them side by side, she couldn't help shaking. She had seen many monsters, and been many more, but not even the demon's predatory hunger matched this man's pure, undefiled will to kill.

Den stepped onto the surf and stopped, surveying the beach. He dismissed Nico at once, focusing on Tesset with a grin that made her chest close up.

"Tesset, wasn't it?" Den said, looking the Council man up and down. "I thought I'd find you alive someday. Finally conquered yourself, did you?"

"Yes." Nico was impressed by the calm determination in Tesset's voice. "To meet you again, master. And to defeat you."

"A worthy goal," Den said. "I can think of none better for a bloody day like this one." He threw out his arms, fists clenched as he grinned wide. "Come then. I let you live in the hope that one day you could give me a fight worthy of my full attention. Let's hope you don't disappoint me."

Tesset smiled back, a tight, controlled turn of the mouth, and then, without warning, he charged.

Tesset flew at Den faster than wind, faster than sound, focusing all his speed, all his strength into the fist that was already inside the Warlord's guard. Before Nico's mind could

357

catch up with what was happening, Tesset's fist landed on Den's unguarded jaw. Sand exploded as the force of Tesset's charge and the blow at the end of it reverberated through the beach.

Nico threw her arms up, her coat swirling over her face just before the sand hit it, but behind the barrier, she was grinning. She'd felt the force of Tesset's blow in her stomach. Famous as he was, if Den hadn't even been able to block such a straightforward strike, maybe they weren't in as much trouble as she'd thought. She knew Tesset's strength firsthand. He was far stronger than he looked. Strong enough to stop her demonseed barehanded. A clean punch with that kind of strength behind it might be enough to end this fight before it started.

The wave of sand passed, and she lowered her arms, looking down the beach to see where Den had landed. But he wasn't there. She looked around, confused, and then she saw it. Den was still standing exactly where he had been, leering at Tesset with a horrible, wolfish grin.

Tesset himself was frozen in place. He was still inside Den's guard, his fist still resting where it had landed on Den's jaw, but his face had changed from quiet determination to open horror. The moment Nico saw it, she knew why. She could read the thoughts in his wide eyes as clearly as print on a page. Tesset had just hit Den with his best blow. He'd hit him with his full strength, unhampered by tiredness and unspoiled by the need to dodge a defense, and nothing had happened. Den was still standing exactly as he had been before the hit. He hadn't fallen, hadn't stumbled, hadn't been pushed back. He hadn't even turned his head. He'd simply taken the blow as though it were nothing, a child's play punch, and that realization had hit Tesset harder than any retaliation.

The seconds dragged on as the men stood there like players in a pantomime fight. Even Nico was frozen. She couldn't help it. The idea that Tesset's strength, the strength that had overpowered her so easily, meant *nothing* to Den had stopped her mind cold. All she could do was watch dumbly until, at last, Tesset stumbled back.

He fell to the sand, panting, staring up at Den with wide, unbelieving eyes. For his part, Den raised a hand to his cheek, rubbing the uninjured skin with a disappointed sneer.

"Is that it?"

It was, and they all knew it. But no one who could master his own spirit was one to give up when faced with the impossible, and Tesset was no exception. Hands clenching in the cold sand, Tesset stood up. He set his stance, his feet solid on the wet beach. His breathing steadied, calm returned, and he raised his fists to face Den again.

Den's eyes lit with a mad gleam as he looked down on his former student. With a joyous shout, Den attacked.

Nico had never seen anything like Den's charge. The enormous man moved like water, each step flowing into the next with the kind of speed she'd seen only in Josef when he was moving with the Heart. His feet hit the beach with such force, such precision, that the sand did not shift beneath his boots. But even as his fists came up to strike, Tesset was already moving. As Den's foot landed to brace the blow, Tesset's landed right beside it. He moved with Den, matching his body to the Warlord's as he stepped inside Den's guard. His arm moved with a speed Nico couldn't follow to catch Den's punch at its farthest, weakest point while his other hand landed in Den's side, right over his liver.

Or it would have.

In the split second before Tesset's hit connected, Den stepped back. Tesset, still holding Den's fist, was pulled forward. He teetered a moment trying to find his balance, and in that moment, Den's knee shot up to knock him in the jaw.

Tesset flew backward and landed sprawling on the sand. Nico held her breath, waiting for him to roll over, to cough out the blood and stand up. His jaw was almost certainly broken, but that shouldn't have been a fight-ender, not for a man like Tesset. And yet he didn't move. He just laid there, glassy eyes staring at the sky, his chest rising in tight little gasps, and she realized he was stunned.

Den walked across the sand, his smile fading. He bent over, grabbing the fallen man by the shoulder and lifting him with one hand until Tesset dangled in front of him. The motion must have snapped him out of his stunned state, for Tesset's head rolled from side to side and then lifted, meeting Den's eyes.

"It wasn't enough," he mumbled, blood dripping from his mouth. "Thirty years of training, becoming my own king, and still, after all that, with everything I had"—a faint smile drifted over his lips—"I lost."

Den sneered and raised his arm, lifting Tesset's body high over his head.

"You lost the moment you called me master."

And with that, he slammed Tesset into the ground. Nico felt the impact through her boots. She didn't even realize she'd run onto the beach until she was falling to her knees at Tesset's side. He was lying on his stomach, his body half buried in the sand, perfectly still. Her hands flew to his face, turning his head, but the second she touched his skin, she knew.

Nico snatched her fingers away, letting his head fall back. It couldn't be. He couldn't be gone. Not like that. Not so quickly. Not Tesset. Not the man who'd stopped the demonseed with one hand.

But it was true. When she looked at him, she no longer saw a man of iron. She saw nothing but dullness, a spirit turned to dumb, dead meat. Choking back a sob, Nico moved away. This thing was not Tesset. She had seen much death in the small parts of her life she could remember, but she had never *seen* death, not like this, and her mind was scrambling to make sense of something a human soul was never meant to see.

"It's a waste, really."

Nico hadn't even heard Den move, but he was standing over her. She tensed, but the Warlord wasn't looking at her. He was frowning at Tesset's body like a child examining a broken toy.

360

"I'd thought for sure he'd be stronger after so long," he said bitterly. "Such a waste. Sorry, little girl." He patted Nico on the shoulder. "I guess I'll go and see if that swordsman can't give me a better run."

Nico's arm shot up and grabbed his hand, her fingers digging into the back of his palm. She felt him tense, and then she heard his voice, very low, right beside her ear.

"You don't want to do this," Den whispered. "I try to fight only strong people, but I will kill you if you get in my way."

Nico held her grip. "If you think I am weak," she whispered back, "you are the one who will die."

Den paused, and his eyes sparked with a new light. "I'd thought you were his daughter, maybe," he said, a smile spreading across his face. "But I was wrong. You were Tesset's student, weren't you?"

"He showed me the way to be my own master," Nico answered, ripping his hand off her shoulder.

Den's eyebrows shot up. "Is that so?" he said. "Well, then, as one free soul to another, let me give you some advice." He leaned in low, bringing his face level with hers. "Run away. You may think you want to try fighting me to reclaim your master's honor, but you should forget that. You can't beat me."

Nico gritted her teeth, her eyes boring into his. "No."

Den leaned back as Nico stood up. "I made a promise," she said, bracing her feet on the sand. "You will not pass this beach."

Den shrugged. "It's your death," he said, planting his own feet. "I just hope you can give me a better challenge than your master."

"He wasn't my master," Nico said firmly. "I have no master but myself."

Den smiled wide. "Good to see you learned better than he did." He beckoned. "Come, then. Let's see whose kingdom is greater. Yours or mine."

Nico didn't answer. Instead, she grabbed a handful of her

coat at her chest. The moment her fingers touched the fabric, she opened her spirit.

"Cover us."

The words were scarcely out of her mouth before the coat obeyed. It sprang off her back, the black fabric expanding, pulling out every inch of the enormous lengths of cloth Slorn had woven into it. It grew and grew, spilling onto the sand behind her and rising overhead like a wave of night. Den held his stance, watching through narrowed eyes as the coat arched over his head. Moments after it started, the coat stopped, trapping Nico and Den inside a large, pitch-black tent of living cloth.

"Clever," Den's voice sounded from Nico's left. "But blinding me won't be enough."

"I didn't do it to blind you," Nico said, fading into the dark. "I did it because I don't want the world to see what I'm going to do."

"And what is that?" Den's voice was curious, not afraid.

Nico didn't answer. She slipped through the shadows until she was facing Den's back. She could see him clearly, but not with her eyes. Her coat was too well made for that. It blocked the light so completely that even her night vision was useless. She could still see with her other sight, though, and now that her normal vision was gone, the world of the spirits was clearer than ever.

Den hadn't moved since the dark had fallen. She could see him holding his breath, waiting for her to give herself away, but more than that, she could see *him* clearly for the first time, not his body, but the actual spirit that was Den. Generally, when she looked at people, wizards or the spirit deaf, the souls beneath their bodies looked jumbled and chaotic. Tesset was the exception. His soul had looked like metal, almost like the Heart's blade.

Den was completely different. Back in the light, she'd seen him as a fortress. Now, in the dark, she saw how much of an understatement that was. Den's body was a vault of power.

Every part of him was perfectly aligned, every angle perfectly set. Strength flowed uninterrupted from his head to his arms to his feet, and when he shifted, everything in his body moved together in perfect unison. For a moment, Nico forgot the fight and simply stared in wonder. Looking at Den, she saw the pure essence of human potential, and with it, the truth of what it meant to be absolutely, completely in control.

"Well?"

Den's voice snapped her out of her gawking, and Nico shrank back reflexively before remembering he couldn't see her. But even as she thought it, Den looked over his shoulder and stared straight at her.

"Come," he said. "I'm getting bored."

Nico fled away through the dark, coming up on his side. Den was still facing the place where she had been, and Nico breathed in relief. Maybe his turn had been just a lucky guess, or maybe he could sense her, but it wasn't instant. Either way, he wasn't looking at her, at least for now. Nico clenched her fist. For now was good enough. All she needed was one good hit.

She exploded out of the shadows low to Den's right, her fist clenched as she flew toward his unguarded side. She was taking a cue from Tesset, aiming for his liver. Fortress or not, Den's body was still human, and no human could take repeated blows to the liver without feeling it. For a thrilling second, she felt her fist connect, and then things started to go wrong.

She could see the shock wave from her blow running through the orderly fortress of his spirit. The force rippled out from her fist, but rather than shooting through the muscle and hitting his liver as she'd intended, the blow began spreading and dissipating the moment it touched him. It all happened so quickly that Nico had to play the strike over in her mind before she realized Den had shifted his spirit the moment she'd touched him, spreading the shock out across his body. Even now, she could see the echoes fading. Every piece of him had taken its part, breaking her blow down to nothing.

She was still staring in amazement when Den grabbed her arm. He snatched her off her feet before she could react and brought her dangling up in front of him, his other hand grabbing her neck as surely as though he were the one who could see.

"I told you," he said, fingers digging into her throat. "Blinding me does nothing."

Nico gasped and tried to kick him in the groin with her dangling legs. He spoiled the blow with his knee, spirit moving instantly to absorb the shock just like before.

"And it's not just that I can hear you," he continued as though nothing had happened. "I can *feel* your killing intent."

He opened his hand, and Nico plummeted, crashing into the sand. The moment she hit, Den's boot was on her back.

"You should have run when I gave you the chance," he said, grinding his heel into her back. "If you don't even know that, then you have no hope of beating me."

Nico gasped in pain, bringing in more sand than air. Den's heel was like an iron spike on her spine, pressing so hard she saw bursts of color behind her eyes. But the dark was still her highway, and the moment her mind cleared enough to slip into the shadows, she sank into dark ground. Relief flowed over her as the pressure of Den's foot vanished from her back. She slipped sideways, coming up in the shadows behind Den as she looked down to survey the damage.

Nico froze in place, all pain forgotten. In the days since she'd first started to see as spirits saw, she'd never once looked at herself without her coat. Now, in the dark, with no coat and no normal sight to intervene between her and truth, she saw herself for the first time.

Above her, Den looked up from the sand where she had been, his face surprised. "Where did you go?" he whispered. "And why are you so afraid?"

Nico did not hear him. She'd forgotten all about Den, about the fight, about her injuries. All she could do was stare in horror as the demon's voice filled her mind.

Now you understand why the spirits panic when they see you?

She didn't. There was no way to understand what she saw inside her own body, beneath the frail mask of human spirit. The only way to describe it was darkness. Living, devouring, hungry darkness. And below that...

Why are you surprised? The demon's voice was like silk against her mind. *You've always known you were a monster.*

"Knowing's not the same as..." She couldn't say it.

Seeing? the demon finished, his smooth voice sharpening to a cutting edge. *I suppose that's true. Poor Nico, don't you wish now you'd taken my offer when you had the chance?*

Nico snarled, snapping herself out of her terrified trance with a burst of defiant rage. She flung open her soul, slamming the demon back into his prison. Across the shadows, Den stiffened and spun to face her. Nico didn't care. She fell panting to the sand, staring up at the blank darkness of her coat, desperately looking anywhere but at her body, if she could even think of that *thing* as her body anymore. But even as the thought of it filled her with fear, another voice spoke in her mind, a voice that sounded very much like Tesset's.

Horrible as it is, it's still your body, isn't it?

Nico blinked. Trembling, she raised her hand, holding it as close as she dared to her face. The blackness below her skin flowed like water. Below it, the shifting yellow eyes stared at her without blinking while the hungry mouths opened and closed in a way that made her stomach clench. Black claws scraped against the thin cage of her flesh, looking for a way out, and on her wrists where her manacles had once rested, she could see the faint outlines of black, jagged teeth waiting for any scrap of food.

Mixed with the liquid darkness, Nico could actually see her own heart pounding in terror in her chest, but she forced herself not to look away. This was her. Her body, her power, her life. She hadn't fought for so long and hard only to be afraid of it now.

Nico flicked her eyes to Den. He'd found the edge of her coat and was pressing his hands against it, looking for the edge. She could see the orderly flow of his spirit tensing. He was losing his patience. Soon he would rip the cloth and return them to daylight, and then there would be no way to stop him going up the beach. That wasn't acceptable. She'd told Josef she would stop him. But Nico was facing a very real dilemma. She couldn't beat Den, not as she was, not even when she had the dark to move through and he had nothing. That left only one path. She had to become stronger, become something Den couldn't stop. Nico looked down again at her own darkness, the clawed hands scraping against her flesh. "Become" was the wrong word, she thought with a grim smile. She already was a monster. All that was left was to embrace it. After all, the monster was hers. She'd ripped it from the demon of the Dead Mountain with her own hands. Now it would fight as she commanded, for it was a part of her, and she was the master of herself.

Before she lost her nerve, Nico looked away from Den and turned her focus inward, sinking down into the pit of her soul. The demonseed leaped to meet her with a vigor that turned her stomach, but she ignored the discomfort and opened her arms, pulling the creature in with a lover's embrace. Power, strong and addictive, flooded her mind. She took it all and held it as hard as she could, letting the slimy black water wash over her, the black teeth bite into her skin and become her own.

When Nico opened her eyes again, she was no longer afraid.

At the edge of her coat's shell, Den froze. He whirled, finding her instantly, but Nico didn't even try to run. After all, it wasn't her killing intent he'd used to find her this time. He was no longer fighting blind, for even a blind man couldn't miss her eyes glowing like lanterns in the dark. She spread her tainted spirit like claws, pushing the demon's fear forward. But Den did not flinch when the fear reached him, not even when she shoved it down his throat, and despite herself, Nico was impressed.

366

"Are you not afraid?" she whispered, wincing at the horrible sound of her own, two-toned voice.

"I have no need for fear," Den answered simply, looking her up and down. "You are a demonseed?"

"I am Nico," Nico said. "I am a monster, but I am also myself."

"A good answer," Den said, stepping into his stance. "I am also a monster. All men are who know no fear. So, monster Nico"—he grinned wide—"why don't you make me remember how it feels to be afraid?"

Nico returned his grin, her mouth opening wider than a human's should to reveal four jagged rows of black teeth, and vanished into the dark.

Den held his stance, waiting.

He didn't have to wait long. The first blow came from above, a black claw reaching down to grab his head, the razor-sharp talons hooking under his jaw. Den grabbed the hand with both of his, but before he could rip it away, another claw appeared from the ground and lashed up, digging into his leg above the knee.

Den grunted and kicked down, spinning sideways out of both claws. The moment he was free, he grabbed the claw from above and ripped Nico out of the shadows. The claw from the ground vanished as she landed in a crouch. The second her feet were on the ground, Nico sprang up, her body shifting back and forth between solid darkness and smokey shadow as she wrapped her arms around Den's shoulders, locking herself to him.

Den's hands went up immediately, but it was too late. She was clutched around his neck. Den froze, his fingers sliding over the black, stone-hard flesh of her arms.

"It's useless," he said, his voice tight and calm despite the pressure she was putting on his throat. "You can't eat me, not without my permission. I am the king of my soul."

"I know," Nico whispered, her dual-tone voice dry as dust. "But I'm not trying to eat you. The demon eats souls. I don't. I'm a human monster, just like you."

"Really?" Den sneered. "Then what are you trying to do?"

The darkness in front of him shimmered and Nico's face appeared, her golden eyes narrowing as she smiled wide. "Hold you still."

Den's eyes widened in surprise as Nico's hold vanished and he looked down to see her black claw buried elbow deep in his chest.

Den coughed, but he did not stumble. Instead, his hand shot out, grabbing for her throat. But his fingers passed through her body like water through sand.

"How," he whispered, hand falling limp at his side.

Nico looked down at her black arm buried in his chest. "Even fortresses have weak points," she said, her voice wafting like smoke. "Your ability to will your body to absorb any damage has held off the ravages of battle and age, but you're still human, Den, with a human's blindness. Blind, you built your fortress to defend against attacks from the outside. Attacks you could see. But in the dark, all shadows are mine, even ones inside your body." She wiggled her claws in his chest. "All I had to do was hold you still long enough to reach them."

Den bared his bloody teeth and began to laugh. He fell to his knees in the sand, still laughing as Nico's claw ripped free. His laughter dissolved into coughing as he collapsed onto his side, looking at her with fading eyes.

"I always knew this was how it would end," he wheezed. "I knew nothing human could kill me."

"You're wrong," Nico said, her glowing eyes narrowing. "I am still human."

"No," Den said, his voice trailing off as the last of his breath left. "You're not."

Not anymore.

"No!" Nico shouted, stepping away from Den, her body flashing between hard flesh and smokey shadow as she tried to push the demon back.

Oh yes, the demon answered, completely ignoring her efforts. *I told you. Every time you used your powers, I would come back. Every time you were weak, I'd be here. You just suffused your body into shadow to beat this man. How can you even dare to say you're still human?*

"*No!*" Nico screamed again, clutching her head between her claws. "I am my own master! My soul is my own!"

That may be, the demon said. *But that doesn't mean you're still human.* The voice paused. *Do you know how new demons are made, Nico?*

Nico clamped her mouth shut, but the demon went on anyway.

I can replicate myself forever through seeds, it said. *Over and over, always the same, little shoots of myself growing in fertile soil. But sometimes, through extraordinary pressure, a seed changes. It ceases to be a part of me and becomes something new. A new demon, a true demon, with its own ambitions and drives. If this was the world that was, the world before, I would now try to kill you. Predators can't abide competition, after all. But this isn't our world, is it? It's her world, and so I think I'll let you be.*

"Her who?" Nico snapped.

The demon laughed. *Our darling jailor, of course. You'll know her when she comes, but by then it will be too late. Maybe she'll actually manage to destroy you rather than just locking you under a corpse, as she did me. But trust me when I say this, little daughter, whatever plans Benehime has for you, the day will come when you would give anything to go back to the time when I was the biggest thing you had to worry about.*

"I doubt that," Nico muttered, pushing the demon's voice down, down, down until it was little more than a whisper.

You'll see, the demon said as he faded. *Talk to you soon.*

Nico slammed the boulder down with a rage she'd never felt before. She was standing in the field, panting as the cool air blew over her face. But even as she realized where she was, she knew something was wrong. Her field, the high golden field of her soul with its rolling hills and enormous sky, was dark. It was night, a cool, still night. Nico looked around in confusion and pictured the sun, the bright noon day that she'd created when she'd made this place.

No sun came. When she looked up at the sky, all she saw was darkness. Endless, endless darkness, and something else. She squinted. High overhead, something was moving against the black sky. A hand, she realized as her blood went cold. A clawed hand, scraping at the sky. From the second she saw it, she could not look away. The hand clenched in the dark above her, clawing faster, harder, until at last it grabbed a great fistful of the sky and, with a horrible, twisting motion, ripped it away.

Harsh, blinding light burned her to ash. Nico fell with a scream, eyes slamming open. She was back on the beach, lying in the sand with Eli standing over her. He was panting like he'd just run a marathon and his hands were gripping the black cloth of her coat, which he'd just torn down.

She blinked at him, confused. "What happened?"

Eli glanced at something beside her. "Looks like you won."

Slowly, painfully, Nico turned her head. Den's face lay a foot from her own, his dead eyes open and staring into hers.

"I won," she whispered.

"You did," Eli said, reaching toward her with her coat. "Now let's try to help you survive it."

Nico looked at him in confusion, and then, hesitantly, she glanced down at her body. Her eyes widened. She was covered in a slick, black liquid. The stuff oozed like hot tar, but it smelled coppery, and it was oozing out of her. Nico's breath caught in what was left of her chest. It was blood, black blood. *Her* black blood.

With a choked scream, Nico started to scramble away on instinct only to find she couldn't. Beneath the tarry slick of her blood, her arms were twisted and broken. So were her legs. She looked like a little ink-filled doll dropped from a great height and shattered on the stone. She didn't even feel pain as she stared at what the demon transformation had left of her body, not at first, and not for the next several seconds.

370

But once it came, it consumed her. Shaking uncontrollably, she fell into the sand, gasping against her panic-frozen lungs, as Eli knelt beside her.

She tried to say something, but her mouth wouldn't work. Eli wouldn't have heard her anyway; he was focused on her limbs. A blinding crack of pain hit her as he pulled them straight, wrapping each one as fast as he could with her coat. She focused on his face as she fought to stay conscious, trying not to think about why he looked so pale and scared.

"Josef is going to kill me," Eli muttered, pulling her coat tight.

That was the last thing Nico heard before the awakened cloth of her coat crawled over her face and she sunk at last into unconsciousness.

CHAPTER
22

The sun hung low over the island as the Oseran ships came around. The fleet was looking ragged. Every runner had arrows peppering its side. Many had dead rowers, struck by a lucky shot, and all the sailors were exhausted. Their tiny supply of clingfire was long gone, but three palace ships were now floundering in the blue water. The first was nearly completely under, her sailors streaming off in lifeboats, which the runners harried whenever they could. The second was burning merrily while the third was taking on water through an enormous gash in its side. Josef had just ordered the flagship to circle back for another strike when his captain shouted, "Sire!"

Josef looked to see the dour old sailor grinning like a boy as he pointed to a thin line of red-tinted signal smoke cutting the evening sky over the beach. Josef lurched forward, rocking the boat as he leaned into the water. Sure enough, the sharp tip of the coral ledge was now clearly visible below their keel.

"We did it," he said, falling back with a grin.

Behind him, the captain began to laugh.

They'd done it. It hardly seemed possible, yet the proof was right below them. They'd sunk only three ships out of a fleet of thousands, but it'd been enough. They'd held the Empress's palace ships over the reef for the two hours they'd needed. Now the tide was rushing out as they watched, bringing the deep-running palace ships ever closer to the rocks below.

"I wouldn't believe it if you told me!" the captain shouted, slapping his king on the shoulder. "We did it! Thirty minutes until this whole strand is nothing but ten feet of surf over coral. Those big hulkers won't even be able to turn around before they run aground."

"Give the signal," Josef ordered, laying the Heart on the deck beside him. "We're going home."

A whoop went up from the sailors, and they leaped into action. The ship jerked as the sail swung around, forcing Josef to duck or be conked in the head. He didn't mind. The moment he'd released the Heart, the exhaustion hit him. He collapsed gratefully on the deck, savoring the wonderful feeling of being flat. Although his body was sending him strong signals it never wanted to move again, he reached up one last time, grabbing the edge of the ship and hauling himself up for a look at the rapidly approaching shore. The crescent beach of the bay was shrouded in shadow as the sun sank behind the mountain, but there was still enough light for him to see what was there. Or, more worryingly, what wasn't.

There was no sign of Den, or Nico. The sand was sundered, and even this far away he could see the dark patches left by blood. Blood, but no bodies.

"What was that, sire?" the captain said.

"I said go faster," Josef grunted, falling back to the deck.

"Yes, sire," the captain said. "Fast as we can."

Josef nodded and lay still as the narrow flagship raced home across the retreating blue water.

The bay filled as the runners returned. Of the ninety-five ships, eighty-two had made it back. A far better number than Josef had expected, and mostly due to the runners' speed. The Oseran archers simply hadn't been able to keep up. All around him, men were hopping from ship to ship, hugging and shouting in joy as they roped in.

Josef's captain steered the flagship away from the crowded docks, beaching it instead. Josef hopped out the second they scraped bottom, sloshing through the water to the beach as he made a beeline for the narrow stair leading up the storm wall. Those sailors already on the beach moved respectfully out of his way, whispering in awe. Any other time, this change would have made him self-conscious, but now Josef was too preoccupied to notice. He reached the top of the storm wall and ran for the watchtower, throwing open the heavy door and climbing the stairs three at a time. Eli met him on the second landing.

Josef pushed straight past him. "How did it go?"

"Den got the worst of the fight, if that's what you're asking," Eli said, keeping right on his heels.

"This isn't the time to be clever," Josef growled. "Did she win?"

"Well, Den's dead," Eli said. "So is Tesset. Nico is alive, for the moment."

"If she's alive, she's staying there," Josef said firmly. "She's a survivor."

"I'm well aware of your confidence in her unkillability," Eli said. "But you really should listen a moment before you barge—"

Josef slammed open the door to the observation room and stopped cold.

"—in," Eli finished, coming to a stop beside him.

Josef said nothing. He just stared.

"I did all I could," Eli said softly. "But I'm not a doctor, and I couldn't get the actual doctors near her without her coat going on the defensive. I don't even know what happened in that fight. I've seen a lot of bloodied people, mostly you, but I've never seen injuries like—"

His voice dropped off as Josef moved away. Josef crossed the room and fell to his knees beside the small, black bundle lying on the floor against the wall.

Nico was completely wrapped in her coat, cocooned like a caterpillar. That much was normal after a big fight. What wasn't normal was the dark pool of thick black liquid seeping into the floor beneath her. Josef swallowed. Slowly, gently, he reached out, brushing the wet cloth with his fingers. The coat twisted away from his touch with a sound that reminded him of hissing, but the sound stopped as Nico's small, pale hand emerged from the coat's folds, her thin fingers reaching for his.

Josef gripped her hand, sucking in a breath when he saw the black stains on her nails. Her pale skin was mottled black and purple, and he could see the beginnings of larger wounds on her arm before it disappeared into her coat. A long, burning stab of guilt cut through him, and Josef winced, opening his mouth before he realized he had no idea what to say. He sat there a moment, clutching her fingers as he searched for the words.

"I'm sorry," he whispered at last.

"Don't be." Nico's voice was thin and muffled by the coat. "I kept my promise."

"You shouldn't have had to," Josef said. "This is my war."

"Your war is my war," she whispered. "You should know that by now."

"Well, you won't have to fight it anymore," Josef said, folding his hands over hers. "Rest, Nico. I'll win it from here."

"I know you will," she said, her fingers going slack.

Josef raised her hand to his lips for a moment and then carefully tucked her arm back into the coat. The cloth rustled, pulling Nico back into its protective swaddle. Josef stood and turned to see Eli hovering in the doorway.

"I'm sorry," he said. "I couldn't help her."

"You brought her here," Josef said bitterly. "That was more than I could do." He met his friend's eyes. "I'm going to win the war, Eli. No matter what, I'm going to win."

"I know you are," Eli said with a grin. "Why do you think I'm still here?"

Josef shook his head. "Come on," he said, starting for the door. "We're not done yet."

"Yes, your majesty," Eli said, his smile widening at Josef's murderous look as they jogged down the stairs.

Nara frowned at the gap left in the line of her palace ships, and her scowl only deepened as she turned to the man kneeling at her feet, his forehead pressed against the tile floor of her balcony.

"Well?" she said. "Did you crush those buzzing gnats holding up our assault? I would like to get close enough to launch the war spirits before we lose the entire front to whatever idiocy is going on at the front."

"The Oserans have retreated, Empress," the general said, pressing his head harder against the ground. "But we must pull back as well. The tide is going out. Your fleet will be stranded on the rocks if we do not retreat."

Nara looked away with a sniff. "I do not retreat."

"But, Empress," the general's voice trembled. "We've already lost three ships. If we do not retreat now, we could lose the rest of the first wave."

"General," Nara said, glaring down. "Do you know who I am?"

"You are the Immortal Empress," the man said, crouching lower. "Queen of all the world."

Nara lifted her chin. "And do you think that the queen of the world fears something as trivial as the tide?"

The general swallowed. "No, Empress."

"You must have faith, General," Nara said, opening her spirit.

The general shook visibly as the enormous pressure landed on him. "I believe," he whispered.

The Empress began to smile as she opened her spirit wider. When her power was roaring in her ears, she reached out, plunging herself into the current that was still waiting below her ships. The mob of water spirits screamed and thrashed as she grabbed it, but her will was absolute.

"The fleet moves forward," she said, her voice thick and resonant with power. "I don't care how many troops it takes. Beach the ships if you have to. We conquer the island by nightfall."

"Yes, Empress," the general said, crawling backward out of her presence all the way to the stairs before standing and running down to the command center to signal her orders to the fleet.

"Well?" Josef said, joining his admiral on the stone walkway above the bay. "How much longer?"

"Not long," said the admiral, dancing from foot to foot in his anticipation. "Tide's nearly out. There's no way they can escape now."

"Good," Josef said, nodding to the crowd of gawking sailors and guardsmen crowding the beach. "Get those men onto the cliffs. Once the ships hit the rocks and start taking on water, the crews are going to head for the shore. If they land, it'll be bad. No one fights harder than men with no retreat. We have to sink their boats before they reach the shore."

"Yes, sire," the admiral said. He saluted and started down the stairs, barking orders as he went. Josef stayed put, glancing at Eli as the thief stepped up beside him.

"You're growing more kingly by the minute."

"Save it," Josef grumbled, glaring at the distant shadows of the palace ships. "We've bought some time, but if the Council reinforcements don't get here before the tide comes in again, that'll be that. I can't sink the whole fleet by myself. All it'll take is one of those ships making landfall and we'll be overrun."

"If it happens, we'll deal with it," Eli said firmly. "You've bought us a reprieve for the moment. That's something to be—"

Eli stopped midsyllable, his face screwing up in a look of surprise.

Josef tensed. "What?" he said. Because Eli looking surprised was never good.

"It's just—" Eli bit his lip. "I'm no sailor, but isn't the water supposed to be moving toward the *sea* when the tide goes out?"

Josef blinked and looked down. Sure enough, the ocean was rushing into the bay, pushing the line of the surf back up the beach.

"Don't tell me the Empress can even change the tides," he whispered.

"No," Eli said. "Look." He pointed, moving his finger back and forth from the sea to the bay, tracing a faint line of darker, deep running water running in through the Rebuke's protective cliffs. "It's a current. She's pushing against the tide with a current."

Josef cursed and ran for the stairs. "Admiral!"

The admiral, already halfway down the storm wall on his way to deliver Josef's orders, looked up. "Yes, sire?"

It would have taken too long to explain, so Josef jumped the short wall onto the stairs and ran down himself, grabbing the admiral's shoulders and pointing the man at the sea. The admiral struggled a moment, and then his body went slack as a look of pure dread crept over his face.

"Powers help us," he whispered.

Josef let him go. "What can we do?"

The admiral ran a trembling hand through his thin, gray hair as he watched the ocean swell back up nearly to the storm wall's base. "She's pushed us nearly back to high tide," he said, his voice despairing. "More than enough to get her ships over the reef. After that, it's a straight shot to us."

"You think she'll hit the Rebuke?" Josef said.

"Undoubtedly," the admiral said. "This is the most strategically valuable spot on this side of the island. It's also where our fleet is and a clear path to the city itself. She'd be a fool not to take this bay, and I very much doubt the Immortal Empress is a fool." The old man clenched his teeth. "We can't let her enter the bay. If they land a ship on us here, we're done."

"Can we take the fleet out again?" Josef said. "Sink the ships as they come in?"

The admiral shook his head. "It took you two hours to sink three ships. By the time you cut one down, we'll be overrun."

Josef cursed loudly. "So what do we do?"

The admiral licked his lips, but before he could answer, another voice spoke up.

"Abuse your advantages," Eli said, walking down the stairs to join them.

The admiral frowned, but Josef turned to face the thief. "Go on."

"This is a nice, deep bay," Eli said. "But those palace ships are ten times the size of the biggest Council freighter. They're heavy, loaded for conquest, and running deep. Even with the current lifting them, they'll have to enter the bay carefully to avoid scraping bottom. But raise that bottom a little, and you make a difficult task impossible."

Josef stared at him. "How am I supposed to raise the bottom of the sea?"

"Put something on it," Eli said, glancing pointedly at the ships filling the bay.

The admiral almost turned green. "You can't mean—"

"Are you suggesting I sink my fleet," Josef said over him. "My *only* fleet, to make a wall?"

Eli nodded. "That's exactly what I'm saying."

"*Are you an idiot?*" the admiral screamed.

"No," Eli said, crossing his arms. "But I might start to think you are if you can't see that your runners are no longer useful."

"Majesty!" the admiral cried. "You cannot listen to this

378

madness." He flung out his hand toward the boats. "Those runners are fine, precision-crafted warships. You can't sacrifice our naval strength on one foolhardy gambit!"

"Actually, I don't see why not," Josef said, rubbing his chin. "Eli's right. Without clingfire, the runners are only good now for drawing fire and dodging between palace ships. Dodging doesn't win wars. If we can block the bay, we can buy time for the Council to arrive."

"But, sire," the admiral said, his voice cracking. "That fleet was your mother's pride!"

"And my mother would throw it away in a heartbeat if it served her country," Josef said. "We can't be sentimental if we're going to have a hope of surviving."

The admiral looked like he was about to cry. "If you sink the fleet, we'll be defenseless against the next naval attack."

Josef smirked. "Fight the sword at your throat, admiral, not the sword in the sheath. If sinking the fleet gives me the luxury of missing it later, I'll count that a victory. Man the runners, skeleton crews only, and tell the men to line them up at the mouth of the bay. I want everyone else to get a bow and get to the cliffs. This is now a siege."

The admiral clutched his head in his hands. "I can't believe this is happening."

"Believe it," Eli said, giving the old man a gentle push. "Off you go now. We don't have much time."

Too shocked to realize he was taking orders from the prince's layabout friend, the admiral nodded and ran down the stairs, calling orders in a mournful voice.

The sailors of Osera lived up to their reputation. Not fifteen minutes after the plan was hatched, the runners were moving out. Four men crewed each ship, rowing hard against the current until they reached the mouth of the bay. They worked quickly, throwing the wrist-thick docking lines from ship to ship. As one pair of men tied the lines, the other worked the anchor, dragging the chain back and forth across the seabed to catch the rocks. One by one, the boats linked together,

379

forming a floating wall between the bay and the sea. When the ships were all tied in position, by rope to each other and by anchor to the ocean floor below, the sailors kissed the prows good-bye before pulling the bilge plugs. As the sea rushed in, the sailors jumped into the bay and swam for the trawlers waiting to take them to shore.

Josef watched it all from the cliffs where the royal guard and those sailors not tasked with sinking the fleet had positioned themselves with crossbows taken from the watchtower armory. The admiral was there as well, his face pale and drawn.

When the last ship had been scuttled, Josef examined the battlefield. The mouth of the bay was now a spiky wall of sunken ships. Each runner had been scuttled prow first, its iron-tipped nose shoved deep between the craggy rocks of the bay floor with its long body pointing up and its narrow mast stabbed into the water behind it like a brace. Even so, the wall of scrapped boats looked like little more than flotsam before the enormous palace ships.

"Will it work, you think?" the admiral whispered.

"We'll know soon enough," Josef said. "Are the archers ready?"

The admiral nodded. "Everyone's in position. The scuttle crews will get bows and get up to the cliffs as soon as they land."

"Good," Josef said. "Because the enemy's on its way."

The Empress's fleet had cleared the reef and was now plowing across the span of deep water that ran parallel to the coast. The front line of ships was already within striking distance of the sea cliffs, but the fleet slowed as it neared the island, turning off the Empress's current to form a ring around the mouth of the bay. Lights flashed on the decks as the ships signaled to each other, and then one of the palace ships from the circle's northern end broke off from the group and began slowly moving toward the wall of sunken ships.

"They'll stop," the admiral said as the palace ship crept toward the barrier. "They have to stop. They'll break their hulls and strand themselves if they don't. No admiral would waste a ship like that."

"And no woman would give up life as a princess and betray her homeland for the love of a ruler she's never met," Josef said bitterly. "Don't underestimate the Immortal Empress, admiral." Josef looked up, raising his voice as he grabbed his crossbow from the ledge. "Stations! Here they come!"

The order was scarcely out of his mouth when the enormous palace ship crashed into the sunken remains of the Oseran fleet.

The squeal of wood on wood echoed off the cliffs, followed by the horrible crunch of breaking timbers. At the mouth of the bay, the line of sunken ships was bowing, dragged inward by the momentum of the enormous ship. The water churned as the sunken runners plowed along the seabed, and then, with a great clang of metal on stone, the tangle of anchors and knotted chains reached the end of its slack. The line caught, and the palace ship jerked to a halt.

The bay held its breath as the ship stopped. On its deck, the soldiers were sliding, thrown off their feet by the sudden stop. Some fell hundreds of feet into the water below as the ship tilted with a great groan, its keel well and truly stuck in the wall of the sunken fleet.

A cheer went up from the cliffs and then died out almost as quickly as the prow of the palace ship began to shake. Josef squinted. It was possible the crash had broken something inside, but the soldiers on the deck weren't running with the sort of panic he'd expect from the crew of a damaged ship. He was still watching their movements for a sign of their plan when the prow of the palace ship fell forward.

The great pointed nose fell like an ancient tree, crashing into the bay with a splash that echoed off the cliffs. It bobbed once in the water before a network of ropes wrenched it tight. Josef bit back a curse. The prow hadn't broken. It was designed to fall, forming a launch ramp for the troop boats Josef could now see waiting inside the ship's enormous belly. The second the ramp was steady, the boats began to roll out, pushed by men carrying long wooden shields over their heads, their dark faces set in grim determination as they hauled the boats down the ramp and into the bay.

Three ships were in the water before Josef realized his army was gawking and not firing.

"Shoot!" Josef shouted, arching his neck to look up at the sailors on the cliffs. "*Now!*"

The men jumped at his voice, and at once a ragged volley launched from the cliffs. The short, black crossbow bolts flew from all directions, falling on the boats like rain. The enemy raised their shields over their heads, but it wasn't enough. Men fell screaming into the water with bloody splashes as the Oseran arrows struck true, but it did not stop the torrent of boats pouring out of the palace ship.

"Keep firing!" Josef shouted as he reloaded his own bow. "Don't let up!"

Wave after wave of bolts shot down from the cliffs, covering the enemy ramp in a bristle of wooden quills. The bolts struck hard, hard enough to punch holes in the troop ships that were already in the water. But for every boat the Oserans sank, two more appeared from the palace ship's maw, sliding down the ramp into the bay whose blue water was now a sickly shade of purple.

"How many of the bastards are in there?" the admiral shouted.

"Too many," Josef said, tossing his empty quiver down and reaching for another. "But they're not the real trouble. Look."

The admiral followed Josef's gaze past the palace ship's open nose to its back, and his ashen face turned even grayer.

On the rear deck of the palace ship, ten men stood in a circle around a glowing sphere of iron and stone. The sphere grew brighter by the second, until it hurt Josef's eyes to look at. When it was as bright as a small sun, the men threw out their hands in unison and the glowing ball launched into the sky. It arced above the bay and started to fall, hurtling toward the watchtower with a high-pitched scream.

"War spirit!" the admiral cried. "Get a team down there!"

"No!" Josef shouted. "Keep firing! The war spirit is covered!"

The admiral stared at him. "Covered how?"

Josef nodded at the storm wall. "Time for that lazy bastard to do his part."

The admiral turned and nearly dropped his bow. Eli was standing on the storm wall, staring up at the falling war spirit with a calm smile as he unbuttoned his shirt. With each button, black smoke rose to curl around him, flashing with sparks. Overhead, the war spirit was picking up speed, its scream ratcheting up to a deafening wail even Josef could feel in his bones. Just before it crashed into the tower's tile roof, the fire over Eli's head exploded and an enormous, glowing hand snatched the war spirit out of the air.

Heat poured over the bay as Karon roared to life. He stepped out of the smoke, his great feet searing the stone of the storm wall. The lava spirit's glowing face was split in a wide grin as he hefted the war spirit in his hand and, after a windup, threw it back. The war spirit shot out of the lava giant's hand like an arrow. It flew screaming, leaving a streak of smoke behind as it barreled across the bay and landed with an enormous crash in the palace ship's hull.

The palace ship rocked under the impact, slamming into the seafloor with so much force Josef felt it through his boots. The Empress's soldiers screamed as their ramp tipped into the water, capsizing the launching ships and toppling their passengers into the bay. Up on the cliffs, an enormous cheer went up from the Oserans. Down on the wall, Eli held his arms up in answer.

"Stop cheering and keep firing!" Josef shouted. "We're still under attack and you're only puffing up his head!"

The men scrambled to obey, sending another rain of arrows down on the invading ships. The wizards on the palace ship were running madly now, too busy patching the hole from the returned war spirit to launch another. Meanwhile, the flow of soldiers from the open nose of the palace ships slowed to a trickle as the crews retreated to help deal with the damage. This left those already in the water unguarded as the Oseran arrows rained down like black hail, and for a moment, Josef almost believed they'd stopped the charge.

"Sire!" a voice shouted, shattering the illusion. "South!"

Josef turned just in time to see a second palace ship crash into the wall of the sunken fleet at the bay's southern tip. The crack of wood drowned out every other sound as the boat ground forward. This ship was going much faster than the first, cleaving into the bay in an attempt to break the barrier. But for all its power, the stubborn tangle of anchors held, and the enormous ship slammed to a stop, sending soldiers skidding off her decks.

Josef gave a triumphant shout. But even as cheers began to ring from the cliffs, the second ship's prow fell, and a fresh surge of soldiers poured into the bay.

"Don't stop!" Josef roared, firing his crossbow at the new boats. "Keep firing! Don't let them reach the shore!"

The sailors on the cliffs answered him with a rain of arrows. The bolts whistled as they flew. Some hit nothing but water, others landed in the heavy shields the enemy took shelter beneath as they pushed the line. A few lucky shots struck true, sending soldiers toppling out of boats. But with so many firing from the cliffs, those few lucky shots had been enough. Just barely. But now, as the second palace ship began disgorging its troops in earnest, the Oserans started to fall behind.

"Keep firing!" Josef shouted again, grabbing another quiver of bolts. "Focus on the ones in the water!"

He had just launched another bolt when he heard a crash above him, and Josef looked up to see Eli's lava spirit grabbing the edge of the cliff. Karon's glowing hands cut easily through the stone, carving out an enormous boulder. Down on the storm wall, Eli was shouting words Josef couldn't hear, pointing at the new palace ship. Karon nodded and hefted the boulder in his hand. He closed his fingers, firing the stone to a red-hot ember before launching it at the second ship.

The boulder struck true, hitting the palace ship's enormous tower of a mast. Josef covered his ears against the crack of shattering wood as the mast snapped and fell, its top plummeting into the deck below. This, plus the impact of the stone itself, was enough to crack the ship's keel against the seabed. The palace ship broke with a scream of wood, and then the air was filled with a rushing roar as the water began to gush in.

Josef screamed in triumph, raising his arm to Eli, who bowed in return, a huge grin on his face. Karon was grinning too as he reached out to cut another boulder from the cliff.

Nara clutched the railing of her balcony, glaring furiously at the enormous, glowing giant sinking her ships. Even at this distance, there was no mistaking the lava spirit for anything other than what it was, and that raised a new problem. No mere wizard could command the fire that ran through the heart of the world. The Oserans had a star fighting for them.

She clenched her teeth. What star would dare oppose her? She was no longer the favorite, but she was close enough that it shouldn't matter. Even forgetting that, how could there be a star here when Benehime herself had ordered this island burned to the ground?

Nara paused, thinking quickly. Perhaps the Shepherdess didn't know? For all her power, she wasn't omnipotent. Maybe she wasn't aware that one of her stars had turned rogue? It wouldn't be the first. The Lady had been forced to put down the Great Bear not long before this. If a star was interfering with the invasion, the wise thing to do would be to call the Shepherdess and get her blessing before continuing, but Nara hesitated.

The Lady loved her as a conqueror, an Empress. An Empress ruled with absolute authority. An Empress rolled over everything in her path. An *Empress* did not run crying to the Shepherdess whenever trouble appeared. Nara pursed her lips. Until the Lady told her differently, the order to burn Osera stood. Whoever this star was, they would soon learn what it meant to challenge the soon to be recrowned favorite.

Smile returning, Nara opened her spirit again and sank down into the sea. This time, she ignored the great current, grabbing a smaller one instead. The current cried and begged, but it obeyed like all the others in the end. As it fled to do her bidding, Nara sat back on her couch to see what the star would do.

Josef didn't notice the admiral's absence until the old man returned, his face grim.

"Sire!" he yelled over the roar of snapping bows. "We're running out of bolts!"

"Can't be," Josef said, launching the last bolt from his quiver. "Finley had six months' worth laid up."

"Six months of normal fire," the admiral said. "Not for this."

Josef turned and looked, his heart falling. He hadn't had time to notice in the heat of battle, but the crate he and the other men on this part of the cliff had been using was empty. So was the crate it sat on.

"They're on the last box on the south side as well," the admiral said. "A runner just came asking for more. I had to turn him away."

"So there's nothing left?"

The admiral shook his head. "We emptied the tower armory as you commanded. Every last bolt was here."

Josef cursed and looked down at the bay. He could hear it happening already. The whistling roar of the bolts was shrinking, the light on the bay brightening as the rain of arrows began to dissipate.

"Send runners to the other cliff," he said, tossing his now-useless crossbow on the ground. "Tell the men to finish the bolts they have and get down to the wall."

"What can we do on the wall?" the admiral said. "We've a hundred royal guard left, but the rest of these men are sailors, not infantry."

"Then it's time to switch vocations," Josef said. "We've five hundred men here. That many of the enemy are lying facedown in the water already, and we haven't even made a dent in their numbers. But we've still got terrain on our side. If Eli's message got through, the Council fleet should be on its way right now. All we have to do is hold a little longer."

"If we go down there we'll be slaughtered!" the admiral shouted.

"We'll be slaughtered anyway!" Josef shouted back. "If you want to roll over for it, be my guest, but I mean to die as an Oseran should: fighting."

And with that, he left the admiral gaping and stomped down to the storm wall.

Eli was waiting for him at the base of the cliff, though he didn't look as smug as Josef had expected. He was smiling, but his face was pale and his eyes were dark with exhaustion.

"You all right?" Josef said as the thief fell in beside him.

"Fantastic," Eli said.

Josef didn't buy it. "You look like you've been running for three days straight. If you can't keep it up, say something. I'd rather fight without a lava spirit than have it go out on me at a bad time."

"I can keep this up as long I have to," Eli said firmly, glancing up at the lava giant as it stepped aside to make room on the storm wall for the gathering troops. "It's just that there's not much for Karon to burn for energy here, so I'm having to feed him some of my own." He laughed. "It's disgustingly Spiritualist-like, actually. My only comfort is that Miranda isn't here to see it."

"Just don't push yourself," Josef said. "I can't have you and Nico down at the same time."

"Don't worry about me," Eli said, his voice suddenly

serious. "Think of this as my chance to pay a little back for all the blood you've spilled for me."

"I don't reckon debts in blood," Josef said, reaching out to grab Eli's shoulder. "Watch yourself, thief."

"You too, king," Eli said, breaking off from Josef with a salute.

Josef shook his head and jogged over to join the soldiers.

The Oserans crowded the storm wall. The royal guardsmen were already in formation by the stair, but the rest of the men stood in loose knots, some still clutching their empty crossbows. They parted to make a path for Josef as he climbed onto the storm wall's lip and turned to face his army, such as it was.

"Listen up!" Josef shouted. "I'm not going to waste time with kingly speeches. All I'll say is this. We did our best to hold the enemy back, but it was never more than a dyke against the flood. Now we're up to our necks, and the only chance we have to stop the Empress from crushing this island and our lives under her feet is the stone under ours." He stomped hard on the storm wall. "We are not dead yet. Reinforcements are coming from the mainland even as I speak. Our job now is to buy those slow Council bastards time enough to get here. Fortunately, Osera herself is on our side. We've got a choke hold." He pointed at the narrow stair leading up from the beach. "We've got the sun at our backs, and we're forcing them to fight uphill. These are our weapons, and with them, we are going to hold this wall."

But even as he pointed out their terrain advantage, many of the men still looked doubtful. Some even looked like they were about to cry. Josef took a deep breath. The storm wall might be strong, but the men were a brittle barrier, easily broken. He was going to need them to be stronger if this was going to work, and so, with nothing left to lose and Eli too far away to hear him, Josef decided to throw it all in.

"Men of Osera!" he shouted, doing his best to infuse his voice with the deep, proud sincerity he remembered from his mother's speeches. "I've been a horrible prince to you my entire life, but though I might be your king for only another few minutes, I mean to make them count. As a swordsman, I learned that the two most dangerous enemies are the desperate man and the man defending his home. Right now, we are both. We are the worst enemy the Empress has ever met. We will hold this wall and make her remember the cost of fighting Osera!"

The cry that came when he finished made Josef jump. The men screamed with a fury he could feel to his bones, raising their blades as they did. Josef raised his sword in answer and shouted for them to get in position. The men scrambled to obey, the sailors lining up on the storm wall while the guard fell in around Josef at the top of the stair. The royal guard saluted their king as he passed, following Josef as he climbed down the stair until he was halfway between the beach and the top of the storm wall. Here Josef stopped, planting his sword as the guard fell into formation behind him.

Down below, the first boats had made it to the shore. The enemy jumped into the surf with a blood-curdling scream, surging up the beach like a black tide. They hit the storm wall and began crowding into the bottleneck of the narrow stair. When the first enemies came in range, Josef stepped forward, swinging the Heart with a shout. Behind him, the Oserans answered with a scream that shook the stones of the storm wall itself.

"Eli," Karon rumbled, pressing his hand to the ground. "The rock says there are ships coming across the channel from the mainland."

"Please tell me it's the Council," Eli moaned.

"Sad showing if it is," Karon said. "Only two boats."

"I'd take a rowboat and a mule at this point," Eli said. "Meanwhile, you ready to give our swordsman some cover?"

"Sure," Karon said, grinning as he grabbed another boulder from the cliff. "Where do you want this one?"

"I'm thinking middle of the bay," Eli said, his voice breathy. Karon was pulling hard on him now. "Make some waves. See if we can't capsize a few boats."

"Easy enough," Karon said, firing the stone in his fist until it was red hot. But as he reached back to throw, a crash made them both jump.

Eli spun around, eyes wide as a spout of water erupted from the sea. It thrust from the bay like a spear, shooting up the storm wall straight at Karon. Eli threw out his hands, but the water was too fast, and he, exhausted, was too slow. The geyser of water hit his lava spirit full in the chest. Some of it hit Eli as well, and he gasped as the icy-cold shock took his breath away. This was no mere ocean water; it was a deep-sea current flowing full force, thrown up from the sea.

Karon fell as the water drenched him, screaming as his light went out. The ground trembled when he landed, and the impact threw Eli off his feet. He landed on the sandy ground by the road, tumbling hard. But before he was done falling, he was scrambling to his feet. Beside him, Karon's body was no longer glowing, but a black heap of steaming rubble. Eli rushed forward with a curse, plunging his hands into the hissing stone. It burned as he touched it, but not nearly as much as it should have. Cursing louder, Eli dug down, stabbing his spirit through the cooling rock as he dug toward Karon's molten core.

He caught it just in time. Eli tugged his hands out of the stone and pressed the lava spirit's flickering heart to his own chest. His skin burned when Karon touched it, but Eli had never welcomed the pain so much. He clenched his teeth and pushed harder, forcing the lava's heart into his own. Karon went without a sound, and, for a long moment, Eli knew he'd lost him. Then the lava's heat flashed as Karon's pulse merged with Eli's, and the burning heart began to beat.

Eli fell to the soaked ground, panting and clutching his burning chest. "Karon," he whispered. "Say something."

The silence stretched on.

"Please," Eli pleaded. "Please say something."

But the lava spirit didn't answer. Eli could feel Karon's heat in his chest, but it was so small, so fragile. Before he could panic further, Eli forced himself to stand. He teetered toward the watchtower, desperately searching for somewhere to collapse. If Karon was going to survive, he needed all of Eli's strength, which meant Eli couldn't have any of it for a while.

"Hang on," he whispered, pushing open the watchtower door. "I promised I wouldn't leave you, but that cuts both ways, you know? Don't go out on me now."

His only answer was silence as he pulled himself up the watchtower stairs.

Meanwhile, halfway down the storm wall, Josef met the first of the Empress's soldiers with a clash that echoed across the bay.

CHAPTER
23

"Hold the line!" Josef screamed, swinging the Heart at the seething wall of soldiers.

The enemy covered the beach in a solid mass, but only a few could go up the stairs at a time. These Josef held off easily, but the enemy, realizing the obvious path was blocked, was now climbing the jagged stone of the storm wall itself.

"Spread out!" Josef shouted to the soldiers behind him. "Half left, half right! Knock them off as they climb. Don't let them reach the top!"

The orders were swallowed as he gave them, overwhelmed by the war cries of the enemy as they surged forward and the dying screams of his soldiers as they shot the last of their bolts at the climbers only to find that the enemy had bows of their own.

Josef swung again, knocking three enemy soldiers down the stairs with a curse. For every man he knocked down, two more popped up. The crashed palace ships were still vomiting up troops, and the bloody bay was full of boats. The storm wall was alive with the enemy. They swarmed the stairs, swarmed the wall; some were even climbing the cliffs themselves, pulling themselves hand over hand up the vertical stone toward the abandoned archer lines. Meanwhile, the Oseran sailors had spread themselves thin in an attempt to hold the storm wall. They screamed as they fought, their eyes wide with the wildness of men pushed past their limits. The only place the enemy sailors weren't attacking was the blackened stretch where Karon had stood, but the lava spirit himself was nowhere to be seen. Instead, a great pile of black stone blocked the storm wall, the boulders still and quiet. Josef knew little of wizardry and nothing about the link between Eli and the giant, but even he knew those dark, cold rocks were not a good sign.

Unfortunately, Josef had bigger worries than the lava spirit. As more and more soldiers began to climb the storm wall, the Oserans were starting to fold. The fragile line he'd drawn as their last stand was cracking. Any second now it would break completely and he would fail his mother one last time.

The Heart jerked in his hands, bringing him back to the fight in front of him. He could feel the blade thrumming against his fingers, and Josef blinked as the Heart's plan became clear in his mind. It was risky, but he trusted the Heart to know its own limits, and they had precious little else to call on. Decision made, Josef swung wide to scatter the enemy and then brought his sword back, holding the blade in front of him with both hands. Down the stairs, the Empress's soldiers hesitated, watching for the strike. When it didn't come, they surged into the opening, swords rising to cut him down. When they were a step away, Josef slammed the Heart into the stair. Iron hit stone with a resounding *gong*, and the weight of a mountain fell on the beach.

As far as he could see, the Empress's soldiers collapsed, slammed to the ground by the pressure. The Heart's force spread wider than Josef had ever seen. It filled the bay, sweeping the soldiers off the storm wall and crushing them into the hard sand below. Infantry boats sank into water pressed glassy by the enormous weight, and a sudden, deafening stillness descended. Even the Oserans were silent, staring down the storm wall at the prone bodies of the Empress's troops in dumb amazement.

Finally, a guardsman behind Josef snapped out of the trance, reaching out to press his shaking hand against the invisible wall of the Heart's weight. "Are they dead, sire?" he whispered, eyes wide.

Josef raised his head, careful to keep his hands on the Heart's hilt. "No," he said. "The ones forced underwater may drown, but no one will die from the pressure. I don't understand it myself, but my wizard friend says it's impossible to kill a human with spirit pressure alone."

The sailor blinked. "Spirit pressure?"

"Don't ask me," Josef said. "I don't do that wizard stuff." He looked over his shoulder, raising his voice. "Everyone!" he shouted. "Stop gawking! We're falling back to the watchtower."

"But we have no more bolts!" a sailor cried. "What are we going to do in the tower?"

"You want to stay out here?" Josef bellowed back.

The man didn't answer, and Josef took the chance to push the guards behind him up the stairs. "Get the wounded to the tower. The rest of you, prepare to hold the road. We'll fight these bastards for every inch!"

The men sprang into action, grabbing the wounded and dragging them back. They swarmed the watchtower, carrying their fallen comrades on their backs as they climbed the stairs. Those who could still fight gathered at the head of the road

393

to the city and began piling barrels, empty arrow crates, anything they could find into a makeshift barricade.

Of the Oserans, Josef alone did not move. He watched his men climb the stairs, hands clenched around the Heart's hilt. Down in the bay, nothing stirred, but as the minutes ticked by, the Heart began to quiver against his palm. Josef gripped it harder and stood firm, trying to press his strength into the Heart as the sword had done for him so many times before. He didn't know if it worked, but the Heart held. Five minutes. Seven minutes. At ten minutes Josef knew as surely as though the blade had shouted that time was up. It was just enough. The sailor's retreat was finished. He was now alone on the stairs with the flattened invaders.

In one smooth motion, Josef ripped the Heart out of the step and turned to run, charging up the stairs toward the Oseran line. Behind him, the sword's weight vanished like mist, and the silent air filled with the angry, confused roar of the Empress's army as it got to its feet and began to give chase. Josef reached the top of the stairs and ran full-out toward the makeshift barricade. Yelling for his men to get out of the way, he jumped the piled barrels. The second his feet hit the dirt, he turned and took stock of their new position.

It was bad. Osera's primary defense on this side had always been the sea and the cliffs. Here, behind those walls, they had precious little. The tower with its thick stone and reinforced doors was safe, but the road was another matter. The wall of junk the soldiers had cobbled together wouldn't stop a charge, only delay it. After that...

Josef glanced over his shoulder. The road ran up the mountain behind him, through the shoddy neighborhoods of the eastern slope to the castle and the city beyond. A straight shot. Josef gritted his teeth. He could feel his men watching him, their eyes wide and terrified. Raising his sword, Josef forced himself to look confident. He wasn't sure if it worked. The men didn't look reassured, but they didn't run away either.

That would have to be good enough, Josef decided. He wasn't his mother, after all.

"We hold here," he said, planting his feet firmly on the sandy road. "Get ready."

He felt the line tighten around him. The royal guardsmen moved to take the road's center, locking together in tight formation with their short swords ready. The sailors hovered at the edges, clutching their knives with wild-eyed intensity as the first enemy reached the top of the storm wall.

For a few seconds, it was just one man, and then the Empress's army poured over the wall. They came in a black wave, armor rattling like an avalanche, their raised swords gleaming in the last rays of the evening sun. When they opened their mouths to shout, the air itself seemed to thicken with the rage of their battle cry.

"Hold!" Josef shouted, but the command was lost in the enemy's roar. It didn't matter. His men were frozen in place by fear. They couldn't have moved now if they'd tried, not even to run. All they could do was bunker down and scream their last defiance as their death charged forward to crush them under a thousand booted feet.

Josef gripped the Heart. Even his sword couldn't beat so many, but he would hold as long as he could. The Heart weighed heavy in his hands, echoing his resolve. They would go down as a swordsman should, in glorious battle surrounded by the bodies of their enemies. But even as he braced for his final stand, Josef heard a cry that stopped him cold. It was a high-pitched shout, not panicked or afraid, but commanding. A woman's shout, and as it sounded, a great wave of water shot through the air above his head and landed on the charging army.

The wave swept the soldiers off their feet, washing them back over the storm wall and down to the beach in the space of a breath. Josef lowered his sword, staring dumbfounded at the now-clear storm wall. He was so shocked, he didn't even flinch as the lithe, silvery, canine shape sailed through the air and landed right in front of him.

Gin landed neatly and turned to flash Josef the smuggest, toothiest grin he'd ever seen, but the dog's grin was nothing compared to the haughty smile on his rider's face.

"Well, well," Miranda said, looking down on him from her ghosthound's back. "If it isn't Josef Liechten."

"Miranda," Josef said, leaning on his sword. "Took you long enough."

Miranda sniffed. "Is that any way to greet your savior?"

Josef shrugged. "Better late than never, I suppose."

She shook her head and turned Gin back toward the city. Josef moved to follow her and stopped, eyes wide. The road from Osera, which had been empty not a minute before, was now filled with the strangest creatures he'd ever seen. There were cats made of living wood, birds shaped from clouds, and even what looked like a long, flat snake made of mud. There must have been a hundred at least, each different, and each carrying a rider whose hands flashed with enormous, gaudy rings.

"Powers," Josef whispered. "What in the world is that?"

"*That* is your salvation," Miranda said proudly. "The Spirit Court comes to face the Empress."

"Lucky us," Josef muttered, taking a step back as the lead rider, an intense man mounted on an enormous jade horse, came to a halt beside Miranda.

"Who is this?" the man asked, looking Josef up and down.

"A criminal, Master Banage," Miranda answered. "But one on our side, for now at least."

Josef looked the old man over. So this was the Rector Spiritualis she was always going on about. He'd have to remind Eli to change his alias.

Banage arched an eyebrow at Miranda's introduction and then moved on to business.

"Miranda, with me," he said, dismounting. "The rest of you"—he looked over his shoulder at the waiting Spiritualists—"form a perimeter and wake the local spirits. This island is now under the Court's protection."

"Yes, Rector!" The shout rose from a hundred throats in unison, and the wizards began to dismount. One by one their creatures disappeared, flowing back to the rings on their riders' fingers. Josef noted that the Rector's own mount had vanished into the large oval of polished jade on his index finger. Banage didn't even seem to notice. He and Miranda were already walking toward the sea wall.

"Hold it!" Josef shouted, leaving his poor, shocked sailors standing dumb on the road as he ran after the two wizards. "What are you, crazy? There are a thousand soldiers down there!"

"Shoo," Miranda said. "Go back to the others. We've got it from here."

"Got what?" Josef yelled.

"Young man," Banage said calmly, not even looking at Josef as he walked. "A thousand soldiers are of little concern. Whom do you think you are dealing with?"

"A pair of suicidal idiots," Josef snapped back.

"I see only one of those," Miranda said, glaring at him.

Josef threw up his hands as Miranda and the Rector Spiritualis stepped out onto the edge of the storm wall. Gin sat down beside his mistress, tail lashing back and forth. Down on the beach, the enemy was regrouping. Soldiers from the boats were trading places with the men down the wall by Miranda's wave. Meanwhile, a mass was gathering at the wall's base with archers taking up position to cover the next push to retake the wall.

Josef cursed and reached to pull Miranda out of arrow shot at least, but she smacked his hands away.

"Just stand back," she said, raising her voice over Gin's growling.

Josef had a pretty nonkingly answer for that, but Miranda had already turned back to face the beach. She stood still a moment, feet pressed against the storm wall's edge, her red hair blowing in the sea wind like a painted archer target. Josef cursed, but before he could yank her down to safety, dog or

397

no dog, Miranda held out her hand and a wave of water exploded into the air.

The torrent poured down the storm wall, sweeping it clean. It blasted the soldiers into the sand before turning like a snake and rushing down the beach until it reached the northern cliff. There it shot up again, defying gravity in a geyser of white spray to knock off the soldiers scaling the cliff face, shucking them from the stone like barnacles before turning back toward the beach, knocking those soldiers who'd tried to stand back onto their faces as it rushed to clear the southern cliff.

But while Miranda's water was sweeping the beach, the soldiers in the boats were on the move. Archers brought up their bows while those with shields gave them cover, and the air filled with the snapping of bowstrings. A volley of arrows launched from the water, whistling toward the two wizards on the storm wall's edge.

Josef moved on instinct, raising his sword. He couldn't cut all the arrows down, but maybe he could stop enough to keep the idiot wizards from getting themselves killed. But as he stepped into position, the Rector Spiritualis raised his arms, the ruby on his thumb glowing like a furnace. That was the last thing Josef saw before a blast of light drowned his vision.

A wave of blistering hot air caught Josef in the face. He stumbled away, cursing as he blinked against the swimming shapes the light had left on his vision. As his eyes cleared, he looked up to see a great ball of fire hovering in the air before Banage. Its edges burned like liquid gold, and its center was so bright Josef couldn't look at it. The fire roared and twisted like a living thing, the flames turning until they settled at last into the shape of a great, golden bird.

The bird opened its mouth, roaring like a furnace as it devoured the arrows. The shafts were consumed instantly, transformed into a harmless rain of ash that pattered at the Spiritualists' feet. When the last arrow had been consumed, the bird began to beat its wings. Each wing beat hammered Josef with a wall of heat, and with each flap, the bird grew larger until its fire filled the sky. The light was so intense now, Josef could barely see, but he could make out the shadow of Miranda crouching on the wall, her water surrounding her and her dog in a protective barrier against the heat. Banage, however, had no protection. He stood at the heart of the fire, a speck of black against the inferno. With a great sweeping motion, the Rector Spiritualis threw out his arms, shouting words that were instantly lost in the roar. The bird screamed in answer and fell, plunging down the storm wall in a river of fire.

For a moment the Empress's army just stood there, staring at the blinding bird. And then, in unison, the invasion force turned and fled. The men on the beach threw themselves into the water, scrambling over each other to get their heads below the waves as Banage's fire spirit swept over them. Everything the bird touched was consumed. Its heat was so intense it blackened the sand and boiled the surf. Those caught in its flames turned to ash in an instant while those who'd made it to the water began to scream as the bay itself became a scalding pot beneath the bird's heat.

Out in the deep water, the landing boats rocked as the soldiers fought to turn them back to the crashed palace ships, but the ships' men were pulling up the landing ramps in a desperate attempt to put anything they could between themselves and the fire. The men in the boats screamed curses, but their voices were drowned out by the roar of the bird as it flew low over the bay, sending the invaders leaping into the sea to avoid its fiery wings.

Josef stood on the wall, scarcely daring to believe his own eyes. Minutes ago he'd been prepared to die in Osera's last stand; now he was watching from safety as the enemy fell over themselves in desperate retreat. He cast an almost sheepish glance at the Spiritualists. Miranda was on her feet again, holding out her hand as her water spirit returned, the cold blue tide vanishing into her palm. Banage was standing beside her with his fingers pressed against the enormous ruby glowing on his thumb, eyes following his bird beneath brows furrowed in concentration.

When every one of the infantry ships had been capsized, the bird turned and flew back to the storm wall. It grew smaller with every foot before finally vanishing into Banage's ring with a puff of smoke. The Rector smoothed the stone with his fingers as the jewel's glow faded.

"How high can Durn lift the bay line?" he said, voice calm and quiet, as though he were discussing a change in his schedule.

Miranda flexed her hand as the last traces of water vanished into her skin. "Three feet?" she said. "Maybe a little more."

Banage nodded, moving his fingers from the ruby to a deep-green stone wrapped in delicate gold filigree on his thumb. "Three feet will be fine. Be ready on my mark."

Miranda nodded and closed her eyes. A second later, the storm wall began to rattle under their feet. Josef cursed, but Banage didn't even seem to notice. He was looking at the bay, eyes locked on the line of sunken ships.

"Steady," he said, clutching his ring as the closing prow of the last palace ship locked into place. "Now."

The heavy ring on Miranda's thumb lit up with a green flare. Far in the distance, over the screams of the panicking soldiers and breaking waves, Josef heard the sound of stone grinding. He followed it and found himself staring at the line of sunken ships. That line was now churning, the sea bubbling like a boiling pot. Josef squinted, leaning out over the wall to see what was happening below the water. In the end, however, it was the sound that told the truth. The bay filled with the groaning of stone as the line of scuttled ships began to rise from the water. Josef stepped back in awe, eyes wide as he looked at Miranda to see her clutching the enormous green stone on her thumb with her eyes closed, her face furrowed in deep concentration as sweat ran down her cheeks. Banage, however, was cool and collected. He stood steady, watching the rising line of ships, his fingers hovering over the green ring on his own thumb.

The grinding rumble went on and on until, at last, Miranda gasped and stumbled, catching herself on Gin as the green light faded. The moment her ring flashed out, Banage stepped forward, holding up his hand as his ring flashed to life, glowing like a green sun on his finger as the grinding of the stone gave way to a great creaking moan of splitting wood. Josef turned back to the bay, but he saw nothing. The sunken fleet was well out of the water now, resting on a line of exposed seabed. Even the two grounded palace ships were several feet higher, their front halves pushed up like matrons with their noses in the air. But that was all Miranda so far as Josef could tell. Banage was obviously doing something as well, but whatever it was, Josef couldn't see. He could hear it though, and he kept his eyes on the bay as the sound of splitting wood grew louder and louder.

Without warning, a wall of green erupted down the line of scuttled ships. It started at the edges where the bay met the cliffs, leaves exploding from the sunken runners as a line of oak trees sprouted from the raised seafloor. The trees spread across the bay like green fire, their canopies popping open like paper lanterns before Josef's eyes until a wall of dense foliage cut the bay off from the sea.

But as the trees' growth slowed, the sound of splitting wood grew louder than ever. Josef scowled, confused, and then a flash of motion pulled his eyes north, toward the first palace ship, and he gaped in disbelief. The grounded ship was moving, its enormous hull rising up as graceless as a bull on its hind legs. Soldiers slid off the decks as the front half of the ship's hull rose out of the water, pushed up by an enormous tangle of tree roots. The same thing was happening to the second palace ship on the other side of the bay. The tree roots dug under the ships' broad bottoms, forcing them up until their noses were in the sky. Finally, with one last, enormous crash, the two palace ships slid backward, off the roots, out of the bay, and into the ocean. They landed in the open sea with a crash, both ships slamming into the water and then sinking almost immediately as the ocean surged in through the shattered hulls.

But that was all Josef saw. The moment the palace ships were dislodged, the trees surged in. Huge oaks shot up like arrows to fill the gap, branches exploding from the trunks as the new canopies spread until the ocean was completely obscured behind a wall of solid green.

The men in the water, those who remained after Banage's fire bird, swam frantically to the line of trees and began to climb, picking their way through the branches and throwing themselves into the ocean beyond in a desperate attempt to escape. Banage watched their struggles with a smile before turning to Miranda.

"Well done," he said, helping her back to her feet. "I'm going to provide some cover. Lend me your mist?"

"Of course, Master Banage," Miranda said, reaching to touch one of her smaller stones. It flashed blue the second her fingers passed it, and Josef smelled the clean, predawn wetness of a mountain valley as a thick mist filled the air. Meanwhile, Banage rubbed his fingers against a white stone set in a thin band on his wrist, and a second smell, salty and cold, joined the first as a thick sea fog rose up from the bay. Fog and mist rose together, intertwining and expanding until the bay vanished beneath a thick, gray blanket. But the fog wasn't finished. It spread up the stairs, around the tower, and along the cliffs, spilling up the mountain toward the mainland. By the time Miranda and Banage finally stepped down from the sea wall, the entire island of Osera was shrouded in cloud.

"That should buy us a little time," Miranda said, glancing at Josef before her eyes darted to something over his shoulder. Josef turned to see his soldiers standing on the storm wall behind him, staring in amazement at the two wizards who, in a little under five minutes, had completely reversed Osera's fortunes.

"Not much time," Banage said. "The fog gives us cover, but they don't need to see to launch war spirits. Frankly, I'm surprised Osera isn't knee-deep in them already. We need to speak with Queen Theresa immediately." He turned to the gathered soldiers. "Who's in charge here?"

The men looked at each other, and then at Josef.

"I am," Josef said with a sigh.

"Don't be absurd," Miranda scoffed. "I don't know what kind of scam you people are running, but we don't have time for your games. Where's the queen?"

"In the palace," Josef said coldly. "Won't do you any good, though. Queen Theresa is dead. I'm king of Osera now."

Miranda's face went very pale. "If you think for one moment I'm going to buy that load of—"

"He's speaking the truth, ma'am," one of the soldiers interrupted, standing a little straighter.

Miranda blinked. "You've got to be *kidding*!" she roared. "Do you know who this man is? He's a wanted criminal! A thief! A bounty hunter, pride fighter, and right-hand man of the most notorious—"

"That'll be enough," Josef said, putting enough edge in his voice to ensure that it really was enough. Miranda snapped her mouth closed, but her scowl only grew deeper.

"How are *you* king?" she said at last.

"Because my mother was queen," Josef answered, turning around and walking toward the tower. "And as I said, she's dead. Now come on. If our time's limited, I don't want to waste it on things that don't matter."

Miranda and Banage exchanged a tight-lipped look and followed.

Down in the bay, hidden by the fog, the last of the Empress's soldiers climbed through the wall of trees and dove into the sea, swimming through the waves and toward the line of palace ships waiting on the other side.

CHAPTER
24

B anage stopped them at the foot of the tower to hear reports from the other Spiritualists, but Miranda was too enraged to listen. Josef Liechten? A king? Of *Osera*? It was absolutely impossible. This had to be one of Eli's scams. How he could trick an entire kingdom, queen included, Miranda had no idea, but she intended to find out. That thief could not be allowed to meddle with something this big.

By the time they entered the tower, Miranda had worked herself into a cold fury. For all his talk about not wasting time, Josef set a maddeningly slow pace. They climbed the winding tower steps carefully, stepping over the wounded as they went. The gristly scene only sharpened her rage. She wasn't sure how, but she was positive Eli was somehow to blame for all this. And while she couldn't actually pin the Empress's sudden appearance on him, she was absolutely sure Osera would have been in a better position to defend itself if he hadn't been here running whatever con he was running.

The stairs finally ended at a large watch room ringed with windows. There were wounded here too, but the half of the room overlooking the bay was clear, though the view of the bay itself was completely obscured by Allinu's mist and Banage's fog spirit. She could feel her mist straining to keep the island covered against the light of the setting sun and the stiff wind from the sea, and Miranda sent a small pulse of power down to Allinu's ring. The strain eased a bit, and she turned her full attention back to the task at hand.

A large table was set up under one of the bay-facing windows. Beside it, an older man in an officer's coat was waiting with a map, which he handed to Josef. Josef took it and leaned over the table, seemingly forgetting about them entirely. The older man looked stricken for a moment by Josef's indifference and then stepped forward, bowing before Banage.

"Rector Spiritualis," he said. "On behalf of all Osera, please let me thank you. You arrived in the nick of time."

Banage nodded. "It was our duty." He paused.

"Admiral Hawthorne," the man supplied in a hurried voice. "Commander of her majesty's navy. *His* majesty's now, of course," he corrected himself. "Though there's not much left of it."

"Wouldn't be *any* left if these two hadn't shown up," Josef said, standing. He looked Miranda in the eye, then Banage. "Thank you," he said, his voice surprisingly sincere. "I really thought that was the end. Thank you for the fog as well. Maybe it'll buy us enough time for the Council reinforcements to arrive."

"Don't count on it," Banage said. "Product of nepotism he may be, but Myron Whitefall's an experienced general. His objective is the preservation of the Council, not Osera. He won't waste time sailing troops out here when he can use your fall to buy the time he needs to fortify the continent."

Josef's face grew very dangerous. "If that's how it is, then why are you here?"

"Because we are not the Council," Banage said. "Much as some would like to claim otherwise, the Spirit Court is an independent body with its own priorities, and right now those include stopping the Empress's advance. If you are indeed king of Osera, then we are prepared to offer you our full cooperation toward that end."

Josef nodded. "What have you brought?"

Banage began to rattle off the Court forces—the number of Spiritualists, the capabilities of the spirits at their command, so on and so forth. Miranda stopped listening almost immediately and began scanning the room. There were many prone shapes lying in the dark around them. Miranda examined each of their faces, looking for the boyish, infuriating one. If Josef was here, Eli couldn't be far away. He was probably watching right now...

Even as the thought crossed her mind, she spotted a familiar shape. At the far edge of the room, a small bundle lay pressed against the wall. Miranda had spotted it only by chance, and even now, when she was turned to look straight at it, the bundle seemed to fade into the shadows. But nothing could hide the white, feminine, skeletally thin hand peeking through the folds. Miranda sucked in a breath. She'd know that hand anywhere. It was the same hand that had dug into Gin's back in Mellinor, and considering Josef was standing a few feet away, there was no doubt in her mind. It was Nico, and if she was there— Miranda's eyes jumped to the lanky soldier sitting slumped beside the demonseed, his unruly black hair falling down to hide his face.

"Eli Monpress!" she shouted, interrupting Master Banage midsentence. "Come out now. You're not fooling anyone."

Everyone turned in surprise to see what she was pointing at. Across the room, the slumped man heaved a long sigh and looked up.

"Nothing gets by you, does it?" Eli said.

Miranda ignored him, turning to the admiral. "That man is the thief Eli Monpress," she said. "He must be arrested at once."

The admiral stared at her, his face strained and white as paper. "Lady Spiritualist," he said at last. "I fear you are mistaken. That is Lord Eliton Banage, best friend and adviser to King Josef Liechten of Osera."

For several seconds, Miranda was too shocked to speak.

"Banage?" she said at last. "Eliton *Banage*?" She turned back to Eli, who was on his feet by this point, neatly picking his way toward them through the lines of the wounded. "Of all the..." She almost couldn't find the words. "Slanderous, outrageous, *presumptuous*—" The list dissolved into enraged sputters. "How *dare* you try and hide behind the name of the most respected wizard on the continent! I don't care if we're at war or if the Empress is coming up the stairs as we speak, I'm taking this criminal in *right now*. Master Banage!" She turned to face her Rector. "I'll handle this. He won't..."

Her voice trailed off when she saw Master Banage's face. He was standing perfectly still, his eyes open so wide she could see the whites all the way around. He was staring at Eli like another man might stare at a corpse suddenly come to life.

"There is no slander," Banage said, his voice thin and almost trembling. "It's been a long time, Eliton."

"Fifteen years," Eli said, stepping up to stand beside Josef.

Miranda couldn't even speak. She just stood there, looking from Banage to Eli and back again. "Impossible," she whispered. "*Impossible*. There is *no way*—"

"Miranda," Banage said, his voice suddenly as sharp as a razor. "Go downstairs and command the front until I return."

Miranda blinked. "What?"

"Now," Banage snapped.

She stared at him stupidly as the command sank in. Then, without a word, Miranda obeyed. She turned and walked down the stairs, the click of her boots and the moans of the wounded the only sound in the tower. She didn't stop walking until she reached the edge of the sea wall. She stood on the precipice, staring out into thick fog, her mind whirring so fast she didn't even notice Gin until the ghosthound pressed his nose into her back.

"Eli is Master Banage's son." The words tumbled out of her before she could stop them.

"Really?" Gin said, sitting down beside her. "I always thought they smelled kind of similar."

"This has to be some kind of joke," Miranda went on as though she hadn't heard him. "Master Banage is a man of duty and integrity. I've never heard him tell a lie, and I don't even think he's capable of stealing. Eli is the most irresponsible, conniving, *sleazy* excuse for a wizard I've ever met. How can they possibly be related?"

407

"Morality isn't an inherited trait," Gin said, flicking his ears. "Look at things objectively and it's really not surprising. I mean, they're both dark haired, tall for humans, thin built, and powerful wizards."

Miranda didn't even want to go down that path, but now that Gin had put the idea in her head, her mind would not stop finding similarities. The way Eli and Master Banage both talked with their hands, for instance, or the particular way their eyes would narrow when they were angry. The little details kept coming, piling up until even her outrage couldn't overpower the mountain of evidence.

"Powers," she muttered, flopping against Gin. "Why didn't Master Banage just *tell* me?"

Gin snorted. "Can't blame him. Can you imagine anyone willingly owning that thief as a son?"

Miranda rubbed her eyes. "I don't even know anymore. I can't believe—"

She stopped when she felt Gin's paw nudge into her side. The ghosthound was looking over his shoulder. Miranda turned as well and saw one of the young Spiritualists, a girl whose name she couldn't remember, standing timidly several feet away with a look on her face that screamed, *I have an important message but I'm too shy to interrupt.*

Miranda sighed. "What?"

"Spiritualist Lyonette," the girl said, bowing low even though she and Miranda were technically the same rank. "Someone's approaching from the city."

"Someone?" Miranda said, frowning. "What kind of someone?"

"We're not sure," the girl said. "It's hard to see with the fog, but it looks like two people leading ten wagons."

"Two people leading ten wagons?" Miranda's scowl deepened, and Gin began to growl. "All right," she said, jumping off the wall. "Let me have a look." Because, really, how much stranger could this day get?

The girl smiled in relief as Miranda and Gin walked to the

head of the road. Sure enough, squinting through the mist Miranda could just barely make out ten wagon-shaped shadows coming down the mountain with surprising speed. Gin raised his nose, sniffing the air in a loud huff.

Miranda waited impatiently. "Well?"

"You're not going to believe this," Gin said, lowering his head with a snort. "And you're not going to like it either."

"What?" Miranda said pointedly.

Gin told her, and he was right, she didn't like it one bit. Biting back a curse, she grabbed the Spiritualist girl and sent her up the stairs to warn Master Banage that things had, against all odds, gotten worse.

Eli hung back, keeping Josef between himself and Banage. The king and the Rector were talking strategy, something about leveraging Josef's ability to sink palace ships, but Eli was too distracted to pay much attention to the actual plan. The Rector's eyes never left Josef or the map, but Eli could feel the old man watching him without watching, just like he used to. Eli crossed his arms and glared pointedly out at the fog. He'd known the moment he decided to send Miranda the message that it would come to this. He didn't regret calling for help, even this beat asking Benehime for aid, but that didn't mean he had to like it.

He was staring as hard as he could at the blank, gray spot where the beach should be when he heard someone enter the room. He looked up to see a girl about Miranda's age, though with only a fraction of Miranda's rings, standing in the doorway. She bowed nervously and went straight for the Rector, whispering in his ear. Banage's already stern face fell into a deep frown as she spoke. When she finished he nodded and waved her away, turning to Josef with a dour look.

"It seems the Council is here."

"Council?" Josef said expectantly. "Troops?"

Banage shook his head. "I imagine troops are coming, but

409

right now you'll have to content yourself with the Council's head wizard."

Despite his best efforts, Eli's breath caught.

Thankfully, Josef didn't notice. He was glaring at Banage, turning this latest development over in his head, looking for the trap. "I thought the Spirit Court split from the Council," he said. "That's what you told me."

"We have," Banage said. "But we face a common enemy. I should think you'd welcome the help."

"That depends on the help," Josef said.

"For that, you'll have to ask her yourself," Banage said, his voice cold. "The Court does not involve itself in her methods."

Josef looked at the Rector with a curious scowl, but he started toward the door all the same. He paused when he reached it, looking over his shoulder at Banage, who had not moved.

"Go ahead," the Rector said. "Eliton and I have things to discuss in private."

Josef's eyes darted to Eli, but the thief shook his head. It would have come to this sooner or later. Might as well be sooner.

Josef turned and started down the stairs, leaving Eli and Banage staring at each other. Thanks to the thick fog, the tower was very dark now. Eli could barely make out the wounded lying on the other side of the room. Banage, however, he could see clearly thanks to the light that was still emanating from his rings. Eli grimaced and looked away.

"If you're here to arrest me, don't bother," he said. "I'm under the king's protection. Last time I checked, Spiritualists don't break local laws."

"I'm not here to arrest you," Banage said quietly. "Though I am happy you remember some of the doctrine I tried to teach you."

"How could I forget?" Eli grumbled. "Sometimes I think you taught me to read only so I could study Spiritualist laws."

410

He paused, waiting for Banage to start raging, but the room was more silent than ever. The quiet stretched on and on until Eli could bear it no longer. "You wanted to discuss things in private," he said, sitting on the edge of the table. "So discuss."

Banage took a deep breath. "Why didn't you come home that night?"

Eli didn't have to ask which night he meant. "I had no reason to," he said. "What was there for me to go home to? You didn't want me unless I was ready to be an obedient Spiritualist."

"That's not true," Banage said. "I was trying to teach you discipline. Responsibility. You were always powerful, and there are rules that—"

"Oh, yes," Eli said, surprised at how bitter his voice sounded. "How could I forget? You cared more for rules than you ever did for me."

"I was trying to teach you respect for the spirits!" Banage shouted. "Obviously, I failed. Look at you, a thief and a degenerate, using spirits for your own selfish purposes." He clenched his fists, his rings glowing brighter as his spirits reflected his anger. "When I think of what you could have been. What I could have made you—"

"I don't have to listen to this," Eli said, hopping off the table. "I freed myself from your expectations years ago, old man. If you're going to be disappointed in someone, save it for yourself. You were a terrible teacher and a miserable excuse for a father. If I didn't turn out the way you wanted, that's entirely on you."

Eli started to leave, but Banage moved to stand in his way. Eli reached out to push his father aside, but his hand stopped an inch from the old man's arm. Banage was looking at him with an expression Eli had never seen on his face before. If it had been anyone else, he would have said the old man was on the verge of tears.

"I am more disappointed in myself than you will ever know,"

Banage whispered. "When your mother refused to leave White-fall's Council, I took you away from Zarin and tried to raise you as best I could. Every night since you vanished, I've been haunted by regret for all I could have done to prevent it. I've hated you, Eliton. I've despised you, blamed you, but I never, ever stopped loving you." His hands reached out, fingers trembling, to clutch Eli's shoulders. "The day I first saw your bounty poster was the happiest day of my life, because that was the day I knew you were still alive."

"And you sent your apprentice after me," Eli said.

Banage flinched. "I had to. Whatever you may think, I am responsible for you, as a father and as Rector. I could not let you go on abusing spirits and flaunting the rules of the Court."

Eli reached up and pried Banage's fingers off his arms. "I've never abused a spirit in my life," he said. "Ever. Ask Miranda, she knows. So would you, if you knew me at all."

"And you think for that I should just let you do as you like?" Banage said, his voice growing heated again. "You're one of the most powerful wizards I've ever seen, and yet you insist on being a criminal. If you will not willingly accept the responsibility and self-control that power demands, then it is my duty to make you. If you want to throw your life away, that's your decision, but you can't be angry with me for doing my duty!"

"*Throwing my life away?*" Eli roared. "You finally find me after fifteen years and that's all you want to talk about? How I'm wasting my power as a wizard? *Powers*, father." He looked away in disgust. "All I ever wanted was for you to see that I was worthy of your interest. Me. Not my power as a wizard or my future as a Spiritualist. Just me, Eli, your *son*."

He glanced back out of the corner of his eyes, but Banage's face was sterner than ever. Eli sighed and shook his head. "Obviously that's too much for you," he muttered, pushing past Banage and stomping toward the door. "Next time you want to have a private chat, don't bother unless you've got something new to say."

"Wait."

Eli paused. He could hear Banage moving, but he didn't turn back. He didn't even want to look at the man anymore.

"Your mother is outside," Banage said, his voice strangely thick. "Will you say something to her?"

"No," Eli said, stomping down the stairs. "I have even less to say to her than I had for you."

If he'd looked back then, he would have seen Banage put his head in his hands, but he didn't. He ran down the stairs two at a time, ducking out at the second-to-last landing, the only landing that had a window. He wiggled through the narrow slit and dropped to the walkway along the sea wall, keeping the tower between himself and the gathered Spiritualists standing at the tower door. He could hear voices on the wind, Miranda's, Josef's, and another, a smoky, haughty voice from his memory. Eli stopped, nearly overcome by the memory of fragrant smoke. Then the wind shifted and the voices vanished. Free again, Eli walked to the very end of the sea wall and sat down in the crevice where the wall met the cliff. The fighting had been lighter here, and he was able to find a clean stretch of stone. The fog hid the ravaged battlefield, and staring into the blank grayness, he was almost able to forget where he was and why.

You should have known better, love.

Powers, Eli thought, closing his eyes as the voice filled his mind. Not now.

His ribs burned through his tattered shirt as Benehime's white arms snaked around him.

I don't even know why you stayed to talk, she whispered in his ear. *To Banage you're just another duty, another mess to put right. Did you really think it would be any different?*

Eli dropped his head. He hated Benehime's voice at the best of times, but he never hated it as much as when she spoke sense. "Good thing I didn't call the Spiritualists to go over ancient history," he muttered. "So long as Banage fights the

413

Empress, I don't really care what he does with his private time."

Oh yes. He could hear Benehime's smile. *How goes the good fight? Not well, I'm guessing, considering the sorry state of your darling lava spirit.*

Eli set his teeth and said nothing.

He's going to die, you know, Benehime whispered. *Such a waste. I could save him, of course. Him, your swordsman, even your little demon. I could save them all, but oh—* She paused. *That's right. You're not going to ask for my help...*

Her voice trailed off, letting the words hang. In the silence, her finger slid across his chest to hover just on the edge of Karon's burn. The moments ticked on, but Eli didn't break his silence. Finally, Benehime sighed in his ear.

I'll be waiting, she whispered, her hands pulling back through her cut in the world. *And unlike Banage, who wants you to be something you're not, or Miranda, who just wants you to disappear, or even Josef, who wants you to save his kingdom, all I ask, all I've ever wanted, is your love. Come home, Eliton. Let me help you. Love me again as I love you and I'll give you everything—your lava spirit, your friends' lives, safety for this land, everything.*

Eli closed his eyes as the Lady's presence began to fade.

When you're ready, love, I'll be here. I'll always be here for you.

The words echoed in the fog, and then the Lady was gone. Eli closed his eyes as her pressure vanished, clutching his fingers against Karon's burn.

"I'm sorry," he whispered. "I'm so sorry. I'll find another way to save you. But you know I can't go back." He felt the water on his cheeks before he realized he was crying. He scrubbed his eyes fiercely and tried to look away, but everywhere he looked, he saw the ravages of war. The dead were little more than shadows in the fog, but he felt them just as he heard the terrified whispers of the spirits all around him, the moaning fear of the winds above, and though he knew it was his imagination, Eli could almost taste the reproach in their voices.

Eli bowed his head. "I'm sorry this is happening," he said, rubbing his eyes on his sleeves. "I'm sorry I *let* this happen. I'm letting everybody down. It's my fault."

And it was. It was his fault. His fault for thinking Benehime would actually be above starting a war over her stupid obsession. His fault for letting it continue. He could stop it right now. One more lie, that's all it would take. But...

"I'm sorry," he said, choking on the words. "I can't go back to her. I'm so sorry, so, so sorry, but I can't. *I can't.*"

The sob shook him this time, and Eli clenched as his burned chest seized. Despite the motion, Karon didn't move. Eli swore under his breath and let gravity slide him down the cliff and toward the cold, wet stone, curling into a ball on his side as the mist swallowed him whole.

Miranda stood at the foot of the watchtower with her arms crossed and her mouth set in a stubborn line. Gin stood beside her, growling deep in his chest as he kept his eyes on Sara and, more important, Sparrow, who was standing beside her. Sara stared right back, smoking her ever-present pipe in long puffs. Sparrow simply looked bored, lounging on the wagon with a sleepy expression like ghosthounds growled at him all the time. Of course, for most of the last two months, that had pretty much been the case.

Miranda ignored the flamboyant man completely, focusing on Sara, head wizard of the Council of Thrones, inventor of the Ollor Relay, and Eli Monpress's mother. Powers, she thought with a stifled groan, that explained so much. But at least it meant Eli came by his scheming honestly, most likely making it the only honestly gotten thing he possessed. She studied Sara as the wizardess took another puff of her pipe, trying to see what Master Banage had ever seen in the woman. Whatever it was, it must be long gone. Miranda had been ready to strangle her from the first moment they'd met.

The door of the tower creaked and she turned gladly to greet Master Banage. But it wasn't the Rector who emerged from the tower. It was Josef, and he did not look happy.

"What's all this?" he said, eyes moving up and down the spectacle gathered at his door.

"All this" was a line of wagons, the same wagons from the Council's assault on the Spirit Court Tower earlier that morning. Each was large enough to carry eight men with room to spare and filled with lumpy objects hidden beneath a cover of thick, tied canvas. There were ten wagons in total, all identical, and none with a driver or animals to pull them. They rolled on their own, much like Slorn's wagons, though with wheels instead of legs. But these weren't like Slorn's wagons; Miranda was positive of that. One, Sara wasn't that nice, or a Shaper, and two, the wagons didn't move and fidget like Slorn's awakened creations did. These wagons followed Sara's instructions with a sluggishness that reminded Miranda more of bad puppetry than spirit work. Still, strange as this was, Miranda put it out of her mind. The threat, if there was one, wouldn't come from wagons that moved themselves but from whatever Sara was hiding under their cloth covers.

Sara met Josef with a smile, her eyes flicking to the enormous sword on his back. "You must be Josef Liechten, master of the fabled Heart of War. I hear you're king of Osera now. Congratulations, and my sincere condolences on the loss of your mother."

Miranda snorted. Sara didn't sound sincere at all. Fortunately, none of this seemed to faze Josef.

"Right," he said. "And why are you here?"

"To honor the Council's duty to Osera," Sara answered with a shrug. "And to offer a new weapon in the war against the Empress."

That got Josef's attention. "What have you got?"

Sara smiled. "You'll see for yourself as soon as the fog clears, which should be any moment now."

"What are you talking about?" Miranda said.

Sara looked surprised. "Can't you hear it, Spiritualist? Listen. The mist is straining. Something's pushing on it."

Miranda shifted her attention immediately to her mist, but Allinu felt fine. Nothing was different. Miranda frowned and pushed softly on the thread of power connecting them. The thread pushed back, but the push was weak and thin, and Miranda's breath caught.

"Allinu!" she shouted, looking up.

"Sorry, mistress," the mist whispered around her. "We're holding as best we can, but the Empress has a wind. I don't know how much longer we can keep this up."

"A wind?" Miranda scowled. "How big a wind?"

"Big enough to blow your mist away," Sara said, glancing up. "Look."

Miranda looked. Sure enough, she could see patches of the evening sky overhead.

"I'm sorry, mistress," Allinu whimpered. "We tried."

Miranda made a soothing sound and held out her hand. The mountain mist spiraled down, sinking into her ring with a sigh. Banage's fog was dissipating as well, and Miranda turned, staring out at the sea as the air cleared.

"Powers," she muttered, blinking against the strong, unnaturally steady wind from the sea.

Behind her, Josef added a more powerful curse.

Just beyond the line of trees and wrecked ships was a wall of palace ships. There were seven in all, pulled so close to each other that their crews could step from one boat to the next. Their decks were black with soldiers arranged in alternating lines, the first row kneeling, the next standing just behind them. All of them were holding larger versions of the curved bows the soldiers who'd invaded the bay had been carrying, and every bow was drawn. Miranda swallowed as the full force of what she was seeing hit her. Thousands of arrows, notched and drawn, and all of them pointed at the top of the storm wall where the Oseran forces were standing.

"Durn!" Miranda shouted, but her rock spirit's name was

417

lost in the deafening snap of the bowstrings. A black wall of arrows shot over the bay. There wasn't time to duck, no time for Miranda to do anything except to raise her hands in a pathetic shield as the arrows whistled toward her.

When the arrows were close enough that Miranda could see the fletching, everything suddenly went black. She blinked in surprise and then winced at the thud of the arrows striking something solid and smooth. Miranda stepped back, and then she began to grin. Durn towered over her, a great stone wall covering a ten-foot-long span of the storm wall. She grinned wider and slapped her hand against the stone. "Thank you."

"Of course," Durn answered, his gravelly voice thick with pride.

Beside her, Josef lowered his sword. "Nice trick."

Miranda looked over her shoulder. By luck of where she'd been standing, Durn's wall had also sheltered the road, the door to the tower, and most of their forces. Outside the stone's reach, arrows lay everywhere. They stuck in the ground, lay broken on the stone, and a few were even embedded in the wooden shutters of the watchtower windows. Miranda swallowed. If Durn hadn't shielded them, that surprise attack might well have been the end. Back on the road, the sailors and Spiritualists stood in a stunned clump, their eyes glassy as everyone realized how close they'd come to death.

"They're notching another volley."

Josef's voice fell through the stunned silence like an iron weight. Miranda turned her head to see the swordsman at the edge of Durn's wall, peering out at the enemy.

"Get to cover!" she cried.

She didn't have to say it twice. Soldiers and Spiritualists scrambled for the safety of the tower's shadow. They used the broken arrows as markers, crowding into the lee of the tower where no arrows had landed. Sara, however, did not move. She stood calmly beside her wagons, and Sparrow stood calmly beside her, though his face was paler than usual as he kicked a stray arrow that had landed inches from his boot.

"They're not going to shoot again," Sara said when she caught Miranda's alarmed look. "The arrows are just to keep us huddled. I'd get your Spiritualists back out here. The real attack is about to start."

"What do you mean?" Miranda said, crouching behind Durn. "How do you know?"

"I've fought the Empress before," Sara said, lifting her chin. "Look. Here they come now."

Miranda pressed her hand against Durn's surface. The stone softened under her fingers, letting her push a small hole through the wall, just enough to see that Sara was right. On the deck of the center palace ship, behind the line of archers, a circle of ten people stood around a ball of stone and metal. The circle of figures raised their arms, and the ball began to glow red hot. Miranda felt her mouth go dry. She'd never seen one before, but there was no question that the thing at the circle's center was one of the Empress's war spirits. But even as she recognized what she was looking at, the circle of wizards threw their arms toward Osera and the glowing ball launched off the deck. It flew through the air with a deep, wailing scream, leaving a trail of smoke behind it as it arced up and then down, straight toward Durn's wall.

Miranda ran back before she knew what she was doing, throwing out her hand as Mellinor surged out of her. The water flew up in a spout at the falling war spirit, and they collided midair in a burst of steam. A second later, she felt Mellinor's triumph echo through her as the jumble of metal and stone, now black and dripping, slammed to the ground at the watchtower's foot, followed by a shower of icy cold water.

Miranda held out her hand as Mellinor flowed back into her. "Good catch!"

"Don't celebrate yet," Mellinor said, his voice dire. "Look."

Miranda glanced back to see the war spirit stirring in its crater, and then the spirit began to unfold. Stone and iron shifted, forming four sturdy legs, a solid, low-slung body, and a broad, flat head with a great hanging jaw of sharp, steel teeth. The moment the transformation was complete, the war spirit rolled smoothly to its feet, steam rising as it started heating itself up again.

"I'll handle this," he said. "Get your wizards ready to stop the rest."

"The rest?" Miranda said, bewildered.

Josef nodded and jerked his head toward the water. Miranda turned, and her heart sank. The sky was full of smoke trails as countless red-hot spirits launched from the decks of the palace ships. Most were already flying high overhead to fall on the city behind them. Miranda could only watch in horror as the first one crashed into the mountain, landing in the houses on the eastern slope with an impact she felt through her boots.

But even as the first wave hit, more war spirits were launching. The second volley hit the palace itself. One struck the crumbling tower at the top, taking it clean off. Another crashed into the palace's eastern face, cracking the wall as it tore into the inner halls.

"Miranda," Mellinor whispered in her ear. She barely heard him. She was staring in horror as a war spirit crashed through the palace roof, shattering the floors below with a distant boom of pulverized stone.

"*Miranda!*" the sea spirit shouted.

She snapped out of it. "Right," she muttered, running for the lee of the tower where the Spiritualists were hiding.

"All of you!" she shouted, pointing to no one in particular. "Get to the city and get those spirits under control!"

The Spiritualists stared at her dumbly.

"Go!" she shouted again.

This time, they obeyed. The air was full of flashes as they called their mounts and took off toward the burning city, but Miranda didn't see it. She was already marching back toward Durn's wall.

"We have to stop those ships," she said. "Where's Master Banage?"

"Still in the tower, I think," Gin said, hunching down behind the stone spirit.

Miranda bit back a frustrated groan. "What's he doing? We need him."

"Don't know," Gin growled. "Look sharp, Sara's on the move."

Miranda snapped her head to see her dog was right. Sara had all ten of her wagons lined up along the edge of the storm wall. She and Sparrow were beside the first one, untying the canvas cover.

"What are you doing?" Miranda shouted, marching over.

"What does it look like?" Sara said, undoing the last knot with a snap of her fingers. "I didn't come here to enjoy the show. The war spirits that have already landed are more than enough to overwhelm your small force of Spiritualists. If we're going to save this island, we can't have them launching any more, which means we have to sink the ships."

"Sink the—" Miranda said, coming to a stop beside her. "How?"

"Same way you sink anything," Sara said. "Put a hole in it."

She flashed Miranda a thin smile and tugged the canvas aside. It slid off the wagon, revealing...Miranda wasn't actually sure. The wagon was full of straw and raw wool, like a packing crate, and nestled neatly in the padding were five black orbs. Each one was slightly larger than a man's head, perfectly round and as shiny black as a puddle of freshly spilled ink. The sun was well down now as evening shifted into night, but Miranda could see the orbs well enough thanks to the grim glow of the burning city behind her. The spheres glistened wetly in the fire light, and though she could hear nothing, something about the orbs made Miranda very uneasy.

"What are those?"

"You'll see soon enough," Sara said, picking one up.

The orb fit neatly between her small hands. As Sara rested

421

it against her chest, Miranda swore she saw the orb's black surface tremble.

"Sparrow," Sara said, lowering the orb. "Ready yet?"

"Almost," Sparrow answered.

Miranda glanced up at his voice to see that he'd uncovered the next wagon. This one held no soft packing or strange orbs. Instead, the wagon contained a miniature catapult. The weapon was very cleverly made, with several different levels of tension to fit the most power into the smallest space. So cleverly made, in fact, that Miranda was only slightly surprised when it greeted Sara in a calm, professional voice.

"Hello, Sara. What is our objective today?"

Miranda gaped. "You brought an awakened catapult?"

"Of course," Sara said, placing the black orb in the small depression at the end of the catapult's arm. It didn't look big enough at first, but the catapult shifted as the sphere settled, moving the grain of its wood to hold the glassy ball neatly in place.

"Shaper-made," Sara said with a smile. "What's the point in slaving for the Council if you can't spend some money once in a while?"

Miranda stared at her, eyes wide. "Why do you need a Shaper-made catapult?"

"Because I put far too much effort into these to waste them on bad shots," Sara said dryly, running her hand over the orb. "We'll start with the center ship."

This last bit was directed at the catapult. It obeyed instantly, turning the wagon until it was pointed at the palace ship in the very center of the line. "Ready on your mark," it said, gears creaking as the arm wrenched back.

Sara held out her hand, checking the wind. The moment it fell slack, she gave the order.

"Fire."

The catapult slung, and the black orb flew silently through the air, vanishing almost instantly into the dark. Miranda held her breath, listening for... she wasn't sure. An explosion, perhaps. But all she heard was the slight, musical sound of glass breaking, so soft it was nearly hidden by the waves. But what followed couldn't have been hidden by anything. Miranda bent double, slamming her hands over her ears as the night began to scream.

CHAPTER
25

The scream was high and terrified. It cut through Miranda's skull, drowning out even her own thoughts. But horrible as the scream was, it was nothing compared to what Miranda saw out in the water. At the center of the Empress's line, the prow of the middle palace ship was gone. Not wrecked, not cracked, *gone*. The place where it had been was now solid darkness. No, Miranda squinted, not solid. It was more like a shadowy cloud, but there were glints inside it, tiny flashes of fast-spinning light.

The cloud crept down the ship, screaming as it went. The Empress's soldiers rushed forward, but when they reached the cloud, they vanished as well. After that, the soldiers turned and fled, running for the wizards at the stern of the ship. Miranda watched in horrified amazement as the shadow pushed forward, slowly consuming the enormous ship while a rain of sawdust and powdered metal fell like snow into the sea below.

When her body could move again, Miranda turned to Sara. "What is that?"

"I should think you'd recognize it," Sara said, picking up the next orb. "I got the idea from your report."

"No," Miranda said, shaking her head. "It can't be."

"Of course it can," Sara said as she lovingly loaded the

glassy black ball into the waiting catapult. "Clever idea, actually, compressing a sandstorm. So much power and destruction at your fingertips." She shook her head. "Only problem was the deadline. It's not like I can just make storms. What you see here is my entire stock. Now do you understand why I didn't want to risk them on a nonawakened launcher?"

Miranda was barely listening anymore. "You copied Renaud's glass storm?" she screamed. *"Are you out of your mind?"*

Sara gave her a sideways look. "It was very effective."

"It was *Enslavement!*" Miranda roared.

Sara winced. "Not so loud, if you don't mind." She turned to the catapult. "Next shot will take out the second-to-last ship on the left."

"Yes, Sara," the catapult said, dutifully turning itself.

"Hold that order!" Miranda shouted, grabbing the catapult with both hands. It stopped, confused, and Sara gave Miranda a cutting look.

Miranda was too angry to care. "Did you Enslave this storm?" she said, jabbing her finger at the ball loaded on the catapult's arm.

"No," Sara answered. "If I had, I could have gotten it down to the marble size you wrote about. The smaller size would have been more difficult to aim, however, so it wasn't necessary."

Miranda blinked in disbelief. "You didn't Enslave it because you were worried about size?"

"That and Enslaved spirits are far too unstable," Sara said. "Would you let go of my catapult?"

Miranda tightened her grip. "If you didn't Enslave these sandstorms, how did they get like this?"

Sara heaved an enormous sigh. "I understand this is difficult for a Spiritualist to comprehend, but there are more ways of being a wizard than servants and Enslavement. Sandstorms are nothing but sand and air spirits whipped together, a roving

424

spirit brawl without any real kind of mind. All I had to do was lean on them a little, give them some firm direction. Stupid spirits take a strong hand."

"If all you did was lean on them, how did they end up as glass?" Miranda said hotly.

Sara shrugged. "I can lean fairly heavily, and they might have been a bit upset about it, but it's a sandstorm's nature to be upset. I only concentrated that anger, pressed them together into something a little more effective, and now I'm giving them an outlet." She shook her head at Miranda's furious expression. "Honestly, you're as bad as Etmon. There's no real harm done."

"*No real harm?*" Miranda roared. "You took an innocent spirit and pressed it so hard you changed its substance! It was a *sandstorm*, not a glass storm."

"An improvement," Sara snapped, but before she could say more, a crash echoed over even the sand's screaming, and they both looked up to see Banage barreling out of the tower. Relief rushed over Miranda like a cool wave. Banage's face was strangely drawn, his eyes red and sunken, almost like he'd been crying, though that couldn't be. But whatever had caused him to look that way was gone now, burned away by pure, unadulterated rage.

"*Sara!*" he bellowed, breaking into a run.

Sara rolled her eyes. "Here we go again," she said with a sigh. "Fire."

Pain exploded through Miranda's hand as the catapult obeyed, launching the next black orb into the night. Miranda followed it as long as she could, clutching her injured hand to her chest as the orb exploded and a new, equally horrible scream joined the first as the released glass storm enveloped the next palace ship.

That was when Banage reached them. He grabbed Sara by the jacket, nearly lifting her off her feet as he brought her up to face him. But before he could do more than sputter, he froze. After a second of confusion, Miranda saw why. Sparrow

425

was standing right behind him, a long, slender knife pressed into the back of Banage's neck.

"Unhand the lady."

Miranda's hand moved in a flash, rings lighting up like lanterns as Gin snarled, but Banage moved first. He dropped Sara and stepped back. Sparrow lowered his knife and moved to Sara's side as she straightened her collar.

"That was very unlike you, Etmon," she said coldly.

Banage took a deep breath. "I find it hard to control my temper when I see the head of the Council wizards using Enslavement. I will see you hanged for this."

"I very much doubt that," Sara said. "We are at war, and my spirits are the only thing holding the line at the moment. But maybe you should ask the Oserans? I'm sure they'd love to die with you to save a few idiot storms."

"War or not, there are rules that cannot be broken!" Banage shouted. "Morals are not flexible. They don't change to fit your convenience. You never understood that, Sara." His arm shot out, finger stabbing at the cartful of orbs. "You will stop this at once, or so help me—"

"Or what?" Sara said. "You'll leave? Fine, go ahead. You're already a traitor to your country. What's one more?" She grabbed Miranda's shoulder, pushing her into Banage. "Run away," Sara said. "And take your little parrot with you. There's no room for idealists in war. I'd have thought you'd learned that years ago."

Banage didn't answer. Instead, he clenched his fist. As he did, Miranda caught a flash from the large, black stone on his ring finger, and the ground began to rumble. Sara's eyes widened, but even she didn't have time to react as an enormous stone hand exploded from the ground below the awakened catapult. The stone fingers, eight in all, closed over the wagon, crushing it instantly with a crash of splintering wood and a soft cry from the catapult as its launching arm snapped in two. Banage opened his palm, and the stone hand retreated back into the ground, leaving the whimpering catapult crooning over its broken arm.

For a moment Sara just stood there, mouth open, and then she turned on Banage with a cold fury that could have killed a weaker man. "That was bald treason."

"That was my duty as a Spiritualist," Banage said, setting his hands at his side.

Miranda stood beside him, grinning so hard her face hurt. But the joy was short lived. The screaming glass clouds on the palace ships were still going, but those ships without mad sandstorms were regrouping. On their decks, circles of wizards were moving in unison, and the decks of the ships began to glow. Miranda stepped back, swallowing against the fear that clenched her throat.

The palace ships' decks were full, absolutely full, of war spirits. They glowed like bonfires, waiting their turn as the wizards moved from spirit to spirit, launching them one after another until the sky was full of bright burning dots.

Their light was so bright Miranda could see the annoyance on Sara's face clearly.

"Well," she said, sticking her pipe between her teeth. "You've certainly done it now."

Banage ignored her and turned to Miranda, his face terrifying in the strange red light.

"Every spirit," he said softly. "Bring out every spirit you have."

Miranda nodded and closed her eyes, sinking immediately into the well of her soul. Her spirit opened with a roar. Beside her, she felt a wave of pressure as Banage's spirit opened as well. It was intense, but unlike an Enslaver's, Banage's spirit didn't press down on the connection she shared with her spirits. Instead, it buoyed them, power feeding on power as they stood together, spirits ready as the bright burning amalgams hurtled down.

"Empress," the general said. "That black weapon of theirs is powerful. We should pull back and continue the bombardment from a safe distance."

Nara heard him speaking, but she did not listen. He was just a distraction, a buzzing that interfered with what was truly important. She stood at the very edge of her balcony. Her spirit was open, though only slightly, and she was using it to reach out toward Osera. The island was burning merrily, a sight that should have pleased her, but she was focused on the dark below the fires, searching for a flash of white.

She could feel the Lady on the island. Feel her like the beloved Benehime was part of her own flesh. But where? And why? Nara clenched her teeth until she could taste her bitter anger. Why was the Lady on the island and not with her? Did it have to do with the star controlling the lava spirit she'd drowned earlier? And if so, why? Didn't the Shepherdess see who was winning?

"Empress?" the general said again, his voice hesitant.

"Why does she not answer me?" Nara growled. "Whom does she think this war is for?"

The general blinked. "Empress," he said timidly. "I'm afraid I do not under—"

Before he could finish, the Empress vanished. The general blinked, staring at the place where she had been, but nothing was left except the fading afterimage of a long, white line, hovering in the air.

At that same moment, Nara stepped onto the deck of her foremost palace ship, much to the terror of the soldiers. They jumped back when she appeared, raising their swords and then dropping them just as quickly to throw themselves on the ground.

"Empress!" The cry rose from hundreds of throats as the realization of who was standing on the deck spread through the ship. Everywhere, men stopped their attack and fell to their knees, pressing their heads to the deck.

Nara ignored them all. She stomped to the prow of the ship. Ahead of her, the swirling black madness of the storm blocked her view, screaming as it tore through the ship's nose. Irritated, Nara let a flash of her true nature show. The glass storm froze when it saw her, all anger gone. She dismissed it with a wave of her hand, and the black glass fell pattering to the water, disappearing into the dark sea below with a soft cry. Even before it hit, the Empress was walking forward. For anyone else, this would have been suicide. The raging glass had consumed the prow, leaving a sheer, hundred-foot drop to the sea below. But Nara was the Immortal Empress, a star of the Shepherdess, and the ship knew its place. Boards flew from the lower decks as she walked. They came from the outer hull, the railings, anywhere that was still stable. They piled on top of each other, forming a solid, if makeshift, ramp beneath her feet. When she reached the place where the end of the prow had been, Nara stopped. The boards creaked below her, stretched to the very edge of their ability to hold. Nara ignored the sound and leaned forward, toward the island.

She paused, listening, watching, seething. The feel of the Shepherdess was stronger than ever. Nara followed it as a dog follows a scent, reaching past her ships, across the bloody bay, and up the steep, rocky wall to the lone figure sitting with his back pressed against the cliff. She could see him in her mind as her will touched him—a young man, thin and gangly with shaggy, dark hair. He was hunched over, his arms wrapped around his knees, but she could feel the burning trace of the Shepherdess's touch all across his body, and the realization stabbed her like a sword in her gut.

"You," Nara whispered, her voice shaking with hatred.

What's wrong, Nara? The Lady's voice seemed to float on the wind. *Are you so surprised? You knew there was another star here, and I only have two among the humans.*

"Why is he here?" Nara roared, forgetting herself in her rage.

He's here because you're here, the Shepherdess whispered. *You said you would do anything to be first in my heart, Nara. Now's your chance. Fight for my favor. The boy has set himself up as defender of this island. Crush his forces and take it from him, and I will know once and for all who loves me best.*

"If you want a fight, I will give you one!" Nara shouted into the wind. "Watch me, Benehime! I will show you the difference between that boy and an Empress."

Her voice echoed across the water, but the only reply was the Lady's laughter, chiming like glass bells in the night.

"Captain!" the Empress shouted, looking over her shoulder. Sure enough, the captain was there, kneeling at the end of the makeshift plank. "Tell the wizards to prepare another volley and signal the fleet to ready the assault boats. We conquer this island within the hour."

"But, Empress." The man's voice was shaking. "The wizards on the shore—"

"Will mean nothing in a moment," the Empress finished for him, turning back to the front. "I am about to teach this land what it means to defy the Immortal Empress."

She heard the soft thunk of the captain's head on the deck as he bowed deeper still and assured her that her orders would be followed. Nara barely listened. Instead, she closed her eyes, reaching down into the well of her soul and giving her spirit a hard, sudden twist.

A ripple of power flew out of her, soaring silently over the dark sea, over the new-grown trees blocking the bay, over the bloody water and the forgotten bodies of her soldiers. Her will struck the island like a tidal wave, suffusing the land. All at once, the air was thick with the proof of who she was, *what* she was.

On the shore, the effect was immediate.

In the minutes before the Empress struck, the storm wall was still in chaos.

Miranda crouched panting against Durn's solid wall, Mellinor coiled around her in a rope of glowing water. Banage

430

had his own stone spirit out and was holding the war spirit down with three granite shackles. The war spirit strained against his hold, its sharp claws rending enormous gouges in the road, but Banage's spirit held it firm. Now, it was Miranda's turn.

"Hit it high and hard!" Banage shouted, his voice straining. "We may not get another shot!"

Miranda closed her eyes, focusing on what she was about to do next. "Durn?" she whispered, accompanying the whisper with a surge of power. "Mellinor?"

"Ready," Durn said behind her.

Mellinor just tightened the spinning of his water, forcing it to race faster and faster.

That was all Miranda needed. She shot up, pushing off the dirt as she threw out her arm, throwing all her power along with it. At the same time, Durn surged forward, joining her power and riding with it. Mellinor joined a moment later, sharpening his water to a swirling point at the end of Durn's sharpened fist.

The power from the three of them, Durn, Mellinor, and Miranda, hit the trapped war spirit at the same time, and it screamed as Durn's fist, sluiced with Mellinor's water, dug into the tangle of metal and stone at its center. The spirit's body flashed red hot, boiling Mellinor's water away, but this just made the attack worse. Water, stone, and steam now forced their way into the Empress's war spirit like a drill, tearing everything in their path until, with a deafening shriek, the war spirit's head and front left leg fell to the ground, ripped from its body by the sheer force of her blow.

Miranda flopped to the ground, gasping with relief. Durn and Mellinor fled back to her, and she welcomed them with open arms. She was beaming with pride, but as she opened her mouth to shout her joy, the ground shook.

She scrambled back, raising her hands against the blast of heat as the war spirit tore itself to its feet, breaking through the granite rings of Banage's stone spirit. She heard Banage cry out somewhere in the dark, but she didn't have time to look for him. Her eyes were on the war spirit as it teetered on its three remaining legs, its headless torso listing sideways as its metal began to glow red hot yet again.

"These things are impossible to kill."

Miranda glanced to see Gin beside her with Banage on his back. The Rector Spiritualis hopped down and moved to Miranda's side, clutching the cloudy-gray gem that had been his stone spirit's black ring.

"He'll be fine with time," he said before Miranda could ask. "Dunerik is nothing if not resilient."

"None of us will be fine if we don't find a way to make these things stay down," Gin growled. "Even that pigheaded idiot's still fighting."

Miranda could only guess the dog was referring to Josef. She didn't have a look to spare for the swordsman, but the constant clang of metal on stone from the walk in front of the tower told her everything she needed to know. If the Heart of War couldn't carve these monsters... She clenched her teeth, forcing the thought from her head before it could finish. No point in going down that path. She'd do better to stay focused on the spirit in front of her.

The war spirit was burning full tilt now, and the heat pouring off it was enough to make Miranda's hair crackle. It moved slowly backward, its three feet taking small, careful steps toward the pulverized remains of its head and fourth leg.

"It's trying to put itself back together," Miranda said, sending a pulse of power to Durn. "I want a pillar underneath it. Shoot it up, we're going to knock the head and the leg into the bay."

But as she gave the order, she realized something was wrong. The surge of power she'd sent down the thread that connected her stone's spirit to her own had reached its destination, but Durn had not answered. A cold cringe of fear curled in her stomach, and Miranda looked to see Durn standing behind her, still as the ground under their feet.

"Durn," she said again, adding a little force to her voice.

"I can't," the stone whispered, his voice full of fear. "We're too late."

"Too late?" Miranda asked, but even as the question left her lips, the wall of power crashed into her. Miranda gasped as the enormous weight forced her to her knees, and she wasn't alone. Every one of her spirits had gone perfectly still. Even Gin was on the ground, facing the bay with his head on his paws, almost like he was bowing.

"Durn's right," her hound whined, pressing his nose into the dirt. "We took too long. She's here."

Miranda didn't have to ask whom they meant. Straining against the power, she lifted her head just enough to see the palace ships. She didn't know what she was looking for, what to expect, but she knew the Empress the moment she saw her.

She was smaller than Miranda would have thought, narrow boned and pale, her black hair piled in an elaborate knot on top of her head. Her golden armor shone brighter than her war spirits, but it was not the brightness that drew Miranda's gaze, nor was it the fact that the woman was standing on a seemingly impossible line of wooden boards stretching out from the palace ship's destroyed prow. What drew Miranda's attention was the same thing that drew the attention of everything in the bay, large and small, awakened or asleep. It was power. Pure, unadulterated, undeniable power radiated from the woman like light from a lamp. Even as a blind human, Miranda could almost see it burning, and her heart began to sink.

"That's it then?" she said, almost laughing at the absurdity. "We've lost."

"We never had much chance to begin with," Banage replied. "We set ourselves against a star, after all."

Miranda did laugh then, a dry, humorless sound of utter disbelief. Across the bay, those palace ships that still had prows began to lower them. The moment the ramps hit the water, ships laden with troops began to pour out. Hundreds of ships, thousands, more ships than Miranda could count, all rowing toward the bay.

The Empress watched her ships with haughty pride. Miranda was too far to see her expression, but she didn't have to. The woman radiated triumph as a fire gives off heat. With a great sweeping motion, the Empress swung her hand down and the wall Durn had raised across the bay tore itself apart. Trees and ship hulls flew in every direction as the seafloor rent itself to let the Empress's boats pass.

For one endless moment, Miranda could only watch as the Empress, with one motion, undid all the ground they'd gained that day. Despair like she'd never felt filled her mind as the boats began to pour into the bay. Despair so thick, so overwhelming, she didn't hear Mellinor the first time he spoke.

"I said let's go," he said again, his voice surging through her mind like a deep current.

"But she's a star," Miranda whispered. "She has the will of the Shepherdess. We can't stand against her. Nothing in the world can. That's what the Shaper Mountain said."

"No," Mellinor said. "Nothing in the world *will*. There's a difference between can't and won't." As he spoke, Mellinor's voice shifted, and Miranda could hear the echo of the enormous sea who'd spoken to her in the dark throne room so long ago. "I am the Great Spirit of the inland sea," he boomed in her mind. "I am still myself, with my own mind and my own soul, and I have no love for the stars or their White Lady. Any one of them could have freed me from Gregorn's prison, but they didn't. They left me to rot and madness in a pillar of salt for *four hundred years*." Mellinor's voice was racing with rage now, and Miranda could feel his power flowing through her, filling her.

"You have shown me more care and protection in the last year than my Shepherdess ever did," Mellinor said finally. "If you're not ready to roll over and give up like the rest, then I am with you, mistress."

Miranda put her hands to her face to stop the tears flowing down her cheeks. "Thank you," she whispered. "If we can try, we must. But how?"

Mellinor told her, and Miranda fell still. It was dangerous, very dangerous. It also went against everything she stood for as a Spiritualist, sworn to keep her spirits from harm. But as she turned it over in her mind, something flinched inside her, snapped like a bone being set into place, and she knew what she had to do.

She turned on her heel and started to run. Gin, still bowing, didn't follow. Banage called her name, but Miranda didn't look back. She kept running, feet pounding across the ruined paving as she ran along the storm wall's edge, straight toward Josef.

CHAPTER
26

Josef clutched the Heart of War, blinking against the sweat that dripped into his eyes. In front of him, the metal-and-stone creature hovered over its two severed legs, still not dead. Josef lifted his wrist to his face, rubbing the sweat and dirt away as best he could. This was taking too long. Cutting the Empress's war monster was easy, but keeping it down was another story, and he was getting tired.

Tired was, as Eli would say, the bedrock of understatement. He was exhausted. His fight with Adela, becoming king, sinking the ships, defending the beach, and—his mind grew dark—the death of his mother, it was all adding up. He'd been fighting in one way or another since midmorning, and now this. He watched as the war creature rolled back to a defensive position, its severed legs already crawling back toward its body. He had to finish this quickly and go help the Spiritualists with the others before the whole island was overrun. Assuming, of course, it wasn't already.

He glanced up at the city. The mountain above him glowed like a sunset. Everywhere he looked things were burning and falling. Even at this distance he could hear the screams of the people, now his people, as they tried to fight the fiery monsters destroying their homes. Rage built up in his chest, but before he could give in to it, the Heart grew heavy, calling his attention back to the fight at hand. Josef obeyed, letting everything else fall aside as he focused on the war spirit, which was nearly finished pulling itself back together. The Heart's hilt pressed against his sweaty palms, pulling him forward, urging him to finish it now, while they still could.

Josef obeyed. He lunged forward, letting the sword's weight pull him into a low sweep. The Heart caught the war spirit's left front leg just as it reattached, and the war spirit opened its great, steel-toothed mouth in what Josef could only guess was a scream of pain. Sometimes being spirit deaf had its advantages.

The Heart jerked in his hands, and Josef refocused. He was beneath the creature now. The blasting heat dried his sweat instantly, baking his skin hard. Josef coughed at the reek of smelted metal, but before he could flee between the creature's legs to cool, dark safety, the Heart jerked again. Josef nodded and shifted his stance, turning with the Heart as the sword flew up to strike the monster's exposed, red-hot belly.

The black blade cut upward, slicing through the glowing metal like a razor through snow. The war spirit jerked above him, a belated dodge, but it was no use. The Heart was lodged at the center of its great, lumbering torso. But Josef was now at the limit of his reach. He stood on his toes, fully extended below the writhing creature with the Heart buried to the hilt in its body. He had no leverage to continue the blow up or strength to knock the spirit over. So he did the only thing he could. He planted his feet and brought the sword down in an arc in front of him.

436

The Heart cut cleanly down and burst free with an explosion of heat as the war spirit's torso tore open. The spirit was thrashing now, and Josef rolled away before one of those writhing legs could skewer him by accident. The second he was clear, Josef spun to face the monster again. The war spirit was on the ground now, rolling and thrashing as it tried to pull its split torso back together. The Heart of War shook in Josef's hands, but Josef didn't need to be told twice. He darted forward, dodging the spirit's thrashing metal legs as he swung the Heart over his head with both hands. Then, gritting his teeth, he swung it down.

The first blow slammed the spirit to the ground. The next drove it into the stone. Josef swung the Heart as hard as he could, shivering with power as the black blade came alive in his hands, hammering the war spirit into the stone of the storm wall with the weight of a mountain. Finally, on the tenth stroke, the war spirit lay still.

Josef fell backward, nearly dropping the Heart as he gasped for air. In front of him, the Empress's monster lay at the bottom of the crater left by the Heart's rage, beaten beyond any recognition. Stumbling, Josef pushed himself up, ears still ringing with the fading power of his sword. Because of this, he didn't hear the woman yelling until she standing right beside him.

"What?" he shouted, turning to see Miranda. She looked terrible, clothes ripped and stained, hair bedraggled and clinging to her sweaty, soot-streaked face. She also looked determined, and that worried him. In his experience, Miranda looking like that meant something terrible was about to happen.

"I need you to cover me down to the beach," Miranda said, her voice exasperated, as though she'd already said this many times.

Josef blinked. "The beach? Why?" He looked over the storm wall and winced. Apparently that crash he'd heard earlier had been more than just the war spirits. Something had punched through the wall that protected the bay. The water was full of boats now, some with their soldiers already out and wading toward the shore.

"Forget it," he said, turning away. "The beach is a lost cause. Fight the battles you can win. We should regroup at the top of the stair and—"

"No." Miranda's voice was determined. "I'm not going down there to fight the soldiers. I need you to protect me from them so I can get to the water."

"The water?" Josef said. "What are you going to do in the water?"

Miranda lifted her head stubbornly. "I'm going to do my best to save your people."

Josef ran a hand through his sweaty hair. "Where's that dog of yours? Can't he do it?"

"No spirit can help me with this," Miranda said, shaking her head. "The Empress is a star. That's why I need you."

Her words made no sense, but then most wizard talk made no sense to Josef, so he didn't bother asking for an explanation. Instead, he leaned back and studied her face. She looked as she always did: utterly determined, completely implacable. Powers, it would probably be more work to fight her off than to fight for her. And who knew? Maybe her plan, whatever it was, would be what they needed. He glanced at the dead war spirit lying in the crater beside them. Anything would be more effective than hammering down the rest of the Empress's metal monsters one at a time.

"All right," Josef said, jogging toward the stairs. "How much time do you need?"

"Not much," Miranda said, running beside him. "Success or failure, I have a feeling it'll be over soon."

Josef paused when he reached the top of the stairs. Down below, the first line of soldiers had just reached the sand. He hefted his sword, leaning forward. "Let's go."

He didn't wait for her reply before he charged. The soldiers on the beach were focused on their landing, pulling the boats in and watching the air for arrows. They didn't see him coming until it was too late. He half fell, half ran down the storm wall and landed in the sand swinging. The Heart's power sang through him, washing away his tiredness. His first blow tossed the closest soldier into the cliffs, his next threw two more into the water. The fourth man had time to draw his blade, but the steel shattered the second it met the Heart's black edge, and he went flying as well, slamming into the boat he'd been in the middle of hauling onto the sand.

Josef moved in a circle, swinging the Heart back and forth like a scythe to clear a small stretch of beach. The moment the opening was made, Miranda rushed into it. She ran straight for the water, wading in until it reached her knees. As she splashed into the dark bay, Josef could see more water pouring out of her. Beautiful, glowing blue water cascaded from her outstretched hands, falling into the waves lapping at her knees. It was so beautiful, the shimmering, glowing water mixing with the black surf, that Josef nearly lost his arm to a well-aimed stroke. He cursed and resumed swinging, sending the enemy scuttling back. But even as he drove them off, more came. Hoards of black-armored soldiers jumped from their boats, swords drawn. Josef was panting now. He could feel the fatigue in his muscles now even with the Heart's power roaring through him. That was a bad sign. Even the greatest awakened sword had limits, and he was fast approaching them.

"Spiritualist!" he shouted as the Heart broke another sword. "Whatever you're going to do, do it quickly!"

If Miranda answered, he didn't hear. He caught a glimpse of her as he came back around. She was kneeling in the bay, her face inches from the lapping waves. The glowing water was gone, but he could still make out a small, shimmering line of it running from her out into the bay. That was all he saw before he had to turn back to the fight. He cursed louder than ever, forcing his tired muscles to keep moving, keep fighting. Whatever that fool girl was doing, he hoped she was as right as she always seemed to think she was.

439

That was his last conscious thought before he abandoned himself to the fight completely.

Miranda knelt in the bay, her fingers digging into the sand below the water. The bay was freezing cold, but she didn't feel it. Battle raged all around her, but she didn't hear it. All her focus, all her attention, everything she was flowed with Mellinor as he pushed out to sea.

When the inland sea had first told her what he meant to do, she'd balked. After all, it was the threat of being sent to the sea that had driven him to accept her as his mistress in the first place. Sending him there now violated the core of their Spiritualist pact, yet Mellinor had insisted, and Miranda, having no other options, had agreed, but only if they did it right.

She'd made their plan clear as Josef had led the way to the beach. The sea was a mass of unruly water spirits, too large to have names or souls of their own. Any water spirit, even a great one like Mellinor, would be torn apart if he entered the sea on his own. But he wasn't on his own. Miranda was with him, and her spirit would act as a wall to protect him against the pounding currents. So long as they kept in physical contact, she should be able to pour enough strength into Mellinor to keep him together long enough to do what needed to be done. Or that was the theory, anyway.

"Just stay with me, Miranda," Mellinor whispered, his voice trembling up the thin tendril of water that connected them as he rushed across the bay. "Don't leave the water, no matter what."

Miranda nodded and opened her spirit wider, reaching out with everything she had. She'd never been this close to a spirit. Her mind seemed to blend with Mellinor's, and suddenly she could feel the ocean all around her as though she *were* Mellinor. When it happened she nearly fell forward at the shock, sputtering as she took in a great mouthful of bitter seawater. But the burning taste was far away. She was flying with Mellinor through the water, clinging to him as the sea tried to rip them apart. Water pounded her from all directions, cold and sharp and filled with tiny, babbling voices. They pushed her, pulled her, beat her soul like a drum as they tried to break through her and join Mellinor's water with their own, but Miranda would not let go. She clung to her inland sea with everything she was, her will an iron wall around him as they pushed out of the bay.

The moment they entered the open sea, a current hit them at high speed, sending both Miranda and Mellinor reeling.

"Hold tight!" Mellinor cried, clinging to her as they tumbled with the stampeding water. "Don't let go!"

Miranda didn't. She held on, wrapping herself in and through Mellinor's spirit until she could no longer tell where she ended and he began. After a few moments, Mellinor righted them and they started upward again, cutting through the churning water like an arrow.

This tied together with her inland sea, Miranda could almost see the currents. They reminded her of flocking birds—great packs of water spirits moving as one, screaming with a million voices. They rushed Mellinor whenever he came near, and Miranda felt each tiny spirit strike her like a needle shot at high speed. Any one alone would have been nothing, but there were thousands of them, hundreds of thousands, and they would have torn her apart had Mellinor not been whispering in her mind.

"You're doing fine," he said, his own voice strained so thin she could hardly make it out. "Just a little farther."

"It's horrible." Miranda didn't realize she was crying until the sob strained her chest. "How can anything survive here?"

"It can't," Mellinor said bitterly. "At least, water can't. Right now, with me, you're as much water as human. That's why you can feel it." A tremor of fear ran through her, and she realized she was feeling an echo of Mellinor's terror. "The sea tears us all apart," he whispered. "It is the horrible end that awaits all water that loses its shore. Now do you see why I was so thankful when you saved me from being sent here by Monpress?"

"If I'd known what it was like, I'd have killed him before I let him send you here," Miranda whispered back.

"Glad it didn't come to that, then," Mellinor said. "Prepare yourself, we're here."

"Here?" Miranda whispered. It felt like any other place in the water.

"Yes," Mellinor said. As he spoke, Miranda could feel the slick, heavy weight of the wood as though she'd hit it with her own back. She looked up, seeing as though she were standing inside Mellinor. Great, black shapes loomed overhead, their edges outlined by the shifting, distorted torchlight. They were below the palace ships.

"I'm going to need to take over a very large amount of water to do this," Mellinor said. "More than I can take on my own, even if I weren't in the sea. This is the most crucial point, Miranda. I'm counting on you to hold me together. Whatever happens, do not leave the water. If you step out of the sea, our connection will weaken and I won't be able to hold together. Do you understand? Do not move, no matter what."

Back in her own freezing body, surrounded by the clanging of swords, Miranda dug her hands deeper into the sand, lying in the water with only her head still above the waves.

"I won't move," she whispered, ignoring the taste of salt that filled her mouth as she spoke. "So long as I can, until I die, I will never, ever abandon you."

"I believe you." Mellinor's voice seemed to flow through her, filling her completely. "Here we go."

Miranda saw what happened next two times, one far away through her own human eyes, the other from Mellinor's perspective as though she were floating at the center of his water. Mellinor was spreading out below the boats, pulling the tiny sea spirits into his own flow. They screamed as he ripped them from their currents, and then fell silent as they were absorbed. His water grew and grew, spilling off in all directions until Miranda could feel the entire sweep of the Oseran island against her body. Mellinor's spirit was straining now,

442

thinning, and she strained as well, holding him together. Finally, just before they both broke, Mellinor stopped taking in water. For a moment he hung there, a vast sea inside the ocean. And then, with a great, undulating roar, he surged upward, taking Miranda with him.

The palace ships began to creak. From her body in the surf, Miranda was dimly aware that the fighting around her had stopped. Everyone, even Josef, was staring across the bay as, with a great groan of creaking wood and the sea's own moaning, the line of the Empress's palace ships lurched to the left.

The ships tilted in unison as Mellinor's sea surged beneath them in a great, vertical wave. Sailors scrambled as the decks turned sideways. Some managed to grab the railings in time; others were not so lucky. Miranda felt them splash into the sea as though they were landing in her own body, but she paid them no mind. Only one body mattered.

From both her perspectives, she looked up at the woman standing on the long plank at the prow of the center palace ship. The Empress stood steady even as her ship tilted beneath her, but her head was turned down toward Mellinor. That was all the warning Miranda got before the Empress's spirit hit them.

The force of the Empress's will knocked Miranda's breath out. It landed on the sea like an iron, crushing Mellinor's wave beneath a wall of immovable, unconquerable power. The sea flattened, its surface pressed glassy smooth by the Empress's will. As the wave vanished, the palace ships crashed back to the water, bobbing back and forth as they righted themselves. The Empress smiled haughtily and turned back to the island, already confident in her victory, and had Mellinor been alone, a simple spirit, it would have been a victory indeed. But he was not alone, and his spirit was not only water. Miranda's will ran through him like a steel net, holding him together even as the Empress pressed him down, for, immortal as she was, powerful as she was, the Empress was still human, and she was still subject to the one immutable law of wizardry: One human spirit cannot control another.

"Go!" Miranda shouted, scrambling to get her head above water as the wave from the palace ship's landing washed over her. "Now!"

Mellinor answered with a roar, and his water surged upward with four hundred years of pent-up rage. This time, though, the wave did not move the boats. It rose in a solid whip of high-pressured water, flying straight for the Empress.

Now it was the Empress's turn to be surprised. She whirled around, her face open with shock as Mellinor crashed into her. The lance of water shattered her golden armor, knocking her off her perch like a bird shot off a treetop. For one glorious moment, the Empress plummeted toward the water, Mellinor's wave rising to meet her with a roar of victory. And then, just as quickly, everything changed.

Seconds before she hit the water, a wind howled down from the sky to catch her. The Empress bounced on the cushion of air and then shot up, riding the wind back to her ship. She landed on the deck and fell to her knees, clutching her chest as the scales of her golden armor fell around her like rain. Down in the water, Mellinor roared with frustration, but Miranda lay still, watching from both viewpoints as red blood covered the Empress's hands.

Their blow had hit. The Empress was wounded, but even as the rush of victory sent her head swimming, Miranda saw the Empress stand. She straightened up, tossing her sundered golden armor to the deck. Her chest was covered in bright red blood, but even as Miranda saw it, the wound began to heal. The edges of the Empress's broken skin glowed blinding white, closing up as Miranda watched. The blood vanished, leaving her pale skin clean and whole. In a matter of seconds, the Empress's wound was completely gone.

Mellinor's rage caught Miranda by surprise. The Great Spirit exploded from the sea, flying over the ship to strike the Empress again. Miranda clung to the water, throwing everything she had into Mellinor's blow, but this time, the Empress was ready.

444

She raised her hand, and Mellinor's wave stopped as though it had hit a wall. Mellinor screamed in fury, pounding on the Empress's barrier with every drop of water he'd absorbed. Miranda screamed with him, pouring herself into the attack. They were so close she could see the Empress's face less than a foot from their water, her ancient, dark eyes shifting away to look...

Miranda gasped, bringing in a lungful of water as her perspective shot back to her own human body. She coughed and blinked the burning seawater out of her eyes as she raised her head. She couldn't see anything, but even at this distance she could feel the Empress staring at her. A spike of terror plunged into her mind as Mellinor's voice washed through her.

"Hide, Miranda!" he screamed. "Hide!"

But it was too late. Across the water, the Empress raised her arm, the one that wasn't holding Mellinor back, and flicked her finger. The second the motion was complete, the sand below Miranda exploded.

The force blew her backward, ripping her from the water and sending her flying through the air with such power she couldn't even move her limbs to flail. She landed hard in the sand, rolling up the beach until she struck the sharp stones at the base of the storm wall. For a moment the world went completely black. She could feel nothing, hear nothing, and then, with a deafening roar, it all came back. Josef was standing over her, the great, black, bloody blade of the Heart glistening in his hand. He was knocking the soldiers back without looking, shouting at her to get up. Miranda stared at him, literally struck dumb. She couldn't make sense of what was happening, but she felt empty, like something was missing.

Then, in one, cold, horrible moment, she realized she could no longer feel Mellinor.

She scrambled away from Josef, running all out toward the bay. Soldiers grabbed for her, but she kicked them aside, scrabbling on her hands and knees through the sand until she reached the water at last. She threw herself into the surf, slamming her body beneath the cold waves. Her soul roared open as she submerged, reaching out until her mind was on the edge of breaking. She yelled Mellinor's name, screaming with her spirit and her voice until both were raw. She screamed again and again, taking in great gulps of seawater with each shout, but it was no use. Nothing answered.

Hands closed on her shoulders, pulling her out of the surf. She fought wildly, writhing in the man's iron grip even as she recognized Josef's voice telling her to calm down or they wouldn't get out of here alive. But she didn't want to calm down, she didn't want to get out alive.

"No!" she shrieked. "Let me go! I promised! *I promised I wouldn't leave him!*"

Josef ignored her. She fought as he dragged her out of the water, but her punches and kicks bounced off him. He tucked her under one arm and ran for the stairs, keeping the Heart high in his free hand, ready to swing. He didn't have to. The enemy was keeping their distance now, unwilling to engage him even when he was burdened with a hysterical woman. Perhaps it had something to do with the dying men lying scattered across the sand. Whatever it was, Miranda didn't care.

"You don't understand," she screamed, the words broken by sobs. "I let him go. I left the water! *I failed him!*"

"That may be," Josef said, charging for the stairs. "But we're still alive, though not for long if you don't stop fighting me."

Miranda went limp, her body flopping in his grasp. She was sobbing violently now. She couldn't help it. She'd poured too much of herself into Mellinor, and what she had left was barely enough to keep her lungs working, let alone stop the tears.

She was still crying uncontrollably when the force hit her, but it wasn't until Josef stopped that she recognized what it was. After all, she'd felt the Empress's spirit just moments

446

before, but that strength, strong as it was, was nothing compared to the wave of pressure that rolled over her now.

All around them, the soldiers were dropping to their knees, pressing their foreheads into the sand. The beach grew silent as everything went still. The fighting on the wall above them silenced as well, and Miranda got the feeling that if she could somehow climb up to look at the city of Osera, she'd find that even the fires had stopped burning. With the sole exception of the waves lapping on the shore, everything in the world seemed to have gone still, and in that stillness, the Empress spoke.

"Osera," she called, her voice clear and ringing through the air. It came from every direction, filling Miranda's ears with its hated smugness. Slowly, painfully, Josef turned them, and Miranda found herself looking out at the sea she never wanted to see again and at the woman standing in midair above it.

"You have fought bravely," the Empress said, standing on a swirl of wind above her ship. "I admire strength, but the time for fighting is over. You have lost. Your army is broken, your wizards defeated, your city burning. Put down your weapons and surrender, and I may be merciful."

"She's got to be kidding," Josef said, though his voice was quiet. "Oserans don't surrender."

There was no way she could have heard him, but the Empress answered in the most effective way possible. She opened her spirit fully.

Miranda seized up as the true power of the Shepherdess's star struck her. Even Josef gasped, his arm clutching painfully around her waist. But it wasn't just the spirit pressure. Out over the water, the Empress had begun to glow. Light shone through her skin, filling her body until she glowed like the morning, but brightest of all, brighter than the sun, brighter than anything Miranda had ever seen, was the mark on the Empress's chest. The moment she saw it, Miranda knew exactly what it was and what it meant.

Bow down.

The Empress's voice echoed through Miranda's mind,

through the very fabric of the world, and as it faded, the world obeyed.

The soldiers around them were already bowing, but now the sand under their knees joined them. All along the island, the spirits were lowering themselves before the Empress. The winds bowed, the stone bowed, even the fires shrank back in obedience, burning low before the star. Even the spirit deaf felt her presence. Oseran soldiers fell to their knees without knowing why, their spirits obeying on instinct alone. Only the wizards remained standing. Up on the storm wall, Banage clutched his rings, staring at the Empress in astonishment and growing terror. Even Sara had lost her jaded expression. She was looking about in open amazement, her eyes wide as she watched the world change itself to honor the Empress.

Miranda's own spirits were bowing as well. She could feel them pressing on their rings, but she barely noticed it. The enormous pressure of the Empress filled her mind, impossibly bright, impossibly glorious, and strangely familiar. Miranda clenched her teeth, forcing her mind to work. She knew this feeling, this light. She'd felt it before. Suddenly, the memory came back clearly, her kneeling in King Henrith's throne room floor beside Nico and Josef's bodies with Gin at her back, staring in amazement that she was not dead while all around her pressure just like this thrummed through the air. And at its center, walking through the ruined hall that bowed only for him, crushing Mellinor's fury with only his presence...

Before she could think about what she was doing, Miranda yanked herself from Josef's grasp and bolted for the stairs. The swordsman didn't seem to notice. His attention, like everything else's in this corner of the world, was on the Empress.

Miranda ran as she had never run before. She clambered up the stairs and hit the top of the storm wall running, dodging the bowing war spirits as she charged the watchtower door. She banged it open and threw herself at the stairs. They were empty now, and a distant part of her mind realized that the common soldiers had had the sense to move the wounded when the war spirits arrived. Good, she thought bitterly, less for her to trip on. She was taking the stairs three at a time now, her lungs heaving as she pushed herself with all her might.

She hit the door to the upper room like a battering ram, and it slammed open. She wasn't sure how she'd known he would be there. Maybe some tiny part of Mellinor still remained, pointing her toward him. Whatever had led her, it had been right. The man she had come for was standing by the window, staring out across the silent beach at the Empress. He didn't even have the good grace to jump when she came in. He just turned slowly, mouth opening to say something.

Miranda didn't give him the chance. She charged him, barely aware of what she was doing as her fingers dug into his shoulders and slammed him into the wall beside the window. He let her, his body going limp under her hands.

She was shaking so hard she could barely keep her grip. Her mind was choked with loss, guilt, failure, and blinding anger, all mashing together until she could no longer form coherent thoughts. When she opened her mouth, the words came out in a trembling, ragged sprawl.

"You're one of them, aren't you?" she whispered. "You're a star."

Eli leaned back against the wall without a sound. Behind him, the Empress's fleet started forward yet again.

CHAPTER
27

Eli stared down at Miranda, ignoring the pain as her fingers dug into his shoulders.

"You are, aren't you?" Miranda said again, her voice quaking. "I saw you, back in Mellinor. It all makes sense now. I never understood how you could get spirits to listen just by talking to them. Why no spirits would ever tell me about you after you left. I knew you had to be something special, something more than just a wizard. Now I see. Nothing can disobey you, can it? You just give an order and your Shepherdess will—"

Eli's anger exploded without warning. He lunged forward, yanking her hands off his shoulders. "That's not how I work and you know it!" he yelled, his voice raw.

Miranda stepped back in shock, and then her face flushed red as her anger rose to match his. "Shut up and answer the question! Are you a star or not?"

"Oh, *fine*," Eli said through clenched teeth. "You win. I'm a bleeding star. Cover that with sugar and eat it, if it makes you happy."

"*Makes me happy?*" Miranda roared. "You're a *star*. What are you doing, hiding up here while—" Her voice began to quiver, and she took a shuddering breath. "If you're really a star, how did any of this happen? You knew the Empress was coming. You *knew* it would be like this. I thought Josef was your friend. How could you let this happen to his country?" She flung out her arm, pointing at Nico's bloody bundle, still lying exactly where he'd laid her this afternoon. "How could you let *any* of this happen? What kind of a coward are you?"

Eli swallowed against the guilt she was hammering down his throat. "I tried to make them leave," he said lamely.

"Tried to make them leave?" Miranda shouted, shaking with rage. "How selfish can you be? Don't you see that this is bigger than your little gang? An entire country is falling, and the continent is next. Hundreds of men have lost their lives today, and—"

She cut off, and Eli winced as tears began to pour down her face. Powers, she'd lost one of her menagerie, hadn't she? He hoped it wasn't the dog. She really would rip his head off

450

if she lost her dog. But though he steeled himself for the worst, her answer still hit him like a punch in the gut.

"Mellinor," her voice broke as she said the spirit's name. She looked at him, her eyes so full of hatred Eli couldn't help but hate himself along with her. "My spirit is *dead*, and it's *all your fault!*"

Eli cringed as her voice hit him and bumped into the wall behind him. She had him cornered. There was nowhere to run.

"Everything is your fault," she said, her voice breathy and raw. "You could have stopped this at any time, couldn't you? Mellinor wouldn't have had to fight, wouldn't have had to die if you weren't hiding in here like a filthy, selfish *coward who won't lift a finger to—*"

Eli moved in a flash. He dropped, reaching out with both hands. The first grabbed her head to hold it still; the second covered her mouth, stopping her voice.

"That's enough," he said.

Miranda tore away from him and lashed out with her fist. Her swing caught him by surprise, and he didn't have time to move before her punch landed in his ribs, her sharp rings digging into his skin. He let her go, falling back with a grunt as he clutched his side. Miranda stood over him, panting as she raised her fist again.

"That's not nearly enough," she said. "I can't believe you're Master Banage's son. You have all the power in the world, but you're too selfish to use it for anything other than taking what other people have worked for. You know nothing of duty. You don't even know what it means to be a responsible wiz—"

"Shut up!" Eli shouted. The anger in his voice shocked them both. Eli stared at her a moment and then dropped his head to his hands. "Powers, Miranda, do you think I *wanted* this? I never wanted to be a star. Look at the Empress. Does that look like the kind of power it does the world any good to have?" Eli shook his head. "I hate it. I hate the way the world turns over and shows its belly to that woman. I hate the way everyone has to dance on her

451

string, even the Immortal Empress. I've spent my whole adult life trying to get away from her, to make my own way on my own power. To make my life *worth* something, even if it's just a bounty."

"You think your bounty makes you worth something?"

Eli sucked in a tight breath. He couldn't see her face from where he was sitting, but he didn't have to. He could feel her disgust bearing down on him like a weight.

"It's nothing," Miranda said. "Less than nothing. All that matters is action, Eli Monpress. If you're sitting on your power, if you let Mellinor die just to keep your *self-worth*. If you're going to let the Empress put her boot on every spirit on this continent all to save your *pride*, then you are even worse than I thought you were."

He heard the floor creak as she turned away.

"You're not worth a drop of Mellinor's water," she said, her voice thick with hatred and loss. "But what more could I expect from a thief and a con artist and a selfish, irresponsible—"

The list went on and on, and Eli sat on the floor and took it. He couldn't even argue with her anymore. She was right. He could have stopped this. He could have saved her spirit, saved Josef's men, saved Karon, saved everything, but he hadn't. He'd sat there and let it happen all because he couldn't stand to go back. Couldn't stand to let that woman win.

But I have won, love.

Eli sucked in a breath. He shouldn't have been surprised, he thought bitterly. Of course she would be here. She was always here.

I told you I'd win in the end, Benehime said. He could feel her now, kneeling beside him just on the other side of the veil that separated the spirit's world from her white nothing. *After all your valiant efforts, this is your reward, known forever far and wide as the man who doomed a continent to keep his pride.* She made a tsking sound. *You've let everyone down—your father, Josef, Nico, even Miranda, who never expected you to be anything more than a thief. But I'm different. I will*

452

always treasure you, darling star. I love you more than anything else in this sad, tiny world.

The skin of his ear began to tingle as Benehime's lips pressed against it through the veil. *Look at the wizard girl. Her loss is already suffered, but hers can be the last. You can still save things. All you have to do is stop being stubborn. Give in, embrace your position as the favorite again, and you can be the hero.* Her voice fell to a shivering whisper. *Come home to me, Eliton, and everything will be put right. I swear it.*

And just like that, Eli gave up.

He stood in one smooth motion, and Miranda stumbled back, surprised out of her tirade.

"What do you think you're doing?" she shouted, glaring at him with red-rimmed eyes.

Eli didn't answer. He stomped past her, shrugging off her hand when she tried to grab him. He kicked open the watch room door and started down the stairs. The boards creaked as Miranda started to follow him, but Eli didn't look back. He kept his eyes straight ahead as he clattered down the tower steps and burst through the door at the bottom into the silent, bowing world.

The door to the watch room slammed shut with a crash that made Miranda wince. She stood there panting, too exhausted to chase the thief down the stairs but too furious to give up. As a compromise, she went to the window, reaching it just in time to see Eli emerge from the bottom of the tower. He walked across the storm wall and down the stairs in quick, angry steps. The world was silent around him, every spirit cowering before the might of the Empress, but Eli paid it no mind. He hit the beach with a stomp and kept walking, stepping over the kneeling bodies of the soldiers. When he passed Josef, Miranda thought she saw him slow, but then he was moving again as fast as ever, marching toward the sea.

Miranda caught her breath when he reached the surf. The

waves were still lapping despite the Empress's pressure, but the moment Eli's boot touched it, the ocean froze. Miranda blinked at the deathly silence that descended on a shore where the sea had gone completely still. The water stood motionless as far as she could see. Even the great breakers on the horizon were frozen midcrest. Overhead, the air was perfectly still as well, the winds holding their breath as Eli walked forward, striding across the smooth water like it was stone.

When he reached the center of the bay, Eli stopped. He folded his arms across his chest and glared up at the towering wall of palace ships. High overhead, the Empress looked down at him with a haughty sneer. In that whole, still world, they were the only two who moved.

"Well, well," the Empress said. "The rat emerges."

Miranda blinked. The Empress hadn't raised her voice, but Miranda could hear her as clearly as though the woman were standing beside her.

"Come to meet my challenge at last?" the Empress continued, drawing a shining sword from the scabbard at her hip. "Come then, boy. I'll show you who is truly worthy of the Lady's favor."

"Nara." Eli said the name like an insult. "You want her? Take her. Love her for another eight centuries. But this?" He pointed his thumb over his shoulder at the shore. "This land is mine. Go home. No one wants you here."

"I am not yours to send away," the Empress hissed. "You claim this land? Fight to keep it. The Shepherdess has no love for the weak."

Eli tilted his head to the side. Miranda could feel the impatience radiating off him even at this distance, but Eli didn't answer the Empress's challenge. He just stood there, staring up at the woman with a smile so defeated it made Miranda's chest ache. And then, without warning, he opened his spirit.

Eli's power exploded out of him. It filled the beach, filled the sky, and swept over the Oseran mountains to fill the channel behind them. It expanded and expanded, pressing down so hard Miranda had trouble breathing. And then, at its center, a light brighter than any Miranda had ever seen broke like the sunrise.

All at once, the world, already bowed in homage to the Empress, turned its back on her and prostrated itself before Eli. Miranda clutched the window's edge, staring in amazement. She'd seen this once before, in Mellinor, but the scale was totally different now. Everything Eli's spirit touched woke, and every spirit that woke praised him. The sea flattened to glass below his feet and the winds circled him in supplication. On the island, the mountain woke and began to tremble, the very rock bowing in obedience. The sand on the beach swelled in reverence, burying the soldiers in its eagerness to show its respect, and even the stones of the tower were singing praises. Their song was little more than a buzzing under her fingers, but its meaning was clear. Miranda stood perfectly still, her eyes so wide they hurt. She had been amazed when the Empress opened her spirit, but this was so much more. Terrifyingly more.

When she found her voice at last, the question was a whisper, more air than sound. "What is he?"

For a moment nothing answered, and then Durn, sturdiest and calmest of her spirits, spoke.

"He is the favorite."

Miranda caught her breath, trying to remember where she'd heard that term before, but too many new things were tumbling through her head and she couldn't make it all fit together. It didn't matter though, for in the next moment, something happened that put everything else out of her mind.

Out on the glassy sea, the Empress fell as the wind abandoned her. She landed on the deck of her palace ship, crashing into the wood with an impact that made Miranda wince. For a moment the woman lay stunned, and then the Empress curled into a ball, burying her head in her hands as she began to weep. Down on the water, Eli, barely visible beneath his own light, shook his head in disgust and raised his arms.

455

All along the Empress's fleet, from horizon to horizon, white lines began to appear in the air. They fell like unraveling thread, the long, white slits growing until they were as large as the monstrous ships themselves, one for each boat. Miranda swallowed as the sea filled with white. Until this moment, she hadn't actually realized just how large the Empress's force was. The sight almost made her laugh. How had the Council ever thought it could win?

A few seconds after they appeared, the white lines stopped growing. For one breathtaking moment they hung in the air beside the ships, each a shining, pure white beacon. Their light lit up the night, each line reflected in the beautiful, still water below. Tears pricked Miranda's eyes as the scene the Shaper Mountain had shown them flashed again through her mind—the night sky lit up with a million lights, the things called stars. Unbidden, her eyes drifted up. The sky looked as it always had, enormous and black, the crescent moon hanging almost sulkily just above the horizon. She'd never thought of the sky as empty, but now, compared to the beautiful lights below, Miranda couldn't see it as anything but.

Below the blank curve of the night sky, Eli stood before the endless lights, the brightest of them all. He looked around at the white lines, almost like he was counting, and then, with a careless motion, he brought his arms down. In that one movement, the white, glowing lines vanished, taking the fleet with them.

Miranda rubbed her aching eyes, but when she opened them again, the view was the same. The ocean stretched out to the horizon, dark and empty. Of the Immortal Empress's innumerable fleet, not a single ship was left.

Down on the glassy water, Eli's light was the only one left. Without meaning to, Miranda found herself leaning forward, drawn to his light. But as she stretched for a better look, she saw that Eli was staring back, his eyes pinned on hers despite the distance. She smiled at him, a great, relieved grin. Five minutes ago she'd been ready to kill him. Now he'd just done the impossible and saved them all. But Eli didn't return her smile. He glared at her, his face bitter and drawn as another light flashed beside his.

Two white lines appeared on either side of Eli's head. They fell to his shoulders, shimmering in the night as his own light faded. A second after they appeared, two white arms emerged, long and perfect and glowing like white fire. They reached out, folding around Eli's neck until they were almost choking him in their embrace. Eli winced as though in pain, but his eyes never left Miranda's. She stared at him, confused, and then she saw his mouth move.

It wasn't like earlier. She couldn't hear him now. Actually, she wasn't sure if he was making a sound or just mouthing the words. But his lips were expressive as always, and she could see the words plainly even at this distance.

Hope you're happy, he mouthed. *Good-bye.*

And then the white arms pulled him back, and Eli vanished without a sound.

Darkness fell with a physical force as his light snuffed out, leaving the world blacker than anything Miranda had ever seen. She could dimly hear a familiar sound repeating in the distance, but it took her several seconds to realize it was the waves lapping on the beach. The wind howled gently over the tower, a land breeze moving out to sea, carrying with it the smell of fire and smoke, but the sounds of battle were gone. As her eyes adjusted to the new dark, she looked down at the beach to see the Empress's soldiers standing dumbly. Several simply dropped their swords in the sand and sat down, too stunned by the defeat of their Empress and the disappearance of their fleet to do anything more. In their midst, Josef stood and began rounding them up, calmly announcing that the war was over.

Miranda wasn't sure how long she stood there. Half an hour, maybe more. She certainly didn't know when Nico joined her, but as she turned at last to go downstairs she found the girl standing at the window beside her, staring out at the dark sea with her coat wrapped around her shoulders.

Miranda winced and backed away. Nico looked terrible. Her pale skin was mottled with bruises all the way to where it vanished beneath her coat. Dried blood caked her hair, and both her eyes were blacked. Her expression, however, wasn't one of pain, but of dread. Miranda hovered a moment, unsure what to do, and then Nico spoke.

"The light woke me up," she whispered, her voice fragile and raw. "Where's Eli?"

Miranda bit her lip, trying to think how best to answer. After several moments, she settled on the truth.

"I think he's gone."

Nico licked her lips, but she didn't move. Miranda didn't move either. They just stood there, side by side, staring into the dark, looking in vain for what was no longer there.

ACKNOWLEDGMENTS

Thank you to Lindsay, whose edits, observations, and refusal to pull punches made this book five times what it was when I first gave it to her. Also, a huge thank-you to the hardworking people at the Watkinsville Jittery Joe's. You are all coffee-making saints. Thank you for letting me take up the corner chair indefinitely.

THE SPIRIT'S END

*For Jeffrey, who has done more for me
than words can ever express.*

PROLOGUE

At age thirteen, Eliton Banage was the most important thing in the world, and he knew it.

Wherever he went, spirits bowed before him and the White Lady he stood beside, Benehime, beloved Shepherdess of all the world. In the four years since the Lady had found him in the woods, he had wanted for nothing. Anything he asked, no matter how extravagant, Benehime gave him, and he loved her for it.

She took him everywhere: to the wind courts, to the grottoes and trenches of the seafloor, even into the Shaper Mountain itself. All the places Eli had only dreamed about, she took him, and everywhere they went, the spirits paid them homage, kissing Benehime's feet with an adoration that spilled over onto Eli as well, as it should. He was the favorite, after all.

For four happy years this was how Eli understood the world. And then, the day before his fourteenth birthday, everything changed.

It began innocently. He'd wanted to go to Zarin, and Benehime had obliged. It was market day and the city was packed, but the crowds passed through them like shadows, unseeing, for Eli and the Lady were on the other side of the veil, that silk-thin wall that separated the spirits' world from Benehime's. As usual, Eli was walking ahead, showing off by slipping his hand through the veil to snitch a trinket or a pie whenever the shadows of the merchants turned away. He was so fast he could have done it without the veil to hide him, but Benehime had ordered he was never to leave the veil without her explicit permission. It was one of her only rules.

He'd just pulled a really good snatch, a gold-and-enamel necklace. Grinning, he turned to show it to Benehime, but for once she wasn't behind him. Eli whirled around, necklace dangling from his fingers, and found the Lady several steps back. She was perfectly still, standing with her eyes closed and her head cocked to the side, like she was listening for something. He called her name twice before she answered. He ran to her, giving her the necklace, and she, laughing, admired it a moment before throwing it on the ground and going on her way.

This was how it usually went. Benehime hated everything humans made. She said they were like paintings done by a blind man, interesting for the novelty but never truly worth looking at. Eli had long since given up asking what she meant. Still, she liked when he gave her things, and making her happy was the most important thing in his life.

She stopped twice more before they made it to the main square. By the third time, Eli was getting annoyed. Fortunately, her last pause happened only a dozen feet from his goal—the Council bounty board.

"Look!" Eli shouted, running up to the wall of block-printed posters. "Milo Burch's bounty is almost a hundred thousand now!" He stared at the enormous number, trying to imagine what that much gold would look like. "He's like his own kingdom."

Benehime woke from her trance with a laugh. *Come now,* she said, stepping up to join him. *You saw five times that in the gold veins under the mountains just last week.*

"It's not *about* the gold," Eli said, exasperated. "It's about being someone who's done things. *Big* things! Big enough to make someone else want to spend that much gold just to catch you." He took a huge breath, eyes locked on the swordsman's stern face glowering out of the inked portrait. "What kind of man must Milo Burch be for his head to be worth that much money?"

Who knows? Benehime said with a bored shrug. *Humans have so many laws.*

"I'm going to have a wanted poster some day," Eli said proudly. "And a bounty. The biggest there's ever been."

Nonsense, love, Benehime said, taking his hand. *Whatever would you do with such a thing? Besides*—she kissed his cheek—*no one could ever want you more than I do. Now come, it's time to go home.*

"But we just got here!" Eli cried, trying to tug his hand away.

Before he'd finished his sentence, they were back in Benehime's white nothing.

Now, she said, sitting him on the little white bed she'd ordered the silkworms to spin just for him. *Wait here and don't move. I have to take care of something, but I won't be long.*

Eli glared. "Where are you going? And why can't I come with—"

Eliton.

Benehime's voice was sharp, and Eli shut his mouth sulkily. She smiled and folded her hands over his.

I'll be back soon, she whispered, kissing his forehead. *Wait for me.*

Eli squirmed away, but the Lady had already vanished, leaving him alone in the endless white. He sat down with a huff, picking at his pillow with his fingernails while he counted down the seconds in his mind. When he'd sat just long enough to be sure she was really gone, Eli reached out and tapped the air. At once, a thin, white line appeared. It fell through the empty space, twisting sideways as it opened into a hole just wide enough for him to wiggle through. Grinning, Eli crawled forward and slipped through the veil after the Shepherdess.

She was easy to follow. Everywhere the Shepherdess went, the world paid attention. All he had to do was follow the trail of bowing spirits. The first few times he'd tried this she'd caught him easily, but Eli had quickly learned that if he was quiet, Benehime didn't always see him. And so, keeping himself very still and very silent, Eli slipped through the world until he saw the Lady's light shining through the veil. He stopped a few feet away, lowering himself into the dim shadows of the real world before opening the veil just wide enough to peek through.

What he saw on the other side confused him. When the Lady had left so suddenly, he'd thought for sure she was going to deal with some spirit crisis. A flood maybe, or a volcano. Something interesting. But peeking through the tiny hole in the world, he didn't see anything of the sort. Benehime was standing in a large, dirty study, her white feet resting on a pile of overturned books. In front of her, a thin, old man sat on a single bed. The sheet was thrown back as though he'd gotten up in a hurry, but his eyes were calm as he faced the Shepherdess, his rings burning like embers on his folded hands.

Eli frowned. Why was Benehime visiting a Spiritualist? She disliked the stuffy, meddling wizards even more than he did. Yet the man was almost certainly a Spiritualist; no one else wore jewelry that gaudy, and the study they were standing in was clearly the upper level of a Spiritualist's Tower. It looked just like his father's, Eli thought, though Banage would never let his room get so cluttered. He never allowed anything to fall short of his expectations, the old taskmaster. Eli glowered at that, but before he could fall into thinking about all the things his father had done wrong, the old Spiritualist spoke.

"You're her, aren't you?" he said, his voice full of wonder. "The greatest of the Great Spirits?"

I am no spirit.

Benehime's voice was so cold and cruel, it took Eli several seconds to recognize it. She leaned over as she spoke, bending down until her eyes were level with the old man's. Her presence saturated the air, as cold and heavy as wet snow, but the man didn't even flinch.

Who told you?

"Doesn't matter now," the Spiritualist said, waving his hand, his rings glittering with terror in the Lady's harsh, white light. "You're here, and I have questions."

Typical human arrogance, Benehime said, crossing her arms. *To think I would answer your questions.*

468

"If we are arrogant, it is you who made us so, Benehime," the old man said, his voice growing every bit as sharp and cold as hers. "We are your creation, after all. Or, should I say, your distraction."

Benehime sneered, her beautiful face twisting into a terrible mask. *It seems the whispers of treason were grossly understated. I came here to deal with a spirit who didn't understand my very simple doctrine of silence and find a full-blown rebellion. Tell me, human, when those spirits who've stupidly thrown their lot in with you were spilling my secrets, did they also tell you that the price for such knowledge was death?*

"And what do I have to fear from death?" the Spiritualist said. "I am old, my life well lived. I have spent sixty years in duty to the spirits. I consider it an honor to die asking the questions they cannot."

With that, the old man pushed himself off the bed. He creaked as he stood, rings burning on his fingers as his spirits poured their strength into his fragile, old limbs. When he spoke again, his voice was threaded with the voices of his spirits.

"What is on the other side of the sky, Shepherdess?" he asked. "Why is it forbidden to look at the hands that scrape the edge of the world? Why do the mountains ignore the claws that scrape their roots? What secret horror do the old spirits hide from the young at your order? What are you hiding that is so dangerous that speaking of it, or even just looking its way, is cause for death?"

His voice rose as he spoke. By the time he finished, he was nearly shouting, and yet his calm never broke. The Spiritualist's soul filled the room, its heavy power steady and tightly controlled. His spirits clung to it, cowering in their master's shadow from the Shepherdess's growing rage. Eli could feel the Lady's cold fury seeping through the veil itself, but when she spoke at last, it was a question.

Why do you care? she asked. *Even if I told you, you couldn't do anything. Why waste your life on knowledge that means nothing?*

Eli held his breath. Benehime wasn't talking to the man but to the trembling spirits on his fingers. Even so, it was the Spiritualist who answered.

"I ask because they deserve to know," he said, raising his rings to his lips. "And while you may control my spirits utterly, you cannot control me, and you cannot control the truth."

The Shepherdess bowed her head, and Eli clenched his fists. If this man had made his Lady cry, he'd...He was still figuring out what he would do when a sound rang out through the still room. It was musical and cold, colder than anything he'd ever felt, and Eli realized the Shepherdess was laughing.

Do you know how many times I've been told that? She giggled, raising her head with a smile that made Eli's blood stop. *You think that you're the first to demand answers? Please. I've been Shepherdess for nearly five thousand years now. I can't even remember how many times I've been asked those same questions, but I've never once answered. And do you know why, little wizard?*

For the first time since she'd arrived, the Spiritualist was speechless.

Let me tell you something about spirits, Benehime whispered, reaching out to trace the old man's jaw. *Spirits are panicky, stupid, and willfully ignorant. They knew what was on the other side of the sky, and they chose to look away and say nothing, to let the truth be lost under the press of time. They chose safety. They chose ignorance. The only one who didn't get a choice was me.*

She sighed deeply, trailing her fingers down the old man's neck to his sunken chest, tapping each rib beneath his threadbare nightshirt. *You want the truth, Spiritualist?* she said, her white eyes sliding up to lock on his dark ones. *I'll tell it to you. The truth is your precious spirits don't want to know what's out there, because if they did, their panic would tear them apart.*

"I don't believe you," the Spiritualist said, though his voice was far less sure than before. "The spirits deserve—"

The spirits deserve exactly what they have, Benehime snapped back, anger cutting through her voice like an icy wire. *This is their world, created for them, and its rules, my rules, are for their protection.*

As she finished, her hand slid into the old man's chest. Her white fingers parted his skin like a blade, and the old Spiritualist gasped in pain. He would have fallen to his knees had Benehime's hand not been in his ribs, lifting him up until his face was an inch from hers.

That may not have been the answer you thought you were dying for, she whispered. *But that's the problem with demanding the truth, Spiritualist. It doesn't always come out as you'd like.*

With that, she slid her hand out of his chest, and the old Spiritualist fell. His body changed as he plummeted, growing thinner, the skin shriveling. Eli pressed his hand over his mouth to keep from screaming as the old man, now little more than a skeleton, hit the ground and crumbled to dust. His rings hit a second later, the gold and jewels landing on the wooden floor with hollow clinks.

Benehime flicked her hand in disgust, and the Spiritualist's blood fled from her skin, leaving her fingers clean and white. When her hand was purified to her satisfaction, she reached down to pick up the largest of the Spiritualist's rings, a great onyx band the size of Eli's thumb. The spirit began to sob the second Benehime touched it, and she silenced its blubbering with a sharp shake.

You, she said. *See what you've done? This is your fault, you know. Why did you tell him?*

The ring did not speak. Benehime scowled, and her light grew brighter. Even through the veil, the pressure of her anger was enough to make Eli's ears pop. He clung to the veil, watching in horror as the ring trembled. Just when he was sure it was about to shake itself apart, the ring spoke one word.

"No."

Benehime arched a thin, white eyebrow. *No?*

471

"I'm not afraid of you, Shepherdess," the black stone whispered. "No, not Shepherdess. Jailor, for that's what you really are. You say you're our Shepherd, our provider, but our wizard gave us more than you ever have. He fought for us, fought to learn the truth, and you killed him for it."

Benehime's white eyes narrowed. *You want to share his fate?* she said. *You're a strong stone, Durenei. Bow and beg forgiveness, and I may yet overlook this transgression.*

The ring trembled in her hand, but its voice was stone when it spoke at last. "I hold true to my oaths and my master," it whispered. "And I will never bow to you again."

Benehime's face closed like a trap. She clenched her hand in a fist, crushing the ring with a snap of cracking stone. The spirit gave one final cry, and then Benehime opened her hand to pour a thin stream of sand onto the floor.

After that, the Shepherdess didn't offer her forgiveness again. She stepped forward, stomping her bare, white foot on the Spiritualist's rings one by one. Each one died with a soft cry, and when her foot lifted, nothing was left of the old man's spirits but dust. When they were all destroyed, the Shepherdess snapped her fingers.

The veil rippled, and Eli tensed, ready to run, but she wasn't calling him. Instead, the Lord of Storms stepped through the hole in the world to stand at the Shepherdess's side. He looked around the Tower as he entered, and his face settled into an even deeper scowl when he saw the piles of dust on the floor.

Erase this man and his spirits from the world's memory, the Shepherdess said, waving at the dust. *I don't know his name, and I never want to.*

The Lord of Storms folded his arms over his chest. "That's not my job."

The words were barely out of his mouth when the Shepherdess's arm shot out, her white fingers grabbing his throat.

I've had enough insurrection for today, she whispered. *You are my sword. I made you, and you will do whatever I ask. Do I make myself clear?*

"Yes, Shepherdess," the Lord of Storms whispered around her hold.

She released him with a disgusted sound and turned away, walking toward the center of the tower. The world was silent around her, holding its breath. When she reached the middle of the room, she stopped and held out her arms. When she brought them down again, the tower fell with a sigh. Great stone blocks crumbled to sand as Eli watched. Books fell to dust. Wood splintered to nothing. The spirits died without a sound, too terrified even to cry out, until Benehime and the Lord of Storms were floating alone in the empty air above a dusty clearing, all that was left of the Spiritualist's two-story tower.

I'll leave the rest to you.

"Yes, Shepherdess," the Lord of Storms said, but the Lady was already gone. She vanished like the moon behind a cloud, leaving the night darker than ever. The second she was gone, Eli fled as well, scrambling through the veil to beat her back home.

He barely made it, winking into place on his pillow just as she appeared. She looked for him at once, and he beamed back at her, but his heart was thudding in his chest. She looked like she always did, white and beautiful, but when Eli gazed up at her now, all he could see was her foot coming down, her hand leaving the dead man's chest.

What's the matter, love? Benehime whispered, sinking onto the pillow beside him. *You're shaking. Are you cold?*

Not trusting his voice, Eli shook his head. Benehime sighed and pulled him into her lap. Eli cringed from her touch before he could stop himself, and the Shepherdess froze.

Never pull away from me, she said, her voice cold as glacier melt. *You love me.*

"I love you," Eli repeated automatically, letting her move him as she liked. They sat like that for a while, tangled together, and then Benehime spoke.

Always remember, love, she said softly, kissing his hair, *the*

*world is a horrible place without gratitude or understanding.
No matter how hard you work, you will never be thanked and
you will never be loved. But we will always be together, darling.
I will always love you, and you will always love me. Now, tell
me you love me.*

"I love you," Eli said again.

Benehime nodded and pulled him closer, crushing him
against her chest until he could barely breathe. *Whatever
happens, my favorite*—she kissed him again and again—
*whatever comes, remember, I am all that matters in the world
for you. I am your hope and your salvation. Love me forever
and I will raise you up when all others are cast off. Though
the world may end, no harm shall ever come to you. I swear
it.*

Eli nodded, letting the White Lady kiss him, but even as
her lips landed again and again, all he could think of was her
face, cruel and unrecognizable, as she crushed the Spiritualist's
onyx ring in her fist. And it was that moment, in the space
between one kiss and the next, that Eli knew things could
never be the same again.

After that night, Eli knew no peace.

Nothing changed at first. He continued as always, following
Benehime wherever she needed to go, entertaining her when
she was bored, telling her he loved her whenever prompted,
like a little parrot. But he didn't mean it, not anymore.

Now that he'd seen the truth once, he saw it all the time—
the cruel shadow that lay behind her white smile. The way
she held him just a hair too tightly. The faint threat in her
voice every time she told him to say he loved her. But worst
of all were the spirits.

Before, when they'd trembled in front of Benehime, Eli had
always thought it was from awe. He now saw the shaking for
what it really was: pure terror. He would stand beside the Lady
as she dealt with the spirits, hating every second of it. Hating
her for being that way. Hating himself for not seeing it sooner.

474

It hurt to think how childish he'd been, how naive. He'd thought he was important, having spirits bow to him as they bowed to her, but he was nothing but a shadow, an afterthought of their fear. It made him sick. Living with his father in the tower, the spirits had been his friends. They'd been kind to him when Banage had driven all kindness out in the name of discipline, and this was how he repaid them? Following their tyrant around, lapping up her attention like a little lovesick dog?

The truth of it ate at him like a worm. Everything Benehime did now—the forced kisses, the constant promises she wrung out of him—made Eli furious. Every day he felt more used and helpless, more disgusted, but what could he do? Benehime was always with him. She didn't sleep, only sat beside him while he did. She never let him out of her sight save for those times when she vanished mysteriously.

Eli didn't follow her anymore; he'd seen as much of her true nature as he cared to. But even if he had taken those chances to open a hole and escape, she would find him. Assuming the spirits didn't report him at once, Benehime had told him many times that his soul shone like a beacon. All she had to do was look at her sphere and pick him out. No, if he wanted to escape for real, for good, Eli would have to convince Benehime to let him go. Of course, he had about as much chance of that as of convincing gravity not to pull him down, but even at fourteen, Eli was never one to let impossibilities stand in his way.

It took eight months before he finally came up with a plan that had a chance of working. He spent another month refining it, and yet another being the best possible boy Benehime could ever ask for just to make sure she wouldn't be suspicious. Finally, when the plan was firmly cemented in his mind and Benehime was in the best mood he could manage, Eli sprang.

They were in the jungle far, far south of the Council Kingdoms. Eli had suggested the place because it was at the other end of the world from the Lord of Storms' fortress, and he'd needed as few variables as possible. They were perched in the branches of an obliging tree, their feet dangling lazily in the air. Eli was using the tree's flowers to make Benehime a crown while the Lady watched, her face beaming with love at the seemingly spontaneous show of affection.

The moment he laid the crown on her head, Eli said the words he'd been rehearsing to himself for the past eight weeks.

"Do you remember the story you told me once," he said, his voice perfectly casual, "about when you first found Nara?"

Don't speak her name, Benehime said, adjusting the flower crown with loving fingers. *She's forgotten, my treasure. Only you matter now.*

Eli smiled his best bashful smile and pushed a step further. "Yes, but do you remember how you gave her a wish?"

Benehime laughed and drew him into her lap. *Is that where this is going?* she said, kissing his cheek. *Do you want a wish, too, love? Silly boy, you know I'll give you whatever you want.*

"It's not so much a 'what' as something I want to do," Eli said, reaching into the pocket of his beautiful white shirt and taking out the folded piece of paper he'd so carefully snitched the last time they were in Zarin.

Benehime's smile faded as Eli spread the paper across their laps. It was a wanted poster for Den the Warlord. His terrifying face glared up at them, daring anyone to try for the enormous number written in block capitals below him: five hundred thousand gold standards.

What is this?

"You remember just before my birthday?" Eli said. "When I said I wanted to be on a wanted poster? Well, I've been thinking about it more and more lately, and I think I'm ready."

Benehime leaned back to stare at him, her white face genuinely confused. *Ready to do what?*

"Get on a poster," Eli said. "I've decided. I want to be a thief. Not just any thief, the world's greatest thief!"

Love, Benehime said patiently, *if you want something, I'll give it to you. You don't have to steal.*

476

"It's not about wanting anything," Eli said. "It's about being the best. Bounties are a measurement: the bigger the bounty, the better you are at whatever you did. Den was the best betrayer, and his face is known across the Council Kingdoms. Milo Burch was the best swordsman, and now he's worth more dead than some nobles see in a lifetime. Den's bounty alone is five hundred thousand gold! One hundred thousand would buy you a good-sized kingdom. How many people can say, 'My life is worth five kingdoms'?"

Benehime sighed and pulled the flower crown from her head. Her brows were furrowed, a bad sign. She was losing interest. Eli licked his lips. He'd have to play this next part just right.

"I'm going to beat that," he said, grabbing her hand. "I'm going to be the best thief ever. I'm going to steal everything worth stealing. I'm going to be famous all over, and I'm going to get the biggest bounty that's ever been, twice as big as Den's. That's my wish. I want to earn a bounty of one million gold."

It was the largest, most impossible number he could think of. Across from him, Benehime shook her head.

You have the silliest ideas, she said. *Why would you want to be a thief?*

"Because stealing's the only thing I'm good enough at," Eli said, smiling as he raised his hand.

Benehime blinked. Eli was holding the flower crown that, a second before, had been safely grasped in her now-empty hands. Suddenly, she began to laugh, reaching out to ruffle Eli's dark hair with her white fingers.

I can't deny you anything, she said. *All right, tell me what I have to do to get you your poster.*

Eli took a silent breath. This was it.

"That's the thing," he said, leaning into her touch. "If the bounty's going to mean anything, I have to earn it myself."

The laughter vanished from Benehime's eyes.

Eli's hands began to shake, but he kept his attention locked on the Lady. If he couldn't finish this now, he would never escape. "I want to find a thief to teach me," he said, enunciating each word to keep his voice from trembling. "I'll learn the trade right, and—"

Enough. Benehime's voice had changed. It was cold now, and sharp as a razor. *Do you think you can outsmart me?*

Eli began to sweat. "I never meant—"

I may not pay much attention to the affairs of humans, but even I know you're setting up an impossible situation. A million gold? From stealing? You'd have to steal everything of value on the continent.

Eli swallowed. "I—"

You think I can't see what you're doing? Benehime's voice dripped with disgust as she took the crown from Eli's hand and threw it on the ground far below. *I've known for some time now that you were changing, Eliton. You tried to hide it, but I know you better than anyone. I knew you were growing distant. The Lord of Storms tried to warn me. He said you'd change, that you'd turn on me. He told me to make you immortal at the beginning, when you were still an innocent child. But I wanted to wait.*

Her hand rose to his chin, delicate white fingers running down the line of his jaw. *I wanted to let you grow into your true potential,* she whispered. *I wanted you to learn how to truly appreciate what you have here. I trusted that even when you knew everything, you would choose me above all else, as I chose you. And now, this is how you repay my faith? A transparent ploy?*

"It's not a ploy!" Eli lied.

Of course it is, Benehime said, slapping his face lightly. *You know as well as I do you could never earn a million gold. You thought I was ignorant of things like money and bounties, and you meant to play on that ignorance, getting me to agree to let you run off in pursuit of an impossible goal. Let me guess, the next part was that you'd return to me once you'd earned your bounty and we'd be together forever, right?*

Eli winced before he could hide it. She'd seen straight

478

through him. The woman sitting across from him now was not the Benehime he knew, but the true Shepherdess—ruthless, cruel, and very, very dangerous. His heart began to pound as the hand on his cheek slid down to his throat, the slender fingers moving to press gently on his windpipe.

Come, dear, she whispered. *Don't look so afraid. I still love you more than anything. In fact, I like you best when you're being sneaky. But we'll have no more of this leaving talk. You're mine. My pet. My comfort. My favorite. Now, come and make me another crown and we'll forget all about this idiocy.*

She lowered her hand and Eli gripped his neck, rubbing the bruised skin. If he'd been older, more experienced, he would have dropped the subject and started picking flowers for a new crown, but he was young. Young and desperate, and as he watched what could be his last chance at freedom vanishing before his eyes, he could not help making a final, desperate grab.

"You're wrong," he said softly.

Benehime froze, her white body perfectly still. *About what?*

"I wasn't lying to you," Eli answered. "I do want to become the world's greatest thief, and I can earn a million gold bounty. You told me I could have whatever I wished for. That's it. I want the chance to prove you wrong."

Benehime sighed. *Now you're just getting desperate, love. The only way you could possibly earn a million gold bounty is if I helped you.*

"You're wrong!" Eli said, speaking his mind for the first time since the night she'd killed the Spiritualist. "I don't need your help, and I'm not your pet. I'm a wizard and the best thief around. I can earn a million gold on my own."

Don't be stupid, Benehime said. *You think you're some kind of savant thief because you've snatched a few trinkets? The only way you got any of it was because I let you open the portals and steal through the veil. Part of growing up is learning to face the truth, Eliton, and the truth is that you're nothing without my favor. Just a charming boy with quick*

479

hands. How could something so small possibly be enough to earn a million gold?

Eli swallowed against his pounding heart. "Want to bet?"

Benehime scowled. *What?*

"I'll make you a deal," Eli said, speaking quickly before he lost his nerve. "Give me the chance to prove I wasn't lying before. Let me go learn to be a thief and try to earn that million gold bounty on my own skills. If it really is impossible, if at any point I have to ask for your help, then you win. I'll come back to you and be everything you want me to be. But if I'm right, if I get a million gold without your help, then you have to let me go free."

Benehime leaned in until she was so close Eli could feel her cold breath on his skin. *Why would I ever take a bet like that?* she said. *I hold all the cards. Why should I take a risk?*

"Because if you don't, then there was no point in letting me grow up," Eli said, his voice trembling. "You said you wanted me to learn to appreciate you, right? Well, how can I do that if I never get to experience life away from you? If you keep me here, then you'll never know if I'm lying when I say I love you because I've never had the chance to experience life without your love."

He leaned forward, closing the tiny gap between them so that their foreheads pressed together. "Let me go," he whispered, staring into her cold, white eyes. "Let me try it on my own. If I fail, then I'll have learned how much I need you and I'll never, ever try to run again. And if I do somehow succeed, then I've proven that I love thieving more than I love you, and that sort of man isn't worthy of being your favorite anyway."

I decide who is worthy of my favor, Benehime said, but Eli could hear the consideration in her voice. Behind the blank wall of her white irises, he could almost see her thinking it over, testing the angles, looking for her edge.

She must have found it, because the Shepherdess leaned in and kissed him. It was a hard kiss, crushing his lips against her burning skin, but when she leaned back, the distance between them felt final. Real.

I always did like you best at your most defiant, she said, smiling. *Very well, you've got your chance. But I'm warning you, Eliton, I will hold you to every letter of our deal. You have to do it all yourself, no using my power, no showing your mark. And the moment you get in over your head, the second you have to ask me for help, you belong to me. Forever.*

"Fair deal," Eli said, a smile spreading over his face. "But you should know better than anyone how stubborn I can be."

Benehime almost laughed at that, but caught herself at the last moment. She reached up, resting her white hands on his shoulders. For a moment, Eli thought she was going to pull him into a hug, but then, without warning, she pushed him.

He toppled off the tree, falling fifteen feet before landing on his back in the wet cushion of leaf litter at the tree's base. The impact knocked the wind out of him, and for several moments all he could do was gasp for air. When his lungs finally started working again, he sat up with a groan, looking around at the endless forest. Overhead, the tree branch was empty. Benehime was gone.

He froze a moment, waiting for her to say something. But the forest was silent. Then, like someone opened a door, the sounds came roaring back as the spirits recovered from the Shepherdess's presence. Eli sat in the muck, trying to get himself to believe what his senses were telling him. Benehime was gone. His gambit had worked. He was free.

He stood up with a whoop that echoed through the forest, and for ten minutes he danced like an idiot, bouncing off the trees in celebration of his glorious, glorious freedom. The white world was gone. Everywhere he looked he saw color. Spirits buzzed all around him, their noises calm and without fear, and Eli fell to the ground, greeting them with pure joy. The spirits, alarmed at this wizard who was suddenly shouting at them, clammed up immediately, but Eli was too happy to care.

After almost half an hour of this, Eli realized he'd better get going. He had a bounty to earn, and he couldn't do that in the middle of nowhere. Brushing the leaves off his white clothes, Eli reached out to tap the veil and make a door to somewhere useful.

He caught himself a second before the cut opened. Oh no, it wasn't going to be that easy. No using the Shepherdess's gifts, that was the deal, and Eli would stick to it if it killed him. They were enemies in the game now, and if she got even an ounce of leverage on him, she would push on it with everything she had, just as Eli would. Now that he was still, he could almost feel her waiting on the other side of the veil, watching him, urging him to make a mistake, to give her something she could use.

With a sly smile, Eli drew his hand back and slid it into his pocket. He picked a direction almost at random and began to walk through the forest, whistling as the evening rain began to fall.

Giuseppe Monpress, the greatest thief in the world, had retired to his northern retreat for a little well-earned rest and to plan his next heist. He was just sitting down to his first dinner in solitude, a splendid roast duck with shallots and an excellent bottle of wine he'd lifted from the Whitefall family's private cellar, when he heard a knock on his door.

Monpress froze. This was one of his most secure hideouts. He was high in the Sleeping Mountains, deep in bandit country. But he had an understanding with the local gang, and anyways, bandits didn't knock. He swirled the wine in his glass, considering his options as the knock came again, louder this time.

With a long sigh and a sip from his glass, Monpress decided he'd better answer it.

He pushed his chair back and walked to the door, grabbing his dagger from the mantel, just in case. The knock was sounding a third time when Monpress opened the door and glared down at his most unwelcome visitor.

It was a boy. Monpress pegged him at a young fifteen. He was scrawny and short for his age with untrimmed black hair and a face that was too likable to mean any good. He was dressed in rags, his feet shoved into ill-fitting shoes that were far too thin for the half foot of snow on the ground, and he looked as if he hadn't had a good meal in weeks. But, hungry as he must have been, the boy didn't even glance at the succulent duck sitting on the table. Instead, he looked Monpress straight in the eye and flashed him what the boy probably considered a deeply charming smile.

"Are you Giuseppe Monpress?"

Monpress leaned on the door, framing the duck behind him with his crooked arm, just to be cruel. "That depends," he said slowly. "Unless you can give me a very compelling reason why you know that name, you can think of me as your death."

To his credit, the boy's smile didn't falter. "I heard from a reliable source that Giuseppe Monpress was the greatest thief in the world, so I set off to find him. Took me the better part of a month to pin him down to this part of the mountains, but I couldn't get an exact location, so I've been checking each likely valley."

"Impressive," Monpress said. "And what were you going to do when you found him?"

The boy straightened up. "I'm going to ask him to take me as an apprentice."

"I'm sorry you've wasted your time, then," Monpress said. "Giuseppe Monpress doesn't take apprentices."

"Since only Giuseppe Monpress would know that, I think you've answered my question," the boy said. "And I can assure you, Mr. Monpress, that you'll take me."

Despite himself, Monpress began to chuckle. "And why is that?"

"Because I'm going to be the greatest thief in the world," the boy said proudly. "And because, if you don't take me, I'm going to sit on your doorstep until you change your mind."

Monpress smiled. "Assuming, for the moment, that you're

483

right, you can hardly expect the greatest thief in the world to be trapped by a boy at his door. What will you do when I give you the slip?"

"Find you again," the boy said with a shrug. "As many times as I need to."

"I see," Monpress said. "Why are you so determined, if I may ask?"

The boy looked insulted. "I told you," he said. "I'm going to be the greatest thief in the world. You don't get to the top by apprenticing yourself to amateurs."

"So you're serious about just sitting there?" Monpress said.

"Absolutely," the boy said, and then, to prove his point, he sat down on the icy step, propping his legs up in Monpress's door. The position only helped to highlight how pathetically thin he was, and Monpress felt a tiny twinge of pity. Fortunately, it was easily quashed.

"Well," he said, stepping back, "then I hope you have a lovely night."

He held just long enough to see the boy's smile begin to crumble before he shut the door in his face.

Nodding at a job well done, Monpress slipped his dagger into his belt and returned to the table. As he sat down in his chair, he braced himself for a racket as the boy began to demand to be let in, but none came. Except for the howl of the wind outside, the cabin was silent. If Monpress hadn't just shut a door in his face, he'd have never known the boy was outside.

He glanced sideways at the shutters, rattling in their grooves as the storm blew back up, and then he looked back down at his rapidly cooling dinner. He'd just raised his knife and fork to carve the duck when the wind gave a low, mournful howl. Giuseppe rolled his eyes and set his silverware down with a sigh. He stood up and marched over to the door. Sure enough, the boy was sitting on the doorstep just as Monpress had left him, only his black hair was now full of snow.

"Change your mind?" the boy said, looking up.

"Not as such," Monpress said. "Happy as I would be to let you sit out there until you starved, it seems that my conscience is heavy enough without a boy's life weighing on it. I'm not agreeing to anything, mind you, but since it's clear you're the suicidally stubborn type, you might as well come in and eat."

The boy grinned from ear to ear and rushed inside so fast Monpress was nearly knocked off his feet. The boy sat down in Monpress's chair and began devouring the duck like he'd never tasted food in his life. The thief sighed and walked over to rescue his wine before it, too, disappeared into the boy's maw.

"What's your name?" he said as he spirited his drink to safety.

"Eli," the boy gasped between bites.

Giuseppe frowned. "Eli what?"

The boy shrugged and kept eating. Monpress sat down with a sigh, sipping his wine as he watched the boy reduce his fine roast duck to bones. The child was cracking them to suck the marrow when he caught Giuseppe looking.

"What?" he said, shoving a leg bone into his mouth.

"Nothing," Monpress said. "Just trying to shake the feeling that I've let my doom in by the front door."

"I wouldn't fret about it too much," Eli said. "I was planning to come down the chimney once you'd banked the fire anyway." He flashed Monpress a smile before spitting out the bone in his mouth and reaching for another. "When do we start training?"

Monpress drained his glass and poured himself another. He briefly thought about continuing his denials, but he was rapidly running out of energy to fight the boy's seemingly endless optimism. "Tomorrow morning," he said, taking a long drink.

Eli's eyes widened, and his face broke into an enormous grin. "What am I doing?"

"Fetching a cask of whiskey from my stash up the mountain."

Eli's face fell dramatically. *"Whiskey?* Why?"

"Because, if you're going to be staying here, I'm going to need it," Monpress said. "Finish your supper. I think a speck of duck still exists."

Eli gave him a skeptical look before turning back to the far more important task of making sure no bit of duck flesh escaped his attack.

Outside the little cabin, far from the cheery light of the little fire, the white shape of a woman vanished into the deep, drifting snow.

CHAPTER
1

Eleven Years Later

The vast desert that stretched across the Immortal Empire's southwestern tip was still and quiet in the moonlight. At its edges, the coast was calm, the ocean lapping tiredly against the beaches. The great storm that had raged for weeks up and down the continent's seaboard had died as suddenly as it began, the clouds dissipating in a handful of seconds to leave the night sky clear and blank as though there had never been a storm at all. Only the wreckage of the sea towns and the wall the Empress had raised to protect them remained, an improvised barrier standing awkwardly at the edge of the placid sea.

Suddenly and without warning, a light cut through the stillness. All across the dark desert, white lines appeared. They sliced high in the air, forming long needles of light that dangled several dozen feet above the sand. One after another they appeared until the sky was full of them, their white light filling the desert until it was bright as noon, and then the quiet shattered as the Immortal Empress's invasion fleet fell through the white lines and crashed into the dunes below.

The palace ships slammed into the sand, their great keels cracking against solid ground. Without the water to keep them upright, the boats toppled immediately, rolling onto their sides like falling horses. The night was full of cracking wood as hulls splintered and masts snapped like twigs, and then, as the white lines faded and the ships settled into their deathbeds, the cries of men rose to drown out the groaning of the boats as the Empress's army, the largest army ever raised, began to pick itself up.

At the head of the now grounded fleet, a large crowd was gathering around a boat that had lost its prow. Even in the chaos, word spread quickly, and the soldiers surged like ants from their toppled ships to gather around the palace ship with the broken hull at the very front of the fleet where, rumor had it, the Empress herself was buried under the wreckage. Up on the deck, the ship's captain was already at work, shouting orders to a crew of fifty strong men as they hauled the top half of the broken mast off the deck where the Empress had fallen.

They found her lying in a crater of broken wood. Her golden armor was shattered and the cloth beneath was stained bright red with blood. When they saw her, the soldiers fell silent, struck dumb at the possibility that the Immortal Empress, the undying, unquestioned divine ruler of the world, could possibly be *dead.*

But then, with a groan, the Empress opened her eyes. The men flinched back. Some fell to their knees, others simply stood, shocked. The Empress paid them no mind. She just pushed herself up, throwing off the remains of her golden armor to free her arms.

"Empress?" her captain whispered.

The Empress didn't answer. She didn't even look at her men. Her attention was entirely focused on getting to her feet. When she was standing at last, she reached out and tapped the air in front of her. No sooner had her finger moved than a new, thinner white line flashed in the dark, dropping through the air to just above her feet. The moment the line stopped growing, the Empress stepped through it, leaving the dark desert full of broken ships and moving into a world of pure white light. When she was through, the line shimmered and faded, leaving her soldiers staring in vain at the empty place where their Empress had been.

Opening a door through the veil to Benehime's private world without the Shepherdess's permission was forbidden even to stars. Nara didn't care. She stomped through the portal, blinking as her eyes adjusted to the blinding white. But even before she could see, the Empress knew exactly who was waiting.

Benehime lounged in the air, her white hair falling over her body like a cloak. Behind her, the Lord of Storms hovered like a glowering black shadow. A small, distant part of Nara's brain noted that the Shepherdess must have pulled him back together not long ago. Bits of him were still shifting between flesh and cloud, giving him that wild look he always got when he was fresh from his true form.

His expression, however, was solid as sharpened steel and locked on her with a look of pure disgust as Nara stumbled forward. But even as she registered his presence, Nara put the Lord of Storms out of her mind. He was beneath her notice. All that mattered was the Lady and the creature she held in her arms.

The thief sat in Benehime's lap like a dog. The travel-stained clothes he'd worn on the beach were gone, replaced by a pure white fitted jacket and trousers tucked into tall white boots. The Shepherdess held him close, one hand around his waist, the other brushing over his thigh like she was petting him. The thief had the good sense to keep his eyes down as Nara approached, but the Shepherdess looked straight at her, absently stroking the boy as she regarded her former favorite through narrowed, white eyes.

I do not recall summoning you here, Empress.

For the first time in her life, Nara's rage was so great that even the sound of the Shepherdess's voice couldn't shock her out of it. She stopped right in front of the Lady, breathing the cold, white air in great gasps until, at last, she managed a single, coherent word.

"Why?"

Benehime tilted her head, laying her ear against the thief's chest. *He is my favorite,* she said simply. *I thought I'd made that clear.*

"I'm your favorite!" Nara screamed. "I've always been your favorite! For the last eight hundred years I've given you my utter devotion. I gave you half the world as a peaceful, prosperous Empire! I raised you an army and sailed across the Unseen Sea. I destroyed an island, sacrificed my men, all for *you*! Everything I've ever done has been for you! So *why*? Why am I so summarily replaced by this disobedient, arrogant, faithless—"

The words froze in her throat as the air around her solidified. Suddenly, Nara couldn't move. She couldn't even breathe. In front of her, Benehime's white mouth curled in a disgusted sneer.

You will not speak so of my favorite.

Completely frozen, Nara could only stare in response.

The Lady reached down and took Eli's wrist. He flinched when she touched him, but didn't say a word as the Shepherdess lifted his hand and held it out to Nara.

I am the Shepherdess, the Lady said, turning the thief's hand palm down and pushing it forward until his fingers were half an inch from Nara's frozen lips. *A Power of Creation, given dominion over all spirits by the Creator himself. There is no opinion in the world that matters save mine, no will save my will. Now, do you love me, Nara?*

The frozen air thawed just enough for Nara to take a breath. "Yes," she whispered, tears running down her face. "But—"

And do you wish to stay by my side forever?

489

"I do." The words burned in Nara's throat.

The Lady smiled a cruel, beautiful smile. *Then know your place.* She pushed Eli's fingers closer to Nara's lips. *Kiss my favorite and apologize for hurting his lava spirit and putting his friends in danger.*

Nara stared at the Lady, her battered body perfectly still though the frozen air had already released her.

Benehime's smile faded. *Do it,* she snapped. *Prove you love me. Honor my favorite and take your place at the bottom of my stars.*

Nara glanced at the thief's fingers, now barely a quarter of an inch from her lips. On the Shepherdess's lap, Eli's face was a calm, bored mask, his gaze fixed on some unseen spot on the ground. But as much as he tried to hide it, Nara saw the truth. The thief's eyes were full of pity. He pitied her, and in that moment, Nara hated him more than she knew she could hate. But even so, even though it boiled her blood to do it, she leaned forward until her lips touched the thief's outstretched hand.

"Hail the favorite," she whispered.

Eli flinched as though the kiss were an arrow in his chest, but the Shepherdess looked pleased. She dropped Eli's hand and reached out to lay her fingers gently on Nara's head.

Poor Nara, the Shepherdess said, stroking her hair. *You probably think I've played you unfairly these last few days.*

The Empress resisted the urge to lean into the Lady's touch. "You used me," she said, glaring daggers at Eli. "To get to him."

That I did, the Shepherdess said. *But it was you who said you would do anything for me. What could be a greater honor than being a tool in the pursuit of my happiness?*

Nara clenched her teeth and said nothing.

Unfortunately, the Shepherdess went on, *all tools outlive their usefulness eventually.*

Nara blinked. "What?"

Times are changing, Nara, the Shepherdess went on,

stroking the Empress's dark hair absently, like she was petting a cat. *There's no room anymore for the disobedient.*

"What?" Nara said again, louder this time.

The Shepherdess's fingers suddenly curled, tangling in Nara's hair, and the Empress cried in pain as Benehime wrenched her head up.

You shouldn't have thrown that water on my favorite's lava spirit, she whispered, her white eyes boring into Nara's. *You shouldn't have come here uninvited, and you should have kissed my Eliton's hand the first time I told you to. One disobedience I could overlook; three is simply insulting.*

Nara's eyes watered at the pain of Benehime's grip on her hair. This was all wrong. This was not how it was supposed to be. The Shepherdess was her beloved, her everything.

"No," she whispered, reaching up to grab Benehime's hand. She clutched the Lady's white wrist, arching her neck painfully as she tried to kiss it. "I love you. If I was ever disobedient, it was from love of you. Tell me what to do, tell me how to change to make you love me again." Her voice rose to a frantic shriek. "Tell me how to love you and I'll do it!"

The pain in her head faded as Benehime's fingers released their grasp. The White Lady snatched her hand away and looked down with a disgust so intense Nara barely recognized her.

Why would I need you? she said, her voice cold as a glacier's heart as she pulled the thief closer. *I already have someone to love me. Good-bye, Empress.*

Nara doubled over as something inside her, something deeper than she'd ever known her soul could go, twisted and broke. All at once, she could no longer feel her body. She tried to breathe, but her lungs wouldn't obey. Looking down at her shaking hands, Nara saw her skin turn gray, then white, then vanish altogether. Her bones shrank before her eyes, growing smaller and brittler until they snapped under their own weight. Her chest ached, and she looked down to see that it was caving in.

She would have screamed then, but there was no longer

491

breath in her crumbling throat. As her vision went dark, her last thought was a memory. She was kneeling in the swamp again, and Benehime was reaching out, her lovely fingers curved in an inviting gesture, her light lighting up the world. Before Nara could rise and go to her, the moment was gone, and she fell to dust with Benehime's name on the last remnants of her lips.

Well, Benehime said, shaking her hand as though she could shake the last feel of Nara from her skin, *that's that.*

On her lap, Eli was staring at the pile of dust that, seconds ago, had been the most powerful ruler in the world. "What did you do?" he whispered.

She was no longer worthy of being my star, Benehime said. *So I removed my blessing and allowed age to catch up with her at last. Eight hundred years is a lot to handle all at once. I guess she couldn't take it.*

Eli's voice was shaking so badly he could barely get the words out. "But she loved you."

Everything loves me, the Shepherdess said with a shrug. *Even you. Isn't that right, darling?*

Eli said nothing, and the Shepherdess tightened her grip, her sharp fingers biting into his ribs.

None of that, she whispered. *I won. You're mine, remember? Now, don't you love me, darling?*

Eli turned to her with a slow smile. "Of course I do."

Benehime smiled back and gave him a kiss on the nose. Then she motioned for him to get off her lap. Eli moved to sit where she motioned, leaving the Shepherdess some space as she turned to talk to the Lord of Storms.

Their conversation was low and tense. It sounded like an old argument, and though Eli tried to listen, his attention kept drifting to the Lady's floating sphere, which was hanging in the air by his elbow. Particularly, his eyes kept going to one small island off the coast of the western continent where the fires were still burning in a destroyed city as dawn broke over the eastern sea.

* * *

492

Josef Liechten, King of Osera, was spending the twentieth hour of his reign in the still-smoking shell of Osera's throne room, listening to old men argue.

He sat on the steps of the throne beside the one remaining iron lion. The other lay toppled on the floor, its head melted to slag by the foot of the war spirit whose cold corpse lay collapsed in the rubble of what had been the throne room's western wall. The throne was crushed as well, the carved stone bench and backboard pounded into gravel. That was probably for the best. Sitting on the stairs listening to his mother's advisers bicker over Osera's future was bad enough. If Josef had been forced to sit in her chair for it, he probably would have walked out.

He was close enough to walking as it was. The advisers weren't even talking to him, just yelling at each other over his head about what must be done. Apparently, there were a lot of musts. Disgusted, Josef turned and looked out the crushed wall of the throne room. Through the large hole the war spirit had left, he could see the whole of the royal city, or what was left of it.

The stylish stone buildings and narrow lanes that had once covered the western slope of Osera were now little more than blackened piles of rubble. Entire blocks had shattered when the war spirits fired from the Empress's palace ships had landed, leaving craters of blasted, burned dirt where houses and shops had once stood. The Spiritualists had managed to get most of the fires under control, but a few stray lines of smoke were still rising from the docks, and, of course, there were the war spirits themselves. Their corpses were everywhere. After Eli had done...whatever it was he'd done and the Empress's fleet had vanished, the war spirits had toppled over and gone cold. They hadn't moved since, but the damage was done. Everywhere Josef looked, Osera was destroyed, and try as he might to remember that his island had rebuilt before, it was hard to feel any kind of hope.

Josef sighed and rested his chin on his fist. Eli's eternal

optimism usually grated on him, but he could have really used some right now. How long did the useless thief mean to disappear for, anyway?

"Sire?"

Josef flinched and glanced up. All the old men were staring at him. Powers, he'd missed something again, hadn't he?

Seeing his panicked look, the oldest of the ministers, a man Josef remembered seeing with his mother in court as a child, though he couldn't remember the old bastard's name now to save his life, repeated the question.

"Minister Archly was asking your opinion on how we should prioritize our emergency response. Should we focus on evacuation or should we concentrate our attention on saving what we can of our remaining structures?"

"We must do all we can to help the people, of course," put in another minster, whom Josef could only guess was Archly. "But our infrastructure is Osera's most valuable asset. We should—"

"Can't have infrastructure without people," Josef said, glad of a simple question. "Our first priority is to make sure we save as many people as possible. We've given the Empress too many Oseran lives as it is. I'll not give her any more."

"Of course, sire," the old minister said, his voice strained. "But what about—"

"Figure it out," Josef growled, standing up. The old men all started talking at once then, but Josef just pushed past them, stalking off toward the blown-out doors.

The Oseran palace had been as hard hit as the rest of the city, but, remarkably, the royal wing was still intact. Josef stomped through the empty corridors. He'd sent the servants to help with the recovery, and so far he didn't miss them. After all the noise and chaos of the last two days, the silence in the empty halls was much more comforting than having someone around to make his fire. Josef jogged down the hall and quietly opened the door to his chambers, tiptoeing through the parlor and into his bedroom, where he stopped to let his eyes adjust to the dark.

Nico lay in his bed, a dark shape buried beneath the covers. He'd carried her here himself when they'd cleared the survivors off the storm wall. She'd been awake then, but was sleeping now. Josef let out a breath. Seeing the steady rise and fall of her chest calmed him better than anything else.

Walking to the bed, Josef eased himself down to the mattress. He kept his eyes on Nico to make sure the motion didn't disturb her, but Nico didn't stir. Smiling, Josef leaned against the heavy headboard and closed his eyes against his own tiredness.

He hadn't slept since the night before last, when he'd fallen asleep on the couch waiting for Adela. Now that he was sitting, he could feel the tiredness in his marrow. Even the Heart on his back felt heavy. He wanted more than anything to lie down beside Nico and let her calm breaths lull him to sleep, but there were still fires in the city below. People were still digging their families out of the rubble, and all the ministers wanted to do was argue over infrastructure.

Josef gritted his teeth. He should have sent the old men down to dig through the broken houses themselves. That would have taught them. But, of course, he'd never do that. He could chop a palace ship in two, but Oseran politicians still made him feel like a stumbling boy. They'd probably taken his "Figure it out" command as a chance to do whatever they liked, but Josef wasn't really sure he cared. After all, they knew more about running a country than he did. Maybe it was for the best if he just stayed out of things.

He must have drifted off in the dark room. One moment he was looking at Nico; the next he was jerked awake by the sound of someone knocking on the door. Stiff and more tired than ever, Josef forced himself to his feet. He walked quietly to the door and opened it a fraction to see one of the guardsmen who'd stood with him on the storm wall.

The young man had bandages on his face and arms, but he was standing, and he bowed when he saw Josef. "Sire," he said, "you're needed in the square."

495

"What's happened?" Josef said, slipping out of the bedroom and closing the door so their voices wouldn't disturb Nico.

The guard grinned far as the bandage across his jaw would allow. "Wouldn't you know it, sire? The reinforcements have finally arrived."

"About bleeding time," Josef said, motioning for the guard to lead the way.

Since most of the palace meeting rooms had been either burned or crushed in the attack, the palace guards, those who were left anyway, had brought the newcomers to a hastily set up tent in the stable yard. A dozen soldiers in Council white stood crammed into the narrow space. Josef wasn't surprised to see Sara there as well. The Council wizard was talking animatedly to a large, middle-aged man in an ornate military coat who seemed to be the troop's leader. So far, the only Oserans present were a few bandaged guards. They saluted as Josef approached, and he saluted back, keeping his eyes on the Council man and Sara as he entered the tent.

"Shall I fetch your advisers, sire?" whispered the guard who'd brought him.

"No," Josef said. The last thing he needed when he was dealing with the Council were old men making him feel like a tongue-tied teenager. "They have their jobs already. I'll fill them in later."

The guardsman nodded and moved to take up position behind his king. Meanwhile, Josef himself took a seat on the folding stool, leaning forward so he could rest his weight on his knees. Sara arched an eyebrow at this, but the man in the military jacket looked almost ill with insult.

"You're the new Eisenlowe?" he said at last, looking Josef up and down, his eyes lingering on the rips in Josef's shirt and the bloodstains on the bandages beneath.

"I am," Josef said. "Who are you?"

The man pulled himself straight. "Myron Whitefall, Commander of the United Council Forces, come to offer Osera the Council's aid against the Empress."

496

"You're a little late for that," Josef said. "The Empress is gone, but if you'd like to stay and help clean up, you're welcome to."

"As much as we'd like to help, the Merchant Prince gathered the Council army to march against the Empress, not to act as janitors," Myron said testily. "You have our thanks and admiration for turning back her initial assault, King Josef. You should rest and regather your armies. We will take up position on the coast for her next attack."

"I already told you. There won't be a next attack," Sara said, blowing a line of smoke into the air. "The boy's right; we've already done all the work. The Empress is gone. Defeated. Sent packing. You've come too late, Myron dear, as you would know if you listened to any of the Relay messages I sent you *or* the last five minutes I just wasted trying to keep you from looking like an idiot."

Myron's face went scarlet. "Do you honestly expect me to believe that you defeated the Immortal Empress with a handful of wizards and a few hundred Oseran troops?"

"What you believe is your business," Josef said. "The truth is what it is. The Empress vanished. We saw it with our own eyes, and all her ships vanished with her."

"*Vanished?*" Myron shrieked. "How does an armada *vanish*? And how do you know it wasn't a trick?"

"We don't," Sara said. "But if it was a trick, it was a badly timed one. She *was* winning, after all."

Myron looked affronted, and Sara heaved a long sigh. For a moment, she looked almost sad, and then the expression was gone as she went on brusquely as ever. "Much as it pains me to say it, I believe we were merely the lucky recipients of a miracle. A miracle I intend to thoroughly investigate, but a miracle nonetheless."

Josef listened with growing anger. Sara's flippant words seemed like an insult to what had happened last night. He could still see it clearly—the dark, frozen sea, the glowing lines, and Eli standing in the middle of it all with that horrible,

497

defeated look on his face as the white arms dragged him through the world. He'd be back, of course, Josef reminded himself. Eli would never pull something like that unless he had a plan.

Somewhat appeased by that, Josef turned back to Myron. The Council commander had lost his look of confident superiority and was now standing bewildered, his eyes begging Josef to let him in on the joke. But there was no joke, and all Josef could do was try and bring the Council man around to his side.

"There may be no Empress to fight," he said. "But we still need your help. As I'm sure you saw on your way up, Osera was nearly flattened last night." He glanced down the mountain to where the Council's ships were moored to whatever docks were still above water. "A dozen warships full of hands would mean a lot to us right now."

Whitefall bristled for a moment, but then his shoulders fell. "Of course," he said at last. "The Council will of course offer aid to Osera in her time of need."

"Good," Josef said. "I'd hate to think we were paying those dues for nothing."

This earned him a nasty glare from Myron, but Josef was already looking over his shoulder to where his advisers had gathered on the stairs. All of them were leaning in to hear what was going on in the tent. When Josef waved his hand, the old men hurried forward.

"The Council has offered to help us clean up," he said as they entered the tent. "Can you work with him?"

Since he said this to no one in particular, every one of his advisers thought the king was addressing him personally, and they all agreed in unison.

"But of course—"

"Your majesty is too gracious—"

"It would be an honor to serve—"

"The Council is a valued ally—"

The cries dissolved into argument almost immediately, and

Josef, realizing he was going to have to do something, started making assignments at random, dividing the city's five districts between the five younger advisers before putting the oldest in charge of working directly with Whitefall on logistics.

Surprisingly, everyone seemed reasonably happy with this setup. They immediately started working things out among themselves, and Josef took the chance to make his escape.

He motioned for a guard and lowered his voice. "I'm going to grab some sleep while they work this out. Spread the word, whoever wakes me up without a good reason loses his head."

"Yes, sire," the guard said, bowing. "Rest well."

Josef nodded and turned away, disappearing up the stairs toward his room, Nico, and the cool, welcoming dark.

Sara sat back, puffing on her pipe and watching with bemusement as Myron was set upon by a swarm of Oseran officials eager to prove their worth to the new king. Despite the horrible things she'd heard about Theresa's son, he seemed to be adapting to his new life quite well. He'd certainly learned how to delegate. He'd learned how to make a quiet exit, too, possibly an even more useful skill, and certainly one that served her purposes at the moment. The boy didn't seem to be any great friend of Banage or his darling apprentice, but she had the feeling the next hour would be much simpler without the king's interference.

Once Myron had extricated himself from the mass of officials, Sara waved him over. He gave her a dirty look, but he came.

"To hear those Oserans talk, you'd think I'd laid the wealth of the Council at their feet," he grumbled, sinking down onto the stool beside Sara. "I can't grow buildings out of the ground."

He gave her a sideways look, and Sara chuckled.

"Neither can I," she said. "I'm no Shaper. And don't look at me like that. You can't be sneering at wizard tricks one week and begging for them the next."

"You're the one spouting nonsense about miracles," Myron said bitterly. "Are you going to tell me what actually happened here?"

"I don't think you'd understand if I tried," Sara said, tapping the ashes out of her pipe. "I'm not sure I understand yet, but I intend to."

Myron snorted. "And I suppose your little fop is working on that?"

Sara laughed. "Sparrow? No, he's asleep. Even he needs his rest sometimes. Unfortunately my curiosity will have to wait just a little longer. For now, you should reserve a squad of soldiers before the Oserans set them all to picking up bricks. We have unfinished business to wrap up."

"We?" Myron said. "What do you mean?"

Sara looked pointedly at a knot of Spiritualists talking to a building across the square. "The Empress may be defeated," she said, "but treason is still treason, Myron."

Myron's expression darkened as he caught her meaning. "I'll get some men. Do you at least know where we're going?"

"I have a very good idea," Sara said, glancing east, over the mountain, toward the sea.

Myron shook his head and called for his escort.

Miranda stood with her bare feet in the cold surf. Her soul was open, reaching through the water as far as she could for what she knew wasn't there. Behind her, Gin and Master Banage sat at the base of the storm wall, watching her with matching worried expressions.

She'd been in the water since before dawn. At first, Banage had been content to let her deal with Mellinor's loss in her own way. Now, after hours of watching her stand in the water with her open spirit straining far past the point of exhaustion, he decided enough was enough. He stood up slowly and walked across the sand. When he reached his former apprentice, he said nothing, just put his hands on her shoulder and gave her a stiff pull.

After two days without sleep, a raging battle, losing her sea, and now hours of pushing her spirit beyond its limits, one pull was enough. Miranda toppled backward, landing in the sand. She tried to stand up even before she hit, desperate to keep her feet in the water, but Banage was too fast. He slipped between her and the surf, using his larger body as a wall to block her.

"Miranda," he said softly. "You have to rest."

Miranda glared at him, but she stopped struggling. She simply didn't have the strength. "How can I rest?" she said, staring down at the sand, its battle scars already erased by the tide. "How can I just walk away? It's my fault Mellinor's—"

"It's not your fault," Banage said firmly. "Mellinor knew the risk and asked you to stand against the Empress with him anyway. Now she is defeated, in no small part by your efforts. Rather than mourning, you should be proud that you accomplished what he so wanted so badly."

"I didn't do anything!" Miranda cried. "It was Eli who stopped the Empress, and now he's gone, too." She rubbed her eyes with her hands. "I sent everybody to their deaths."

Banage's eyes narrowed. "That is talk unbecoming of a Spiritualist," he said. "You did exactly what you should, your duty. You protected the spirit's will from the human who would have crushed it. But our duty is never done, Miranda. The Empress is gone, but we have as much ahead of us as behind. If you let guilt over what you could not change cripple you, then Mellinor's sacrifice will have been in vain."

His hand shot forward, hanging in the air inches from Miranda's face. "Get up, Spiritualist Lyonette."

Still crying, Miranda took her master's hand. Banage pulled her to her feet and turned her away from the sea. Gin trotted over to meet them, sliding his broad head under Miranda's arm. She smiled a little then, tangling her fingers in his coarse, shifting fur as he helped her to the stairs from the beach.

But when they reached the broken walkway at the top of the storm wall, Banage stopped suddenly. He was staring up the hill, his face, pale and drawn from the night's horrors, going paler still. Still on the stair, Miranda leaned on Gin to peer around her master to see what had stopped him. Given how still he'd gone, Miranda was braced for something horrible—a reactivated war spirit, or the fires bolting up again. What she saw was even worse: a squad of soldiers in the Whitefall family's white and silver riding down the mountain with Sara at their head.

Her hand went for Banage's sleeve at once, but the Rector just shook his head. "It was only a matter of time."

Miranda refused to believe that. "They can't mean to keep pressing the charge of treason," she said. "You defied White-fall's initial order to fight the Empress for the Council, but you helped defeat her in the end. Surely that makes things even."

"The end doesn't matter," Banage said.

"How does it not matter?" Miranda cried. "The Council got what it wanted. You fought! If they bring a charge of treason against you for this, it'll break the Spirit Court between those who are loyal to you and those who want to join the Council. The Merchant Prince *needs* us, he needs the Court whole and functioning. Why would he keep forcing the issue now that everything has already worked itself out?"

"I might have fought the Empress at the end," Banage said, reaching down to brush his rings as the riders closed in. "But I defied Whitefall's command."

"That's worth wrecking his greatest wizard allies?" Miranda said.

"The Merchant Prince risks more than the Court by appearing weak on traitors," Banage said calmly, raising his glowing rings.

Miranda cursed under her breath and reached for her rings as well. She didn't know what good it would do. She had nothing left to give her spirits. Anything stronger than her moss might well knock her out for the day. Still, she intended to back her Rector no matter what. But, to her great surprise,

Master Banage didn't call any of his spirits. Instead, he pulled the ring from his left middle finger and reached out, pressing it into Miranda's palm.

She looked down in amazement. It was the heavy gold band set with the perfect circle of the Court that all Spiritualists received the day they took their oaths. Banage's ring was larger than her own, warm, and surprisingly heavy. Far heavier, in fact, than it should have been.

"It's not gold," Banage said, as though reading her thoughts. "Look inside."

Miranda turned the ring in her hand, and her eyes widened. The gold ended there, worn off by years of use to reveal the white stone core beneath.

"That is the Rector's Ring," Banage said. "The direct link between the head of the Court and the spirit of the Tower."

"But," Miranda whispered, remembering the heavy gold collar set with the flashing gems, Banage's mark of office, "I thought—"

"The collar is a tool," Banage said. "It makes feeding power to the Tower easier, but it is not necessary. That ring is the link that forms the heart of the Rector's power. It's difficult to use, but I expect you to master it before you need it in earnest, which may well be very soon."

"No," Miranda said, thrusting the ring back at him. "Why are you giving it to me? You're the Rector. If that ring is the connection to the Tower, then it belongs with you. I can't—"

"Now is not the time to be willfully ignorant, Miranda," Banage said, his voice dangerous. He glanced at the riders, now only a hundred feet away. "I defied the Council knowing very well how it would end, but I did what I did because I thought it the right thing to do, and I have no qualms about paying for it. But the world is changing quickly. Now more than ever, the Spirit Court must be united. We must make peace among ourselves and the Council if we are to uphold our duty in the days to come." He met her eyes again. "Whatever you believe, the Council sees me as a traitor now. A traitor cannot make peace. But a young woman, a Spiritualist beloved by spirits great and small as well as a former agent for the Council, she could."

"No, she couldn't!" Miranda cried. "It's you we need, Master Banage. You're our Rector. I won't leave you to Sara!"

Banage grabbed her hands, and Miranda stilled at once. She was so tired, so weak, she couldn't fight him. She had no will to fight Banage anyway. He peeled her fingers apart, pulling off her own golden ring from her left ring finger before deftly sliding the Rector's ring down in its place.

Banage's ring hung below her knuckle. The masculine gold circle was far too large for her, but even as Miranda was wondering how she would ever keep it on, the ring began to change. The gold-covered stone slithered like a living thing, warm and fluttering against her skin as it cinched itself to a perfect fit. When it was settled, the ring lay still against her skin as though it had always been there. Miranda tensed, waiting to feel something, a brush of a spirit across her mind, a voice, but there was nothing. The moment the ring stopped moving, all proof that it was anything other than a simple gold ring vanished save only for the suspicious warmth and oppressive weight.

Banage nodded and released her hand. "It won't fully open for you until you're confirmed as Rector," he said, turning to face the riders. "That may or may not happen, depending on the Tower Keeper's vote, but it will do for now. You must call the Conclave as soon as possible."

"Conclave?" Miranda whispered. The Conclave was the most sacred Spiritualist gathering, called only in dire emergency. Every Spiritualist had to attend or forfeit their oaths. "How could I call one? There hasn't been a Conclave in nearly a hundred years."

Banage smiled. "High time for one then, I'd say." The Council troops were almost on top of them now, and Banage pulled himself straight. "Wipe your eyes. Sara preys on weakness."

Startled, Miranda scrubbed her eyes as the riders circled

504

them. Sara pulled her borrowed horse to a stop a few feet from Banage and dismounted stiffly. The man beside her, a middle-aged officer Miranda recognized as the one who'd helped Sara surround the Spirit Court Tower before the Court had left Zarin the day before, stayed in his saddle, watching with the bored detachment of a soldier doing his duty as Sara faced her husband.

"You were wise not to run, Etmon," she said. "You've spared your Court the indignity of watching their Rector be hunted down like a common criminal."

Banage lifted his chin. "Considering how bad the Council is at catching common criminals, perhaps I should have taken my chances."

Sara sniffed. "Your agents haven't done much better, as I recall."

"At least my agent managed to actually make contact once in a while," Banage said, holding out his hands. "Shall we get this over with?"

Sara pushed his hands away with a smile. "Don't be silly. We both know no common restraints can hold you." She stepped forward, sliding her arm around Banage's. "Until we return to Zarin, I am your manacles. It'll be just like old times, won't it, Etmon?"

Banage said nothing, but Miranda saw his shoulders sink at Sara's touch.

"Now," Sara said, lifting Banage's hand to get a look at his rings, "Myron here brought the loyalist Tower Keepers with him. Alber would prefer if you named one of them as interim Rector. Where's your ring?"

"With her," Banage nodded over his shoulder at Miranda. "Spiritualist Lyonette has agreed to serve as Rector and lead the Spirit Court until a vote can be taken."

"*Her?*" Sara glared at Miranda. "Really, Etmon, playing favorites to the end? It won't look good, you putting another traitor at the head of the Court. The Council may start believing that all Spiritualists share your rebellious tendencies."

"I don't care what the Council believes," Banage said. "The Spirit Court is an independent body, and it will govern itself as its members see fit."

"Yes, yes," Sara said, looking away from Miranda with a superior smirk. "We'll see how long that lasts."

She motioned, and the soldiers fell in around them. Banage climbed onto the horse Sara had ridden down and Sara climbed up behind him, wrapping her arms around the Rector's waist in a way that reminded Miranda of a hawk's talons wrapping around a rabbit.

Miranda started forward, her mouth open to object, but Banage's eyes stopped her in her tracks. She stood frozen as the Council troops turned and galloped up the mountain, taking Banage away toward the city. When they were gone, Gin pressed his cold nose into her side.

"I would have eaten them for you," he said.

"I would have eaten them, too," Miranda answered, rubbing her eyes. "Come on, we have to find the others. I've got some tough news to deliver."

Gin knelt. As soon as Miranda was safely on his back, he took off up the hill. Miranda clung to his fur as they passed the Council guards. She didn't look at Banage as they rode by. She didn't look at the sea behind her. She only looked forward, toward the city, the core of loyal Spiritualists who waited there, and all that must be done.

CHAPTER
2

Nico opened her eyes and saw nothing but blackness. For a long moment she lay perfectly still, fighting to keep the panic from overwhelming her mind. Then something moved over her face and she realized she was staring into the wraps of her coat. She sank into the soft bed with a relieved, almost embarrassed sigh and tilted her head. Her coat obeyed instantly, sliding off her to reveal Josef's bedroom.

She sat up, pushing back the covers, then paused. The blankets next to her were rumpled. She slid her hand over them. The coverlet was warm, as though someone had been lying on top of it, and from the sloughed-off pile of throwing knives on the chest at the end of the bed, she had a pretty good idea who.

Pulling her hood up to hide her blush, Nico swung her legs around and stood up. The room was dark, not that it mattered to her, but the flavor of the dark suggested it was night. A line of yellow light shone under the door leading to the sitting room, and Nico could hear soft voices on the other side, followed by the clink of silverware.

She crossed the bedroom, bare feet silent on the wooden floor, and paused at the door. For a moment, she considered stepping through the shadows so she could see what was waiting before she entered the other room, but something held her back. Something was different now. She could see the world of spirits clearer than ever, but even they couldn't hide the darkness that seeped along the edges of her vision. It was swirling like inky water, the tendrils reaching for her whenever she looked away.

She'd noticed them when she first woke up the night she and Miranda had watched Eli vanish. Then she'd thought it was a side effect of her injuries, but she felt fine now, and the darkness was still there. She slid her eyes to the side of her sockets, trying to catch more, but the tendrils slid away every time she tried to look at them straight on. But the more she tried to catch a glimpse of it, the more Nico realized the swirling dark wasn't actually new. The blackness had always been there. She was just noticing it now, because now Nico knew what it was. She'd seen it for herself when she'd looked down at her body during the fight with Den. The swirling

507

darkness was *her*. Her true form. The malicious, grasping shadows weren't some trick of the demon or the seed repairing her injuries. She was seeing the edges of her own *eyes*.

You wish it was me, don't you? The demon's voice seeped through the back of her mind like cold water. *At least then you'd have someone to blame. But whom do you blame now that you're the monster?*

Nico clenched her teeth and slammed her will down hard. The demon's voice vanished, leaving only silence. When she was certain she was completely in control, Nico turned away from the shadows and seized the door handle, pushing it open with a loud *click*.

Josef and the other man looked up in unison. They were sitting at the table by the fireplace. Josef was eating dinner, and his side of the small table was buried under a plate of roast beef, a pitcher of water, and a basket with bread with a vial of flavored oil. The other man was far older, though much of that age may have been an illusion caused by the lamps casting shadows into the deep, deep worry lines that crossed his face. His side of the table was covered in ledgers and reports, and neither he nor the king looked happy with their contents.

Josef's frown deepened the moment he saw her. "Nico, go back to bed. There's no way you should be up yet."

"I'm fine," Nico said, eyeing his plate. "Hungry more than anything."

Josef grabbed a spare chair and pulled it up beside his. "Eat," he said gruffly. "And then back to bed."

Nico bit her lip to hide her smile as she walked over and took her seat. Josef piled a plate high with meat and bread before plopping it in front of her. Only when she'd taken her first bite and was well on the way to her second did he turn back to the man with the ledgers.

"Continue."

The old man began to drum his fingers nervously against his papers as he made every effort not to look in Nico's direction. "My lord, these are matters of Osera's national—"

"If you can say it to me, you can say it in front of her," Josef said, shoving a fresh roll into his mouth.

"I'm sorry, your majesty." The old man shifted uncomfortably. "But I don't believe I know your young lady, and I'm afraid I cannot divulge information this sensitive to—"

"Powers," Josef muttered around his mouthful of bread. He jabbed his thumb at Nico. "Nico, this is Lord Obermal, my, um—"

"Keeper of the treasury of Osera," the old man supplied.

"Right," Josef said. "Treasury Keeper, Nico. Nico, Treasury Keeper. Now that we all know each other, can we get on with this?"

The old man went paler still, and Nico had to take a large bite to keep from laughing. Actually, she knew exactly who Lord Obermal was. She'd kept an eye on him while Eli and Josef had infiltrated the castle that first night in Osera. She just hoped the old treasurer didn't connect the strange case of the missing audit officials with his prince's sudden appearance, or, if he did, that he had the good sense not to mention it.

"Very well, my lord," Obermal continued at last, pushing a ledger toward Josef. "As I was saying, your mother, may she rest in peace, extended nearly all of Osera's reserves preparing to meet the Empress. Our gold supply is at a critical level, and with the extensive damage to the city, especially to the docks and roads, we cannot expect to levy enough tax revenue to meet our basic obligations, much less the needs of Osera's citizenry for repairs to the basic infrastructure required for—"

"So we're broke," Josef said. "Too broke to rebuild, but we can't get money until we rebuild because everything's too wrecked to do business."

"Yes, your majesty," Obermal said with a long sigh. "As I just said—"

"So how do we get money?" Josef interrupted again.

Lord Obermal stiffened. "If my lord would allow me to finish." He waited until Josef nodded before continuing. "We

509

have no choice but to borrow from the Council. Until the full damage reports are in, I can't say for certain how much we'll need, but if the numbers so far are any indication—"

"No," Josef said, crossing his arms.

Lord Obermal blinked. "No to what, my lord?"

"No, I'm not going to go begging money from the Council," Josef said. "Whose skin do you think we saved stopping the Empress? If it wasn't for Osera, it'd be their houses on fire, not ours. They should be falling over themselves to help us."

"That's not the way the Council works, sire," Lord Obermal said, his voice taking on the patient air of a tutor with an exceptionally stupid child. "The Council of Thrones is an economic and defensive agreement for the mutual benefit of all countries. Though I'm sure our fellows in the Council are very grateful to Osera for stopping the Empress and will almost certainly grant us a very favorable rate of interest in any loan for rebuilding, you can't possibly ask them to just give—"

"*Interest?*" Josef roared, slamming his chair against the floor as he lurched forward. "You mean those bastards want to make a profit off rebuilding the country that saved their lives? Are you *kidding me?*"

"There are several precedents, my lord," Obermal said gently.

"Forget it," Josef said, shaking his head. "Forget the whole thing. There is no way I'm borrowing money from that Council of vultures who couldn't even be bothered to show up to fight their own war until eight hours after the Empress was gone."

"But the repairs must be made!" Lord Obermal cried. "And there's simply no other way to raise that sort of capital. The Council's the only body large enough to offer the amounts we will require."

"How much?" Josef said.

Obermal paused. "Pardon?"

"How much are we talking about?"

Obermal began riffling through his papers. "I couldn't be sure without—"

Josef rolled his eyes. "Guess."

"Yes, sire." Obermal ran his fingers down a list of figures. "If I had to guess, and mind you, this is almost certainly a gross underestimation, but if I *had* to make a blind guess based on incomplete information for the cost of rebuilding the docks and all the infrastructure in Osera, I'd say it could be anywhere from a hundred and fifty to three hundred thousand gold standards."

"Oh," Josef said, sitting back. "Is that all?"

"*Is that all?*" Obermal cried, forgetting himself as his face turned scarlet. "I don't know how much money you handled as a murderer for hire, Thereson, but Osera is one of the most prosperous countries in the Council, and we pull in, at most, a hundred and twenty thousand per year, *including* our tax on sea traffic. Even if my lowest estimates were correct, which I can assure you they aren't, it would take one and a half years of Osera's pre-Empress income to save that much money, assuming of course we didn't pay for anything else during that time, so no guards, no servants, no social services, no garbage men or lamp lighters. And let's not forget that level of income is impossible now since our docks are destroyed." The treasurer shook his head. "It can't be done. We cannot raise that kind of money on our own, not unless you want the repairs to take twenty years. Your mother borrowed Council funds the last time the Empress destroyed Osera, and it was the salvation of our island. The least you can do is try to follow her good example."

Josef leaned back, glaring at the old man as he finally fell silent. "Are you done?"

Obermal went very still, his eyes growing wide as he realized what he'd just done. "Yes, sire," he whispered. "Forgive me. It's been a very stressful time for our office, and—"

"It's been a stressful time for everyone," Josef said. "Forget it. I'd rather you say what you think rather than have the truth all muddled up with flattery. Anyway, I've got an idea that could make this all very easy. Nico?"

511

Nico looked up from what was left of her slab of roast.

Josef flashed her a huge grin. "It seems Osera's short on cash. Since Eli's not around for me to shake down at the moment, can I borrow your prize?"

"My prize?" Nico scowled in confusion, and then, like a flash, she got it. "Oh," she said, returning his smile. "Of course."

"Right." Josef turned to his treasurer. "That's settled then. Go get what's-his-name, the Whitefall, and have him meet me downstairs."

"Lord Myron?" Obermal looked appalled. "What do you need him for?"

"He's the highest ranking Council man here, right?" Josef said, standing up. "I have business with the Council, so he'll have to do. Just send him down and we'll handle it. Believe it or not, I actually have some experience with this sort of thing." His grin grew feral. "I did used to be a bounty hunter, after all."

Nico couldn't help smirking at that as she shoved the last of her dinner into her mouth. Meanwhile, Josef ducked back into the bedroom for his knives. Lord Obermal just watched, his eyes growing wider and wider, like he was waiting to see how things could get any worse. "Are you sure I can't assist—"

"What part of 'go get Whitefall' didn't you understand?" Josef said, picking up the Heart from its resting place by the fire.

Lord Obermal jumped up. "Yes, my lord. I'll have him sent to you at once."

Josef nodded, watching the old treasurer as he gathered his ledgers and excused himself, bowing deeply before shutting the door. When he was gone, Nico stood and stretched, popping her joints.

"If Eli were here, I think this is where he'd say that you should try being a little nicer to your staff," she said.

Josef snorted. "If Eli were here, I'd ignore him. Anyway, if there's one thing I did learn from my mother, it's that

512

sometimes you have to roll over people if you want to get anything done." He stopped a moment, checking his knives again. When he was confident they were all accounted for, he jerked his head toward the door.

Nico nodded and fell in beside him, following the king into the hall and down the stairs toward the burned-out western wing.

Myron Whitefall looked up from his dinner with an incredulous scowl. "He wants what?"

"The servant said King Josef wants to meet with you," his guard repeated. "Says it's urgent."

"It better well be urgent," Myron grumbled, pushing back from the table with a shove that almost toppled his wineglass. "I finally have a moment's peace now that Sara's taking her freak show back to Zarin, and the vagabond king of Osera wants me to spend it with him? He'd better have the Empress on a leash."

The guard smiled. "Do you want us to escort you, sir? Just in case he does?"

"I should only be so lucky," Myron said with a laugh. "Stay and finish your dinner. You deserve it after the march you boys pulled to get to this ungrateful speck of an island. Arrived just in time to be insulted, didn't we? I think I can handle the king on my own. He probably just wants to tell me again what a horrible job the Council's doing."

"Thank you for your sacrifice, sir," the guard said, grinning as he saluted.

Myron chuckled and clapped him on the shoulder. "As you were, as you were."

He left his men laughing as they returned to their dinner and followed the Oseran servant down the stairs. The short trip took far longer than it should, mostly because the palace was so badly damaged they had to keep taking detours around broken walls and collapsing floorboards. The servant wasn't helping things, either. He set a maddeningly slow pace,

513

stopping every few steps to apologize for the state of the castle and the lateness of the king's summons.

This last type of apology was delivered with such sincerity that Myron got the distinct impression the man was ashamed not just of his king's rudeness but of the king himself. Myron couldn't blame him. It was common knowledge across the Council that Theresa's son was a disgrace to her kingdom, a runaway turned thief or vagabond or some such unpleasantness. Osera had had a double swing of bad luck to get such a king and the Empress at the same time. So unlucky that it might well be better if the Council took over the island until a more suitable ruler could be found. Annexation would be unpopular, but anything was preferable to letting an incompetent king kick over an already weakened state. Myron made a mental note to discuss the subject with Alber as the servant finally ushered him into what was left of the palace's west wing.

He froze as the door opened. The servant had taken him to the very bottom of the palace, into a large, long room that looked as if it had been built to serve as a cold cellar. Whatever its original purpose, however, it had been superseded by the grisly needs of Osera's current crisis.

Myron had been raised to be a soldier. He'd seen conflict since he was a boy, but even the life of a professional warrior hadn't prepared him for the sheer number of corpses piled into what was now Osera's makeshift morgue. Oseran soldiers lay in rows, their bodies respectfully covered with clean, white cloths. Some had names painted across their chest; others had not yet been identified. There were civilian dead here as well—men, women, even children, covered and waiting for their mourning families to identify them.

Though the cellar was cold and most of the bodies were less than a day old, the air was still full of the smell of decay. Myron cursed and covered his face, wishing the messenger had come before he'd started eating. He looked around for the king, eager to get this over with and get out of this cold, foul-smelling place of death. He spotted the towering King Josef immediately, standing at the far end of the morgue with another, much shorter figure in a coat whose gender and face Myron couldn't make out.

The servant bowed one last time and made himself scarce, leaving Myron to pick his own way through the bodies to the king. Josef didn't even have the good grace to greet him, just looked up and nodded, motioning for Myron to join him.

"This had better be important," Myron said, holding his hand over his nose as he glared at the king. "If you brought me down here just to garner sympathy for Osera's fallen, you're wasting both of our time. The Council has already offered ample assistance as stipulated by the treaties."

"Don't worry, I didn't call you down for a sob case," Josef said. "This is a business matter. These poor souls will be burned tomorrow, once we've finished purging the Empress's filth."

Myron thought of the billowing pillar of smoke he'd seen rising from the eastern side of the island. Burning the enemy first was typical. With no one to mourn them, they could be disposed of faster, leaving more time to honor your own dead. But that smoke had been rising since he had arrived that morning. If they hadn't started burning Oserans yet, how many of the Empress's troops must they have slaughtered to keep a pyre that large going all day?

"Business, eh?" Myron said, his voice a shade more respectful. "What business needs discussing in a morgue?"

"It wasn't like we had anywhere else to put him," Josef said, nudging the nearest body with the toe of his boot. "But I would have hauled him up for you if I'd known you were squeamish."

Myron bristled and glared down at the corpse by Josef's feet. It was different than the others, set off on its own and covered with a square of old sail rather than a white sheet. The dead man had been enormous in life, obviously a warrior, and he'd died a warrior's death if the blood clotted on the sail was any indication.

Before he could ask, Josef leaned down and grabbed the edge of the cloth, pulling the shroud back just enough for Myron to clearly see the dead man's face. Myron wasn't sure what to expect, but the face he saw was enough to shock even him into silence. After all, it was a face every Council citizen knew. There, lying dead on the floor of an Oseran cellar, was Den the Warlord, the first and greatest criminal in Council history.

The king smiled at his expression and pulled Den's poster out of his pocket, its corners freshly ripped from being pulled off whatever bounty board Josef had snatched it from.

"Dead or alive," Josef read. "Five hundred thousand gold standards."

Myron looked from Den to Josef and back again. "You killed Den the Warlord?"

"Not me," Josef said. "She did."

He nodded to the figure behind him. Myron squinted in the low light, and then nearly laughed out loud as a thin hand pushed back the hood to reveal the face of a young, frail girl.

"She?" Myron couldn't help himself; he started to laugh. "You're telling me a little girl killed the greatest fighter in the Council? Do you think I'm an idiot?"

"I'm beginning to," Josef said flatly. "You can try her yourself if you want proof."

Behind him, the girl closed her hand into a fist, cracking her knuckles as she did. All at once, Myron began to feel very cold, weak almost, and strangely afraid. Myron Whitefall was many things, but he wasn't a fool. As the feeling started to build, he decided to drop the issue.

"Who killed him isn't important," he said, rubbing his suddenly clammy hands on his trousers. "What matters is that Den's dead."

"Glad we agree," Josef said, dropping the cloth to cover Den's face again. "Now," he smiled, "about the money..."

Myron began to sweat. This was bad, far too bad for him to handle. Better stall and pass it to Alber, he decided. Make the old stuffed shirt work for his title.

"I'm afraid I don't have anything to do with the bounties," Myron said in his most official voice. "You'll have to bring him to Zarin and submit your request through the proper channels."

To his surprise, Josef nodded. "Fair enough. Couldn't really expect you to have that kind of cash on hand. Thank you, General. We'll bring him to Zarin immediately. In the meanwhile, I hope you'll keep this in mind as you plan your aid for Osera's rebuilding."

Myron sighed through clenched teeth. The threat in the king's voice wasn't even veiled. Did this oaf know nothing of statecraft? Still, he smiled and made all the correct polite noises, excusing himself from the king's presence. The second he was out of the morgue, he started to run. He made it back to the room he'd been given in a third the time it had taken the servant to lead him down, shouting for his Relay point before he was properly through the door.

His soldiers brought it at once. Myron grabbed the glass sphere and shook it violently. The second it turned the bright blue that meant it was working, he began shouting for Alber. He had to warn the Merchant Prince, or it was very likely that the bounty no one ever expected to come home could ruin them all.

As the tiny ball of the sun sank below the horizon inside Benehime's sphere, the Lady pulled the man in her lap closer, nuzzling his neck.

Are you tired, love?

Eli kept stone still and said nothing.

You must be tired, the Shepherdess said, running her lips up his neck to nuzzle the edge of his hair. *You've been up for over a day now. Your bed is just as you left it. Wouldn't you like to sleep?*

517

Eli was tired, so tired that the only reason he wasn't asleep already was the constant burn of Benehime's touch. He longed to pass out and forget everything, if only for a few hours, but he didn't answer immediately. Something about the way Benehime asked bothered him. After a day spent clinging to him like a possessive cat with a piece of fish, she suddenly seemed almost eager to be rid of him. The change made him curious, and against his better judgment, Eli decided to push a bit.

"How could I be tired?" he said, looking at her with a blinding smile. "I'm with you."

Benehime arched an eyebrow. *Now's not the time to be clever, love. You must sleep. You just came home. I can't have you jeopardizing your health first thing, can I?*

She reached out and plucked the air. Instantly, a white bed appeared beside them.

Eli nearly groaned. The white silk bed he'd slept on for four years looked exactly as it had when he'd left. He remembered how impressed he'd been when she'd first presented it to him, how he'd fawned over the downy softness and the subtle pattern woven into the silk by the worms themselves. Now, the soft square on the floor reminded him of nothing so much as the sort of bed rich ladies in Zarin had made for their pampered dogs to sleep in. But being with the Shepherdess in her white world had brought the old habits back, and Eli hid his disgust behind a warm smile as he sank down onto the soft cushion.

There, Benehime said, leaning over to kiss his head one last time. *Rest, love. Maybe tomorrow you'll remember that living with me isn't so bad. I'm not far if you need me. See you in the morning, my darling.*

She stroked his head a final time and turned to walk back to her sphere. Eli shivered as the air solidified behind her, locking him in. That was new. She'd never bothered locking him up before, but then, a lot had changed.

He reached out experimentally, running his hand over the invisible wall. There was just enough space for him to sit up

518

without knocking his head, but that was it. He lay back on the bed with a sigh, grateful at least that she'd made it so large all those years ago, seeing as he was a foot taller now than he'd been at fifteen. Even so, it was a tight fit, and he propped his feet up on the invisible wall as he wiggled out of the ridiculous white coat she'd made him wear.

He glanced sideways at Benehime. She was sitting by her sphere about fifteen feet away, staring intensely at the floating world and not, for once, at him. Eli sighed in relief and spread the coat over his chest like a blanket. When it was in place, he slid his hands beneath it and began unbuttoning his crisp white shirt. He shoved the cloth aside, leaving his chest bare, and then, hands shaking, he ran his fingers over Karon's burn, touching the lava spirit hesitantly with his will at the same time.

From the moment she'd brought him here, Eli hadn't felt the lava spirit stir. But despite his fears, the Shepherdess had been true to her word. Karon woke instantly, his heat rising to meet Eli's touch. The rush of relief hit Eli so hard he was forced to look away before he cried again. Once was bad enough; twice in a twenty-four-hour period was unforgivable.

"Welcome back," he said when he could trust his voice again.

Karon didn't answer. His fire trembled in Eli's chest, pulling back as deep as he could into Eli's body. When he spoke at last, his voice was a trembling, smoky whisper.

"Why are we in the Between?"

It took Eli a minute to remember that the Between was what the spirits called Benehime's white world, when they spoke of it at all.

"I ran out of escapes," Eli said, staring up at the endless white as he pressed himself deeper into the bed. "Caught at last, and by my own hand no less. Some thief, eh?"

"We shouldn't be in the Between," Karon whispered. "It's too close. We need to leave."

"Yes, well, tell that to the Shepherdess," Eli said bitterly. "She's the one who locked us in here."

"Here?"

Karon's voice was thick with confusion, and Eli sighed. The spirit probably couldn't even see the walls. They were a nice little pen made just for a human.

"Karon," he said, kicking the invisible wall at his feet. "What do you see in front of us?"

"Nothing," Karon said. "Just white forever and forever and..." His voice trailed off. "Wait, there is something." The heat intensified as Karon's smoke curled up from the burn, brushing against the invisible barrier like curious fingers. "There's a wall," the lava spirit said. "It's so white I couldn't see it. I think it's all around us."

"You think correctly," Eli said. "I see nothing, but we're trapped all the same."

"Can't you make a door?" Karon said. "I mean, if you're here, then you're back to being the favorite for real, right? So it shouldn't be a problem anymore."

Eli laughed out loud. "Not that simple, friend. You were out, so you missed my glorious defeat, but the long and short of it is that I lost, and now I'm back to being a good little dog. Probably forever." He winced at the thought and turned his head, pulling the jacket up to cover his face in a vain attempt to shut out some of the blinding white. "Powers, how did I ever sleep like this?"

"You can't be serious," Karon said. "Eli Monpress? Roll over? I refuse to believe it."

Eli peeked over the coat at Benehime, but she was completely absorbed in whatever she was doing with her sphere.

"Believe it," he said quietly. "Even if I found a way out, I wouldn't take it. Not now. The woman proved she was willing to start a war just to make me give in and ask for help. Can you imagine what she'd do to Nico and Josef if I ran away?"

Suddenly, he was so angry he was shaking. "I have no more illusions," he whispered. "Benehime's crazy. Maybe she's always been crazy, but I know she wouldn't hesitate a moment to do whatever she had to in order to keep me here. If I ran, she wouldn't even think before killing Josef or Nico, killing you, killing anything she thought could get me to come back. And since I gave up my freedom to save your hides, I'm not exactly in the mood to throw them away again on an escape attempt." He closed his eyes. "What I want to know is, when did I become the bloody hero?"

"You can't stay here, Eli," Karon rumbled. "It'll kill you. She'll break you for good."

"I'm not *that* fragile," Eli said, rolling over so that his back was to Benehime.

It was a good lie, but as he stared off into the blank white of Benehime's world and thought of his future, Eli had to admit he was starting to feel a little suicidal. However bad the mists were, they couldn't be worse than this endless, changeless future of being Benehime's lap dog.

"It can't last forever," he said, trying his best to sound confident. "As the Lord of Storms loves to point out, I'm not the first favorite, and I won't be the last. I'm sure she was just as devoted to Nara at the beginning." And just look what happened to her, he thought grimly.

"Eli, please," Karon said. "Benehime is my Shepherdess and I cannot speak against her, but I can speak for you, and I'm begging—don't give up. Don't let her beat you like this. The Shepherdess has changed over the last few centuries, and not for the better. Do you remember how you found me?"

Eli smiled. "How could I forget?" Lava spirits weren't stone or fire, but a mix of both. That dual nature made them extremely argumentative, especially with each other, and before too long the great stone spirit who held them would get fed up and kick them out, which is why volcanoes were constantly blowing. "Your volcano threw you out right on top of our heads while Giuseppe and I were robbing the King of Ser blind. Cost us two golden lions, though the chaos left by the fire made for a nice escape."

"The volcano didn't throw me out," Karon said quietly. "We

521

were forced out. The volcano wanted to go dormant and it forced us out so it could sleep. But it's a volcano's purpose to hold us lava spirits. That's why it exists. Used to be if a spirit did something like that, violated its purpose and left the spirits in its charge to die, the Shepherdess would be there to knock some sense into it. But she wasn't. Of all my brothers, only I survived, and only because you were there to take me in before my fire died out completely."

"Never let it be said the Shepherdess took her job too seriously," Eli said bitterly.

"It's not just negligence," Karon said. "Gredit was right. She's ignoring the world on purpose. It's almost like she actively hates us now. The only one she doesn't hate is you, and that scares me, Eli. The Shepherdess is supposed to be our guardian, our caretaker, but she was willing to crush all of Osera just to get you to give in." Karon fluttered nervously in his chest. "I don't know what's happening, but I don't like it. I don't like it at all."

"Add it to the list," Eli said, rolling onto his stomach with a sigh.

"You have to do something," Karon hissed. "If you won't save yourself and escape, then maybe you can get the Shepherdess to change, but you can't just sit here and do nothing."

"You think I like this?" Eli snapped. "I hate being here. I hate every second of it, but I told you, that woman is crazy. I was the one who made myself weak. I was stupid enough to get attached to that dumb swordsman and his demonseed and the Spiritualist and all the other poor saps I care about. The whole war was my fault. I could have stopped it at any time, just like Miranda said, but I didn't. I held out for my pride and people died, so now I'm going to sit here and be a good dog and maybe everyone I've cursed by calling them friend will get to live a little longer. Including you."

"Don't do this to yourself, Eli," Karon said. "Don't make yourself a martyr."

"You think I'm selfless enough to be a martyr?" Eli said,

punching the bed as he rolled over again. "Whose body have you been living in all these years? I'm the thief, remember? I'm just taking the path of least resistance."

"Yeah, right," Karon hissed, and Eli winced as his burn began to ache with the lava spirit's anger. "Well, I'll just leave you to your misery, then, *favorite*. When you're done sulking, let me know, and we'll figure out how to beat this together. Until then, I'm going to sleep. Maybe this will all turn out to be a dream."

"I didn't know spirits had dreams," Eli grumbled into the bed.

"We don't," Karon said. "But I'd kill for one right now. Anything to get out of here."

Eli closed his eyes as the lava spirit sank into him and fell into a grumbling sleep. Karon was probably right. He probably should be planning an escape, or at least a new plot to get Benehime to let him go of her own will again, but he just couldn't summon up the energy to care. He could almost feel Benehime's hand on his throat. She had him good and tight now, and every time he tried to think about the future, all he could see was endless white.

He'd been so arrogant, thinking he could run forever. He'd forgotten the first rule of thievery: no one runs forever. That was why you had to fence your goods and move on. But he'd just kept running, thinking he was smart, thinking he could do it all on his own. Now Josef's island was destroyed, Nico was nearly dead, Mellinor was lost, and that was just the tip of the iceberg of things that were his fault.

Unbidden, his mind went back to that day in the forest when he'd tricked Benehime into letting him go. He'd thought of that moment daily since then, usually with pride. His freedom was what he'd always fought for, but now he saw that first con in a different light. If he'd known how bitterly things would end, would he still have made the deal?

Eli rolled violently, kicking the wall with his feet. He didn't like the way this was going, and he didn't want to think about it anymore. He tossed and turned, throwing the white jacket into the corner. As always, the temperature in the Between hovered just slightly cooler than was pleasant, but he couldn't stand having her white all over him. He flopped over again, slamming his head angrily into the soft, white pillow and found himself facing Benehime.

She was sitting in front of her sphere exactly as she'd been since he lay down. Her profile was toward him, probably so she could keep an eye on him while she watched the world, he realized sourly. But her eyes weren't looking at him now. They were locked on the sphere, and her mouth was moving.

Eli's eyes darted back and forth, but he didn't see anyone, not even the Lord of Storms. Didn't hear anything, either. Thankful to have something to puzzle over besides his own misery, he scooted to the edge of the bed to get a better look.

It was night inside the glistening globe. The sea was dark and calm, the mountains still. The moon rode high in the sky, its light a pale reflection of Benehime's own as her hands rested on the curve of the sky. Her gaze was fixed on the ocean, but other than her mouth, she wasn't moving at all. After five minutes of this, Eli was about to dismiss the whole thing as another of her eccentricities when her lips stopped moving, curving instead into a smile that turned his blood to ice water.

Without warning, her hands pressed down, passing through the sphere's sky like she was pressing through the surface of a soap bubble. Her white fingers turned transparent the second they entered, but Eli could still make out the edges of her hands as they descended through the night and plunged into the dark sea below.

Eli watched in stunned silence as Benehime reached into the sea up to her elbows, going down so far that her fingers must have scraped the very bottom of the ocean floor. Her hands fished around for a moment, and then Eli saw her muscles clench, tightening her fingers into a fist. Her sickening smile grew wider as Benehime began to pull.

And that was when her eyes moved toward Eli.

Only years spent as a thief let him react fast enough. In the blink of an eye he was asleep, his body splayed, his breaths even and deep, his eyes closed. The white world was silent, but he didn't dare move. He stayed that way until his muscles were aching from stress. Only when he was sure not even Benehime could draw a connection between the movement and what had just happened did he risk a look.

Body as slack as a rag, he rolled over, cracking his eyes as he did. Benehime was sitting exactly as she had been before, but her hands were at her sides now, and her mouth was closed in a quiet smile. The sphere floated same as always, and though the ocean looked a little choppy, there was no other sign that anything had happened.

Frowning, Eli turned again, trying for a better look, but then Benehime glanced at him. This time he didn't have a chance to fake, so instead, he caught her eye and gave her a sleepy blink. She smiled indulgently and mouthed, *Sleep.*

Eli nodded and turned to lie on his back. His heart was thudding in his chest, but he kept his eyes closed. His whole body was wired, and he didn't feel the least bit sleepy. Even so, he forced his breathing to remain deep and even. He was a good dog now. Good dogs obeyed their mistresses.

Just the thought made him feel ill, but Eli kept it to himself. He lay perfectly still, focusing on his breaths until exhaustion finally took him for real, and he fell into a deep sleep full of white, terrifying dreams.

The minute he drifted off, Benehime rose from her seat beside the sphere, walking silently to stand over her sleeping favorite. When she reached him, she laid her hands on the invisible wall. When Eli didn't stir, Benehime's face broke into a wide, sharp smile. Without a sound, her hands passed through the barrier and began to descend toward Eli's bare chest.

And in his safe haven beneath Eli's skin, Karon began to scream, but it made no sound at all.

CHAPTER
3

It was midnight when Gin finally trotted through the white gates of Zarin and started up the hill toward the Spirit Court's Tower. Miranda clung to his back, blinking blearily at the rowdy late-night crowd scrambling to make way for her panting ghosthound. Gin's trot slumped to a walk as they got closer, but Miranda didn't try to speed him up. The dog was exhausted. With the run down from the mountains and then the mad dash to Osera and now a night run back to Zarin... well, even ghosthounds had limits.

Of course, Miranda wasn't doing much better. She'd spent seven hours clutching Gin's back for dear life as the hound forced his way through roads crowded with soldiers and Oseran refugees. Add to that the hours she'd spent reaching in vain for Mellinor this morning and the battle before that and she was wrung out completely. Clinging to Gin as they wove through the Zarin streets, she felt fragile and stretched, but as the Tower's moonlit spire came into view, she forced herself to sit straight. She had work to do. Banage had entrusted her with the fate of the Spirit Court. She could not let him down.

When they reached the gate separating the Spirit Court's district from the rest of Zarin, she motioned for Gin to stop. He lay down for her to dismount and didn't get up again as she stretched the ride out of her joints.

"Good work," Miranda said, rubbing the short, coarse fur on the bridge of Gin's muzzle. "The stables should still be open. Go and get some sleep. I'll have them bring you a pig as soon as I can."

"Two pigs," Gin said and groaned, pushing himself up one last time. "Fat ones."

"Fat ones," Miranda promised as the ghosthound walked

slowly between the buildings and toward the stables, his patterns swirling sluggishly.

When she was satisfied he would make it to the stables without falling over, Miranda turned and started down the wide boulevard toward the Tower itself. The Spirit Court's district was silent and empty. All the non-wizards who made a living serving the Court's human needs had distanced themselves as soon as the Court fell into the Council's bad graces. The wind whistled between the closed-up buildings, rattling the bolted shutters with a lonely sound. Ahead, the Tower rose like a white bone from the ground, smooth and straight and, Miranda saw with dismay, still sealed against the world, just as Banage had left it after his confrontation with Whitefall's army.

She climbed the wide steps with trepidation. The great red doors were still lying where they had fallen. In their place, the Tower's grand entry was a smooth wall of stone. Hesitantly, Miranda laid her knuckles against the cold rock, tapping the Rector's ring against the Tower's surface.

Nothing happened.

She tried again. Nothing. Not even a flicker of movement.

Miranda pulled her hand back and stood there a moment, focusing her mind on the Rector's ring. Waiting for...she wasn't sure what. A sign, maybe. A direction. Some hint of what she was supposed to do. Nothing came. The gold ring sat sullen and silent, its stone underside as cold as the Tower against her skin.

Miranda heaved an enormous sigh. She was too tired for this. All she wanted was to get inside to Krigel and call the Conclave before things got any worse than they already were. Holding that goal firmly in mind, Miranda balled her left hand into a fist and slammed it into the stone.

The golden Rector's ring hit the Tower with a deep, ringing sound, just as hers had when she'd first returned to the sealed Tower days before. That time, the ringing had faded and a tunnel had opened through the stone. This time it only grew louder. The sound doubled and redoubled, filling the air until all of Zarin seemed to be vibrating. And then, without warning, the ringing simply stopped, and as it stopped, the Tower opened.

Stone peeled away from the great doors, the white rock curling like unfurling petals before vanishing again into the smooth stone walls. Gleaming windows winked open up and down the Tower's spire as the protective layer of stone slid away. At the Tower's peak, the enormous windows of the Rector's office reemerged, the thick glass catching the moonlight until the Tower's top shone like a lighthouse.

The whole transformation took less than a minute, but it was a minute more before Miranda could stop gawking. She looked down at the golden circle of the Rector's ring. She hadn't felt anything the whole time—no draw of power, no spirit pressure, just a faint heat against her skin. But the ring was already cooling, and Miranda, too exhausted for mysteries, stumbled gladly into the now-moonlit entry hall where Spiritualist Krigel was running down the stairs to meet her.

"Miranda!" he cried. "What are you doing back so soon? Where's Banage? Why did he open the Tower?"

Each question came on the heels of the one before it, and Miranda, too tired to form coherent answers, just held up her hand. The Rector's assistant stopped cold when he saw the ring on her finger, his eyes growing wide and horrified.

"Powers," he whispered. "He's not—"

"He's alive," Miranda said, lowering her hand. "But we've still got problems. We have to call a Conclave right away. Let's move somewhere private and—"

She'd taken a step toward him as she spoke, but it proved to be one step too many. As her foot hit the floor, her legs gave out. She toppled sideways, landing on her side, too tired to catch herself.

She'd gone limp before she hit, so the fall didn't hurt like it should have, but even as she realized she was on the ground, she knew for certain she couldn't get up again. She heard Krigel's voice giving orders, and then something hard and sweet smelling slid under her body, lifting her off the ground. She looked up to see the lovely crown of a linden tree spreading overhead, its branches cradling her body like a mother's arms. Krigel was right beside her, the bright green ring on his index finger illuminating his worried, wrinkled face. He said something to the tree, and Miranda felt herself begin to sway as they moved toward the stairs.

The tree's roots rolled over the smooth stone floor with one wrapped around Krigel's outstretched hand. He was feeding it, Miranda realized with a flash of worry. Krigel wasn't a young man anymore. Feeding a tree who had no place to dig its roots was a tall order, especially if you were making it move as well. She should say something, she thought, tell him to stop so she could get one of her own spirits out to carry her. But as she opened her mouth, Krigel gave her a look so sharp it skewered the words before she could speak them.

"If you so much as imply I am too infirm to do my duty as your assistant, Rector Lyonette, I will drop you down these stairs."

"But I'm not Rector," Miranda said, or tried to. The words came out in a garbled mumble.

Krigel seemed to understand well enough. "The Rector's ring doesn't go to just anyone," he said. "If Banage gave it to you and the ring accepted the transfer, then you're Rector enough for me. Now shut your mouth for once and let me do my job."

Miranda licked her lips. "Pigs," she whispered.

This time it was Krigel's turn to look confused. "Excuse me?"

"Gin's in the stable," she whispered, enunciating each syllable. "He needs pigs."

"I'll see to your dog," Krigel said. "Now go to sleep before I have Ellinell knock you over the head."

The tree shook with laughter, swaying Miranda back and forth. She leaned into the motion, falling into a deep sleep before they'd reached the second landing.

* * *

529

Miranda woke suddenly to bright light in her face. She closed her eyes and rolled away, bumping her nose into the pile of pillows behind her. Raising her hand as a shield, she tried again, opening her eyes slowly as they adjusted.

She was lying on a narrow bed in the corner of a small, neat room. Her dirty boots were off, so was her jacket, leaving her in her shirtsleeves and pants on top of the embroidered bedspread. She also realized with a bit of a shock that her hair was wet. She moved her hand up timidly, running her fingers through damp curls that smelled faintly of the mountains.

"I took the liberty of asking my spring spirit to wash it," said a deep voice. "I thought you'd sleep better if you were clean."

She looked up with a start to see Spiritualist Krigel rising from a deep armchair beside the bed. He took a covered tray from the table beside him and plopped it unceremoniously onto Miranda's lap.

"You'll be relieved to know that your ghosthound has been taken care of. He ate three pigs and passed out in a fat stupor in the stable yard. Since you already had your pass out, I'm hoping you'll take care of the eating part so we can move on to what exactly happened in Osera that sent you running back here with Banage's ring."

Miranda pushed herself up and uncovered the tray. A lovely smell wafted up, and she grinned in delight at the large bowl of egg soup and the round loaf of walnut bread.

"Thank you for looking after Gin," she said, tucking the napkin under her chin. "And me, I should add. I'm sorry to impose—"

"I've been the assistant to the Rector Spiritualis for close to thirty years now," Krigel said. "It is my job to mother you. Now"—he sat down in the deep chair again—"talk."

Miranda took a mouthful of soup and a bite of bread. Once those were down, she told him. Krigel listened impassively as she described the mad ride down to Osera, how they'd broken the Empress's siege and retaken the beach only to lose it again.

He didn't even flinch at her description of the war spirits, though his eyebrows did furrow when she reached Banage's meeting with Eli and his argument with Sara.

That part still felt unreal. Even two days later, she wasn't able to fully wrap her brain around the idea that Master Banage was Eli Monpress's father, or Sara's *husband*. But Krigel took all these things without comment and told her to get on with it.

She told him about the burning of Osera next, and Sara's counterattack, but when she reached her and Mellinor's attack on the Empress, and how it had ended, her throat closed up. Eventually, she choked out enough of the important details to get to the Empress herself.

That was also hard to tell, but in a different way. How did you explain a star to someone who'd never seen one? Eli's role took longer still, mostly because Miranda wasn't sure what had happened, exactly. Even so, no matter how unbelievable Miranda knew her story must sound, Krigel's expression didn't change until she reached Sara's apprehension of Banage on the beach this morning.

"I always told him Sara would never give up," Krigel said, leaning back in his chair. "So he made you Rector and let them arrest him?"

Miranda nodded, staring down at the dregs of her soup.

"A good move," Krigel said. "We knew his days as Rector were numbered the moment he told me he'd rejected Whitefall's compromise. A Spiritualist must stand on ideals, but it is the Rector's job to be a uniting force between us wizards and the rest of humanity, and you can't do that when they're calling you traitor."

Miranda's head snapped up. "So you think he should have just given in to Whitefall, then?"

"Of course not," Krigel said. "But Banage knew as well as any of us that taking a stand meant ending his time as Rector. Still, it was his decision. I am sorry to lose him, but we in the Spirit Court don't force men or spirits to act against their will."

"Well," Miranda said. "I don't mean to let him rot in a Council jail, especially not with Sara as his jailor. We have to free him."

"On what grounds?" Krigel said.

Miranda stared at him, disbelieving, but Krigel just laced his fingers together. "He's made himself a traitor to the Council," the old Assistant Rector said. "And he must answer for that. If we try to spare him his punishment, all we'll do is widen the rift between the Court and Whitefall."

"But we can't just leave him there!" Miranda cried.

"We can and we must," Krigel said, his voice infuriatingly calm. "He gave himself up as a traitor to save the Court. By turning himself in, he confines his crimes to one man rather than dooming our entire organization. In going with Sara willingly, he's freed the Court to make peace with the Council and mend the schism."

Miranda slumped against the pillows. She hadn't thought of it that way. Honestly, the idea of Banage under Sara's thumb without anyone to help him made her so angry she couldn't see past it. But as Krigel spoke, she could hear Banage's voice on the beach as he pressed the ring onto her finger, telling her to mend the Court. And, as much as she hated it, she knew what she had to do.

"We must call a Conclave," she said. "We must bring all the Spiritualists together again and unite the Court. That's what Banage told me to do."

"Already done," Krigel said, smiling at her surprised look. "I sent the messages while you were sleeping. The Conclave is set for the day after tomorrow."

Miranda blinked. "So soon? Can we even gather the Court on such short notice?"

"Conclaves are always short notice, as I understand it," Krigel said. "And Spiritualists move very quickly when they have to."

Miranda bit her lip. It made her nervous to rush something so important. "But—"

532

"Calling the Conclave was the entire reason Banage gave you that ring," Krigel said. "Only a Rector can call a Conclave, and if we're to avoid charges of favoritism over his appointing you as interim Rector splitting the Court further, we must move as fast as possible. The Court exists to bring order to wizardry, and we can't do that if we can't bring order to ourselves."

Miranda lay back, covering her tired eyes with her hands. "Very well, what do I have to do?"

"For the moment, nothing," Krigel said. "Except try and stay out of trouble, if you're even capable of such a feat."

Miranda laughed at that, but then her face grew serious. "I wish I could stay here and not move for the next two days," she said. "But the world is changing, Krigel. Greater forces than I knew existed before a few days ago are moving. Banage told me that the world needs the Court now more than ever, and I believe him. The Court must be united to do whatever must be done."

"And we will be," Krigel said, pushing himself up. "One way or another." He reached to take her tray and paused. "You realize, of course, that many of the Tower Keepers were very unhappy with Banage at the end. When the Court comes together for the Conclave, the first thing the Tower Keepers will do is call for a vote for a new Rector."

"That's fine with me," Miranda said. "I became a Spiritualist to help spirits, not play politics."

"That may be for the best," Krigel said solemnly as he gathered the tray. "The Rectorship is often the worst thing that can happen to a good Spiritualist. Just look at Banage."

Miranda couldn't argue there.

When Krigel had everything stacked, he turned toward the door. "There was a Spiritualist who wanted to see you earlier. I told her you were resting, but she was very insistent. Shall I show her in, or would you rather sleep?"

Miranda wrinkled her nose. "What did she want to talk about?"

"Something about the river," Krigel said. "Should I tell her to wait?"

"No," Miranda said, pushing herself up again. "Send her in."

Krigel nodded and vanished into the hall. A few moments later, a woman Miranda had never seen poked her head in. "Rector? May I enter?"

"Of course," Miranda said, fidgeting self-consciously. Answering to "Rector" would take some getting used to. Fortunately, the woman didn't sit on ceremony. She let herself right in and shut the door behind her.

She was middle aged, plump in an active, good-living sort of way, but what really caught Miranda's eye were the woman's rings. She had several, an impressive collection for any Spiritualist, but where most of the Court had a variety of colored stones marking a wide array of servant spirits, this woman's rings all seemed to be cut from the same watery blue stone.

"Sorry to bother you while you're resting, Rector," the woman said. "I wouldn't have intruded, but Rellenor was very insistent."

"Rellenor?" The name was familiar.

"The river running through Zarin," the woman answered, staring at Miranda like she was stupid.

"Oh, the Whitefall," Miranda said. She regretted it instantly.

"She has her own name, you know," the Spiritualist said in a huff. "Honestly, Rector, it is a disgrace to hear a Spiritualist using the name imposed upon her by the Whitefall family's hubris!"

"I'm sorry," Miranda said. "I'm afraid I never had the pleasure of meeting Rellenor. How can I help you, Spiritualist..."

"Brennagan," the woman said. "Jenna Brennagan. I'm the head of the Court's Committee on Water Relations."

Which explained the blue rings, Miranda thought.

"But I didn't actually come here to talk to the Rector," Jenna said. "I came here to talk to Miranda Lyonette." She paused. "You *are* Spiritualist Lyonette?"

"I am," Miranda said.

"Oh good," Jenna said with a sigh. "Everyone kept calling you Rector, so I wasn't sure. Anyway, I was paying my daily visit to Rellenor this morning and found her all in a tizzy. Some foreign water spirit had invaded her river, you see. A *sea* spirit, if you can imagine. He was being frightfully rude, getting salt everywhere, but Rellenor said he kept asking for you by name."

Miranda's heart skipped a beat. "A sea spirit?"

"Yes," Jenna answered. "I told him I'd pass on the message, but only if he promised to...Where are you going?"

Miranda was already up. She ran past the woman, sock feet sliding on the polished stone.

"Thank you, Spiritualist Brennagan!" she cried as she ran down the stairs. "I'll take it from here!"

"Right," Jenna said, staring bewildered as the Rector Spiritualis ran down the stairs yelling for her boots. "Thank you for your prompt action."

Miranda was already too far away to hear.

Ten minutes later, Miranda was dressed and in a carriage clattering toward the river. She sat impatiently on the bench seat, drumming her fingers on the window as the hired driver worked his way through the crowded street. It would have been faster to wake Gin, but with all she'd put her ghosthound through already, Miranda hadn't had the heart. Now, she wished she had.

It was early morning and Zarin was in full swing. Everywhere Miranda looked, people were out doing their morning shopping at the market stalls as though the war had never happened. Of course, for these people, it hadn't. The Immortal Empress had come, triumphed, and fallen without causing Zarin so much as a hiccup. Mostly the crowds seemed happy to have their streets to themselves again now that the soldiers were in Osera. Normally, this would have made Miranda smile. Today, they were in her way.

Three crowded blocks from the docks, Miranda gave up on the carriage. She paid the driver for the full trip and set off on foot, taking the back way down the cargo ramps to the water. After some finagling and more than a few dirty looks from the barge men, she climbed down a steep-graded stone ramp toward the black water of the Whitefall River. Rellenor, she reminded herself.

The river that cut through the center of Zarin was swift and deep. Centuries of city planning had squeezed the once broad waterway into a narrow, stone-walled channel riddled with docks and shadowed by bridges. Boats of all sizes crowded the intakes, but one boat slip was empty, and Miranda scrambled down it to the water's edge. The white stone of the ramp was slick with green slime where it met the river, but Miranda fell to her knees in it without thinking, plunging her hands into the cold water up to the elbow.

"Mellinor?" she whispered, her voice hesitant.

Nothing happened. As the seconds ticked by, dread filled Miranda's stomach. Had she missed him? Had she taken too long? Maybe the invading sea spirit wasn't her Mellinor at all. Maybe she'd let wild hope cloud her judgment. Maybe she'd rushed all the way down here for nothing.

She'd nearly worked herself into a full-blown panic when the water answered. "You must be the Spiritualist."

It wasn't Mellinor's deep voice but higher pitched and faster, the words clipping into each other.

"I am Miranda Lyonette," Miranda answered, getting a firm grip on her emotions. "You must be Rellenor."

"About time you got here," the river replied in a snippy voice. "I was about to kick him out, Great Spirit or no. The nerve, bringing salt water into *my* current."

"Thank you for your patience," Miranda said. "Can I speak with him?"

The river burbled noncommittaly, and then the black water around Miranda's hands grew clear, the river muck separating out to reveal a current of blue, beloved water.

"Miranda," the water whispered in a deep, relieved voice. "I found you."

"Mellinor..." It took every bit of self-control Miranda had not to burst into tears right there. Instead, she leaned down, lowering her face until her nose was brushing the clear, salty water. "I thought..." She couldn't even say it. "I'm sorry. I'm so sorry. I let you down. I left—"

"Don't start," Mellinor said. "We went in together knowing the risks. I can't have you taking all the blame for something we both decided."

"But how did you survive?" Miranda said, running her hands through his cold water. "And why are you here, in a river?"

"The answer to both those questions is the same," Mellinor said. "After the Empress knocked you out of the water, the sea currents tore me apart. I lost nearly all my water, but I managed to preserve my core. I don't know how, exactly. My best guess is that four hundred years in a pillar followed by my time with you gave me a greater sense of self than most water spirits. But even though I was able to hold the last bit of my soul together, I was trapped by the currents and eventually sank."

"You sank?" Miranda couldn't imagine it.

"Like a stone," Mellinor answered. "I didn't have the strength to go against the crashing waters and I was too heavy to flow above them, so I fell down into the black abyss." Mellinor's water trembled against her fingers. "I've never been anywhere so dark, so cold. I didn't even have the strength to flow. All I could do was keep falling. I've never felt so helpless, even in the pillar."

"I'm sorry," Miranda whispered again. "I'm so, so, so—"

"Enough," Mellinor rumbled. "Didn't I say it's not your fault?"

Miranda clenched her fingers. "But you suffered."

"I did," Mellinor said. "But I'm only telling you about it so you can understand why I did what I did next. Listen, and stop interrupting. I don't have much time."

Miranda nodded and motioned for the water to continue.

"I sank for a long time," he said. "Until, finally, I hit something. At first, I thought it was the bottom of the sea, but then I realized it was moving."

"Moving?" Miranda said, forgetting her promise not to interrupt. "Was it a leviathan?"

"Far bigger," Mellinor said. "I'd landed on the Deep Current, the backbone of sea."

"But I thought the sea was a mad mass of water?" Miranda said. "Too large and chaotic even for Great Spirits. That's what you said."

"It is," Mellinor said. "But it wasn't always that way." The water paused. Had Mellinor been human, Miranda could almost picture him looking side to side before leaning in to whisper, "You remember what the Shaper Mountain showed us? About the time before?"

Miranda nodded.

"Back then, the sea was different," Mellinor said. "It used to be that the ocean was home to the greatest spirits, the enormous forces who kept the sea moving. Now, only one remains, the Deep Current that runs from the northern ice down to the warm southern seas. It's the largest water spirit in the world, the only one big enough that the now-mad ocean can't rip apart. Its flow is what drives the other currents and prevents stagnation."

"And you landed on it?" Miranda said. "What happened then?"

"What else?" Mellinor said. "I was sucked into its flow. Even I can't fight a spirit that large."

Miranda trembled at the thought. "How were you not destroyed, then?"

"Because the Deep Current doesn't absorb lesser spirits," Mellinor said. "It must remain pure and whole because it is one of the most ancient spirits, and, in turn, one of the stars."

"Mellinor!" the river's voice cut in, horrified. "You dare speak the Lady's business to a—"

538

"She already knows," Mellinor snapped back. "Quiet."

To Miranda's great surprise, the river fell silent.

"I thought that was the end, then," Mellinor continued. "The Deep Current runs along the base of the world. Once you're caught, there's no escape. You don't get absorbed, but you can't escape, either. You can't do anything except roll along forever until you finally give up and let your water go. But before I could resign myself to my fate, the current vanished."

Miranda blinked in surprise. "Vanished? But you said—"

"I know," Mellinor said. "Old, ancient, enormous, how could it vanish? It was a star. But it did. One moment I was flowing through the dark with the Deep Current; the next it was gone. Just disappeared, like it was yanked out of the ocean."

"I don't understand," Miranda said. "What did you do?"

"The only thing I could do," Mellinor said. "The bottom of the sea was still for the first time ever. I was surrounded by abandoned water without a will or mind of its own. It had to go somewhere, so I took it over."

"You took it over?" Miranda repeated dumbly.

"Yes," Mellinor said. "Without the Deep Current to push it, the sea's cycle was slowing. It would eventually stop altogether. The moment the current vanished, the lesser water spirits began to panic. I had to do something. I did spend several thousand years as a Great Spirit, you know. That kind of obligation doesn't just go away."

"You took over the water left by a star?"

"Yes," Mellinor said again. "That's what I came to tell you. Until a bigger spirit comes to take the job, I'm the Deep Current, and we have a serious problem."

"You can't be the Deep Current?" Miranda said, her head spinning.

"No," Mellinor snapped. "That part's fine. I'm talking about the fact that a *star vanished*. The Deep Current, the king of the sea, one of the largest, oldest, steadiest spirits in the world. A water spirit so large that it drove the ocean *disappeared*, Miranda. It was only by chance that I was there and had retained enough of myself to take over the gap it left before the ocean went stagnant."

Miranda took a deep breath. "All right," she said. "How long can you do the Deep Current's job?"

"Long as I can bear the dark, I suppose," Mellinor said. "I'm an inland sea, I'm used to warm water and sunlight. But I can stand it for a while, especially since the currents are treating me like they used to treat the old Deep Current."

"They're treating you like a star, then?" Miranda said.

"More or less." She could almost hear Mellinor's smile. "How else do you think I was able to get a river to take my water into Zarin to find you?"

"Certainly not my first choice," Rellenor said with a splash that drenched Miranda to the chest. "I don't care if you took over the Deep Current's position; how can you calmly break the Lady's law to this human? It's blasphemy, and if you think I'm going to keep quiet about this, then—"

"I don't think a river could be quiet if its waters depended on it," Mellinor snapped. "You can go crying to the Shepherdess if you want, but before you do, you should know that Miranda here is a friend of the favorite."

The river suddenly went very still. "Friend of the favorite?" It sloshed quietly. All at once, the water began to gently lap at Miranda's boots. "Why didn't you say so, my lady?"

Miranda almost declared that she had never been friends with that irresponsible thief, but she caught herself at the last second when Mellinor's cold water pressed against her hand.

"I'll hold out down here as long as I can," the sea spirit said. "Meanwhile, you have to help me discover what happened. Stars don't just vanish. Something bad is brewing, Miranda, and I fear it'll only get worse."

"Of course I'll help," Miranda said. "I couldn't call myself a Spiritualist if I didn't. Even if I wasn't one, I made you a promise, Mellinor—strength for obedience, power for service. My soul is still your shore, and whatever is happening, I'll protect you however I can."

"I know you will," Mellinor said, his voice fading. "I have to go. I've held against the tides too long. I'm counting on you, Miranda."

"I won't let you down," Miranda said as the blue water ran away from her fingers. "Not this time."

This last part was a whisper, and the words were lost in the sound of the river as Mellinor's water vanished downstream. The moment he was gone, the emptiness came roaring back almost as strong as when she'd first lost him, and Miranda nearly fell into the water. The river caught her, pushing back against her hands until she was steady again.

"I'm sorry about before," Rellenor said. "I didn't know you were a friend of the favorite. I'm sure the Deep Current simply had business with the Lady. Don't worry, the ocean's star will return and your sea will come home. Just keep flowing and everything works out, you'll see."

Miranda nodded and straightened up, but she couldn't help remembering Mellinor's insult to the river Fellboro so long ago. Rivers, always taking the easiest route. That snatch of memory almost made her cry again, but she steeled herself, wringing the water out of her soaked sleeves and trousers as she set off up the boat ramp to catch a coach back to the Tower.

Even if the reason turned out to be innocent, a missing star was worrisome news indeed. It was good she'd already called the Conclave. She had a feeling she would need the whole Court before this was over.

All these thoughts tumbled through her head as she climbed the steep streets away from the river, and Miranda gave herself over to them completely—planning her actions, making lists, putting things in order—but once she'd found a cab willing to overlook her soaked clothes in exchange for a handsome tip, she collapsed onto the cushions and allowed herself to focus on the one thought she'd been holding back until she was alone.

Mellinor was *alive*. He was alive and he'd found her.

Shrinking back into the corner of the coach, Miranda finally let herself break down as all the guilt and fear and sadness of the past two days washed through her. The roar of the city covered her crying as the coach wound its way slowly through the packed streets toward the Spiritualist Tower.

CHAPTER
4

Eli woke to the feel of burning fingers stroking his cheek. He was lying on his side, curled under his coat against the cold of the Between. He could feel Benehime beside him, her white body shining through his closed lids like a beacon. He took a deep slow breath and opened his eyes, plastering his face with the warm, sincere smile that worked best with her. The first thing he saw was Benehime sitting on the bed beside him, watching him with the all-consuming love that made his stomach clench into a tiny, icy marble.

Sleep well? she whispered, leaning down to kiss his forehead.

"Well enough," Eli said, clenching his jaw so he wouldn't flinch.

I've brought your breakfast. She leaned back so Eli could see the breakfast tray on the floor, the enormous platters of sweet meats, pastries, and breads all steaming hot.

Eli sat up without comment, sliding his jacket back over his shoulders. As usual, his clothes were clean. He never knew quite how that happened, if Benehime changed them in the night or if she simply ordered the dirt to leave. As he pulled his coat square, he sincerely hoped it was the latter. The idea of Benehime dressing him while he slept made his skin crawl.

When he was fully dressed again, the Shepherdess reached

down and picked up the tray. The silver platter practically leaped into her hands, but Benehime didn't pay attention to its fawning. Instead, she selected a frosted bun and held it out to Eli.

Eat, she commanded. *I won't have you so thin.*

Eli obeyed. The food came from Zarin, snatched through the veil on its tray with the crest of an extremely prestigious inn stamped into the metal. She always got him the best. Too bad the frosted cake tasted like ash in his mouth under the Shepherdess's scrutiny. He ate mechanically, shoving the food down and doing his best to look grateful, but as he woke up fully, he couldn't shake the feeling that something was wrong...

That thought almost made him choke on a piece of ham. Who was he trying to fool? *Everything* was wrong. He was right back where he'd started, back in the prison he'd worked all his life to avoid. And this time there was no con, no game, no hope of escape. This time, he was here *forever*.

Eli shook himself and forced his attention back to the food that was going down his throat before he could get really depressed. It did no good to fret. He was the only one who would suffer if he let himself get bent out of shape over this. Best to make the most of it, he thought, taking a muffin from Benehime's hand. Be a good dog, stay out of trouble, and maybe if he was boring enough Benehime would forget her obsession in time. He glanced sideways at the Lady, who flashed him an adoring smile. Sure, and maybe he'd be the Heart of War's next wielder.

He chewed violently and swallowed, but the food sat like lead in his stomach. Eli closed his eyes. Powers, he wished that feeling of wrongness would go away. If he had to eat, he'd rather not be sick from it.

When he'd cleared the tray enough to satisfy her, Benehime took his hands and stood them up. The bed vanished the moment they were on their feet, leaving them standing alone in the white nothing. He was about to ask what she wanted to do when he caught the Lady staring at him, her lips curved in a loving smile.

I'm so glad you're home, she said, drawing him close. *You have no idea how dull life has been without you, pet.*

Eli winced at the endearment, but his face was hidden against her white hair, and she didn't see.

It's just like old times, she murmured, stroking her hands over his back, her fingertips gliding up and down his spine. *Just the two of us.*

And that was when Eli realized what was wrong.

He pushed her away and reached down, pulling his jacket apart. He unbuttoned his shirt, calling out in his mind for Karon. Nothing answered. He cursed and popped the middle button, staring down in horror at his smooth chest, the pale skin whole and unmarred, as though it had never been burned.

For a long moment, he could only stand there and force the breath in and out of his lungs. Anger like he had never felt before rose in his throat, threatening to overwhelm his well-honed instinct for self-preservation. Across from him, the Shepherdess stood playing with her hair, smiling innocently as she watched him fight for control.

"What did you do to him?" Eli said at last, grinding each word through his clenched teeth.

I removed him, Benehime said, her voice light and casual. They could have been talking about the weather for all the care she showed.

Eli closed his eyes. "Why?" he whispered. "Did I not come when called? Have I not been a good favorite?"

You are perfect, Benehime said, reaching out to stroke his cheek. *And that's why he had to go.* Her fingers traced down his jaw to his neck, following the line of throat to his chest. *I can't have such an ugly burn marring my beautiful favorite, can I?*

"He was my friend!" Eli roared, catching her hand and forcing it away. "Where is he? Tell me, Benehime!"

Benehime's smile vanished. *Don't be bossy with me,*

darling, she said, grabbing his hand and bending it backward before he could react. Eli gasped in pain, cursing himself. He always forgot how strong she was.

You made the rules of the game, she said, bending his hand farther and farther. *But I won. The time for defiance is over. You're mine, every last bit of you, forever. I decide who your friends are, what you can do and when, what you eat, when you sleep.*

She stopped bending his hand just before his wrist snapped. Eli clamped his jaw, fighting not to cry out as she loomed over him. *Forget the lava spirit*, she whispered. *My happiness is your only concern now.*

Panting from the pain, Eli glared up at her. Every instinct he had was screaming at him to keep his mouth shut. To let it go. But he couldn't. Not this time. Not Karon.

He leaned forward, bringing his face up to hers. "What. Did. You. Do?"

Benehime sneered down at him, and her grip on his wrist vanished. Without the support, Eli stumbled, falling at her feet. The moment he was down, she grabbed his head, forcing him to look at her.

I've sent him away, she said, her fingers digging into his jaw like claws. *He was a bad influence, keeping you up all night with talk of disobedience.* She laughed at his startled look. *What? Did you really think I'd put you somewhere I couldn't hear you? Don't be stupid, love. I heard it all. But you needn't worry, darling, I'm not mad at you. How could I be? You're my everything. But I couldn't let such talk just slide, could I?* She sighed deeply. *Someone had to pay, love. Someone always pays, and I could never let it be you. And anyway, I couldn't bare seeing his filth clouding your beauty any longer.*

Benehime smiled down at him and dropped her head, brushing her burning lips against his. *I tore him out and tossed him down with the rest of the spirits*, she murmured, nuzzling her lips back and forth over his. *Now you're beautiful again. As beautiful as the first time I saw you.*

Eli wrenched his face away from hers. "You sent him out on his own?"

The Lady's look grew cold. *It's no longer your concern where—*

"Are you *crazy?*" Eli shouted. "He's a *lava* spirit. They need constant energy. He'll *die* without me. Why do you think I offered to let him live in my chest in the first—"

Benehime's hand struck his cheek before he could finish, slamming him to the white ground at her feet.

No more of that, she hissed. *I'm what matters to you, not him.*

Eli reached up to rub his throbbing jaw, but his fingers had barely made it before white hands grabbed arms. The Lady lifted him like he weighed nothing, setting him back on his knees as her hands moved up to cup his face again. *There, there, love,* she said, stroking him, her white eyes soft again. *Let's not fight. The lava spirit's gone, a payment for your disobedience. It's finished, everything swept clean, so say you love me and I'll take you somewhere nice, all right?*

Eli said nothing. He just knelt there, staring at her, his body trembling like a plucked wire. He knew what he should do, of course. He should kiss her, lie to her, tell her she was his everything and then go look for Karon later once things cooled down. That would be smart; that would be best. He knew how to placate her better than anyone, after all. It was a life skill he'd honed to perfection. All he had to do was bow his head, but his neck would not budge.

Eliton? the Lady said, her voice heavy with warning.

Shaking with rage, he said the only word he had left.

"No."

The Shepherdess's eyes widened, but Eli didn't care. He was so sick of this. Sick of being afraid, sick of lying, sick of *her.* Before he could think, he was standing up, pushing her hands away.

"How can I love you?" he cried, backing away. "You're cruel and petty and vicious. The only reason I came back is because you threatened to destroy everything I *actually* loved." He pressed his hands against his empty chest. "If you're going to punish someone for what *I* said, then punish *me*, because those words were probably the only true things to come out of my mouth since you brought me here."

He bared his teeth at her, letting all the fury that had been building since Osera come roaring out. "*I hate you*," he said. "I would have hated you from the first moment I saw you if I hadn't been so young and stupid. You're not my Lady, and you never will be. I wish I'd never met you."

His words echoed in the empty white, and for once, it was Benehime who was shocked into silence. She stood perfectly still, her eyes stretched wide, her mouth pressed into a thin, white line. It was several seconds before she could move, but when she did, she moved faster than anything Eli had ever seen. In less than a second she was on him, her weight knocking him flat. The air thickened to cement around his arms and legs, pinning them down as she straddled his chest and grabbed his neck, her shaking thumbs pressing into his windpipe like twin icepicks.

At that moment, Eli was sure Benehime was going to kill him. Just rip his head right off, or cut off his air and watch him suffocate, but she didn't. Gradually, her shaking subsided. The rage faded from her face, leaving it tired and drawn as she glared down at him.

I don't think you understand how this works, love, she whispered, her voice terrifyingly calm. *You blame me for everything, but you made the bet, remember? Do you know how much it hurt when you tried to trick me into letting you go?*

The fingers on his throat relaxed, sliding up his neck to tangle in the hair behind his ears.

I died a little that day, she whispered. *But I took your bet, just like you wanted. I played along, just like you wanted me to, but did you think I wouldn't be playing for keeps? That I wouldn't do whatever was necessary to get you home?* She leaned down, pressing her cheek against his. *Do you think my love is that shallow?*

Eli moved his face as far from hers as he could. "I don't think you know what love is."

Benehime slammed his head into the floor so hard he saw spots. *I know more of love than you could ever comprehend!* she screamed. *I am the Shepherdess! I am the most beloved thing in the entire world! Everything loves me, must love me, and you will, too.*

"Why should I?" Eli snapped. It was suicidally stupid to keep antagonizing her, but he couldn't stop. He was so fed up with every part of this ridiculous affair, the senseless loss of Karon, the loss of all his friends, his life, everything she'd taken from him. He was going to speak his mind now even if she killed him for it. At least then he would be free.

"Why should I love you?" he said again. "What have you ever done to deserve it?"

Everything! Benehime's voice roared in his ears. *I gave you everything you have! Had I not taken notice of you, you would have died that night in the woods. It is my favor alone that makes you worthwhile. You are* nothing *without me!*

"*You're wrong!*" Eli shouted back. "I learned to be a thief on my own. I met Josef and won his friendship on my own. Same with Nico. My bounty is my own! I'm Eli Monpress, the greatest thief in the world, and I did it with their help, not yours!"

Benehime stared at him, mouth agape, and then she began to laugh. *You really believe that?* she said, incredulous. *Do you honestly think any of those spirits would have listened to you had it not been for my mark? Are you actually egotistical enough to believe you were just so charming that the world fell over for you?* She laughed harder, falling across him. *How preposterous! Even when you were trying to do things on your own, I was always there. It was never you, love. It was me. It was always me.*

She shook her head and tilted it sideways, her voice growing sweet and patient, like a teacher explaining numbers to a silly child. *I protected your pet demonseed from the League,* she said. *I saved you in Mellinor. I let you make a portal to save your swordsman when you'd sworn never to use them again. I even stopped the Lord of Storms' blade right in front of your face.*

Eli flinched. "I didn't ask you to do any of that."

But you knew I would, Benehime scoffed. *You counted on it. You took those big risks because you knew I would be there to bail you out, just like I always do. I could have called you in at any of those times, but I didn't. The truth, darling, is that I've bent over backward time after time to help you. I've healed you, comforted you. I've done everything you've ever asked of me, and all I asked in return was your love. And yet you still have the gall, the* arrogance *to say you did it all on your own?* The Shepherdess lifted her lip in a sneer. *Get over yourself, Eliton. Everything you are is because of me.*

Eli sat up as far as he could with the heavy air pinning him down. "Everything I am is in spite of you," he said, spitting the words at her. "I never asked to be your favorite. You've played me and dangled me like a puppet ever since I met you, and you abused your power over the spirits to do it. I don't love you, nothing does. The only reason the world obeys anything you say is because the spirits are afraid of you, just like I was, but not anymore." He lay back, his face breaking into a wide smile. "I'm done being afraid of you, Benehime, and I'm done being your favorite."

As he finished, Benehime began to tremble on top of him. When she spoke, her voice was an icy knife. *You don't get to make that decision.*

"Yes, I do," Eli said. "Because, while you can force everything else in this world to dance for your delight, you can't make me do the one thing you need above all else. You can't make me love you."

Benehime dug her nails into his head. *You will love me,* she snarled.

"If you wanted love, you shouldn't have killed Nara," Eli snarled back. "Because you'll get none from me."

The rage on Benehime's face was a horror to behold, twisting her lovely features into a hideous mask. But then, as fast as it came, the rage was gone, replaced by something worse.

Slowly, terribly, a smile began to spread across Benehime's lips. She sat up, staring down at Eli from her perch on his chest. And then, in a beautiful, fluid motion, she rolled off him. Eli didn't move as she stood, not even to test the bindings on his limbs. He just lay there, meeting her white eyes with his own unwavering glare. *Show no weakness*, a voice very much like Josef's whispered in his mind. *Hold your ground.*

Benehime straightened to her full height. She loomed over him, white and terrible with that cold smile on her lips, and the air grew thick with the pressure of her will. It surrounded Eli like tar, pressing in until he could scarcely breathe.

You think you are anything without my love, arrogant boy? she whispered. *You're nothing without me. The only worth you have is what I give you.*

Eli rolled his eyes. He'd heard that one before. "You're wrong," he said, grinning wide. "I'm worth two hundred and forty-eight thousand gold standards. Now that Den's dead and Josef's king, that's more than anyone else in the world."

Benehime closed her eyes. *I should have known better than to expect sense from you, but to choose a bounty over my favor...* Her voice trailed off, and then, without warning, her face softened.

I love you, Eliton, the Lady whispered, opening her eyes. *Despite all you've said, all the insults, all the selfishness, I love you. Nothing can change that. But since you would choose a bounty over my favor, even in jest, it's obvious you need to be reminded of the value of my love. All these years living in the light of my good graces have made you forget how easy you have it. I think it's time for you to relearn the harsh realities of the world.*

Before Eli could answer that, Benehime reached out and

touched his chest. Her fingers burned through the cloth of his shirt, and Eli didn't even have time to brace before the pain exploded through him. It flooded his mind, burned over every inch of his skin, ground into his bone, but then, as quickly as it had started, the pain was gone.

Benehime's hand left his chest, leaving only the feeling of emptiness and the knowledge of what he'd lost. The mark of the Shepherdess, the sign of Benehime's favor that had been inside him so long he couldn't remember life without it, was gone. Suddenly, Eli felt painfully weak and small, like he'd deflated. It must have shown, for Benehime began to laugh as she straightened again.

Let's see how you live up to your words, she said haughtily. *But don't worry, darling, I haven't taken everything from you. After all, you still have your bounty.*

Eli opened his mouth to say she was bloody right about that, but before he could make a sound, he realized he was falling. Above him, Benehime's face shone down like the moon, her lips curved into a cruel smile.

I hope it's everything you dreamed of.

Her voice rang in his ears as the white world vanished, slipping away through the cut in reality she'd opened under his back. Suddenly, he was surrounded in a whirl of color— blue sky and green trees and tall white spires topped with gold. That was all he caught before he crashed into something cold, hard, and uneven. Eli rolled on instinct, clutching his chest as the breath was knocked clean out of him. When his lungs were working again, he opened his eyes to see the tip of a sword hovering right in front of his nose.

Eli raised his hands on instinct. He was on his back in some kind of paved yard surrounded by soldiers in white surcoats, all of whom had their swords out. Overhead, a great citadel rose like a mountain, its seven, gold-tipped spires scraping the pale morning sky.

"You've got to be kidding me," Eli muttered, lowering his hands to rub his aching eyes.

"Arms up!" the soldier barked.

Eli raised his hands again, smiling at the guards. It wasn't his best smile, but it was all he could manage. Of course, of all the places Benehime could drop him, where else would she choose but the front gate of the Council of Thrones?

"That's him, all right," one of the guards said, nodding toward the wall of the guardhouse where Eli's poster was pasted prominently. "Looks just like his picture."

If the fact that the most wanted criminal in the Council had literally fallen from the sky bothered them, the guards hid it well. They hauled Eli to his feet without fanfare and marched him into the citadel through a side gate. Once inside, they said something to another guard who was wearing a long white coat, and then took Eli down a long set of narrow stairs as though following long-standing orders.

Despite all the jostling, Eli saw little of the journey. His mind was still reeling from how quickly his situation had changed. It was a strange realization to have while he was surrounded by guards marching down a seemingly never-ending stair into the dark underbelly of the Council of Thrones, but it was slowly dawning on Eli that he was free. The mark was gone. He'd done it. He didn't know how long it would last, but for now, in this moment, he was *free*.

His face broke into an idiotic grin, and Eli practically floated as the guards pushed him along a suspended walkway through a huge, dark, cavernous room. He was so lost in his happiness, he didn't even notice where he was going until the guards sat him down in a worn but surprisingly comfortable chair. And then, to his great astonishment, they left.

Shocked out of his happy daze by his sudden abandonment, Eli looked around, casing his surroundings with the attention to detail Giuseppe Monpress had drilled into him. He was alone in a small, windowless office with strange, curving metal walls held together by rivets. Desks covered in papers took up most of the space. The walls were covered in papers as well, drawings mostly, but one wall, the wall he was facing, was different.

There, pasted in neat rows from the ceiling to just above the desks, hung every bounty poster he'd ever had, starting when he was only worth five hundred and going all the way to the current sum of two hundred and forty-eight thousand. The sight of his own smiling face repeated over and over was so puzzling and unexpected that Eli didn't realize there was someone else in the room with him until she spoke. But even though he hadn't seen her, the scratchy, smoke-stained voice told Eli exactly who it was.

"Hello, Eliton." Sara stepped out from behind him, her pipe dangling between her teeth. "Been a while."

Eli took a deep breath. "Not long enough."

His mother smiled, and Eli felt the joy of his freedom shrivel away to nothing.

CHAPTER
5

Miranda leaned back in the padded chair and ground her palms into her eyeballs. Powers, she was tired. Six hours of sleep was not enough for this nonsense. All she wanted to do was lie down and never get up, but she couldn't rest now, not when there was still so much to be done.

From the moment she'd gotten back to the Tower after leaving Mellinor, Miranda had been trying to figure out what to do about a disappearing star. The problem was overwhelming, mostly because she knew so little about the stars or the Shepherdess who ruled over them.

The Shaper Mountain had told her stars watched over other spirits that were like them, sort of like a Great Spirit but on a much larger scale. She knew that most of them were ancient, though not as ancient as the Shaper Mountain, and that they had a great deal of free will and awareness compared to the smaller spirits. Other than these few basics, though, she knew nothing. She didn't know where to find the stars, how many existed, or even how to recognize one if she saw it. With so little to go on, Miranda had had no choice but to start at the beginning and proceed methodically.

Before she could worry about what a star's disappearance meant, though, she had to know if this was an isolated incident. Had something happened to the Deep Current alone, or was this a larger epidemic? And how would she know if it was? She needed more information. Specifically, she needed to know how many stars there were and where to find them. Once she knew that, she could figure out which ones had disappeared (assuming the Deep Current wasn't an isolated incident), and then she could start looking for patterns.

Identifying and locating the stars had seemed like a simple and reasonable starting point. Surely, if stars were so important, they would be well-known. All Miranda had to do was ask her spirits. Her rings had been with her every step of the way; they understood the need. But while her spirits were perfectly willing to break the Shepherdess's edict of silence (yet another mystery she intended to unravel), what they'd had to say hadn't actually been very helpful. In hindsight, Miranda shouldn't have been surprised. Spirit politics were about as transparent as baked mud.

"I don't see why you're so upset about it," Kirik crackled from his place in the lamp at her elbow. "It's not like we need to know who our stars are. They're supposed to watch over *us*."

"Well, excuse me for expecting a large and intelligent spirit to know who was in charge," Miranda grumbled, glaring at the flame. "You'd think you would at least know whom to complain to."

"That's what Great Spirits are for," Kirik flickered. "I don't even think I have a star, actually. Any fire that big would burn the continent to ash. I'm probably under the watch of one of the great volcanoes down south."

Miranda's glare grew belligerent, and the fire puffed up. "What? It's not like it's ever been an issue before now. And I'd know my star when I saw it. You can't miss the mark, after all."

"You missed it on Eli," Miranda huffed.

"That was different," Kirik said, his crackle defensive. "You humans keep your spirits closed up all the time."

Fortunately, not all her spirits were so willfully ignorant. Her stone spirit Durn, for example, had named his star right off. Too bad it was one of the few Miranda already knew: Durain, the Shaper Mountain.

But while the stars were universally powerful, they seemed to have wildly different policies on how to manage the spirits under their care. Some were very involved, like the Shaper Mountain, or another Durn had named, Gredit, the Lord of the Bears. Others seemed downright indifferent, like the Great Ghosthound. From what Gin had told her, the Great Ghosthound cared for nothing but the hunt, and would even kill other ghosthounds who got in his way. Gin seemed to take this as a matter of course.

"He's a ghosthound," he said at Miranda's look of horror. "What else can you expect?"

"Nonsense," she said. "You wouldn't act that way."

"I'm not like other ghosthounds," Gin said, tucking his nose under his tail. "That's why I'm with you." And that was all he'd say about the matter.

So it had gone all morning. Miranda had grilled her spirits one by one, and while she'd learned things about them that she'd never thought to wonder over before, like how her mist spirit Allinu was actually a member of the Wind Courts and thus had no star at all, she got precious few of the answers she was actually after. Around lunch, she'd finally given up on her own spirits and gone for the one source of information she had left—the Spirit Court's Restricted Archives. That's where she was now, three fruitless hours later.

The Restrictive Archives dealt exclusively with the Court's

555

interactions with stars. Of course, they were never *called* stars, either by the spirits or the Spiritualists who'd written the records, but the truth was plain if you knew what to look for. She'd skimmed the archives the morning before Master Banage had ordered the Court to Osera; now she dug in deep, plucking out the details the dry reports did their best to dance around—names, places, and, most important, the star's past relationships with the Court. It was slow work, but thanks to her stint working for the Council before she'd chased Eli up north to Izo's, Miranda had gotten surprisingly good at picking the important bits out of bureaucratic writing.

Despite this advantage, however, she had precious little to show for her hours. Her list of stars, so optimistically penned on a piece of paper as long as her arm, had a grand total of ten names on it, four of which she'd known before she started her research: the Shaper Mountain, Eli, the Immortal Empress, and the Deep Current that Mellinor had replaced. From her own spirits she'd added Gredit, the Lord of the Bears, her moss spirit Allinora's star, a huge cave lichen that supposedly lived in the Empress's lands, and the Great Ghosthound, whose actual name Gin hadn't mentioned, probably because he didn't know it. And there was one more, a surprise confession from Skarest, her lightning bolt, who claimed none other than the Lord of Storms himself as his star.

"You're telling me the Lord of Storms is *actually* a storm?" Miranda said, aghast. "How? I mean, he's human. I've seen him."

"So have I," Skarest crackled from his ring. "That's how I know he's my star, not that he's ever done anything for me," the lightning bolt finished sulkily.

"How does a storm, and a star no less, run a human organization like the League?" Miranda wondered out loud, tapping her fingers on the table.

"I don't know," Skaraest said. "He's different from the other stars, though."

Miranda frowned. "How so?"

The lightning dimmed a moment, and then he spoke in a humming whisper that ran up Miranda's arm, making her hair stand on end. "The Lady's mark is different on him than on the Shaper Mountain. The Mountain's mark is like a stamp pressed onto the surface of the older spirit. But the Lord of Storms bears the Lady's mark on every part of his essence. Like it's woven in."

"What do you mean woven in?" Miranda whispered back.

"I can't explain it any better," the lightning crackled in frustration. "Even if you could see it, I don't think you'd understand. I don't understand it myself. One thing is certain, though. Whatever the Lord of Storms was before the Shepherdess touched him, he's hers now. When the Lady made him, she gave him a purpose, and it wasn't to take care of lightning. Does that makes sense?"

"It will if I think on it a moment," Miranda said, working this new information through her head. "The Lord of Storms is the demon hunter, master of the League. If the Shepherdess made him for a purpose, it must have been that. Of course"— her voice turned bitter—"he certainly doesn't seem to give much effort to demon hunting, judging by what we saw at Izo's and how he's let Nico run around loose. If he's not doing his bit as your star, either, I don't know what he does with his time."

"I don't want to know," Skarest said with a shiver. "He's very dangerous, mistress. Wherever this investigation leads, please don't cross him. I won't be able to act if you do."

"I have no plans to," Miranda assured him.

But that had been three hours ago, when she'd known eight stars off the top of her head without so much as opening a report. Since then, she'd managed only two more: Ell, the mother river far to the south, and Frejesll, the great coral reef off the pirate islands. The slow pace made her want to kick things. She'd promised Mellinor she'd find out what was going on with his disappearing star. If she was going to keep that oath, she needed to get everything rolling before she lost her powers as Rector and access to the Court's aid. At this rate, she'd still be looking up names when the Conclave convened tomorrow.

Miranda glanced again at her pathetically short list. Of the ten names she had, three—the Empress, the Deep Current, and Eli—were certainly gone. Three out of an unknown number wasn't much to go on, but her spirits had all insisted that they didn't *feel* that their stars were gone.

Of course, none of them had ever been without their stars, but Durn had been adamant that they would know if something had happened. That meant the Shaper Mountain, Kirik's unknown star, the Lord of Storms, Allinora's lichen, and Gin's ghosthound were all still around, at least for now. Discounting the stars she knew were gone, that left two on her small list still unaccounted for: the mother river and the coral reef.

The river had been easy enough to check. Miranda had simply sent Spiritualist Brennagan to ask Rellenor. The Spiritualist had returned an hour later with an extremely long report. It seemed that the river, despite being sorely put upon by Mellinor's salty presence and the constant strain of the boats and the narrow channeling of the docks and dire concerns about the amount of trash in her waters, was otherwise fine. Certainly not a spirit who'd lost its star. That left the coral reef far down south.

Going down to check it herself was out of the question, and this far from the coast there was no one in the Court with a coral spirit for a servant. In the end, she'd sent her wind, Eril. According to the archives, the reef was over five hundred miles from end to end, spanning the entire southwestern corner of the continent. If something had happened to it, her wind would be able to tell even from the air. She'd sent him as soon as she'd realized the reef was her last lead, but even Eril couldn't fly down to the end of the continent and back in an hour. So, sick of records and with no way to check on a new star even if she did find another, Miranda decided it was time for a break.

One of the perks of being Rector was that she never had to fetch anything for herself. Miranda closed the record she'd been reading and called the apprentice who'd been assigned to her for today. The girl entered meekly, all wide eyes as usual. Miranda smiled her best "I don't bite" smile and asked for something to drink.

The girl bowed and left, returning not five minutes later with an enormous tray loaded with sweet breads, cookies, biscuits, and a carafe of steaming hot tea. For a moment, Miranda wanted to ask the girl just how much she thought a Rector ate, but one look at the girl's pale face decided her against needless antagonism. Thanking the girl profusely, Miranda poured herself a cup and tucked in.

Thirty minutes later she was feeling pleasantly stuffed and decidedly more optimistic. She was sipping her third cup of tea and working up the willpower to dive back into the archives when the window on the wall began to rattle. Miranda sprang from her chair, tea forgotten. Running to the other side of the room, she flung the window open. Eril blew in as soon as the glass was out of his way, scattering her papers in the process.

"That was fast," Miranda said, bending down to snatch her list off the floor.

"Of course," Eril said smugly. "It's me, remember?"

Miranda smiled, and then grew serious. "What did you find? How is the reef?"

"I wouldn't know," Eril sighed, spinning into her hands. "It wouldn't talk to me. I *told* you it wouldn't. Even if I could get through the water, why should a reef talk to a wind?"

"I didn't ask you to learn its life's story," Miranda said, exasperated. "Was it *there*?"

"Yes," Eril said. "From what I could see through twenty feet of water, the reef looked fine."

Miranda heaved a sigh that was half relief, half frustration. She put her list on the table and leaned over, carefully marking a check beside the reef's name.

"That's everyone," she said. "Not that it means anything with such a small sample."

Eril blew after her as she stomped back to her chair and flopped into it.

"Maybe I'm overreacting," she grumbled, rubbing her temples. "Maybe Mellinor just happened to fall onto an isolated incident and stars aren't vanishing after all."

Eril blew through her hair. "I wouldn't say that just yet."

"Why not?" Miranda asked, looking up. "You said the reef was fine."

"The *reef* was," Eril said, spinning in a little circle. "But I blew over a lot of country on my way down, including the rain forest."

"The Allva," Miranda said. She'd never been that far south, but she'd seen maps enough to know roughly what the wind was referring to. "Go on."

Eril spun faster and dipped, fluttering Kirik's flame. "Before I threw my lot in with you, I used to spend most of my time flying for the Lord of the South. I flew over that forest a lot, and I remember there was this one tree that was bigger than the others. Much bigger."

Miranda shrugged. "The forest's Great Spirit?"

"No, bigger," Eril said. "There are trees there that stand taller than this tower, but this tree was twice the size of any other. It was enormous, a king of the forest. A king of all trees."

"A star," Miranda said, eyes wide.

"I think so," Eril said, his breeze dipping in a nod.

"What do you mean you think so?" Miranda said, crossing her arms. "I thought you could see this kind of thing."

"I can, *if* I'm looking," Eril said defensively. "The South Wind's not like the Lord of the West. Illir encourages his winds to look at everything, but when you blow for the south, well, you don't put your air where it isn't wanted, if you get my meaning. I had no business with the tree, so I didn't look at it. That's why I took a detour this time."

Miranda smiled. "You wanted to look at the tree."

"I was curious!" Eril cried.

"That's fine," Miranda said, putting up her hands. "So, now you've had your look. Is the tree a star or isn't it?"

"I don't know," Eril said. "It wasn't there."

Miranda froze. "Was it cut down?"

"No," Eril said. "There was no sign of the tree at all, just an enormous hole in the ground."

Miranda sucked in a breath through clenched teeth. "It *was* a star," she said. "A forest star, and now it's missing."

"Can't say for sure," Eril said, blowing across Miranda's face. "But that's the conclusion I came to. Also, whatever happened to it, it happened recently. The upturned dirt was still fresh."

Miranda hopped up and strode to the table, leaning over to write "Allva tree" on her list of stars, along with a thick, black X. "You asked the trees, didn't you? What did they say happened?"

"I *tried* to ask the trees," Eril said. "But I couldn't get a word in edgewise. The whole forest was in a panic."

Miranda's head whipped toward the wind's voice. "Panic? What do you mean panic?"

"Panic panic," Eril said. "The way they were carrying on, you'd think a demonseed had built a tree house in their branches." The wind puffed against her. "If that's what losing your star does to you, then I'm glad the winds don't have one."

Miranda turned away from the table and began to pace. Now that she thought about it, Mellinor had said the sea spirits were panicking when he took over for the Deep Current. If loss of a star sent its spirits into an uproar comparable to demon panic, then this situation was even more dangerous than she'd initially thought. What would happen if the Shaper Mountain vanished? Or Kirik's great lava spirit? Would the mountains quake and the volcanoes erupt?

"I hate to say this," Eril put in, "but do you think Eli might be to blame?"

"How do you figure that?" Miranda asked.

"He is a thief," the wind whispered. "And things are missing."

Miranda could only blink in amazement. "You think Eli Monpress is stealing stars?"

Eril puffed up around her. "It's not *that* far a stretch. He's the favorite, after all. Nothing is beyond his reach."

"What does that mean, anyway?" Miranda asked. "Whose favorite is he?"

The room fell into an uncomfortable silence. Finally, Kirik answered. "He is the star the Shepherdess favors above all others," the fire crackled softly. "Her beloved."

Miranda closed her eyes. Now *that* was a terrible prospect: Eli Monpress, boyfriend to the most powerful force in the world. But the more she thought about it, the more the idea rang hollow. When she remembered Eli as she'd last seen him, all she could see was his defeated face as the white arms wrapped around his neck and dragged him through the hole in the world. That was not the face of a smug thief getting what he wanted.

"I don't think we can blame this one on Monpress," she said at last. "Whatever else he may be, Eli's never been an enemy to the spirits. And besides"—her face broke into a smile—"it doesn't raise his bounty. He'd never waste his time on anything that didn't make his number bigger."

"Come on," Eril said, "his bounty can't be everything."

"Want to bet?" Miranda asked, but there was no laughter in her voice. "I worry Eli may be a victim, just as much as any of the others," she said quietly. "I also worry that the thief may be in over his head this time."

"Well," Eril huffed, "if the favorite's not behind this, then what's going on?"

"I don't know," Miranda said. "But I mean to find out."

Her wind moaned. "How? We've tried everything."

"Nonsense," Miranda said. "We haven't even begun to try." But even as she said it, Miranda was keenly aware that she didn't know where to look next. She could keep plowing through the archives and hope she got lucky, but time was so short, and there were still shelves and shelves to go. The Conclave was tomorrow. If she was going to have sufficient proof to convince the Council to act by then, she needed something faster. But what? Her spirits and the Shaper Mountain were the only ones who dared to break the Shepherdess's edict of silence, and even Gin couldn't run to the Shaper Mountain and back before the Conclave, which brought her right back to the archives.

Miranda's thoughts were still circling madly through the same dead ends when, out of the blue, she realized she was overlooking an important source of information. The idea hit her like a slap, and she froze, frightening Eril, who was still hovering above her. He hissed, but Miranda barely noticed, she was too busy examining the new idea from every angle, looking for the flaw. But the more she thought about it, the more sense it made, and soon the only flaw she could find was that it had taken her so long to think of this.

Grinning widely, Miranda hopped to her feet, scaring Eril again.

"Mistress," he said, "what's wrong?"

"Not a thing," Miranda said. "Just a change of plans. It's clear now that I can't do this on my own, not with the resources I have."

"But what else is there?" Kirik asked, orange flame leaning out of the lamp.

Miranda grabbed her list off the table and shoved it into her pocket. "I'm going to ask the West Wind."

"The West..." Eril's voice trailed off, horrified. "You can't just call down the *West Wind* like some common spirit!"

"Why not?" Miranda said, holding out her hand so her fire spirit could return to his ring. "We brought the Court to Osera for him. He owes us. Besides, Illir's a confirmed meddler. If anyone can get us answers, it's him."

"*Confirmed meddler?*" Eril blustered as Kirik's fire flowed out of the lamp into the ruby on Miranda's thumb. "He's one of the Wind Lords! Mistress, I mean no offense, but you're human. You don't understand. If something's big enough to affect stars, then the Shepherdess is involved. Even if Illir does know what's going on, he's not going to risk her anger by telling you."

"That may be," Miranda said, "but it doesn't stop me from asking, does it? Anyway, I don't think Illir is much of a fan of the Shepherdess. Maybe he'll be more helpful than you think."

The records fluttered as Eril spun in nervous circles.

"Relax," Miranda said. "I'm not going to be sending you to him."

"You're not?" The wind in the room fell off as Eril's circling stopped. "Oh, well, that's different."

Miranda rolled her eyes and held out his pendant. Eril returned in a rush, but just before he reached his pearl, he paused. "Remember," he said nervously, "I had—"

"Absolutely no part in this," Miranda finished for him. "I know, Eril. I'll take full responsibility. Now get in. We've wasted enough time as it is."

The wind gave one final huff before returning to his pendant. The moment he was in, Miranda turned and started for the door.

She hit the stairs and began the climb to Banage's office at the top of the Tower. Her office now, technically. Miranda blanched at the thought. Master Banage had sent her here for this, to find out what was happening in the world and bring the Court together so they could face it. Eril's story blended with Mellinor's in her mind. Stars disappearing, leaving their spirits in upheaval and panic. Two were bad enough, but if this kept going, it could do serious damage to the Spirit World she was sworn to protect.

Miranda set her jaw stubbornly. If Illir couldn't tell her what was happening, she'd find someone else. She'd do whatever it took, but she would not let this go without a fight. She would not be forsworn in her duty, not when Master Banage had put so much faith in her, and not so long as she called herself a Spiritualist.

With that thought, a new burst of energy flowed through her body, and Miranda picked up the pace, taking the stairs two at a time, then three. She moved faster and faster until she was running full tilt up the Tower. So fast, in fact, that she didn't even see the Tower Keeper until she ran into him.

Miranda stumbled back as she bounced off the robed man, her conviction forgotten in a wash of mortal embarrassment.

"I'm *so* sorry," she said, reaching to help the Spiritualist she'd knocked over, but her hands froze when Tower Keeper Blint's cold eyes met hers.

The Tower Keeper took his time standing up. He pulled his formal robe straight and steadied his feet before dropping the shallowest bow he could get away with. "Rector, how fortunate. I had just gone to your office in search of you."

He said her title like it was the worst insult imaginable, but then, for Blint, it probably was when he had to apply it to Miranda. Blint had been one of Hern's cronies before the Gaol Tower Keeper's crimes had been exposed. He'd also been the first to answer Whitefall's call to betray the Court and the head of the Spiritualists who'd left for the Council. He'd never made any attempt to disguise his hatred for Banage or anyone who was loyal to him, especially Miranda. Of course, the dislike was mutual, and it was only Miranda's respect for the decorum of the Court that kept her from pushing past the Tower Keeper without a word.

"You should have asked Spiritualist Krigel," she said, her voice cooling to match his icy tone. "He could have told you I was in the library and saved you a trip."

"Slipped my mind," Blint said. "But I should have known you'd take full advantage of the perks of your ill-gotten power."

Miranda sighed silently. She didn't have time for this. "What do you want, Blint?"

"Nothing from you," Blint said haughtily. "I came only as

565

a point of procedure. Doctrine demands that the request for emergency session be delivered to the sitting Rector in person."

He held out his hand, and Miranda glanced down to see a letter, bound and sealed, between his fingers. She took it without a word, cracking the wax with her thumbnail. The message itself was short, but by the time Miranda's eyes reached the list of names at the bottom, she was angry enough to spit nails.

"A demand for an emergency gathering of the Tower Keepers to vote on a new Rector?" she cried. "You *do* know I've already called a Conclave, don't you? The entire Court's going to be here by tomorrow afternoon. You can't possibly get enough Keepers in for an emergency session before then, so why even bother gathering the signatures?"

"To prove a point," Blint snapped. "You might be Rector now, but the Court won't tolerate Banage's dictatorship any longer. The man is a traitor, and so far as I'm concerned, you are as well. It may be within your power to call a Conclave, but you wouldn't be the first appointed Rector to use the emergency rules of the Conclave to bypass a vote and cement your position without the approval of the Tower Keepers."

For a moment, all Miranda could do was blink at him. "What are you talking about?"

"The Conclave is the Spirit Court's most sacred gathering," Blint said. "Called only in dire emergency. It is also the only way for a nonelected Rector to legally maintain her seat beyond the mandated week by using the Conclave to declare a state of emergency." Blint's lip lifted in a sneer. "Really, Miranda, did you think we wouldn't see through such a transparent play by Banage to keep his power even while he's facing the Council's justice? It's a nice try, but it won't work. That letter bears signatures from over half of the sitting Keepers, more than enough to force a—"

"*Is that what you think this is about?*" Miranda roared, crushing the letter in her fist. "You think . . . you actually *believe* that I called the Conclave because I wanted to keep my position as Rector? Are you paying attention to *anything* that's been going on?"

For a split second, Blint's haughty expression faltered. "I speak for all the Keepers—"

"Get out of my way," Miranda said, pushing past him.

"Enjoy it now, Lyonette!" Blint shouted as she ran up the stairs. "Tomorrow I'll see you stripped of your rings and kicked out of the Court for good! A fitting end for a traitor!"

Miranda stopped midstep and whirled around, drawing herself up to her full height. "Blint," she said, "do yourself a favor. Shut up long enough to listen to your own spirits, and maybe then you'll understand why I called a Conclave. Meanwhile, stay out of my Tower and stop distracting my Spiritualists from their duties with your idiotic petitions."

"You can't order me out of the Tower!" Blint shouted. "I'm a Spiritualist!"

"Really?" Miranda said, throwing the crumpled letter at his feet. "Then start acting like one."

With that, she turned and stomped up the stairs, leaving Blint staring after her, his face turning redder with each step she took.

How dare he, Miranda seethed. How *dare* he think she was like him? All that man cared about was position. He wouldn't care if the whole world was falling apart so long as he was wearing the Rector's mantle. If it wouldn't have meant the doom of the Court, she would have made Blint Rector right there on the steps just to get him out of her hair.

She sighed in frustration, slamming her boots down on the steps as she climbed. At least it would all be over soon. Those Spiritualists who hadn't answered Banage's call during the war were pouring in now for the Conclave. Tomorrow afternoon, the entire Court would be gathered, and the first thing they'd demand was a vote for a new Rector to be chosen. Good, Miranda thought, stomping harder. Let someone else deal with the Court. She had enough to worry about.

When she reached the last spiral before the Tower's top,

Miranda shoved Blint out of her mind and focused on running. She passed the door to Banage's office, going instead to the wall on the other side of the landing. The stair leading to the Tower's roof was exactly where Master Banage had left it the day they'd gone to Osera at the West Wind's behest. Or maybe it was always there and Banage simply closed it off when it wasn't needed. Whatever the truth, Miranda threw herself up the stairs gladly, opening the little stone door at the top with a touch of the Rector's heavy ring.

As soon as the door was unlocked, the wind came barreling in. It blew the stone door wide open, nearly taking Miranda off her feet. Gripping the wall, she crept through the door and out onto the tiny ledge at the very top of the Spirit Court's Tower.

She huddled there a moment, looking down on Zarin as it glowed in the bright afternoon sun. The wind buffeted her, nearly prying her off the Tower as it whipped her hair in all directions. Pressing herself against the stone by the door, Miranda waited, letting her now-tangled hair act as a weather vane. The wind shifted and blustered, muttering as it blew over her, but Miranda said nothing. She simply stood, letting the wind toss her until, at last, a strong western wind blew up. The moment she felt it, Miranda cried out.

"Hail Illir, Lord of the West!"

That got the wind's attention, and the gust slacked just a little. Sensing her opportunity, Miranda continued. "I am Miranda Lyonette of the Spirit Court, and I ask an audience with the West Wind. If you serve the Lord of the West, then tell your master that I am calling in our debt. Ask him to come to the Spirit Court's Tower. I will stand here until he arrives."

Her words were gone as soon as she spoke them, snatched by the wind. But though she could not hear her own voice, Miranda felt its effect. All around her, the winds grew smooth, whispering to each other. They blew over her curiously, running over her body, over her rings.

Miranda stood tall and kept her calm. Being Eril's mistress

had taught her never to show weakness before a wind. They weren't cruel, but it was their nature to delight in upsetting things. They respected strength and stability, however, and once it was clear she wouldn't fall down, the curious winds stopped pushing her.

As the air calmed, Miranda took a deep breath and let herself relax a fraction, leaning back against the entrance to the stone stair as she waited for the West Wind to appear.

And waited.

And waited.

An hour later the afternoon sun was noticeably lower, but Miranda still hadn't moved. After so long it had become a point of pride not to give an inch. Still, time was short, and she couldn't stand here forever. After another twenty minutes had ticked by, Miranda was seriously considering making a try for the Shaper Mountain instead when she heard a sound behind her. It was a soft noise, like a bird landing on cloth. It wasn't a sound that winds made, but Miranda turned anyway and nearly fell off the Tower in surprise.

An old man stood on the Tower's peak just behind her. A white sheet was wrapped around his bony body, and a pair of spectacles sat on the bridge of his long nose. The cloth's edges fluttered madly in the high wind, but the man himself seemed unaffected, standing casually despite his tenuous perch.

"Hello, Spiritualist," he said, smiling at Miranda with the polite, slightly patronizing smile of a scholar who'd rather be doing something else. "I bring you greetings from my master."

Snapping out of her surprise at last, Miranda crossed her arms at the West Wind's human servant. "What are you doing here, Lelbon? I called Illir."

"The Lord of the West is indisposed," Lelbon said. "But I'm sure I can offer whatever assistance you require." He glanced at the city below. "Should we go inside? The winds are keeping themselves low as a courtesy, but I'd hate to strain their hospitality. Especially with such a long drop."

Miranda nodded and motioned for Lelbon to follow as she

ducked back through the little door into the Tower. Light as a falling leaf, Lelbon hopped down after her.

"This way," Miranda said, starting down the stairs. "Your master owes us a great deal. I hope you're ready to answer some questions."

"I will do everything in my power to meet your expectations," Lelbon said, climbing down after her.

Miranda scowled inwardly at his neat dodge, but her face was all politeness again as she led the West Wind's human representative into the Rector's office and shut the door behind them.

CHAPTER
6

S ara sat down on the edge of her desk, studying Eli through the trail of smoke rising from the pipe she was working between her lips.

"You're looking well," she said at last. "Better than the last time I saw you. Though, considering the last time I saw you, you were being pulled through one of the League's white portals, that's not saying much." She paused. "I don't suppose you're going to tell me what actually happened in Osera."

"Wasn't planning on it," Eli said flatly. He nodded at the poster-covered wall behind her. "I see you've been keeping up with me."

"Of course," Sara said with a smile. "I've been following your career since the very beginning. I'm very proud of you, Eliton."

"Proud?" Eli said, cocking an eyebrow. "That's not something a thief usually hears from his mother."

Sara shrugged. "I refuse to dismiss brilliance simply because it falls outside of the preset moral structure." She took a deep draw and held it before finally letting the smoke out in a puff. "Unlike some."

Eli didn't have to ask who she meant. "So," he said, "how hard is old Whitefall laughing now that the Council gets to keep my bounty?"

Sara shrugged. "I wouldn't know. I don't pay attention to money. But if you're worried about your trial, don't be. You're going to serve your debt to society under my care."

Eli sank into the chair. "Lucky me."

"Least I could do," Sara said, taking the pipe from her mouth and placing it in the ash-filled bowl beside her. "You're my son, after all."

Eli rolled his eyes. "You can lay off the caring mother act, *Sara*. Do you think for a second I believe you had me brought here for a tender reunion? You left before I was old enough to remember what you looked like."

"I didn't go anywhere," Sara said hotly. "It was Etmon who took you away."

"And you who made no effort to visit," Eli countered. "I've seen you, what? Six times in my entire life? *Counting* today?" He shook his head. "You never even remembered my birthday. If you wanted to play the doting parent card, you should have started laying the groundwork years ago. You can hardly expect me to go all misty eyed now."

"What, you're angry that I wasn't there to tuck you in at night? Tell you stories and give you kisses?" Sara scoffed. "Grow up, Eliton. What was I supposed to do? Abandon my research so I could make you eat your carrots and teach you the alphabet? Look around. You are sitting at the center of the largest spirit experiment ever attempted. I am doing amazing things here, things no one even thought to attempt of until I came along. I am reinventing what it means to be a wizard, stretching spirits in ways no one thought possible, and you're in a huff because I wasn't a good mother?" She shook her head in disgust. "*Any* woman can be a loving mother, Eliton.

571

There's no one else in the world who can do what *I* do."

"So what do you want me for, then?" Eli said. "You seem to have your hands full as it is. Why take on a criminal?"

Sara smiled. "You're a little more than a criminal, Eli Monpress. Don't forget, I saw you stop the sea itself and make an entire fleet disappear with a single motion not two days ago."

"Everyone has their time to shine," Eli said, careful to keep his expression bored.

Sara saw right through him. "All you do is shine, or so I hear," she said, smiling down at him as she swung her legs, clunking her low heels against the back of the desk. "You forget. I've been keeping tabs on you for years. I knew something was different about you almost from the beginning. Even if I hadn't had a personal interest in you, the stories of your thefts were too grandiose to ignore. Even after accounting for the sort of exponential embellishment one expects in such tales, your exploits went far above even the flair for the dramatic you inherited from your father. And then there's the matter of Miranda."

Eli frowned. "Miranda?"

"Banage's little pet is no slouch wizard," Sara said grudgingly. "She has the loyalty of several very large spirits and the personal power to back that up, not to mention her unassailable dedication to the Court. The perfect apprentice for Etmon, truly." Sara smiled brightly. "She's the child he always wanted you to be."

"How lucky for them," Eli said, though the words came out more sulky than he'd meant. Thankfully, Sara didn't seem to notice.

"When I first heard she was chasing you to Mellinor, I thought it was over," she went on. "Other than Banage himself, Miranda's the best the Court has to offer. But I was wrong. You ran circles around her, even to the point of convincing the Great Spirit Mellinor to move into her body."

"You've got that bit backward," Eli cut in. "She convinced me."

"But you gave her the idea," Sara countered. "No Spiritualist would ever think of using their own mortal shell to hold a spirit."

When he didn't deny it, Sara slid off her desk. "Almost from the moment of your birth, I knew you'd be a strong wizard," she said, walking toward him. "How could you fail to be, with your parentage? But what you do goes beyond wizardry, Eliton. I can't explain the way the world reacts to you, or how the spirits talk of you, when they'll say anything at all." She leaned over him, eyes flashing. "That sparks my curiosity."

Sara reached out and touched his chin, gently lifting his head until he was looking at her. Eli let her move him, meeting her studying look with a flat glare.

"Something happened to you, didn't it?" Sara said. "After you ran away, but before you became a thief. The signs were there from the first time I heard the name Eli Monpress, but Mellinor sealed it. You command Great Spirits like they're pebbles. I want to know how you do it."

"Easy," Eli said breezily. "I ask. It's amazing how obliging the world can be when you're not being an overbearing, pompous jerk."

"Really?" Sara said. "And did you just charm the Lord of Storms into letting you use his portals as you see fit?"

Eli shrugged. "The Lord of Storms is another matter, isn't he?"

"I don't think he is," Sara said, straightening up to reach for her pipe again. "Something's watching out for you, Eliton. Something bigger than any spirit, and that intrigues me greatly. So, I'm going to make you a deal."

"A deal?" Eli asked, incredulous.

Sara just smiled as she blew the embers in her pipe back to life. "I may not have spent much time with you, but even I remember how you always did love a deal."

"Go ahead then," he said, smiling back. "Dazzle me."

Sara gave him a droll look and took a fresh draw of smoke.

573

"I'm prepared to offer you a clean slate," she said after she'd blown the smoke at the ceiling. "Officially, you'll be hung as a thief for your crimes against the noble members of the Council. This is a huge waste of time, but in order for Alber to keep his precious bounty system flowing, I'm afraid you have to die, at least in the public eye. It's amazing how much of politics is nothing but theater." She stopped for a long sigh. "Anyway, after the farce, you'll come here and live with me as a part of my team. I'll get you a nice salary, a suite in the citadel, and anything else you desire within reason. You'll be an agent, not a prisoner, and you'll answer only to me. Otherwise, you'll have complete freedom within the Council."

"That's quite the large piece of bait," Eli said. "What will it cost me?"

"Only the truth," Sara answered. "I have dedicated my entire life to the study of spirits. What are they really? Why do humans have power over them? Why are we blind? So many questions, but no matter how hard I press, there are some things spirits won't talk about. That's where I think you can help me. I think you know the answers, or enough of them to point me in the right direction."

"And that's what you want?" Eli said. "Answers?"

"That's it," Sara said, nodding. "Help me, Eliton. Work with me. Tell me what you know and I'll make all your problems with the Council go away. Together we might finally be able to unravel the mysteries that have held wizardry back, and who knows? You are my son, you might even enjoy it."

"I doubt that," Eli said, settling back into the chair again. "I don't care much for work of any sort. But let me ask you a question, Sara. Supposing you're right, and I am so greatly in the know, what's to stop me from letting you fake my execution and just vanishing through a portal as soon as it's done?"

Sara laughed. "Because, silly boy, you're still here. If you could have escaped you would have done it ages ago."

Eli's smile grew wider. "And what if I'm bluffing?"

"Then you proved you care enough about me to bluff your way into this conversation," Sara said. "And as much as such a thing would warm my heart, I'm not so blinded by mother love to think you'd waste your time on sentiment."

Eli looked away. He didn't have anything to say to that.

Sara took a final puff and tapped out her pipe in the bowl. "Either way, the offer stands," she said, sliding the pipe into the pocket of her long jacket. "I don't care about justice or restitution or any of that backward-looking nonsense. You could be the worst murderer in the Council and it wouldn't matter a jot. All I want are answers. You don't even have to stay here if you don't want to. Tell me what I want to know and I'll let you go free tonight."

Eli almost laughed at that. "How lucky the Council is to have such a loyal servant. Would you open the Whitefall treasury for me as well?"

"If you wanted," Sara said. "Don't be mistaken, Eliton. The Council needs me far more than I need it. I have no qualms about doing whatever is needed in order to reach my goals."

"I don't doubt that for a moment," Eli said. "Thank you for the generous offer, Sara, but I'm afraid I'll have to decline for the time being. Let me think it over in my cell for a bit and I'll get back to you tomorrow."

Sara scowled. "What makes you think this conversation is done?"

"Because I'm not going to give you anything," Eli answered. "That means any further effort on your part would be a waste, and one of the few things I can remember about you is how much you deplore wasting your time."

Sara's mouth twitched. "Fair enough," she said. "Sparrow!"

The door clicked open and Eli winced as a canary-yellow coat came into view.

"Mr. Monpress and I are done for the moment," Sara said. "Could you escort him to his room?"

"My pleasure." Sparrow leaned over and snatched up the rope that bound Eli's hands. "Together again!" he said cheerily.

"Do I have to drag you this time, or will you deign to walk?"

"I'll walk, if it's all the same to you," Eli said, standing up. "It's much easier now that Mellinor's not trying to drown me."

"I'm sure," Sparrow said. He smiled at Sara and turned Eli around, marching them out of the office. The last thing Eli saw was Sara reaching for the box of blue Relays on her desk before the heavy door closed, blocking her off completely.

Sparrow gave him a little shove, and Eli picked up the pace. As they walked across the broad wooden platform, he arched his neck to get a good look at the details he'd missed on the way down. They were at the center of a large cavern below the Council Citadel. It was almost certainly not natural. He'd never seen a cave with walls this straight, but there were no chisel marks on the stone. Wizard-made, then, he realized with a low whistle. He'd thought only Shapers could craft things this large. Sara had been busy indeed.

But high as the ceiling was, Eli wasn't even standing on the floor. Sparrow was leading them down a suspended walkway that ran between a grid of strange, large, metal objects. Each one was enormous, made of black metal and cylindrical. They spread out in all directions in a grid that ran all the way to the walls.

As Sparrow led him away from Sara's office, which Eli could now see was built into an enormous version of the metal cylinders around them, he leaned sideways and peered over the walkway edge. Despite the light of the lamps burning on the railing, the black cylinders vanished into the thick shadows far sooner than they should have, leaving him nothing to guess how far down they went or where the cavern's floor lay.

He would have looked longer, but Sparrow nudged him forward, guiding Eli down one of the many suspension bridges that branched off of Sara's office.

"So," Sparrow said as they walked in the dark, their boots thumping on the suspended wood. "Why did you turn yourself in?"

"Who said I turned myself in?" Eli said. "This is quite an involuntary incarceration."

"So you just fell out of the sky?" Sparrow laughed. "Well, you picked a good time to do it. Word is that Den the Warlord was killed in that scuffle in Osera. The Council's going to need the cash on your head to pay that tab when the king comes to collect. Say, didn't the king of Osera used to be your swordsman? That must be terribly awkward."

"I don't know what you're talking about," Eli said cheerily. "My only experience with kings is stealing them."

"Of course," Sparrow said. "How could I forget? You should know that they're keeping your capture very hush-hush at the moment. The Merchant Prince has put the soldiers who caught you on lockdown, but that's only a temporary sop. The Council is a sieve for information. I wouldn't be surprised if the story wasn't all over the continent by day after tomorrow. After all, it's not every day you catch the greatest thief in the world."

"Flattery will get you everywhere," Eli said, his voice echoing strangely off the dark metal cylinders. "But what makes you think I care about how Whitefall's handling my capture?"

"Just didn't want you to blow your escape early," Sparrow said. "I know you like to make an impression. If you escape tonight, before anyone knows the Council has you, it would be a waste."

"Escape?" Eli scoffed. "Impossible. I am a model prisoner. Though I must say you're being an uncommonly thoughtful jailor."

"I'm a very thoughtful man," Sparrow said, bringing them to a stop at a gap in the railings. "Watch your step, please."

They descended down a narrow stepladder into the dark. The great tanks rose around them like iron trees, dark and foreboding. Every noise Eli made seemed muffled, and the farther he climbed, the worse it got. It was like the deeper they went, the more the silence swallowed them, until, finally, they reached the cavern floor.

577

Eli's boots hit the stone without a sound. Far overhead, the lanterns on the walkway shone like lights from a distant shore, but down here there was nothing. Only a blackness so heavy it pressed the air from Eli's lungs.

Tugging his rope, Sparrow led Eli between the tanks. He tapped each one with his fingers as they passed, like he was counting. Eli tried counting, too, but he lost it quickly. The air around them was so oppressive it was actually distracting. It took all his attention just to walk without falling. They went on like this for close to a minute before Sparrow stopped without warning and began feeling around on the floor with his foot.

When he'd found what he was looking for, Sparrow kicked his leg up before bringing his heel down on something large, metallic, and hollow. The blow landed with a muffled *clang*, and almost at once, something scraped in answer. The grind of stone on metal was shockingly loud in the dense silence as the floor in front of them slid away to reveal a darker, circular patch of blackness two feet across.

"Right," Sparrow said. "In you go."

"Down there?" Eli said, leaning over to peer into the abyss.

"'Fraid so," Sparrow said. "I suggest you get climbing, because in another five seconds I'm just going to push you and be done with it."

Eli gave him a nasty look that was sadly lost in the dark. Finding the ladder with his feet, he started to climb down. But just as his head was about to vanish through the hole, he felt Sparrow's cool hand close on his shoulder.

Eli froze, waiting. For one long second, he thought Sparrow really was going to push him, but nothing happened. Instead, Sparrow's smooth voice whispered in his ear.

"She offered me a deal, too," he said. "I took it."

"Really?" Eli said, keeping his voice calm. "How's that working for you?"

It was too dark to tell properly, but Eli got the distinct impression Sparrow was baring his teeth. "I just spent two weeks chasing a girl, a dog, and a bear-faced man through howling wilderness. Before that, I spent nearly as long trying to lay a trap for you in a city full of savages. I almost died both times. This was nothing out of the ordinary. How do you think it's working?"

"Right," Eli said. "I get it. You don't like it here. But why are you telling me? I have absolutely no intention of taking up Sara's offer."

"Neither did I," Sparrow said, patting him on the shoulder. "Keep that in mind, Mr. Monpress."

Sparrow's grip vanished after that, and Eli resumed his descent. It was so dark he couldn't see an inch in front of his face. He navigated by touch alone, climbing the rough metal bars down, down, down, until, after thirty rungs, his feet hit stone.

The sound of his boots hitting bottom must have been the signal Sparrow was waiting for, because as soon as he stepped down, Eli heard the metal door fall shut.

"See you tomorrow for breakfast." Sparrow's voice was muffled as he stomped on the metal again, locking it in place. "Meanwhile, enjoy the company."

"Company?" Eli shouted. He held his breath, but no answer came. Either Sparrow was waiting to see what he would do or he'd left too quietly for Eli to hear. Both were likely. Gritting his teeth, Eli turned away from the known enemy to face the unknown.

What kind of company had Sara arranged for him? Probably something to keep him too busy to escape, pit of snakes or something of that sort. Well, Eli smirked, he'd dealt with pits of snakes before. He just needed to—

A soft scrape cut his thoughts off cold. The sound was very close, maybe a foot away. Eli dropped to a crouch without thinking, his hands going for Karon's burn before he remembered it wasn't there. Dropping his arms with a silent curse, Eli put his back to the wall. He was staring into the inky black, ears straining as he considered his very limited options, when a light flared.

He blinked at the sudden brightness, covering his eyes. When he could see again, he dropped his arms and risked a glance to see who, or what, had caused the light.

Etmon Banage was sitting on the floor across from him, a candle flame flickering in the air above his palm. "Eliton?" he said softly, blue eyes going wide.

Eli cursed again, loudly this time. Why couldn't it have been snakes? As the Rector Spiritualis started to get up, Eli flopped back against the metal rungs and wondered what he'd done to deserve his horrible, horrible luck.

After dropping the thief into the second half of this impromptu family reunion, Sparrow turned to more pressing matters. He jogged back to Sara's office at the chamber's heart, dropping his speed to nothing the second it was in sight. His footsteps became like cat feet, and even his breathing slowed to a whisper. Utterly silent, Sparrow removed his garish coat and hung it on the railing, leaving him in only a plain white shirt and brown trousers.

Without his coat to announce his presence, none of the dense clusters of technicians so much as glanced at him as he let himself into the lower level of Sara's primary tank. Usually, when he entered the more delicate areas of Sara's operations, the wizards made a great show of snubbing him. They hated that a spirit-deaf criminal had better access to Sara, greatest wizard of the age, than they did. Now his presence didn't even draw a sideways look, not even when he walked directly behind them. Their obliviousness was almost enough to make Sparrow smile. His curse was the joy of his life, sometimes.

Unseen and unnoticed, he walked right down the middle of the room, passing workbenches filled with glass decanting pipes and trays of empty crystal spheres. Everything here was spotlessly clean, from the polished metal walls and floor to the white coats and gloves of the wizards to the sanded tables themselves. Sara's wizards worked in pairs; one held a glass pipette filled with a tiny amount of water so blue it almost seemed to glow. The other held an empty glass ball just below the pipette's sharp mouth, catching the blue water as it dripped. As each drop fell, the wizards whispered together.

"Quiet, quiet, quiet."

The words sounded more like droning than human speech, but the wizards always looked so intense while they said it that Sparrow suspected there must be a great deal of mental effort involved. That seemed to be the case with most wizardry, actually. Yet another reason to be glad he didn't have to worry about any of that nonsense.

He wound through the gauntlet of droning wizards to the heavy, padded door at the room's far end. Sparrow pulled the handle gently, opening the heavy contraption just enough to slip through. The door didn't make a sound as it swung, but Sparrow knew better than to congratulate himself on this. This door was Sara's, and it wouldn't have made a sound if he'd kicked it off its hinges. Any noise at all was anathema for the door to the Quieting Room. Beyond the silent door there was nothing but darkness and a set of padded stairs leading down. Sparrow followed them, his soft boots falling as silently as everything else.

From the doorway, the Quieting Room looked little bigger than a closet, but it went down forever, digging deep below the cavern's floor into the heart of the black granite outcropping that supported the citadel above. It was also dark, nearly as dark as the space between the tanks with the same stiflingly, oppressive feel. Sparrow suspected the two were related, but he'd never gotten curious enough to risk the lecture Sara would give him if he asked. Instead, he used the quiet to his advantage, creeping down through the dark until the stair opened up into a second, smaller cavern about the size of a large bedroom.

Unlike the cavern above, which was irregular, this cave was perfectly round, ringed in on all sides by smoothly cut stone. Its ceiling was smooth, too, save for the hole that let in the spiral stair, but this cave had no floor. Instead, a pool of water filled the room to its edges, the liquid black in the dark, sinking down farther than Sparrow could see.

The spiral stair stopped just above the water, and at its base was a small, suspended platform held inches above the pool's surface by the stair's thick, central support. Below the platform, the water's surface was still as glass. Stiller than anything in nature had a right to be, except for one part.

Sara was kneeling at the platform's edge with her hands hovering just above the water's surface. Beneath them, the water was bubbling, and the commotion showed off its true color, a deep, deep blue. Such a motion should have sent ripples through the entire pool, but the rest of the glassy water didn't so much as wobble as Sara lifted her hands, bringing a small ball of water up with her. She cupped the water in her hands, moving it gently as a mother with a new baby to the hinge-lidded silver bucket sitting on the platform beside her.

She lowered her hands into the bucket's wide mouth, letting the blue water fall before snatching her fingers back and closing the bucket's lid as fast as she could. She snapped the latch shut and reached for a metal wire that hung from the stairs above. Threading the wire through the hooks on the bucket's sides, Sara began to murmur commands. The wire obeyed, curling itself around the bucket before it began to rise into the dark, the thin wire curling in on itself to prevent any jostle from touching its precious cargo.

Sara watched the bucket rise until it vanished, and then she turned on her heel, fixing her glare on Sparrow.

He flashed her his best smile and sat down on the stairs.

Sara's glare intensified, but she didn't speak. Instead, she walked to the edge of the platform and reached out to pull a lever set into the stone wall. At once, the cavern's silence was broken by the hushed scrape of metal as a protective sheet emerged from the walls. The metal slid into position like a thrusting knife, sliding under the platform to cover the pool with a protective shield. Only when the metal cap was safely in place and the water completely separated from the air above did Sara turn to face her servant.

"The Quieting Room is not a place to play, Sparrow," she said, her voice cutting. "Are you even aware of how much damage you could cause?"

"I'm very well aware," Sparrow said, resting his elbows on the stair above him. "You tell me every time. Of course, if you would stop hiding down here every time you got angry, I wouldn't have to come after you."

"I'm not angry," Sara said, grabbing the ledger from its hook on the wall to record the water she'd just sent up. "Just disappointed."

Sparrow shrugged. "Why? It wasn't like you were expecting him to come running into your loving arms."

"No, but I had hoped he would show a *hint* of interest," Sara said, pencil scratching furiously. "I'd hoped that *my son* would have enough natural, inborn curiosity to at least listen with grace before saying no. Even the Lyonette girl showed some enthusiasm about learning the secrets of the world before turning me down. If he can't exhibit more interest about magic's inner workings than a closed-minded, hide-bound Spiritualist, I fear there's no hope for him at all."

"Maybe it's not as bad as you think," Sparrow said. "There is always the chance Mr. Monpress is sentimental enough to let his abandonment issues stand in the way of his rightfully inherited curiosity."

"Powers forbid," Sara said, slapping the ledger back into place. "If I have to play mommy, this is going to be a very long week."

"If that's how you feel, why did you put them in the same cell?" Sparrow said. "Banage is only going to make things worse, you know. And then there's the part where you're leaving two of the most powerful wizards in the world alone together." He shook his head with a *tsk*. "Sounds like a recipe for disaster on all fronts."

"It was the best of a few bad options," Sara said defensively. "I have only one cell capable of holding a wizard of Eliton or Etmon's power."

"And only one cell that Alber doesn't know about," Sparrow added. "Really, Sara, it was very unmotherly of you to lie to the boy like that, acting like Whitefall was already on board with your plan to fake an execution and hire the world's most notorious thief."

"It was necessary," Sara said with a shrug. "I didn't have time to get Alber's permission. I'll bring him around later, after I've got Eliton well in hand. Did you drop the hints like I told you?"

"I did," Sparrow said. "He is fully informed that there will be no audience for his escape until at least tomorrow. But do you really think that will be enough to keep him in? Not to cast doubt on your skill as a jailor, but Eli Monpress has a reputation for being difficult to contain."

"I'm well aware of my son's prowess," Sara said proudly. "Just as I am equally aware of his near pathological need for attention. Monpress will stay put until he's sure his escape will draw the proper level of attention, and by that point I'll have brought him around."

"And what of Whitefall?" Sparrow asked.

Sara shrugged. "I've taken care of the witness. Alber can live in ignorance a little longer."

Sparrow shook his head. "You can lock up soldiers all you like. Whitefall *always* finds out. The man is a hunting hawk when it comes to secrets in his castle, and he is not going to be happy you kept this from him."

"What do I care about Alber's happiness?" Sara said. "He can rage all day, but in the end, the truth is that he needs the Relay, which means he needs me, and *I* need Eliton. And it's not like this secret is hurting him. I only need to keep Monpress's capture quiet for a day, two at most, just enough for me to gather the proper leverage to make him accept my ridiculously generous offer."

"I don't know if any leverage will be enough," Sparrow said. "He loathes you quiet openly."

Sara shrugged. "He'll come around. Eliton's a thief at heart, and all thieves have their price. Fortunately, I have the feeling my leverage is about to improve dramatically. A little birdie told me that the Lyonette girl has been using her newfound power as Rector to investigate certain very large spirits."

Sparrow nodded as expected, face neutral, but alarm bells were sounding in his mind. Knowing Sara, she'd probably gotten the information from an *actual* bird, and he wasn't about to go chasing bird tips again. Never trust an animal with a brain the size of a walnut to make an accurate assessment.

"Word is that she's calling down the West Wind itself," Sara continued. "Considering the Spirit Court's position—the Rector imprisoned for treason, its membership split, and a Spiritualist not three years out of her apprenticeship holding the reins— you'd think the girl would be focused on Court matters, not poking after spirits who've been stable for hundreds, maybe thousands, of years. I want to know what emergency has upset her priorities."

"Which means you want me to find out," Sparrow finished.

"What else do I keep you for?" Sara said with a shrug.

"How is this going to help with the Monpress problem?"

"Eliton's proven on several occasions he has a soft spot for spirits, and the Spiritualist girl," Sara said. "I'm sure you'll find something we can use. Now, I suspect the girl's behavior has something to do with the events in Osera and the disappearance of her sea spirit, but I can't be sure. The Relay point I had you plant on her isn't responding anymore, so I'm afraid we have to do things the hard way. Go find out as much as you can about what's going on. I'll expect a full report tomorrow morning."

Sparrow could feel his body tightening with long-checked anger. "And it didn't occur to you that, after months on the road, followed by a war in Osera, I might not be up for sneaking around the Spirit Court?"

"It did," Sara answered, leaning over to glance at the water record again. "But I don't much care. I ask no more of you than I ask of myself."

Sparrow crossed his arms over his chest. "And what if the standard you set for yourself is inhuman?"

"Then I would be dead," Sara said. "Which, as you can see, I'm not. Now stop complaining, and don't even think of shirking. Remember"—she reached into her coat—"I can always find you."

As she spoke, she drew a small, round object out of her inside pocket, and Sparrow's chest began to constrict. Between Sara's fingers was a Relay point. It looked like all her others, a small glass sphere on a chain, but where the other points were blue, this one was a deep, deep crimson. Her fingers tightened on the glass as he watched, and suddenly it felt like someone had dropped a weight on his lungs. The pain sent spots dancing across his eyes, and it was all Sparrow could do to keep from doubling over.

"Really, Sara," he said, fighting to keep the effort out of his voice. "A threat? We've been together almost ten years now. I thought we were past all that."

"So did I," she said, rolling the red orb between her fingers. "But then you started complaining again. I ask very little, Sparrow. Just that you do your job. If that proves too difficult, I can always give you back to Alber. Now that the war's done, he's running short on favors. I'm sure he'd love to earn some back by offering his family another chance at the head of the only man to kill a Whitefall and live."

"I'm very aware what a treasure my head is," Sparrow said, his voice growing thin as he fought the pain. "No need to twist quite so hard, Sara dear."

"Apparently, I need to twist harder," Sara said. "You're still here."

Sparrow stood with effort. "Just on my way out."

Sara nodded and finally slid the orb back into her pocket. Sparrow steeled his face against the rush of relief as the pressure on his chest vanished, determined not to give her the satisfaction of seeing him wince. Instead, he smiled as wide as ever and started up the stairs, slipping out the door as quietly as he'd entered.

The wizards outside took no more notice of him as he left than they had when he'd come in, but Sparrow took no joy in their ignorance this time. His mind was wholly focused on the lingering pain in his chest. It wouldn't be too much longer, he told himself as the pain finally began to fade. He'd been patient for a long, long time now, playing his role, waiting for his opening. Now, at last, he was almost there. Banage had always been Sara's weakness, the chink in her cold, logical armor. Her son was even worse, and now they were both here, together.

Considering how edgy Sara became at their mere presence, going so far as to use her control over him for the first time in years for a relatively minor disobedience, it wouldn't be long before something pushed her out of her usual caution. Soon, very soon, one of the Banages would do something to make Sara angry enough to forget what she should never forget, and when that happened, Sparrow would be there.

By the time he made it back to where he'd left his jacket, Sparrow was smiling again. He pulled on the glaring yellow coat and yanked the collar up rakishly before shoving his hands into the magenta-lined pockets. Then, whistling, he started down the suspended walkway.

With every step, the plan in his mind grew clearer, simpler, the pieces clicking into place. By the time he reached the turnoff that led to the service door, his usual exit when Sara sent him to spy on the Spirit Court, everything was set, and he passed the turning without so much as a glance. Instead, he headed up the stairs toward the citadel proper.

When the time came, Sara wouldn't have a chance to use her control, Sparrow thought as he reached the Citadel's main floor. When he was done, Sara wouldn't know what hit her. That thought made him grin until his face ached, drawing suspicious glances from the noble hangers-on that clogged the Council hallways. Sparrow happily ignored them, picking up his pace as he started up the stairs leading to the tallest of the Citadel's seven towers, his whistling growing louder and more cheerful with every step.

The Lady's summons came as they always had, quickly and without warning. And, as he had done since the beginning of memory, the Lord of Storms answered immediately, leaving Alric midsentence to open a door into her white world.

Her back was to him when he entered. She was standing by her orb, bent over the curve of the sky like a woman at her spinning wheel. Her white hands were deep inside, digging through the bedrock and magma that made up the foundation of the miniature world. He could see her fingers pushing against the veil as they moved, and he wondered, briefly, if the spirits felt her passing through them. He didn't think so; otherwise the bedrock would be shaking the world to pieces in its rush to bow. Still, it was a strange sight, the Shepherdess up to her elbows in the world she'd been ignoring for so long.

If Alric were here, he'd probably be curious. He might even ask a question. The Lord of Storms knew his deputy was bold enough for it. But Alric was not here, and the Lord of Storms did not bother with questions. So long as the Lady's actions didn't interfere with his hunting, he didn't much care what she did.

She dug for sometime before going stiff, and then her hands withdrew. The Lord of Storms stood at attention, watching with growing impatience as the Lady pulled something from the sphere. From where he stood, it looked like a root. Like a root, it was long and spindly with branches curling off in all directions, but no root was ever that beautiful, golden color. The thing in the Lady's hand shone like a river of sunlight, hanging on her fingers with a weight far greater than the Lord of Storms would have expected given its size. A gold vein, he realized at last. An enormous one.

He mulled this over as the Lady lifted the vein to her lips, whispering sounds sweet as pure water across its beautiful surface. As the gold vein shook in delight, the Lady closed her hands, pressing the vein into the skin of her fingers. No, not her fingers. The Lady was holding something.

The Lord of Storms scowled. It looked almost like a soap bubble, a translucent, shimmering sphere no larger than the top joint of the Lady's thumb. She pushed the gold vein into it as he watched. The Lord of Storms wouldn't have thought the thing would fit into such a small, delicate space, but the vein entered willingly, singing to the Lady all the while in a heavy, ringing voice.

When the last golden gleam had vanished, the Lady lowered her hands and turned to face him. She looked tired, he thought, her white eyes nearly gray with fatigue. He scowled. It was dangerous for the Lady to tire herself. Dangerous for her and very dangerous for everyone else. Her temper was deadly when she was tired. Even so, her voice was surprisingly sweet when she spoke to him at last.

I have a task for you.

"I should hope so," he said, resting his hand on the hilt of his sword. "Your League held together well in my absence. We are ready to act."

What do I care of the League? The Lady's voice turned scornful. *Did I not just say this was a task for you?*

The Lord of Storms stiffened. "What would my Lady have of me?"

A hunt, the Shepherdess said, her white lips turning up in a slow smile. *One you've been after for a long time now.* She reached out for her orb, laying her free hand, the one that wasn't still cradling the tiny pearl, on the vault of the sky. *The time has come to rid the world of the demon's protégé.*

The rush of anticipation left him shaking. "You would let me hunt the Daughter of the Dead Mountain?"

I demand it, the Lady said. *You've been very loyal, my sword. Even in your rebellion, everything you've done has*

589

been for me. As a reward, I give you leave to track down this threat at last. She turned, gazing at the world below her fingers. *I would have my sphere clean of the demon's filth before my brother returns.*

The Lord of Storms blinked. The Hunter, of course. The days ran together when he was a storm even more than they did when he was a man. In the confusion, he'd forgotten that the Hunter's day of rest was close at hand. Unlike her other brother, the Weaver, whom she despised, the Shepherdess honored the Hunter. It made sense that he should be the one to finally make her see what the Lord of Storms had been saying all along.

But even if she hadn't come to her senses, the end would have been the same. Unlike his siblings, the Hunter was a warrior. He would never abide a demon at his back. He would slay the Daughter as soon as he entered the sphere, robbing the Lord of Storms of his rightful prey. But that crisis was averted. Finally, the Lord of Storms would hunt as he had been created to hunt.

"All shall be as you say, Lady," he said, his deep voice rumbling with pleasure. "I will destroy anything that threatens your sphere."

The Lady didn't answer immediately. Instead, she turned away from her sphere and walked to him, reaching up to cup his face in her burning hand. *Do it quickly, my Lord of Storms*, she whispered, her fingers tightening on his face. *Strike down the demon's daughter and bring me her seed. Bring it to me. Do you understand? It must be large and powerful by now, far too great for your vault. Bring it here and I shall take care of it myself.*

The Lord of Storms strained against her burning touch. He wanted nothing more than to take her permission and run, throwing everything into the hunt. But he'd been too long in the company of Alric's prudence, and he knew the question he must ask just as surely as he knew how much he would regret the asking.

"What of the thief? He still favors the demon's company. What would you have me do if he gets in the way again?"

Benehime's fingers froze against him, and the Lord of Storms braced for her inevitable anger. But, though her eyes narrowed, she didn't strike him or scream. Instead, she stepped back, regarding him with a fury so cold it froze the air.

The thief is nothing, she said, her voice like ice in his ear. *Do what must be done. Get the seed, and do not return here or bother me again until you have it.*

The Lord of Storms' face split into an enormous grin of pure, mad joy. So simple, so beautiful, just as it had been at the beginning. At last, after so long, his Lady was back. "As you say," he rumbled. "So it is done."

The Lady nodded and turned away, walking back to her orb with small, tight steps, her shoulders set at a furious, bitter angle as she leaned over the sky again. The Lord of Storms barely noticed that she was upset. Already, he was lost in the hunt. With one swipe, he tore his way out of the Lady's white world, reappearing in his Deputy Commander's office with a crack of thunder.

To his credit, Alric didn't jump. He simply turned and looked up. "Well?"

"We hunt!" the Lord of Storms roared, marching to the window. He flung it open, cracking the glass with his force, and leaned into the wind. Outside, those League members not on assignment were gathered in the yard for practice. They looked up as one at the sound of breaking glass and saluted when they saw it was the Lord of Storms. He grinned back, feral as a wolf.

"Drop everything and get to the hall," he bellowed. "The League hunts the Daughter of the Dead Mountain!"

A shout went up, but the Lord of Storms had already ducked back inside. Behind him, Alric was on his feet, buckling what was left of his golden sword to his hip. "A good meeting, I assume?"

"The best we could have hoped for," the Lord of Storms

said, crossing the room in two long strides. "Come, we've work at last."

Alric nodded and followed the Lord of Storms into the corridor to join the stream of League men already flowing toward the great hall.

CHAPTER
7

Miranda had been avoiding Banage's office since she'd come back to Zarin. Going in now was even harder than she'd expected, but there was nowhere else she could talk to the West Wind's human representative the way she needed to, as the Rector of the Spirit Court. The room looked exactly as it had the morning they'd left for Osera. As she held the door for Lelbon, she almost expected to see Master Banage sitting at his desk like always. But the desk was empty, and, after a short hesitation, Miranda walked over and slid behind it, sinking into the Rector's high chair with as small a grimace as she could manage. Lelbon took the seat in front of the desk, the one that was usually hers.

"You've been promoted since last we spoke, I see."

"Considering the last time we spoke I was exiled from the Court, that's not saying much," Miranda said, straightening up in a vain attempt to keep from being overshadowed by the enormous desk. "But it's been made clear to me that I won't be here long, so I'll just get right to the point. I have reason to believe we're facing a crisis the likes of which has never been seen in the Court's existence. How much has your master told you of the Shepherdess and her stars?"

Lelbon tilted his head. "My master would never tell me anything the Lady did not wish humans to know," he said cautiously. "However, what I deduce on my own is outside of his control. Considering I've spent the last twenty years of my life in service to the winds, most of them are comfortable enough to forget I'm there half the time. As a result, I've heard enough to draw my own conclusions."

"Good," Miranda said. "Then you know that stars are at the very top of the spirit world. Ancient spirits, some even older than the Shepherdess herself, chosen by the Lady to guide those spirits beneath them."

"And fixed with her mark of authority," Lelbon added. He smiled when he saw Miranda's brows furrow. "That's the part of the story the spirits themselves focus on. Benehime's mark is what makes the stars so powerful, even outside of their areas of control. That mark allows them to act in the Lady's name. For a spirit, disobeying a star is the same as disobeying the Shepherdess herself."

Miranda nodded. She hadn't heard it phrased quite that way before, but considering her own spirits' reactions to the stars they'd met, it made sense. "Well," she said, "if you understand all that, then you'll understand the crisis we're facing. I have reason to believe that stars are disappearing."

She paused, waiting for his reaction, but Lelbon just nodded. "Go on."

"Do you need more?" Miranda said, pulling herself forward until the edge of the desk cut into her stomach. "The largest spirits in the world are vanishing without a trace and leaving the spirits who depend on them in a state of panic. This isn't some minor emergency."

"Have any of your spirits been affected?" Lelbon said.

"Not yet, but that's hardly the point," Miranda said. "The Spirit Court stands for *all* spirits, not just the ones who serve us. If stars are vanishing, it's a problem for all the spirits below them, and we need to stop it." She held up her hand, counting off the questions on her fingers. "We need to know why they're disappearing, where to, how many are already gone, and how we can stop this. That's why I need Illir's help. He may not

593

be a star himself, but he's certainly powerful enough to know what's going on."

"And what will you do with that knowledge?" Lelbon asked.

"I'm going to use it to mobilize the Court," Miranda answered. "Even if we can't stop the stars from vanishing, we might be able to help prevent the panic. But I need to know what's going on so I can explain it well enough to get the Tower Keepers moving; otherwise idiots like Blint are going to claim I'm making this up as an excuse to hang on to power."

Lelbon raised his eyebrows. "Blint?"

"One of the sort of Spiritualist who'd sit around arguing over the Rectorship while the world crumbled under his feet," Miranda said bitterly, leaning over the table at him. "I need *answers*, Lelbon. I swore an oath to protect the spirits, and I will not be forsworn."

Lelbon leaned back with a long sigh. He'd watched her carefully while she was speaking. Now he looked down at his hands resting on the folded cloth of his robe.

"Your dedication is a credit to your organization," he said. "But I'm worried you're missing an important point." He glanced up at her. "Stars are beloved by the Shepherdess. They are her lieutenants, overseeing their segments of her flock. If you're right, and they are disappearing without explanation, would it not be logical to assume that she had some hand in their disappearance?"

Miranda set her jaw stubbornly. "My wind spirit mentioned something to that effect," she said. "But I thought the Shepherdess's purpose was to care for the spirits? Why would she do something that throws them into such chaos? It doesn't make sense."

"It doesn't," Lelbon said matter-of-factly. "But who else could make stars vanish? They are enormous spirits with an echo of the Lady's own authority, unassailable by any save a demon as large as that which waits under the mountain. So, either the Master of the Dead Mountain has made his escape at last, in which case I'm sure we'd already know, or the Shepherdess is stealing her own stars."

"But"—Miranda was openly gaping now—"*why?* The Deep Current was vital to the function of the oceans. If my Mellinor hadn't taken it over, the sea would be falling stagnant even as we speak. And what about the tree at the heart of the Allva? Its loss has thrown the entire forest into a panic. If a demon did half so much, the whole League would be down there. How could the Shepherdess condone such actions? What end could possibly justify such painful means?"

"I cannot presume to tell you the Shepherdess's mind," Lelbon said. "One thing, however, is deadly certain. The Shepherdess's attention is on us, now more than ever. All spirits, especially those large enough to know the consequences of her wrath, are minding her rules to the letter. To do otherwise under such scrutiny would be suicidal folly."

Miranda stiffened. "Now I understand why you're here and not Illir himself," she said. "The Shaper Mountain may have let the cat out of the bag, but the West Wind can't very well come and talk to a human about the Shepherdess's affairs, can he?"

Lelbon smiled delicately. "My master did not share his reasoning with me, but I think that is a safe assumption."

"And what am I supposed to do?" Miranda shouted. "Let it go? Sit back and watch while the Shepherdess yanks her stars out and leaves the world helpless and panicked?"

"Could you do that?" Lelbon said.

Miranda glared daggers at the old man. "Of course not."

"Then I suggest you find another way," Lelbon said. "One that works around the Shepherdess, rather than against her."

Miranda sat back with a disgusted harrumph. "I'm open to suggestions."

"Well," Lelbon said, "the first step is to figure out exactly what you want to do."

"Help the spirits," Miranda said.

Lelbon sighed. "A bit more specificity would be helpful, Miss Lyonette."

595

Miranda rolled her eyes. "Fine. Our problem is that stars are disappearing. When they disappear, they disrupt the world and leave their spirits in chaos. So, the first thing I'd want to do is stop any more stars from vanishing."

Lelbon shook his head. "If the Lady's the one calling them back, stopping the disappearances isn't within the realm of our influence. What's next?"

Miranda frowned. "If we can't stop stars from vanishing, then we'll need to respond to the disappearances themselves. The panicking forest, for example. If I had a team down there, we could ease the strain. Of course, to do that we'd need a way to know which stars have vanished and where so we could get there before the panic could do lasting harm."

"You'd have to move very fast for that," Lelbon said quietly.

"I know, I know." Miranda ran her hands through her hair. "But I don't know what else to do! I can't just stop trying."

"A noble sentiment," Lelbon said. "But let us think practically for a moment. The stars are scattered all across the world. Many are in places people never go, like the bottom of the sea or high in the mountains. Even if you knew exactly where and when a star disappeared, could you get there in time to do any good? And even if you could, many stars' spirits are spread out all over the world. Say the star of fish vanished, what would you do? Send your Court to comfort every mackerel who was tearing out his gills in terror because he thinks the world is ending?"

"Are you trying to dissuade me from my duty?" Miranda cried, clenching her fingers so hard her rings dug into her skin.

"I am trying to be reasonable," Lelbon said. "Has it never occurred to you, Miss Lyonette, that perhaps this time you are in over your head? That the scope of these problems is simply beyond what the Spirit Court can handle, and that by attempting to blindly follow the right path, you risk doing more harm than good? It is true, the spirits suffer when stars vanish, but they won't suffer forever. Even the greatest panic fades in time."

He watched her reaction, and when her glare refused to soften, Lelbon pressed a hand to his chest with a deep sigh. "Let me tell you a story," he said. "Long ago, before I entered the West Wind's service, I was a scholar of history for the Immortal Empress."

Miranda jerked back. "*You* worked for the Immortal Empress?"

"In as much as any junior official can be said to work for an immortal being," Lelbon responded with a dry smile. "But that's neither here nor there. You are very young, Miss Lyonette. I don't say this to downplay your competence, only to point out that your worldview, like most young people's, tends to center on the present. This isn't to imply that the current situation isn't bad, possibly even disastrous, but when you look at the entire sweep of history, you see that bad things happen all the time. Is it not wise, then, to consider what is best in the long run, even if that goes against your feelings in the short term?"

Miranda closed her eyes. "It's been a very long few days, Mr. Lelbon. I'd appreciate it if you got to the point."

"My *point*," Lelbon said, leaning forward, "is that, as much as you want to help spirits, the Court is simply not equipped to handle this scale of disaster. Say you were to hop on your hound this instant; it would take you, what, four days to reach the Allva rain forest?"

"Three," Miranda said flatly.

"Three days, then," Lelbon said. "Now, it's my understanding you're one of the faster Spiritualists, but let's assume for the sake of argument that everyone in the Court could move at your speed if pressed. The Allva is enormous, hundreds of miles of dense trees spread over three river basins that eventually braid together into the Ell, the mother river. If the entire forest is in a panic as you say, it would take thousands of wizards to cover that much ground. Even if you rallied every Spiritualist to your cause, you still wouldn't have the manpower to handle a single lost star, assuming you could even get your people there fast enough to do any good for a panic that is already in full swing."

Miranda clenched her teeth. "So I should just ignore my oaths and turn away?"

"You are the Rector Spiritualis," Lelbon said, leaning back in his chair. "I would never presume to tell you how to run your Court. I can only suggest that you consider the larger picture. Even I know the Spirit Court is fractured. Noble as your intentions may be, *think*. Is it worth pushing an already battered Court past its limits to offer aid that will be too late and too little to do any good?"

Miranda closed her eyes and buried her head in her hands. "I can't do nothing," she whispered through her fingers.

"The Spirit Court is the single greatest human organization for the good of spirits that has ever existed," Lelbon said. "I would hardly count its rebuilding as doing nothing."

"You don't understand," Miranda said, pushing her head up. "The only reason I'm Rector is because Banage made me. I'm not the one who will rebuild the Spirit Court. The Conclave will reunite us, probably under Blint, who'll waste no time turning us into an arm of the Council. That's what we are now, just more of Whitefall's cronies. I knew the Court was changing when they kicked me out for aiding a Great Spirit, but I thought it was just Hern's influence. Now, I'm not so sure."

"If that's how you feel, why continue as Rector?" Lelbon said. "Why not give it to whoever wants it and strike out on your own?"

"Because I can't do anything on my own," Miranda said. "That's why I need proof. My only hope at this point is to gather enough information about what's happening with the stars so that when I present it at the Conclave, the Court will realize what it has to do, no matter who's leading it. They might have gotten caught up in the power of the Council, but every Spiritualist takes the same oaths to protect the Spirit World from harm, even Blint. We may not be able to fix everything, but we can still try. Even if we can protect only a few, that's better than nothing, and maybe in the process of trying we'll remember what the Spirit Court's really about: spirits, not humans."

Lelbon stared at her. "And do you think it'll work?"

"It better," Miranda said, rubbing her tired eyes. "I'm all out of cards, otherwise."

"I applaud the effort, in any case," Lelbon said. "What is the minimum you need to convince your Court?"

Miranda took a deep breath. "I can start with proof that stars are vanishing, and that it's a problem, but that's just the beginning. To really show that this is a true emergency, I have to show the scope of what we're dealing with. I'll need to know how many stars there are, where they are, and how many are missing, all before tomorrow. You've already made it clear that Illir can't give me this information. If you can't tell me, either, then please forgive my rudeness, but I don't have any more time to chat."

"A fair assessment," Lelbon said. "I'm afraid I cannot give you the information you seek, Rector Lyonette. At this point, I think you can name more stars than I."

Miranda fell back in her chair. She'd been so sure that would work, that the old windbag would drop the act and just tell her if she pressed directly. But before she could fall completely into despair, she realized Lelbon was still talking.

"What?"

"I said there are other ways to find what you're looking for," Lelbon repeated. "Ways that are beneath the Shepherdess's notice."

Miranda wanted to throw up her hands. "Why didn't you just say that earlier?"

"You're not the only one with a duty to fulfill," Lelbon said. "I was sent to give you my advice and experience as well as to answer my master's debt. Whether you use them, however, is up to you."

Miranda sighed. "Right. So what's the trick, then?"

"You'll see," he said, standing up. "Shall we be off? You did say you had no time to spare."

Miranda blinked at the sudden change. "Where are we going?"

"Not far," Lelbon said. "You will need a nondescript conveyance and some money."

"Money?" Miranda froze halfway out of her chair. "How much money?"

"A great deal, I'd imagine," Lelbon said. "Brokers aren't known for giving discounts."

"You're taking me to see a broker?" Miranda was almost shouting now. She couldn't help it; this was too absurd even for her. "Brokers are for finding stolen goods and spreading gossip. How is a *broker* going to know about stars?"

"Miss Lyonette," Lelbon said with a long sigh, "if I didn't think this was worth your time, I wouldn't have suggested it. Now, are you coming, or should I leave?"

Miranda took a deep, calming breath. "Let me ask Krigel how much we have on hand. If you want to wait downstairs, I'll meet you there."

"Very well," Lelbon said. "I'd bring a hundred gold standards at least. More, if you can manage it. This isn't an answer they're going to have on hand, after all."

"Right," Miranda grumbled. She walked her guest to the top of the stairs. Once she was out of sight, she walked back into the Rector's office and began yanking as hard as she could on the rope pull that rang down to Krigel's desk.

Thirty minutes later, Miranda and Lelbon were in a hired carriage bumping down a steep, uneven backstreet toward the river. Miranda sat sideways on the bench, clutching a large, leather satchel in a white-knuckled grip. Across from her, Lelbon watched with an amused expression. Miranda scowled back and clutched her satchel tighter, wincing at the jingle of coins every time the carriage hit a pothole.

Two hundred and fifty gold standards was all Krigel had

been able to pull together on such short notice. Even so, it was way more money than Miranda had ever personally carried, and she was absolutely certain something horrible was going to happen. Not that forking it over to a broker wasn't horrible enough. In fact, the more she thought about it, the more she felt this was a bad idea.

The carriage rocked violently and then creaked to a halt. Miranda peeked out the window. They'd stopped in front of what looked like an abandoned shop. The old building was half stone, half timber, both black with tar and torch smoke, and the whole structure seemed to be leaning backward into the river behind it. She was about to ask why they'd stopped when Lelbon began climbing out of the coach. Miranda's eyes flicked to the clusters of barge workers and drunks loitering on the docks down the road, and her frown inched lower. She *knew* she should have brought Gin.

But done was done, so she hefted the strap of the heavy money sack onto her shoulder and followed Lelbon out of the carriage and up the rickety steps to the building's warped door. Lelbon knocked once and stood back. The door opened a few moments later, and Miranda found herself staring at a short, broad woman in a leather vest and workman's trousers. She jumped when she saw them, which Miranda considered a natural reaction to opening your door to find a Spiritualist and an old man wearing a bedsheet, but then, to Miranda's surprise, the woman lowered her eyes respectfully.

"Welcome, Voice of the Wind."

Lelbon thanked her and stepped inside. Miranda followed hesitantly, clutching her bag as the woman bolted the door behind them. Inside was a narrow waiting room with benches on either side of the door and a potbellied stove in the corner. The tiny space was further crowded by a large desk, which the woman slid herself behind before turning to Lelbon and Miranda.

"What can we do for you, sir?" she said, opening a large, ink-stained ledger. "Have you come to check the accounts?"

601

"Not today, Emma," Lelbon said. "I've brought you a customer."

He gave Miranda a little push, sending her stumbling up to the desk. She recovered quickly, pulling herself up to her full height and fixing the woman with her best no-nonsense look. "I understand you answer questions."

"That we do," the woman said, giving Miranda a shrewd once-over that was worlds apart from the awed obedience she paid Lelbon. "The price depends on what you want to know. Simple questions are cheap, difficult ones less so."

"And what if you can't answer the question?" Miranda said.

The woman turned up her nose with a sniff. "We're all licensed brokers here with a century of experience between us. Our price is dear, but our service is the best you can receive. There's no question in the world we can't answer."

"I meant no offense," Miranda said. "I've never used a broker before."

The woman gave her a "well that's obvious" glare and flipped the ledger around so it was facing Miranda. "Write your question here," she said, pointing at the top of the page. "After that, we'll agree on a price, and then we'll find your answer."

"What if I have more than one question?" Miranda said, taking a metal quill from the cup at the woman's elbow and dipping it in the large inkpot.

The woman tapped the empty lines with her fingernail. "Write them all down, one per line, and then we'll talk."

Miranda obeyed, scratching her questions onto the paper. When she was finished, the woman flipped the book back around and read out loud.

" 'How many stars are there? Where are they located? Which ones are missing?' " She glanced at Miranda. "Just those three?"

Miranda blinked. Considering she was asking openly about stars, she'd expected some kind of reaction, but she might have been after the names of the last five merchant princes for all the woman seemed to care. "Yes, that's it," she said. "Can you do it?"

The woman didn't even bother to answer. Instead, she grabbed another sheet of paper and began working out figures. Miranda had no idea where she was pulling the numbers from, but they were growing at an alarming rate. The woman checked her math and then circled the number at the bottom before sliding the paper over to Miranda.

"Three hundred gold standards?" Miranda cried, snatching the paper off the table. "Is that what you normally charge?"

"Hundred gold per question seems a fare rate considering we're going to be getting answers for the whole Spirit Court," the woman said, crossing her arms. When she saw Miranda's startled look, she rolled her eyes. "We're Zarin brokers, Rector Lyonette, not some small-town operation. It's our business to know who you are and what you're up to."

She reached over and grabbed the ledger again. "What we've got here is really one question with three parts—you want names, locations, and verification. Since you've come to us, that means this information is either too big for the Court to gather on its own or you don't want anyone knowing you're after it. Both carry a premium. If you don't like it, you can go somewhere else, but there ain't any other broker worth the name going to give you a better deal than that."

She put her hands on her hips as she finished, and Miranda knew she was defeated. "Fine," she muttered, hauling the sack of gold onto the desk. "I've got only two hundred and fifty with me."

The woman smiled. "Seeing as you're with the Voice of the Wind, I'll spot you the rest. Just have it here by tomorrow morning and there won't be no problem."

Miranda sighed. Krigel was going to kill her. The Court wasn't exactly flush these days, and that two hundred and fifty was next month's operating budget. But she was in this up to her neck now, nothing to do but keep going and hope it worked. "When do I get my answers?"

"Soon as we do," the woman said. "Which means it'll take as long as it takes." She lifted the sack of gold off the table and set it down behind her desk with a grunt of effort. "You can wait in the back, if you'd like, sir," she said, straightening up. "It's nicer than up front, and more private."

This last bit was directed at Lelbon, who accepted graciously. The woman led them behind her desk and through a small door into a much larger room full of the strangest contraptions Miranda had ever seen. Each was the size of a large loom, but rather than lines of yarn, these were strung with squares of cloth in a rainbow of colors sewn onto ribbons at various heights. Each cloth strip had two sides, and each side was stamped with a symbol Miranda didn't recognize.

There were four of the contraptions in total, all alike and each set well apart from the others. Three other women, all about Emma's age, stood clustered in the far corner around a table set with sandwiches and a battered kettle. They all bowed when they saw Lelbon, and he waved politely as Emma led them between the strange machines and through another door to a small, cozy room overlooking the river.

"There you are," she said, motioning for Lelbon to take a seat in one of the worn but very comfortable-looking chairs under the window. "You can stay here as long as you like. I'll bring you your answer when it's ready."

"Thank you, Emma," Lelbon said, sinking into the closest chair.

Emma beamed at him and retreated back to the large room, shutting the door firmly behind her.

"I didn't know you were such a celebrity," Miranda said, sitting down in the chair beside Lelbon's.

"All part of the job," Lelbon said with a smile.

Miranda arched an eyebrow. "So," she said, leaning back. "The West Wind runs the brokers."

The old man shrugged. "What gave you that impression?"

"It's pretty obvious," Miranda said. "Come on, they called you 'Voice of the Wind.'"

As though in answer, a gale began to bellow inside the room they'd just walked through, howling against the warped board walls and rattling the door on its hinges. Miranda smiled triumphantly, but Lelbon's face was unchanged.

"Your assumptions in this are entirely your own, Spiritualist Lyonette," he said, glancing out at the river. "Isn't the water lovely today?"

"Why would a huge spirit like the West Wind care about running an information-selling organization?" Miranda said, completely ignoring the attempted subject change. "Brokers have nothing to do with spirits that I know of. I've never even heard of one who was a wizard. Why would a Wind Lord put his efforts into spreading information for spirit-deaf humans?"

Lelbon gave her a dry look. "You're not a subtle woman, Miss Lyonette."

Miranda crossed her arms over her chest with a glare.

"As a loyal scion of the Wind Courts, I cannot answer your questions," Lelbon said at last. "You know that, so stop asking."

"So don't answer me as a servant of Illir," Miranda said. "You were an historian first, not to mention a wizard so interested in the Wind Courts you actually convinced one of the four winds to employ you. I'm asking your opinion as a fellow knowledge seeker. We do have some time to kill, might as well fill it with good conversation."

Lelbon's mouth twitched. "Very well, Spiritualist, let me put it this way. The Wind Courts are different than other spirit hierarchies, mostly because they have no lands to call their home. Other than that technicality, however, three of the four Wind Lords are much like any Great Spirits—sleepy, overbearing, sure of their own way, and fanatically loyal to the Shepherdess."

"But Illir is different," Miranda said.

"Very," Lelbon said. "Of all the spirits I've met, Illir is the only one I've found with a real sense of curiosity. He's especially interested in humans."

Miranda frowned. "Why?"

"Because of all the spirits, humans are the only ones created by the Shepherdess," Lelbon said. "We are unique. Unlike everything else in the world, our strength is not bound by our size but by our will, and though over ninety percent of us are deaf and all of us are blind, we are the only souls in creation with the power to dominate other spirits. You can see then how studying such creatures would be of great interest to my master."

Miranda frowned. "But why brokers? I mean, I can see how making your winds into a conduit of information would be a great way to learn about humanity, or its underbelly at least, but why charge for it? What's a wind going to do with three hundred gold standards?"

Lelbon's mouth twitched. "There are other forms of power besides wizardry, Spiritualist. My master likes to keep his interests diverse."

"Is he bribing politicians?" Miranda said, laughing at the idea. "Running merchant empires on the side?"

"I don't pry into my master's private affairs," Lelbon said. "But I do know he's contributed to certain criminal bounties."

Miranda's smile fell instantly. "You can't be serious."

"Monpress has provided him with a great deal of entertainment over the years," Lelbon said. "My master likes to pay for a good show."

Miranda clenched her jaw and said nothing, glaring out the window at the river below.

"He also writes from time to time," Lelbon added, almost as an afterthought.

"Writes what?" Miranda said, still looking at the river.

"A variety of things," Lelbon said. "Histories, travelogues. You might have heard of him, actually. His books are under the name Morticime Kant."

"*Are you kidding me?*" Miranda roared, nearly launching out of her chair. "The *West Wind* is the source of that overwrought, misleading, misinformed, horribly written nonsense about wizards? The books that say we wear pointed hats and robes and do nothing but brew frogs into potions all day? *That* Morticime Kant?"

"I hadn't heard the bit about the frogs," Lelbon said, trying hard not to laugh. "But yes, that Morticime Kant. It was part of a long-running experiment to see if he could influence human behavior through suggestion."

"That's absolutely insane," Miranda huffed. "You don't see any members of my Court wearing pointed hats."

"Not in *your* Court," Lelbon's grin widened. "Others are less prejudiced."

Miranda snorted. "Thank goodness other spirits aren't as curious as your master or we'd be up to our noses in ridiculous ploys."

"It's not that spirits aren't curious," Lelbon said, his voice growing suddenly bitter. "Curiosity isn't a quality the Shepherdess values. She prefers obedient silence to questions, and since she is the Power, what she prefers becomes the way of the world."

Miranda frowned, tucking that knowledge away for future use. "That still doesn't explain why Illir runs the brokers, though," she said. "You'd think he could learn everything he needed to know about people from watching. He is a wind, after all."

"Knowing what people want to know tells you more about them than any simple observation," Lelbon said sagely. "Watching a man bake may tell you he's a baker, but learning what he would pay to know tells you infinitely more about the man himself."

Miranda sighed. "Well, it seems like an overly elaborate setup to me."

"It is," Lelbon said. "But my Lord Illir enjoys it immensely. Plus, it keeps the winds busy. They can be a handful if left to their own devices."

Miranda thought of Eril and agreed heartily. "So," she said, scooting to the edge of her chair. "Now that we're on the subject, how do the big looms work? Since the brokers are spirit deaf, I'm guessing the machines help them interpret the winds without hearing them? Do they read combinations from the symbols on the cloths?"

"That I certainly could not tell you," Lelbon said. "Industry secret."

"Seems like a lot of hassle," Miranda said. "Why not just use wizards?"

Lelbon closed his eyes as the warm sunlight drifted over his face. "Because that would defeat the whole purpose."

Miranda flopped back into her chair. "Are you deliberately being infuriating?"

"Quite the contrary," Lelbon said. "I'm being very open. More open than I should be. You, however, seem to be making an effort to be thick."

Miranda glared at him and said nothing. Finally, Lelbon sighed. "I'll add this, and no more. The Shepherdess watches her spirits closely and her wizards when they catch her fancy, but she completely ignores the spirit deaf. They are beneath her notice altogether, and she certainly would never take the time to learn any sort of code a wind or other spirit could devise to communicate with them. With that in mind, consider, if the winds wanted to pass on information they usually couldn't say without attracting her anger, what would be safer? Whispering to a wizard or flipping a piece of cloth?"

Miranda's eyes went wide, but before she could say anything, Lelbon cut her off with a wave of his hand. "Let's leave it there."

She nodded, and they lapsed into silence, listening to the howling wind on the other side of the wall.

CHAPTER
8

After five minutes of listening to the wind howl in the broker's room, the urge to get up and peek was almost overwhelming. Miranda desperately wanted to see with her own eyes how the pieces of cloth on ribbons worked, but she stayed put, fingers locked on the battered arms of her chair. The West Wind was already doing her a lot of favors; now wasn't the time to press her luck.

To get her mind off the sound, Miranda leaned back in her chair to contemplate what she'd learned of Illir. She'd always known he wasn't a spirit that did things in the normal way, but using the spirit deaf to pass information right below the Shepherdess's nose was brilliant, and the more she thought about it, the more brilliant it got. How many other events had Illir influenced through his brokers, feeding the right information to the right people at the right time?

She sighed loudly, causing Lelbon to look up in alarm. Miranda shook her head. No need to tell him how much it stung to finally realize how little she actually knew about the spirit world she'd given her life to. If Illir was secretly behind both the brokers and Morticime Kant and she hadn't known, how much else was she missing? She didn't even want to think about it, but it all came down to the same mistake: underestimating the spirit world.

Every time she thought she had spirits figured out, they did something that turned her on her head. Even seeing the truth of it in her servant spirits every day, it was easy to forget in the rush to do her duty that spirits weren't some faceless mass to be saved but a complex network of individuals all trying to make their way in the world. They had their own ambitions, their own wants and needs and likes. Thinking of it like that, the fact that she could control them, overpower them with her will, just seemed...wrong.

For some reason, that thought sent her back to the vision the Shaper Mountain had shown her, his memories of the world that had existed before the Shepherdess. There'd been no wizards then, no people at all, just spirits and the demons who preyed on them. The spirits had been awake then. All of them, even the little ones. Miranda closed her eyes, trying to imagine a world where everything was as awake as her own spirits. A time when the world was enormous, and spirits fought their own demons. A world of free, independent souls without a Shepherdess or her stars to watch over them. Unbidden, Miranda's hand sank down to brush her rings. If such a world existed now, would humans have any place in it?

She was still mulling this over when the wind on the other side of the wall died out, falling from a roaring gale to nothing in less than a breath. Miranda blinked and turned to look at Lelbon. It couldn't be time yet. They'd been sitting here less than half an hour, but Emma was already walking through the door with a surprised look on her face and a sheet of paper in her hands.

"Luck is with you today, Spiritualist," she said, handing the paper to Miranda. "Here you are, names and locations, just as requested. The ones missing are marked with asterisks. I think you'll find everything to your satisfaction."

Miranda snatched the paper from her hand. As her eyes ran frantically over the scribbled names, the first thing that struck her was how long the list was. There must have been hundreds of names, each with a place listed beside it, just as Emma had said. The only star without a location was the one at the very top, Eli Monpress.

Reading that name was harder than she expected. All at once, she was back in the Tower at Osera, staring across the dark, still water as the white arms tightened around Eli's throat, pulling him out of the world. Miranda shook herself out of the memory, scrubbing her blurry eyes with the back of her hand. There was no sense worrying about the thief. If there was one thing Eli Monpress excelled at, it was looking out for himself. Setting the past firmly out of her mind, Miranda plunged ahead, reading as fast as her eyes could move.

All the names from her own investigations, the Shaper Mountain, the Great Ghosthound, and so on, were listed, with one exception. The Immortal Empress's name was missing. Miranda read the list twice over, searching for Empress or

610

Nara, the name Mellinor had mentioned on the ride down to Osera, but she found neither. That confused her, but Miranda didn't have time to worry about the Empress.

As she read the list through again and again, a realization began creeping over her mind. From the very beginning, she'd known there must be several stars. A few dozen, maybe a hundred, but the list in her hands was well over that. And then there were the missing stars. Coming in, she'd expected to see the Deep Current and the Allva's tree, plus a few more. Now, staring at the paper between her shaking hands, Miranda felt like she'd stepped off the edge of a bottomless pit.

"How is it?" Lelbon said, peering over her shoulder.

Miranda shoved the list at him. He took the paper from her shaking hand, his wispy eyebrows climbing. Of the nearly two hundred listed names, a full thirty had the sharp, black asterisk beside them.

"I thought four, five at the most," she whispered. "Ten at the very worst. But *thirty*? How do thirty stars vanish without our knowing?"

Lelbon's pale face went a little paler. "Look," he said, pointing at a cluster of names marked with the black asterisks. "They're mostly stone spirits, or spirits involved with the sea." He glanced at Emma, who was still hovering. "Have there been reports of earthquakes?"

"Aye," she said. "Several, mostly down south."

Lelbon shook his head, muttering under his breath.

"Look here!" Miranda cried, pointing at one name toward the bottom of the list. "It's the coral reef I sent Eril to check on just this morning." She looked up at Emma. "Are you sure this one's missing?"

"Everything you see there is correct as of five minutes ago," the woman said, insulted.

Miranda mumbled a quick apology and turned back to Lelbon, who was reading the list over again. "Sea spirits, corals, a rain forest, bedrock, the humans," he muttered, resettling his spectacles on his long nose.

"Is there a connection?" Miranda said.

"There must be," Lelbon said. "These are all spirits whose loss won't be felt by the world at large immediately." His frown deepened, and his voice dropped to a whisper. "It's like she's picking off the hidden ones, the stars whose spirits are either isolated or locally clustered. And since human souls can't dominate each other, we wouldn't feel the loss of Eli or the Empress." The paper list fluttered as his hands began to shake. "She's taking the ones who won't be noticed."

"Hold on," Miranda said. "You're saying that the Shepherdess is out there grabbing stars, and she's trying to keep it secret?"

"There's no one else who could," Lelbon said. "Not on this scale. But what could she be hiding from? Nothing in this world can stop her from doing whatever she wants." He scratched the white stubble on his chin. "Maybe she *is* trying to prevent a wide-scale panic after all? But then, if she cared enough to show that kind of caution, you'd think she'd say something before ripping a star away from its spirits."

Miranda had no idea. The more she tried to think about what all this meant, the heavier the feeling of being helpless, *useless*, became. The weight grew and grew until it physically forced her back down into her chair.

"It's hopeless," she whispered, shoulders sagging. "Even if every wizard in the world mobilized, thirty stars vanished in one day. How can anyone stop that?" She scrubbed her hands over her face. "You were right. I'm in over my head. I can't do *anything*."

"Now hold on," Lelbon said. "It's still possible we're jumping to conclusions. After all, we don't know for sure how long this has been going on, or if the Deep Current was first. Maybe this has been building slowly."

Miranda didn't believe that for a second, but she had no proof, so she kept it to herself. Instead, she studied the list, paying close attention to the stars who weren't yet missing. "If she's trying to keep things quiet, she can't do it for much longer. Look, she's already pulled every ocean and stone spirit save the Shaper Mountain itself."

"You're right," Lelbon said, pulling the list toward him. "She's finished the easy targets."

Miranda shook her head helplessly. "Whatever goes next, it'll be big. But there are, what, a hundred and fifty, hundred and sixty stars left to choose from? There's no way we can cover them all before the next one vanishes. But if we wait until the next one pops, we'd most likely arrive too late to do any good, just like you said."

Lelbon looked at her sadly. "I didn't tell you these things to weigh you down, Spiritualist."

"No," Miranda said. "You told me the truth."

"At least you now have the proof to convince the Spiritualists that the world needs them united," Lelbon said. "If the list isn't enough, the panic and chaos following whatever spirit goes next certainly will be."

Miranda blanched. "Forgive me for not jumping for joy at that thought." Even the idea of sitting back and waiting for a panic to galvanize the Court felt like a betrayal of everything they stood for. "It can't be all dead ends," she muttered. "There has to be—"

A sound exploded before she could finish, stabbing into her mind and cutting every other thought free. It started like a shot, an arrow of pain plunging deep into her flesh before widening into a high, keening wail of loss. Miranda gasped and clutched her head, trying in vain to keep her skull steady as the scream vibrated through it.

The sound was cold and sharp, but the terror in it turned Miranda's bones to jelly. She would have fallen if Lelbon had not been there, catching her arm even as he grabbed his own temple in pain. The sound went on and on, changing and deepening from a keening scream to a roaring torrent of sorrow and abandonment, and Miranda realized that she had to pull herself together. If she waited for the sound to end on its own, she'd be here forever.

Gritting her teeth, she forced herself to stand. Lelbon was still clutching her chair, his wrinkled fingers wrapped around her arm. Across the room, Emma was slumped against the door frame, and behind her, Miranda could see the other women were doubled over as well, clinging to their machines for dear life.

That threw her. The scream going through her certainly belonged to a spirit. How could the spirit deaf be crippled by it as well? But before she could puzzle over the impossibilities, the floor began to shake under her feet.

The windows bucked in their frames, and the walls shook and groaned as the tiny, sleeping spirits within them woke. Woke, and began to scream, their tiny voices joining with the wail that was still hammering through her skull. When the air itself joined them, the atmosphere tightening like the empty space was bracing for impact, Miranda's blood went cold. She'd seen this before.

"Lelbon," she whispered through gritted teeth. "Demon panic?"

It had to be. Nothing else could wake this many spirits with such fury. She cursed loudly. This was just what they needed now. But Lelbon was shaking his gray head.

"No," he whispered hoarsely. "The river."

He jerked his head at the window, and Miranda's eyes followed on instinct, her breath catching in her throat. Outside, the Whitefall River that flowed behind the broker's had stopped. No, she realized, not stopped. The river was pulling upstream, the water sucking in like a breath. It roiled and foamed as it flowed backward, taking the boats with it, and as it churned, the river rose.

Brown, frothy water spilled over the narrow channel, flooding into the street. Screams went up as street carts vanished under the muddy flood. Still lurching under the endless wail, Miranda pulled herself to the window for a better look. She'd barely made it to the wall when the floor under her feet stopped shaking and started to groan.

She looked down in alarm. Brown water was welling up between the floorboards. It rushed up in little gushes, flooding over Miranda's boots, but even this was wrong. Miranda had dealt with floods before, but she'd never seen water behave like this. The river's water wasn't just rising; it was spitting up, almost like the water itself was jumping to escape something.

Outside the window, the river was screwing itself into knots. Whirlpools spun all across its surface, all turning different directions in a terrifying, unnatural spectacle. But worst of all was the scream.

It was still going, still stabbing through Miranda's mind, growing louder and louder, harsher and harsher. Each swirling eddy and gushing spout added its voice to the rest, flowing faster and faster as the sound rose. The building was screaming as well now, the stone foundation babbling in fear as the water overwhelmed it, and Miranda realized with a start that she had to do something before they were all swept away.

Purpose pulled her out of her panic, and Miranda slammed her eyes shut. The practiced calm fell on her like a stone, and her spirits rallied to her silent call, each going still and ready in its ring. When her mind was quiet, she opened her spirit.

Grief hit her like a wall. Grief and loss and fear and all the things that had been in the initial scream were still there, only now they battered against her naked spirit rather than the shell of her flesh. Miranda stumbled under the onslaught, but she found her ground again and opened her spirit wider, throwing her arms out to take in the full wave of the scream. As it broke over her, she realized with a shock that it wasn't a single, nonsensical wail, but a word. One word, repeated over and over and over.

"Gone!" it shouted. "Gone! Gone! *Gone!*"

"Who is gone?" Miranda shouted back, kneeling in the water, which was now up to her calves. "Rellenor!"

At the sound of her name, the river pitched, sending its water even higher.

"Our source, our guide," the water sobbed. "Our everything, the mother water, the mouth of the world." The names came on top of each other, tumbling together like flotsam in the flow of the river's panic. One word, however, was crystal clear. "Ell! Ell!"

Miranda knew that name. She'd seen it on her list just moments ago. Ell, star of the rivers, whose water wound from the plains through the rain forests before finally spilling into south sea in a delta so wide you couldn't see its end. But Ell's name had been one of those without the asterisk, one of the stars still present. Miranda cast a frantic glance at the backward-flowing river. It seemed that had changed.

"Gone!" the river screamed again as it pounded against the building. "Gone! Gone!"

Outside, the river barges were now level with the windows and the water was full of debris, some of it moving. People, Miranda realized with an icy shock. Men and women, little children caught up in the river's sweep before they were sucked down beneath the swirling brown water.

"Gone!" Rellenor's scream crashed against her. "Lost! We are all—"

"Be still!"

The command rang like a bell through the whole of Miranda's spirit. It was not an Enslavement. She did not grab the river or force it down, but she leaned on it as hard as she could, using the whole of her will as a weight to press on the water until, at last, the terrible wail sputtered to a stop.

"Who are you?" the water said bitterly. "Who are you to stop our grief?"

"You know me, Rellenor," Miranda said slowly, never letting up on her pressure. "I'm Miranda the Spiritualist, Mellinor's shore. I can help you, but I need you to let go of some of your water before you destroy the docks."

Laughter filled her mind, cold and bitter and stinking of mold. "What do I care?" the river cried. "My star is gone! All water flows through Ell. We rivers are only tributaries of the

616

greatest water. The Mother River has been with us since before the beginning of this world, but now her voice is silent and her banks are dry. Without the connection of her water, I can no longer feel the other rivers, no matter far I reach. I am *alone*, human. What can I do but flood?"

The river's voice rose as it spoke, building again into the heart-wrenching wail, and the water rose with it. Miranda ignored the icy swirls beating against her knees and slammed her will down harder.

"Stop!" she commanded, and then eased her voice into a plea. "Please, Rellenor, stop. It is your right to flood, but do the spirits around you deserve to be washed away? Lower your waters. The Spirit Court knows stars are vanishing, and we are doing everything in our power to bring them back."

"Bring Ell back?" Scorn flooded the river's voice. "Are all you wizards so arrogant? What can you hope to do? Ell is a *star*."

Miranda pulled herself ramrod straight. "I am the Rector Spiritualis!" she shouted. "There is no spirit I will not serve, and no crime against them I will not seek to undo! So I have sworn, and so I will do until I die. Even if the Shepherdess herself stands in my way, I will do everything I can to bring your star and the others back to their places."

The River seemed momentarily stunned by this outburst, and Miranda went on, softer now. "You flow through the city of wizards, Rellenor. You should know better than any spirit the tenacity of the Spirit Court. We will serve you well, I swear it, but please, *please* do not destroy the innocent in your grief. The loss of Ell is loss enough. Do not add these poor spirits as well."

For a long moment the water hung, and then a watery sigh went through her, as cool and soft as evening rain.

"You humans are as stubborn as you are blind," the river muttered as the brown water began to sink back through the floorboards. "But I have long flowed through the white city of the Tower, and those years have taught me better than to go against the Tower's master. Still, you can do nothing, human. Ell is gone."

Miranda reached down to plunge her hand into the retreating water. "I can't speak for my race," she whispered. "But *I* will not desert you, nor will any other Spiritualist. All you have to do is flow as you have always done and we will do the rest."

"I don't see much point." The water's voice was deep and bitter. "What good is flowing if you flow alone?"

"Just keep flowing," Miranda said, gently lifting the weight of her spirit. "We will make things right. I swear it."

The river didn't answer; it just cried, folding itself back into its banks with a soft sobbing sound. Miranda caressed it one more time before closing her spirit and shooting to her feet. She rushed past the brokers and out of the building, shoving the list of stars into her pocket as she went. Lelbon followed hot on her heels, his voice low and buzzing like a wasp in her ear.

"Spiritualist!" he hissed. "I realize you're upset right now, but think about what you're saying! The Lady's own hand is in this! You can't fight the Shepherdess's will. If you charge ahead, she will cut you down. She cares nothing for humans save those she favors. You can't just make promises—"

"What else was I supposed to do?" Miranda shouted, bursting into the street. "Look around!"

She flung out her arms, forcing Lelbon to stop and look. He did, his face paling.

The river district was a scene of chaos. A layer of slimy mud lay everywhere the river had flooded. Barges had been washed up into the street. Many had crashed through houses, dropped there by the racing water. People lay scattered as well. Some were lucky. They sat on muddy doorsteps, filthy and half drowned but alive. The still shapes washed into the gutters showed that others weren't so fortunate.

"And Zarin was lucky," Miranda said, taking quick, shallow breaths through her mouth to avoid the smell of the river bottom as it mixed with the growing smell of death. "How many rivers are there, Lelbon? How many of those places didn't have Spiritualists standing by to calm the water? How many people will die today? How many spirits broken and drowned? And you still say I shouldn't try?"

"I'm saying you shouldn't go blithely to your death!" Lelbon cried, his wrinkled face drawing into a terrible scowl. "This is larger than you. Larger than the Court. There's a line between honoring your oaths and throwing your life away. Even if you did somehow find a way to undo this, we're not talking about some rogue Enslaver, Miranda. This is the Shepherdess, the Power whose will rules the world. Even the favorite couldn't defy the Lady. What hope do you have?"

"I don't intend to defy the Lady," Miranda said. "In fact, in a roundabout way, I mean to ask for her help."

Lelbon's scowl fell into a look of utter bewilderment. Miranda didn't blame him. The insane thought had struck her dumb as well. It had come just a second ago while she was running out of the building, but the more she thought about it, the more certain she was that this was the best chance they had. She might not be able to make everything right as she'd promised the river just now, but if this worked, she could make things *better*, and any improvement was worth taking a chance for at this point.

Miranda put her fingers to her lips. Grimacing at the stench, she took a deep breath and blew an ear-splitting whistle. It rang in the air, echoing off the low buildings. Across the city, another call rose in answer, a long, ghostly howl. Miranda grinned at the sound and turned back to Lelbon.

"I'm not the only one who cares for the preservation of this world," she said. "But to get my help, I'm going to need to call in my favor from your lord."

Lelbon sighed. "I thought I made it quite clear that Lord Illir could not—"

"He can do this much," Miranda said. "All I need is transportation. The wind doesn't even have to stay."

Lelbon scowled. "And where would you be going?"

Miranda told him, and Lelbon's eyes went wide as eggs. She set her jaw, ready to argue, but he just turned and raised his arm. A wind rushed down in answer, making his white robe flap like a flag. He whispered something to it, and the wind spun back into the sky. By the time Gin arrived, panting from the dash but looking rested and much improved, an enormous wind had come to Zarin, a great howling gale that nearly knocked Miranda off her feet.

"I hope you know what you're doing," Lelbon shouted over the wind's roar.

"Not at all," Miranda shouted back, climbing onto Gin's back and clutching her legs around the ghosthound's barrel chest. "But if I stay here I'll fail for certain. What have I got to lose?"

Lelbon's eyes narrowed, but he waved his hand. The second it moved, the great wind swept down, lifting Miranda and her ghosthound into the air. She dug her fingers into Gin's fur, pulling herself down to his back as the ground sank away below their feet.

"This is going to be a long trip, isn't it?" Gin growled, kicking his legs in the air. "Wish you'd told me about this before I ate."

"If your belly wasn't full of pig, you'd never have let me do this," Miranda said. The wind bucked around them, and she pulled herself tighter to his back. "Hold on."

"To what?" Gin cried, his orange eyes going wide.

All around them, the wind began to laugh, an enormous sound that made Miranda's teeth rattle. And then, with a stomach-churning lurch, they were off, spinning through the sky north and west toward a distant, stormy shore and the lonely citadel where Miranda had pinned her last, desperate hope.

The Oseran royal carriage creaked to a halt a half mile outside Zarin's towering south gate. The driver cursed and arched his neck, looking with dismay at the enormous clog of traffic running back from the gatehouse. Cursing again, he glanced down at the ring of king's guards riding close escort. "Mind going to see what we're in for?"

The guards exchanged a look, and then the youngest of the group turned his horse out into the fields beside the road, riding around the clot of carts, carriages, and angry farmers to see what the problem was.

"Why did we stop?"

The driver rolled his eyes and looked down to see the Royal Treasurer climbing out of the coach. The old man looked terrible, but then anyone would look like death warmed over after being locked in a small carriage for a day and a night with the king.

"Seems there's trouble in the city, my lord," the driver said. "Just sent a rider up, so we should know in a moment."

He heard hoofbeats as he finished and turned to see that the boy was already riding back.

"It's a flood," the young guard called as soon as he was in earshot. "River just wiped out the center of Zarin."

"*A flood?*" the Treasurer cried. "The ground's bone dry! How do you have a flood with no rain?"

"Could have been rain upriver," the driver said, and then snapped his mouth closed at the Treasurer's poisonous look. "Yes, my lord. If we're fast, we can cut west along the ring road and beat the crowd to the north gate. Shouldn't take more than an hour."

"Just get us there," the Treasurer snapped, stepping back inside. "The king's impatient to get this over with."

The king was impatient about everything, the driver thought with a scowl. Not that he was going to complain, of course. He'd been at the storm wall; he'd seen what the king could do with that hunk of metal on his back.

The driver whistled to the riders to fall back in. He was about to turn the horses off onto the grass when he felt the carriage shift. The driver cursed and reined his team back in just before the carriage door burst open and the king himself climbed out.

All the guards froze in place, saluting as King Josef hopped down onto the grass. For his part, the driver was doing his best to make himself as small and inconspicuous as possible.

Powers, the king was large. Large and deadly and dangerous; the kind of man you'd cross the street to avoid day or night. The girl he kept with him was no better. She jumped down after him, a leather sack swinging from her hands, her pale face hidden by the creepy coat she wore. He swore he'd seen it moving on its own sometimes, twitching like a sleeping animal even when she sat perfectly still, the cloth black as a nightmare no matter how bright the light.

"Your majesty!" The Treasurer scrambled out of the carriage, chasing the king like a mother after her toddler. It was a pathetic sight for a minister of Osera, and overbearing as the old bastard had been during the trip, the driver almost felt sorry for him.

"Please get back in the carriage," the Treasurer pleaded. "It will be only another hour."

"A minute in that coffin on wheels is like an hour anywhere else," the king growled. "Forget it. We walk."

The Treasurer went so pale the driver worried he would faint. "*Walk?* You are a sovereign monarch on an official visit to the Council of Thrones! You can't just *walk* in!"

But the king was already striding down the line of traffic, his long legs quickly taking him out of sight behind the other wagons. As always, the girl stuck to him like a shadow, jogging to keep up.

The Treasurer cursed loudly and turned to the riders. "Follow the king! Make sure he comes to no harm."

As the six horsemen took off, the driver was tempted to point out that, seeing how the king had killed half the Empress's army with his own hands, the riders' presence would likely be more of a hobble than a help if an actual threat did emerge, but the Treasurer was already climbing back into the carriage.

"Drive on!" he shouted through the little curtained window. "We'll meet his majesty at the Council Citadel."

"Yes, my lord," the driver said, snapping the reins.

The carriage creaked forward, bouncing over the grass as they turned off the road and cut west through the open field. As he eased the horses into the grass, the driver leaned back, enjoying the sunlight that suddenly seemed far warmer and cheerier now that the monster king and his monster girl were out of his coach. Laughing at the thought, he urged the horses faster, whistling an Osera fishing song as they bounced onto the narrow, rutted cart track that circled Zarin and turned north toward the hopefully unflooded, uphill side of town.

CHAPTER
9

"Eliton?"

Banage's voice broke on the last syllable. Eli rolled his eyes. "Who else?"

The candle flame flickered as Banage stood, his eyes wide and bright in the shaking light. "It is really you?" he whispered.

Eli started to say something snarky, but the words vanished as Banage did something completely unexpected, something he'd never done before in Eli's memory. The Rector Spiritualis reached out, grabbed his son, and clamped him to his chest. The fire hovering on Banage's hand danced wildly as it skittered to avoid catching Eli's clothes, but the Rector didn't seem to notice. He hugged Eli with a bone-crushing fury, and Eli, feeling decidedly off balance, stood and took it, his hands resting awkwardly on his father's shoulders.

Several long seconds later, Banage finally drew back. "Forgive me," he said, surreptitiously wiping his eyes with the back of his sleeve. "It's just—" He stopped, taking a deep breath. "It's not many fathers who get to see their sons come back from the dead twice."

"Well, no one's happier I'm not dead than me," Eli said, wincing at how awkward his voice sounded. "What are you doing here?" He glanced at Banage's empty fingers. "Where are your rings?"

"Later," Banage said. "How are you alive, Eliton? What happened? We all saw you vanish, but afterward nothing would talk about it. What was that light? Where did you go, and how did you return?"

Eli scrambled to think of a good lie, something plausible enough for his father to believe without giving too much away. But just as he started picking through his options, he stopped. What was he doing? The whole reason he was here right now was because he'd decided he was done being the Shepherdess's dog. If that was true, then why should he continue lying for her? Why should he bother hiding her secrets?

The realization broke over him like a bucket of cold water, and Eli's lips peeled away into a wide smile. He'd been so busy with his capture, he'd forgotten for a moment that he was *free*. Eli almost laughed out loud at the idea. Free. He lifted his head to look Banage in the eye, and then, with a delicious breath, he told the truth.

"I went to the Shepherdess," he said. "That was the deal. I used her power to make sure the Empress's fleet wouldn't bother us anymore, and she got to take me back. But when she realized I'm not as easy to live with as I used to be, she kicked me out on the Council's doorstep. She thinks it will bring me around to her way of thinking, but she doesn't understand that I'd rather rot in the worst prison the Council can devise than spend another minute in her company. At least here I can escape." He reached out to knock on the prison wall with a cheery smile. "Big improvement."

He stopped there, waiting for Banage to comment, but his father just stared at him, utterly bewildered. Eli sighed deeply and tried again. "You remember when you asked me why I didn't come home that night?"

Banage nodded.

"It's because that was the night the Shepherdess found me," Eli said. "I was just a kid, and I was so mad at you." He shook his head at the memory. "She was kind to me, treating me like I was some kind of treasure. I thought she was my savior. We lived together happily for a few years, but then I grew up. Or, rather, I woke up to what she really was. After that, I decided it was time to get away, and I convinced her to let me go. It was also around that time I decided I wanted to be a thief, so the second I was out of her care I apprenticed myself to a master and started learning my trade. The rest is public record."

"Hold a moment," Banage said, his voice quivering with disbelief. "You mean to tell me that you lived with the *Shepherdess*? You're saying that the greatest of all Great Spirits, the force that controls this world, isn't some giant, sleeping mother spirit but a real woman who took care of a little boy?"

"I don't know about the real woman part," Eli said. "She's not human. She's not a spirit either. She's something else altogether, a Power of Creation."

He stopped a moment to enjoy the sight of his father gaping in amazement, but to his surprise and disappointment, Banage only nodded, his eyes dropping to his empty fingers where the small fire still burned. "Miranda told me something very similar."

"Miranda?" Eli couldn't quite wrap his mind around it. "What does Miranda know of the Shepherdess?" Unbidden, a memory of his childhood welled up inside him: the Shepherdess standing cold and terrible before the Spiritualist whose name he'd never learned. Miranda would ask the same questions, he was certain, and for a moment he saw her hanging on the Lady's hand, staring down in disbelief at her own death. Eli shook his head and forced the thought away.

Banage didn't notice. "After the events with Izo the Bandit King, Miranda went with Slorn to the Shaper Mountain," he said, his voice full of worry. "There she learned of the stars and the Shepherdess. Afterward, Slorn stayed behind so she could escape. The knowledge she brought allowed us to answer the West Wind's request to come to Osera and help in the fight against the Empress." He raised his eyes to Eli. "Later, when everything was done, she also told me that you gave yourself to save us."

Eli gritted his teeth. Of course Miranda would see it that way. She would never understand what it meant to lose like that, to give up. And since Banage thought he was dead, she must, too, which gave more credence to the whole martyr story. The idea of Miranda spreading fabricated stories of his selflessness annoyed Eli so strongly that he completely missed what Banage said next.

"What?"

"I said I'm proud of you," Banage repeated. "I'd thought you were lost to even the concept of responsibility, but it seems I was wrong."

For several seconds, Eli just stood there, blinking. *"What?"*

Banage's face darkened. "If my gratitude means so little to you, Eliton, you don't have to accept it."

"No, it's not—" Eli stopped, dragging his fingers through his hair. "I just never thought I'd hear you say that."

"I never thought I'd get the chance to say it," Banage answered, his eyebrow arching into a skeptical glare.

Eli decided to leave it at that. Any more pushing and this bizarre world where both his parents said they were proud of him in a single day would surely shatter.

"So," Banage said, clearing his throat. "The Shepherdess just dropped you here, did she?" He folded his arms over his chest with a glare. "What did you do, Eliton? It must have been terrible to make her so angry she'd hand you over to the Council."

"I'm sure she thought it was," Eli said, his voice snippy. "But I didn't do anything except speak my mind."

Banage made a disbelieving sound, and Eli decided it was time to change the subject. He wasn't quite ready to throw away this strange new respect his father had for him by falling right back into their old ways.

"What are you doing down here, anyway?" he said, leaning back against the cold stone. "I'm used to jails, but they're not the sort of place you expect to find the Rector Spiritualis. Did Sara decide it was time to get the family back together and have you kidnapped?"

Banage's face fell, and what warmth there was in the room fell with it. "I am no longer Rector," he said. "I refused to allow the Council to use the Spirit Court as a weapon, and for that I have been charged with high treason."

Eli's eyes widened. "But you were at Osera before the Council could send a fishing boat."

"Because the Lord of the West asked for our assistance," Banage said. "The Court fights for the good of the spirits, not because Whitefall is worried about his borders."

Eli dropped his head and began to rub his suddenly aching temples. "No offense, but that sounds like a pretty small distinction to lose your office and go to jail over."

"It is the small distinctions that matter, Eliton," Banage said solemnly. "If we do not stand on our morals in all matters, small or great, then we are no longer moral men, and no longer worthy of the spirits' trust."

Eli sighed deeply. This was more like the Banage he remembered. "So what now? Will there be a trial, or did Sara just lock you down here and throw away the key?"

Banage gave him a flat look. "Guess."

"Good old mom," Eli said. "At least she's consistent."

"Actually, I'm pleased with the way things worked out," Banage said. "Though I was named traitor and stripped of my position as Rector, there were issues I lacked the freedom to pursue as part of the Court. Now that I'm in disgrace, I mean to set things right."

"Like what?" Eli said, genuinely curious.

Banage's eyes drifted up to the darkness above them. "Do you know how the Ollor Relay works, Eliton?"

Eli arched an eyebrow at the sudden change of subject. "You speak into one ball, sound comes out the other."

"I meant how it really works," Banage said with an exasperated sigh. "How it moves sound like that?"

"No," Eli said. "But that's kind of the point of a state secret. Why, do you?"

"No," Banage said softly, lowering his eyes until he met Eli's again. "Not for sure. But before Sara and I were married, she showed me, just once, how she made a point."

"She always was a show-off," Eli said with a shrug.

Banage laughed. "At least you come by it honestly."

When Eli refused to dignify that with a response, Banage continued. "You saw the tanks above us?"

Eli nodded. How could he have missed them? The cylindrical tanks filled the cave beneath the citadel like the eggs of some enormous insect.

"Each of those tanks is one Relay point," Banage said. "Every Relay point is really three parts: two orbs, one that's kept by the Council, usually by Sara, and another that's out in the field, and the tank is the third part. It lies in the middle, connecting the other two. Words spoken in one orb echo through the tank to the other, allowing communication across any distance."

"Come on," Eli scoffed. "I'm no Shaper, but even I know that can't be how the Relay works. For words spoken in one end to be heard through the other, the orbs and the tank would all have to be part of the same spirit, and that's impossible. I mean, *maybe* if you were working with a very large, very strong water spirit *and* you were a Shaper with a deep understanding of Spirit Unity, you could possibly divide the water into three separate vessels and still keep it as one spirit for a few minutes, but it would never work long term. A spirit separated becomes two spirits. That's a fact of reality. If you pour a water spirit into two blue marbles and a tank, you're going to end up with three spirits. It's just how the world works. Claiming otherwise is like saying rocks fall up when you drop them."

Banage shrugged. "Then you tell me. How does she do it?"

"I don't know," Eli said. "It's probably some kind of stupid trick. Or maybe she's got a Great Spirit on the line." She was egotistical enough to try it.

"She can't," Banage said, shaking his head. "No Great Spirit would let itself be used like that willingly, and the only Enslaver who ever kept one longer than a few hours was Gregorn. But whatever she's doing, she's hidden it very well. I've been looking into the Relay discreetly for years. Every time I came down here, I tried to question the tanks, but I never heard a thing back. It's like the entire cavern is asleep."

Eli remembered the strange, thick silence and shuddered. "Still, that's good," he said. "If they're asleep, then you know she's not Enslaving anything."

"I almost wish she was," Banage said darkly. "Enslavement is straightforward. Enslavement I could end right now. But I don't understand what Sara's doing, or how, and that makes me afraid."

"If you're so worried about it, why didn't you stop her before?" Eli said. "I thought protecting spirits from abusive humans was what Spiritualists did."

He stopped there, bracing for the explosion that always came whenever he criticized the Court, but Banage just ran his hand over his tired eyes.

"I've asked myself that many times," he said quietly. "At first I did nothing because she was my wife and I was sure she'd tell me eventually. Later, I did nothing because I was furious and wanted to keep you away from her. And then, when I became Rector, I still did nothing because the Spirit Court needed the Council of Thrones. I have lived with this growing guilt for twenty-six years now, Eliton, but for all my excuses, the truth was that I still loved her. Despite everything, I couldn't look at her without remembering the brilliant girl she'd been, and I could not bring myself to believe she would do something truly awful, even as the evidence of it became overwhelming."

629

He stopped there, his face hidden behind his hand. Eli bit his lip. He'd never seen his father like this. Banage never got emotional. He shifted back and forth, wondering if he should say something, but before he could think up anything good, Banage resumed his story.

"When the Empress returned, I thought I'd found my chance at last," he said, lowering his hand with a sharp breath. "The Council needed the Court desperately. I thought I finally had the leverage to force Sara to open up. I thought surely, *surely* whatever she'd done to make the Relay couldn't be so bad she'd risk losing the Court's support during a national emergency to keep it hidden. But it was. Whatever secret she's keeping down here, she needed it more than she needed me."

He raised his head, and Eli was surprised to see that his father's face was calm and determined. "But things are different now," Banage said. "As Rector, I had everything to lose. Now I have nothing, not even the duty a husband owes to his wife. Sara and I have nothing left between us but the truth, and the truth, Eliton, is that there is right and wrong in this world, and even Sara with all her brilliance cannot escape justice forever."

Now it was Eli's turn to drop his head. "How are you still this arrogant?" he muttered. "Just because she won't show you her experiments, you let yourself get captured thinking you're going to shine the righteous light on her sins?" He glowered at his father. "Powers, old man, you don't even know if she's actually doing anything wrong. You just assume she is because she won't share her secrets with you. Maybe she's just tired of your lectures, ever think of that?"

"Don't take that tone with me, Eliton," Banage said, his voice full of the old warning. Eli nearly climbed the ladder right then just to get away from him. But when Banage kept going, his voice had softened again with that strange tenderness.

"You're right, though," he said. "Had I been a braver man, I would have found out the truth of the Relay years ago. But I was a coward. A coward and a fool, clinging to forsworn promises under the cover of duty."

He looked at Eli, and his face broke into a sad smile. "One of my many failings, as I'm sure you can tell me. But though you call me arrogant, believe this. There would be no greater joy in my life than to find out I'm wrong. Wrong about the Relay, about your mother, about everything. That's why I chose to leave the Court and let the Council take me as a traitor. I still hope to find out I'm mistaken, you see."

"And what if you're not," Eli said, his voice barely more than a whisper.

Banage's expression grew hard as iron. "Then I will do what I must, and I will do it myself. I owe her that much. Whatever wrongs Sara has done, I loved her once. And besides"—that sad smile returned—"she gave me you."

Eli looked away and kept his mouth shut. The room fell into a deep, deep silence, punctuated only by their breathing. But Eli was never one for silence, and less than a minute later he couldn't help but ask the other question that had been weighing on his mind.

"So," he said, leaning back, "if you're here, who's running the Court?"

"I gave it to Miranda," Banage said.

Eli gaped at him. "You *what*?"

"I had very little time," Banage said in a measured voice. "Sara was coming to arrest me and I had to do something to keep Hern's faction from—"

"You threw her to the wolves!" Eli shouted. "Miranda's cut from the same goody-goody moral idiot cloth as you. They'll eat her alive for trying to claim the title of Rector. Why didn't you just leave it to some power-hungry Tower Keeper? Then at least you'd tie their lust for power to the Court's preservation and Miranda would be free to keep helping Slorn or saving puppies or whatever other high-and-mighty missions you've lined up. But no, you just gave her the ring and sent her in, didn't you? And she's duty bound enough to keep charging straight ahead even if it kills her, just because you asked."

He stopped and waited for Banage to get angry, but the former Rector just dropped his head.

"I thought about that, actually," he said. "Miranda has family of her own, but I think of her very much as my daughter. I knew giving her the Rectorship would put her in danger, especially in times like these, but I had to do it for the good of the Court. In any case, even if I had appointed some 'power-hungry Tower Keeper' as you suggest, she'd never stand aside and let him turn us into an arm of the Council. Even if I'd ordered her to keep her head down, she'd fight all the way. It's her nature."

Eli rolled his eyes. That was certainly true. Counting on Miranda not to go butting her nose in where she shouldn't was like betting on a bottomless boat not to sink. Still. "You should have been more careful," he scolded. "She'd just lost a spirit. Couldn't you have given her a little time off?"

"She wouldn't have taken it if I did," Banage said. "Miranda's stronger than you think. She'll do the right thing."

"I don't doubt that at all," Eli grumbled. "What I question is her ability to not get herself killed along the way."

"She's survived so far," Banage said. "Have a little faith in the girl, Eliton."

Eli huffed and leaned back against the wall, crossing his arms over his chest as he stared up into the dark. They'd been talking for a while now. Well long enough for Sparrow to get bored and move on if he had decided to lurk. Time to get to work.

"Well," he said, standing up, "lovely as this little father-son bonding session has been, I've just managed to escape the Shepherdess, and I don't mean to spend my freedom rotting in a cell."

Banage looked up. "What are you going to do?"

Eli smiled and held up four fingers. "Find Josef and Nico." He folded one down. "Find out what the Shepherdess is up to." He folded the next. "And find out how to get out of her way." Down went the third. "First rule of thievery," he said with a wink. "Don't be a hero. Of course, before I can do any of that"—he wiggled the fourth and final finger at his father—"I'm getting out of here."

Banage laughed out loud. "Impossible. Sara had this place put together specifically to keep powerful wizards under control. Look around." He held out his arms, sending the flickering light dancing over the rough stone walls. "This rock isn't part of the Tower. It's a separate bedrock spirit, and it's so deep asleep I don't think we could wake it up even if we both stood here for days with our spirits wide open. So that's the walls, as for the door…"

He pointed up into the dark where a silver gleam was barely visible in the candlelight. "It's solid steel, Shaper-made, and deathly loyal to Sara. You'll never get it open. If I had my rings it would be another story, but alone like this…" Banage sighed deeply. "The only way out is to wait for Sara to slip up."

"Or Enslavement," Eli said, craning his neck back.

Banage went rigid. "Eliton!" he cried. "Don't you dare even think—"

"Relax," Eli said. "I've never Enslaved anything, and I don't mean to start now. I wouldn't need to anyway. This looks pretty straightforward."

Banage stared at him, aghast. "Did you hit your head on the way down? I told you, I tried everything. This is a wizard prison designed by the most brilliant wizard inventor of our age, maybe ever. There's no way out."

Eli laced his fingers together and stretched his hands, popping his knuckles one by one. "Just who do you think you're dealing with?" he said, flashing his father an impossibly smug grin. "I'm Eli Monpress, the greatest thief in the world."

And with that, he started to climb the iron rungs hand over hand, leaving Banage staring dumbfounded as he vanished into the dark.

Twenty minutes later, Eli was starting to wish he had been a little less cocky. He was hanging upside down under the circular door, knees looped over the second rung of the metal ladder for support while his hands ran over the door's overlapping rings of polished steel. Each ring was fitted so tightly into the next he couldn't get so much as a fingernail between them. What's more, the door, though obviously awake, wasn't responding to polite inquiries.

For a terrified moment, Eli had thought that he'd lost his touch. That Benehime had actually been right and the spirits really had paid attention to him only because of her mark. But then he'd seen the door twitch almost like it was turning up its nose after one particularly entreating prod, and Eli had come to a new conclusion: This door was a jerk.

"Come on," Eli whispered, careful to keep his back to Banage, who was waiting expectantly below. "I just want to talk to someone with some sense. Don't leave me alone with *him*."

The door pressed itself more firmly into the stone and began to emanate a silence so saturated with smug superiority it almost made Eli gag. He flopped back, dangling from the wall by his knees so the door wouldn't have the privilege of seeing him fume. This just made the door cinch down tighter with a haughty *clink*, and Eli gritted his teeth. Yep, definitely a jerk door.

He was working up the will to try again when he heard the door tremble against the stone. Quick as a monkey, Eli dropped, swinging down the ladder to land at Banage's side. The second his feet hit the ground, something hit the door with a resounding *clang*, and the metal swung open.

Banage stared at the opening door, and then his eyes flicked to Eli, wide with wonder. "You weren't just bragging," he whispered. "That was amazing."

Eli shook his head. "As long as I've waited for such a compliment, I'm afraid that wasn't me. Look lively, I think we've got a bird."

As though on cue, Sparrow's head appeared above them. "Sorry to interrupt family time," he called cheerily. "I need Banage the younger. Quickly, please."

Eli crossed his arms. "What's my motivation?"

"Well," Sparrow said, "if you don't come up on your own, I can always go get Sara and let her think up a way to get you out."

Eli grimaced. He had no interest in being on the receiving end of Sara's creativity. With a long-suffering sigh, he shimmied up the ladder once more. Sparrow's hands met him at the top, gathering Eli's wrists together and deftly tying them behind him with a supple length of steel cord.

To Eli's surprise, Sparrow wasn't alone this time. Two guards in the Whitefall family's personal dress stood a short distance away, staring at the surrounding forest of tanks with obvious discomfort.

When Sparrow was finished trussing him, he turned Eli over to the guards before going back to the metal door. In one swift motion, he lifted his leg and kicked the door hard with the heel of his boot. The impact sent a ringing reverberation through the metal, and the door fell gracefully back to its locked position. Eli got one last look at his father's worried face before the door landed, settling back into its stone groove with a solid crunch.

Sparrow took Eli by the elbow. "This way, little Eliton."

Eli began ambling forward. "That was a neat trick with the door, Sparrow. Tell me, do you have to kick it every time?"

"It's the most convenient way to get its attention," Sparrow said, pulling him into a faster pace. "But I don't know if it's strictly necessary. I do my best not to get involved with Sara's contraptions."

Eli nodded, letting Sparrow drag him between the tanks. Sparrow probably didn't know how the door worked at all, he reasoned. The kicking was most likely a trigger, something to let the spirit-deaf Sparrow communicate with the awakened door. The real question was, could anyone kick the door and have it open? Eli filed this thought away for later testing as the guards fell in behind them.

He expected they'd head for the ladder leading up to the

suspended walkway, but Sparrow led them in a different direction, setting off between the tanks at a quick pace. They walked this way for several minutes until, suddenly, the tanks ended and Eli saw they'd reached the wall of the cavern.

Sparrow didn't miss a beat. He skirted the wall for a dozen feet before leading them up a metal stair set that had been bolted into the stone of the cavern itself. At the top, they passed through a guarded door and into a long, spiraling tunnel of a hallway leading up. Eli quickly lost all sense of direction. The tunnel seemed to be tying itself in knots, twisting in and over on itself before finally ending at a nondescript door that opened into a very well-appointed hallway lined with heavy wooden doors, each bearing a gold nameplate and a small flag. Eli licked his lips in anticipation. They must be deep in the inner offices of the Council of Thrones if this much money was lavished on a hallway.

Sparrow led them forward without pausing, and the guards made sure Eli kept pace, their boots falling soundlessly on the rich carpet. The hall ended at a graceful stair, and Sparrow led them up two more floors until the stairs ended, letting out into the richest, most tasteful waiting room Eli had ever seen. Eli began dragging his heels, buying himself time to take in the fine furniture and classic paintings before moving on to the vulnerabilities he would exploit the next time he was here. Privately, he decided that would be very soon. Those crystal decanters on the left end table were far, far too fine to leave in the hands of bumbling Councilmen.

He was just deciding which house at Home would make the best use of the embroidered curtains when Sparrow jerked him out of his happy thoughts, pulling Eli up beside him as he knocked on the heavy door at the far end of the waiting room. The door opened immediately, and Eli took a deep, appreciative breath.

If the waiting room had been fine, the office before him was truly the center of the treasure trove. It was large, spacious, and set all around with windows looking down on the city.

The walls by the door were lined with handsome bookcases while the stretch of space between the two picture windows was filled with a mechanical clock, the first of its kind Eli had ever seen. But while he was gawking at that, Sparrow was nodding to the genteelly handsome older gentleman sitting at the broad mahogany desk set dramatically at the office's center.

"Mr. Monpress," said a soft, well-bred voice. "An honor to meet you at last."

Eli looked away from the clock in surprise, but as soon as he saw the man, all surprise vanished. Even though he hadn't grown up in Zarin, he'd spent enough time looking at Council-issued coins to know the face of the Merchant Prince of Zarin.

"Alber Whitefall," he said with a broad grin. "Never thought I'd have the pleasure."

Whitefall smiled and then glanced at Sparrow. "Thank you, you may go."

Sparrow bowed lavishly and, after handing Eli over to one of the guards, turned on his heel and walked out of the room. Eli craned his head, staring at Sparrow's retreating back in surprise. It was just sinking in that, while Whitefall was here, Sara was not, and now Sparrow was leaving and she still wasn't here. He licked his lips and turned back to the Grand Marshall of the Council of Thrones. Whatever this was about, he couldn't imagine Sara letting other people have access to him without her oversight, which meant either he was wrong or Sara didn't know he was here. Considering how quickly Sparrow had left, Eli was leaning toward the latter.

If Whitefall noticed his confusion, he didn't comment. Instead, he turned his smile to the guards. "Please make Mr. Monpress comfortable."

The guards saluted and moved Eli to the chair in front of Whitefall's desk. They sat him down slightly harder than was necessary, and then the first guard took a length of rope from his belt pouch and started tying Eli down.

"Oh, come on," Eli said. "Rope? Really? Don't you know who I am?"

"I respect your reputation as an escape artist, Mr. Monpress," Whitefall said, his voice unfailingly polite. "But we do have appearances to keep up. I promise not to keep you long."

"Take your time," Eli said, tensing his muscles against the rope as the soldiers tried to pull it tight. "It's not like I have pressing business in my cell. Why did you bring me up here, anyway? Didn't feel like climbing all the way down to the basement?"

"It is a bit of a challenge for a man of my years," Whitefall said. "But that's not the reason. I brought you up here, Mr. Monpress, because unforeseen circumstances have put me in a rather delicate position. One that, unfortunately, prevents me from leaving you in the shelter of your mother's loving bosom."

It might have been Eli's imagination, but he thought he detected a hint of anger in that last sentence. He couldn't say for sure, though, so he filed it away for pondering later. "I'll have to revise my opinion of you," he said, leaning against the ropes as the soldiers finished their knots. "I didn't think you let yourself get into delicate positions."

Whitefall's smile didn't even flicker. "Even I get caught unawares sometimes. Fortunately, I have you to get me out. I'm afraid you're going to be my bargaining chip, Mr. Monpress. An ignoble fate to be sure, though one you must be used to by now."

"I'm getting there," Eli said, wiggling his arms to test the knots. He started to ask what sort of problem was so huge that the Merchant Prince of Zarin needed a thief worth nearly three hundred thousand gold standards as a bargaining tool, but before he could think of the right wording, the door burst open and a page in crisp white livery strode into the room.

"The king is here, my lord," he said. "He arrived just minutes ago."

Whitefall tilted his head. "If he arrived minutes ago, why hasn't he been brought to my office?"

The page flushed. "Apologies, Merchant Prince. His arrival was very...unconventional, and we had a bit of trouble

638

confirming his identity at first. We're sure of him now, but I'm afraid the guard captain is having a hard time convincing him to comply with your law prohibiting weapons in the Citadel."

Eli's eyebrows shot up. Suddenly, things started to click together.

"If that's the king I think you're talking about," he said, "no amount of protocol is going to convince him to disarm. If you want to have your meeting today, Alber, I'd suggest you give in and let him keep his weapons. None of you look like master swordsmen, so I doubt he'll use them."

The page went pale with horror, though whether it was from Eli's casual use of the Merchant Prince's given name or the suggestion that a king be allowed to enter the Grand Marshall's office while armed Eli couldn't tell. Whitefall, however, didn't seem to care.

"Mr. Monpress makes a good point," he said. "Tell the king he is welcome to keep his weapons. I know he will behave himself as a gentleman."

The page's face went paler still, but he was too well trained to object. After a moment of shock, he bowed and hurried out the room, closing the door softly behind him. The guards on either side of Eli shifted nervously, but the Merchant Prince offered no reassurances. Instead, he stood up and reached into his pocket, taking out a long, white handkerchief.

"I did not ask my guest to disarm," he said, all politeness. "But I'm afraid I cannot take such luxuries with you, Mr. Monpress."

"I don't see what you mean," Eli said, looking desperately pathetic. "I'm a prisoner, tied down and at your mercy. If you disarmed me any further, I wouldn't have any arms left."

Whitefall chuckled and strode around his desk, balling the handkerchief in his hand as he stopped in front of Eli. "Come, Mr. Monpress, I've followed your exploits for many years now, even more so since the disaster with Izo. I like to think that I am a man who can learn from the misfortunes of others. Sparrow and Miss Lyonette made the mistake of not securing

639

you properly. I do not intend to be so foolish, especially when dealing with a commodity worth..." His face crumpled, folding into a frown like he was fighting to remember something. "I'm sorry," he said. "Remind me again, how high was your bounty?"

Eli straightened up and opened his mouth to recite his bounty down to the last gold standard, but before he could get a word out, Whitefall's hand swooped in to shove the balled-up handkerchief between his teeth. Eli gagged, eyes bulging. Whitefall snatched his hand back as the soldiers moved in, wrapping a length of rope around Eli's cloth-stuffed mouth before he could spit the handkerchief out.

"Your youth betrays you, Mr. Monpress," Whitefall said with a slow smile. "Cleverness is inborn, but guile is the providence of the aged. A few more years and you would have seen that coming a mile away."

Eli made a furious sound, but Whitefall had already started back toward his seat. "I apologize for any discomfort. If it makes you feel better, I don't expect this to take long. Turn him around, please."

This last bit was directed at the guards, and Eli grunted in surprise as his chair was suddenly lifted and turned sideways so he could see the door and Whitefall. By the time he was safely back on the floor, the Merchant Prince had returned to his chair and was shuffling papers on his desk, tapping the piles into neat squares.

"Remember," he said softly, "no matter what happens, do not take your eyes off the thief. I will do the talking."

The soldiers saluted. "Sir!"

Eli said something as well. Fortunately, though, it came out as a series of muffled grunts, because that was not the kind of language one used in the presence of the Merchant Prince.

Whitefall had time to give him one last smile before a soft knock sounded. He lifted his head to answer, but the door flew open before he could get a word out and two familiar figures swept into the room. When he saw them, Eli was really afraid he was going to cry.

Josef came in first. He looked the same as always, but tired, with dark circles under his hard blue eyes. His swords, all of them, were in their places, strapped awkwardly over his expensive jacket and well-tailored trousers. The familiar, battered hilts of his daggers peeked over the edge of his glossy polished boots, and Eli felt a kind of peace settle into his bones. No matter how much else changed, this part of the world at least was still as it should be.

Nico was likewise unchanged. She followed Josef like his shadow, her coat wrapped up to her neck with the hood drawn forward. Beneath its shadow, she looked tired as well, but where Josef projected a weariness born of eternal annoyance, Nico looked like she'd been pulled too tight.

Her skin was pale, even for her, and her eyes were dark and sunken under furrowed black brows. Still, Eli was happier than he cared to admit to see that the injuries from her fight with Den seemed to be healed. Strangely, she was carrying a large satchel over her shoulder, but before Eli could get a better look at it, Nico and Josef both froze in the doorway, staring at him like they'd seen a ghost.

Eli tried to smile, but all he managed was to scrape his lips against the rough rope that kept the hated cloth in his mouth. He settled for a slow wink at each of them before looking pointedly at Whitefall. Keep going, he thought at them as hard as he could. Don't fall for his trap.

And this was where years spent in constant company paid off. One look was all it took. Josef nodded, a bare duck of the chin, and then ignored Eli completely, turning to the Merchant Prince with a deadly glare. To his credit, or perhaps due to his vast experience with being glared at, Whitefall didn't even flinch.

"King Josef," he said. "Welcome to Zarin. My condolences on the death of your mother. Queen Theresa was an old ally and a dear friend. She will be greatly mis—"

"You're the Whitefall?" Josef interrupted. "Head of the Council of Thrones?"

641

Whitefall stopped, mouth open, and Eli was almost glad of his gag at that moment. It helped stifle his laughter.

"I am," Whitefall said, sounding a little less self-assured. "I suppose we're cutting straight to the point, then?"

"You political types seem to make an art of wasting time," Josef said with a shrug. "Thought I'd save you the trouble." He jerked his head at Eli. "Why's he here?"

Whitefall's smile returned. "So you recognize him, then?"

"Course," Josef said. "Can't turn a corner anymore without seeing his smug face cluttering up a perfectly good wall. Any kid in the Council could tell you that's Eli Monpress."

Whitefall leaned back in his chair. "You're the one wasting time now, King Josef," he said, his voice as smooth and cool as polished wood. "Let's not play. I already know that you and Mr. Monpress have a deeper relationship than posters. I know, for instance, that you two, and I believe the girl behind you, worked together at the events in Mellinor and Gaol. You were certainly together when Izo's camp was destroyed, or did you forget that it was Council agents who subdued your little trio?"

Josef shrugged. "Considering how badly those agents failed, I didn't know if they'd told you. I never denied knowing or working with Monpress. I just asked why he's here, which you have yet to answer."

"He was caught this morning," Whitefall said. "Usually, that would be the news of the year, but then I got a message from my cousin that you, King Josef of Osera, were bringing in a bounty that eclipsed even the famous Eli Monpress. Bearing that in mind, I thought it would be prudent to delay the announcement of Monpress's capture until we could talk."

Smiling at Josef's stony expression, Whitefall turned to Eli's guards. "You may go."

The guards did not look pleased with this order, but they obeyed, walking past Josef with a great deal of posturing and bravado before finally slipping out the door.

"Such delicate matters are best discussed in private,"

Whitefall said after the latch clicked. "Now, do you have proof of the bounty to show me?"

Josef glowered at him a few moments more, and then nodded to Nico. She walked forward, hefting the bag off her shoulder. When she reached Whitefall's desk, she stopped and unbuckled the flap. Her hand went in and came back out with her fingers tangled in a mess of dark hair. With no more care than anyone else would show a pumpkin, Nico plopped the head of Den the Warlord down on Whitefall's desk. The Merchant Prince shrank back, eyes wide with horror as the old, black blood adhered to the wood.

"Charming," he said finally, reaching for his handkerchief only to find it gone. He sighed and padded the sweat from his brow with the edge of his sleeve. "Thank you. I've witnessed the bounty. You can put it away now."

Nico grabbed the head and shoved it back into the bag. On the other side of the office, Eli slumped in his chair. Of *course* they would bring a severed head to the Merchant Prince of Zarin. It made perfect sense in Josef logic. Powers, he had to get back to them before Josef decided that sending Nico to terrify the daylights out of the opposition was a valid political strategy.

Now that the head was gone, Whitefall's color was returning. "Den the Warlord, dead at last," he said. "No small feat. Who defeated him?"

"She did," Josef said, tilting his head toward Nico.

Whitefall gave him a deeply skeptical look. Eli could see the old man examining the angles, trying to figure how Josef could benefit from such a lie. He must have come up blank, though, because he sighed and leaned on his desk, careful to keep his elbows well away from the blood smears.

"I suppose it doesn't matter," he said, glancing at Nico. "You're giving the bounty over to this man, then?"

Nico nodded.

"May I ask how you intend to use the reward?" Whitefall said, eyes going back to Josef. "Five hundred thousand gold standards is a great deal of money, more than enough to destabilize the Council. You can see why we have to be careful, especially after the panic we've had this last week."

"I'm not building an army, if that's what you're asking," Josef said. "The Empress destroyed my country. Osera is a smoking ruin, and after paying for the war, we have no money to fix it. That's where he comes in." Josef pointed to the bag where Den's head rested. "I mean to use Den's bounty to rebuild my island. Anything left over will be put in the treasury to guard against future disaster."

"How extremely reasonable," Whitefall said, lips tilting up like the words were some kind of private joke. "Maybe we should appoint more swordsman kings?"

Josef shrugged. "Seemed fitting to me that the man who helped wreck Osera twice should be the one whose head pays to fix it. How long until the Council can pay up? We need the money as soon as possible."

"And that's where we find our problem," Whitefall said slowly. "Yours is not the only country that's had to pay for a war, King Josef."

"We're the only country that had to fight one," Josef said, crossing his arms.

"I'm not arguing with you there," Whitefall said. "But armies have to be fed, clothed, and paid whether they meet the enemy or not, and it all adds—"

"Stop," Josef said, putting up his hand. "You're telling me that the Council is broke, too?" When Whitefall didn't answer at once, he threw his head back. "Powers! Does *anyone* actually have money in this little club of yours?"

The gag reduced Eli's cackle to a safely muted grunt. Whitefall, however, did not look amused.

"Not being able to produce five hundred thousand gold standards on command hardly counts as broke, King Josef," he said crisply. "The Council of Thrones would be hard-pressed to do that at any time. Now, however, it is particularly difficult. So difficult, in fact, that were it not for a certain

644

windfall, we'd be unable to offer you any meaningful assistance at all."

He tilted his head toward Eli as he spoke, making it painfully clear what windfall he was talking about. Josef didn't answer, but his eyes also flicked to Eli, and Whitefall's face lit up.

"Let me put this as simply as I can," the Merchant Prince said. "If the Council does not claim the Monpress bounty, there's little chance of Osera getting a red cent. Of course, this would mean Mr. Monpress would have to stand for his crimes. Though since there's little question of his guilt, any trial would be a mere formality on his way to the gallows."

Eli swallowed against the pressure of the gag.

"But it doesn't have to be that way," Whitefall said, his voice softening. "You'll find I'm a very understanding soul. I know you and Mr. Monpress are old friends. Who could expect you to condemn your dear companion to death in order to placate a country that's never made a question of how much it disliked you?"

Josef's face darkened, and Whitefall moved in for the kill.

"Come, King Josef," he said kindly. "We are grown men. Let's not bicker. Compromise is the foundation of good governance. Here's my offer. I'll give you Eli Monpress, no strings attached. I will let him walk out of this office as your guest and never ask after him again. And to honor the great debt we owe Osera for her bravery, the Council will keep its fleet at Osera to help with the rebuilding as long as necessary. You will get back your friend and your country, and all I ask in exchange is that you leave that head here and never speak of it again. Let Den remain what he's always been, a black specter from the past. Such things have no place in our modern world. Forget him, forget the bounty, and take friendship instead: Eli's, mine, and the Council's. What do you say, King Josef? Is that not fair?"

Eli glanced at Josef, but the swordsman didn't look at him. His glare never left his target, the old man smiling behind his large desk.

"I give you what you want, or you send my friend to the gallows," he said, scratching his chin. "That sounds very much like a threat, Whitefall. I didn't know the Merchant Prince of Zarin made threats."

"Then you must not have been in politics very long," Whitefall said drily. "Which is good, actually, because it gives me the chance to do something truly unheard of for a man in my position."

Josef arched an eyebrow. "Which is?"

"Be honest with you," Whitefall answered. He sat up straight, and for the first time his voice grew deadly serious.

"When I set Den's Bounty, I made a gamble. The Council was a fledgling mess then, a dozen countries united in terror against a common enemy. When the Empress's first fleet was defeated, we immediately began to fall back into the endless infighting and petty quarrels that have divided this continent since the first man called himself king. Even the promise of the Relay wasn't enough to make the kingdoms forget their old enmity. As someone who's sought to unite this land all his life, I could not let my hard-won consensus fracture, so I found another common cause—our mutual condemnation of Den's betrayal."

Whitefall glanced at the sticky bloodstain on his desk, and his voice began to tremble with old anger. "The night Den turned traitor, he killed men from every kingdom. He betrayed us all for no reason other than his own bloodlust. Den's treason was an act everyone could condemn without reservation, and setting his bounty was the first unified action of what became the Council of Thrones. That debt bound us together, and from that first binding, I forged another, and then another. I built this Council on Den's blood, piling each pebble of common ground one on top of the other until there was enough for all of us to stand on."

"With you at the top," Josef said.

"But of course," Whitefall said, lips curving in a thin smile. "I built the Council, after all. I found Sara, I funded the research that became the Relay, I was the first to unite with Osera against the Empress the first and the second time she came, and I was the one who held everything together at the end."

Josef tilted his head. "And did it never occur to you that you might have to pay if your gamble fell through?"

Whitefall shrugged. "It did. But you have to understand, when he betrayed us, Den was in his late fifties. At the time, we assumed he would either return with the Empress herself in the next year to finish us off, in which case the bounty would be the least of our problems, or he would die across the sea and we'd be rid of him forever. Either way, it seemed a safe bet."

Josef snorted. "Any gambler knows that even the safest bets can come back around, Whitefall."

"You're right," Whitefall said. "But gamblers also know that you can't get blood from a stone. The simple, honest truth, King Josef, is that the Council can't pay what you're asking. Even after we handed over the Monpress bounty, we'd still be nearly a hundred thousand short on Den's. But even if we could clear the total amount, the Council still might not pay. You see, the damage of collecting Monpress's bounty may well be far worse than defaulting on our debt to you."

"How do you figure that?" Josef said. "Eli's bounty isn't some giant, made-up number like Den's. It's backed by pledges from dozens of countries. Just call them in."

"That's precisely the problem," Whitefall said. "There's not a country in the Council at this point that hasn't involved itself in some way with the Monpress bounty, and several, including Gaol and Mellinor, are in far deeper than they should be. It's gotten to the point now where collecting the bounty pledges could destabilize the entire Council."

Josef rolled his eyes. "Then why did you suggest it?"

"Because you left me no choice," Whitefall said heatedly.

He stopped and took a deep breath. When he spoke again, the Merchant Prince's voice was low and earnest. "As much as Osera thinks of itself as an isolated island, the truth is we're all in this together. Osera needs the Council for trade and food, and we need Osera to protect our sea lanes. If you continue to demand what I cannot give, you'll doom us all, including your own people. And that *is* a threat, King Josef."

Josef sneered, but Whitefall just leaned back in his chair. "I've been very generous," he said. "I've offered you your thief, I've promised to help rebuild your kingdom, and my ships are yours as long as you need them. What more do you want?"

Eli glanced at Josef. The swordsman was standing in first position, his eyes fixed on Whitefall with that cold, unwavering intensity usually reserved for serious duels. Eli grimaced. This was going to be bad. But when Josef finally spoke, his voice wasn't the deep, threatening growl that usually came out of him when he looked like that. It was calm and measured, filled with a resolution as deep as mountain roots.

"I haven't been king for long," Josef said. "But I've made promises. Promises to people who lost their country and their children protecting your Council. Promises to my mother. Promises to all of Osera. I didn't want this crown, but now that I've got it, I won't betray it. Not for Eli, and certainly not to make your life easier." He relaxed his stance, crossing his arms stubbornly. "I promised to bring five hundred thousand gold home to Osera, and I mean to keep that promise. Anything less is unworthy of my island."

Whitefall's eyes narrowed. "For being so new to kingship, it seems you've picked up the basics fairly quickly," he said. "Making promises you can't keep and being overly generous with other people's money are certainly kingly qualities."

"I wasn't finished," Josef said sharply. "You want a compromise? Fine. Here's *my* offer. Osera still gets the full bounty, but we'll give you fifty years to pay it. In return for our generosity, Osera will pay no Council taxes, tariffs, or dues for the entire fifty-year period."

"No tariffs…" Whitefall's eyes widened. "That is a hefty rate of interest, King Josef."

Josef shrugged. "If you don't like it, I can always take my bounty claim public. I'm sure everyone who pays Council taxes would love to see you default."

Whitefall's jaw tightened in fury. Eli didn't blame him. If Den's bounty was the uniting act that formed the Council, then failing to pay it could shatter the public's trust, not to mention the trust of the member kingdoms. But if Whitefall did try to make good on the pledge, those countries that joined in the years after the first war with the Empress would balk at having to pay for such an enormous bounty they had no part in setting. It was a bitter fruit any way you cut it, one even Whitefall didn't seem to know how to swallow.

"That is a bald threat indeed," the Merchant Prince said at last, thrumming his fingers on his desk.

"You started it," Josef said.

Whitefall did not look amused. "You realize that if I go by your terms, I'll have to keep Monpress? The Council's going to need all the leverage it can muster to handle such a long-term debt."

"Do what you have to do," Josef said. "A king has no use for the world's greatest thief."

Eli put on a great show of looking deeply distraught. Whitefall, however, didn't have to put on airs. He looked positively stricken as he reached into his drawer for a clean sheaf of paper.

"I find myself at a loss," he muttered, glancing at Eli. "You turned out to be a very poor bargaining chip indeed, Mr. Monpress."

Eli shrugged, but Whitefall's eyes were already back on the paper. "It will be a few hours before I can have all of this formally drawn up," he said, jotting down notes. "I trust you don't mind waiting."

"Actually, I do," Josef said. "This is a simple agreement, Whitefall. I don't want some Council bureaucrat turning it into a thirty-page treaty full of loopholes. Write it out now, just like I said, then we can both sign and put all of this behind us."

Whitefall's pen stopped midscratch. "You can't be serious."

"I'm always serious," Josef said. "Get writing."

Whitefall's fingers clenched the paper, crumpling it into a tight ball, and for a moment, Eli thought the old man was going to order Josef out. But then the Merchant Prince's shoulders slumped, and he bent down to pull a fresh sheet from the drawer. He set it on the table and, as Eli watched in amazement, began to write out the contract.

Not that he had a choice. Smart and experienced as Whitefall was, he hadn't seen Josef coming. Any other king would have taken the first offer and gone home dancing that he had the Council so deeply in his debt, but not Josef. Whitefall was simply unprepared for a king who didn't care about political power or the Council's goodwill or even, seemingly, the life of his friend. Josef had come to Zarin to claim five hundred thousand gold standards for Osera, and that was exactly what he was going to do. In the face of such simple, bald determination, even Whitefall's expert maneuvering was useless. Of course, just because he'd lost didn't mean Whitefall was done fighting.

"I'm setting Monpress's trial for noon tomorrow," he said casually as he wrote. "The execution will probably be that night, considering the overwhelming evidence. Should be quite the event. I do hope you'll still be in town to see it."

He glanced up, but Josef's stony expression hadn't changed a hair, and Whitefall returned to his writing with a sigh. "So much for honor among thieves."

He wrote in silence for another minute before handing the paper to Josef. The king read it twice and then leaned over the desk, signing his name on the line Whitefall had drawn below the last paragraph. Whitefall turned the paper around and signed as well, stamping his seal in ink at the bottom.

"That it?" Josef said.

"That is it," Whitefall said tiredly. "Unless you mean to kick me while I'm down as well?"

"No need," Josef said.

He turned to leave, avoiding Eli's eyes as he did, and left the Merchant Prince's office without another word. Nico followed him silently, a shadow behind her swordsman. As the door shut behind them, Whitefall leaned back in his chair and tossed the contract on the table.

"And to think Theresa posted two hundred thousand gold standards trying to get *that* back."

He glared at the door a moment longer, then reached back and pulled a velvet rope hidden behind his bookcase. The guards entered immediately, rushing to Eli. They hauled him up straight in his chair, though he was still sitting as straight as when they'd left. When Eli grunted in protest, the larger guard bent his arm back painfully. Eli went limp at once, giving the large man his best pathetic look.

"Take him away," Whitefall said. "And tell the pages I need to see the Revenue Board, the Bounty Committee, and the Judiciary as soon as possible. Also, Sara is not to be admitted to my office for the rest of the day."

"Yes, Merchant Prince," the guards said, cutting Eli free.

Eli stood gratefully, stretching his arms before the guards caught them and tied him again for the trip back. When they cut the gag from his mouth, he pushed the handkerchief out with his tongue and glanced over his shoulder.

"Pleasure to finally meet you, Alber," he called.

Whitefall didn't even look up as the guards dragged Eli out of his office.

CHAPTER
10

Sparrow was waiting just outside. He fell into step with Eli's guards as they marched down the stairs, but when they reached the end of the spiraling hall, he told the guards to return to the Merchant Prince; he would take the prisoner from here. The guards didn't look happy about this. They hadn't looked happy since Whitefall had first sent them out of his office, but, now as then, they obeyed, and Sparrow led Eli down through the doorway and into Sara's cavern alone.

As they climbed down the metal stairs, Eli saw that Sparrow was dragging a little. His already uncharacteristic silence was punctuated with sharp gasps, as though breathing hurt him. The gasps only got worse when they reached the ground, and Eli decided it was time to pry.

"All right," he said, slowing down. "I give in. What's wrong?"

"You mean right now, or with this situation in general?" Sparrow said, his voice thin and strained.

"I mean why do you sound like you're having a heart attack?" Eli said. "I can't take pride in an escape if the only reason I got out was because my guard dropped dead."

"Your compassion is touching," Sparrow said, pushing Eli to make him go faster. "If you must know, your mother is rather angry with me at the moment."

"And that's making it hard for you to breathe?" Eli said, dragging his feet along the dark stone as best he could. "How does that work?"

"Terribly well, actually," Sparrow said. "Here we are."

He stopped them at the shiny door to the cistern prison Eli and Banage shared.

"Hands out, please," Sparrow said. "Now hold still while I figure out what new knot those Council idiots invented this time."

Eli shoved his hands back, waving them up and down to make the untying as difficult as possible. Meanwhile, he took the precious opportunity to study the lid to his cell from this side. His eyes, already adjusted to the dark from the walk, picked out the same interlocked concentric circles he'd seen inside. They were probably a pressure system, he realized. A

652

kind of spring that helped the metal bounce itself open. Very clever, and very like a Shaper to use the metal's natural tension to help it move.

His eyes traced the outer lip, sliding along the polished surface until, finally, he found the hint he was looking for. An intricate mark had been pressed deep into the upper circle, the maker's seal of the lid's Shaper. There was no time to study it, so Eli burned the image into his memory as Giuseppe had taught him, focusing only on seeing, not understanding.

Understanding takes time you do not have, the old thief's voice droned in his mind. *Focus only on the physical act of observation, Eliton, and save the understanding for later.*

It had been one of the harder lessons of being a master thief, but Eli had learned it, and he used it now, memorizing every detail of the mark in the time it took to blink and then looking elsewhere before Sparrow could catch him staring.

"There," Sparrow said, pulling the rope free. "Down you go."

He raised his foot, slamming his heel down at the dead center of the door's concentric circles. The metal boomed at the impact, and the door bounced up like a dog standing for a treat. When it was all the way up, Sparrow gave Eli a little push, and Eli, taking the hint, began to climb down.

"I want you to know it's been a real pleasure," Sparrow said, kneeling on the prison's edge as Eli descended into the dark. "It's not every day you see the famous Eli Monpress crawling down a hole like a rat. I very much doubt we'll meet each other again, but I do hope you'll remember our time together well enough to stay clear of me in the future. Not that I don't enjoy your company, understand, but a man of my talents doesn't relish the tornado of attention you seem to attract."

"No worries," Eli said. "If I have the slightest chance of avoiding you, I'll be sure to take it."

Sparrow laughed at this, a bright sound that cut off with a sharp, pained breath.

Eli looked up, half expecting to see Sparrow keeling over the pit, clutching his chest in pain as he fell. But the hateful man was still perched on the ledge like his namesake, smiling wide through clenched teeth.

"Good luck, Eliton," he called. "And good-bye."

Eli frowned in confusion, but before he could ask what Sparrow meant by that, the man stood and hit the door again. It dropped closed with a soft hiss, plunging Eli into a darkness so deep it felt like he was drowning. The feeling lasted less than a breath. The moment the door was fully closed, Banage's small candlelight flickered to life.

"Nice trick," Eli said, smiling at the dim, flickering light. "How'd you sneak that spirit past Sara?"

"It's not my spirit," Banage said. "Sara left me one candle when she first locked me down here. The wax is long gone, but I've been keeping the flame alive as best I can on my own energy."

"Seems a little unorthodox," Eli said, dropping to the ground.

Banage's voice grew defensive. "It was a fair exchange. He would have gone out otherwise. I've promised to join him with my fire bird." He lowered the flame. "Enough. What was that about?"

"I don't know," Eli lied, dusting off his now badly smudged white suit. "And I don't think I care. I've had about enough of Council politics. What do you say we get out of here?"

"I think that's the most sensible thing you've ever said."

For the first time in a very, very long while, Eli gave his father a genuine smile. Banage gave a surprised jerk and then slowly smiled back. The situation was so unbelievable, Eli just shook his head as he dropped to a crouch and set his mind on the task at hand. It was time to try the new angle he'd thought of on his way down. Grinning, he felt along the wall until his fingers found the one spirit he and Banage hadn't considered in their initial assessment.

The hole Sara had stuck them in hadn't always been used for

keeping pesky wizards locked up. Before it was a cistern prison, it had been an actual cistern, catching the water that gathered here at the lowest point in the cavern. But with a hole this deep, the stone couldn't be counted on to keep itself up. It needed a brace, and in this particular case, that brace was a flat piece of metal the width of Eli's palm that ran in a U shape up both sides of the prison and across the pit's floor.

Eli seized on the metal like a child grabbing a present, running his fingers eagerly over the brace's cold, rust-pitted surface. The metal was locked in deep, deep sleep against the silent stone. It didn't stir at Eli's prodding, not even when he knocked his knuckles over the rivets that held it to the stone. Undeterred, Eli sat down and reached out with both hands, softly thrumming his fingers up and down the metal, scratching the rust like he'd scratch an itchy spot on a dog's back.

Minutes ticked by, but Eli didn't stop. He just kept moving his fingers, whispering encouraging sounds laced with just enough power to draw the sleeping spirit's attention. It was tiring work. The stone he sat on was hard and cold, and keeping his spirit cracked open a tiny fraction for such an extended period of time was like trying to hold a bucket of water at arm's length without letting it drop. But Eli was a professional, and he didn't let up until, finally, the metal twitched against his fingers.

Eli stopped his movements at once, holding his hands still in the air.

"What are you doing?" Banage whispered, his voice hoarse, as though he'd been holding the question back for a long time.

Eli put his finger to his lips. On the floor, the metal twitched again, and then a tiny, rusty voice whispered, "Well?"

"Well what?" Eli asked.

"Keep going," the metal said, arching up a millimeter. "That felt nice."

Eli winked at Banage, who was staring at him like he'd just turned into a ghosthound, and lowered his hands back to the metal. "Like this?"

"Yesssssss..." the metal hissed, vibrating under his scratching fingers.

"Hasn't anyone been down to rub you?" Eli said, his voice thick with scornful astonishment. "Don't they take care of you here?"

"No," the metal said, wiggling. "That feels lovely."

"They do this to metal upstairs all the time," Eli said, intensifying his scratching. "Don't they?"

This was directed at Banage, who, after several seconds of stunned hesitation, nodded. Eli rolled his eyes, and Banage quickly changed his answer from motion to verbal.

"Yes, of course they do," he said in the most unconvincing lie Eli had ever heard.

He shook his head and made a note not to involve his father any further. Thankfully, the metal wasn't familiar enough with humans to notice the bad acting.

"Really?" it said, its creaking voice tinged with jealousy. "Must be nice."

"It's more than nice," Eli said. "I'd say it's mandatory. Are you *sure* no one's come down to rub you?"

"No," the metal said sullenly.

"Criminal," Eli said, his voice grave. "Absolutely criminal. And to think, they spent all that effort putting in a new door when they can't even be bothered to come down and take care of the metal they've got."

"Yeah." The metal shook against his hands.

"It's not right," Eli said zealously, scratching harder. "That's a Shaper-made door, too. They're terribly full of themselves. Entitled. They think the world owes them something just because they spend all their time awake."

"It's from the Shapers?" The metal creaked, arching almost like it was trying to look up. "I didn't know that. Why would something like that be all the way down here?"

"Taking attention and resources away from others, apparently," Eli said, disgusted. "I bet it's not even grateful."

"Yeah," the metal grumbled as the support beams running

656

along the cistern wall started to creak. "That door thinks it's so great. I'm the one holding up all the weight."

"I just can't believe this," Eli said. "Hang on, I'm going to go have a talk with it. You stay here and let Banage scratch you. I'll get us some answers."

"Yeah!" the door said again.

Eli stood up, motioning frantically for Banage to take his place. After a slight hesitation, the former Rector leaned over and started running his fingers over the metal just as Eli had been doing. The brace sighed contentedly, rolling back and forth like a dog angling to have its belly rubbed. When Eli was sure Banage could keep it up, he turned and shimmied up the ladder to the door.

The polished steel surface was perfectly still, but Eli could almost feel the door leaning away from him. He smiled and hooked his legs under the top rung of the ladder so he could lean back and look at the door directly.

"You're not talking to me," he said gently. "I understand. You're just doing your job, after all. But since we're going to be together for a while, and seeing as you're a Shaper door, I was hoping I could ask you a question."

The door creaked suspiciously.

"I'm no expert on Shapers," Eli continued undeterred. "But I did notice the mountain swallow in your maker's mark. Isn't that the mark of Heinricht Slorn?"

"Absolutely not," the door answered, its voice surprisingly loud after so much stubborn silence. "Heinricht is a traitor to the Mountain. I was Shaped by Jonath Findel, master blacksmith and loyal student of the Great Teacher."

"Findel," Eli said, stroking his chin. "I've seen some of his work. Fantastic stuff, really brilliant designs."

Eli didn't know a Findel from a fondant, but it didn't matter. The door was rolling now.

"Absolutely brilliant," the door agreed, its metal rings humming with pleasure. "I'm a prototype for a new kind of locking mechanism designed specifically for Lady Sara. Of

657

course, I was originally made to stand upright, but as you see, Findel's design works either way thanks to the coils. True brilliance is utterly adaptable."

"So when she needed a door, she came to you," Eli said.

"Of course," the door rattled with pride. "Who else could switch directions to act as an emergency prison door? Thanks to my Shaper's work, I'm miles beyond the dull, ordinary metal you find around here." The door stopped suddenly, and Eli felt himself being looked over. "Just so you know, wizard, I'm completely loyal and utterly unbreakable. You'd have to be Gregorn himself to Enslave me, so don't even try."

Eli pressed his hand to his chest. "I would never dream of such a thing. I'm a thief, not a spirit abuser. But"—he raised his voice—"surely a door such as yourself must get bored just sitting around with all this quiet."

"Of course," the door said, slumping against the stone lip. "It's an absolute waste keeping me down here. I'm sure you're a very tricky sort of thief, but really, there's no ruse you could pull that would fool me. I'm Shaped." The door's voice swelled with pride. "Awakened! I'm a higher form of spirit than anything else you'll find in this pit."

Eli nodded in commiseration. "No one to talk to, eh?"

"No one worth the effort," the door said. "I mean, look around. There's nothing but the bedrock, who never wakes up, and the metal support, who has the conversational skills of a cockroach. A rather dumb cockroach, I might add."

At this, the metal rungs Eli was standing on, rungs that, it should be noted, were attached to the metal support brace, began to vibrate. All along the walls, stone dust was falling in little cascades where the support beam met the stone. The door didn't seem to notice.

"I'm just biding my time until I can get back to a real use of my talents," it said, turning its interlocked rings in a motion that reminded Eli of a girl tossing her hair. "Sara promised me a place up top in the citadel proper once this blows over, but at this point I'd take anything to get away from these dullards."

"Dullards?" Eli prompted, moving sideways so he was clinging to the wall instead of the iron ladder.

"These stupid spirits," the door said. "All they do is sleep. Sometimes I don't even think they have minds of their own. Why a door like me should have to pick up the slack for such weak, dull, pathetic little creatures I really can't—"

Eli never got to hear the rest, for at that moment, the cistern's metal supports jerked free from their rivets and surged upward, hitting the door square on both sides. The door squealed in surprise as the force launched it upward with an echoing clang, tearing its hinges from the stone with an explosion of rubble. It landed a few feet away, crashing into the floor of the cavern hard enough to chip a large piece from the sleeping bedrock. Eli shook his head to clear the ringing from his ears and then looked down to grin at his father, who was standing far below with an utterly amazed expression on his face.

"Stupid door," the metal support muttered, sliding back into place.

"Stupid door, indeed," Eli said, giving the metal one last scratch.

The metal purred at the contact and wiggled its rivets back into their holes. When it was securely locked in place once again, the metal went still, falling instantly back into a deep sleep. And down below, Banage was still staring at his son, his mouth opening and closing like a landed fish.

"Eliton," he said at last, "did you just incite a brawl between two spirits?"

"Yep," Eli said, swinging up through the now-open top of the cell. "Pretty clever, eh?"

"*Clever?*" Banage roared. "That was horrible! How dare you take advantage of a poor, gullible spirit's loneliness to trick it into attacking one of its brethren for your own selfish—"

"You can stay down there if you don't like it," Eli said, pulling himself to his feet.

Banage snapped his mouth shut. He stood in silence a few moments, and then, with an air of unassailable dignity, climbed out of the cistern.

"This doesn't mean I agree with your methods," he said when he finally made it to his feet beside Eli. "Only that there are larger wrongs that I cannot right if I'm locked in a hole."

"Spoken like a true Spiritualist," Eli said. "You're welcome, by the way."

Banage pressed his mouth in a tight line and said nothing.

"Well," Eli said. "Not that our time together hasn't been a delight, but I need to get moving. This has already been one of the longest unintended incarcerations of my career, and I'm not looking to push it any further. I'd suggest you take the back exit." He pointed through the dark at where he was reasonably certain the service door stood. "Should be easier for a man of your inexperience."

Banage shook his head. "I'm not leaving."

Eli sighed dramatically. Rings, of course. "You know," he said, "you'd probably have better luck demanding your rings from Sara through an official Court petition. I know Miranda would help you draw one up."

"My rings aren't why I'm staying," Banage said. "Watch."

He closed his eyes, and the weight of his spirit landed on Eli without warning. Banage opened his soul like throwing open a door, and the call that rang through it was deafening.

Far across the cavern, from the direction of the barely visible glow of Sara's headquarters, a chorus of voices shouted in surprise. A second later, the whole cavern shook with the sound of metal tearing. The floor rumbled as the sound solidified into pounding hoofbeats that grew closer and closer until, just when Eli was sure he'd be deaf for life if this kept up one second longer, Banage's jade horse burst from the shadows between the tanks and skidded to a stop before its master.

Banage reached up to stroke its glossy stone muzzle before taking a pile of gold from the spirit's mouth. "Didn't I tell you," Banage said, slipping his rings onto his fingers. "Not a problem."

"If you could do that, why didn't you do it *before?*" Eli shouted.

"Because Durrel couldn't break through the cell door without chipping himself, and I would never knowingly do him harm," Banage said, glancing at his son. "Shouldn't you be going?"

"Well, after all that noise, I guess I'd better," Eli muttered, shaking his head. Powers, what theatrics. Banage's horse would lead everyone right to them. "Do what you want, old man."

But as he started to jog away, he heard Banage's voice softly over the din of shouts that was rising from the walkways above.

"It was good to see you again, Eliton."

Eli heaved an enormous sigh and ran into the dark, waving with one hand before vanishing into the forest of tanks.

At the other end of the Citadel, Sara was busy with a confrontation of a different sort.

"*How dare you?*" she shouted, slamming her hands down on the glossy wood of the Merchant Prince's desk. "How *dare* you take my son for your games, Alber! He is a vital resource for the expansion of the knowledge of magic. He is *not* a bargaining chip!"

"You were the one who tried to keep him from me in the first place," Alber said, not even looking up from the pile of papers his assistant was passing him to sign.

"To keep you from doing something like this!" Sara roared.

Whitefall sighed. "Sara, I am very busy—"

"I don't care," Sara snapped. "You shouldn't, either, not if that business comes at the cost of our alliance. Your precious Council would never have stayed together if it wasn't for me and my work. Work that you've just put in terrible jeopardy, if you care to know. What were you thinking, trying to trade Eliton to that bloodthirsty, no-account swordsman?"

"Considering that bloodthirsty, no-account swordsman pretty much owns the Council at this point, I should think you'd be happier if he'd taken my offer," Whitefall said drily. "Now I'm going to have to sell your son for the bounty so we can make ends meet for the next few years."

"I won't allow it!" Sara cried. "He is not going before the Judiciary today or ever. And I can't believe you thought you could just order me out of your office and keep it a secret!"

"I'm not going to waste my breath pointing out the hypocrisy of that statement," Alber said drily, but Sara bowled over him.

"I have not put up with you for almost three decades to be treated like this now, Alber!" she cried. "This is absolutely unacceptable!"

"I don't care if you accept it or not," Whitefall snapped, slamming down his papers to look her straight in the eyes. "I don't have a choice in this, Sara. I have a government to run, a government that foots the bill for all of your fiddling, I might add. Considering how vital you're always insisting your work is, I'd think you'd take a greater interest in the financial health of the Council that supports it."

"Not everything is about money," Sara said through gritted teeth.

"There's too much money at stake right now for this to be about anything else," Alber said. "I've been a very lenient patron to you, Sara. I built your facility. I pay your staff's wages. I buy whatever equipment you ask for. I even let you keep Sparrow." Whitefall narrowed his eyes in a stinging glare. "Do you even know what that cost me? The man killed my cousin."

"A very distant cousin," Sara reminded him. "One *you* said you didn't like."

"Like has nothing to do with it," Alber said. "Your man killed a Whitefall. His head should be rotting on a spike over the river, but no. You wanted him. Powers knew why, but you wanted that murderer, so I covered it up. Though it jeopardized some of the closest ties in the Whitefall family to do so, I hid

662

Sparrow's involvement and gave him to you. I did this because I believe your work is vital to making this Council the dominant political force for centuries to come, but we are nearing the limit of what I can give, Sara."

Sara started to answer that, but Whitefall cut her off. "Since we've got fifty years to pay Osera, I have time to call in the Monpress bounty slowly and hopefully avoid economic collapse, but I will not take the absurd risk of keeping the greatest escape artist in history locked in a cell. He goes to the noose tonight, and that is not open to negotiation. So if you have something you want from your wayward son, I suggest you wring it out of him in the next few hours, because that's all you're going to get."

Sara slammed her hands on the desk, scattering his papers. "You're going to regret this, Whitefall," she growled.

"I already regret this whole situation," Alber said, gathering his papers back into their piles. "But if you need someone to scream at, I suggest taking your rage out on Josef of Osera. He's the one who decided to let your son hang. I'm just the middleman."

Sara scraped her nails across the polished wood, and then, without another word, she turned on her heel and stalked out, slamming the heavy office door so hard she heard books fall from Alber's shelves. Sara didn't care. Her mind was a seething fury when she spotted Sparrow waiting by the stairs. He was the picture of obedience, and it didn't help her mood one bit.

"*You*," she hissed, glaring murder at her garishly dressed assistant. "You're in more trouble than he is. I told you to watch the Court, and where have you been? Sneaking behind my back and taking my son to Whitefall, of all people—"

"He asked me," Sparrow said, pleading.

"And how did he know?" Sara snapped.

"I told you. Whitefall always finds out," Sparrow said.

"Not that fast," Sara said, eyeing him suspiciously.

Sparrow looked aghast. "Surely you don't think *I* did it? You're the only lifeline I've got, Sara. I'd never betray you."

"Then why did you bring my son to Alber?"

"He's my boss, too," Sparrow said, exasperated. "I can't just—"

He cut off with a wince as Sara's hand slipped inside her coat.

She let him dangle like that a bit, rolling his orb between her fingers before reaching past it to pull out her hastily extinguished, half-smoked pipe instead. "I am the only authority you should worry about, Sparrow," she said quietly, setting the pipe between her teeth. "You'd do well to remember that your capacity to please and serve me is the only thing keeping the ax off your neck. Do you understand?"

"More than you will ever know," Sparrow said, stepping forward to offer her a light.

Sara puffed against the match flame, glaring at him through the rising smoke. "This isn't over," she said once the pipe was going. "It won't come tonight, because that's all I have to learn whatever it is Eliton's keeping secret, but one night won't matter. You're going to be doing penance for this for the next decade. I'll make you wish—"

She froze midstep, her pipe falling from her mouth. Sparrow caught it neatly, holding it between her slack teeth. "What?"

"The door to Eliton and Etmon's cell just cried out," Sara said, snapping her jaw shut. He started to say something else, but she held up her hand. "And there's Etmon's spirit," she said, pushing past him. "Downstairs. Now."

Sparrow followed dutifully, bobbing behind her like a brightly colored shadow. They cleared the citadel proper in record time, bursting through the door at the top of the cavern with a *clang* that was lost in the roar below. Sara stopped cold, clinging to the iron railing as she stared down in disbelief.

The usually dark cavern was bright as day, lit by a bird of fire the size of a ghosthound that was flying in slow circles just below the hollowed-out ceiling. Down on the floor, her wizards were shouting, holding up their hands against what looked like a mass of twisted wood. She could feel their open spirits against her own, but as her staff had always been limited to the Spirit Court's leavings, it was a pathetic showing. The lot of them couldn't stop the roots as they shot out and twisted around the closest tank.

The iron groaned as the roots began to pull, and then it toppled, spilling a flood of beautiful blue water onto the dusty floor. As this happened, another spirit, a great jade horse, ran past her line of sight, its glossy legs splashing through water that was already a foot deep. It reared as Sara watched, kicking the next tank with enough force to puncture the iron wall. Water sprang through the hole, shooting out in a torrent of brilliant color.

For several moments, Sara could only watch in horror. Even under the fire bird's orange light, the water on the floor was bluer than blue, a pure azure shining with its own light, the light she had nurtured, the light that was now dying out as the water mixed with the dust and grime. It flowed down the slight slope toward the center of the cavern, toward…Sara's eyes shot up and froze, caught on the twisted, blown-out ruin of what had been her office. The large tank was almost unrecognizable, the metal plates yanked apart by enormous force to reveal the stairwell that led to the water below, *her* water.

Sara's chest began to ache, and she suddenly realized she hadn't taken a breath for nearly thirty seconds. She gulped in the air as she looked frantically around the cavern, her gaze sliding past the spirits, past her own useless wizards, to lock on the man responsible. The second she had enough air, she screamed at the top of her lungs.

"Etmon!"

The tall wizard standing on the suspended walkway turned. Even from this distance, she could see the look of triumph on his face.

"Your husband certainly can make a mess," Sparrow said, peering over the railing.

"Shut up," Sara spat, tearing off her coat. "I'll handle Etmon. You find Eli."

"Find Eli Monpress?" Sparrow cried. "In this chaos?"

"Do it!" Sara roared, shoving her coat at him.

She didn't even wait for him to nod. She just spat out her pipe and hopped up on the railing, ignoring the protests of her aging knees. As soon as she was up, she fell forward, plummeting toward the water as she gripped the large, polished quartz on the ring of jewels hanging from her belt.

The moment her fingers touched it, the wind sprang forth. It caught her like a falling feather, blowing her up just before she hit the intact tanks below. Sara held out her arms, balancing as the wind set her down on the suspended walkway a dozen feet from Banage. She gripped the handrail to steady herself, the wind returning to its crystal as she raised her head to met Banage's haughty gaze with a look of pure, molten rage.

"I told you it would all come to light, Sara," he said solemnly. "It always does. Sooner or later—"

A blast of wind knocked him off the walkway midword.

Banage fell like a stone for several feet before a tangle of branches caught him, lowering him gently to the ground. Sara pulled her wind back, binding it around her body as she sent a spike of power to the largest of her red jewels. The temperature began to rise as the wind swirling around her filled with embers, wreathing her in red light. The wind spun faster and faster, blowing the fire inside hotter and hotter. When it was as hot as she could stand, Sara jumped the railing again, sailing down through the air after Banage. Another tank toppled as she fell, spilling its blue, blue water without so much as a cry.

Behind her, forgotten, Sara's wizards were fleeing into the citadel. They crammed the stairwell in their panic, rushing toward the safety of the Council. And though they ran right by them, none of the fleeing wizards noticed the two coats abandoned on the railing, one plain and white like theirs, the other a gold-embroidered tapestry of turquoise, their sleeves fluttering in the hot, dry wind.

* * *

666

Eli Monpress was severely disappointed by the security at Whitefall Citadel. He'd expected to have to do some serious legwork, maybe even a little climbing, but in the end he'd been able to walk right out through a side door. Of course, the guards were a little preoccupied by the fit Banage was throwing in the cellar, but still, disappointing. Didn't anyone make a proper citadel anymore?

To be fair, the guardhouse would have been harrier if he hadn't managed to nick a fine military overcoat, complete with medals, from the coat check. As it was, he'd had no problems. With all that authority on his chest, the soldiers had opened the gate without a second glance, letting Eli Monpress stroll leisurely into freedom.

It was far too fine a day for heavy clothing, so he ditched the military coat as soon as the citadel gate was out of sight and snatched a nice, broad farmer's hat from a tragically unattended shop front. He ditched Benehime's white coat as well, stripping down to his shirtsleeves in the alley between two buildings.

He put his back to the wall and ran his shirt along it, staining the fine, white fabric with grime. His hands, already filthy from climbing around in the cistern, he wiped across his shirtfront until it was hopelessly smudged. When he'd stained himself to his satisfaction, he rolled up his sleeves and kicked off his white boots, letting his pants, which were already acceptably dingy from his imprisonment, hang down over his bare feet.

Eli smiled at his efforts and slapped the straw hat on his head. Then, dirty and barefoot with his head down beneath the broad brim of his hat, he turned onto one of Zarin's busiest streets. Though his smiling face was plastered across nearly every wall, Eli walked through the crowd without causing a ripple, just another poor, dirty farmer, passing right under people's notice. If the snobbery hadn't been so advantageous, Eli might have been insulted.

He made it as far as the wharf without a hitch, but then his plans stumbled. Something must have happened while he'd been in prison, because the roads down to the river were a chaos of soldiers and soggy, bedraggled boat workers. A few seconds of listening told Eli that the river had flooded, which, considering there had been no major rains lately, he found very surprising. Still, the river district was clearly out of the running, so Eli slipped away from the crowd between the buildings and started up toward the workman's quarter high on the city's northern ridge.

The farther he went from the Citadel, the smaller and rougher the buildings became. Carriages were fewer and more storefronts were open instead of glassed. When he finally reached what he judged as the right part of the wrong side of town, Eli slowed down and started looking in earnest. He walked in a weaving pattern, studying and dismissing several taverns before he found the one that was just the right sort of seedy. Ducking under the faded sign, he pushed open the swinging door and slipped inside without a sound.

The place was dead. This close to dinner time, even drunks were home with their families. The lone barman didn't even look up as Eli walked through the empty taproom toward the darkest, farthest corner table tucked away between the fireplace and ale casks where two familiar figures sat playing cards.

"Took you long enough," Josef said as Eli took the empty chair with its back toward the room. "Nice hat."

"Thank you," Eli said, motioning for Nico to deal him in. "I hope you weren't waiting long."

"We just got here," Josef said. "Oserans are tenacious bastards, took us forever to shake them."

"I have to admit I was a little worried you wouldn't show," Eli said, picking up each Daggerback card as Nico dealt it. "After that display in Whitefall's office, I almost believed kingship really had lured you in. If I'd known you could act like that, I would have worked out more two-man cons."

"Who said I was acting?" Josef grumbled. "I meant it when

I said I wasn't going to trade my people's money for a thief, and I promised my mother I'd take care of Osera."

"So what are you doing here, then?" Eli said, frowning at his hand.

Josef leaned back, fanning out his cards while his free hand fiddled with the collar of his expensive coat. To a causal observer, he probably looked like a roughneck on a lucky streak. Certainly not the king of a Council Kingdom. "I think five hundred thousand gold standards is more than enough care for any country," he said slowly. "It's no secret I'm a pretty terrible king, so I figured now that money's not an issue I should just get out of the way and let the people who want to rule have a go."

"Very prudent," Eli said. "I mean, it's painfully obvious you don't know anything about the niceties of politics."

"I thought we did pretty well," Josef said with a shrug.

Eli gave him a flat look. "You brought a *severed head* to a meeting with the Merchant Prince of Zarin."

"What other proof am I supposed to bring?" Josef said. "His body was too big to haul around."

Nico covered her mouth in a cough that sounded suspiciously like a laugh. Eli just rolled his eyes.

"Now that that's settled," Josef said, "where to?"

Eli scowled, suddenly serious. He'd been thinking about that question ever since he got out of the Citadel, and no matter how many angles he tried, there seemed to be only one answer he could live with. "The Shaper Mountain," he said at last. "Karon is missing."

Nico looked up. "Your lava spirit?"

Eli nodded. "Benehime took him away for helping me, but the Shaper Mountain will know where he is. Lava spirits are as much rock as fire, so they fall under the Mountain's star as well as the great Lava River that minds all the fires. The Shaper Mountain knows as well as I do that Karon will die unless he finds a volcano willing to take him or I get him back. The old rock pile might put on a good front as a loyal star, but I know for a fact he's not as law abiding as he pretends, especially not when one of his children, however distant, is on the line."

Josef sighed. "Should I be concerned that I understood none of that?"

"Nope," Eli answered. "Not unless you have a problem with going back to the mountains."

"Mountains are fine," Josef said. "While I know Osera will fare better without me, the rest of the country doesn't seem to agree. I'm sure they'll come around once they realize that not having a king actually sitting on the throne doesn't mean the world is ending, but for right now the farther away from Osera we get, the better I'll feel."

"That makes things easier," Eli said. "Nico?"

Nico shrugged. "If Josef doesn't care, I don't. I lost my fear of the mountains months ago."

"Easier still," Eli said, tossing his cards on the table. "It's decided then. Let's get out of here. That was a lousy draw anyway, and I've had more than enough of Zarin to last me another twenty years."

"Figures," Josef said, handing his cards to Nico. "The one time I get the Shepherdess."

"She's not all she's cracked up to be," Eli said, slapping his hat back onto his head.

Josef tossed some coins on the table as Nico tucked the Daggerback deck into her coat. The barkeep nodded to them as they left, never realizing that he'd just let the three most wanted criminals in the Council stroll out his front door.

"Do we need to pick up any operating funds?" Josef asked, adjusting the wrapped shape of the Heart on his back as they walked.

"Nope," Eli said. "I've got it covered."

He turned them down an alley and reached into his shirt, drawing out a set of tiny golden spoons. Josef's eyes widened as the spoons were joined by a silver-wrought paperweight, a pair of delicate porcelain horses, and a miniature landscape still in its gilt frame.

"Where were they keeping you?" he asked as Eli piled his wealth in Nico's hands. "A museum?"

"Oh, come on," Eli said, fishing around in his pockets. "I was in the Council Citadel. I couldn't leave empty-handed, could I?"

Josef rolled his eyes as Eli added several rare coins, a jeweled curtain pull, and an inkwell bearing the Whitefall family crest to the pile.

"That's all I could fit," he said with a regretful sigh. "We have to go back, though. Whitefall has amazing taste, and we could really use a wider collection of porcelain at Home."

"Put it on the list," Josef said. "Now, let's find a fence and get going."

Eli held out his arms in a grand gesture for Josef to lead the way, and they set off down the street toward a square filled with exactly the sort of dark, seedy stalls that would suit their purposes. Behind them in the distance, the Council Citadel's golden spires trembled, sending pigeons fleeing across the sunset sky.

CHAPTER
11

Sara lashed out. A wave of fire followed her motion, washing Banage under. For a moment he was lost in the flames, but then cool mist fanned out around him, quenching the fire in midair.

When the flames were gone, the mist returned to its master, circling his body in a protective blanket. Sara drew the remains of her fire back, the wind and flame hissing together as they retreated. Behind his wall of fog, Banage glared and stretched out his hand to touch the metal wall of the closest, unspilled tank.

"Stop!" Sara cried, holding up her hands. Her eyes went wide as Banage's fingers pressed against the metal, the great black ring on his thumb glowing like the sun through smoked glass. As the ring's light grew, the cavern floor started to rumble as a great stone hand yanked itself from the ground. It rose up with a grinding sound, folding its dark, rocky fingers in a mirror of Banage's own around the tank's metal supports.

"Etmon, *please*," Sara begged, eyes locked on Banage's stone spirit as her tank began to wobble. "Do you even know what you're destroying?"

"Oh, I know." Banage's voice was as cold as his fog. "For the first time, Sara, I know. I always suspected, but I thought surely, *surely* I couldn't be right. You were a Spiritualist once. You couldn't possibly have strayed that far. Now, I know better."

The metal tank groaned as the stone hand began to push.

"This isn't the Spirit Court," Sara said calmly. "You have no right to come in here and shove your morals—"

"I have every right!" Banage roared. "Morals don't change with location! There is truth in this world, Sara. Right and wrong. These things don't vanish when you close your eyes, and you can't make them go away by burying them in a cave."

Sara flinched at the scorn in his voice. "I've nothing to be ashamed of."

"Of course you do," Banage said, his deep voice rich with power. "Or you wouldn't be hiding down here. You always were a show-off. You'd done the impossible, created a spirit that could be broken into three parts separated by any distance and yet still be connected enough to pass words between them. The Relay is possibly the greatest innovation in the history of magic, and yet you've never said anything about how it works. Nothing. That alone was proof."

"Proof of what?" Sara snapped. "That I was guarding the Council's secrets? The Relay is the base of the Council's power. *Of course* I hid it."

"So you really think you've done nothing wrong?" Banage

said, looking at the tank. "Well then, since I'm a traitor and no one will listen to me anyway, it won't matter if I see for myself."

"Etmon," Sara said, her voice ringing with warning. "Etmon, *no*."

She flung out her hand, too late. Banage's ring flashed as his stone spirit pushed up, breaking the tank's metal supports like straws. The tank fell with a groan of twisting metal. The floor shook as it hit, and the metal casing broke with a loud, cracking pop. The only thing that didn't make a sound was the water that spilled from the tank's sundered side.

The water shone bluer than blue as it fell. Heartbreakingly clear, even as it mixed with the dust and grime on the floor below. It made no sound as it fell and no sound when it landed, not a splash, not a burble, nothing at all. Banage was just as silent as he watched it pour, but when he raised his eyes to Sara again, they were full of fury.

"I thought it would be happy," he whispered. "When I broke the first tank, I thought the water would leap to freedom. Even then, I didn't realize how bad it was. I didn't know you'd taken everything from it, even its voice."

Sara watched the blue water pouring from the tank stoically, resisting the urge to scrub her eyes. All her work, gone.

"You collected the water," Banage went on. "You picked the small spirits, the ones too weak to have a full consciousness of their own." His voice grew disgusted. "I saw the *hole* where you combined them below your office. You poured the water together in utter, oppressive silence, quieting and mixing them in that stone hole in the ground until you had a new spirit large enough to be awakened. And you did awaken it. That's the worst part. You kept the water awake, but you never let it speak. You never even let it discover its name, did you? You couldn't. In order for the spirit to be quiet enough, still enough, *empty* enough to transfer voices clearly, it had to be isolated. *Stunted.*"

"It's not like that," Sara said. "You're skipping several key—"

Banage's hand shot out, his finger pointed accusingly at the silent fountain flowing from the broken tank. "You created something pure, a distilled water spirit, and *you locked it in the dark.* It's water's nature to flow and mix and create new spirits wherever it pools, but you, *you* trapped it in a tank and pushed it down. You and your wizards took a newborn spirit and locked it away like a child in a closet."

"There was no other way," Sara snapped. "I needed to transmit a human voice instantly between one place and another. *Any* human voice, wizard or spirit deaf, and the only way to accomplish that was through vibrations. Water worked excellently, but I couldn't just run a hose between whoever was talking. If my plan was going to work, I had to divide the water, but even the largest, most alert spirits forgot about their water as soon as it left them. I'd take a bucket from an awakened fountain, and by the time I'd lifted it, the water in the bucket was its own spirit, disconnected from the first and utterly useless."

"That is the nature of water," Banage said scornfully. "To disconnect and reconnect, to *flow.*"

"It was a problem," Sara said, standing straighter. "A problem *I* solved. Quieting spirits is nothing new. Your own rings are quieted to make room for the spirits they house."

"Rings are different!" Banage shouted. "Jewels and metal are still by nature. Water moves constantly. To quiet water is cruel."

"It was brilliant!" Sara shouted back. "I was the one who discovered that if you took a water spirit and isolated it from everything from the moment you woke it, something extraordinary happened. The quieted water never realized it was part of a larger world. It never learned its name, and it never connected with the greater spirits above it. This disconnection gave the quieted water an extraordinary property. With only its own spirit for comfort in the world, the water had Spirit Unity like nothing else I've ever seen. I could chop a tank in half and sail it across the Unseen Sea and it would still be one spirit with the half I'd left behind."

Sara took a step forward, her voice trembling with the excitement of finally being able to explain her Relay to someone who would understand, if not appreciate, her cleverness. "Don't you see, Etmon? It was perfect. The quieted water was still enough to pass voices, and its ignorance of other spirits besides itself meant I could divide the water up and send the pieces across the Council. I could pass voices instantly over thousands of miles, and even better, I could do it without wizards. Oh, I kept wizards with the points to make sure the water stayed isolated, but the Relay passes sound, not will. Even Sparrow could use them. It was *brilliant*. The only downside was how long it took me to make a point and how much water was required. I needed enough to make sure the spirit was big enough to have a cohesive soul, but in order to preserve the isolation, the majority of the water had to be locked in silence. That's where I got the idea for the tanks. Hundreds of spirits all held together, and each one thinks it's alone in the world."

Sara took a deep breath. "Absolutely brilliant. Someday I hope to find a way to make the tanks smaller, but even if I never figure it out, the Relay was the discovery of a lifetime. The foundation of my career. Even you have to admit it's genius."

"It's cruelty!" Banage screamed. "Inhuman, unforgivable cruelty! I'd call it Enslavement, but you found a way to subjugate a spirit without touching it. You've shackled living spirits with their own ignorance, their fear of being alone, and for *what*? Sending trade deals? The business of running a Council?"

Sara heaved an angry breath. "Powers, Banage, it's only water."

"*Only water?*" Banage's cry was horrifying. "Are you truly that far gone, Sara? Look around you!" He threw out his hands at the remaining tanks, the water lapping at their feet. "Every one of these has a mind. They feel pain, loss, *suffering*. Far more than their share of suffering, thanks to you. What if you'd had to Enslave a person for your Relay. Would you have done it then? Would you have kept a child locked down here alone in the dark if it served your career? Would you have done this to Eli?"

"Don't be stupid, Etmon," Sara said, forcing her voice to stay measured, stay calm. "There's a world of difference between people and spirits, even between the spirits themselves. You said it yourself, water flows. Its ability to flow in and out of itself is unique in the spirit world. Cut a rock in half and you have two spirits with half the power and intelligence of the original. They can never be rejoined, only reforged and born again in the molten fires beneath the mountains. But water is *different*. Pour out half a bucket of water and the half that remains is diminished. But, unlike a rock, you can pour that water back *in*, and the spirit is restored. Or you can pour the whole bucket into a river and it becomes the river, which becomes the sea."

She pointed at the water that covered their feet. "All this water is draining away. Maybe it will flow to the Whitefall River. Maybe it will evaporate and become rain. Maybe it will just stay here forever. But whatever happens, this water you're so deathly concerned about will eventually become part of something else, and anything I did to it will be forgotten. An abused child is damaged forever, but water can forget a hundred years of torment between one wave and the next."

"So if suffering is forgotten, that makes it forgivable?" Banage said, his voice low.

"There's nothing to forgive," Sara said, crossing her arms. "The water is ignorant. It doesn't even know it's being wronged. And when you look at the larger picture, even you should see that I've actually been doing a great good. Think about it, the Relay gives the Council of Thrones power the individual kingdoms cannot touch. This power provides a lasting peace and prosperity that will ultimately make everything's life on this continent, spirit and human, better. So yes, I think the temporary suffering of water spirits who will forget all about

676

it as soon as they're released is perfectly forgivable considering what we all get in return."

Banage's face twisted into a look of pure disgust. "I would never believe anyone who'd bound a spirit in service could think such thoughts."

"Well, you never were any good at knowing what I was thinking," Sara said bitterly, crossing her arms. "And I only ever bound one spirit."

"I remember," Banage said. "I was there. Ollor was a calm, deep water spirit. When I first heard that the Relay's full name was the Ollor Relay, my heart lifted. I thought it was proof that a part of you remembered your oaths. Now, I'm not so ignorant." His eyes darkened as he stepped forward. "Which tank is he in, Sara?"

Sara stiffened, then forced herself to relax. There was no point in lying anymore.

"The center one," she said. "He was the first, the spirit who helped me learn how to make the Relay work. It seemed only fitting the final product should bear his name."

Banage closed his eyes. "After such loyalty," he whispered. "That spirit stayed with you when you renounced your oaths. He followed you here, let you experiment on his water. He served you faithfully, and this was how you rewarded him?"

"I put him to sleep," Sara countered. "I've seen your own protégé do as much to the sea she shoved down her throat. And now that sea is lost to the waves while my Ollor is the anchor for a network of spirits that are helping to bring world peace." She lifted her chin with a haughty stare. "Who served their spirit better, Etmon?"

Banage looked away in disgust. "Enough," he said, raising his arm. "This ends now, Sara."

"And what will you do?" Sara said. "Destroy everything I've built? Make yourself a true enemy of the Council? Whitefall will have to kill you for this, you know. The Spirit Court won't be able to stop him, not that they'll want to. The Relay

677

is the heart of the Council. Destroy it and you'll be known forever as the man who killed our best hope for peace."

Banage hesitated then, and Sara bit her lip, reaching down to call her fire spirit for a surprise attack on his open back. But before she could reach the red jewel at her waist, a slow smile, the same one she'd once found so handsome, spread across Banage's face.

"Better to be the man who destroyed peace than the man who saw suffering and did nothing," he said, clenching his fist.

"No!" Sara shrieked, but she was too late. Even as her fire spirit roared forward, Banage brought his fist down.

As it fell, the ground began to rumble, the quiet water shaking in delicate waves that grew larger and larger, soaking her legs. All across the cavern, the tanks were shaking, bobbing back and forth like corks. And then, with an enormous rumbling crack, Banage's fully opened spirit struck her like a hammer, and the ground exploded.

Deep black stone shot up from the floor, but it wasn't her bedrock. It was Banage's stone spirit in its full glory, the huge rocky outcropping he'd won over years ago, when they were still in love. Then, it had been the size of a small castle. Now, with the help of his will, the rock had broken itself into hundreds of enormous hands, and each one was gripping the bottom of a tank. High overhead, the fire bird screamed. The jade horse galloped through the water, bucking in triumph while the tangled roots retreated to form a ring around her and Banage, a barrier against what would happen next.

Banage flexed his fingers, and the black stone hands responded in kind, filling the air with the squeal of crumpling metal. Etmon's eyes never left hers as he flipped his hand over, his wrist turning in a quick, snapping motion, like he was breaking a neck.

The stone hands mirrored his movement, and the tanks collapsed, each one falling like a felled tree. They hit the cavern floor with a deafening *clang* that knocked Sara to her knees.

She fell hard, too stunned to catch herself, and then curled in a ball, her face inches from the dirty water as the silent tide poured out. The water hit the ring made by Banage's roots with a soft rush, but otherwise there was no sound at all.

If Sara had not known already, she would have had no hint that her life's work, the great discovery that had launched every other, was draining away. Ollor was somewhere in that flood, but she didn't call him. She'd given up that bond long ago, just as she'd given up another.

When Sara raised her eyes at last, Banage was standing over her. His face was hard, set in firm approval at the rightness of his actions, the justification of his wanton destruction.

"You have no idea," she whispered, staring up. "No idea at all what you just destroyed. What you've *done*."

"None of us know the full extent of our actions," Banage replied. "But I know I was right, Sara. I know I was right."

And it was those words, spoken with such conviction, such blind, mindless faith, that undid her.

"*Right?*" she screamed, heaving herself off the ground. "You've undone the work of nations, set us all back decades, and all you can say for yourself is that you were *right*? Right by what? Some water that won't even remember to thank you? Do you even understand the concept of the greater good?"

"Good built on exploitation is no good at all," Banage said calmly. "And you know it."

He would have kept preaching forever, but Sara didn't give him the chance. The moment he closed his mouth, she threw open her spirit.

It had been a long time since Sara had opened her spirit fully. She preferred more delicate instruments, and besides, opening her spirit in the presence of the tanks would undo all the effort she'd put into keeping them quiet. But Banage was a blunt man. Blunt tactics were needed, and the tanks were already broken beyond repair. So, with nothing left to lose, Sara threw herself open and let her power pour out, doubling and tripling until she filled the room.

Sensation flooded through her. She could feel the weight of the stone, the heat of Banage's fire bird, the cold water of her broken tanks. More important, though, she could feel the lines of power, thin as thread but stronger than steel, connecting Banage to his spirits, both those who were out and the ones still in his rings. Focusing on those thin lines, Sara kept going, opening herself as far as she dared. And then, when the power was throbbing through her, surrounding and filling every inch of the cavern, she shoved it down.

The effect was immediate. Banage's spirits slammed to the ground when her power crashed into them. The root wall collapsed, the stone horse fell to its knees, the stone hands crumbled, and the fire bird plummeted, its light going out in a puff of smoke. The room went pitch black for a moment before a red glow bloomed from the ring of tiny rubies at Sara's waist.

She stood in the red light, her soul still roaring open, and glared down at her husband lying prone on his stomach, pinned by his connection to the spirits she was grinding under. His head lay sideways in the water that was beginning to leak through the sundered wall of roots, the flood slowly rising to cover his mouth and nose.

"I should let you drown," she whispered, panting under the strain of her own power. "How fitting it would be if you died under the water you'd worked so hard to free. It wouldn't even notice, you know. It would fill your lungs just like any other crevice and drown you without a second thought."

"As it should be," Banage said, rolling his eyes up to look at her. "If you think I did this with a care for my own life, then you understand nothing, Sara Banage."

Her whole body went rigid. How long had it been since anyone had called her that? Twenty years at least. Not long enough.

"I never should have married you," she hissed. "I never should have let you near my work. You break everything you touch."

"It's not my fault your work breaks when it is held to a standard of morality," Banage said, coughing a bit as the water filled his mouth. "You were the one who chose to build your greater good on a flawed foundation. If I did any wrong in this, it is that I did not act sooner."

Sara closed her eyes. Her open spirit was vibrating with her rage. Through it, she could feel the water flooding through the cavern, still creeping along under the pressure of her will. How easy it would be to lift her hand and let it rush over Banage, silence his arrogance forever. But as soon as she thought it, Sara shrank away from the idea. Even in her fury, she couldn't do it.

She sighed bitterly, trying to decide her next step when she felt a familiar but unexpected twinge against her chest. She welcomed the signal with a smile and turned her head just in time to see Sparrow slip silently out of the cover of a fallen tank. Without his coat to draw her attention, she had trouble keeping her eyes on him, but she could see well enough to know he was alone. Her smile faded.

"Sparrow," she snapped. "What are you doing back? Where's Eliton?"

Sparrow shrugged and kept walking, his feet moving silently through the still water.

Sara scowled. She didn't have time for his games. "Forget it," she muttered, returning her attention to Banage. "You can give your excuses later. For now, I need you to help me secure the former Rector. There should be some rope on the floor." She glanced at Banage, lips lifting in a haughty sneer. "This time we're going to throw his rings in Whitefall's vault. Let's see them get out of *that*."

She paused, waiting for the splash of Sparrow's hands moving through the water for the rope, but she heard nothing. "Sparrow, this is not the time for—"

The knife was in and out before she felt it. It slid into her back, between her ribs, twisting up once before pulling out. She gasped as she realized what had happened, only to find she couldn't. Her lung, her mind scrambled as the left side of her chest blazed up like a fire. He'd hit her lung.

Sara didn't realize she'd fallen until she felt the cold water lapping against her burning skin. It was a bad fall, her arms hadn't moved to catch her, but she felt no pain. Or, if she did, it didn't matter. Nothing mattered except reasserting her control. Her hands shot up, patting her chest, fumbling under her coat through the half-dozen Relay points she kept on her at all times, but the one she was searching for wasn't there.

As she began to panic, her eyes drifted up, squinting against her darkening vision to see Sparrow standing over her, his mouth curled in a smile. One hand held the knife, still dark and dripping with blood. Her blood, she realized with a twinge, but she dismissed the thought as soon as it came. None of that mattered. Her eyes darted to Sparrow's other hand, the one clenched in a fist. A deep red, viscous liquid dripped between his fingers, and Sara's burning blood went cold.

Sparrow's smile widened at the realization in her eyes.

"What?" he said, opening his hand. "Looking for this?"

A chain dangled from his fingers, and at its end was a shattered glass shell no thicker than a soap bubble. Deep red liquid dripped from its broken edge, falling into the water below. Sara blinked in disbelief. She hadn't even felt him take it. But then, she hadn't felt the knife either.

"You never were any good at seeing what was around you," Sparrow said, dropping the remains of the broken orb into the water. "Especially when you have your spirit open."

Sara stared at him, her mouth moving to shape a word. *Why?*

"Why?" Sparrow sneered. "Because I'm done taking your orders. Because I don't want to spend the rest of my life as the Council's errand boy. And because, in the whole Council, you're the only one who could ever be my jailor." He wiped her blood off his knife, smearing it across his dull pants. "I'd say it's nothing personal, but I can't think of anyone who deserved that stabbing more than you. And the best part of this is everyone will think *he* did it." Sparrow pointed his newly clean blade at where Banage was lying.

Sara rolled in the water, gathering her spirit as she struggled to breathe. Sparrow just sheathed the knife in his boot and dropped to his knees beside her.

"Catching Eli was your fatal mistake, you should know," he whispered, leaning down so she could hear. "Banage was bad enough, but the minute you decided to reason with your son instead of handing him over to Whitefall, I knew I had my chance at last. All I had to do was make sure Whitefall knew enough to push you. Of course, the idiot Oseran king almost ruined everything. How was I supposed to know he'd move that fast? But everything worked out in the end."

Sparrow gave her a blinding smile. "Eli was sent back to his cell with no more reason to stay. True to his reputation, once he decided to escape, he was out in a matter of minutes, and with both Banage boys on the lam, you were far too busy to keep your eyes where they should be." Sparrow's smile turned cruel. "On me."

Sara's mouth began to work, trying to form any of the biting responses she had to that, but Sparrow was already rocking back on his heels.

"I'd give you some parting advice about the dangers of hubris," he said, his voice so glib it was almost singsong. "But since you're not going to be around to use it, I don't think I'll waste my breath. Good-bye, Sara dear, and remember—you deserve every bit of this. Let that be the last thought that takes you to the mists."

He patted her cheek and straightened up, his face leaving her field of vision. Sara tried to follow him, but her body had gone rigid. The pain was finally starting to bleed through her shock, and it was quickly crowding out every other concern.

Powers, she hurt. The world was spinning now. She blinked hard, trying to see around the dark shape swimming across her field of vision, but it wasn't until she heard his voice that she realized the shadow wasn't an illusion caused by her failing eyes. It was Banage.

He was on his feet, hands out, his rings shining like miniature suns. Of course, she realized, her spirit had closed when she'd fallen, freeing him. Banage was shouting something. She couldn't make out the words over the ringing in her ears, but his voice was full of command and, unexpectedly, rage.

She was still trying to puzzle it out when stone hands burst from the floor, breaking through the water with a great crash. They grabbed for Sparrow, but he dodged them neatly, laughing. Sara frowned in confusion before she remembered Banage's spirit couldn't see Sparrow. None of the spirits could. She heard Banage swear above her, calling another spirit as he dropped to Sara's side.

His hands, surprisingly hot, pressed into her back, fingers fumbling to stop the blood. A shock of pain went through her as he touched her wound, clearing her mind. The world, which had seemed so far away only seconds before, suddenly snapped into focus, and she knew with absolute clarity that if she did not pull herself together right this instant she was going to die.

The realization was like another knife in her chest. At once, with the discipline she'd learned as a Spiritualist and perfected in her own work, she forced everything out of her mind and turned all her power, all her will, toward the only two goals that mattered.

From the outside, what happened next probably looked like a miracle. All at once, Sara's convulsions stopped. She lay still, her eyes closed, and then, quietly, she took a deep, deep breath. Banage froze. Gingerly, he lifted his hands from her back. Her wound was still open, but the flow of blood had slowed to a trickle. When Sara took another breath, it stopped altogether.

But a few feet away, the story was very different. Between the stone hands that were still blindly looking for him, Sparrow fell to his knees, grasping his throat. His handsome face turned red and then blue as his mouth opened and closed, desperately trying to force air down his throat.

It didn't work. He started to flail, his eyes bulging as he fell onto his back. He rolled in the water, but as the seconds ticked by, his thrashing slowed until he lay still, his head slumped beneath the dark, dirty water. He didn't move again.

Banage stared at Sparrow's still body for several seconds, and then he looked at Sara, his face pale as paper behind his graying beard. "What did you do?"

Sara shook her head and closed her eyes. Each breath came easier than the last, but she didn't dare relax her control. She kept her focus inward, turning all her concentration onto her own soul now that Sparrow was down. She wasn't nearly as good as Tesset at this sort of thing—her initial panic proved that much—but she'd learned enough from him to patch up a little knife hole. Ah, Tesset, she thought longingly as the pain began to fade. How I miss you.

She opened her eyes just enough to steal another look at Sparrow's still body. If Tesset had been here, this never would have happened. Despite the fact that she had saved his life, it was no secret that Sparrow hated her. Still, they'd worked through it for a decade thanks to her vigilance and Sparrow's refusal to take any opportunity that wasn't a sure win. But between the extra workload Tesset's death had left and this business with Banage, she'd gone sloppy, and now look at things. Sparrow was dead, her workshop was destroyed, Eliton was gone off who knew where, taking her answers with him, and her Relay was crushed under the weight of Banage's moral hardline.

All her work, everything she'd dedicated her life to, had been washed away in a matter of minutes, and all she had left now was Banage hovering over her like a mother hen. Sara blew out her hard-won breath in a huff. He was probably staying only because he couldn't stand the thought of her dying before he'd dragged her before the Court, the pompous, self-righteous fool.

685

Even so, her frown softened a little, it was nice to know Etmon still cared.

When she had her bleeding under control, Sara opened her eyes to find herself lying on her side on a dry stretch of stone. Etmon's roots had surrounded them again, blocking off the flood, and Banage himself was using his mist spirit to evaporate the last of the water over the barrier. His rings glowed as he worked, lighting him in a rainbow of color. It was a nostalgic sight, and Sara smiled before she could stop herself.

Gingerly, she rolled onto her back. It didn't hurt as much as she'd feared, but the movement sent her into a coughing fit. Banage jumped at the sound.

"Sara?" he said, grabbing her hand as he knelt beside her.

"I'll live," she muttered, glancing at their entwined fingers. She thought about breaking free, but then relaxed. Etmon's hand was warm. Comforting, she realized, lying back. How long had it been since she'd felt his hand like this? Not since Eliton was a baby.

Sara winced. Her brush with death must have taken more out of her than she'd realized if *she* was getting sentimental. She was about to tell Banage to help her up when he rolled her onto her side without so much as a warning, peeling back her ripped coat to examine her wound. His breath hitched when he saw it was closed, and Sara smirked. It was about time the man was impressed by something she'd done.

"Let me down," she said, forcing her voice to be stern. "I told you, I'll live."

"How—" Banage began.

"A trick of Tesset's," Sara answered, cutting him off for time's sake. Whitefall's troops would be down soon enough, and she wanted to savor the pleasure of explaining her cleverness before she was forced to order around a bunch of frightened guardsmen. "If the only human soul a wizard can touch is her own, then it's a shame not to control it thoroughly. I never quite managed his level of mastery, but I can stop small things like this."

She arched her shoulder to show him, ignoring the painful hitch of the wound that was not quite as closed as she was making out. Banage, however, just folded his arms over his chest. "That much I can understand," he said. "What I don't get is him."

He nodded across her, beyond the wall formed by his roots where, Sara knew, Sparrow's body lay still in the water.

"A wizard cannot touch another human soul," Banage said. "It's the core rule of magic. How in the world did you break it?"

"Are you sure you want to discuss this now?" Sara asked. "The guards are coming."

"I might not get another chance," Banage said. "And I've blocked the guards for the moment." He sat on the ground beside her. "Humor me."

Sara frowned, searching for the best way to describe what she'd done without sending Banage into one of his fits of morality. She didn't want to destroy the momentary truce that had grown between them, and she actually relished the idea of explaining Sparrow. He was, after all, one of the most interesting puzzles she'd ever stumbled across, and bombastic as her husband could be, Etmon always had been one of the only people who could understand the intricacies of her work. Provided she could distract him from his moralizing, of course.

"Sparrow is, *was* an anomaly," she said finally. "Most human spirits encompass their bodies naturally, and these are what spirits see when they look at us. Wizards shine brighter, so I'm told, but even the spirit deaf have some kind of presence. Not so with Sparrow. For whatever reason, he was born with a soul so small, so faint, as my spirits would say, that he's basically invisible. Unless he wraps himself in something they can see, spirits look right through him."

Banage eyes widened. "The hideous clothes?"

"Exactly," Sara said, nodding. "A simple, elegant solution. Though even wrapped in bright spirits, he's hard to focus on. Or so I'm told, anyway. But that wasn't what I was interested in. The most interesting part of Sparrow is that, when he wears dull clothes, he's basically invisible to humans as well."

She stopped to let this knowledge sink in. Banage hovered over her, his brows knotted, deep in thought. She could almost see him putting the pieces together—*click, click, click*—in rapid succession, coming to the same conclusions she'd ended on. It made her smile. Ah, if only he weren't so stubborn. What a pair they would have made.

"If humans have trouble seeing him just as spirits do..." Banage trailed off. "Sara, are you implying that, on some level, we see as spirits see?"

Sara's smile spread. "That's exactly what I'm implying. Sparrow is a known blind spot for all of us. If we share this blindness with spirits, then perhaps humans are not completely unseeing as spirits say we are. Maybe we do see, but we don't know it, or something blocks our sight."

"It makes sense," Banage said, scratching his beard. "The spirits call us the Shepherdess's creations, but I don't think that's quite right. Miranda told me that the Shaper Mountain claims the Shepherdess does not truly create. If we can see as spirits see at all, even if it's only in a shared blindness, then maybe we're not newly created spirits, but changed ones, modified to fit whatever it was the Shepherdess wanted us to be."

"Slorn told me much the same thing once," Sara said. "Though the real question now is, if we could see at the beginning, why would this Shepherdess go through so much effort to take the sight we already had away?"

"Make us blind, you mean?" Banage said. "If you're right, then all we have are more questions. Why would the Power who was created to watch over the world make a race that can control everything else and then actively take our sight away? That sounds more like destruction than preservation."

"It's a heady problem, isn't it?" Sara was grinning now. Talking like this with Banage, exploring the possibilities of magic freely, without his dogma getting in the way, made her feel like a teenager again. She gripped his hand. "Now do you see why I risked so much to keep Sparrow with me?"

Banage's face darkened. "I see," he said. "But I don't understand. You must have known from the beginning that that man could not be trusted. I can see keeping him for research in a cell, but what possessed you to let him roam free?"

"Because he was useful," Sara said. "And I was always in control."

He gave her a suspicious look. "How?"

Sara bit her lip. For a moment, she considered lying. It had been so long since she'd had a civil conversation with her husband, she'd forgotten how pleasant it could be. But Banage was glaring at her now, and she knew the look well enough. He'd never let up until he had an answer he was satisfied with, and she didn't have a lie ready that was good enough to trick him. The truth, then, she decided with a sigh. Such a pity. Their truce had been nice while it lasted.

She settled back on the ground, bracing for impact. "I could control him because I'd bound him as a servant spirit."

"What?"

Sara winced at his roar. Banage loomed over her, dark and terrible, his rings glowing like multicolored suns. Then, unexpectedly, he eased back down.

"How?" he said as curiosity finally overcame his inherent rage. "Even if it was as faint as you claim, his soul is still human. How did you bind a human soul into service?"

"I didn't bind *his* soul," Sara said. "Remember what I said earlier about how a human's soul usually encompasses their entire body? Well, Sparrow's didn't. It wasn't large enough. This meant that the vast majority of his physical body wasn't actually part of his soul."

"Impossible," Banage said. "Everything has a soul."

"It did," Sara said. "Just not a human one. As I said, Sparrow was an anomaly. He had a human body, but not enough human soul to fill it. So his body developed a unique coping mechanism to keep itself alive. Each organ developed a tiny soul of

689

its own. That was why spirits never saw Sparrow as human. To their eyes, he's closer to a pile of pebbles."

"That still doesn't explain how you bound him," Banage said.

"I told you," Sara huffed. "I didn't bind *him*. I bound his lungs."

Banage blinked. "His *lungs*?"

Sara nodded emphatically, smiling at the memory of that genius idea. "It was really simple, actually. I called in White-fall's surgeon and took a tiny piece of Sparrow's lung. I kept it with me, feeding power into it just as I would a Spiritualist spirit. I had to fudge things a bit, but in the end I basically made Sparrow's lungs into a servant spirit who was always out of its ring. That way, if I ever needed to find him or discipline him, I could just tug on the thread connecting us. After all, he can't go anywhere without his lungs, can he?"

She finished with a grin, but Banage wasn't smiling. He just stared at her, his face horrified. "You made a Spiritualist pact with a spirit too small for consciousness, with a man's *lungs*..." His voice trailed off.

Sara put up her hand. "Before you start to lecture, remember, the lungs were a part of Sparrow, and he gave his consent to be my servant in exchange for salvation from the Whitefalls. I just took him a little more literally than he intended."

Banage's face grew even more severe. "Then I suppose the red orb he crushed was the equivalent of his ring?"

"More or less," Sara said. "But as you saw, I didn't need it anymore. His lungs still knew who their mistress was." She set her jaw at Banage's scornful look. "Powers, Etmon, it wasn't like I wanted to kill him. After all the work I put into that man? But he tried to kill me, and he would have died anyway when Whitefall—"

"Enough," Banage said, running his hands over his face with a long sigh. "I don't want to hear any more about how you've twisted the most sacred bond of the Spirit Court. Honestly, Sara, how can you be so clever and yet understand

690

nothing about what's actually important?" He shook his head. "Truly, Eliton is your son."

Sara arched an eyebrow. "Really? From his stubbornness, I'd say he's more yours."

Banage laughed at that, and the noise made her jump. It was such a nostalgic sound, and such a sad one.

"We're a miserable excuse for a family," he said, leaning back on his hands beside her. "A traitor, a thief, and a woman who'd give her right arm for a hint at the secrets of the universe."

"Left arm," Sara said, fumbling for her pipe before remembering she'd left it upstairs. "I'm right-handed."

"Left arm," Banage repeated. "Or another man's lungs."

"It *is* all a bit monstrous," Sara admitted. "But it was necessary, Etmon."

"Was it?" Banage said, his voice soft in the dark. "Did you ever think about maybe not striving so hard?"

Sara's only answer to that was a scoff, and Banage sighed.

"You know," he whispered, "I didn't set out to be Rector. What I really wanted was to live with you and Eliton together. To be a family. A real one."

"Well," Sara said, "if that was what you wanted, you could have had it at any time. I was always willing. You were the one who left because you didn't approve of my work, remember?"

"How could I forget?" Banage said. "You rub my face in it every chance you get."

"Well, we none of us are quitters," Sara said. "I don't think I could have loved you were it otherwise."

Banage reached out and grabbed her hand, squeezing her fingers so tight against his that his rings cut into her skin. For a moment, Sara could feel his power in the air, warm and heavy and wonderfully familiar. Then it was gone, and a great scraping of metal and stone filled the silent chamber.

"The soldiers will be coming now," Banage said. "I wanted to make sure the water had a chance to drain away before they arrived."

691

"Can't have it falling back under my evil ways, eh?" Sara said, lying back against the stone.

Banage didn't answer. But then, without warning, he leaned down and pressed his lips against her cheek. It was a soft, sad touch, filled with regret. It lasted a few heartbeats, and then Banage was standing, his shape vanishing into the dark.

"I'm sorry."

The words were out before Sara could stop them. She didn't even know what she was apologizing for. Hurting him, maybe, or putting him in prison, or just not being the person he wanted her to be. Maybe it was everything, but it didn't matter. His answer came quickly, the words so sad they ached.

"So am I," he whispered. "Good-bye, Sara."

She tried to speak, but her voice wouldn't come. Her throat was stuck, her tongue dry and useless. Powers, she wanted a smoke. A good pipe on a sunny balcony somewhere far away from the ruined shambles of her life. Instead, she got glaring lanterns and the thunder of boots as the soldiers surged into the cavern.

"Down here!" someone shouted. There was a string of curses and clanging metal as the men climbed over the downed tanks, and then she heard a man shout her name. The light moved to shine right in her face as a pair of young guardsmen dropped to their knees at her side.

"Lady Sara!" the one in the officer's coat cried, holding his lantern high. "What happened?"

Sara pressed her fingers against her eyes, trying in vain to blot out the glare. "Too much," she muttered. "Help me to the Merchant Prince. It looks like I get to ruin his day twice over."

There was a chorus of shouts as the soldiers ran to obey. Sara let them lift her, too tired to protest when the pair of guardsmen slung her between them like an oat sack. She closed her eyes as they carried her past the destruction, past Sparrow's body, still lying where it had fallen. Only when they'd climbed the stairs and emerged into the noise and light of the Council Citadel on high alert did she let herself look ahead to the long, painful, hateful, slow process of rebuilding, or at least patching over, everything that had shattered today.

"What was that, Lady Sara?" her guard asked, looking down.

"I said, get me a new pipe."

"Yes, Lady," the guard said, and then he turned to shout the order over his shoulder.

Sara scrubbed her eyes, breathing shallow against the growing pain in her back. Through the windows she could see the sunset painting the white walls of Zarin in bright oranges, as bright as Banage's fire bird. Feeling slightly ill, Sara turned away, letting them haul her up the endless stairs to Whitefall's tower.

Powers, this was going to be a long night.

CHAPTER

12

Eli woke up to the familiar feeling of Josef's boot in his ribs. He rolled over with a grunt, blinking in the dark.

"Hour till dawn," the swordsman whispered. "Time to go."

With a noncommittal grumble, Eli sat up off the board floor and rubbed his aching eyes. Oh, the comforts of home. He arched his shoulders to get the kinks out of his back and looked over. Josef and Nico were standing under the tiny street-level window set high on the wall. The street lamps's glow filtered down through the wood-thatched shutter, the only source of light in the small basement they'd taken over for the night. When Josef saw him looking, he tossed Eli something small and dark. The thief caught it by reflex and looked down to see a round loaf of dark bread.

"Eat," Josef said, eyes narrowing as Eli took a small bite. "*Quickly.*"

"It will be faster if I don't choke," Eli said, chewing thoughtfully.

Josef's scowl deepened. "It would have been faster if we'd used the night to get out of town."

"Some of us haven't been living like a king," Eli said pointedly, breaking the bread in two. "And unlike you two monsters, I need normal, human amounts of sleep. I've had a very rough few days, thank you very much."

Josef shook his head and turned back to the window, glaring suspiciously at the passing feet of the early-morning traffic. Beside him, Nico leaned against the wall staring intently at the Heart of War's blade, which was leaned up beside her.

Eli shoved the bread in his mouth, wondering what the demonseed saw when she looked at Josef's sword. Not for the first time, he wished he could see as she did, as spirits saw. He'd been curious his whole life, but when he'd asked Benehime, back in the days when he still asked her for things, she'd just laughed and told him there was nothing to see.

That line of thought brought him right back to the place he didn't want to go. Eli slumped on the ground, chewing mechanically. The first rule of thievery said that the only person you had to be honest with was yourself. It was the rule he broke more than any other, and he always, *always* regretted it.

Eli's hand slid under his shirt of its own volition, feeling the smooth, unburned skin of his chest. Yesterday he'd almost believed that all he had to do was get to the Shaper Mountain, get his lava spirit back where he belonged, and then everything would be fine. He'd have Karon, he'd have his freedom, he'd have Josef and Nico, and the world would be roses. No more dealing with his past, no more walking the edge of Benehime's displeasure. Paradise, or as close as he could hope to come. Now, with the rush of his escape gone, the truth was getting harder and harder to ignore.

Eli closed his eyes and forced himself to face reality. There was no way Benehime would actually let him go. They'd argued before, never that badly, but if Benehime could be convinced with words alone, he'd have been rid of her a long time ago. Whatever freedom he felt was an illusion, nothing but slack in his long leash. Any moment, she'd pull it taut and he'd be right back in her lap again.

Eli grimaced and tongued the bread that had gone to sawdust in his mouth. How stupid, getting his hope up. He should know better by now. She was the only prison he could never escape.

Across the room, Josef said, "What?"

Eli jumped. "What?" he repeated dumbly.

"You're looking uncharacteristically gloomy," the swordsman said, folding his arms over his wide chest. "That's usually a bad sign."

Eli sighed. If Josef was noticing, it *must* be bad. "Just feeling sorry for myself," he said, all smiles as he polished off the last crumbs of the bread. "I'm a tragically heroic figure, you know."

"Yeah, yeah," Josef grumbled, pushing off the wall. "But if you're done with your sulk, we need to talk business. I'd like to know how we're getting to the Shaper Mountain without walking halfway across the continent. You said you had a plan."

"Yes," Eli said, clearing his throat to buy some time. Josef was staring at him like a hawk, his whole body poised like he was about to charge. Nico was looking at him as well, one skeletal hand picking idly at the coat that pooled around her like spilled ink. Under such scrutiny, Eli couldn't help but think how many times they'd sat like this, hidden in some hole while he laid out his brilliant plan to turn everything around. Trouble was, this time he didn't know what to say.

He took a deep breath and started with the truth.

"We have to move fast," Eli said. "I saved Karon from the volcano who expelled him years ago. My body was the only home he had left. Unless Benehime sent him to another volcano, which I doubt she was thoughtful enough to do, he's fighting for his life as we speak. If conditions are right, he

695

can keep his core alive for several days, but if Benehime dumped him somewhere cruel, like into the sea or under a glacier, he's already snuffed out. The only way to know for sure is to ask the Shaper Mountain. If there's a chance Karon's still alive, I need to get to him fast. Anything less would be an insult to all the times he's saved our lives."

"If that's how it is, why did you go to sleep?" Josef said, crossing his arms.

"Because I was tired," Eli said, rubbing his eyes. "Because running off on no sleep is a quick way to make mistakes we can't afford, because I need every bit of my mind together before I try to get the Teacher to do me any favors, and because if we can do this like I'm hoping we can, Karon'll be back in my chest by this afternoon."

"This afternoon?" Josef said, loud and incredulous. "Powers, Eli. We couldn't fly there that fast. What the..."

His voice trailed off when he saw Eli wasn't looking at him but at Nico. Josef looked back and forth between them, his scowl deepening, but it was Nico who spoke.

"The white gate in the air," she said softly, her dark eyes boring into Eli's. "You're going to open the hole through the world again."

Eli shook his head. "I can't do that anymore." He stopped a moment, surprised at how strange it felt to admit that. But it passed quickly, and he pressed on. "The only one who can help me now is you."

Nico's eyes went wide, and Eli held his breath. She knew what he was asking. He could see it on her face. But before she could answer him, Josef's voice fell like a sword stroke, cutting the silence clean through with a single word.

"No."

The anger in Josef's voice made Nico cringe. She shrank back, feeling like a coward as she hid beneath her hood. Across the room, Eli's eyes flicked to the swordsman, his boyish face falling into an uncharacteristic scowl.

"Josef," he said, his voice as light and pleasant as the morning breeze. "I respect your opinion, I really do, but this isn't your call."

Josef didn't move. He didn't have to. Nico could feel the tension rising in him, ready to spring. "Do you even know what you're asking?"

"If I didn't, I wouldn't *be* asking."

Eli smiled and stood up, walking across the room to fall to a crouch in front of Nico. He reached out and snatched her hand before she realized what he was doing, clutching her thin palm between his long, nimble fingers. She stared at him, thrown off guard not just by the contact but by Eli himself. This close, she could see the faint glow of the light he'd shown her up on the roof back in Osera, when they'd first found out she could see as spirits saw. His spirit wasn't open now as it had been then, but Nico could see that the mask he usually kept so smooth was beginning to fray. She stared at him, gripping his hand just as tightly as he gripped hers. What had happened in the days he was away from them? What had that woman *done*?

"Nico," he said, his voice earnest. "I know you can take people with you through the shadows. I saw you do it in Osera with Josef. Den also carried me that way, back in the mountains when he took me from Izo's. He carried me hundreds of miles over impassible terrain, and then he took me back again, walking through the shadows like they were his own private highway. That's how I knew I could ask you. You're stronger than Den ever was."

Nico began to tremble. "I'm not—"

"You *are*," Eli said fiercely. "I saw you in the valley outside Izo's. Even when you were lost in the demon, you stopped yourself from hurting Josef. You saved him even though you didn't know yourself, and then you beat the demon. You conquered the enemy even the Shepherdess couldn't best, and you did it on your own. That's the only reason I'm asking this, because I know you can do it."

He inched closer, pushing her hand against his chest, his blue eyes earnest and pleading as his heart thudded against her fingers. "All Karon did was care for me," he whispered. "Because of that, and because he spoke his mind, the Shepherdess threw him away. I couldn't do anything to stop it, but I refuse to let him die, not if there's the slightest chance I can save him. I'm begging, Nico, if I've ever done right by you, please take me through the shadows to the Shaper Mountain. I know it's far and I know it'll be hard, but I'll help you any way I can. Just please, *please* help me undo this wrong. Help me save Karon, if there's anything left to save."

Nico closed her eyes and stared at the darkness behind them, the endless, empty blackness. The Demon of the Dead Mountain waited there for her. She'd beaten him inside her own head, but the shadows were his world, not hers. Alone, he couldn't touch her, but she wasn't sure she could protect Eli and Josef from the demon's grasp. Even if she could open her spirit wide enough to shelter them, the Shaper Mountain was a long, long way away. They would have to cut the journey into several small jumps, and there would still be long periods in the dark where the demon could work his way in.

But that wasn't all. Something had stirred in her yesterday when Eli said they were going to the Shaper Mountain, something far below her conscious mind. A deep, throbbing pain, the kind that meant she was treading dangerously close to memories she'd suppressed. The pain was there even now, bleeding through the wall of her memory.

She took a ragged breath. Whatever the memory was, she didn't want it. She'd locked her past away for a reason, and the pain alone was enough to warn her that going to the Shaper Mountain was a bad, bad idea, however they got there. And yet...

Nico opened her eyes to see that Eli hadn't moved. He was still crouched in front of her, his face so full of hope and trust she wanted to cry. How could she disappoint him? He and Josef were so strong, and she was always so weak. Always the soft spot, the brittle link, and now he was counting on her. Depending on her.

She didn't realize her hand was shaking until Eli moved his other hand to join the first, pressing her trembling fingers against his shirtfront with both palms. She was the one who could see souls, but his eyes were the ones that looked through her, reading her fears like posters.

"I know you can do it," he said again. His thumbs rubbed against her skin as he spoke, a soft, soothing motion. "All you have to do is get me there. I'll do the rest."

"You can't." The words were so tremulous, so afraid that Nico almost didn't recognize her own voice. "The shadows are the demon's realm. You don't understand, the fear—"

"How can I be afraid if you're with me?" Eli said, his face breaking into a smile. "You beat the demon already, remember? If you can master your own soul, you can kick him out of the shadows." His voice warmed as he spoke, suffusing Nico with confidence and hope. "This is your chance to take his final stronghold, to beat the demon once and for all. You can do it, and we'll do it with you. You're not alone, Nico. We're a team, now more than ever. All you have to do is help me get—"

He never got to finish. One moment he was in front of her, gripping her hand, the next he'd vanished. It was over so quickly Nico didn't realize what had happened until she saw Josef was standing beside her with Eli dangling in front of him, his wrists bound in the vise grip of the swordsman's fist.

"Josef!" Eli shouted, his feet kicking. Josef didn't move. Nico couldn't see his face from where she was, but she knew from the set of his shoulders that he was furious. Killing furious. Behind her, the Heart of War began to shake.

"Don't. You. Dare." Josef's voice was low and cold, and each word was sharp as a dagger. "Don't you *dare* try to con her."

Eli's eyes widened. "I wasn't—"

Josef dropped him before he could finish. Eli fell with a grunt, hitting the floor hard. He scrambled to his feet and stepped back, putting a foot between himself and Josef, who'd moved in to block Nico with his body.

"Josef," Eli said, his voice pleading. "I don't know how you got the impression I was—"

"You don't?" Josef growled. "Then you must think I'm an idiot. I've been with you on a lot of jobs, Monpress. You think I don't recognize how you work?" His hand whipped back, finger pointed directly at Nico's face. "You were talking to her just now like she was a damn *door*. Powers, man, you were even stroking her hand."

Eli closed his eyes, throwing his head back in frustration. "It's not like that."

"Oh *sure*," Josef said. "You had nothing but Nico's best interests at heart while you were trying to convince her that helping *you* get where *you* want to go was the next phase of her battle with the demon. Like taking you to the Shaper Mountain was her damn *destiny* instead of your self-serving idiocy."

He took a step forward, looming over Eli, and for the first time ever Nico was glad she couldn't see Josef's face.

"I warned you before," Josef growled. "Don't ever try to con me. You're not stupid, so I'd figured you'd understand that that warning extended to Nico as well, but guess I underestimated what a selfish bastard you could be."

"Josef, come on," Eli pleaded. "I wouldn't do that to you, to either of you. I'm your friend. I'd die for either of you. You *know* that."

"I do," Josef said. "But I also know that you're a con artist, a thief, and a stubborn bastard who doesn't take no for an answer, even from us. Now shut your mouth before it runs you any deeper into trouble. Nico's not one of your idiot spirits, and she's not taking you anywhere."

"I've never thought of her that way!" Eli shouted, clenching his fists. "You're the one treating her like an idiot, Josef. You think she needs you to stand up and say what she will and won't do? You've been all mother hen with her ever since you

700

found her, but Nico's her own person, and she can make her own decision."

Josef clenched his fists as well, his white-knuckled hands moving to his sides where his twin swords rested. "She has enough to fight without adding you to the list," he said, his voice thick and dangerous. "Now back off, thief, before I—"

"Stop it."

Both men jumped as Nico stomped forward, pushing herself between them. She grabbed Josef first, wrapping her hand over his shoulder and pushing him down with a burst of her demon strength. He folded like a collapsing chair, his legs buckling as he landed on his rear with a slam. She did the same to Eli, though more gently. The bewildered expressions on their faces as they hit were so similar that Nico almost laughed.

She suppressed the urge at the last second. Laughing would ruin the moment, and she only had the nerve to do this once.

"Josef," she said. "Your support and protection are dearer to me than you can ever know, but this time it's not necessary. Eli wasn't conning me. He was trying to make a point and getting carried away like he always does, but that doesn't mean he was wrong. We *are* a team, now more than ever."

She stopped. Her voice was faltering and she didn't want to lose her courage. Breathing as she'd heard Tesset do so many times, she found her calm again. Only when she was utterly in control did she speak again.

"We are a team," she repeated, her eyes flicking back and forth between them. "And you two are the only family I've ever had." She looked at Josef. "Eli might be a con artist, but he stood by me in Osera when you were out cold and no one else thought I'd make it. His voice was the one I heard in the dark. You saved me on the mountain years ago and you've saved me countless times since, but so has he. He's saved you as well, and you've saved him. We're all tied together by so many life debts now we can't begin to untangle them, but there's no need to. I don't need debts to help either of you. When friends are so close they're blood, you don't need

701

anything but a request to walk into a sword with your head held high." She turned back to Eli. "That's how I feel, but I don't need to ask to know you agree. After all, you already walked into the sword for us in Osera the night you stopped the sea."

Eli shook his head. "That was different," he whispered. "I'm not—"

"It wasn't," Nico said, drawing strength from the iron certainty in her own voice. "And you are. So go ahead. Ask me."

Eli glanced up at her. "Ask you what?"

"Ask me to take you through the shadows to the Shaper Mountain."

Eli took a hissing breath, glancing at Josef, but the swordsman's face was closed, his eyes focused on Nico. "All right," Eli said, turning back to Nico. "Take me. Please."

"I will," Nico answered without hesitation. "And I'm not doing it because I want to face down the demon or because I think it's a good idea. I'm doing it because you need to get there, and because you asked."

The look Eli gave her then was so bewildered Nico couldn't stop the enormous smile from breaking over her face. She fell into a crouch beside him, bringing her head level with his. "Of course I'll do it, stupid thief," she said, punching him softly on the shoulder. "We're a team, aren't we?"

For three heartbeats Eli didn't move, and then his face broke into the most beautiful, joyful expression Nico had ever seen.

"That we are, Nico," he said. "That we are."

"Well, I'm not going."

Nico's and Eli's heads both snapped toward Josef. The swordsman was leaning back on his hands, but his face was deathly serious.

"Nico's a free woman," he said. "She can take you wherever she wants. But I'm not moving a step until I get a promise."

Eli went very pale, and though his body was still, Nico could see his spirit trembling. "What kind of promise?"

702

"If we're a team, you need to act like it," Josef said flatly, looking Eli up and down. "I've followed you for years now, no questions asked. I'm not saying we should change that. I kept my secrets as tight as either of you, after all, and I'll never forget that you were the first ones at my side when my past caught up with me. But this isn't another heist. I don't know what you're wrapped up in, Eli, but even I can see it's big. Bigger than us. Too big to walk into blind. So before I agree to throw my lot in with you once and for all, I want your word that, from here on out, you're going to tell us what's going on. No more secrecy, no more glib brush-offs when I ask you a question. I don't care if you're the prince of the spirit world or just a big-mouthed idiot who talked himself in over his head. From now on, you tell us what's coming as best as you can, and when either of us asks a question, you answer it straight. Promise me that and I'll follow you to the end of the world or wherever it is you're headed." Josef raised his hand, holding it in the air between them. "Deal?"

Eli glanced at the offered hand, and then he raised his own, clasping Josef's palm. "Deal."

Josef gave Eli's hand a hard shake as his glare dissolved into a smug grin. "I would have come even if you hadn't promised," he said as he released him. "You know that, right?"

Eli's jaw dropped, and then he kicked Josef in the shin. "You are such a jerk. You know *that*, right?"

"You've told me as much before," Josef said as Eli's kick bounced off him easy as a child's. "I'm glad I got the promise, though. Despite all your other faults, you've always been a man of your word."

"Gee, thanks," Eli grumbled, glancing at the window. "Now, if you're done being a pain, can we get going? Daylight's burning and we've got a long way to go."

Josef shrugged and stood up. He grabbed the Heart of War and slung it onto his back, fixing the strap over his other blades. Nico grabbed their bag and started to put it over her arm when Eli stopped her.

"I've got it," he said, sliding the bag over his shoulder so that it rested on his hip. "You just worry about getting us there."

Nico nodded, fighting the icy spike of fear that stabbed her stomach at the mention of leaving. But she'd made her promise, and nothing was going to stop her now. For the first time in many months, maybe the first time ever, the three of them were all on the same page, united in purpose. She was going to do her part or die trying.

"Grab on, then," she said, steeling her voice against the fear.

Josef's arm was around her waist before she'd finished, pulling her close. Eli latched on next, wrapping himself around her shoulders.

"Isn't this cozy?" he said, smiling over her shoulder. "Wrapped up together like coins in a cloth."

"Just make sure you stay that way," Nico said, planting her feet. "And whatever happens, whatever you feel, whatever you see, *do not let go.*"

She waited until both men nodded, and then, with a final, deep breath, Nico stepped them backward into the shadows and vanished without a trace.

Eli gasped as the darkness ate them whole. The first thing he noticed, aside from the black shutter that had closed over his eyes, was the cold. It sank straight to his bones, as sharp as broken glass. So sharp, in fact, that he had trouble breathing. But the biting, breathless cold faded to a minor inconvenience once the fear hit him.

Pure terror gripped him like a giant's hand. He could actually feel the weight of it pressing on his heart, stopping it cold between one beat and the next. Lungs frozen, heart stopped, Eli's body sank, a dead weight sliding down Nico's arm. His fingers twitched uselessly as they slipped from her coat, and he started to fall. In the parts of his brain that still worked, he cursed himself and fought to grab hold again, but it was no use. His body was a wooden doll, an empty vessel crushed by fear. Another second and he would fall into the dark entirely, and the grasping mouths that nibbled at his arms would fall on him in earnest and eat until there was nothing left.

But just before he fell away altogether, something strong and warm shot around his chest, pulling him tight. He looked up to see Nico looming over him. There was no light, but he could see her pale face clearly. Her eyes were as bright as lanterns, and her arm was wrapped around him, holding him up as they slid through the dark.

Eli didn't know how long they traveled. It could have been minutes or days or lifetimes. The dark had no end. Nico's arm kept the cold away, and though the fear never abated, Eli found he could manage it if he clung to Nico's small, wiry body with his face buried in her coat like a child's.

He couldn't see Josef, but he could feel the swordsman's arm wrapped around Nico's waist. His fingers were pressed as tight as Eli's own into her coat, and Eli took some bitter comfort that Josef felt the fear, too. The only one who didn't seem to feel it was Nico. She stood above them, her pale face calm and determined below her glowing eyes as she stared into the dark ahead of them.

And then, just when Eli was sure he'd never see daylight again, they burst out of the blackness and into blinding light.

The three of them stumbled and fell as one, landing on something soft and sweet smelling. Eli blinked rapidly, willing his eyes to adjust, fearing they wouldn't. He wouldn't have been surprised to find he was blind. It seemed impossible that he could face so much darkness without suffering some consequence. But his sight slowly returned, and the first thing he saw were his hands digging into newly plowed dirt.

A field. They were lying on a tilled field in the shady lee of a stone shed. The land was rolling, a gentle country of undulating hills. There was a low, red farmhouse on the ridge above them, and above it, Eli could see the shadow of mountains in the distance.

"We're three days' ride north of Zarin."

Eli jumped. Nico's voice was surprisingly loud, and he rolled to see her and Josef standing over him. Nico frowned at his surprise. "Sorry," she said.

"Not your fault," Eli assured her, pushing himself up. "Are we in the foothills yet?"

"Almost," Nico said, nodding at the mountains. "We'll be there after the next jump."

Eli eyed the distant mountains. "That's a long jump."

"It's good to do the large ones first," Nico said. "Before we get tired." She held out her hand. "Ready?"

Eli wasn't, but he grabbed her hand anyway, pulling himself tight against her. Josef did the same, wrapping his arm around her waist again. As Nico took a deep breath, Eli examined her face covertly under lowered lashes. She was pale, but that was usual for Nico. Her breathing was steady and her shoulders were straight, all good signs. Still, he could see the first hints of dark shadows under her eyes, and he was about to suggest they should rest a moment when Nico pulled them back into the dark.

This time Eli was prepared for the cold and the fear, but it didn't help a jot. He went stiff just like before, and he would have fallen again had Nico not gotten a good grip on him this time. He could feel her spirit now. It was open and roaring, surrounding them in a bubble of her will so solid Eli felt like an idiot for not knowing she was a wizard from the very first time he met her. Nico's will didn't ward off the dark or the cold or the fear, but as he clung to her coat, Eli had the strong suspicion that, were it not for her protection, they would never have made it through with their souls intact.

This time, their trip through the dark was noticeably shorter. Just as Eli had dug in to weather the terror and the cold, it was over. They popped back into the light like a surfacing cork and toppled over onto the pine-strewn floor of a dark, mountain forest.

Eli rolled as he fell, landing on his back in the soft, cool

706

loam. His vision returned more quickly this time, and he looked around to take stock. It wasn't good. Josef was up as usual, but Nico was still down beside him. She was lying on her back in the pine needles. Her eyes were closed, and her pale face was the color of chalk. Josef was hovering above her, his brow set in a permanent scowl.

"We're resting here," he announced, looking at Eli like he was daring him to object.

"Fine with me," Eli said, letting his weight press him into the ground. "Where's here?"

Josef glanced up. "Going by the trees, I'd say we're exactly where Nico said we'd be, in the forest covering the foothills of the Sleeping Mountains. The road we took across the northern kingdoms on our way to Gaol cuts through here somewhere, probably south of us."

"Ah, memories," Eli said, pushing himself up with a groan.

With some difficulty, he scooted himself over to the nearest tree and propped his back upright against its scaly trunk. Josef did the same, laying the Heart across his knees. Assuming the swordsman was right about their location, they were already halfway to the mountain.

Not bad, Eli thought with a grin. The morning sun was still low. At this rate they'd be knocking on the Shaper Mountain's slopes by noon. But then, they couldn't keep up this rate, could they?

He glanced at Nico. She was lying perfectly still on the forest floor, the gentle rise and fall of her chest the only sign she was alive. In addition to the usual deathly pallor of her skin, the dark circles under her eyes were now deep and pronounced, and her cheeks looked hollow. Worse, her coat was twitching.

The movements were small and subtle, so small that Eli would have dismissed them as a trick of the wind if a wind had been blowing. But the forest floor was still. The coat was moving on its own, inching around her like it was trying to fold her into a cocoon.

Eli bit his lip. That was bad. The coat Slorn had made was as loyal as a Spiritualist's spirit, and it knew Nico's body better than she did. If it wanted to wrap her up, she was in a bad way. But the movements were still minor, and despite the dark circles, Nico's face was peaceful. A good thing they didn't have much left to go, then.

An hour later, Nico suddenly opened her eyes and sat up. Josef's arm shot out just as fast, steadying her shoulders. "You all right?"

Nico nodded. "I'm rested enough. We should go. Next time might be longer."

Eli cursed under his breath. "Nico, we can take as long as you—"

"I can do it," she said, cutting him off as she stood up. "Come on, let's go."

Eli took a deep breath and reminded himself that if Karon's core hadn't faded by now, the lava spirit could certainly wait until nightfall. With that truth firmly in his mind, Eli made a great show of not hurrying as he stood up, stretched, brushed the pine needles and dirt from his clothes, and finally stepped in to stand with Josef at Nico's side. He took his now customary position at Nico's shoulder and looked up, filling his mind with daylight as Nico leaned back into the tree shadow and the darkness ate them once more.

This jump was even shorter than the last, but when they emerged again, Nico collapsed in a heap. Josef fell to his knees beside her, pulling her into his lap while Eli slumped to the ground and focused on assessing their surroundings.

His eyes were getting faster at recovering, and almost immediately he saw they were in another forest, a familiar one this time. They were sitting on the sandy bed of a dry creek. The banks were crowded with beautiful, spindly, golden-leafed trees, their dove-gray trunks ringed with white. Nico had brought the three of them out in the shadow below a large outcropping of water-worn stone at the center of the dry stream bed. Off to their left was a long, flat sandbar strewn with leaves and feeling somehow empty, as though it were missing something.

Which, of course, it was. This was Slorn's Awakened Wood, and Slorn was what was missing. While Josef pulled Nico out of the rock shadow into the sun-warmed sand, Eli wondered briefly what happened to the house on chicken legs with both Pele and Slorn away. Did it wander on its own like a dog waiting for its masters? Or did it sit empty like any other building, gathering dust as its awakened parts fell asleep?

"Eli!" Josef's voice snapped him out of his dreaming. "Get over here."

Eli was at Nico's side in an instant. "What?"

"I was afraid," Josef said, looking at him pointedly.

"Josef," Eli said tenderly. "She's going to be fine."

"No," Josef said, rubbing a frustrated hand through his cropped blond hair. "I meant when I was moving her, I felt a small flicker of fear." He leaned in close and dropped his voice. "Demon fear."

Eli stiffened. That was a different matter. He looked down at Nico. Her coat was moving more than before, bundling itself tight around her until all he could see was her face.

"Her coat's in place," he said. "That should block any fear. Are you sure it wasn't just left over from the jump?"

Josef shook his head. "I specifically felt it when I touched her."

Eli bit his lip. "She's tired. It's possible her control is slipping."

"Powers help us if it does," Josef said, his hand flicking to the Heart's hilt. "If the League finds us now, she'll be a sitting target."

Eli could only nod and nudge the coat tighter around Nico's body. "Let's sit in the sun for a while," he said softly. "When Nico wakes up, we'll see what she wants to do."

Josef nodded and sat down by Nico's head. Eli took a similar position by her feet, pulling his legs up in front of him and resting his knees on his chin. They sat like that for a long time, neither saying a word. Still, it was hardly silent.

As always, the Awakened Wood was buzzing, the trees whispering together like gossipy old ladies. Eli fought the urge to roll his eyes. At this rate, the entire northern forest would know where Eli Monpress, the girl in Slorn's coat, and that man with the Heart of War were. Fortunately, the three of them would be long gone before that became a problem. Eli glanced at Nico again. Should be, he amended, squeezing his hands tighter.

An hour later, Nico still hadn't moved. Eli fidgeted in the warm sand, glancing at Josef whenever he dared. The swordsman was still as stone, watching Nico from beneath hooded lids. Eli was about to suggest a game of Daggerback just to break the tension when he realized something was wrong. He froze for several seconds, listening as hard as he could, and then he shot to his feet and started marching toward the tree line.

"What is it?" Josef called behind him.

"The forest is silent," Eli called back, breaking into a jog.

The Awakened Wood was never silent. Ever. In all the times Eli had been here, he'd never heard all the trees fall quiet at once. Something was wrong. He could actually see it as he came closer. Despite the stiff breeze blowing down from the mountains, every one of the narrow trunks was perfectly still, their branches frozen in place.

Even the leaves were motionless, their narrow, golden shapes as still and sharp as knives against the pale blue sky. Frowning, Eli reached out to touch the closest trunk. The wood was tense beneath his fingers, taut as a drawn bowstring just before it snapped. Eli snatched his hand away, but before he could think of what to say, the silence shattered.

It broke like glass, and the trees surged together as one word echoed through the forest.

"Gone!"

The trees screamed in a single ragged voice so loud that

Eli clapped his hands over his ears on instinct, even though he knew it would do no good. Nothing physical could stop that raw terror, that crippling, hopeless despair.

"Gone!" they roared again. "Gone, gone, *gone!*"

With each repetition, the unified voice began to splinter. The tremendous roar sent Eli stumbling back, putting several feet of distance between himself and the trees that were now thrashing furiously, transforming the graceful, golden Awakened Wood into a storm-wracked sea.

"Eli!" Josef shouted. Eli turned to see the swordsman sheltering Nico with his body, staring at the rocking trees in confusion. "What is going on?"

Eli had no answer for him. He could only cringe in horror as, with a final, sobbing wail, the trees tore their roots from the ground and began to rip each other apart.

CHAPTER
13

Alric, Deputy Commander of the League of Storms, sat at his desk behind a mountain of reports, rubbing his temples in a futile attempt to forestall the massive headache that was building at the front of his skull. There had been many, many times in his long career with the League when the Lord of Storms had demanded the impossible, and every time, Alric had delivered. That used to make him proud, but as the years rolled by, he'd come to realize that the problem with always doing the impossible was that people came to expect it. You had to keep performing miracles over and over again until you finally hit a task that was truly impossible and were forced, at last, to fail. He glanced up again at the stack of waiting reports. Had his time come at last?

As though in answer, a cluster of thin, white lines opened in the air above his desk and another half-dozen reports fell onto the pile below, sending the rest of the papers sliding. Alric closed his eyes and wondered if he should just retire now, while he still could.

On the surface, the task was a simple one: find and kill the Daughter of the Dead Mountain. Alric still shuddered at the name, remembering what he'd seen a few years ago at the Shaper Mountain, and then again recently in the forest on the outskirts of Den's bandit city. Alric had seen her clearly both times, but even for him, a longstanding League member, fear made his memories hazy. He could recall only glimpses: the endless black shadows, the wings, the millions of mouths...

Even these few details were enough to make him shake. The Daughter was the largest demonseed he'd ever personally encountered, perhaps the largest in the League's history, but strangely, it wasn't the killing part that had him worried. Even the Daughter of the Dead Mountain couldn't stand against the unified efforts of the League of Storms now that the Shepherdess had withdrawn her favor from the man who had harbored her, Eli Monpress. No, it was the *finding* part of the mission that was giving Alric fits, and the Lord of Storms was swiftly growing impatient, even more so than usual.

And it was all Alric's fault, too. That was the worst bit to swallow.

Alric had, of course, been keeping an eye on the girl on behalf of the League from the moment Monpress and his companions had left the bandit's camp. Her thrice-cursed coat made it impossible to actually watch her through the network of spirits who reported to the League, but keeping track of her companions had been almost laughably easy.

Josef Liechten in particular had been making quite the name for himself, and if the events at Izo's had taught Alric anything, it was that wherever Liechten was, the Daughter of the Dead Mountain wasn't far behind. So when the Lord of Storms had called them all together to announce the hunt, the first thing

Alric had done was check Liechten's location. And, he recalled with a deep sigh, the second thing he'd done was convince the Lord of Storms to wait.

He'd done it with the best of intentions. Liechten had been in Zarin at the time. Alric was not squeamish about the spilling of innocent blood if it got the job done, but this was simply too much. Any fight between the Lord of Storms and the Daughter of the Dead Mountain was sure to destroy anything it was near, and Zarin was the largest city on this half of the world. If the League had gone after her there, it would have been a massacre of unimaginable proportions.

So, using every trick he'd learned in the several lifetimes he'd spent as the Lord of Storms' second, Alric had convinced his commander to wait. They knew where the demonseed was, he'd argued, and she still reckoned herself safe. They just had to draw her out to somewhere less populated, an easy task requiring little more than a duel challenge from the Lord of Storms to Josef Liechten. The swordsman would never turn down a duel against a superior opponent. Liechten would go, the demonseed would follow, and then it would simply be a matter of closing the trap.

Such a good, simple plan. But then, between one hour and the next, everything had changed. Without so much as a warning, the rivers had gone mad, and in the confusion that followed, Alric's agents had lost both Josef Liechten and the Daughter of the Dead Mountain. That was almost eighteen hours ago, and since then, nothing. It was like the girl and her swordsman had just vanished into thin air, which, considering she was a demonseed, wasn't actually impossible. As the night wore on, Alric had expanded his search to the entire continent, but the answer was always the same: no sign of the girl or her swordsman.

Alric leaned back in his chair with a long sigh. He was working up the will to go through the newest batch of reports that had just landed on his desk when his body froze. As always, he smelled the Lord of Storms the second before he appeared. The sharp tang of burning ozone brought the Deputy Commander to his feet, and Alric fell into a low bow just in time as the white portal winked into existence.

The Commander was shouting before his boots hit the floor, his voice thundering with a fury that still made Alric cringe even after so many years.

"Have you found her?"

"Not yet, my Lord," Alric said. "I have every agent looking as we speak."

The Lord of Storms gave him an accusing look. "You told me she'd fully awakened in the mountains while I was away. I don't care what she did to cram herself back down after, her damn coat can't have kept up completely. How have you not found her yet?"

"I don't know," Alric said truthfully. "Even stretched beyond its limits, Heinricht Slorn's craftsmanship remains superb."

The Lord of Storms bared his teeth. "I'm going to skin that bear man."

"That wouldn't help matters," Alric said. "The coat is no longer her only cover. She's learned to dampen herself somehow, to clamp down on her own demonic nature. I have reason to believe she used her powers quite heavily in Osera, and yet there was little more than a blip so far as the spirits were concerned, though any panic might have been lost in the chaos caused by a war between stars."

The Lord of Storms settled his long fingers on the hilt of his sword. "I'm hearing a lot of excuses, Alric. That's not like you."

Alric closed his eyes. "I apologize, my lord. But, if I may speak plainly, even if the girl's coat was off completely, I don't think we could find her given the present situation."

"What do you mean?" the Lord of Storms growled.

Alric cleared his throat, searching for the most politic way to phrase their current predicament. "Our network relies on responding to spirit fear, but over the last day we've had a great deal of...interference."

"What?" the Lord of Storms said. "Are we not hearing the panics?"

"We're hearing them too well," Alric said, pointing at the pile of papers on his desk. "Every time the Lady calls in a star, we have a massive influx. I can't even keep up with the reports, much less decide which ones should be investigated. The Daughter has always been a quiet demon. Looking for her under these circumstances is like trying to separate the whispering voice out of a choir of screaming maniacs."

"Oh," the Lord of Storms looked considerably relieved. "Is that all?"

"That's *more* than enough," Alric said, not quite managing to keep the exasperation out of his voice. "With all due respect, sir, the Shepherdess asks the impossible. Telling us to hunt the Daughter of the Dead Mountain at the same time she decides to call in her stars without warning is practically inviting us to fail. How are we supposed to—"

"If we'd acted when she called the hunt, this would not have been a problem," the Lord of Storms said, his voice cold.

Alric snapped his mouth shut. A fair point. But still. "If the Lady had warned us about the incoming panics, I would never have suggested the delay," he said quietly. "That is no excuse, I know, but I cannot change the past. The truth of our current situation is that the Daughter of the Dead Mountain is missing, and there is simply too much fear for the League to find her. For pity's sake, sir, I've got our agents combing Zarin like common guardsmen. If the Lady would consent to hold off calling her stars for a few hours, it would be enough to—"

"The Shepherdess tends her flock," the Lord of Storms' voice said, rolling over him. "That's her job. Killing demon-seeds is ours."

Alric clenched his teeth. "And how are we to do that when—"

"*I have spoken!*" the Lord of Storms roared.

Alric stepped back, his face pale. "Yes, sir."

The Lord of Storms nodded. "Forget Zarin," he said. "The

Daughter of the Dead Mountain cannot be trusted to stay in one place. Check every panic. I don't care how many there are, have the men investigate every single one. If the demon is not there, they move on, no matter how upset the spirits are. Our only priority is the hunt."

"Yes, sir," Alric said, lowering his head. "What will you do?"

"I'll hunt as well," the Lord of Storms said. "She can't hide forever. Now get to work. We're running out of time."

"Yes, sir," Alric said again, but the Lord of Storms was already gone, his enormous black form vanishing in a crack of lightning.

Alric fell back into his chair with a sigh. He hadn't expected the Lord of Storms to shut down his suggestion quite that quickly, but looking back, he wasn't surprised. It was times like this that he had to remind himself that the Lord of Storms was not human. His body was an illusion created by the Shepherdess for her own amusement and to make it easier for him to interact with his human followers, but his mind was that of a spirit, one shaped from its very beginning to have a single purpose: to be the Shepherdess's sword against the demons.

No matter how much the Commander railed against the Lady in private, unless her actions directly impeded his work, he would not question her. So what if the Shepherdess was sending the whole world into a panic, picking out stars like she was picking flowers? To the Commander's mind, that just meant they had to look harder. He had balked against her order to leave Eli Monpress alone because it had put a wall between him and his purpose, but now that she had given him the freedom to hunt the Daughter of the Dead Mountain despite the thief, the Lord of Storms didn't care how difficult the Shepherdess's actions made things. So long as he got to hunt, to serve his purpose, the Lord of Storms wouldn't care if the Lady ordered him to do it without hands. He'd just take it as a challenge to rip the creature's throat out with his teeth.

Alric shook his head. It had taken him many years to

716

understand the Lord of Storms' nature, but no amount of understanding could make him like it. Still, there was little he could do. The Commander had given his orders, and Alric would obey. That was how the world worked.

He allowed himself a full thirty seconds of sulking before turning back to his desk and the impossible task the Lord of Storms had set before him. He grabbed the latest report and ripped it open, reading it quickly before laying it down on the bottom of what would become a stack of dead ends. Alric read the reports one by one, scratching off replies, sending his men after every panic, just as he had been ordered. They would go without question, do their duty to their utmost just like always, just like him.

"The Shepherdess's will be done," he muttered, laying another dead end on the pile.

An hour of furious work later, Alric had almost caught up to the current reports when a bright white light flashed in the paved yard below his window. A minute later, a brisk knock sounded at his door.

"Enter."

A man in the League's long black coat opened the door and stepped into the room without a sound. He was dark skinned and tall, and the sword at his hip shone as red as the setting sun. Alric smiled. Chejo was one of the League's oldest and most trusted members. An efficient man who didn't waste his time. If he was here, it was important, and Alric put everything else aside to hear his report.

"Deputy Commander," Chejo said. "Eli Monpress has escaped from the Council."

Alric frowned. "I wasn't aware he'd been captured."

"They got him yesterday morning," Chejo said. "Whitefall's good at keeping secrets."

"Though not as good at keeping prisoners, it seems," Alric said, tapping the paper in front of him. "But to be fair, this *is* Monpress we're talking about. When did he escape?"

"Yesterday evening," Chejo said. "Right after the incident with the rivers."

Alric's mouth pressed to a thin line. The timing lined up far too well for his liking. "Well, that explains the sudden disappearance of Liechten and the demonseed quite nicely, doesn't it?"

"That's why I thought you'd like to hear it in person," Chejo said, his frown deepening. "Sir, does the thief's presence change the mission?"

"No," Alric said without hesitation. "The orders stand, but this does make things more complicated. Monpress always was the cunning one of their little group. If the demonseed is wrapped up in whatever scam he's running, finding her could prove more difficult than we thought."

"Don't see how, considering it's already nigh impossible," Chejo said with a sneer. "The whole world's in a panic these days."

Alric sighed. "I know, just do your best."

He motioned that the League man was dismissed, but Chejo didn't leave. He stayed put, his eyes as sharp as the sword at his side. "Permission to speak freely, sir?"

Alric could guess what the man wanted to say, but he nodded anyway.

"We're pledged to protect the world from the demons," Chejo said, gripping his sword hard. "But what the Shepherdess does now with her stars is worse than any demon fear I've seen in all my years with the League. I serve the Lord of Storms and his Lady without hesitation, but I have to wonder if we aren't landing on the wrong side of the problem this time around."

Alric looked down at his desk. Chejo's words were dangerously close to insubordination. It was also a fair point, one that occurred to him every time he opened a report of a new panic.

"The Shepherdess has guided our world since its beginning," he said calmly, locking his eyes on Chejo's dark glare. "We

718

must trust that she knows what she's doing. Spirits are panicky by nature. Most of them are little smarter than animals, but even the big ones are prone to attacks of irrational fear. It's only natural; spirits are prey. They are helpless, weak sheep, while demons are predators. The sheep must go where the Shepherdess leads, and we as her dogs must protect the flock and ensure it follows. That is why we are here, Chejo, to protect and corral. Not to question."

"It is human to question," Chejo said, crossing his arms.

"An urge we must suppress on occasion if we are to serve the spirits," Alric answered tiredly. "Is that understood?"

Chejo's glare grew icy, but he lowered his head. "Aye, sir."

Alric nodded. "Have you anything else to report?"

"Yes," Chejo said. "There's a woman here to see you."

Alric's eyebrows shot up. "A woman?"

Chejo smiled. "Pretty little Spiritualist with a ghosthound. She arrived a few seconds after I did. Asked for you by name. I left her arguing with the quartermaster, but I thought you would like to know."

Alric leaned back and resumed rubbing his temples. It did little good. "I would, thank you, Chejo. I'd like you to return to Zarin and see if you can't learn more about where the thief might have gone. Could you send the Spiritualist up before you leave?"

"Of course, sir," Chejo said, turning on his heel. "Good luck, sir."

Alric waved him off and stood up, carefully moving the remaining unopened reports to a side table. There was only one Spiritualist with a ghosthound he knew of, and if he was going to deal with her without losing his temper, he needed to remove all other sources of frustration. When his desk was bare, he sat down, folded his arms, and waited for the knock.

Miranda stood in the courtyard where the League man had left her, leaning on Gin and trying not to look as wobbly as she felt. Though she'd never admit it, she was vaguely disappointed. She'd always thought flying would be more freeing, or at least more fun. But after a night and a morning spent hurtling through the air, she'd never been happier to be on solid ground. From the way Gin had pressed himself into the stone the second they touched down, she knew he felt the same. Her stomach certainly did, though this particular stretch of ground wasn't helping much on that account.

Against her better judgment, her eyes drifted up again. The League's fortress was perched on a lonely jut of land in the far, far northwest corner of the continent, a desolate country well beyond the Council maps. The sea, iron gray and choppy beneath the cloud-heavy sky, surrounded them on three sides, and the land wasn't any more hospitable with its wet stone and wild nettles.

The fortress itself looked as though it had been pushed up from the rock during some great argument among the lava flows and then forgotten completely. Its surface was black and pitted save for the sea-facing walls that had been worn smooth by the endless wind. The stern black battlements, the sharp, jutting towers, the harsh military efficiency of it all was dreadful to look on and even worse to stand under. Already, after less than five minutes of waiting for Alric, her stomach was a quivering mess of nerves far worse than the man deserved.

Miranda closed her eyes, missing Mellinor terribly. Diminished or not, he had still been a Great Spirit, and his presence, not to mention his advice, would have been very welcome now. As it was, all she could do was clutch Gin's fur and try to keep her mind calm, for her other spirits if nothing else.

She could feel them shaking in their rings, even Eril, and the wind spirit was usually the cockiest of them all. Miranda couldn't blame them. The longer she waited, the more she realized that it wasn't the fortress or the anticipation of meeting Alric that made her uneasy. The League's Fortress was just a building, and she'd dealt with the Deputy Commander before, but the growing dread that gnawed at her resolve was something

720

greater. She could feel it rising in her throat even now, an icy bile of fear, completely irrational and so omnipresent it seemed to radiate from the black stone itself.

"It's the vault," Gin whispered.

Miranda jumped and looked down to see her ghosthound was crouched low on the ground, his pointed ears pressed flat against his skull. "It must be right below us," he whispered again, softer this time.

"What?" Miranda whispered back.

"The vault of the demonseeds," a strong voice answered.

Miranda whirled around to see the tall, dark League man who'd been there when the wind had dropped her into the courtyard. The one who'd told her to wait. He'd been gone awhile, but now he was back, standing only a few feet from her. His hand rested on the red sword at his hip as he looked her over, its hilt glowing as red as an ember between his fingers.

Miranda winced. She hadn't heard him return, but from what she'd seen of the League, that was normal. The man's lips curved into a smile that didn't touch his eyes and he nodded to the ground at her feet. "The dog is right. The fear you're feeling comes from the vault. This citadel is built on the great cavern where the League stores the seeds of the demons after we cut them from their hosts."

Gin whimpered and pressed himself flatter against the paving stones, but Miranda stepped forward in alarm. "Why would you keep such things?"

"Demonseeds are indestructible," the man said with a shrug. "All we can do is pile them up and lock them away. If that's how it must be, then what safer place is there for them than beneath the Lord of Storms' own fortress?"

Miranda frowned. She didn't have an answer to that. Fortunately, the League man seemed to have lost interest. "The Deputy Commander will see you in his office," he said, pointing at the gate behind him. "Second floor, first door on the right."

"Thank you," Miranda said, but before she'd gotten to the "you," the man was gone. She stood a moment, staring at the shimmering white line as it faded from the air, and then, setting her shoulders, she marched across the black-paved courtyard. "Stay here," she ordered.

For once, Gin didn't argue. He just put his head down, his orange eyes following her as she vanished into the fortress.

It was just as cold inside the fortress as it was outside, but at least the black stone walls blocked the endless wind. Still, Miranda shivered as she climbed the stairs, blowing on Kirik's spark to keep her hands warm. When she reached the top, she went to the door the League man had indicated and knocked purposefully.

Alric's voice rang clear and immediate through the heavy, metal-bound wood. "Enter."

She opened the door to see a spare but surprisingly normal office. A large, worn desk took up most of the room. Alric sat in a high-backed chair behind it, looking the same as he ever did. On the wall above his head, a sheathed sword rested on a mounted stand, its swooping, golden hilt shining like the day's last sunbeam in the dim, cloud-shrouded light that filtered through the tall window. Outside, she could see the courtyard where Gin was still crouching and the sea beyond, an endless swath of ash-gray water and white peaks running to sky's edge.

"Spiritualist Lyonette," Alric said. "Or, forgive me, Rector Spiritualis. Please"—he held out his hand toward the carved wooden chair in front of his desk—"sit."

Miranda sat, folding her hands in front of her so that her rings would catch the gray light. "Why am I not surprised you've already heard about that?"

"I try to stay informed," Alric said with a tight smile. "And on that note, would you mind telling me how you arrived at our headquarters today? Chejo was vague on that point."

When Miranda frowned, Alric held up his hands.

"I don't ask just to be nosy. We guard many things here,

so you can understand how an unexpected guest, no matter how welcome, would be a matter of some concern."

That made sense, Miranda thought, and there was little point in trying to keep the West Wind's involvement secret after his wind had blown her across half the continent. "One of Illir's winds brought me," she said. "Payment for a favor."

"Must have been some favor," Alric said thoughtfully. "Thank you for your honest answer, Rector, but I'm afraid you've caught us at a rather busy time."

"I thought you might be busy," Miranda said quickly. "That's why I'm here."

Alric gave her a strange look. "Really?"

Miranda nodded emphatically. "I think we can help."

If Miranda had known the Deputy Commander better, she would have known how rare the look of pure confusion on his face was. He leaned forward, resting his elbows on the table. "Maybe you should explain from the beginning," he said. "Just to be sure we understand one another."

"I don't see that there's much that needs explaining," Miranda said. "Surely the League is aware that stars are vanishing." She paused, watching Alric's face. His polite smile fell at once.

"Ah," he said. "You're here about the panics."

"Why else would I be here?" Miranda asked, exasperated. "Maybe you haven't noticed, but the world is tearing itself apart out there. The spirits who lose their stars are convinced the world is ending, and frankly, I don't think they're too far off. Not when the stars who form the foundation of the world are vanishing without a trace."

"How do you know about—" Alric stopped and took a long breath. "Never mind, I'm not going to ask who told you. It doesn't really matter. I suppose, then, you'd like to know *why* the stars are vanishing."

Miranda nodded. "It would be a start."

"Then that makes two of us," Alric said, spreading his hands helplessly. "All I can tell you is that the Shepherdess is the one who calls her stars away. As to the why of it, your guess is as good as mine."

"But you work for her, don't you?" Miranda said. "I heard you say it before, in Izo's camp. The League does the Shepherdess's work."

"The Lord of Storms serves the Shepherdess," Alric said flatly. "And the League serves the Lord. We know only what the Lady sees fit to tell her demon hunter, which has never been as much as most seem to believe."

"So you don't know why she's doing it?" Miranda said hotly. "Why she's ruining the world she's supposed to be guiding?"

"No," Alric's voice grew sharp and cold. "Only that it is for the best."

Miranda gaped at him. "How can you possibly believe that?" she cried. "Open your eyes! There is no way this kind of panic is good for the spirits. How do you know she's not ruining everything and counting on her doctrine of ignorance and fear to discourage questions until it's too late?"

"I don't," Alric said. "But I've trusted my life to the Lord of Storms and his mistress for a long, long time now, Lady Rector. In that time, the Shepherdess has done many things I did not agree with or understand, and yet the world has continued."

"Not like this," Miranda said. Her anger was boiling now, and her head was full of the memory of the river's screaming voice.

Gone! Gone! Gone!

She forced herself to stop and take a breath. Only when her temper was firmly back under control did she let herself speak again.

"When I first decided to come here, I meant to demand that the Shepherdess stop whatever she was doing," she confessed. "But while I was stuck in the air, I had time to calm down and think, and I realized I was asking the impossible. The Shepherdess is the top authority in this world, isn't she? No one stands up to her, not the Shaper Mountain, not the Lord of the West, no one."

Not even Eli, her mind whispered, but Miranda forced the thought out of her head. "I am a Spiritualist," she continued. "My oaths demand that I serve the spirits, protect them from abuse, and try to make the world better for them. I don't know why the Shepherdess is taking her stars away seemingly without a care for the spirits who depend on them, but I understand now that I can't stop her. All I can do is try to control the damage as best I can."

Alric was looking down at his empty desk when she finished, tracing the worn grain of the wood with his fingertip. "That is unexpectedly wise of you, Rector," he said quietly. "But while I can understand why you came here initially, I don't yet see what you want from the League now."

"I want to help," Miranda said. "I've seen the League work twice now, once repairing the damage in Mellinor and once in Izo's camp. I saw your power firsthand both times, how you calm panicked spirits and repair damage like it never was. I've also seen how you can move easily through the world using those white lines. All over the world, on this continent and I'm sure on the Empress's as well, maybe even in the frozen north, spirits are panicking. With every star that vanishes, the spirits who relied on it lash out in fear and despair, hurting themselves and everything around them. If we don't stop the panic quickly, the spirits will do enormous harm in their fear. I've seen it already with the rivers, and it's only going to get worse as more stars vanish."

"It can't be helped," Alric said. "Spirits are panicky by nature."

"Anything would be panicky if it thought the world was ending!" Miranda cried. "The only reason *people* aren't tearing their cities apart is because we're too blind and ignorant to know what's going on. The Shepherdess holds all the power. The spirits have no choice but to depend on her. How can you fault them for panicking when she rips the floor out from under their feet?"

Alric took a deep breath. "I'm not blaming them," he said. "Believe it or not, Rector, I'm on your side, but the League has other priorities at the moment. We are not a large organization—"

"I know that," Miranda said. "It's not your job to guard the common spirits, but it is mine." She pulled herself straight in her chair, fixing her gaze solidly on Alric's. This was it. "The League is small, far too small to deal with a crisis of this scale, but the Spirit Court is over a thousand strong, and every one of us has sworn the same oath to serve the spirits and protect them from harm. What I'm proposing is a partnership. If you will share the League's powers with the Court for the extent of this emergency, we will take over calming all the panicked spirits gently and with understanding, in accordance with our oaths."

To her surprise, Alric smiled. "You don't think we'll be gentle?"

"I think you'll be rushed," Miranda answered. "The League doesn't have the manpower to handle every panic. We do. If we don't have to worry about travel time, my Spiritualists will be able to take the care needed with each outburst. With us handling the panic caused by the lost stars, your membership will be free to pursue your 'other priorities.'"

Alric drummed his fingers on his desk, his brows furrowed in thought. "You propose an interesting plan, Lady Rector," he said at last. "But I wonder, could you follow it through?"

Miranda jerked back. "What?"

"You forget I am well informed," Alric said, his voice bland. "The Court is fractured, and you are Rector only until those who balked at Banage's leadership organize to kick you out. Even if it were in my power to wave my hand and give you everything you ask, you're hardly in a position to be making deals on behalf of the Spirit Court."

"That doesn't matter," Miranda said, holding her head high. "I know which way the Court will go once the situation is properly explained. We may quibble about how the Court is run, but to stand back and abandon the spirits to panic and fear goes against the very nature of our purpose and our oaths. No Spiritualist would allow that, no matter who wears the Rector's mantle. So long as there are rings on our fingers, we will honor our oaths and do our duty. *That* I swear to you, Deputy Commander."

Alric leaned back in his chair, his face closed, considering. "It is a bold offer," he said at last. "Bolder than I'd ever expect from the Court, but I can find no guile in it."

"Of course not," Miranda said, insulted. "I'm not a liar."

"No, you're not," Alric said, looking at her with a faint smile. "Your offer is a good one, Lady Rector, and would actually solve a great number of my problems if you were successful. Unfortunately, the League's power is not mine to dole out. It, like all else we have, flows from our commander, the Lord of Storms. He's the one you'll have to convince."

Miranda sighed, frustrated. "Fine, when can I talk to him?"

Alric's smile widened. "I believe he's already here."

Miranda started and looked around, but the office was empty. The only change at all was a faint smell of ozone in the air. And then, without warning, the white line opened right in front of her face, and the Lord of Storms filled the room.

Miranda jerked back without thinking, nearly falling out of her chair. Her eyes saw a tall man stepping out of the air between her and Alric, a man with long black hair that fell well past the high collar of his black League coat, pale, intense eyes set in a pale, intense face, and a long, gently curved sword at his side, its hilt somewhere between blue and silver, like a lightning bolt glimpsed suddenly on a clear night.

That was what she saw, anyway, but her other senses were screaming at her that this was wrong. She'd *felt* the man appear, felt the air thickening, tightening with the anticipation that came just before a storm. The room was still, and yet she could smell the storm on the air, cold and wild and dangerous, and it took every bit of pride she had to resettle herself in her chair instead of running for cover like her body was screaming for.

The Lord of Storms, for who else could it be, was saying something to Alric, but Miranda couldn't make out the words. They rumbled through her like distant thunder, and then the Lord of Storms turned to look at her, and his lightning-colored eyes narrowed. All at once, the pressure relented and the Lord of Storms seemed to shrink. It was like he was pulling himself in, resettling the human shell that contained the full extent of...whatever he was. Miranda swallowed and forced herself to be still, but she couldn't stop the beads of sweat rolling down the side of her face or the deepening feeling that she was now not only in over her head, but so far out that the bottom had vanished completely.

"You." The Lord of Storms' voice was softer now, more human, but Miranda could still feel the words vibrating through her ribs. "Wizard girl. Alric tells me you have an offer?"

Miranda swallowed. "Yes," she said, proud that her voice trembled only a little. "I understand you are having problems containing the spirit panic that is—"

"*You understand?*" the Lord of Storms' sneering voice cut her off. "You understand nothing, human. We are in the middle of the greatest hunt of your age. I have no time for your ignorance. Tell me the offer, if you have one, but don't waste my patience reaching above your place."

Miranda tensed in anger, glaring up at the Lord of Storms. Who did he think he was? She'd faced down the Shaper Mountain; she'd taken in Mellinor and answered the Lord of the West's call for aid. She wasn't some *wizard girl* for him to kick around.

"My *offer* is a simple one," she said, standing up to meet the Lord of Storms' glare with one of her own. "The world is in a panic and the League does not have the resources to quell it. I can help you. As acting Rector Spiritualis, I offer you the Spirit Court's aid. We have over a thousand wizards with centuries of experience handling spirits between us. If you will consent to grant my Court limited access to the League's gifts, namely instant travel throughout the world and the ability to still and reconstruct spirits, we will handle the panic caused by the vanishing stars, leaving you free to continue your hunt."

She'd expected the Lord of Storms to be angry at her disrespectful tone, but the tall man only put his hand to his chin, considering. "I give your Court temporary access to the League's power, and you'll handle the spirits?" He frowned. "Why do you take so much on yourselves? What are you after?"

"Survival through this crisis with the least amount of life lost, along with the continued peace and stability of the spirit world," Miranda said hotly. "The same thing we've been after since the Court was founded. We've already tried smoothing things over ourselves, but we're only human, as you're so quick to point out. We can't be everywhere at once. The League can. So let's help each other."

She finished with her chin up, looking at the Lord of Storms dead-on, but he wasn't paying attention to her anymore. He was staring out the window at the stone-paved yard where Gin was waiting, his face set in a deep scowl. "Do you know how we hunt the demonseeds?"

The question caught Miranda off guard, but before she could collect her thoughts, the Lord of Storms answered it himself.

"We listen," he said, tapping the fall of black hair covering his ear. "When a demonseed awakens, a wave of fear is born with it. When that fear hits the spirits, a great cry arises, and it is that which calls us to our duty. But a cry of demon fear and a cry of loss for something as precious and vital as a star sound very much the same, especially when so many cries happen at once." He turned to glare at her. "The demon we hunt is a quiet prey. She's hard enough to track under normal circumstances, but this racket has made the task nearly impossible."

Without warning, the Lord of Storms leaned down, his face hovering dangerously close to Miranda's own, and it took everything she had not to duck away. She could feel him all around her, now. The pressure was almost painful, the air alive with the quick pulse of lightning about to strike.

"I tire of waiting while my League wastes its time sorting through frightened spirits," he said, his low voice booming. "If your Court can quiet the field long enough for us to find and conquer our quarry, I will grant you whatever power you need."

"My lord," Alric said, his voice taut with warning.

"It is already done, Alric," the Lord of Storms said. He straightened up, and Miranda shivered as the enormous pressure subsided. "I've decided. The hunt is all that matters. Anyway, they can hardly make things worse, can they?"

"Things can always get worse," Alric said tiredly. "But if you've decided, then that's that. We'll still need a pledge for the transfer, though. When can we address your Court?"

It took Miranda several moments to realize this last question was for her. "The Spirit Court gathers for the Conclave this afternoon," she said. "Everyone alive who's taken the Spiritualist oath will be there."

"Conclave?" Alric's voice shifted from weary to interested in a flash. "Isn't that the Court's great meeting, called in times of dire crisis? And doesn't it usually start with a referendum on the Rectorship?"

Miranda's cheeks flushed again, with shame this time. "It does," she said quietly.

The Lord of Storms' glare swept back to her. "I hope you have not promised more than you can deliver, girl."

"The Spirit Court will do whatever it needs to ensure the protection of the spirit world whether I'm Rector or not," she snapped. "We will keep our end of the bargain, Lord of Storms."

The Lord of Storms laughed then, a great, terrifying sound like thunder cracking directly over her head. "I love it," he said, grinning wide. "Alric, get it started."

"Yes, Commander," Alric said, bowing.

The Lord of Storms nodded and vanished in a flash of

lightning. Miranda covered her eyes a hair too late and was left blinking against the afterimage of clouds pouring through a long, white line.

"Well," Alric said, standing, "shall we get going?"

"We have some time," Miranda said slowly, glancing out the window as she pulled herself together. "It's still morning. The Conclave doesn't start until noon."

"Then we should certainly get going," Alric said. "It's twenty past already."

Miranda blinked at him. "But the sky," she said lamely, looking again at the gray morning clouds.

"It's always like that here," Alric said. "This is the citadel of the Lord of Storms. The sky reflects his moods, not the time of day."

Miranda took a deep breath and saved the cursing for later. "Do I have time to get Gin?"

"He's already in Zarin," Alric said, taking the sheathed gold sword down from the stand behind him and buckling it to his belt.

Miranda's head whipped back toward the window. Sure enough, the ghosthound was gone. So was the man who'd introduced himself to her as the League quartermaster when she'd first come tumbling out of the sky.

"We in the League take good care to jump *before* the Lord of Storms says frog," Alric said with a smile. He reached out, his hand hanging in the air before her. "Shall we be off?"

Rather than answer, Miranda reached out and took his offered hand. His skin was surprisingly cool and dry to the touch, and as his fingers closed over hers, a white line opened in the air in front of them.

"After you, Lady Rector," the Deputy Commander said with a smile she would have called wry were his face less serious.

Miranda nodded and, after only a tiny hesitation, stepped through the hole in the world.

CHAPTER

14

Spiritualist Krigel rubbed his knotted hands across his wrinkled face. He was too old for this, he reminded himself. The ache in his chest was constant now, forcing him to take his breaths in short, tight gasps. His heart had been through too much already. Another hour of this kind of stress and he would be dead.

Against his better judgment, he lowered his hands and looked out at the crowd. The circular assembly hall of the Spirit Court was packed to the rafters. As demanded, every Spiritualist who had ever sworn an oath, from the most influential Tower Keepers to the newest crop of apprentices, had answered the call of the Conclave. They filled the raised gallery that surrounded the hearing room floor. Those who'd arrived early and those whose rank demanded deference sat on the benches. The rest piled in wherever they could, a great mass of red robes and nervous shifting.

Below the ring of benches, the white floor was empty, as was the witness stand at the room's center. This was a formal meeting of the Court, not a trial. Of course, Krigel sighed, you'd think it was *his* trial the way Blint and his ilk were glaring at him.

The Tower Keeper had a large contingent, too. A good third of the Spiritualists on that side of the room had come in with him, probably from one of those secret meetings he was always holding. The man was as bad as Hern. Blint had jumped at the chance to go over to the Council when Banage was declared a traitor, and though he'd dressed it up afterward, saying he'd just been doing his duty to the land of his birth, the bald truth was that Blint had grabbed for power the moment he saw weakness. From the naked hunger in his eyes, he was clearly ready to do so again, and given the current situation, Banage's supporters weren't in much position to oppose him.

Rubbing his aching chest, Krigel let his glare drift up to the place everyone else was studiously avoiding. High above him, the Rector's chair stood empty. Miranda has been missing since yesterday afternoon. Considering how she'd been acting over the last two days, Krigel shouldn't be surprised, but seeing as she was the one who'd called the Conclave in the first place, he'd assumed she'd at least show up for it. But here it was, thirty minutes past noon, and there was no sign of her.

Krigel gritted his teeth. If it were anyone else he'd have wagered she'd skipped town, but not Miranda. The girl was too stubborn to run from her own execution. She was probably off doing something she considered frighteningly important. More important than being Rector. Hopefully whatever it was would give her some comfort when she lost her position and Krigel was torn to pieces as Blint rushed the Rector's seat. Assuming, of course, his heart didn't give out first.

Krigel was sinking deeper down that bleak line of thought when a cracking sound shocked him out of his gloom. At the other end of the enormous room, the double doors flew open. A hundred long benches scraped as all the Spirit Court leaned forward, looking to see if this was Banage's protégé at last. But their gasp of anticipation faded to a hiss as, alas, not the Rector but her ghosthound strode into the room.

Gin trotted across the empty assembly floor, his claws clicking on the polished stone. He'd barely gone three steps before the room exploded. Spiritualists shouted over each other, demanding to know where his mistress was. The ghosthound ignored them completely. He simply made his way to the spot directly below the Rector's chair and sat down, wrapping his tail around his feet as he glared at the assembled Spirit Court, most of whom were now very close to rioting.

"Order!' Krigel shouted, jumping to his feet as he banged his hand on the heavy banister.

The wizards ignored him. A few were already up and

making their way to the doors. Blint was on his feet as well, but he was headed for the Rector's chair, his face set in a predatory smile of long-held ambition nearing its fulfillment. Krigel cursed under his breath and leaned over the railing.

"Where is the Rector?" he hissed at the ghosthound, who was sitting directly below him. "Everything is falling apart!"

"She's coming," Gin said, his quiet voice picking up the hint of a growl as his orange eyes locked on Blint. "Just a bit longer."

"We don't have a bit longer," Krigel snapped. "We haven't had a bit longer for the past half hour. You tell her to get here *now*, or I'll—"

A brilliant flash of light cut him off. Blinded, Krigel fell backward, his mouth working dumbly in his shock. He wasn't alone. The light cut through the chaos in the room like a falling ax, leaving the chamber silent except for Gin's growl. When Krigel's blindness faded at last, he looked up to see the Spirit Court gaping at him in shocked silence.

No, he realized belatedly, not at *him*. Their eyes were locked on the seat above him, the Rector's raised pulpit. Swallowing against the sudden tightness in his throat, Krigel braced his hands on the banister and turned, his eyes going wide.

A white line hung in the air in front of the Rector's throne-like seat. It was no thicker than a thread, but it flashed as bright as a sunbeam off a mirror. He saw it for only a moment, and the world split open as Miranda stepped into view.

She stepped through the hole in the world as though she did it every day. Her face was set in an utterly implacable frown, and her clothes were wrinkled and travel worn, but that mattered little. What *did* matter was the enormous golden chain that lay across the neck and shoulders of her tattered coat.

Krigel's breath caught. She was wearing the mantle of the Tower, the sacred mark of the office of Rector that he'd laid out for her this morning, back when he'd still thought they'd have time to discuss the Conclave before it began. He had no idea when she'd had the time to go up to her office and put it on, but she had it now, and she wore the golden weight as though she'd been born to it.

When Miranda had both feet on the wooden floor of the Rector's stand, the white line she'd entered through flickered and vanished. But as it died, another flashed, this time to her right, and Krigel felt his poor chest constrict as a middle-aged man with neatly cropped dark hair, a golden sword, and a long black coat stepped out of nothing to stand at Miranda's right. By this point, the stunned silence was as thick as cotton. Krigel himself had never seen the man before, but there wasn't a soul in the room who didn't recognize the long black coat with its high collar trimmed in silver, or what it meant.

Krigel raised a shaky arm to wipe away the sweat beading on his face. The Rector Spiritualis and the League of Storms, standing together. Powers, what had the fool girl gotten herself into?

The scrape of the Rector's chair was offensively loud as Miranda pushed it aside to stand before the podium. The League man hung back, his cold eyes moving over the assembled Spiritualists, judging each of them in turn. Outside, despite the clear sky, a roll of thunder crashed in the distance.

Krigel closed his eyes as the rumble shook the Tower. Forget the girl, what had she gotten the *Court* into? His only answer was another peal of thunder as the sunlight faded from the Court's high windows.

Miranda faced the gathered Spirit Court with iron determination. The Court stared back at her, a sea of faces packing the ring of benches. She'd never seen so many people in the Court's chamber, and for several moments the sheer weight of their stares threatened to send her curling into a ball. But she steadied herself against the Rector's wide podium, keeping her back straight as a beam. Now was not the time for weakness. Now was the time to perform the task Master Banage had entrusted her to do. On her left hand, the Rector's ring gripped her finger like a vise, trembling with the thunder that shook the Tower. The Lord of Storms would be here soon. She had to move quickly.

"Spiritualists of the Court," she said, and then stopped. Even with the crowd, her voice boomed through the chamber. It rang in her ears and echoed in her stomach, not just loud but clear, like a brass bell. The chamber's high walls and polished stone took her voice and made it a proclamation. The mantle on her shoulders rang with the words as well, and Miranda realized that the Tower itself was helping her. Immense gratitude flooded her mind, and Miranda began to speak in earnest.

"I am sorry for the delay," she said, her voice ringing in the air. "Thank you all for responding so quickly to the call for Conclave. For those of you who don't know me, I am Miranda Lyonette, former apprentice to Rector Banage, who was arrested three days ago for supposed treason against the Council of Thrones. Knowing he could not perform his duty from the Council dungeon, Master Banage conferred upon me the role of emergency interim Rector Spiritualis for the sole purpose of calling the Court to Conclave."

The crowd shuffled and began to whisper. On her left, Blint leaned over the railing and opened his mouth to speak. Miranda didn't give him the chance.

"Master Banage's arrest by the Council violated the neutrality of our order," she said hotly. "Whitefall's attack on our Rector was an attack on all of us, but this was not the reason Rector Banage ordered the Conclave convened."

She turned slowly, fixing her eyes on Blint. "The war with the Immortal Empress lasted only one night, but in the run-up to that night, great damage was done to our Court. Our strength was splintered, our ideals muddied. Rector Banage ordered me to call the Conclave because he hoped to heal this division so that the Court could once again stand united against the trials to come. In hindsight, this was immeasurably wise. For in the last two days a disaster of unprecedented scope has fallen upon the world. A crisis even Etmon Banage did not foresee."

"But you did?" Blint's voice shot through the room like an arrow. All eyes turned to the Tower Keeper as he leaped to his feet, glaring at Miranda like she was a stain on his robes.

"You fancy yourself a wise leader, girl?" he cried, his face blotchy with rage as he spat the words at her. "You dare stand at the Rector's podium and lecture us on Etmon Banage's goodness? Have you forgotten that it was Banage's ego that broke the Court in the first place? And now you say a crisis is upon us. Let me guess, is it a crisis only you can face? One that requires you to remain as Rector so you can continue Banage's doctrine of destructive absolutism?"

The room erupted as he finished. The benches rocked as the Spiritualists turned on each other, shouting and arguing. Miranda banged her hand against the wood of the podium, but her calls for order were lost in the chaos.

She felt Alric shifting beside her. There wasn't much time before the Lord of Storms arrived. If he saw the Court in such disagreement, he could rescind the deal. She had to get control, and she had to get it now. Clenching her fingers, she brought the Rector's ring to her lips. *Please*, she mouthed against the smooth, warm gold, *let me be heard.*

The ring began to buzz against her finger, and Miranda had the curious sensation that the room was bending toward her. When she spoke again, her voice fell on the crowd like a torrential rain, drowning out all else.

"This isn't about Banage!" she cried, the words booming loud as thunder cracks. "Not anymore. Forget your politics for one moment and *think*. Something horrible is happening, something far greater than Banage or the Council or even this Court. You've all felt it, haven't you? Your spirits launch into a sudden panic and won't tell you why. The Whitefall River overflows its banks in a screaming terror with no provocation. All around the Council Kingdoms, reports flow in of earthquakes and floods, of spirits turning on each other in terror, and none will say *why.*"

She stopped, her unnaturally loud voice echoing in the

newborn silence, but all around the room, heads were nodding. Hands crossed over rings turned inward, and faces drew tight with worry. Strangely, Miranda felt a swell of relief. They knew what she was talking about, and they were as afraid as she had been.

"Your spirits won't tell you what is happening because it is forbidden for them to speak of such matters," she said, her voice gentle. "But it is not forbidden for me."

And then she told them. She told them as the Shaper Mountain had told her, about the stars, about the Shepherdess. After that, she told them about Mellinor and his warning, and then she told them of her own research and calling the West Wind, about her trip to the broker and her promise to Rellenor, the Whitefall River. She told her story in a rush, letting the last three days pour out of her, stopping just before she'd left for the League's stronghold. When she finished, the room was as silent as a tomb. Only Blint's face was unchanged. But for all his haughtiness, his fingers were clutching the dark green ring on his right thumb, and Miranda knew that, whatever else lay between them, he believed her.

"I don't have to tell you the scale of the disaster we're facing," she said slowly. "You saw it for yourselves yesterday, when the rivers flooded. You've felt it in your own spirits. The stars are the foundations of this world, but one by one, they are being pulled away, leaving the spirits who depended on them in free fall. As they unravel, so does the world we've sworn to protect."

She leaned forward, and her voice dropped low. "Spiritualists," she said, letting the title shake with emotion. "I don't have to remind you of your oaths or your duty. When Rector Banage told me to call the Conclave, he meant it to reunite the Court. But *I* say that no matter our past squabbles or petty politics, we have always been united in our core purpose: the protection and preservation of the spirit world. For every ring I see in this chamber, I know your dedication, and I'm asking you now to act on it. I'm asking you to stand with me, to stand together as a Court, and do what must be done."

738

"And what is that?"

Miranda turned to see Blint leaning out toward her, but though his face was screwed up in its usual glare, his voice was more pleading than angry. "You just told us this was the Shepherdess's doing," he said. "Before tonight, I'd heard of her only in the abstract, a spirit so enormous as to be completely separate from the scope of human magic. Now you tell us she's not only real but she's turning the world on end, ripping out the largest spirits in creation like weeds and leaving the rest to fend for themselves. A terrible problem, I'll grant you, but what can we do about it? Every wizard in this room stands by their oaths, but there's a bit of a jump between defending the spirit world and performing miracles."

A smattering of nervous laughter went up from the crowd at this, and Blint crossed his arms with a smug smirk. Miranda tightened her grip on the podium's worn wooden lip.

"We can't take the place of the lost stars," she said. "But we can help to calm the panic caused by their disappearance. The floods that devastated Zarin and every other riverside community weren't caused by the vanishing river star but by the panic of the rivers once they realized their star had gone. That panic is the danger. We can't stop the stars from vanishing, but if we could calm the spirit's fear before it became dangerous, if we could have reached out to the rivers before they flooded, we could limit the damage, maybe even prevent it altogether."

"And how do you mean to manage that?" Blint said. "Catching the panic means reaching the spirit the moment the trouble starts. We can't be everywhere at once. Do you mean us to only comfort spirits in Zarin? Or is that why *he's* here?" Blint's hand shot out, finger pointed directly at Alric. "The League of Storms are demon hunters, last I heard. Their members are said to have strange powers, a rumor that was just proven by your own flamboyant entrance." His eyes narrowed to slits. "Have you sold out the Court, Lyonette?"

Miranda clenched her teeth against her growing rage. "Must

739

you see everything I do in the worst light possible?" she snapped. "Whatever you may think of me, this isn't a power play, Blint. Yes, as you can all see, I went to the League, and yes, I went to make a deal. I saw just as you did that there was no way we could handle a problem this enormous as we are. We move fast, but not that fast. What good is it to go to calm a panic if you arrive days after the panic occurs? It is our duty and our calling to offer our help to the spirits, but for that help to be of any *use*, we need more than we can muster on our own." She raised her hand, motioning to Alric. "The League also suffers from this crisis. No one wants this panic, and the League has agreed that we should combine our efforts to fight it."

"Combine how?" Blint said. "What, do you mean to swear them in? Give them rings and pledge them to service like apprentices?"

"Not quite."

It was Alric who spoke, his quiet voice booming thanks to his position beside Miranda. He smiled at Blint with the same tight-lipped politeness he showed everyone, but his eyes were burning with banked anger.

"If I may?" he said, looking at Miranda. When she nodded, he addressed the Court. "I am Alric, Deputy Commander of the League of Storms. This morning, Rector Lyonette came to us with an offer of aid. The League exists to prevent the spread of demonseeds. To this end, we have been given certain powers to help in our hunt. However, the current situation prevents our organization from operating as it should, and we find ourselves overwhelmed by the scale of the panic we are facing. With this in mind, the Lord of Storms has offered a deal to your Rector and the Spirit Court she represents."

He raised his hand, holding it out palm up like he was making the room an offering. "We will grant you temporary use of our gifts, namely the power to open portals through the veil to any location in the world, the ability to hear the ripples of spirit panic so that you can respond to any outbreaks as soon as they occur, and the command to instantly crush any panic deemed dangerous to a spirit or those around it. The League will make these gifts available for as long as this crisis persists, and in return, the Spirit Court will supply the manpower needed to properly deal with the panics. This is the agreement tendered between my commander and your Rector."

As he finished, the room began to buzz. Miranda let it. This was the crux of all her work, the pinnacle of these last, horrible days. Alric's words were simple, but the ideas behind them were enormous and so far removed from the day-to-day life of the Court that some pushback was inevitable. She was a polarizing figure, Banage's protégé, a reminder of the recent strife, but Alric was neutral, and the League of Storms, while mysterious, was highly respected. Better they should whisper over his words without her speaking up and dragging the discussion back to the bitter anger of Blint and those like him.

Better still, with this, her role was over. The truth has been told. Alric had laid out the deal and the Court knew enough to make a decision. It was done. She'd fulfilled her promise to Banage and her pledge to Mellinor. Maybe now she could rest.

Miranda closed her eyes. The weariness went all the way to her bones, but though the Rector's chair was right behind her, she dared not sit. First, it was Master Banage's chair and she had no right to take it. Second, if she did sit down, she had no real conviction she'd ever be able to make herself get up again.

As a compromise, she let herself slump against the podium. The gold mantle of the Rector was heavier than she'd ever imagined, but the gold and gems were dull on her shoulders. There was no sign of the light she'd seen when Master Banage wore it, and somehow that was a relief. Rectors served for life. If it had flared up for her, it would have been a sign that Master Banage really was never coming back.

Better the mantle stayed dull, she thought, fingers clenching. Better if everyone saw her for what she was—a stand-in who was going back to her real duty as soon as the Lord of Storms came to take their pledge. The second he did, she'd throw the mantle at Krigel and use her new abilities to find and free her true Rector from wherever Sara had hidden him. She would bring him back to the Court in triumph, and then they would both work to settle the panic before the world tore itself to pieces. After that, she would rest. She would stuff herself full and sleep for a year. She deserved it after the last few weeks. Powers, she'd been fighting looming disaster for so long now she almost missed eating Eli's dust.

It would all be over soon enough, though. Already, the conversation in the room was dying down. As the Spiritualists stilled, she could see their resolve solidifying. Thank the Powers, she was almost done. She was almost *free*.

"Rector," Alric whispered. She looked over to see the Deputy Commander had leaned down so his head was even with hers. "How long?"

"I can call the vote at any time," Miranda whispered back. She would have liked to wait a little longer to let the Court come around completely, but Alric's expression was tense.

"Do it," he ordered. "He's nearly here."

As though in answer, a flash of lightning lit up the windows, followed immediately by a peal of thunder so strong it rocked the Tower beneath their feet. That was warning enough, and Miranda pushed herself straight. But as she opened her mouth to call the question to order, a flash of lightning so bright it sent her hands flying to shield her eyes filled the Court chamber.

For a second, Miranda could see nothing but white. The smell of ozone burned her nostrils, but all she could feel were her rings as they vibrated against her fingers, the warning trilling up every connection. She dropped her hands with effort as the thunder crash came and turned to face the man who now stood at the center of the Court.

The Lord of Storms was standing in the witness stand, the same stand where Miranda had made her case what felt like years ago. Though he looked no larger than usual, leaning casually against the stand's railing with his arms crossed as his silver eyes raked over the crowd, his presence filled the room to bursting. The Spiritualists cowered before him. Even Blint pulled back, his skin gray with fear. This reaction seemed to please the Lord of Storms, for his face broke into a smug smile as his gaze moved to Miranda.

She took a deep breath and banished her fear, pulling herself to her full height. "Welcome, Lord of Storms," she said, her voice stiff and formal. "The Spirit Court extends its friendship to you and yours in good faith."

The Lord of Storms shrugged and pushed himself up. He walked across the floor toward the Rector's stand, the click of his boots on the polished stone the only sound in the deep, terrified silence. When he reached the stand's base, he vanished. There was no white line this time, no lightning; he simply vanished in a swirl of cloud only to reappear instantly right beside Miranda.

A gasp went up from the crowd, but Miranda barely heard it. She was too concerned with not falling over as she scrambled to give the commander room in the narrow space. This close, he towered over her, and it took every ounce of her pride not to flee down the stair at the back of the platform. As Miranda held her ground, the Lord of Storms' smile grew, and he sat down in the Rector's chair like it had been set out just for him.

"Well?" he said, his voice as loud and deep as the thunder that rolled outside. "Are you ready for the binding? Because I don't have all day."

"Almost," Miranda said, trying to keep the anger out of her voice. "I was just about to take the vote."

He waved for her to go ahead. Miranda glowered and turned back to the Court. But as she lifted her voice to call the vote, a throat cleared right below her. Miranda jumped at the unexpected sound and looked down to see Krigel trying to catch her eye.

"A point of procedure, Rector," he said, his quiet voice clear in the terrified hush.

Miranda frowned, confused, but Krigel's stare was unwavering. When she nodded, he turned sideways so that his face could be seen by both her and the Court beyond. "By rules of the Conclave as stated in the Court's founding pledge, this is not actually a voting matter."

Miranda clamped her mouth closed right before the question *It isn't?* popped out. Breathing a silent breath of relief at avoiding looking like an idiot, she clenched her teeth and waited for Krigel to continue.

"Were this a standard hearing, we would now vote on the matter of whether or not we should offer our aid to the League," Krigel said, his voice dry and formal. "But this is not a standard hearing. It is a Conclave. Conclaves are held only in emergencies, and are thus governed by emergency rules. Since a Conclave has not been called in fifty years, however, I feel it is timely to refresh the Court's memory that all proclamations made by the Rector Spiritualis during a Conclave become law immediately."

For a moment, Miranda could only gape. "What?"

"Conclaves exist to galvanize the Court in times of crisis," Krigel continued. "At such times, our founders felt it imperative that we be united in purpose and speak with one voice, that of the Rector. Therefore, as this is Conclave and you are Rector, all you have to do to ally us with the League is say so. Speak the decree and it becomes law. Well"—he tilted his head—"for five weeks anyway, at which point the matter returns to debate among the Tower Keepers who can either—"

Miranda closed her eyes, unable to follow Krigel's legal lecture any further. She'd never paid much attention to the finer points of Conclave procedure because it had never seemed important before. How stupid, she realized with a flush, going into Conclave without even reading the rules. If the Rector got to just make laws during a Conclave, it was no wonder Blint had reacted so badly to the news. Of course, part of her argued that this made things easier since she wouldn't have to worry about a vote, but a much louder part argued back

744

that this was actually much, much worse. She probably would have won a vote, but no one was going to take her decrees for law because she wasn't even—

"The girl's not even properly Rector!" Blint shouted, finishing for her. "Conclave or no, you think this Court will obey anything she spits out?"

"That is a valid point, Tower Keeper Blint," Krigel said gravely. "And that is exactly why all Conclaves must, by law, begin with a ratification of the sitting Rector or an election if the position of Rector is unfilled. A step, I might add, that has been overlooked in the current proceedings." He turned and gazed up at Miranda, his face curiously blank. "Seeing this, I must demand that we vote at once on the office of Rector to prevent any future dispute on the legitimacy of Conclave decrees."

Miranda had to bite down hard to keep from screaming. Why was Krigel pushing this *now*? The Lord of Storms was practically standing on her toes. If they'd called a vote, this would already be done. Now what should have been a simple decision to make both the Court and the League's jobs easier was going to get lost in the massive crash of politics and ego surrounding the office of Rector. The exact same crash that had torn the Court apart in the last crisis with the Empress. Powers, what was Krigel *doing*?

As though in answer to her question, Krigel's voice rang out. "Who wishes to serve the Court as Rector?"

Blint's answer was immediate. "I do."

A murmur of approval rose from his half of the room, and Miranda fought the urge to bang her head against the podium.

"Anyone else?" Krigel asked.

The question hung in the air. Benches creaked as the Spiritualists shifted, but no one said a word. No one was stupid enough to stand against Blint, Miranda realized. She glared at the crowd, noting that the men around Blint were grinning like schoolboys. Miranda gritted her teeth. If there was a way the situation could get worse, she couldn't see it.

When the silence had stretched long enough, Krigel shook his head. "By law, there must be a contest for the position of Rector," he said. "As assistant to the office of Rector, I claim the privilege of nominating the second candidate."

Without warning, he turned his back to the crowd and looked up at Miranda with an expression of smug pride. "I nominate Miranda Lyonette, friend of the West Wind, Savior of Gaol, Master of the Great Spirit of the Inland Sea and Deep Current Mellinor, War Hero of the Second Battle of Osera, apprentice and chosen successor of our former Rector, Etmon Banage, and, as Rector Banage often said in this very room, the pride of this Court."

A cheer erupted at this, causing both Miranda and Blint to jump. They turned in unison, staring at the surprisingly large group of clapping Spiritualists standing across the hall from Blint's entourage. Miranda's brain didn't get much further than that, however. She was too busy fighting the terrible clenching in her stomach.

"Why?" she said, her voice cracking. "I don't want—"

"That is why we chose you," Krigel said, his voice rising to fill the room. "The Rector gives her life in service to the Court. It is a position that demands absolute dedication to the ideals of Spiritualists' oaths. The Rector must never be swayed by human politics and never abandon the spirits for landed power. The office of Rector must be above reproach, or we risk losing the faith of those spirits we are sworn to serve."

He turned away from her then, sweeping his arms out as he faced the crowd. "With this in mind, I ask the Court, who is more suited? A man who has coveted the Rector's power all his life, who colluded with Hern, the traitor who helped Enslave all of Gaol? Or the woman who has never once violated her oaths? Who, in fact, continued her duty to the spirits even after the Court kicked her out? Who would serve our ideals better? A Tower Keeper who has spent the time since his Rector's arrest plotting his own ascension, or the Spiritualist who has used her emergency powers as Interim Rector to work without rest to find a solution to what may be the greatest threat to the spirit world since the Enslaver kings this Court was founded to fight?"

Krigel pulled himself straight, his voice so full of pride it trembled. "It was Spiritualist Lyonette who went to the League of Storms, Spiritualist Lyonette who forged the very bargain before us that may well be our only salvation in this crisis. Therefore I ask you, Spiritualists, who but Miranda Lyonette is fit to lead us through it?"

Blint began to shout then, but Krigel's voice rolled over him. "It is time the Spirit Court remembered its purpose!" he cried. "We have allowed ourselves to be swept up in Whitefall's Council for too long, and I say it is time to prove that we are beholden to none save the spirits who depend on us. If you would be worthy of the oaths you swore, if you would have a Spirit Court that truly serves the spirits, and not the Council of Thrones, then do as I do." He thrust his hand in the air, his rings glowing like lanterns on his bony fingers. "Raise your hand for Miranda Lyonette, and let this Court be what it should again."

"Krigel!" Miranda hissed, leaning over to grab the old man's hand out of the air. "Powers, man, stop..."

Her voice trailed off as she faced the Court. In the packed benches of the hearing room, nearly every hand was up. Hundreds of rings glittered in the white light of the lanterns overhead, and every face mirrored Krigel's determination. Even on Blint's side, hands were raised. Blint himself looked ready to explode, and Miranda didn't blame him. That had hardly been a fair election, and if the Court's will had been less clear, she would have made Krigel do a formal vote. But the Spirit Court had spoken, loudly, and even though Miranda was ostensibly at the heart of it, she could no more deny its will than she could send a wave back to sea. Defeated, she slumped down, her elbows cracking on the Rector's podium. Below her, Krigel lowered his hand with a look of pure triumph.

"I believe that settles it," he said. "If anyone objects, it is their right to speak now."

With a great clatter, Blint shot up from his bench and marched out. A few of the men who'd been sitting beside him scrambled to follow, but it was nowhere near the crowd that had been whispering with him at the beginning. Most of those men were now doing their best not to look at the Tower Keeper as he vanished through a side door, his formal robes swirling behind him in an angry riot of red silk.

"As there are no objections," Krigel said, "the Spirit Court offers the office of Rector to Miranda Lyonette." He turned slowly, fixing Miranda with his eyes. "Do you accept the Court's call, Spiritualist?"

Miranda very seriously considered saying no, but old Krigel was looking at her with so much pride. The same pride that lit his face when he looked at Banage, she realized. That line of thinking brought her back to her lost master. As Rector, she'd have the clout to fight for his release. Powers knew they needed him now more than ever. She glanced sideways to see the Lord of Storms was watching her, his eyes going through her like hailstones as his boot tapped against the edge of the podium.

Miranda set her jaw and turned to face the Court. "I accept," she said, proud that her voice betrayed none of the bone weariness that suddenly threatened to overwhelm her.

The second the words left her mouth, everything changed.

Without warning, the Rector's ring tightened on her finger hard enough to make the bone ache and a presence roared into her mind. Miranda jerked in surprise, her eyes slamming shut in pain and shock. It was like binding a spirit, an enormous one, but she'd given no oath, made no pledge. Yet the connection was there, as strong as Mellinor's had been, but where the sea had been inside her, this spirit was all around her, enormous and steady and, she frowned, laughing at her.

"Of course I laugh, little Rector," the voice boomed in her mind. "Banage always told me you would come."

Her eyes popped open. The golden mantle of the Rector was glowing as bright as noon across her shoulders, a multi-colored light show that, she realized for the first time, was the product of one spirit, not many. That same spirit ran through the floor below her feet, up the walls that surrounded her. It reached up to the Tower's peak and down to the Tower's foundations, which ran deeper than she'd ever imagined, down to the very roots of Zarin itself. She could feel every bit of the stone like she held the whole of it in her hands, and her mind filled with wonder until it was all she knew.

"You are the Tower," she whispered, clutching the gold chain.

"And you are faster than most." The Tower's voice laughed in her head. "Though I'd expect as much from Mellinor's master and one who has seen the truth of Lord Durain's heart."

"Durain?" Miranda repeated foolishly. "The Shaper Mountain?"

"The Lord of all Mountains," the Tower said reverently. "It was he who bade me to enter a pact with your kind many years ago, but it is another lord you should mind now, Rector."

The words were accompanied by a sort of mental prod. Miranda followed it and found herself facing the Lord of Storms, who was looking dangerously bored.

"Can we get on with this?" he drawled, tapping his long fingers on the clawed arm of the Rector's chair. "I have a hunt to finish."

Miranda nodded, grabbing her shocked mind and forcing it back to the here and now. "Lord of Storms," she said, her voice rising as she became mindful of the crowd of Spiritualists who were watching her like hawks. "The Spirit Court is honored to accept your bargain as offered."

The Lord of Storms nodded and vanished in a swirl of cloud only to reappear again on the witness stand at the center of the room. "Line them up here," he said, pointing to the stand's small step. "I'm not bothering the Lady for permission on this, so I'll have to do them one at a time. And be fast about it. I've wasted enough time with Court theatrics for this century."

Miranda nodded and, almost without thinking, turned and stepped off the Rector's elevated platform into thin air. She couldn't say why she'd gone that way instead of taking the stairs, and for a moment she was sure she was going to fall and break her fool head. But as soon as her foot left the platform, the floor of the chamber rose to meet her. The white stone moved like water, flowing up to form an elegant stair, each step coalescing a moment before her foot landed. A gasp went up from the gathered Court, and Miranda began to blush.

"You make me do things now?" she hissed, stomping her way down.

"Not at all," the Tower whispered. "I merely offer suggestions, and your mind, though distracted, seems to know a good idea when it hears one. Besides, I've been an ally of the Court for a long time. I know when it needs a little impressing."

She had to admit the spirit's plan worked. The Spiritualists were watching her with round eyes as she walked across the smoothly polished floor and came to a stop before the Lord of Storms. He held out his hand impatiently, but just before his palm landed on her head, Miranda ducked away.

"Wait."

The Lord of Storms gave her a murderous look. Miranda ignored it and turned to face her Court. "Before we begin, I wish to make a few things very clear. First, even with the power of the League behind us, know that the path we begin today will be a difficult one. You will see spirits suffering as never before, and it may come that you will have to use a strong hand to stop their panic if it becomes violent. The use of force over spirits, even for their own protection, is abhorrent to Spiritualists by nature. Therefore, participation in this operation is entirely voluntary. I want only the willing, and there will be no punishment or shame for those who do not wish to accept the Lord of Storms' offer. Those who do wish to help may come down now to receive the League's gift of

750

power. *However*"—the sudden sharpness in her voice interrupted the scrape of benches—"before anything is given or received, each of you must stand before the Court and reaffirm your oath as a Spiritualist."

The Spiritualists began to mutter angrily, and Miranda put up her hand. "I don't ask this because I doubt your loyalty or resolve. I wouldn't be standing here if that were the case. But the League's powers go far and beyond the normal scope of our Court. If this is to work, we must be above reproach. We must be exactly what our oath requires: servants of the spirits. With that in mind, I want everyone who means to work with the League to reaffirm that loyalty, starting with myself."

She placed both hands on her chest, rings out, just as she had when she was a raw apprentice so many years ago. Now as then, she lowered her head before the Tower and the Court and spoke the words that had guided her life from that moment on.

"I pledge my life to the unseen world," she said, her voice ringing loud and clear. "My soul to the protection of those who suffer. On my life and my soul I swear to never stand quiet before abuse or stay my hand when my strength may aid the world's good. I pledge my life and my soul to the spirits, and those who aid me I will bind in solemn promise: power for service, strength for obedience, a servant to the Court and the spirits it defends until the end of our days. This is my oath, and may my life be forfeit before ever I am forsworn."

As she finished, she raised the solid gold band on her left hand and kissed the center of the perfect circle. Oath spoken, she turned back to the Lord of Storms.

His hand landed on her head like a vise, and her body trembled as a pulse of electricity shot through her. It crawled over her skin, more intense than painful, and then, as fast as it started, it was over. The pressure on her skull vanished, leaving only a faint tingling. She glanced up, confused.

"That's it?"

751

The Lord of Storms sneered. "What did you expect, a speech? Unlike you lot, we don't waste time with ceremony."

Miranda swallowed. Surely there was more than that. Her skin was tingling, but otherwise she felt no different than before.

"It's there," the Lord of Storms said, answering the question she hadn't asked. "All you have to do is hold out your hand and think of where you want to go."

Sheepishly, Miranda obeyed, stretching out her arm as she'd seen Alric do. The moment her fingers rose in front of her, the white line appeared. It fell like a knife, cutting a door in the air that opened onto the beach by Osera. Miranda blinked in amazement. She'd done little more than picture the destination in her mind, but there was the sea, choppy and dark blue under the overcast sky.

As she stared at it, her vision began to blur. On the other side of the white cut was the stretch of shallows where she'd lost Mellinor, and later, Eli. The sea spirit was out there still, deep below the water, but he wasn't hers. Not anymore. And the thief...

Miranda dropped her hand, and the line vanished, fading as quickly as it had appeared. She scrubbed her eyes covertly, though there was no way the Lord of Storms could have missed the tears. But when she glanced up, he wasn't even looking at her. By this point the room was full of the sound of shuffling as the Court came down from the benches to the floor to take part, and he was watching the approaching line with a look of growing annoyance.

"Make them speak quick, girl," he growled, leaning against the railing. "I mean to be back on the hunt within the hour."

Miranda nodded and motioned for the first Spiritualist to step forward. The woman, a Tower Keeper from the south, spoke her oath with pride and did not even flinch when the Lord of Storms touched her head. When he lifted his hand, she looked him straight in the eyes.

"How do we find those in panic?" she said, all business.

"Listen," the Lord of Storms said. "You'll hear it."

The woman nodded and stepped aside to let the next Spiritualist take her place. As Miranda watched, the Tower Keeper closed her eyes and tilted her head like she was straining to hear a distant sound. Almost at once, her eyes popped back open and she held out her hand. The white line appeared instantly, and a blast of icy wind hit Miranda in the face as the Tower Keeper stepped through the cut and into a world of snow, ice, and something terrible. A screaming, howling fear. The hole closed as soon as she was through, cutting off the cold and the sound as though they'd never been.

By this point, the next Spiritualist, a journeyman as Miranda herself had been before the events in Osera, had finished his oath and received the Lord of Storms' gift. He staggered as the Lord of Storms released him, and Miranda jumped to catch the young man before he fell.

"Easy," she said, helping him regain his balance.

The Spiritualist shook his head. "How do you stand it?" he whispered. "Can't you hear the fear?"

Miranda couldn't. She actually hadn't heard anything out of the ordinary since the Lord of Storms touched her. Her frustration must have been plain on her face, because the Lord of Storms laughed.

"What?" he barked. "You think all human souls are the same just because you're all shaped alike? Don't be stupid. My gift fits each person differently. Even in the League we have people who are better at some aspects than others." He nodded to the young Spiritualist who was still shaking in Miranda's grip. "That man has large ears, so to speak. If you weren't so blind, you'd see the difference for yourself."

"So my ears are small, then?" Miranda snapped, helping the Spiritualist over to the wall.

"Not very," the Lord of Storms said, motioning for the next person to hurry up and come forward. "Come on, come on. Move."

The next Spiritualist waited until Miranda nodded before

stepping forward and reciting his oath. The Lord of Storms grabbed his head the second he finished and released it almost as quickly, pushing the man away with a quick jab.

"Next!"

The line moved quickly after that, with each Spiritualist stepping forward just long enough to give their oath before the Lord of Storms grabbed them. Some were like the first Tower Keeper. They seemed to get the powers instinctively and jumped into action, opening their portals to places of trouble without a word of explanation or training. Others were like the young Spiritualist, staggering away, as pale as death.

These Miranda led to the growing group gathered on an empty stretch of floor by the benches. Krigel was already there, helping them sit, encouraging them to talk. Miranda watched him with a worried frown, but she couldn't get away. The Lord of Storms drove the line forward, and she had to move quickly as well, witnessing the oaths one after the other. She was about to ask for a reprieve when a voice spoke in her ear.

"Don't worry about it."

She jumped and turned to see Alric standing behind her, a thin smile on his lips.

"It's the way of the Lord of Storms' power," he said softly, his eyes on his commander as the Lord of Storms grabbed the next Spiritualist's scalp. "Some take to it like fish to water; others take longer to come around. It's the same within the League."

"Shouldn't we be explaining something?" Miranda said. "It seems downright foolish for the Lord of Storms to give his gift and not teach people how to use it."

"That's how it's always been," Alric said with a shrug. "The League's gift isn't some boon or mystical power. It's a sliver of the Lord of Storms' own soul. Think of it as piggybacking on his strength. He's not making something new so much as breaking up what he already has. That's why he doesn't explain how it works. His powers come to him as natural as breathing comes to us, and he could no more explain them than you could explain how you make your heart beat. But this is the way it's been since the beginning, and it works. You yourself were able to make a portal with little more than a cursory explanation, after all."

Miranda scowled. "It's reckless."

"Storms aren't known for their caution and forethought," Alric said, smiling. "Of course, if you don't like it, you could always go to a different spirit for aid."

Her scowled deepened, and Alric chuckled. "Don't worry, Rector," he said. "Even your tremblers over there will come around in time. For now, we should focus on getting as many of your Spiritualists into the field as possible. There's so much panic at the moment I can hardly hear myself think."

"I hear nothing," she said. "Am I doing something wrong, or—"

"You can't 'do something wrong' with an instinctive power," Alric said. At her crestfallen expression, he added, "Think of it this way. Panic rings best in hollow vessels, but your soul is full, isn't it?"

"Very full." The Tower's deep voice rumbled through Miranda so loudly that her bones rattled.

"I begin to see your point," she said, wincing at the sensation. "I suppose it's hard to hear anything through all this rock."

"You should be glad," the Tower said. "It's a storm out there, little Rector. Be thankful of my protection."

"I just hope I'm able to do my job deaf," she snapped.

"Excuse me?" Alric said.

"Nothing," Miranda muttered, a blush spreading over her face as the Tower's chuckle rattled her teeth.

"Don't worry," the Tower said, its voice full of black humor. "You'll hear the panic when it's close, and when you do, you'll wish I could block it all out."

Miranda had no answer to that, and she turned her attention back to Alric. "We'll just have to weather whatever comes."

"Oh, no, my dear," Alric warned. "You're part of the storm

now. There's no more weathering, no more sitting back. You ride with the Shepherdess's favor now, good or ill, just like the rest of us. I only hope this little trick of yours works. If we don't find the demon, I dread to think of the consequences."

Miranda steadied herself, turning to hear the next oath before asking the question that had been smoldering in her mind since this morning. "What are you hunting?"

Alric's answer was so cold she almost didn't recognize his voice. "A demon who should be dead twice over," he said, his hand vanishing from her shoulder.

When she turned to ask what he meant by that, Alric was across the room, standing beside Krigel as he talked with the Spiritualists who hadn't instantly adapted to the change.

She watched him another moment before giving up. She had enough to worry about without pressing into League business. Steeling herself, she turned back to the matter at hand, acknowledging each oath as, one by one, the entire Spirit Court received the Lord of Storms' gift.

It took a good hour before the last Spiritualist left the Lord of Storms' grasp. By that time, most of those who hadn't adapted to the gift at once had come around, just as Alric had predicted. Alric himself had left twenty minutes ago after a brief, whispered conference with his commander. He was probably going to prepare the rest of the League for the hunt, Miranda realized.

The Lord of Storms was certainly ready. As the line dwindled, he seemed to grow larger. He loomed over the platform now, and the room felt colder for his presence. Colder and full of reined-in power. It reminded Miranda of the minutes just before a storm broke, which was appropriate. She just hoped he didn't break in her assembly room.

When the final Spiritualist had received the League's gift and vanished through her portal, Miranda expected the Lord of Storms to vanish with her, but he didn't. Instead, he began to stalk around the room with his eyes closed, as though he were listening. After watching him circle for several nervous minutes, Miranda decided to ignore him and go on with her, which was to say the Court's, business.

The assembly room was nearly empty now. Krigel was seeing off the last of those slow to adapt to their gifts. Miranda held her tongue, waiting until the last Spiritualist vanished before asking for a report.

"It's as you see, Rector," Krigel said, leaning against the wall below the Rector's seat with a sigh. "One thousand twenty-two Spiritualists attended the Conclave today, and of those, nine hundred and ninety-eight renewed their oath and took the League's gift. An excellent turnout, all said, especially when you consider what Blint's influence was not two hours ago."

Miranda bit her lip and glanced around. Save for the stalking Lord of Storms and Gin resting behind her, she and Krigel were alone in the enormous room. Even so, she reached down and gave the Tower's ring a little prod.

At once, the enormous room shifted subtly, the acoustics changing. When she spoke again, the words that should have echoed across the empty stone fell tiny and flat, just as she wanted. There could be no chance of anyone overhearing what she said next.

"Krigel," she whispered. "Why did you do it?"

The old Spiritualist didn't ask what she meant. He leaned against the polished wood and fixed her with a glare that made her feel like a bumbling apprentice again.

"You would have me let Blint make a mockery of all we've fought for?" he said. "All Etmon sacrificed?"

"I don't want to be Rector," Miranda argued. "I want to fight. I should be out there—"

"What you want means nothing," Krigel said. "You have a duty, Miranda. A duty to the Court and a duty to Banage, who's sacrificed more for you than you can ever know. If Blint became Rector, the Spirit Court would be little more than a subchapter of Whitefall's Council."

Miranda knew she should leave it there, but selfish as it

was, she couldn't stop. "But why *me*?" she cried. "Why do *I* have to be—"

"Because there was no one else," Krigel said. "This Court has been too long in the presence of the Council. Men like Blint sway others with power and greed. He had half the Court in his pocket this morning. It didn't matter whom I'd named for Rector. Had the vote been taken when the Conclave began, Blint would have won. That's why I didn't call the referendum at the beginning as I should have. I meant to let you call the vote for the Court's agreement with the League, procedure be hanged. But while you were standing on the Rector's platform speaking the truth of the horrible events taking place around us, flanked by the League's Deputy Commander and the Lord of Storms himself, the power in the Court began to shift. With every word you spoke, the Court forgot its greed. It forgot the promise of power and remembered its oaths and its purpose. At that moment, Miranda, you were more powerful than Blint could ever be."

"So you forced the vote," Miranda said, dropping her head.

"Of course," Krigel said. "Powers, girl, I might be old, but I'm not so great a fool to let an opportunity like that pass me by. With you as Rector, the Court will continue to live up to its purpose. You proved as much just now when you made us reaffirm our oaths. The lust for power that let men like Hern and Blint climb so high is still there, but today at least, the Court's pride won out. With good leadership and a clear purpose, I hope we can keep it that way. This crisis may be the key to finally breaking the Council's hold on us and regaining our true independence. Surely you're not going to let a little thing like a personal aversion to being Rector stand in the way of such a great and noble goal, are you?"

Miranda's answer was a deep sigh, and Krigel's smile spread.

"Glad we see eye to eye," he said, bowing low. "It is my honor to serve you, Rector Lyonette."

Miranda waved him away and slumped down, landing hard

758

on the polished stone. As though on cue, Gin got up from his post to the right of the Rector's podium and padded over to thrust his enormous head into her lap.

"Let's get to business, then," she said, scratching the ghosthound's muzzle. "You can hear the panic, right? So, tell me what's going on."

Krigel snapped to attention. "The fear has already died down considerably thanks to your Court's efforts, Rector. It seems the star of the hardwood forests vanished just before the Conclave, but from what I can hear, the panic has all but vanished in the south and across the sea. There are still screams coming from the north, but they're dying down. At this rate, it's only a matter of time before the Lord of Storms gets his quiet."

"None too soon," Miranda muttered, glaring at the Lord of Storms, who was still stalking back and forth across her assembly floor. She watched him as he walked, his feet slamming down on the stone so hard she felt it through the Tower's connection. She was about to ask him if he would mind stomping more quietly when the Lord of Storms froze.

It happened without warning. One moment he was moving fluid as a panther; the next he was still as the floor beneath his feet. He stayed that way for one endless breath, and then his face transformed.

The change was so dramatic Miranda had no words to describe it. There simply was no human name for such pure, rapturous, purposeful joy. It was a look of completion, as though the entire work of the man's life had suddenly been validated. For one brief second, the Lord of Storms stood transfixed, and then he opened his mouth with a roar that was more power than sound, vibrating through the fabric of the world.

"There you are!"

As the words thundered, the Lord of Storms vanished in a flash of light. Miranda flinched back against the wooden wall, blinking madly against the echo of his power throbbing through her mind. As she struggled to get her thoughts back in order, she felt almost sorry for the demon.

Poor thing wouldn't know what hit it.

CHAPTER
15

"*Get back!*" Eli shouted, waving frantically at Josef.

The swordsman was already on it. He scooped Nico's limp body into his arms and dashed for the shelter of the rocky outcropping at the center of the dry creek bed. Her coat curled around his shoulders as he ran, the cloth circling him like a black tide.

That was dangerous, Eli realized. With Nico out, her coat might mistake Josef for a threat. Unfortunately, he didn't have the luxury of taking that line of thought any further since containing the mess in front of him was taking every ounce of his attention.

He was standing at the edge of Slorn's dry creek, his spirit roaring open all around him. He'd stretched himself to the edge of his strength, reaching as far as he could see until he felt as thin as a thread, and it still wasn't enough to hold back the forest's madness.

Madness was the only word for it. The trees of the Awakened Wood fell on each other like tigers, branches ripping and clawing while roots shot in all directions, breaking everything in their path. They screamed as they tore at each other, their overlapping voices too jumbled to make any sense, but it wasn't hard to guess what they were saying. They'd said only one word since the madness started: *gone*. Something was gone, something fundamental, and they were left behind. Open as he was, Eli could feel the grief that fed the tree's fury, the enormous loss running beneath the anger. What he didn't understand was *why*.

"What's gone?" he screamed, pouring power into the words so they could be heard. "What happened?"

The forest ignored him, or maybe the trees were too far gone to hear even a wizard's words. They were lost in madness, consumed by it. The only thing stopping them from ripping themselves to bits was Eli's will. He stood with his boots planted in the sand, slamming himself down on as many trees as he could reach. And it was working, mostly, but he couldn't keep it up forever.

Sweat poured down his face and plastered his shirt to his back. Holding his will this wide over such a large area was burning his stamina hot and fast, but letting go wasn't an option. He couldn't let Slorn's trees destroy themselves, not while he was watching, and certainly not before he knew what was going on. As his knees started to wobble, Eli thought bitterly how much easier this would be if he still had the Shepherdess's mark. Her command could have stopped this idiocy the moment it began.

Eli thrust that line of thought away with a snarl. Nothing was worth going back. *Nothing.* For all he knew, this madness was Benehime's doing, a ploy to make him miss her power. After the fiasco with Nara, he wouldn't put any cruelty past her when it came to manipulating him, and that was exactly why Eli could never let her get under his skin again. No bait or barb was going to drag him back to her ever again. So, with a silent apology to the poor, mad trees, Eli dug his heels into the sand and opened his spirit wider, hammering the trees down with everything he had.

It was stupid to give so much, and he would pay bitterly for this later, but Eli couldn't stop. If this was Benehime's ploy, then he couldn't let her win again, and if it wasn't, well, they were still Slorn's trees. He'd be a poor friend indeed to let them die just because he wasn't willing to spend a little time on his back.

Gritting his teeth, Eli kept going as the minutes stretched into eternity. The panic went on and on without end, but he braced his legs and held, pushing the forest with his will until they found a sort of balance. Eli took a strained breath, adjusting himself to the pattern of push and push back. But just as he was settling into the rhythm of the forest's madness, another complication appeared.

A white line opened at the center of the dry creek bed. That alone was almost shock enough to collapse Eli's overextended spirit. The League was more bad news than he could handle. But shock became confusion when the figure who stepped through the hole in the air wasn't a black-coated man with an awakened blade but a middle-aged woman in a long red robe. Though the glittering rings on her hand identified her profession as clearly as if she'd shouted it, Eli's poor, overworked brain still took several seconds to piece together the obvious question.

Why was a Spiritualist using a League portal?

Sadly, he never got his answer. The woman had emerged not five feet from where Eli was braced in the sand, and she froze when she saw him, just as surprised by his presence as he'd been at hers. She recovered much more quickly than he had, though, her expression of startled recognition shifting to smug triumph in a flash.

"Eli Monpress," she said, raising her hand, the ruby on her index finger sparking like a firecracker. "Of all the luck."

Eli cursed and swung his spirit in preparation to block whatever it was the woman was about to launch at him... and realized too late that this was one battle too many.

The moment he took his power away from the trees, the forest overwhelmed him. The trees burst through the line he'd held at the bank, their roots plunging into the dry creek bed with mindless screams. The spindly trunks followed, whipping like snakes. The roar caught both Eli and the Spiritualist by surprise, and they turned together, throwing their spirits open in unison to meet the mad tide of the trees. But it was too little, too late. The Spiritualist vanished beneath an avalanche of splintering wood before Eli could even shout at her to move. He cursed and fell back toward the rocks where Josef and Nico were, thinking that if he could just keep them safe, this whole stupid battle wouldn't have been for nothing.

Ignoring the throbbing pain of his overextended soul, Eli pulled inward, shaping his will into a bubble around the shelter of the rock. He didn't need much. He wasn't trying to stop the trees now, just make a barrier that would force the madness to flow around the three of them. But as he turned to run toward Josef, something hit him hard from the left.

Pain exploded through his head, and he was vaguely aware that the impact had sent him flying. That he was, even now, about to land face-first in the sand. It seemed like a minor concern, though. Everything was a minor concern compared to the flashing lights going off in his head.

He should have told Josef to run, he realized as he slammed into the streambed. How arrogant could he be? Telling the swordsman and Nico to hide by a rock while he tried to hold back an entire forest. It would be funny if it wasn't so stupid. Eli only hoped his ego didn't get them all skewered. It would be a crying shame if the greatest thief team in history died to *trees*.

And with that happy thought in his mind, Eli fell into the dark.

The first thing Nico saw when she opened her eyes was Josef, holding her. The second thing she saw was Eli getting hit over the head by what looked like a walking tree. She was about to dismiss that last bit as a fatigue delusion when she felt Josef's chest contract.

"Eli!"

The scream made her ears ring, and then she was dropped on the ground as Josef lunged toward the falling thief. She scrambled in the sand, fighting to get her feet beneath her. The haze in her mind grew thinner with every movement, and

763

she realized with a start that the cold mountain air was filled with terrified screams. Her head shot up so fast her neck snapped, searching for the source of the sound as she willed her coat to cover everything but her eyes.

A sound that terrified had to be demon panic. Had she let something slip? The exhaustion of the jumps hung over her like a pall. It wasn't unthinkable that her control had faltered, but she didn't feel the demon's presence nearby. Utterly confused, Nico looked again at the forest, and this time what she saw froze her solid.

The Awakened Wood was thrashing. The trees spirits, usually a calm, green color, were now a sickening burnt yellow. She could smell their terror in the air, bitter and sticky in her nose, but worse than the smell or the color was the way the trees moved.

The tree spirits were writhing in wild undulations no spirit, not even an awakened one, should have been able to achieve. They jerked like seizure victims, moving in crazy, unnatural spasms. It was as though every tree had suddenly been cut off from whatever anchored them and were now shaking themselves to pieces in their struggle not to collapse.

Nico couldn't explain the sight, couldn't fathom it within what she'd come to understand as the natural order since she'd first started seeing as spirits saw. One thing, however, was perfectly clear. Josef wasn't going to get to Eli before the writhing trees crushed him.

Before she could think further, Nico dove into the shadows. She came out in Eli's own shadow, the one cast below his falling body. Her arms shot out of the ground to wrap around his waist. The second she had him, Nico pulled him down, and they vanished together into the sand just before the trees crashed.

Throwing Eli over her shoulder, Nico stepped out of the shadows again, emerging directly in the path of Josef's charge. The swordsman had no time to stop. He barreled into them, and Nico let his momentum carry them into the shadow of the thrashing forest itself. The moment she hit the dark, she grabbed the men tight and started to run.

It was harder than she'd expected. Her body felt heavy as a mountain as she struggled forward, and the shadows clung to her like tar. In her exhaustion, even she could feel the fear.

The cold seeped into her bones, turning her legs to jelly until she was tripping over her own feet. But even as she felt the demon closing around her, Nico forced her body into submission. Her will was absolute, and she wrapped it around them like a fiery cloak. The cold fled as she reestablished control, but the fear lingered. Nico ignored it, focusing her will like an arrow on the enormous presence looming in the distance, their end goal, the Shaper Mountain. The ache pounding through her mind told her this was probably her last jump. Clutching Eli and Josef, Nico made it a good one.

She stretched herself through the dark, forcing her body forward. Each step felt like her last, but every time she managed to take another and another until, without warning, she hit the end of her strength.

It was like running face-first into a wall. All at once, the darkness began to tilt and spin. Nico didn't even know where they were, but it would have to work. With a final, desperate flail, she burst from the darkness into air that felt cold even after the cold of the shadows.

Snow crunched against her knees as she fell, and she was painfully aware of the loss of Eli and Josef's warmth as her arms gave out. The sky spun into view as she toppled, a dull, cloudy dome marred with sharp, white shapes. Mountains, she realized belatedly. Snowcapped mountains.

Nico eyes fell closed with delicious relief. She'd done it. She'd brought them to the mountains. Victory ran through her, sweet and burning, warding off the biting cold. Her coat was already winding around her, and she felt something else. Arms. Josef's arms. That thought was sweeter still, and she fell gleefully into a deep, happy sleep.

*   *   *

765

Josef trampled the snow down, cursing with each stomp. It did no good. The howling wind stole the words from his mouth, denying him even the satisfaction of his own anger. Just another irritation on top of the mountain of things that had gone horribly wrong in the last half hour.

Kicking the ice off his boots, he reached over and gently picked up Nico again. The demon fear rolling off her was stronger than ever now. It bled through the coat, stealing what little warmth he'd managed to keep. Gritting his teeth, Josef ignored it. He cradled Nico to his chest and turned his back to the wind, shielding her as he inched across the flat stretch of ground to the ditch he'd stomped into the deep snow of the mountain slope.

He fell to his knees and laid her down as gently as he could, turning her so her back was against the packed snow. The short wall was a poor windbreak, but it was better than nothing. When he had her arranged to his satisfaction, he stood and went for Eli.

The thief looked worse than Nico. His face was gray as dirty soap, and there was blood running from his temple where the tree had hit him. Josef picked his friend up gently, mindful of his head, and laid him feet to feet with Nico.

When they were both safely out of the wind, Josef straightened up and started looking for something to burn. Fire was vital if they were going to last more than a few hours in this cold. There was precious little fuel here, but Josef had made fires in the high mountains before. He would find something to burn. He would keep those idiots alive, and the moment they woke up he would tear into both of them for being reckless, self-sacrificing bastards and making him worry.

He'd just spotted a likely lump down the slope where a bush could be growing under the snow when he heard a strange scraping sound. Woodsman routine forgotten, Josef spun to face the noise, the Heart of War leaping into his hands. But as he stepped into first position, he froze, eyes going wide. Eli and Nico were lying under the windbreak just as he'd left them, but there was something wrapped around Eli's chest. Something glowing.

They were bright white and delicate, almost intimate, but so dreadfully out of place that it took Josef a full second to realize the things were *arms*. A pair of woman's arms had wrapped around the thief's chest in a lover's embrace. The realization hit him like a punch in the gut, and suddenly Josef knew exactly what was about to happen. He'd seen it before, in Osera.

"Eli!"

He lunged as he shouted, moving with the Heart's supernatural speed. But even that wasn't fast enough. A split second before his hand caught Eli's shoulder, the white arms jerked and Eli vanished. Josef crashed into the wall of snow where the thief had been, crushing the left half of the windbreak he'd worked so hard to make. He rolled and scrambled to his knees just in time to see the last of the white line as it faded.

Josef dug his fingers into the hard-packed snow and shouted a fresh string of curses into the wind, but even as he howled in rage, the swordsman in him, the ever calm, ever watchful core he'd nurtured for close to fifteen years, raised a warning.

He fell still instantly. All around him, the daylight was growing dimmer. Josef raised his head. The sky, which had been white with snow clouds when they'd first landed, was now a dark gray, and growing darker. With hours until sunset, Josef didn't even bother looking west. Instead, he turned south against the wind, and his eyes went wide as he saw the wall of black clouds rolling toward him like an avalanche.

After that, Josef wasted no more time. Shifting the Heart to his right hand, he scooped Nico up with his left and began to climb down. He half ran, half slid down the mountain's snowy slope, angling sideways along the ledge toward the spot where he'd spotted the bush.

He jumped down a little cliff and pressed Nico's slumped body into the space between the lee of the stone and the woody shrub that was indeed growing from a crack in the stone. It was so dark now he could barely see what he was doing, so Josef left the task to instinct, trusting his hands as they bound the thick, stubborn branches into Nico's coat, pinning her upright to the cliff face. When she was as secure as he could make her, Josef turned and took in the battlefield.

The base of the ledge was flatter than the mountain slope, but it was still steep. There was snow on the ground and ice under that. Treacherous footing, but he could find a way to use that. He could use the wind, too. It was blowing hard up the mountain, pushing him back toward the ledge above him. A good position, Josef decided. The wind would help keep him away from the steep drop down the mountain, and the cold would help numb the pain.

Satisfied, Josef stripped off his bag and the leather pouch at his belt. His swords went next. He tossed them, sheaths and all, on the icy stone. The larger blades were followed by his throwing knives and the daggers he kept in his boots and sleeves. Josef stripped off every bit of excess weight, dropping the lot of it at Nico's feet. Finally, completely unencumbered, he stood and rolled his shoulders, warming and loosening his body as he waited for his enemy to arrive.

He didn't have to wait long. Thunder crashed overhead, a deep roll that grew to a deafening crack as trunks of lightning flashed in the sky, lighting up the world in a blinding blue-white that banished every other color. The second flash came before the first had finished, and as the lightning spidered across the sky, the man appeared.

The Lord of Storms formed from the air itself. He loomed as the light faded, his shape a dark afterimage on Josef's blinded eyes. Josef ignored his lost sight and focused everything on his sword. He might be blinded, but the Heart of War followed the Lord of Storms like a compass needle. He could *feel* the man stepping into position, his boots digging into the icy ground.

"Isn't this nostalgic?"

The deep voice sent tremors of fear through Josef's body,

768

and his back seized up in remembered pain. Josef gritted his teeth and fought it down, the pain and the fear, until his body was still again, a weapon waiting for use, just like his sword. Firmly back in control, Josef opened his eyes and glared at the Lord of Storms. "Where's Eli?"

"I don't know," the Lord of Storms said. "And I don't care. I'm here for her."

He raised his arm, and as his hand stretched out, the lightning crashed again. But instead of fading, the light condensed into a long, curved, blue-white sword. Its hilt rested against the Lord of Storms' palm, and its tip pointed behind Josef at where Nico lay against the ledge.

"Move, master of the Heart of War," the Lord of Storms said, hand closing on the blue-wrapped grip of his blade. "While you still can."

Josef said nothing and held his ground.

The Lord of Storms' eyes narrowed to silver slits, shining in the dark. "I'm not here to play, swordsman," he growled. "I live for a good fight, but today is business only. *Move.*"

"I'm not playing," Josef said. "And you're not taking her. Not while I draw breath."

"Those terms are acceptable," the Lord of Storms said. "I have no problem killing you."

Josef bared his teeth. "I think you will."

The Lord of Storms laughed, a harsh, cracking sound like lightning ripping through a tree. "Really?" he said, grinning wide. "I must have hit your fool head harder than I thought last time if you've forgotten how things ended."

"I'm not the man you fought then," Josef said, boots crunching as he ground them farther into the snow. "And I won't move."

The Lord of Storms regarded him in silence for several moments, and then his broad shoulders arched in a shrug. "As you wish, swordsman."

He swung his sword up, and Josef felt a flash of fear as the blue-white blade whistled through the air. Then he forced the pain away, focusing instead on the heavy feel of the Heart in his hand. Just as he had done in Osera, he threw himself into his blade, giving himself over to the Heart and accepting the sword in turn. Their wills met and began to resonate until the Heart was no longer a weight in his hand but a part of his arm. The scarred black metal became an extension of his own heart, his own soul, binding them inextricably together in one purpose: to cut the enemy.

After all—the Heart's voice was Josef's own—*even lightning can be cut.*

"Impossible."

Josef blinked. He didn't realize he'd spoken out loud until he heard the Lord of Storms answer. The Lord of Storms grinned at his confusion and flipped his sword around, stabbing the tip through his black coat and into his own chest.

Josef flinched instinctively. From where he stood, it looked like the man had just skewered himself, but the Lord of Storms wasn't cut. As the blade met his chest, it became lightning. It forked inside him, lighting up his body like a cloud until the Lord of Storms removed it, turning the glowing tip toward Josef's own chest.

"I am the storm," he said. "The first and greatest of the Shepherdess's servants, the star of storms, bound together from the greatest storm spirits by the Lady herself at the dawn of creation. To cut me would be to cut the Shepherdess's own will."

Josef raised his chin. "There was another man who told me he couldn't be cut," he said defiantly. "I took off his arm."

The Lord of Storms' jaw clenched in fury, and the glowing sword shook in his hand, its tip leaving jagged trails in the dark. "I see your arrogance finally matches that of your sword," he said, his voice as tight as a wire. "Come then, boy. If you're so eager to die, I will not stop you."

Josef's answer was to lift his sword, sliding the enormous blade forward as he set his feet in first position. The Lord of Storms watched him move through slitted eyes, and then he was gone.

It was the same as before, that terrifying speed, the sword that moved like the wind and came from anywhere. But this time, Josef was different. He might not be able to see the Lord of Storms' movements, but he could *feel* them through his sword like the Heart's metal was his own bone. His sword moved without thought, rising to meet the Lord of Storms' blow before the swing could flicker back into existence.

When the Lord of Storms appeared at Josef's left, the Heart of War was waiting. The lightning blade struck the Heart's scarred, black edge with a squeal of metal. The impact nearly sent Josef to his knees, but he forced himself to hold, and then, feet digging into the icy rock, he began to push back. He had one fleeting glimpse of the Lord of Storms' astonished face before the League Commander vanished in a swirl of cloud. He reappeared instantly on Josef's right, his glowing sword falling toward Josef's unguarded thigh.

Even as he saw it, Josef knew there was no time to dodge, and he caught himself saying good-bye to his leg before he remembered what was at stake. The Heart was buzzing in his hands, and Josef had the distinct impression the sword was screaming at him, demanding to be let in. Josef surrendered at once. His body went slack, his fingers relaxed, no longer holding the Heart but being guided by it, his arm following the black blade as it would follow his hand.

What happened next was the fastest thing Josef had ever seen his body do. One moment he was wide open below the Lord of Storms' swing, the next the Heart was there, an iron wall between him and the glowing blade. Now it was the Lord of Storms who had no time to change course. The swords met with a crash, the blue-white blade pulsing as it ground against the Heart's black barrier.

Push up.

The command pounded through Josef like a shot of adrenaline, and before he'd even processed the words, his body obeyed. He shot up, bringing both swords with him in a great upward lunge. Caught off balance, the Lord of Storms had no choice but to rise as well. His sword slid along the Heart's blade, leaving a trail of sparks that faded into forked crackles, but the Heart of War was rolling like an avalanche now. With all of Josef's weight behind it, the black blade shot upward, throwing off the glowing sword like water before slicing into the Lord of Storms' neck.

The blow was so fast Josef didn't even realize what he'd done until he began to fall forward. The stroke's power flowed through him and vanished, leaving him overextended. He slammed his leg down at once, turning and steadying himself in one motion as he looked back.

Behind him, the Lord of Storms stood frozen, his sword flung out at his side. The blue-white blade was flashing wildly, flickering between steel and lightning, but Josef hardly saw it. His eyes were locked on the Lord of Storms' neck, or what was left of it. There, right at the jugular where the Heart of War had passed, flesh gave way to roiling clouds shot through with forked lightning. Above that there was…nothing. The blow had taken his head clean off.

A surge of triumph nearly brought Josef to his knees, but the joy was smothered almost immediately. As soon as he saw what the Heart had done, the clouds on the stump of the Lord of Storms' neck began to rise and coalesce. They swirled together, forming long, dark hair, pale skin, a long, hard nose, and a pair of silver eyes flashing with smug triumph.

"I warned you," the Lord of Storms said, his voice warped as his mouth rebuilt itself from the clouds. Josef got one look at the man's white, white teeth coming together in a smile before his lips re-formed, and then the world exploded into pain.

Josef choked and fell forward, gripping his chest. In front of him, in the space that had been nothing but empty air not a second ago, was a white hole. Through it, the Lord of Storms' pale hand was gripping the hilt of his sword, the blade of which was shoved through Josef's ribs.

For one long, breathless moment, Josef could only stare at

his blood dripping down the blue-white blade and think how impossible it was. The Lord of Storms was behind him with both arms at his side, sword in hand, and yet that was the Lord of Storms' hand in front of him, and his sword. Josef was still trying to work his mind around this when he was interrupted by the hateful sound of the Lord of Storms' laughter.

"You humans really are blind, aren't you?" the commander said, walking around to grin at Josef with his fully re-formed head. "You knew I wasn't human. You've seen me remake myself, seen me pull swords out of the air, and yet you still expect me to have only two arms just because that's what your flesh eyes tell you?"

He threw out his arms in a welcoming gesture, his sword hanging lazily from his long fingers. Meanwhile, the third arm twisted through the cut in the air, wrenching the other sword in Josef's ribs. A fresh wave of pain blackened his vision, and Josef coughed, spitting his blood out on the ground before he choked on it.

Somewhere above him, the Lord of Storms made a *tsk*ing sound. "It's your greatest weakness, you know," he said. "You'd be a real challenge if you didn't have to rely on these blind idiots to swing you."

Lost as he was in the pain, it took Josef several seconds to realize the Lord of Storms was talking to his sword, not to him. That was just as well, though, for it was the Heart who answered.

"It is you who are weak, Lord of Storms." The Heart's voice vibrated through him, the words clear as bells, though Josef wasn't sure if that was thanks to his connection with his sword or the fact that he was racing toward death. Whatever the reason, Josef was glad. The conversation gave him time to process the injury.

The Lord of Storms bared his teeth. "I'm not the one whose champion is *leaking* into the snow."

"Your anger is your weakness," the Heart said. "You were cobbled together by the Shepherdess from other spirits same as the humans you scorn, and yet they are blessed with a measure of her power, while you are nothing but an amalgam, a storm held long past when it should have blown out. You rage on only with the White Lady's fickle favor, but even the smallest of these 'blind idiots' bears more of the Shepherdess's power than you ever could. You are bound by her will, but my swordsman lives through his own. That is why I chose him, why I've always chosen humans, blind though they are. You do not need eyes to cut, only the will to swing."

"And look where that's gotten you," the Lord of Storms scoffed, his voice thick with scorn. "You're about to lose your wielder again, old mountain. How long will you rust up here, waiting for another?"

"I need no other hand," the Heart said, its voice as deep as the roots of the world. "We will not fall."

"Say that when your boy is back on his feet," the Lord of Storms sneered. He shifted his stance as he spoke, and the third hand reaching through the white slit withdrew, taking the sword with it.

As the blade slid out of Josef's chest, it also removed the only thing still supporting him. Josef flopped forward, gasping like a landed fish in the dirty slush of sundered snow and his own blood. The Lord of Storms turned away in disgust, walking across the frozen ground toward the cliff where Nico was slumped.

"Don't you...touch her..."

The Lord of Storms stopped a foot from Nico's crumpled body and looked over his shoulder. "How do you mean to stop me?"

Baring his bloody teeth in a snarl, Josef forced himself back to his knees, then his feet. His body was numb with cold and blood loss, but the Heart burned like a brand against his palm, flooding him with a strength so large he could barely contain it. There was a strange pressure on his chest, and Josef knew without looking that the Heart was binding the wound, staunching the blood flow. After that, he paid little attention.

It didn't matter anymore. Nothing mattered except the Lord of Storms' hand hovering over Nico.

If you want to stop him, the Heart spoke in his mind, *you'll have to cut him.*

"How?" Josef wasn't sure if he spoke the question aloud or silently, but the Heart answered all the same.

He is a spirit, same as I am. Same as the mountain beneath us, same as the wind blowing through your hair. The Shepherdess's will holds him together, but humans are her creatures, and your will is an echo of hers.

Josef looked down at the black blade. It was trembling in his hand. No, that wasn't right. The blade was still; it was his hand that was shaking. "I don't know if I have the strength for another cut."

Muscular strength is meaningless. Your muscles could never have pierced the hull of a palace ship. It was your will to cut that sliced the boards. I will strike the blow, but it is your will that must cut the Shepherdess's binding.

"I'm not a wizard," Josef growled.

You don't have to be, the Heart said, its voice steady and measured. *You're spirit deaf, not spiritless. Will is the birthright of all humans, not just wizards. Just as you learned to listen to me, so you can learn to focus your will. The Lord of Storms' power is enormous, but he is still nothing more than a storm. He is limited by his nature, but you are freed by yours. Human souls are not determined by size or density, but by will alone. So open your spirit to me, Josef Liechten. If you would save your precious demonseed, then you must throw away the knowledge that the Lord of Storms cannot be cut. Forget what you are not and embrace what you are.*

Josef shook his head. "And what is that?"

The Heart's answer vibrated through his bones. *My swordsman.*

Josef stared at the Lord of Storms, his breath thundering in his head. Wisps of cloud were curling at the ends of the man's long black hair, and his eyes flashed like lightning. But as Josef gripped the Heart, he could already see the black blade stabbing through the Lord of Storms' chest, hitting nothing but air, just like before.

"What if I can't?" he whispered.

If you could not cut the Lord of Storms, you would not have the strength to lift me, the Heart of War said. *Look down, Josef Liechten, and know the truth.*

Josef obeyed without thinking, his eyes falling to the black sword in his hand, and the world fell away. It was just like what had happened in Gaol during his first fight with Sted. Josef was floating in the blackness again, and now as then, the image appeared. A mountain taller than any mountain has ever been, its peak cutting the clouds.

Are we one, swordsman?

Josef breathed deep. "Aye."

Then let's finish this.

"Aye," Josef said again, bracing for the lunge. "Together."

In the next heartbeat, they moved as one.

CHAPTER
16

Eli drifted back to consciousness slowly, waking up one bit at a time. His first thoughts were little more than groggy impressions: soft stroking on his hair, musical humming in his ears, warm, still air, and brightness. White brightness that bled through his skin.

His eyes snapped open. Benehime's snow-white beauty filled his vision. Her face hovered over his, her white hair falling in a curtain around them, blocking out the rest of the world. Her white eyes were soft as goose down, full of love, and her cheeks were streaked with sparkling trails. Tears, Eli realized belatedly. The White Lady was crying.

Oh, my darling. Her voice trembled as she fell on him, pressing his body tight against hers. *My love, my only love, I was so worried.*

Eli could only blink. He felt like he'd been hit with the Heart of War. His chest ached, his limbs were useless, and he was so tired it was actually difficult to stay conscious. Even so, the need to get away overpowered him, and he began to struggle weakly against her grasp.

There, there, she cooed, pushing him down. *Be still. The healing isn't done yet. You gave far too much of yourself, but that's over now. I've got you. You're never going to do that again.*

Eli blinked, trying to remember. The haze in his mind made everything fuzzy, but he dimly recalled something being wrong with Slorn's Awakened Wood. The trees, he'd stopped the trees...

He jerked as the memory of their screams came back in a rush. He'd been restraining the mad forest, and then that Spiritualist had surprised him and he'd lost control. After that, things got a bit jumbled. He remembered Nico grabbing him after he fell, but not why he'd fallen. Whatever it was, it must have been bad for Benehime to look this worried. She was hovering over him now, stroking his hair and making little soothing noises, calling him "love" and "darling." Eli closed his eyes as a cold, sinking feeling of dread began to curl in his stomach.

That's right, love, lie still, Benehime whispered, petting him. *You mustn't scare me like this. Oh, it's all my fault. I never should have removed my mark. I meant to teach you a lesson, but I forget how weak you are without me. If I'd lost you, I'd...* Her hand froze as her voice trailed off, and then the petting resumed faster than before. *Don't worry, I'm never letting you go again. Soon as you're healed, I'll replace my mark and then we'll be together forever just as we were meant to be.*

"No."

The word came out as a wheeze, no louder than a breath, but Eli knew that Benehime heard. The moment he spoke, her body went stiff beneath him, her white fingers frozen in his hair.

What was that, love?

The words were sweet, but the threat looming behind them resonated down to Eli's bones. He began to tremble, and for a moment he almost fell back to the old false compliments and appeasements. But then, clear as day, he saw Karon, still lost by her hand. He saw the nameless old Spiritualist, his wrinkled face wide with shock just before he crumbled to dust, his rings crying as Benehime crushed them beneath her white feet. He saw himself lying in her lap, being petted forever. No bounty, no fame, no freedom, no Josef or Nico or even Miranda. Nothing but Benehime's hand petting him like a dog forever and ever and ever.

The horrible vision gave him strength, and Eli pulled himself from her hands. He sat up with a pained sigh, rubbing his eyes hard as his surroundings came into focus. He was in Benehime's white world, no surprises there. Behind him, he could hear Benehime seething. Eli took another breath and turned, steeling himself against her rage, but as he faced her, he caught something out of the corner of his eye that stopped him cold.

Benehime's sphere hung in the air behind her, the miniature seas and forests and mountains tiny and perfect as ever, but it was no longer alone. Floating beside it was a second sphere. It was tiny compared to the original, barely larger than a marble, but inside its delicate curving sky was a tiny world more beautiful than anything Eli had ever seen.

A sparkling blue sea lay along a golden coastline. Jewel-like corals sparkled beneath the gentle waves, and the beach was lined with beautifully colored reeds, each stalk as wispy as spun silk. Beyond the reeds, a field of grass so green Eli couldn't help wanting to roll in it stretched off into gentle hills. Waterfalls tumbled into streams that flowed toward a snaking, shining river whose water was pure and crystal clear.

Above the gentle hills was a deep forest, its tall treetops wrapped in silver mist.

After the forest, the land rose dramatically, forming a beautiful rising line before suddenly going strangely flat, as though something were missing. Otherwise, it was perfect, a dream landscape born of a painter's imagined paradise. Just looking at the soft grass and clear water made Eli's heart ache with longing until it was all he could do not to cry.

Isn't it beautiful?

Benehime's whisper was right in his ear, and Eli jumped only to find she'd pressed herself against his back. Her arm encircled his waist, trapping him against her as she reached out with her free hand to brush her fingers against the tiny, perfect sphere.

As much as he hated to ask her anything, Eli couldn't help himself. "What is it?" he whispered, his voice a hoarse croak.

Benehime dusted a butterfly kiss against his cheek. *Paradise.*

Her white finger slid across the sphere's surface, petting it just as she had pet his hair. *I made it for us*, she whispered, cuddling him closer. *A perfect world all our own, filled with my favorite spirits. It's not finished yet, though. The mountain is the last touch I need. As soon as Durain stops being stubborn, we'll be ready.*

Eli jerked. Durain was the Shaper Mountain, the Lord of all Mountains, the *star*. He thought of the Awakened Wood's panic, the strange flooding in Zarin, and everything became painfully clear.

"You made this from stars?" he whispered, voice shaking.

Of course, Benehime said. *Nothing else is worthy.*

"But what about the spirits?" The words were out of Eli's mouth before he could stop them. He didn't care. All he could think about was Slorn's beautiful golden trees tearing themselves apart.

"The stars are the greatest spirits, the roots of the world." His voice was rising now. "You made this system. You *bragged* to me years ago that you set your mark on the stars and tied the other spirits to them so you wouldn't have to watch everything all the time. You built this house of cards with the stars at the bottom, and now you're just yanking them out? Do you even care about what that will do to the rest of the world?"

No.

The quickness of the answer made Eli jump. Benehime's weight vanished from Eli's back, and he spun around to see she was leaning back with her head lowered, her hair falling over her like a shroud.

I'm tired, Eliton, she whispered. *I've been Shepherdess for over five thousand years now. It was never supposed to be like this. I was never supposed to rule so long. Five hundred years, Father said. A thousand at most, and then he'd be back to save us, to free us from the prison. But he never came back.*

"Father?" Eli said, bewildered. "You have a father?"

Of course, Benehime said. *The Creator brought forth my brothers and me from his own body, each of us created to do our job. The Hunter hunts, the Weaver weaves, and I shepherd the spirits in his absence.*

Benehime's hand drifted to the larger of her spheres, her fingers running along the curve of the sky. *This isn't even the world*, she said wearily. *Creation used to be larger than your mind can comprehend. It stretched on forever, as full of spirits as the sky was full of stars. I was born into that world, and for one shining moment I saw things as they were meant to be.*

Her voice was so full of sorrow and loss that Eli reached out without thinking, brushing her shoulder with his fingers. "What happened?"

Benehime leaned into his touch. *All was lost*, she said. *Everything that is left of the world that was is held in this sphere.* Her hand stroked the larger of the two floating worlds. *A fragile shell, a tiny seed, an ark that was supposed to shelter us until the Creator could restore his creation. That's why he made my brothers and me. We were to maintain and tend what remained in his absence. Just until he could return, he said. But he never did.*

Benehime raised her head, gazing up into the white nothing above them. *I worked for thousands of years in the hope of seeing the night full of stars again, but as the years wore on and the Creator did not return, the spirits began to degrade. Locked in this tiny orb, this cell, they fell deeper and deeper into sleep, and I could do nothing but take the blame.*

I'm tired, she said again, taking her hand from the orb to cup his face. *Tired of hoping, tired of waiting. I'm tired of managing the demon, tired of keeping things calm. I've been so tired for so long, I think I was actually starting to die. But then, without warning, everything changed.*

Her white eyes filled with love. *I found you,* she whispered, stroking Eli's cheek with her burning fingers. *You were the only thing in all the world that loved me without prompt or knowledge, without fear. The night I found you in the forest, you embraced me without hesitation, without knowing what I was. You were so beautiful, so bright, I felt alive again for the first time in a thousand years. I loved you instantly, loved you so much that I would give up the world just to see you smile. That was when I knew it was over.*

Eli swallowed. "Over?"

I'm tired of being the Shepherdess, Benehime said. *So I'm not going to anymore. I'm done.*

Eli stared at her, his brain scrambling for purchase as she turned his world on its head. "You can't be done!" he cried. "You're the *Shepherdess*. You protect and support every living thing in the world!"

I did, and far longer than I was supposed to. The Shepherdess shook her head. *It doesn't matter. Even if I stay, nothing changes. The Great Spirits grow weaker, the weak spirits fall into sleep and never wake, the world crumbles into entropy with or without me. Better I save what I can now.*

Her other hand shot out and wrapped around his shoulders, pulling him closer. *Don't you see, Eli?* she said. *I'm saving the best of creation. The paradise I've built is small enough that I can support the entire thing with my will alone. It will be a world without death or suffering, a world without the demon. A world where everything loves me and I am free to love you with nothing in my way.*

"But what about the rest?" Eli said, trying to jerk away. "What about the seas and the mountains and the plains and the people who aren't stars?"

Why should I care for them? Benehime said, holding him firm. *All I love is safe in the paradise I've made, except for you.* She slid her hands down to his shoulders, her long nails digging into his arms. *Come with me. I can't wait to show you the world I've made for us. A world just for you and me, ours alone, forever.*

Eli went stiff against her, his head tilting up to look at her face.

She smiled down at him, shining with love. *I'm sorry I had to be so cruel before*, she whispered, kissing his forehead. *But that's all over now. Look.*

She beckoned the tiny sphere closer. It floated to her, flying soundlessly through the white until it reached her hand. She took the delicate world between her fingers and tilted it so Eli could see the black stone of the bedrock and the glittering red vein of magma that ran through it. Eli's breath caught as he recognized it, and Benehime's smile widened.

You were so sorry to lose him, she said. *And I hate to see you unhappy, so I brought Karon back and gave him a place of honor. Now do see how much you mean to me, darling? He's not even a star, but I will share my paradise with him gladly if it makes you smile.*

She kissed Eli again. *See how much I love you, darling? Now*—she released the paradise and reached down to seize Eli's hands—*come with me. Leave this dirty, thankless world, and come away to paradise.*

Eli looked up, searching Benehime's eyes for some hint that this was a test, that she was joking, but he found only sincerity and love. She was serious about going through with this, serious about taking him into that tiny sphere and leaving the rest of the world to rot. Eli's eyes flicked to the green fields and blue waters, to the peaceful golden shore and the velvet forest, to Karon.

His chest contracted. The lava spirit looked so happy flowing below the ground again, living as fitted his nature. Could he be happy, too? Eli frowned, trying to imagine an eternity of walking beneath those trees, nothing to steal, no one to talk to except Benehime and her fawning stars for the rest of time.

Bile rose in his throat, and Eli jerked back, putting as much space between himself and the Shepherdess's hands as possible.

"No," he said.

Benehime cocked her head at him. *No?* she repeated, as though she didn't know what the word meant.

"No," Eli said again. "Thanks for the offer, but I'd rather rot here."

Benehime began to tremble. Her shoulders shook, her hair rolled in waves like a storm-tossed sea. The only thing that stayed still were her eyes. They remained locked on Eli's, the white irises widening as the love that had shone in them seconds before burned away to pure, violent fury.

Why? The word roared out of her as she surged to her feet, taking Eli with her. She shook him then, grabbed him by his shoulders and shook him until his neck was snapping. *I've given you everything you've ever wanted!* she shrieked. *I gave you my love, my attention and adoration! Now I give you paradise, and you throw it back in my face!*

Her fingers dug into him like knives as the shaking stopped, and Eli gritted his teeth against the pain, desperate not to cry out as she dangled him like a hooked fish before her. Benehime's face was terrible in its rage, and when she spoke again, her voice was cold enough to burn.

Why? The word trembled. *Why am I never enough? There's someone else, isn't there? Is it the Spiritualist girl or the demonseed? Or maybe your swordsman?* She jerked him close, and this time Eli did cry out. Blood ran down his arms from where Benehime held him, the red painfully bright against the white perfection of her world. *Tell me!*

Eli raised his head, biting his teeth against the pain as he grinned in her face. "If you want me to list everyone I'd rather spend time with over you, we're going to be here awhile."

Why? she whispered again. *You love me.*

"I did," Eli said. "A long time ago, when I was too young and stupid to understand what I didn't want to know. But I wised up. I've seen what you really are, Benehime, and what you are is cruel. You're a cruel, selfish, violent, spoiled brat, and I will never, ever love you again."

Benehime hissed and dropped him. He hit the white ground hard, and the impact left him gasping. He tried to roll over, but Benehime's white foot landed on his chest, stopping him. She crawled over him, forming a cage with her body as her face hovered just above his. For a long moment, she just stared at him, and then, without warning, she leaned down and kissed him hard enough to bruise.

You will have no other but me, she said when she finally raised her head. *I will kill anyone else who dares to touch you. You are mine. Mine forever.*

"I'm *mine*," Eli hissed in her face. "My life is my own and no one else's. But you were right about one thing."

Benehime eyed him suspiciously. *And what is that?*

"There is someone else," Eli said. "Josef, Nico, Karon, old man Monpress, Slorn, even Miranda and Banage. The list goes on and on, and the truth is I'd rather stay and die with any of them than live in paradise forever with *you*."

As his voice faded, the air grew very cold. He could feel Benehime's rage pressing down on him like a physical thing, and the small, realistic part of Eli's mind whispered that this was probably it. He'd pushed her too far, and now she was going to kill him. But even as the truth dawned on him, Eli was surprised to find he didn't care. After all that had happened, he'd rather die here than suck up to Benehime ever again.

But the Shepherdess made no move to attack. Instead, she rolled off him, her long white hair sliding after her. When she was on her feet, she glared down with a look of hatred so intense it took Eli's breath away. And then, without another word, she turned her back on him.

Get out of my sight.

Eli was about to point out that she was the one keeping him here, but before he could open his mouth, the ground beneath him vanished. He plunged down in free fall. Benehime's white form shrank above him, quickly fading into the white. Even so, her final words were as loud as though she were standing right beside him.

Never come back.

With that, the white world exploded into blue sky. Biting cold wind slammed into Eli's body, buffeting him from side to side as he plummeted through the air. He began windmilling his arms on instinct, trying to get his head up. It did no good. He fell like a stone, going faster and faster as the wind ripped past.

Just when Eli was sure he was going to be falling forever, cold white exploded all around him. For a terrifying second, he thought he was back in Benehime's world, but then the white stuff fell on his face, burying him in wet, cold dark. Snow. He'd landed in a snowdrift.

As the snow finally stopped his fall, all Eli felt was relief. He lay still in the freezing dark, so happy to be alive it hurt. No, he was actually hurting, and not from joy. His back ached from the impact, and the weight of the snow above him was crushing his chest. He was buried alive.

At that thought, his body exploded into action. He thrust his feet down and began to swing his arms around, batting madly at the snow. At the same time, he flung open his spirit. That hurt more than anything else. Opening his spirit now was like trying to use torn muscle, but Eli gritted his teeth and kept at it, running a plea through the snow, begging it to move.

For a long time, the snow didn't even seem to hear him.

And then, slowly, it started shuffling. The tiny movements became larger ones as the bank woke up. Eli increased his pleading, and the snow obliged, rolling out of the way to form a tunnel up.

Eli burst out of the snowbank and rolled onto his back, gasping and shivering. He wasn't sure how long he lay like that, sucking in air and reveling in the pure joy of being alive, but eventually the world began to assert itself again. The first thing he noticed was how dark it was. He stared up at the sky, wondering how long he'd been gone for it to be so late. But the longer Eli looked, the more he began to suspect that it wasn't actually night at all. The night sky didn't roil and move like the one above his head. He frowned, squinting up at the blackness just as a wild fork of lightning flashed, lighting the sky up from the inside.

Eli caught his breath, and then he was scrambling to his feet, cursing himself for an idiot for not recognizing it earlier. There was only one force of nature that brought clouds like that, and it didn't take a genius to guess what the Lord of Storms might be doing up here. He floundered in the loose snow, looking for traction. The moment he found it, Eli opened his spirit as far as he could before the pain stopped him.

Sure enough, he felt the Heart of War blazing like a beacon to the west. Eli turned his feet toward it and started running, holding the Heart's position in his mind. He didn't know what he would do when he got there, but whatever it was, Eli hoped against hope that it wouldn't be too late.

Josef gripped the Heart in his hands, blinking against the sweat that poured into his eyes despite the cold. Behind him, Nico was slumped motionless against the cliff, and ahead of him, standing on the flat ledge like he owned it, was the Lord of Storms.

The tall man looked completely unruffled. No sweat stained his brow, and his breaths, if a storm needed to breathe at all, were so calm Josef couldn't see them. The Lord of Storms held his sword high before him, his arm steady with no sign of fatigue, and his body was completely uninjured despite the fact that Josef had been sticking him like a pincushion for the last quarter hour.

Will, swordsman, the Heart's voice boomed in his head. *Concentrate. You have to strike him with—*

"I know!" Josef shouted, shifting his fingers on the black sword's hilt. "I'm trying. I've never done this before."

Then you'd better learn quickly, the sword said, its voice sharpening. *Because I can't keep you up much longer.*

Josef knew that. Even with the Heart's strength roaring unchecked through his body, he was nearing his limit. How many times had the Lord of Storms' blade slipped through his guard? Too many, Josef thought with a wince. He hadn't pulled that third-arm stunt again, thankfully. Probably because, for all his other faults, the Lord of Storms was a warrior. A warrior would consider such tricks beneath him.

It wasn't like the Lord of Storms needed cheap gimmicks anyway. He was standing firm on the icy stone, waiting for Josef's next attack and smiling like he was having the time of his life. Considering how the man was always going on about a fight to make him feel alive, he probably was. Josef sneered. Must be fun to swing a sword around when you were an uncuttable bastard.

Stop thinking that, the Heart snapped. *Thoughts like that are why you can't cut him. Focus your mind, forget what you think you know and strike.*

Josef tightened his grip and lunged. He came in low this time, the Heart clutched at his side until the last second. The Lord of Storms grinned wide and ran to meet him. He didn't bother blocking. Instead, he threw all his weight into a swing that would have taken Josef's arm off had Josef been a hair slower. But Josef wasn't just Josef anymore. He was a true swordsman now, with the Heart's strength and centuries of experience flowing through his veins beside his blood. He shifted at the last second, dodging the Lord of Storms' glowing blade as he swung the Heart down and around to come up with a stabbing thrust straight through the League Commander's side.

Josef knew he'd failed again as soon as the strike connected. The Heart went through the larger man's torso without resistance, leaving Josef to stumble forward, a slave to his own momentum. They'd been at this long enough now that the Lord of Storms didn't even try to take the opening on Josef's back. He just lowered his sword and turned around to wait for Josef's next charge.

"I've got a little bet going with myself," he said as Josef plunged the Heart into the ground and leaned on it, panting so hard his lungs ached. "What do you think? Will I kill you first, or will you faint on me?"

Josef didn't answer. Even if he'd had the breath to waste, there was no point rising to such obvious bait. Instead, he focused on stilling his shaking muscles and clearing his mind as the Heart commanded. It was a near-impossible task. His body was screaming for rest now, and the countless failures made his thoughts twisted and bitter. Josef wanted to beat the Lord of Storms until the man was a cloud-shaped pulp, but he couldn't, and the frustration was making him wild.

Stop it, the Heart said. *You're not learning from your mistakes. You're just swinging like an animal.*

"I know." Josef panted.

No, you don't, the Heart said. *If you knew anything you wouldn't keep doing the same thing over and over again and expecting a different outcome.*

Josef had no answer for that, so he focused on pushing himself up for the next charge.

His body stopped moving before he made it to first position.

No, the Heart said. *No more. Stop for a moment, Josef Liechten. Stop and think.*

Josef slumped against the Heart's hold. What was there to think about? He couldn't do this wizard nonsense. He'd lost. The only reason he was still standing was because the Lord

788

of Storms was having too much fun playing with him to end it.

Shut up. The Heart's voice roared through his mind, drowning out everything else. *This is the last blow I'm keeping you up for, swordsman. After this, it's done. I'm letting you drop. But before that happens, I want you to shut up and think about how best to spend your final strike.*

Josef bared his teeth in a snarl and threw his head back. The Heart had locked his legs, but he could still move his upper body, and he used what was left of his strength to look up at the rolling clouds. The Heart was deluding itself. He wasn't a wizard, wasn't even a real swordsman, apparently. He was just a man, a man in way over his head. A man who couldn't save his most important thing.

Josef's eyes flicked to Nico. She looked so small, pressed back against the ledge. Her coat had wrapped around her completely, hiding her face, but he had the feeling her eyes were open. Shame shot through him. She was watching him fail her. Watching him throw everything he had at the Lord of Storms only to come up short. What a pathetic end this was.

That line of thought made him feel queasy, so Josef tore himself away from Nico and forced his attention back to the sky, the only safe place left to look. The storm stretched out as far as he could see, a swirling vortex above the Lord of Storms. Lightning forked between the black clouds, lighting them up from the inside just as the Lord of Storms had lit his own body with his sword. The clouds' curling edges reminded him of the wounds he'd laid on the Lord of Storms before they healed. The thunderheads moved quickly in the high wind, the same wind that blew the Lord of Storms' long hair back without touching Josef's...

Josef jerked as his mind ground to a halt. Of course. He turned to his opponent. The Lord of Storms was standing as before—feet planted, sword arm raised tirelessly, his smile slipping into an expression of bored disappointment. But Josef

789

saw the body for only a moment before he discarded the image the Lord of Storms projected and looked *deeper.*

He could see nothing special, nothing he hadn't noticed before, but the more he looked, memorizing every detail of the Lord of Storms' pale, unmarred skin, his unflushed cheeks, his sweatless brow, his undamaged coat still perfectly settled on his broad shoulders, the deeper the truth settled into Josef's bones. Of course. How could he have been so blind?

Nature of your race, the Heart said. *Are you ready to take the last swing?*

"Yes," Josef whispered, picturing the strike in his mind.

The Heart's deep laughter filled him like water. *A good blow*, the sword said as Josef raised it to his shoulder. *I am with you, Josef Liechten.*

"And I with you, brother," Josef whispered.

Across the ledge, the Lord of Storms lifted an eyebrow. "If you're done talking to yourself, I do actually have business to get on wi—"

Josef attacked before he could finish. He didn't lunge like the times before, didn't throw himself at the League Commander. Instead, he planted his feet and swung, sweeping the Heart's blade down in an enormous arc from the top of his shoulder to just above his foot. His arms ached as he moved, but it didn't matter that they had no more strength to give. This blow had nothing to do with muscles, and it was not aimed at the Lord of Storms.

Josef swung with everything he had. His mind, his body, his desperation, all of him was focused into this one motion, this single arc of the blade. The blow exploded out of him with a boom that echoed across the mountains, and in the sky overhead, directly in a line from the tip of his sword as it traveled down, the thunderheads split open.

It was as though someone had cut the clouds with a knife. The heavy ceiling of black storms split in two, the storm clouds peeling back to reveal a perfectly straight swath of blue sky running from horizon to horizon directly over Josef's head.

But Josef himself didn't see this. He was frozen at the end of the blow, lungs thundering, his muscles straining to keep him upright. The pain and exhaustion were little more than a buzz, however. Insignificant background noise against the single thought that filled Josef's mind.

From the moment he'd committed to the swing, he'd seen only one thing. The image had filled him, pushing out everything else, every doubt, every pain, until there was room for nothing but the truth. He clung to it even now, unable to do anything except hold on as the final echoes of the blow left his body. He had no thoughts, no knowledge, just that one image held like a candle behind his closed eyes.

It was a memory. Not his own, but one from the Heart of War. The same memory the sword had shown him when it had picked up his dying soul and told him to make a choice: walk out of death a swordsman, or not at all. Even as the last of the overwhelming power left him, Josef clung to the cold, clear vision of the mountain rising taller than any other, its sharp, knife-like peak cutting the clouds in two. The Heart's true self.

Finally, slowly, Josef forced himself to let the image go. He unclamped his mind from the memory as he peeled his white-knuckled fingers from the Heart's hilt. As the vision faded, the world roared back, and Josef stumbled as the pain and exhaustion crashed back down. He was still standing though, his sword still in his hands, his heart still thudding in his chest, full of life. With these things in mind, Josef pried his eyes open to see if his final blow had been enough.

What he saw rooted him to the icy rock. Across the ledge, the Lord of Storms stood, his pale face contorted in disbelieving horror. Overhead, the storm raged, lightning forking from every cloud, but the storm itself had changed. Directly down its center, the strip of clear, blue sky remained untouched, a cut dividing the thunderheads horizon to horizon. And directly below the cut in the sky, a second cut, just as clean, ran across the Lord of Storms' chest, dividing him from shoulder to hip, nearly cleaving him in two.

Josef stared at the wound in disbelief, waiting for it to close as all the others had. But it didn't. Inside the Lord of Storms' body, the thunderheads were churning. Lightning blossomed, lighting him up, but no matter how the storm raged, it could not close the gaps, not the one in the sky nor the one in the Lord of Storms himself. Through it all, the Lord of Storms' eyes never left Josef, but the look in them changed as Josef watched, creeping from shock to raw fury and, buried beneath it, a burning, grudging respect. He saw it for only a moment before the Lord of Storms vanished.

Josef stumbled, looking frantically for his opponent as he fought to raise his sword again. There was no way the Lord of Storms was defeated that easily. Groaning at the effort, Josef wrenched up his sword and spun, letting the Heart guide him toward the electric feel of the Lord of Storms' presence just as the man reappeared behind him, right in front of Nico.

"No!" Josef screamed, but it was already too late. The Lord of Storms' hand was shooting forward even as he coalesced from the cloud, his long, white fingers stabbing into Nico's chest the second they were solid. Her coat's scream was so loud even Josef heard it, but black fabric couldn't stop the Lord of Storms. His hand tore through the screaming coat like paper and slammed into Nico's rib cage, fingers clenching as he found what he sought. Fast as his lightning, the Lord of Storms pulled his arm back, ripping his hand from Nico's chest and bringing the black thing with it.

Even in his fury, the sight of what the Lord of Storms pulled out of Nico almost sent Josef to his knees. It was black as ink in the Lord of Storms' bloody grip and shiny as a beetle's shell. Its surface glittered in the dull light, a thick, black cylinder as long as an infantry short sword and tapered to a wicked point at both ends, and though Josef had never seen one, he knew it at once. It was Nico's seed, the demonseed itself.

Nico made no sound as her seed was ripped from her, but her eyes were screaming beneath the cowl of her hood as the

Lord of Storms stood, holding the seed in front of him. She fell when he let her go, collapsing into a black pile at the base of the small cliff, her white fingers scrabbling in the snow that was quickly turning black as the blood poured from her sundered chest. Almost at once, her movements slowed, and then stopped altogether. The small, pale hands reached out one final time, and then the fingers fell still, lifeless as the rock below them.

After that, Josef saw nothing but red.

With a raw howl of fury, he charged the Lord of Storms, the Heart swinging madly. The Lord of Storms glared over his shoulder at the sound, and Josef screamed louder still, throwing the Heart of War over his head, but the Lord of Storms made no move to defend. Instead, he clutched the demonseed to his chest, his skin smoking wherever it touched the seed's bloody surface, and vanished in a flash of white.

Josef stopped, boots skidding on the icy rock as he spun to look for where the man would appear next, but the air felt strangely empty. Overhead, the black clouds were dissipating, leaving the afternoon sky clear and empty.

"*No!*" Josef howled. "Come back you *coward*! Come back and fight!"

He screamed and screamed until the words faded to gibberish. He screamed until his throat was raw, sword swinging uselessly at the clear sky. His rage was like a river, washing him away, but hard as it held him, he never turned around. Josef was strong enough to rend the sky and cut the Lord of Storms, but he wasn't strong enough to turn around and see Nico's lifeless body.

He might have stayed like that forever had the hands not grabbed his shoulders. The grip was firm, but the fingers were gentle. Even so, Josef spun around, Heart flying and teeth bared like an animal. But the sword grew heavy as an anvil as he turned, and the hilt tore from his fingers. The Heart fell from his grip, crashing into the icy ground, and Josef fell with it.

He landed on his knees with his head in his hands, but even that was too much. Without the Heart, it was exhaustion that calmed him, and he flopped on his side, lungs gasping. As the red haze of fury faded, Eli's worried face came into focus a foot above his own.

The thief's mouth was moving, and from the way his lips shaped, Josef knew Eli was shouting his name. Still, it was some time before the pounding in his ears faded enough to make out anything else.

"What?" he croaked.

"I *said,* 'Get up you blasted *idiot!*'" Eli shouted. "You have to do something!"

Josef just stared at him. How could he tell the thief he'd tried to do something and failed. That Nico was dead and it was all his fault. That he hadn't been strong enough.

Pain shot through him as Eli grabbed his cheek and pulled *hard.*

"Whatever you're thinking, stop it right now," the thief snapped. "Nico needs you."

Josef's voice shook. "Nico's dead."

Eli cursed and grabbed Josef's head, wrenching it up. "Does that look dead to you?"

Josef's fury drained away, the frustrated sorrow and rage giving way to icy dread. At the foot of the ledge where Nico's body had fallen, all light was gone. In its place, a pillar of liquid night rose to the sky. It swirled and seethed like a living thing, and at its center was Nico.

She floated at the pillar's heart, naked and tiny, a splinter of pale white in a river of ink. Her eyes were shut tight, but her mouth was open, stretching in a scream Josef could not hear over and over and over while her hands clutched at the empty, black wound that was spreading across her chest.

The second he could move, Josef went for his sword.

"We have to get her down," he said, grabbing the Heart.

"Tell me something I don't know," Eli grumbled, helping the swordsman to his feet. "Like how we're going to do that."

"How did you get her to snap out of it last time?"

"She snapped herself out," Eli said, holding Josef steady. He sighed. "You know, I wouldn't be so worried about her going crazy if she didn't find a new way to do it every time. I was hoping you'd know what happened."

"The Lord of Storms happened," Josef said. "He took her seed."

Eli went paler still. "Impossible. If he took her seed, she'd be dead. I don't know what she is, but dead ain't it."

Inappropriate as it was, an enormous grin broke over Josef's face. "You should know by now, thief," he said, almost laughing as he tightened his grip on Eli's shoulder, "Nothing kills Nico."

He should have known, too, he added silently. He should have kept faith. "Come on," he said, walking forward. "Let's get her back."

Eli did not look comforted, but he fell into step behind Josef.

And all around them, the mountains began to wake as the dreaded fear rose up.

CHAPTER
17

The Lord of Storms stumbled into the white world, clutching the Daughter of the Dead Mountain's demon-seed to his sundered chest. Pain was making his edges hazy, and bits of him were dissolving into cloud without his permission, proof that he was dangerously close to the edge, but the commander couldn't quite bring himself to care. All he could think of was the fight.

An enormous grin spread over his face as he looked down at the gaping hole that ran across his torso. How long had it been since anything had injured him this badly? A thousand years at least. But this was no child of the mountain. This was a *human*, a swordsman of the Heart of War. Could it be that he'd found his equal at last? The one to give him the challenge he'd sought since Benehime had torn him from the sky and made him her sword?

His eyes flicked back to the black length in his hand. The seed was enormous. Most demonseeds were the size of almonds. When Alric told him Sted's seed had been as wide as his hand, the Lord of Storms almost hadn't believed him. But the Daughter's seed dwarfed anything he'd seen in the five thousand years he'd been hunting.

It was as long as his forearm and only slightly thinner, tapered to a sharp point at both ends. How the thing had fit in the girl's body, he had no idea, but it was good he'd gotten it out. Even separated from its host, the seed's surface burned like a brand against his palm, eating him little by little.

The Lord of Storms shifted his grip with a grimace. He could see why the Shepherdess had wanted to handle it herself. A seed like this was a danger to the entire sphere. Of course, he thought bitterly, it was only fitting she deal with the seed since it was her fault the thing had gotten this big in the first place. If she hadn't prevented the League from going near her precious thief, they would have killed the girl ages ago.

He shook his head and set off across the whiteness in the direction of the Shepherdess. The Lady had been in decline for a long time now, but she took all leave of her duty whenever the boy was involved. Fortunately, that infatuation seemed to be over. Maybe now, with the Daughter of the Dead Mountain safely disposed of, Nara out of the picture, and the thief in disgrace, things could finally get back on track.

The Lord of Storms cleared his thoughts as he approached the White Lady. Benehime was kneeling beside her sphere with her head in her hands, white hair falling across her body. She didn't look up as the Lord of Storms approached.

"The Hunt was successful," he said, coming to a stop beside her.

She stirred at his voice and slowly raised her head. When he saw her face, the Lord of Storms jerked back. The White Lady had been crying.

"Shepherdess," he said, feeling uncharacteristically awkward. "I can return later if—"

You have the seed?

The Lord of Storms held out his hand, offering her the seed. The lingering blood on its black surface hissed when she grabbed it, burning away with white fire wherever her fingers touched. The seed itself, however, was unchanged.

You've done well, my Lord of Storms, the Lady said, cradling the seed in her arms. *It's larger than I thought.*

"I've never seen its like," the Lord of Storms admitted. "How do you mean to dispose of it? Will you give it to the Hunter when he returns today?" The Hunter was the only soul who left the shell that sheltered creation from what lay beyond. Even in the Lady's own care, the seed was far too dangerous to remain here. Throwing it into the void would be perfect.

Benehime lay the long, wicked length of the seed across her bare knees. When she looked up again, her white eyes went to the Lord of Storms' sundered chest, and her mouth pressed into a thin line. He stood at attention and waited for her to say something, but she simply turned back to her sphere. No, he squinted—not to her sphere, but to something floating beside it.

It was the pearl from earlier, the small sphere that she'd pressed the gold vein into, but where before it had been opaque, it was now beautifully clear. Clear enough that, despite its tiny size, the Lord of Storms could easily see what lay inside. The Shepherdess was holding a tiny, perfect world between her fingers, a beautiful, jeweled landscape of sparkling seas and deep forests, and as he saw it, the Lord of Storms felt himself go cold.

"What is that?"

You're overstepping your bounds, my Lord of Storms, the Lady said, stroking the delicate arch of the tiny sphere with one long finger. *Swords do not ask questions.*

"You are the source of my strength," the Lord of Storms said. "And I am the source of the League's. Therefore it is very much within my bounds to question you when your actions seem self-destructive." He crossed his arms over his lacerated chest. "Why were you crying just now? And what is that small sphere? Why are you calling in the stars?"

The Lady glared at him over her shoulder. *I do not explain myself to you.*

"You do if you want me to keep your world safe from the demon," the Lord of Storms said. "You've been causing a panic for three days now that's made my life very difficult and almost cost you that seed. I don't care what you do with your time, Benehime, but if it hurts my ability to do your work, then I need to know. Especially if you mean to keep this up much longer."

The Lady turned suddenly, the black seed clutched in one long hand while the other reached out to grab his face. As she touched him, the air went rigid, trapping him in place. The Lord of Storms could do nothing but clench his teeth as she pulled his head down until their faces were level.

My dear Lord of Storms, she whispered, running her white fingers along his jaw. *How long have we been together?*

The Lord of Storms didn't know this game, but he grudgingly played along. "Little over five thousand years," he growled. "As you well know."

So long, she whispered. *And in all that time, have you ever wished you could do something else?*

The Lord of Storms sneered. "Like what?"

Have you ever tired of this life? she whispered, her lips inches from his as she looked down on him through half-lidded eyes.

"No," the Lord of Storms said. "I am your sword. Swords don't get tired of cutting." And he might have just found the equal opponent he'd been searching for all his life, but the commander kept that bit of information to himself.

The Lady was looking at him strangely, her snowy eyes studying his face as though she were memorizing it. As she looked, her fingers roved up to trace his nose, sliding down the ridge of it before coming to rest on his lips. *I think I shall miss you*, she said quietly. *I would take you with me, but I have no need of storms in paradise.*

Her words made no sense, but the finality in them made him wary. He shifted back, trying to pull away from her touch. "What are you talking—"

She cut his words off with a kiss. It was not the hard kiss she usually gave him when he was caught like this, but a soft brush, gentle as a new lover's. Her lips lingered against his, and when she pulled away, her face was almost sad.

Good-bye, my stubborn, loyal sword.

And then her hand stabbed into the wound in his chest.

The Lord of Storms screamed, the sound turning into a thundercrack as it filled the white nothing. The Shepherdess's hand burned inside him, her fingers searching through his clouds for the threads of power that kept him together. She broke each one as she touched it, undoing the binding she'd laid down at the world's beginning. Every break brought a new flash of pain,·but the worst was the feeling of falling apart. The Lord of Storms was breaking, crumbling, his power splintering beneath the Shepherdess's fingers, and he could do nothing but hang in the air and scream as the White Lady did what no demon had ever been able to achieve.

When she finally released him, the Lord of Storms fell to the ground. His form was more cloud than man now, and he could barely move for the pain. Even so, he forced his head up just in time to see the Lady turn away.

In reward for your years of service, I've left you enough control to choose the location of your death, she said. *Go now, I must prepare for my brother's arrival.*

The Lord of Storms twitched on the ground. The agony

was overwhelming, and yet he had to speak. Even if he died halfway through, he had to know.

"Why?" he croaked. "If I die, the League falls, and the demonseeds will overrun the world. You told me so yourself when you made me. So what are you—" His voice broke as a wave of pain overwhelmed him, but he forced himself to finish. "Why, Shepherdess?"

She looked down, her face full of pity. Not for him, but for herself. *I find I don't much care what happens to the world anymore*, she said. *Now leave, you're bleeding all over my floor.*

Sure enough, a puddle of clear rain water was spreading out around him. The Lord of Storms squeezed his eyes closed, willing it to stop, but he wasn't a human, wasn't the Heart of War, blessed with the Lady's power. He was a storm, a common spirit, and his will could do no miracles. Bit by bit, he was draining away, but he had a little strength yet.

His hand began to creep across the white floor. His fingers, now little more than tendrils of cloud, pulled themselves forward until they reached the Lady's bare white foot. With a final burst of strength, he grabbed her ankle and squeezed with everything he had left.

"I—" he gasped. "Will not. Let you. Betray. Your duty."

She scowled down at him, kicking his hand away.

It is the world who betrayed me, she said. *Get out.*

With that, she raised her foot and brought it down hard on his chest. Pain greater than any he'd ever felt exploded at the impact, and then he was falling. The last thing the Lord of Storms saw was Benehime's back as she turned away, fading into white as her world closed to him forever.

You'd better wake up, little girl.

Nico flinched in her sleep, her abused body going stiff with panic.

Why are you here? she thought frantically. The demon was buried. She'd buried him herself. He wasn't supposed to be able to talk anymore.

I'm always here, idiot, the demon sighed. *I'm part of you. And as part of you, I'm telling you that you need to wake up. Right now.*

Nico's eyes popped open.

She saw nothing but storm. A great primordial storm that spread out as far as she could see. The clouds were as black as char except for where the blue-white lightning shot between them, lighting them up in purple flashes. But right through the middle of the storm, cutting across the black expanse like a razor, was an unnaturally straight strip of blue sky. Clouds rolled at the edges of the divide, cracking and rumbling, but they never moved forward. They could not close it, and Nico could not understand why.

Use your eyes, stupid girl.

Nico blinked in surprise. Suddenly her mundane, human vision reasserted itself, layering over the spirit sight, but what she saw there was no less horrible. The Lord of Storms filled her vision. He was nearly on top of her, his black form towering over her head. He was injured, his chest rent in a great gap lined with the same black clouds she'd seen before, nearly splitting his chest in two. But the wound didn't seem to be slowing him down as he slammed his hand into her chest.

Nico had put her body through a great deal in the years she remembered, but she had never, *never* felt pain like this. The Lord of Storms' hand dug into her flesh, burrowing through her like it was searching. And then, just when she was sure the pain couldn't get any worse, his fingers closed on the hard, stiff mass in her chest she'd never actually felt before he touched it.

The panicked pain that shot through her at the contact would have knocked her to the ground had his hand not been inside her, holding her upright, but Nico couldn't think of that. She couldn't think of anything but the feel of his fingers wrapping around the *thing* inside her. Her seed. He was holding her seed.

I'd help if I could, but it seems a little late now. The demon's voice was almost wistful as it floated through her pain-washed mind. *I would like to say I'm sorry, though.*

That was almost enough to shock her out of what was happening in her chest. The demon never apologized.

I'm sorry I didn't kill you when I had the chance, he continued. *For all our differences, you are still my daughter, and I owed you that kindness. Trust me, you'll hate me for it later.*

Nico found that very hard to believe.

Believe it. You're going to miss me when I'm gone, darling, and I'm not talking about wishing you'd taken me up on any of my hundreds of generous offers.

Why would I ever miss you? Nico thought, gritting her teeth in the hope that she could somehow keep herself from passing out.

Because I've been the only thing holding it back. The words were a whisper, but Nico could hear the demon's smile. *Goodbye, daughter.*

Nico was about to ask what he meant, but then the Lord of Storms began to pull and the pain drove everything else from her mind. The whole world shrank down to the hand in her chest, and then, with a ripping jerk, the Lord of Storms pulled the seed free.

It was like he'd torn out her core. Nico flopped forward, her body spasming against the snow. Her chest was ripped wide open, but that seemed like a minor concern. Without the seed she felt like an empty skin. Even the pain was fading into the distance now, eaten by the yawning emptiness, and it suddenly occurred to her that she was dying. This was death. Normal, human death.

The realization nearly made her weep. She'd never thought she'd be able to just die, to open herself to the emptiness and pass into the mists. But as quickly as it came, her relief morphed into anger. She couldn't die. Not like this, not after Josef had risked so much to save her so many times. She couldn't throw away his efforts, his suffering, and take an easy

802

death. Even if she could, she wasn't ready to give him up. She wasn't ready to give any of it up. She wanted to live. She was going to live.

Her fingers clenched in the icy ground, slowly at first, and then stronger. She could feel the Heart of War's spirit dimly nearby, wrapped around another soul she knew as well as her own. Josef was close, and he was furious. So furious that even the Heart's presence faded beneath his rage. Why? Nico wondered, and then she pushed it aside as unimportant. All that mattered was that she had to get to him. Had to help him.

Slowly, deliberately, she forced her arms to extend. Grabbing the icy rock, Nico pushed herself up inch by burning inch. Finally, she made it to her knees. Only then, when she was firmly anchored, did she let her eyes open again.

Josef was the first thing she saw. He was standing on a ledge with the Heart of War in his hands, screaming in an enormous, wordless, enraged roar. Nico tried to move toward him, but her limbs wouldn't obey. Weeping with frustration, she focused on her legs, trying to make them cooperate, but the more she fought to move, the more she became aware that she was hungry. Frighteningly hungry. Ravenous. Unbidden, her head snapped back to Josef and the Heart of War. She could see both spirits clearly, see the power coursing through them.

A spike of hunger hit her, slicing through her body with such fury it reduced the pain to a whimper. The Heart of War drew her like a beacon, and the need to devour its power was almost overwhelming. She would devour the swordsman as well, and the cliff he stood on, and the mountain below that. She could eat the snow and winds overhead. Eat everything.

Before she knew what was happening, she was on her feet, stalking toward Josef like a predator on the hunt. The moment she realized what she was doing, Nico slammed herself to the ground. As she buried her head in her hands, she noticed that her sundered chest had stopped bleeding. The wound was still open, but it didn't hurt much anymore. It was just a black hole in her chest—

Nico stopped cold. Black. Her blood was black. No. The seed was gone. She should be human, a normal girl with red blood and normal hunger, not this all-consuming need. Why? What was happening?

The answer came to her in the demon's voice, something he'd said to her days ago on the beach at Osera after she'd defeated Den. Rival, he'd called her. A new demon.

Nico clutched her chest with shaking hands. The skin was healing as she watched, the black edges knitting together, and as the wound closed, the hunger rose in her until it was all she knew.

The need to eat was like a madness. It came over her in waves, pushing her will away with careless strength as it strained toward Josef and the Heart. Her mind was emptying until all she could think of was how delicious that power would be, how filling. To hunt, to eat, these things were her right. These things were her nature. The only truth that mattered.

Just before the need to devour took her over completely, Nico slammed her eyes shut. New demon or old, it didn't matter. Nothing had changed. She would beat the hunger, beat anything that stood in her way. This was still her body, her soul, and she was still master of herself. The only master she would ever serve.

When Nico opened her eyes again, she was standing in her field where she'd first buried the demon. As it had been in Osera, her inner world was dark, the hills hidden by a pitch-black, moonless night, but the darkness was no longer the only change. In front of her, the rock she'd used to crush the demon down had been torn free. The pit where he'd lain was now a gaping chasm, the ground ripped away along with the seed. Around it, the grass was gummy and decaying. No wind blew, and a foul smell was rising up from the soil, making her gag.

Rot, Nico realized with a spike of terror. Her field was rotting. No, this was her world. She was master. Nothing happened here without her consent. But even as she thought it, the hunger roared in her mind. The need to eat sent her to her knees. She could almost feel her stomach curling up and vanishing inside her. She had to eat. Had to eat or she would die.

After that, the hunger became all-consuming. It seized control of her mind, bending her to its will. Eat the sword, it commanded. Eat the human. Eat everything. Eat and grow strong. You can't be king if you're weak.

"No!" Nico shrieked her answer. "Weak or strong, dead or alive, this is *my* body."

You'll die, the hunger jabbered. Die die die *die die die.*

Nico shut herself down, refusing to listen. Slowly, mechanically, she crawled up the large stone that had held the demon in his prison and curled into a ball on top of it, wrapping her arms around her wounded chest as she stared into the dark.

Out on the edges of the field, blackness was lapping like water. It rose as she watched, flooding over the rotting grass and fetid ground, pouring into the chasm where her seed had been. It rose until her rock was the only island in an endless, black sea. Rose until the dark waves were lapping at her feet. The darkness was as cold as the space between the shadows. It froze her wherever it touched, but Nico refused to move.

The hunger was gnawing at her bones now, surging with the black water that threatened to drown her. The madness flooded her mind with each wave, but Nico did not budge. If she moved now, if she showed any weakness at all, she knew without a doubt she wouldn't be able to stop herself from attacking Josef and the Heart of War.

So she didn't. She sat perfectly still as the black water rose over her calves, then her knees. Rose to her chest, then her neck. She squeezed her eyes shut when it touched her chin, but her mouth opened despite the bitter, freezing dark that flooded through her lips. Even as the darkness choked her, she opened her mouth and spoke the one truth that must remain though everything else was lost.

I am the master of myself.

I am the master of myself.

She said it over and over until the words ran together. Said it until she was screaming, even though the blackness was pouring down her throat now, eating her voice, dissolving her to nothing. But despite the cold, despite the darkness, despite all that had happened, she kept going. She was the master of herself. The choice to step forward, to take another breath, was hers and hers alone.

This was the lifeline she clung to, her mouth moving frantically, shouting the truth again and again as the black water covered her head.

Josef stood with the Heart planted in the stone between his feet, one hand on the hilt, the other bracing against Eli's shoulder for balance. In front of him, the sword's open spirit was slammed down on the mountain slope with enough weight to press the snow into clear ice. The enormous black pillar, however, howled on as before, completely unaffected.

"It's not working," Josef announced unnecessarily.

"Well, it is helping to keep the panic down," Eli said, raising his voice over the demon's wailing. He pointed at the mountain beneath them. "The stone should be cracking itself in terror by now, but the Heart's weight is keeping it still. Not too elegant, but it should keep the League off our backs for the moment."

"Hang the League," Josef growled. "I want Nico down from there."

They both looked up. Nico was still hanging in the air at the center of the black pillar. The Heart's pressure hadn't even touched the surging darkness. It flowed uninterrupted, shooting from the ground to the sky like a black river. Nico's body was motionless under the flood, her white limbs seized up in terror or pain, probably both. She was so still, Eli wouldn't have believed she was alive were it not for her mouth.

Nico's mouth was moving frantically, her jaw opening and closing like she was screaming the same thing over and over again. It was clearly a full sentence, but with the Heart's pressure and the roar of the dark river itself, Eli couldn't get close enough to read the words on her lips. Feeling utterly useless, he looked down at the shredded black fabric he clutched in his hands, all that was left of the coat Slorn had made for her.

"We need a new plan," he muttered. "You keep up the pressure as long as you can. I'll think of something."

Josef nodded, releasing Eli's shoulder to rest both hands on the Heart. *He trusts you completely,* Eli realized with a start as the swordsman settled into his post. *It has never occurred to him that you won't cook up a way out of this.*

That thought made Eli feel bleaker than ever. He crept away, tromping over the battle-torn snow until he found a reasonably clear spot. He sat down with a sigh and rested his chin on his fist, the very picture of clever man deep in thought, just in case Josef looked over.

Trouble was, though, Eli didn't have a clever plan. For once, his sleeves were completely empty. Up here in the mountains, he was miles away from anyone who owed him a favor, assuming there was a favor big enough to deal with something like this. Demons were League and Shepherdess work, but the League was out for obvious reasons and the Shepherdess wouldn't help him now even if he begged, not that he would. That thought brought the anger flaring back, and Eli closed his eyes, putting Benehime firmly out of his mind. First rule of thievery: one disaster at a time. Always focus on solving the problem in front of you.

Tried-and-true advice, but five minutes of sitting and thinking later, Eli was no closer to a solution than he'd been at the beginning, and he was starting to feel a bit panicky. There really seemed to be no way out of this besides waiting for Nico to win or killing her outright. Neither of those would fly with Josef, and while the giant pillar of darkness wasn't getting bigger, it wasn't getting any smaller, either. Their only protection right now was the Heart's iron grip on the mountain's panic and the fact that the Lord of Storms would never expect a demon to live through losing its seed. But the Heart couldn't keep this up forever. Once the sword failed and the panic got out of control, the jig would be up. The League would come, and with Josef so injured already, that would be that.

Dropping all pretenses, Eli slumped forward, resting his head between his knees. But just when he was starting to feel really hopeless, he heard a sound that made him go rigid, the soft, familiar tearing of a cut opening in the veil.

He wrenched his head around just in time to see the white line finish its fall through the air behind Josef. It happened so quickly, Eli could only watch, eyes wide. No, he thought, not yet. With so much going on, why was the League on the ball *now*?

But while the man who stepped through the white hole in the world was large enough to be a League member, he carried no sword, and he wasn't wearing the League's iconic black coat. He was dressed as a workman in a linen shirt and leather apron, but he could have been naked for all Eli noticed. His attention was on the man's head, or rather the large, brown bear's head where the man's head should have been.

"Slorn!" The name was a jubilant shout as Eli jumped to his feet. Josef turned to stare as Eli ran across the ledge, stopping just in front of the bear-headed wizard. "What are you doing here?"

"Monpress." Slorn's muzzle peeled back to show his yellow teeth. "And Liechten, too. Good. Just the men I wanted to see. Give me a hand with this."

He nodded back to the white hole in the air, which was still hanging open, but Eli was just staring at him.

Slorn cleared his throat. "Quickly, please."

Josef and Eli exchanged looks, and then, since Josef couldn't leave the Heart, Eli went to do as Slorn said. At the Shaper's urging, he reached through the white hole and began to pull on the long, rectangular object on the other side. It was unexpectedly heavy, and Eli ended up having to let Slorn do most of the lifting. The thing was off-white and felt almost like soap against his fingers. It was rectangular, as long as Josef and nearly as wide, its four sides, top, and bottom held together seemingly without pins, hinges, or joints. It actually looked very much like a coffin, Eli thought with a sinking feeling. A smooth, white coffin.

The cut in the veil closed as soon as the box was through. Slorn directed Eli to put it down gently, and then he reached over and opened the top with a creak. Eli swallowed when he saw the hollow space in the middle. It *was* a coffin. And the white material...He ran his fingers over it again, hissing as he finally realized what he was touching.

"This is bone metal," he said, staring at Slorn in astonishment. "What are you doing with a bone metal coffin?"

"Solving your problem," Slorn said, propping the lid so it would stay up.

"Coffin?" Josef said at the same time. He glared at Slorn over his shoulder. "Killing her is not an option. She's still in there."

"I am the last man in the world who needs to be reminded of that, swordsman," Slorn said quietly.

Josef snapped his mouth shut.

"Our only hope is to get her contained," Slorn went on, staring up at Nico. "I don't know why she hasn't gotten larger, but I'll take my luck as I find it. In any event, we should move quickly."

"How do we contain *that*?" Eli said, pointing at the black pillar.

"Demons gain strength by feeding," Slorn said. "So we're going to start by locking her away from her food source, and then we'll see what happens."

Eli glanced down at the white box. Suddenly, it looked pathetically small. "I guess we're about to learn the limits of demons and bone metal."

"That we are," Slorn said. "First, though, we have to get her down."

"Leave that to me," Josef said.

Eli started to protest, but Josef had already left his sword anchored in the stone and started marching toward the black pillar. He walked through the iron weight of the Heart's open spirit like it was nothing, which, for him, it was. He stopped when he reached the base of the enormous pillar, his bare hands clenched into fists as he stared up at Nico.

She floated in the air above him, her bare feet even with the top of his head. Her already thin body looked skeletal in the liquid shadows, and her face was screwed up in intense pain as her mouth moved unceasingly, screaming the same words over and over.

"Nico," Josef shouted, his deep voice cutting through the roar of the flowing dark. "I'm bringing you down. Slorn's going to heal you. I need you to trust me and not fight."

If she heard him, Nico gave no sign, but Josef didn't wait for one. The second he finished speaking, he reached up, grabbing her ankles with both hands. Then, bracing his feet against the stone, Josef began to pull. The dark river roared over Nico's body, the flowing shadows wrapping around her, pulling her back, but Josef pulled harder.

Slowly, Nico began to sink. Soon, Josef was able to grab her knees, then her waist. By this point, he was standing in the pillar himself. The darkness poured over him like a waterfall, but to Eli's amazement, it did not consume him. When he had her low enough, Josef grabbed Nico's shoulders and tugged her into his arms. Wrapping himself around her like a shield, he turned and walked away from the pillar, carrying Nico out of the dark and into the afternoon sunlight.

The second her body left the pillar, the blackness dissolved. The roaring torrent just melted away like snow in the sun. But as the pillar vanished, darkness began to grow around Nico's body. It oozed up from her skin, covering her like black mold. Josef walked toward them, holding her carefully, but with every step his face grew paler. It took years for him to cross the stretch of clear ground, and by the time he reached the

810

bone metal box, Nico's body was nearly invisible under the shadows.

Josef fell to his knees beside the coffin and gently set her down inside. As he lowered her, Eli realized Nico's darkness clung to the swordsman as well. Josef's shirt was rotted away where she'd rested against him, and wherever the darkness had touched skin, his flesh was gray and unhealthy.

But Josef didn't seem to mind his injuries. All of his attention was on Nico as he laid her in the box, his hands peeling away from her skin like letting her go was the hardest thing he'd ever done. The second his fingers were out of the way, Slorn slammed the lid down and the mountains fell silent.

The Heart's spirit lifted the moment the threat was gone, and the sword almost seemed to slump into the stone. Eli didn't blame it. He felt like collapsing himself, but he forced himself to stand and watch as Slorn checked the box's seams. They must have passed inspection, for the Shaper's bear face was calm as he got to his feet.

"We should return to the mountain," he said. "She'll be safest there. As will we."

"Slorn," Eli said quietly. "What is going on?"

Slorn raised his hand, and a white line flashed in the air in front of him, falling to the ground in an instant as the white door opened. "Come with me and you'll get all the answers you want," he said. "Plus some you don't."

Eli rolled his eyes. "Isn't it always that way?"

Josef was silent as he went to retrieve the Heart of War, sliding it onto his back with slow, stiff movements as though he'd aged twenty years. When he returned to them, he grabbed his end of Nico's box without prompting, and together he and Slorn lifted it off the ground and carried it carefully through the hole in the world. Eli followed after, stopping only to whisper an apology to the mountains before stepping through the cut in the veil and vanishing without a trace.

811

CHAPTER
18

A s Eli stepped through the portal, all he saw was white, and his stomach seized in dread. No, Slorn wouldn't have taken him back to Benehime. But the portal, the white, white world...

His chest began to heave as a cold sweat broke out all over his body, but before Eli could ramp himself up into a full-blown panic, he noticed that this white world had walls. They were hard to see, but they were definitely there. Benehime's world had no walls, none he knew of at least. Moreover, Josef and Slorn were still here, fussing over the bone metal box. So was a new man, an older gentleman with a long gray beard wearing the finest robes Eli had ever seen outside—

Eli let out a great breath and looked up, his face breaking into a grin as he traced the tapering curve of the glowing white room. "The heart of the Shaper Mountain," he said, nearly laughing. "Never thought I'd be here again."

"You would not be here if the circumstances were less dire, thief."

The deep, unfamiliar voice made him jump, and he turned in surprise to see the old bearded man staring at him with a murderous glare.

"I'm sorry," Eli said. "Do I know you?"

"No," the man said. "But I know you, Eli Monpress. Or rather, I know what you did."

Eli's smile turned sheepish. "Could you remind me, then? I've done a lot over the years."

The man crossed his arms, his beautiful silk sleeves rustling like grass in the wind. "Three years ago you stole five of the finest tapestries ever woven by Shaper hands from our private collection."

"Oh, yes," Eli said. "One of my first big solo jobs. I still have them, you know." He clasped his hands over his heart. "The memory of their beauty sustains me every day. I feel truly lucky to have touched such workmanship. I've stolen many fine things, but your tapestries are truly the jewel of my collection."

On the floor beside Nico's box, Josef rolled his eyes and Slorn made a little huffing sound, almost like he was stifling a laugh. The old man, however, was not amused.

"Be thankful that the only thing Shapers value more than the work of their hands is their duty to the mountain, thief," the old man said. "Had the Teacher not given you safe passage, I'd be escorting you to one of our cells."

Eli's smile grew wicked. "Well, maybe once this is over, we could give that a try. I'd actually love to see your cells. A prison so shoddy that *Miranda* could break out of it must truly be a wonder of the world."

The old man went pale with rage, his eyes going wide, but before he could explode, Slorn interrupted. "Father," he said, "now is not the time. And Eli?"

Eli lifted his head. "Yes?"

Slorn flattened his small, round ears to his flat scalp. "Shut up."

With a coy little grin, Eli obeyed.

Josef, Slorn, and the man Slorn called father moved Nico's bone metal box to the middle of the white room. The enormous hall was perfectly circular, and there was some fussing on the part of the two Shapers about getting the box exactly at the center. Once it was there, Slorn raised his hand. A white slit in the air opened in answer, and Eli blinked in surprise. On the other side of the hole was Slorn's workshop. It looked just as Eli remembered it, everything neatly shelved and labeled. Slorn stepped through the portal, coming back almost immediately with a long length of shining chain looped between his hands.

It must have weighed a ton. The metal was as thick as Eli's thumb, and the links themselves were as long as his palm, but Slorn moved the chain easily, spreading it out between his arms like common rope. He spoke quietly to the others, and then he, Josef, and the old Shaper lifted Nico's bone metal box. As soon as it was off the ground, Slorn began wrapping the chain around it.

He wrapped the box ten times, five across the width and another five going lengthwise before attaching the final link to the first. The glittering metal snapped open at his touch with reverent obedience, sealing itself again so perfectly Eli wouldn't have believed the work had been done without the aid of a forge if he hadn't just seen it for himself.

"There," Slorn said, wiping the back of his neck with his hands. "That should do it. Lower her down."

Eli moved in for a closer look. He loved Slorn's toys. "What was that?"

"Extra precaution," Slorn answered. "It's an awakened alloy of my own design, stronger than steel and stubborn as stone. It's not inedible like bone metal, but it's close. This way, if the bone metal cracks, the containment will hopefully stay shut long enough for us to do something."

Eli felt the blood drain out of his face. Slorn's voice was as serious as the grave. "This isn't like before, is it?" he said quietly.

Slorn closed his eyes. "No."

Josef's shoulders went tense. "What do you mean?"

"He means she's not coming back from this," Eli said. "It's finally gone too far."

"Eli," Josef growled, but Slorn's voice stopped him.

"It's not a matter of going too far," the Shaper said. "If your fight with the Lord of Storms hadn't been so close to the Shaper Mountain, the world would be a very different place right now. Possibly not at all."

Josef bared his teeth. "What do you mean, bear?"

"We watched your fight," Slorn said, unflinching. "The girl you call Nico has another name here. The Shapers call her Daughter of the Dead Mountain, and if the Lord of Storms hadn't finished her, they meant to."

814

Josef's face turned murderous, and the old man beside Slorn drew himself up. "It would be our right," he said. "Almost three years ago, that creature led the demon's assault on the Shapers. She slaughtered the Teacher's mountains, eating them like sheep as she carved a path from the Dead Mountain to our very slopes. Had the League of Storms not stopped her, she would have attacked the Shaper Mountain itself. She is our enemy, but worse, she was our child."

The old man stopped a moment, and when he continued, his voice was softer. "Before the demon took her, the girl was one of our own daughters. A child of the mountain, precious to us and to the Teacher. Killing the monster she became would not just be vengeance for those she killed, but vengeance for the girl she had been, our daughter whose soul was eaten by the demon and replaced with his black seed."

"Nico's bounty," Josef said, his voice dangerously strained. "That was you?"

"It was," the old man said. "I am Ferdinand Slorn, Guildmaster of the Shapers. I gave the order then just as I would have given it now. Had the Lord of Storms fallen, we would have come forward to kill the demonseed ourselves. But then, things changed."

"The seed was ripped out," Slorn said, picking up the story. "But Nico didn't die."

"Of course she didn't die," Josef snapped. "She's a survivor."

"No, swordsman," Slorn said, shaking his head. "A demonseed's host dies the moment the seed is removed. Always. That's why a demonseed is a death sentence. Even if the seed is small, the moment it is implanted, the seed's life becomes tangled with the host spirit. Removing the seed kills the soul and destroys the host body. This is a universal truth. Or so we thought."

Josef folded his arms over his chest. "Nico proved you wrong."

"Nico is no longer a demonseed," Slorn said. "If she were, she would have died the second the seed left her body. But the seed is gone and her soul still lives. Actually, I'd say she's more powerful now without the seed than she was when I saw her at Izo's camp."

Eli winced, remembering the enormous black monster with its hideous yellow eyes, the black mouth roaring as it devoured the forest. He glanced at the bone metal box on the floor between them. He didn't want to see something more powerful than that.

Slorn took a long breath. "The truth, swordsman, is that we didn't decide not to kill Nico out of kindness or respect to you or her. We *can't* kill her. It's my belief that she is no longer a demonseed inside a human host but a fully fledged demon in her own right. She is the very thing we have feared for so long, the thing the Demon of the Dead Mountain has been striving to create since his imprisonment began. And with this demon as with the other, none of us, not the Shapers nor the Teacher nor the League nor the Shepherdess herself, has the power to destroy her. Not without striking so hard we break the world in the process. The best we can hope for now is to contain her as we contained her father."

"So you're just going to keep her in that box forever?" Josef shouted. "Not a chance! I won't allow it."

"You don't get a choice," Slorn said. "This is larger than us now, Josef Liechten. The thing in that box isn't Nico anymore but a predator capable of devouring everything we call reality. It is by pure good fortune that we had a vessel capable of containing her ready before that happened. Letting her out is simply not possible. We're lucky we got her *in*."

"She's not a monster!" Josef roared, grabbing Slorn by his collar. "And she's still in there. Nico doesn't lose to anything!"

Slorn didn't answer, nor did he pull out of Josef's grasp. He simply stood there, brown bear eyes staring into Josef's until, at last, the swordsman let go. "I'm not giving up," Josef said, sitting down on the white stone beside the chain-swaddled box.

Eli, Slorn, and the Guildmaster exchanged a look and

stepped back, moving quietly to the far end of the white room, giving Josef his space.

"I want to say he'll come around," Eli said, scrubbing his hands through his hair in frustration. "But I don't think he will. I don't know that *I* will. After everything she's been through, all the fights she won, I can't believe Nico's lost now."

"I don't know what her future holds," Slorn said. "Something like this has never happened before. But I do know we cannot afford to take chances, not with things as bad as they are."

"There at least we agree," Eli said. "All this aside, though, I'm very glad you appeared, Slorn. I have some news I need to tell someone, and I think you're the best choice by far, but first"—Eli folded his arms and gave the Shaper a piercing look—"how did you get the ability to cut the veil? Did the Lord of Storms finally convince you to join his club, or does everyone get those now? Because I swear I saw a Spiritualist use one just before everything went south."

"I don't know about the Spiritualists," Slorn said. "But to answer your question, no, I'm not in service of the Shepherdess, League or otherwise. Other than the ability to move through the veil, I am the same as I was last we met. That power was granted me only recently by the Master of the Veil himself in order to make the bitter work we're about to embark on a little easier."

"Wait," Eli said, holding up his hands. "Wait, wait, wait. What work? And Master of the Veil? I know I've been out of the loop for a while, but what are you talking about? Who's the Master of the Veil?"

I am.

Eli jumped a foot in the air. The voice rang through his head just like the Shepherdess's, but where hers was a woman's cold soprano, this was a steady tenor. Beside him, Slorn and the old Guildmaster were lowering their heads in reverence. Eli followed their eyes and found himself face to face with an old man.

817

He was as tall as Josef, but frail with age, his limbs thin and bony. Even so, his shoulders were straight, his hands steady, and his white skin was as luminous and unblemished as Benehime's. His hair was white, too, as was his beard. They covered him from head to toe just as Benehime's hair covered her body when she wished it covered. But even without all this, Eli would have known what he was. There was nothing else in the world with those white eyes, the irises outlined in a faint shadow of silver. The man was one of the brothers Benehime had spoken of. Another Power of creation, but which one?

I am the Weaver, the old man said, answering the question before Eli spoke it. *I am responsible for the world's shell and the veil that hides it from the spirits within, who are the Shepherdess's domain. And you would be my sister's favorite, are you not?*

"Former favorite," Eli said. "But why are you here?"

It is true I have no place within the sphere, the Weaver said. *But I've always held a special fondness for Durain's children, especially his human ones. I consider it vital to my purpose to remember whom my weaving protects, so I have maintained a closeness with the great mountain over the years. Even had I not, though, I would have come now.*

"Because Benehime is calling back the stars," Eli said.

The Weaver's bright face darkened as his fine brows fell into a scowl. *Sadly, that is but the final stroke of her betrayal. The Shepherdess has been negligent in her duties for many years, but after she allowed the Daughter of the Dead Mountain a near total awakening, I knew I could no longer stand aside.*

Eli swallowed. The Weaver was talking about that business up at Izo's. "Well, if you're here to try and talk the Shepherdess into doing her job, I've got some bad news for you. Just before we got here, she took me back to her white place."

The Between, the Weaver corrected.

"Whatever," Eli said with a wave of his hand. "Anyway,

the floating sphere she's always looking at, that's our world, isn't it?"

It is, the Weaver said.

"Well, she's made another one," Eli said. "A smaller sphere filled with the stars she's been yanking up."

The Weaver frowned. *Why would she do that?*

"Because she's going to join them," Eli said. "She told me she was tired of being Shepherdess and that she was quitting to go live in this new paradise she's made."

"Quitting?" Slorn said, horrified. "You don't just *quit* being one of the three Powers of Creation."

"That's what I said," Eli replied. "But she's completely serious. That was why she snatched me up. She wanted me to go to paradise with her."

"But you're still here," Slorn said.

"Of course," Eli said. "Living with Benehime forever in a world full of spirits who worship at her feet? That's not paradise. That's torture."

The Weaver chuckled. *I suppose that explains the "former" part of your status as favorite.*

"She was the one who decided I was her favorite," Eli said, crossing his arms. "I got away from that as soon as I could."

The Weaver's chuckle grew into a full laugh. *I was prepared to hate you, thief. I blamed you for my sister's distraction, but now I think I have gained a greater understanding. As for the news she means to leave this world for another of her own making, we already suspected she had a plan of that sort.*

Eli blinked. "You did?"

"There was nothing else she could be doing with the stars," Slorn said. "And you don't ruin one world without having somewhere else you're planning to go."

"Well, if you know that, why are you still here?" Eli snapped. "She's got just about every star now."

All but one, the Weaver said, his white eyes drifting up. *Durain, Teacher of the Shapers, Lord of all Mountains. He is her oldest star, and the last to answer her call. He's been resisting her pull for days now to buy us time.*

"Buy time for what?" Eli said.

For my brother to arrive.

The Weaver said this with such reluctance that Eli realized he'd been thinking about this all wrong. "Wait," he said. "You're not just going to go lecture her, are you?"

No, the Weaver answered, his eyes sad. *My sister has chosen to abandon the world our father left her in charge of. That is a path that cannot be ignored or forgiven. I would stop her myself if I could, but I cannot. The Creator in his wisdom made his children to live in peace, and to that end, he made us equals. My power is as great as the Shepherdess's and not a hair greater. Any struggle between us would end in stalemate and likely destroy that which we were created to protect in the process.*

"But you're not alone," Eli said. "There are many spirits, powerful spirits, who would be more than willing to rise against the Shepherdess."

That may be, the Weaver said. *And that would be useful were the Shepherdess's realm any other than what it is. But the Shepherdess commands the sphere and the spirits it contains. No soul in this world can raise a hand to harm her, no matter how justified. Even if I had every spirit behind me, they could not act against their Lady.*

"So what are you going to do, then?" Eli asked. Because this was all starting to look pretty hopeless.

I told you, the Weaver said. *We are waiting for my brother, the Hunter. The Shepherdess rules over the spirits who live within the sphere. I, the Weaver, maintain the boundaries, constantly rebuilding the world's shell as it is torn down. The Hunter lives outside the world, defending the shell from those who would break it.*

"Outside the world?" Eli said, his voice trembling.

The Weaver sighed. *You would call it the other side of the sky. This world, all that you know, is but the last, tiny outpost of what was once a vast creation. The shell is the boundary between this world and what lies beyond, a wall against the dark created for your protection, you and all spirits. The Hunter is the one who protects the wall.*

Eli was starting to feel wobbly. "So," he said, "if the Hunter's job is to protect, what's he protecting against? What does the Hunter hunt?"

Such things are not to be discussed and have no bearing on our current predicament, the Weaver said coldly. *The important thing is that the Hunter is returning to our world very soon. His rests are sacred and seldom, but this situation is serious enough to warrant interrupting him. I've already woven a message into the sphere itself for him to come to me as soon as he is inside. When that happens, we shall be two against one, and the Shepherdess will be completely overpowered.*

"And what happens after?" Eli said, staring at the Weaver with growing horror. He hated Benehime, hated her for everything she had done, but he couldn't think of her being killed.

"That's what I was for," Slorn said, his voice low and growling. "I was sentenced to life imprisonment for disobeying the mountain and fleeing with my wife after she became a demonseed. The Teacher offered to rescind that punishment if I helped the Weaver construct a prison capable of holding the Shepherdess."

"Prison?" Eli said, astonished. "You're going to put her in prison?"

We must, the Weaver said. *We are Powers, created from the body of the Creator himself. Even if I wanted to kill my sister, I could not. We can restrain her, overpower her, but nothing in creation can kill a Power.*

"So, what, you're going to lock her up for a few thousand years and see if she won't come around?" Eli said. "What are you even going to put her in?"

The Weaver's eyes fell to the bone metal box, and Eli stiffened. "Ah," he said. "I see."

"I am the only thing in this world that can Shape bone metal," Slorn said. "The Weaver cannot change spirits, so the lot fell to me."

The substance you call bone metal is not actually metal at all, the Weaver said. *At the beginning of this world, as the Creator fought to make the sphere, his hand was torn off. It fell to the ground. His bones are all that is left, and just like the Powers or the black cores of the demons, they cannot be destroyed. This bone is the only substance that the Shepherdess cannot shatter.*

"Hold on," Eli said. "If Slorn can Shape it, why can't Benehime?"

Slorn looked at his hands. "All wizardry comes from the Shepherdess, even Shaping. But to Shape bone metal requires more than will and power. It requires sympathy. Sympathy, and a deep understanding of the spirit's true nature. That's why it is the perfect prison for the Shepherdess. If she was capable of the kind of sympathy needed to bend bone metal, we wouldn't need a prison in the first place."

Eli glanced at the bone metal coffin with an enormous sigh. "That's all well and good," he said. "But aren't you overlooking the part where your box is a little occupied at the moment? Unless you have a second one hidden away somewhere, we're in a tight spot."

Slorn shook his head. "It took all the bone metal known in the world to make that one."

Eli cursed under his breath. He didn't like where this was going.

This is why we told you the truth, Eli Monpress, the Weaver said gently. *You now understand the desperation of what we are about to attempt and how vital it is that we succeed. It was a lucky stroke that we had the box ready when your demon was born, but we cannot keep her there. Once my brother and I overpower our sister, we will have to move the demon to a new cell.*

Eli brightened. "You have a new cell?"

Slorn and Weaver frowned in unison. *We have a vessel that will suffice*, the Weaver said. *But you must understand. When the first demon was discovered within the shell, it took all three Powers to seal it away with the Shepherdess taking the lead. This time, however, our sister will almost certainly not help. As such, down a third of our power, it will be a very delicate operation. There will be absolutely no room for outside forces, especially those who would seek to aid the demon.*

At that, the Weaver's eyes moved pointedly to Josef.

"You must control your swordsman when the time comes, Monpress," Slorn said, laying a large, heavy hand on Eli's shoulder. "Nico must be bound, but with only two Powers to seal the prison, one swing from the Heart would be enough to tip the balance. I wish we could give him more time to come to terms with his loss, but the Hunter is coming very soon. We must move now."

The timing is both fortunate and unfortunate, the Weaver said. *The Hunter is allowed to leave his duties for only one hour of rest every hundred years. That hour falls today. Had Benehime decided to turn traitor at any other point, we couldn't have dealt with it. But my sister and the Hunter were always the closest of us three. I can only guess she still loves her brother enough that she could not abandon him without saying good-bye. That sentimentality may be the only thing that saves us.*

That explanation didn't sit well with Eli, but the Weaver didn't give him a chance to comment. The Power leaned forward, his white presence overwhelming Eli.

That is why we must move now, he said, his deep voice thrumming in the air. *If we miss this chance, the timing won't line up again for another hundred years, and the Shepherdess will be free to make her escape. Even if we could somehow get her back, the world cannot live so long without its Shepherdess or the stars she's taken with her.*

"The demon has already pushed our timetable to its limits," Slorn said. "Once the Hunter enters the sphere, we'll have one

823

hour to work. We must move the girl the moment he arrives so the box will be empty in time for the Shepherdess's imprisonment."

"I understand that," Eli said. "But—"

Your swordsman is now a true master of the sword he carries, the Weaver said right over him. *The Heart of War is very particular about its loyalties. An outburst from them could ruin everything. You* must *restrain your swordsman when the time comes.*

"Why are you so worried about me going crazy?"

Everyone jumped, even the Weaver. Across the room, Josef was sitting beside the coffin, glaring daggers at them. "I have pretty good ears, you know."

So it seems, the Weaver said.

Josef stood up, settling the Heart on his back as he walked with a dangerous grace that made even Eli uncomfortable. When he reached them, he crossed his arms, glaring at each of the men in turn. "How bad is it going to be?"

The Weaver answered truthfully. *If you care about the demon at all, it will be unbearable. She will fight tooth and nail every step of the way, and we will have to crush her. If she is anything like her master, it will be very painful indeed.*

"Nico has no master but herself," Josef snapped. "She'll take any prison you put her in and come out on top, just like always."

"She won't be coming out of this one," Slorn said, his voice gentle and sad. "This isn't a holding cell like Nivel lived in. Nico will be bound as the first demon was, crushed beneath the Weaver's seal as well as the Hunter's, and she will never rise again."

Josef hissed, backing away, but Eli raised his hand. "Wait," he said. "The first demon was bound under the corpse of the greatest mountain in the world whose soul went on to become the Heart of War. With all the stars gone, do you even have a spirit large enough to do that sort of thing?"

Slorn and the Weaver looked helplessly at each other.

Behind them, the Shaper Guildmaster lowered his head in pain. When the silence had stretched on long enough, Eli scowled and opened his mouth to ask again, but before he could get the words out, a great rumble cut him off.

"There is one."

Eli shrank back in surprise. The deep, rumbling voice came from everywhere, echoing off the walls and vibrating through the stone under his feet.

"I will be the prison," the Shaper Mountain said, his words as proud and solid as the stone they came from. "I have lived a half-life in this twilight world long enough. It is my honor to give my body to save those spirits whose stars have abandoned them for the Shepherdess's paradise."

The Guildmaster of the Shapers bit back a sob as the mountain spoke. Slorn's head was bowed as well, his eyes hidden behind his hand. Even the Weaver looked stricken, but it wasn't any of them who spoke next. The Shaper Mountain's rumbling words had barely faded when another voice filled the room. It was a voice Eli had heard only once before, but had never forgotten. You did not forget the iron fury of the Heart of War.

"No, brother!" the sword shouted. It fell from Josef's back, landing on the white floor with a deafening crash. "I gave my stone so that you could live. Would you throw my sacrifice away?"

"We always knew it would come to this, brother," the Shaper Mountain answered, its deep vibrations resigned.

"This is different!" the sword roared. "The Shepherdess will not be here to save your essence as she saved mine. You were always the Teacher, the one who did good for the world, the one who spoke the truth. You are the one who must go on. I will not allow you to do this. I will not let you die."

"This is what must be done," the Shaper Mountain said. "And you cannot stop it. The favorite and my children will restrain your swordsman, and he will restrain you. We are all bound by the inevitable, my brother. Fate has dealt us two horrors that must be contained and only one prison. As a spirit and a star, I cannot hold the Shepherdess, but I can hold the demon just as you did. This is my choice to make, and I will make it no matter how much you rage. This isn't a battle you can win."

The Heart of War shook against the stone, and then, in a voice so low Eli felt the words more than he heard them, it said, "Take my hilt, Josef Liechten. We cannot allow this to happen."

Eli almost laughed then. Was the sword so angry it had forgotten Josef was spirit deaf? But the laughter died in his throat as Josef's arm shot out, his hand wrapping around the Heart's leather-bound hilt.

"There we agree," the swordsman said. "I'm through listening to this nonsense. Nico will be leaving that box, but she's not going under any mountain. She's coming with me, and we will stop anyone who says otherwise."

The Heart of War hummed in agreement, its hilt fitting into Josef's palm as though it had grown there.

Eli slapped his hand over his face. Even his imagination couldn't come up with a way this situation could possibly get worse. But as he was searching frantically for the magical combination of flattery and reason that might be enough to calm Josef down, the Weaver and Slorn stepped into line in front of him.

We must restrain them quickly, the Weaver said. *The Hunter arrives any minute.*

"I'm not joking around," Josef said, taking up position in front of Nico's coffin, the Heart steady in his hands. "Stand down before you get hurt, Eli."

"You must stand with us, Monpress," Slorn whispered. "We cannot risk the whole world on a mountain's love for his brother and a swordsman's love for a demonseed."

Eli didn't move.

Favorite? the Weaver said, staring at him with those white eyes. *We have no time. Are you with us?*

826

Eli's eyes flicked from Slorn to the Weaver to Josef and back again.

"Eli," Josef growled. "Step back."

At the warning, Slorn grabbed Eli's shoulder. The gentle weight of the large Shaper's fingers drove the knife of conflicting loyalties deeper. For one long breath, Eli hung motionless, and then, legs shaking, he stepped out into the open space between them and Josef.

The Weaver's hiss was as sharp as a knife behind him, but Eli ignored it and stepped forward again. Step by step, he crossed the smooth white stone of the Shaper Mountain's heart until he was standing directly in front of Josef's blade.

"I've bet it all on Nico three times now," he said quietly, tilting his head back so he could look Josef in the eyes. "I'm willing to bet it all again if you're in with me."

He reached out his hand, fingers trembling slightly in the white light. Josef didn't even hesitate. His hand shot forward, clasping Eli's painfully hard. "Always have been," he said, his face breaking into a wide grin.

Eli grinned back and moved to stand at Josef's side. On the other side of the room, Slorn buried his bear head in his hands. The Weaver sighed, and the Guildmaster, who had spoken not a word all through this, broke into a righteous sneer. Eli ignored them all, tilting his head toward Josef.

"Stand your ground, thief," the swordsman said. "It's going to be a rough few minutes."

Eli nodded, but as he moved to brace himself, the floor of the Shaper Mountain bucked beneath him, tossing him and Josef off their feet.

Benehime stood motionless at the end of her white world, waiting. In front of her, the clawed hands were scraping, their sharp nails raising long trails on the barrier that marked the edge of her domain. As she watched, the clawing grew faster and more frantic until the curved inside of the shell looked like it was boiling. Just when it seemed like the barrier would burst, a black line fell through the turmoil and the shell split.

All at once, a sucking wind roared up around her, nearly taking her off her feet. The air of her white Between was pouring out through the hole in her wall, vanishing into cold, black, deep, lifeless beyond. As it left, the clawed hands beyond shot out, scrabbling for a touch of the wind's soul, and as they reached, a horrible sound rose in the dark.

It was a scream. An enormous, keening wail layered over and over as though a million throats were splitting themselves raw to make it. There was rage in it, fury and anger and a hunger so deep it made her ache. The terror hit her next, and it took every ounce of Benehime's will to stay standing before the sundered wall. But stand she did, holding her ground as a white figure strode out of the dark.

His body was like hers, but larger, pale, and looming as he stepped through the hole in the shell. His white hands carried a white sword, its blade gently curved, like the Lord of Storms'.

That was no accident. She'd shaped the Lord of Storms in the imitation of the man walking toward her. Behind him, she could see the shadow hands grasping, thin as bone, their claws so black they ate the light. The mere sight of them filled her with dread, and she said a prayer to her father as the black hole closed, hiding them from view.

The sucking wind vanished, and Benehime gave herself a moment to drink in the relief before pushing it aside and returning to her purpose. She turned to the man, and her face filled with love as she held out her arms. *Welcome home, brother.*

The Hunter stepped into her embrace. *Sister,* he whispered.

She winced at his voice. It was always so deep, so weary.

I cannot stay, he said, hugging her gently. *The Weaver requests my presence on some pressing matter.*

The Shepherdess ignored the claim and pressed her brother down onto the white seat she had summoned. *Let him wait a moment,* she said. *You must rest.*

The Hunter did not fight her. He all but collapsed into the chair, his sword falling to the floor beside him. Coming from the dark he'd seemed white as alabaster, but here, against the true white of her world, her brother looked dirty. His whiteness, once a twin of her own, was marred with black scars. They blasted his skin and the fine armor of his hair that wrapped across his torso, shoulders, and down his legs. He was the youngest of them all, but sitting there with his head in his hands, his shoulders slumped, he looked older than the Weaver.

Brother, she whispered.

It never gets better, the Hunter said softly. *They never die, Benehime. No matter how many I strike down, they never die. They've eaten nothing since Father created the shell. They have nothing out there, no food, no light. They were supposed to have starved off long ago, but the hunger only seems to make them stronger.*

His scarred hands went to his face, hiding his ruined features. *I don't know how much longer we can hold out. After five thousand years, I think we can all admit that the Creator is never coming back. We are alone and growing weaker while our enemies endure and strengthen. I see no future, sister. Nothing but slow and crippling death.*

Benehime stroked the hard shell of his hair where it wrapped around his shoulders. *Shh, brother, you don't have to fight. Rest now.*

I do, he said. *I will fight until I am destroyed. So I was made, just as you were made to love the spirits. I could no more stop fighting than you could stop loving, but I'm so tired, sister.*

Relax your hair for me, Benehime whispered, stroking his shoulders. *Let me ease you.*

The hard shell of his hair relaxed at once, the blackened strands going soft as water under her fingers. Gently, she pushed them aside to reveal the still perfect white skin of his back. *There, there*, she said softly, running her fingers across his hard muscles until they began to unclench. *Rest.*

829

The Hunter relaxed under her touch, his head lolling forward. *How many of these reprieves have I taken?* he said. *One hour out of every hundred years. That's all I dare take, but I wish I could see you both more. Seeing my siblings reminds me why I fight. I forget, sometimes, alone out there in the dark.*

You honor us with your strength, Benehime said, lifting one hand from his back. *Father was cruel to give you the most difficult job. We have relied on you too long, borne this endless waiting too long. It is only right that we be tired, you most of all.*

How you ease me, the Hunter said, his scarred face breaking into a smile. The expression made Benehime's heart clench. How beautiful he'd been once, as beautiful as herself. But that beauty was gone now, and the unfairness of the loss, the endless, pointless nature of their existence galvanized her resolve. Slowly, quietly, her hand slipped down to the folds of her hair at the small of her back.

I must go, the Hunter said, moving to stand. *My hour is short, and I must see what our brother wants.*

Not yet, Benehime said, gently pushing him down again. *He can wait one more minute.*

The Hunter hesitated, then relaxed again under her stroking hand. Benehime smiled, bringing the long, wicked black length of the Daughter of the Dead Mountain's seed from the shelter of her hair.

Be at peace, brother, she whispered, brushing one hand across his back as she raised the other high over her head, the seed grasped like a dagger in her fist.

The Hunter nodded and dropped his head, that sad smile still playing over his face, reminding her of all they had lost. She stared at it for one last moment, memorizing the curve of his mouth, the strong line of his brow. When she could picture every bit of him in her mind, she brushed a final kiss against the back of his neck before bringing her other hand up to join the first. Gripping the seed in both fists, she threw back her arms and stabbed the sharp point into the Hunter's exposed back with all her strength.

The Hunter's scream filled her white world, striking her spheres, large and small, with a blast that made the seas slosh and the bedrock tremble. One moment, that was all it lasted, but in that moment the world changed, and everything, from the greatest mountain to the smallest blade of grass, knew it.

CHAPTER
19

Eli fell as the Shaper Mountain pitched under his feet. He would have landed on his face had Josef not grabbed him at the last second. Eli grumbled his thanks as the swordsman set him back on his feet, but the return was short-lived. The mountain was bucking like a bull beneath them, forcing Eli to his hands and knees to avoid getting thrown again.

He shifted his weight with the stone, cursing his own stupidity. Of *course* the Shaper Mountain would join the fight. It was the Heart of War's brother. But as he looked to see what Slorn and Weaver's attack would be, he saw something that confused him utterly.

Slorn, his father, and the Weaver were all on the ground the same as he was, and all three of them were staring up at the white ceiling as though the mountain had gone mad. It would have been comical if their faces hadn't been so terrified. Eli had no clue what was going on, but whatever it was, they hadn't expected it, either. He frowned. Surprises were rarely good in this sort of situation, but before he could figure out how to turn this to his favor, a scream shot through him with the force of a battering ram.

Josef couldn't catch him this time. Eli tumbled forward,

his whole body tightening as the sound punched through him. He was dimly aware of Josef going down beside him, the Heart falling with an iron cry. The Shaper Mountain was wailing as well, a deep vibration that shook through the undulating stone, but all Eli could hear was the unknown man's scream.

The voice was deeper than any Eli had heard before and filled with shock. Shock, pain, and a betrayal so deep it brought tears to Eli's eyes. But that was only the beginning. The scream cut off seconds after it had begun, and as it vanished, the hole it left was filled with a loss deeper than Eli had realized he could feel, and he *knew*, knew in his bones that something vital had died.

No, his breathing hitched, not died. It had been killed. A pillar of the world he never knew existed had been knocked down, and they were all about to go tumbling after it.

Eli was powerless against such a death. He clung to the bucking ground, letting the loss and the anger flow through him. He could have stayed that way forever, but a flash of white caught his eye. He looked up instinctively to see the Weaver standing between the crippled forms of Slorn and the Guildmaster. The Power stood straight and tall despite the mountain's shaking, but his white face was contorted with despair even more powerful than the wave Eli was trapped in. Despair, and a fierce, white-hot rage.

The old man thrust out his hand, and the air tore itself apart. A great rent opened in the world as the veil split before its master. The gateway hung as white as snow at noon in the air, but the Weaver did not step through.

He started to, but stopped right at the portal's edge. For a moment he just stood there, his white hands pressed against the hole in the world, and then the air itself began to vibrate as the Weaver crashed his fists against the white wall of the portal, his fury a crushing weight on top of the loss that had already sent the world to its knees.

Brother! he cried. *What has she done to you?*

Slowly, crawling on his hands and knees, Eli pulled himself across the still-moving floor to the Weaver. When he reached the Power's bare feet, he flopped over and stared up in amazement. The enormous hole in the veil hung above him, dazzling and solid white. The Weaver's hands were flush against it, beating against the brilliant light like a wall. Eli blinked in confusion. That was not supposed to happen. Then again, he was fairly sure none of this was supposed to happen.

"Why does the veil not open?"

It was Slorn's deep voice that spoke. Eli turned to see the bear-headed Shaper pushing himself up as well. "What has happened, Weaver?"

My brother is dead, the Weaver said, his voice breaking as he pressed his white forehead against the glowing wall. *The Hunter has been killed, and it seems Benehime has taken his seed for herself.*

The Weaver closed his eyes in pain. *I am now the odd man out*, he said gravely. *My sister controls the power of the Shepherdess as well as what remains of the Hunter, and she has locked the Between against me.*

He lifted his head from the solid wall of light and looked over his shoulder. *If it were just her, I could still break through. The veil is my domain, the product of my own hands. But she has the remnants of our brother's power now as well as her own, leaving me outnumbered, though I suppose it matters little now.*

Eli gawked at the old Power. "Matters little?" he cried. "She just killed your brother!"

That she did, the Weaver said, sinking down to the stone floor. *The Hunter is dead and we are unguarded. Don't you see, human? All is lost. Even if she had not locked the Between against me, I can't weave the shell faster than our enemies rip it down. Without the Hunter's protection, the wall will fall.* His voice crumbled into a sob as he lowered his head into his hands. *Oh, Benehime...*

No one said a word. The Power's weeping echoed through

the now-still mountain, the only sound in the world. It was Slorn who finally broke the silence, his gruff voice hard and echoing. "How soon?"

An hour, the Weaver whispered. *Maybe less.*

"Wait," Eli said. The agony of the Hunter's loss was fading now, and he pushed himself to his feet. "What happens in an hour?"

When no one answered, Eli clenched his fists and raised his voice. "What is on the other side of the shell?"

The question echoed through the cavern. Eli let it hang, glaring at the Weaver until the old man sighed.

Our shadows, he said. *Before the beginning of time, the Creator formed creation. To every piece he gave a spirit so that the world might know itself as he knew it. But the moment he brought forth the world, a shadow was cast, and a second world was created. If creation is concave, they are convex; they are the opposite world. Where the Creator brought forth life from nothing, they return it to nothing. They are the devourers, the eaters of worlds.* His white eyes narrowed. *My sister named them demons.*

Eli blew out a breath. "You mean there are more of the thing under the Dead Mountain out there? More like Nico?"

The Weaver looked away, but just as Eli stepped forward to demand an answer, the ground shook under his feet. "Innumerably more," the Shaper Mountain said.

Durain, the Weaver said, his voice harsh.

"What point is there in secrecy now?" the mountain rumbled. "Weaker spirits may take comfort in their ability to forget and sleep, but I never will. Anyway, he'll see it for himself in a few minutes."

The Weaver sighed, but the mountain turned its attention to Eli. "Listen, thief, if you would know the truth. My brother and I were created at the birthing of the world, wrought by the Creator's own hands, two small bumps in the spine of a world so large you could not begin to comprehend it. Back then, there were no humans, all spirits were awake, the large cared for the

834

small, and we held our own against the devourers, the demons. The Creator walked the land, creating the world even as it was eaten. There were seasons, then. Time moved forward and stars shone in the sky. We were part of the world, all of us, the spirits and those who preyed on us. For thousands of years we lived in balance, if not harmony, but then something changed."

The mountain wavered and fell silent. It was his brother who continued the story, the Heart of War's deep, iron voice filling the cavern.

"The demons began to overrun us," the sword said. "Small losses at first, but it grew quickly out of control. Creation was being devoured faster than it could be made. If something hadn't been done, the world would have been eaten entirely."

"Out of love of his creation, the Creator devised a last, desperate gambit," the Shaper Mountain said, picking up the story again. "He created a shell around what was left of the world he'd made, a wall that could keep the demons out. But nothing created can stand against uncreation forever, so he took three pieces of his own body and fashioned them into the three Powers. Each was given a portion of the Creator's own power and a job. The Hunter guards the shell from the outside, cutting the demons from the walls. The Weaver weaves the shell, repairing the damage caused by those blows that slip by his brother. It takes both the Hunter's protection and the Weaver's repairs to keep the shell that shields the world from cracking, but it was the third child who held the Creator's most treasured power."

Our sister was fashioned from our father's heart, the Weaver said, his voice trembling. *The Creator loved his creation above all else. He created the Shepherdess to watch over the spirits when he could not. She was made to love the world and guide it in his stead.*

"Three Powers and a shell," the Shaper Mountain rumbled. "This is what the Creator gave us, and then he closed the circle, locking himself outside. As he left, he promised he would return and let us out when it was safe."

"And will he?" Eli said.

No, the Weaver whispered. *That promise was made thousands of years ago. Our father sacrificed everything to lock the demons outside, away from his creation. He thought, as we all did, that the demons would die off if we deprived them of food. Starve them off, that was our plan, but it did not work. The demons do not die. I think they cannot. All our efforts have managed is to starve them to madness.* He raised his head, staring up through the mountain and, Eli wagered, through the sky beyond, glaring with pure hatred at the things waiting on the other side.

There is no food left for them save what lives in this sphere, he said. *This last crumb of the world. They no longer think of anything save eating, but they shall get their meal soon enough. Even if I were able to get to the Between right now and resume my weaving, without the Hunter's aid I could only hold the shell together for a day, maybe less. However long I held, though, the eventual end would be the same. The shell will weaken and crack and the demons will pour in to devour all that remains of the world.*

The Power's words hung in the air like sad music, low and tremulous, and the defeat in them made Eli clench his jaw in fury. "So you're telling me we're as good as dead?" he shouted. "I don't believe it! How did the Shepherdess even kill the Hunter, anyway? I thought you Powers were supposed to be equal."

We are, the Weaver said. *I don't know how she did it. We all heard his scream, so the Hunter must have been inside the shell when he died. Nothing inside the shell should be able to kill a Power, even another Power. But the* how *changes nothing. The Hunter is still dead.*

"On the contrary," Eli said. "The *how* matters a great deal." He tore his eyes off the Weaver and began to pace. "When the Creator first closed the shell, one demon snuck in, didn't it? That's why we have the Dead Mountain."

The Weaver nodded. *We contained it as best we could, but—*

"I know the rest," Eli said, walking faster. He knew he was being rude, but if there really was only an hour left until the shell began to crack, he didn't have time to be nice. "Josef?"

From his spot beside Nico's box, the swordsman glanced up. "If you're going to ask me something, you should know I've heard only about half of the nonsense conversation you've been having."

"Doesn't matter," Eli said. "Tell me, when the Lord of Storms took Nico's seed, did you see it?"

Josef nodded. "It was long and black, about the length of my short sword's blade. Sharp, too." His eyes narrowed. "Why do you want to know?"

Eli ignored the question and turned back to the Weaver. "You said nothing in creation could kill a Power. But demons aren't creation; that was the whole point of your story. The seed inside Nico is part of the demon under the Dead Mountain. Tell me, would a piece of a demon this long be enough to kill the Hunter if he didn't see it coming?" He spaced his hands at the size Josef had said and held them out to the Weaver.

The old man's white eyes went very wide, and he began to tremble. *It would*, he whispered. *Oh, Benehime. Oh, sister, how could you?*

Eli shook his head. "You said earlier that it was our good luck Benehime decided to do all this when the Hunter was coming, but I don't think it was *our* luck at all. It was hers, her plan." Eli dropped his hands and began to pace faster than ever. "You've known Benehime a long time, but I think I know her better than you do these days. Your sister's a schemer. That's why we got along so well at the beginning, I think. She doesn't do anything without an end in mind."

Eli took a deep breath. This next bit was going to be hard. Not talking about his tangled relationship with Benehime was deeply ingrained, but what went for the Weaver went for him as well. The time for careful stepping was over. It was now or never. Eli winced. He'd never used that phrase quite so literally.

"Ever since I found out what Nico was, I've been struggling with the question of *why*," Eli said. "Why did Benehime let her stay with us? With me? I learned early that the Shepherdess did not take unmeasured risks, and Nico was a liability from the moment Josef found her. So why did Benehime tolerate it? Why did she forbid the Lord of Storms from taking down a demon who was such an obvious threat? She always said it was because of me, but Nico and I have been separated several times since we started working together. There were ample opportunities for the League to take her down with no threat to me. Yet when the Lord of Storms tried to do just that, he was punished severely. So, why? Why did the Lady leave her alone until just now?"

"Because you're no longer the favorite," Slorn said.

"I don't think that's it," Eli said. "For once, I don't think this had anything to do with me." He turned and stared at the bone metal box. "I was a handy excuse, a cover. She knew Nico was strong. Strong enough to pull herself back from the brink over and over, strong enough to grow the weapon she needed. All she needed was time."

The room was silent. Everyone, even the Weaver, was gaping at him openly.

You're saying she grew the demonseed for the purpose of killing her brother? the Weaver whispered. *That she defended the seed from her own guards?*

"I'm actually beginning to wonder if it's just coincidence Josef happened to be on the mountain when Nico fell," Eli said. "We can't know for sure how far her plans went, but I know Benehime well enough to guess that she's probably been working on this for years, setting up the pieces in preparation for this day. This was a premeditated murder. She's wanted out of her job as Shepherdess for a long time, but she knew she could never run away while her brothers were both alive. So she created the one set of circumstances that allowed her to circumvent the Creator's will. She grew a demon and killed the Hunter with its seed, and then she sealed the Between to prevent you from interfering while she escapes into her

838

paradise and leaves the rest of us to be demon food." The plan was so selfish, so like her, that Eli could almost hear Benehime's voice explaining it along with him. "I wouldn't be surprised if she were already gone."

No, the Weaver whispered. *Even through the seal, I can feel her presence. She's still here, but why? What more can she be waiting for?*

"Her paradise isn't complete," Slorn said, looking up at the stone ceiling. "She doesn't have Durain yet."

"No," the mountain rumbled. "Her pull on me vanished when the Hunter died. If she is waiting, it's not for me, but I can guess whom she would hold back for."

Eli sucked in a breath, eyes squeezing closed. Of course. How could he ever think she'd actually drop his leash?

"She won't give you up until the very end," the Shaper Mountain said. "You are the tie that will hold her here until the shell shatters, and as such you may well be the only hope we have of reclaiming the Hunter's seed."

Eli blinked, startled out of his self-pity. "Seed?"

The piece of the Creator inside us, the Weaver said.

"You mean like a demonseed?" Eli said.

I told you, they are our shadows, the Weaver said testily. *But where their seeds devour, ours nurture and sustain us. My brother is dead, but the core of the Creator that gave him life can never be destroyed. That is how Benehime is able to hold a part of the Hunter's power even when the Hunter is no more. She has his seed.*

Eli licked his lips. "And could that seed be used to create a new Hunter?"

The Weaver considered. *It's never been tried before, but I don't see why not. Provided the correct soul was found.*

Eli grinned and clapped his hands together, making everyone jump. "All right," he said. "I think I've got a plan."

"I've learned to fear those words from you," Slorn grumbled.

Eli shrugged. "You want to stand around here and wait to die?"

Slorn shook his head and motioned for Eli to continue.

Eli took the cue with a flourish and gathered everyone around, including Josef and the Heart of War. Especially them. Those two were vital to his plan, but while Eli was reasonably sure the Heart would go along, Josef was another story. He made a mental note to play up the heroic warrior parts and straightened up to speak. But just as he opened his mouth to expound what he was sure would go down in history as the idea that saved the world (or the idea that doomed the world, but no one would be around to call him on it if that was the case), a white line flashed into existence right in front of his face.

Miranda forced herself off the floor of the Rector's office. The heartbreaking loss was still pounding in her brain, but she couldn't afford to stay down any longer. Stumbling like a drunk, she made her way to the large windows behind Master Bana— *Her* desk and pressed her face to the thick glass. She already knew what she would see, she could feel it in her own spirits and from the window against her cheek, but she forced herself to look anyway.

Down below, all of Zarin seemed to be pulling in. The white buildings were leaning as though the stone itself had doubled over. The glittering strip of the river, still fragile after its breakdown the day before, was pulling back in its banks, its water swirling into whirlpools so large Miranda could see them even at this distance. Strangest of all, though, were the people.

Everywhere she looked, the citizens of Zarin were on the ground. Spirit deaf or wizard, they'd all felt it just as she had. She slumped against the window. Something vital had died; she knew that fact as clearly as she knew her own name, but what? What in the world could have done this?

"The Hunter." The Tower's voice was little more than a whisper, but Miranda could feel the strain in the gold collar at her neck and the ring on her finger.

"Easy," Miranda said, layering the word with power. "Who's the Hunter?"

Even with her calming weight pushing on it, the Tower's answer was almost hysterical. "Our protector. Our hope. Our wall. We are defenseless, and they are coming. *They are coming!*"

The Tower finished in a deafening wail, and then the floor under Miranda's feet began to buck.

Without hesitation, Miranda opened her spirit and slammed her will down. She slammed it through the Tower's ring, hammering their connection until she was panting from the effort. She could feel her own bound spirits cringing from her fury, but she dared not let up. The Tower was the great bedrock spirit beneath Zarin. If she let it lose control, the city could be destroyed.

The seconds ticked by as she kept up the pressure, sweat rolling down her face. She pushed until she felt she was going to throw up from the strain, but she never let her will slack. Slowly, inch by inch, she felt the Tower relax, and then finally surrender. She kept the pressure up a moment more before pulling back into herself.

"Thank you," the Tower rumbled, and his tone said he meant it.

"You're welcome," Miranda panted. "Now, who's coming?"

The Tower's voice began to tremble so badly that were it human Miranda would have said it was crying. "I can't say," it whispered. "The Lady forbids us old spirits to speak of it. She wishes it forgotten. Even now..." The Tower shuddered. "I cannot act against her edict. All I can say is that the Hunter was the wall that held back the black tide. Now he is fallen and they are coming. *They are coming.*"

"*Easy,*" Miranda said, pressing her spirit down again. It was a gentle, soothing pressure, not the hard slam she'd used earlier, but it worked. Miranda let out a grateful sigh. She didn't think she could manage something like that again.

"If you can't tell me, that's fine," she whispered, petting

the Tower's chain like it was a frightened puppy. "I'll find out another way. Can you at least tell me what's about to happen?"

She got the strangest feeling that the stone was staring at her as it whispered.

"The end."

Miranda shot up from the floor and marched to the door, tearing it open with a bang. Outside, Krigel was curled under his desk in a ball. She dropped to her knees beside him, shaking him by the shoulder.

"Krigel!"

The old Spiritualist looked up, his eyes glittering with terror and newly shed tears. "Rector," he whispered. "What happened?"

"I mean to find out," Miranda said, helping him to a seated position. "I need you to listen and tell me where the panics are."

Locations, she needed locations. Needed to know where to send her Spiritualists to get things under control again. But Krigel was just staring at her, his eyes wide and confounded as if she'd asked him to recite all the kingdoms of the Council in alphabetical order.

"Krigel, *please*," she said. "We have to move now or this is only going to get worse."

"Yes, but…" Krigel's voice trailed off as he stared at her in disbelief. "Can't you hear it?"

"No," Miranda said, fighting to keep her temper under control. "The Tower's presence in my mind muffles the spirit's panic. You *know* that."

The old man looked down, his face falling as he stared at his limp hands.

"Come on, Krigel," Miranda said, shaking him again, gently this time. "I need you. Tell me what we're dealing with."

"I thought you'd be able to hear it," he said. "Even muffled, I thought—"

"I can't," Miranda said. "The Tower does it to protect me. That's why you're so important. Close your eyes and listen. I

842

need to know where the panics are so we can send Spiritualists to calm things down. That's our mission now; that's why
we're here. We're going to serve the spirits and get them what
they need. Now, where are the panics?" She hoped there
weren't too many; she was getting frightfully shorthanded.

"Everywhere," Krigel said at last. "Everything is panicking.
Besides your voice, all I can hear are screams."

Miranda cursed and threw out her hand. The Tower answered
at once, opening a hole in the stone wall to the outside. The
blast of wind nearly blew them both over, but Miranda pulled
herself upright, grabbing the stone and looking out over Zarin.
She almost didn't need to. The second the wind hit her, she
heard it.

The air itself was screaming, the wind crying in terror as
it blew in mad circles. Down in the city, the buildings were
wrenching themselves apart, timbers splitting like matchsticks
as the stones below them rolled in fear. The river was flooding
madly now, filling the lower part of the city with crazed muddy
water. Even the Council's fortress was twisting. One of the
seven golden spires toppled as she watched, screaming as it
fell, and Miranda had to press her hands over her mouth to
keep from screaming herself.

The Tower was right; it *was* the end. Zarin was tearing itself
apart like Izo's town had, only there was no demon running
through its streets, and this was far, far larger. So large she
didn't know how to begin to fix it, assuming something like
this could ever be fixed. All at once, the searing sense of loss
hit her again, but this wasn't grief for the death of the unknown,
beautiful, irreplaceable thing that had struck her earlier. This
was a closer tragedy, a pain that ground her heart to dust.
Everywhere, in all directions, the spirits she'd given her life
to serving were in a mad panic and she could see no way of
making it right. The world was ripping itself to shreds right
before her eyes and there was *nothing she could do*.

The need to cry almost overwhelmed Miranda then. She
wanted nothing more than to throw herself on the floor beside

Krigel and let the bawling sobs ride through her. But even if this was the end of the world, she was Rector Spiritualis still, and she had work to do.

But just as she bent down to try and get Krigel to sit up so they could start regrouping, she felt a familiar prickle on the back of her neck. She froze halfway down, eyes darting to the twisting city below. No, she thought with a frown. It couldn't be.

That was her last thought before Etmon Banage's open spirit landed on Zarin.

His will fell like an iron weight, and wherever it landed, the panic stopped. The twisting spirits lay still, frozen beneath Banage's pressure as a deep, deep silence fell over the city.

For five breaths, Miranda stood dumbstruck, and then she clenched her fingers around her glowing rings. "Where is he?"

The Tower's answer was joyous and immediate. "Front promenade."

Miranda nodded. "Take me there."

The words were barely out of her mouth when the floor opened beneath her feet.

She fell like a stone, hurtling past the floors. The descent was over in seconds, the Tower slowing her gently before setting her down in the corner of the Court's enormous entry hall. Miranda was running the moment her feet touched the ground. The newly repaired red doors sprung open for her before she reached them, and she flew down the stairs into the wide promenade that led from the Tower to the city proper.

All around her, spirits were bowed under the pressure. Even the laurel trees that lined the Spirit Court district's broad streets were bent over like they were bearing up under a deep snow. Miranda saw none of it. Her eyes were fixed on the tall figure standing at the center of the empty road, his hands spread in front of him as though he were waiting to receive a heavy burden, his gray-streaked black hair falling limp around his tired face.

"Master Banage!"

The name flew from Miranda's throat as she charged into him, arms flying around his chest and squeezing him in a vise. He stumbled a little as she hit him, but the weight on the city didn't even flicker. Miranda wouldn't have noticed if it had. Her eyes were too blurry with tears to see anything other than her master.

"Where have you been?" she cried, burying her face in his shirt. She knew she was making an undignified scene, but she didn't care. Master Banage was smiling down at her with one of his rare, true smiles, and the sight of it was almost enough to dissolve her.

"I'm still a criminal," he said. "I thought it best that I stayed away, but now I'm sorry I didn't come sooner."

His voice was low and strained, no doubt from the effort of keeping so much pressure on the city. Miranda dropped her arms at once and stepped back guiltily. Powers, what was she doing? Master Banage was maintaining the largest open spirit she'd ever seen. He was pressing down an entire city; she'd never even heard of such a thing. She beamed up at him, remembering yet again why he was her Rector.

"Here," she said, reaching to take the golden mantle of the Tower off her shoulders. "This is yours."

His hand stopped her before she'd gotten it to her chin.

"No," he said, shaking his head. "I gave up being Rector. But the fact that you're wearing the Tower's chain proves I made the right gamble on the beach at Osera. The Tower and Court are yours by bound oath now. I cannot take them back."

Miranda stopped, stricken. "But you're the—"

"Not anymore," Banage said, looking out over the silent city. "But I am still a Spiritualist, and I mean to hold Zarin as long as I can."

"I can't let you do that alone," Miranda said. Calming the Tower had taken everything she had, and that was just one spirit. How long could Master Banage possibly expect to keep a whole city calm?

"It won't be as hard as you think," Banage said, smiling

again. "I'm not alone in my work. The Tower is here as well, and we don't need the mantle to work together. Do we, old friend?"

"No, indeed," the Tower said, its deep voice buzzing through the gold-wrought chain. "We will hold here."

"That we will," Banage said. Then he caught Miranda's eyes with his, and his look grew deathly serious. "You have greater work to do, Rector. This disaster is the sort of thing this Court was created for. Whatever this is, the spirits are powerless before it. We must stand for them, and you must stand for the Court."

"But what do I do?" Miranda cried.

Banage tilted his head. "What do you think you should do?"

Miranda bit her lip and looked down at her rings. They glittered back at her, each of them keeping strangely silent. She thought about what the Tower had said earlier. The end, he'd called it. Miranda didn't know about that, but whatever this was, it was something the Shepherdess had forbidden the spirits to speak of, something they feared above all else. Something was broken, that much was clear, but she had no idea what.

Miranda's hands curled into tightly balled fists. This worry was getting her nowhere. If she was going to do any good at all, she needed knowledge. She needed answers, real, straightforward ones, and she had a good idea where to get them. Of course, going there would likely get her killed, but if she did nothing she was pretty sure she'd end up dead all the same, along with everything else. In that light, the risk didn't look so bad.

"I'm going," she said, raising her head. "I'll be back as soon as I can."

"We'll hold as long as it takes," Banage said. "Keep the Tower's mantle close to you. He'll need your strength."

"I'll need no such thing," the Tower rumbled. "Go, little Rector. We will hold."

Miranda nodded and looked over her shoulder only to see Gin sitting right behind her.

She jumped in surprise. "How long have you been there?"

"Since about a second after you got here," the dog answered, showing his teeth. "Come on, Banage's spirit coming down on everything? Not hard to guess where you'd be." His orange eyes shifted to Banage. "Though your weight did slow me down, old man. I'd have beaten her otherwise."

"I'm sure you would have," Miranda said walking over to put a hand in his fur. "Ready to jump into the fire?"

"Always," Gin growled, his tail lashing back and forth.

Miranda nodded and closed her eyes, steeling her determination into an iron wall. When her mind was set in stone, she raised her hand and pictured her destination in her mind, lingering on the white stone and the soft, constant white light she still sometimes saw in her dreams. The cut appeared immediately, ripping down through the air. The moment it was clear, she stepped through the world into the Shaper Mountain, her demands ready on her lips...and ran into Eli Monpress.

Eli stumbled as Miranda slammed into him, almost falling over Josef in his rush to get back. She looked just as startled to see him as he was to see her. The Spiritualist scrambled back as soon as she realized whom she'd run into, only to get pushed forward again as Gin stepped through the white hole behind her.

Miranda caught herself at the last second, clinging to her ghosthound. Gin, to his credit, immediately fell into guard position, ears back and teeth bared as he growled at Eli and Josef. Through the hole in the veil, Eli caught sight of his father's tense face looking out at what appeared to be a ruined Zarin before the white portal closed, the line fading away as fast as it had appeared.

Realizing suddenly that he looked like a proper idiot, Eli pushed off Josef and stood on his own two feet. He was about to call the Spiritualist out for barging in like that, but the words died in his throat. Miranda looked terrible, like she hadn't slept in a week. Her eyes were a mix of dark circles and puffy edges, as though she'd been crying, and she looked utterly confused, almost fragile in her bewilderment.

The illusion was gone in an instant. The second she caught him looking, she pulled herself straight, casting off tiredness and doubt like a veil. It was then he noticed that she was dressed in the formal crimson robes of a high officer of the Spirit Court. The intense color was almost painful to look at after the blank white of the Shaper Mountain, and the effect was only enhanced by the glittering rainbow of rings on her fingers and, brighter still, the enormous collar of woven gold and gems draped across her shoulders.

Eli pursed his lips, impressed. Banage really had made her Rector, and she seemed to be playing her part full force. But, for all the trappings, it was still Miranda, a fact that was hammered home as she crossed her arms over her chest and glared icy death in his direction, her curly red hair bristling with righteous fury.

"Eli Monpress," she said, speaking his name the same way most people said *dead skunk*. "Is there any disaster in this world that doesn't have you at its center?"

Eli blinked in surprise. "Now hold on," he said. "What makes you think any of this is my fault?"

"The fact that it's *always* your fault," she snapped. Beside her, Gin's growl swelled in agreement.

"And you always jump to conclusions," Eli snapped back. "I'll have you know I am an innocent bystander." That wasn't completely true, but this was Miranda. Give her a handhold and she'd pull the whole rope down. "And I'm trying to make things better, believe it or not. The real question should be why are *you* here? You're no Shaper, and that was one of the Shepherdess's portals, if I'm not mistaken."

"You are," Miranda said. "It's a League portal."

"Same difference," Eli grumbled, but Miranda was already rolling over him.

"I'm here on behalf of the Spirit Court and all spirits under our protection," she announced. "I demand to know what is going on, and I'm not leaving until I get some answe..."

Her voice faded off as she finally realized that Eli wasn't alone. Her eyes darted across the group, pausing longest on Slorn, but when she got to the Weaver, they stopped altogether. "Are you the Teacher?" she whispered, her voice shaking with wonder.

Overhead, the Shaper Mountain made a disgusted sound. "I would never put any part of my power into a human form. That is the Weaver, a Power of Creation. If you're going to barge in whenever you like, Spiritualist, the least you can do is try to be informed."

"The Weaver?" Miranda sounded more confused than ever. Suddenly, even her self-righteousness didn't seem to be enough to hold her up. Her body began to shake, legs wobbling like jelly. She would have fallen into a heap had Eli not grabbed her arm.

Miranda let him ease her down without comment, another sign of how bad a shock all this must be for her. When she was safely seated on the floor, she looked up again, her eyes flicking between the white man, the bright white wall hanging in the air, Eli and Slorn standing beside him, Josef and the Heart, Nico's coffin, the Shaper Guildmaster, and then she put her hands over her face as though she were dizzy.

"I'm sorry for the intrusion," she whispered, her face almost green. "But will someone *please* tell me what's going on?"

Be at ease, child, the Weaver said, his eyes dropping to the golden mantle on her shoulders. *You are the leader of those humans who have sworn themselves to the spirits?*

She nodded.

Then you must be here because the world is in panic.

Miranda laughed at that, a dry, humorless sound. "The world's been in panic for the last two days, sir," she said, her voice shaking. "We'd just gotten that under reasonable control when... whatever it was that just happened happened." She lowered her voice again. "Who was the Hunter?"

849

Our greatest protector, the Weaver answered gravely. *My brother, killed by the Shepherdess, our sister.*

Miranda went white then, her color fading away until she was as pale as the stone she sat on. Behind her, Gin made a low keening sound.

"The Tower told me our hope had died," she whispered. "Our wall, he said."

The Weaver nodded. *He was all those things.*

Miranda swallowed. "A wall against what?" When the Weaver didn't answer at once, Miranda lurched forward, her hands slamming into the stone. "Something's coming, isn't it?" She demanded, "Something terrible. Tell me what it is."

The Weaver started to answer, but Eli stepped in front of him, cutting him off. "You remember the thing at Izo's?"

Miranda nodded.

"Think that," Eli said. "But larger, and more."

The Spiritualist began to tremble again. "How many more? More than the League can handle?"

Let me put it this way, the Weaver said, pushing Eli aside. Eli winced when the old man's hand touched his arm. The painless burn was the same as Benehime's.

The Lord of Storms and the League were created to answer the challenges of one demon, the Weaver said. *Just one. And a buried, bound one at that. In less than an hour, the wall that guards this world will begin to crack, and they will pour in. Even if every spirit in the sphere were a member of the League, it wouldn't be enough to handle what's coming.*

Miranda stared up at him, utterly still, and then her head dropped. "The Tower was right," she whispered. "It is the end, isn't it?"

"No, it's not."

Everyone turned to look at Eli. He put his hands on his hips and glared back. "We're not dead yet," he said. "We still have an hour, and I don't mean to waste any more of it on doomsaying and hand wringing."

There is a line between hope and self-delusion, the

Weaver said, his white brows drawing together in disapproval. *If we are to stop the shell from cracking, I must weave and the Hunter must hunt. The Shepherdess has made both of those impossible. How can you still play like we have a chance?*

Eli clenched his teeth and fixed the Power with a glare. "First rule of thievery," he said. "Until the noose snaps your neck, there is always a chance of escape. You just have to find it, and I mean to find ours. I didn't work this hard just to sit around twiddling my thumbs while I wait for death."

"The thief is right."

Eli snapped his head down to look at Miranda. She looked just as surprised as he at the words that had left her mouth, but surprise quickly faded into a much more familiar Miranda expression: determination. Grabbing Gin's fur, she pulled herself to her feet. "What's your plan?"

Eli couldn't stop the grin that was sneaking across his face. "You mean you're going to put yourself at my mercy? You always said my plans were terrible."

She arched an eyebrow. "They are. But, as I've mentioned before, your terrible plans have an infuriating habit of working, and I think I'd like that luck on my side for once. Besides, I can't actually see how you could make things worse, for once."

"How very astute of you," Eli said, glancing around at the others. "Anyone else feel like taking an active role in their own survival?"

Slorn sighed and raised his hand. Beside him, the Shaper Guildmaster set his jaw stubbornly, but he nodded. Josef was in from the beginning, which left only one. Eli turned to face the Weaver. "Well, old man?"

The Weaver took a tired breath. *What did you have in mind?*

Eli grinned. Having Miranda burst in might actually make his plan easier. First, though, he had to make sure step one actually worked. He glanced at his swordsman. "Josef?"

Josef stepped forward. "What?"

"You cut the Lord of Storms," Eli said, pointing at the

851

enormous glowing wall of the blocked veil behind the Weaver. "Think you can cut that?"

Josef lifted the Heart. "I can try."

The swordsman walked up to the glowing wall and stood there for a second with his head cocked, like he was listening to a voice only he could hear. At his side, the Heart of War began to vibrate like a tuning fork. A low humming sound filled the Shaper Mountain's white chamber as Josef raised the blade, pulling it up over his shoulder. And then, stepping into the swing, he brought it down with all his strength.

The black blade struck the white wall with a great *gong*, and blinding light exploded over everything. The vibrations rocked the Shaper Mountain, and Eli had to brace to keep from falling over again. Even within the Shaper Mountain's own brightness, the white light flooding from the veil blinded him. Eli blinked furiously, rubbing his eyes hard as he tried to get them working again.

The first thing he saw was the Shepherdess's seal. The mark glowed with phosphorescent fire, shining so bright the other whiteness looked dingy. For several seconds, the mark seemed to float in the air. Then Eli's eyes recovered enough to see the mark was not, in fact, floating but set in a solid white blade the exact size and shape of the Heart of War.

Eli squinted in amazement. The Heart of War was glowing as white as the Lady herself, shining like the sun in Josef's hands. This was the Heart's awakened light at last, Eli realized, the light he'd never seen. But as bright as the Heart was, the mark on its blade shone brighter.

The Shepherdess's seal burned whiter than anything Eli had ever seen, but as he stared at it, Eli realized that, though the sword was straining in Josef's hands, the seal itself never moved. It stayed locked in place, holding the blade a hair's width away from the white wall of the veil. On the other side of the sword, Josef was pushing with all his might, but the sword would not budge.

And then, without warning, the Heart's light snuffed out.

The sword fell like a stone, blacker than ever as its light vanished. Josef fell with it, landing in a sprawl on the white floor. Eli was at his side before he could think to cry out. The swordsman was gasping for breath, his face pale from effort. He flipped over with Eli's help and hugged the Heart's blade to his body, clutching the metal like a wounded limb.

"We could have cut it," he wheezed. "But she stopped us. Never landed the strike. The Heart—" His voice broke off as he launched into a coughing fit. "The Heart says it can't. It's her creation. It can't attack—"

The words vanished into another coughing fit, and Eli saw with a start how stark Josef's face was, how heavy the Heart rested against him. They'd been at their limit after the fight with the Lord of Storms, he realized. How hard had they swung just now? He put the thought out of his mind and helped settle Josef back onto the ground.

What now?

The Weaver's voice made Eli clench his eyes shut in frustration. He left Josef's side and turned to see them all standing there, staring at him.

I told you. Spirits can't stand against her, the Weaver said. *Though the Heart of War had a good chance. After it gave up its body, Benehime re-formed it with her own hands, just as she made humans. That's why it has will as you do, but in the end even that wasn't enough, apparently. So, now what?*

"Give me a moment," Eli muttered, sinking to the floor.

Burying his head in his arms, he tried to make himself think. He'd *really* thought that would work. The barrier was a product of the Shepherdess's will just as the Lord of Storms was. If Josef could cut one, he should have been able to cut the other. The rest of his plan depended on them getting inside. If they couldn't get through the veil, everything else was a wash. He had to find another way, and fast. There wasn't much time left.

Pushing the looming deadline out of his mind, Eli set himself to finding another way in. But the others had started talking, and their voices were distracting him. Miranda was pestering Slorn, asking him about other spirits. She even suggested finding the Lord of Storms, though thankfully Slorn turned down that plan. The League Commander was the Shepherdess's oldest ally; he'd never turn against her. The old thunderhead was probably already relaxing in paradise, Eli thought grimly. His nice, fat reward for a job well done. The fact that the storm would be bored stiff after an hour with nothing to attack was Eli's only consolation, but before he could take any bitter pleasure from it, the Weaver joined Slorn and Miranda's conversation, and they all started talking over each other.

Eli rolled his eyes and gave up, letting the voices bleed over him, mixing together until the words were just sounds. An idea. He needed an idea. A really good—

He stopped suddenly, ears straining. Below the drone of the arguing voices, he'd caught another sound. It was soft as a heartbeat, almost lost in the noise, but it was steady and strong, tapping out a rhythm Eli knew as well as his own breath.

And with that, his idea came to him clear as a trumpet.

Eli jumped up and scrambled over to Josef. The swordsman was still lying on the floor. His chest rose and fell with his deep breaths, as though he were asleep.

"Josef," Eli whispered.

The swordsman's eyes cracked open, and Eli grinned in response. "Hear that?"

For a moment Josef looked confused, and then recognition spread over his face. Eli's grin widened. "Up for one more cut?"

Josef's answer was to pry one of his hands off his sword so Eli could pull him up.

Everyone else was still arguing, so no one noticed as Eli hauled Josef to his feet and helped him walk over to the bone metal box lying forgotten at the center of the Shaper Mountain.

The thumping grew louder the closer they got—three long

beats followed by two short raps, then a silence, then the pattern twice again before a slight variation, four raps instead of two.

Eli had thought of that part himself, a safeguard against imposters. By the time they reached the box, Eli's grin was so wide his cheeks hurt. He looked down at the dull white lid, watching with deep pride as the heavy bone metal vibrated in the unmistakable rhythm of their long-standing all-clear code.

Without a word, Josef let go of Eli's arm and stood on his own before the coffin. He hefted the Heart in his hands, lifting the black blade to his elbow before dropping it in a clean stroke. The blade fell perfectly, sliding between the coffin's edge and the gleaming chains and then pulling out, snapping the chain with one swift motion.

The awakened steel broke with a ringing cry, and the room fell deathly still as the metal links clattered to the floor. Eli didn't have to look to know everyone was staring at them, so he didn't. He kept his eyes on the coffin as the knocking stopped. And then, with a long, groaning creak, the bone metal lid began to open.

CHAPTER
20

Miranda watched in horror as the chains fell from the box that lay like an offering at the heart of the Shaper Mountain. She didn't know what was inside, but anything wrapped in that much awakened metal couldn't be good. This observation was reinforced by the stricken expressions on the faces of the men around her.

Even Slorn looked terrified, his bear eyes wide and his ears back. Beside her, Gin was growling so loudly she could feel the vibrations in her bones. His muzzle was pulled up, revealing all his teeth, and his nose was twitching, sniffing the air in a way that told her he'd caught a scent. She wanted to ask what he smelled, but her body was so frozen with fear she couldn't speak. She could only watch as the white lid opened.

From here, all she could see was darkness. The box was filled with shadows so deep not even the white light of the mountain could penetrate them. As the lid slid off and fell to the ground, the shadows seemed to slosh, almost like water, and then something extraordinary happened. A thin, white hand emerged from the darkness, followed by a bony arm. The hand reached up blindly, the fingers grasping at the empty air.

Josef moved faster than her eyes could track. His arm shot out, grabbing the hand with his own. The white fingers gripped his tanned, scarred skin, and then Josef pulled up, ripping Nico from the dark.

Her body was thinner than Miranda remembered, though that could have been because she'd never seen the girl without her coat. There was nothing to hide her frailness now. Nico was naked as she burst from the shadows, her body little more than pale skin and thin bone dangling from Josef's hand. She was so thin, Miranda almost thought she was dead, but then she caught sight of the girl's eyes.

Nico's dark eyes were now golden yellow, and they looked only at Josef. The second she was free of the dark, the swordsman crushed her against his chest and turned, carrying her to the base of the box he'd pulled her from. He reached down, grabbing a small, sad black pile from the floor and wrapping it around her body. The second the black cloth touched her, it began to writhe and change, growing and reforming into a shape Miranda recognized.

When Josef turned again, Nico was dressed in her coat. It should have been a familiar sight, but the eyes changed everything. Nico's yellow gaze lit up the deep shadows of her cowl, and at once Miranda remembered the yellow eyes of the creature at Izo's. The endless glowing eyes with the dancing shadows behind them. But there were no shadows behind Nico's eyes now and, Miranda realized with a start, no fear. Just the intense, golden stare as it moved across their group.

What have you done?

Miranda shrank away from the terrible fury in the Weaver's voice. Suddenly, the old man was looming over them, large and threatening and cold as new-fallen snow, his white face alien in its rage.

You have freed the demon! he shouted. *As though things weren't bad enough. Is this your plot, favorite? Do you mean to hurry us to our deaths?*

"I am not your death." Nico's voice rang pure and clear, but there was something in it that put Miranda's teeth on edge. The words echoed with a strange double harmonic. It wasn't unpleasant, but it also wasn't a noise that should ever come from a human throat.

Nico whispered something to Josef, who nodded and set her down. She swayed a little, but then she planted her bare feet and fixed the Weaver with a glare.

"I am not your death," she said again. "Nor am I your enemy, lest you make me one."

Impossible, the Weaver boomed. *You are a demon. Your very nature makes you an enemy of everything we know. We saw you change; we bound you in that box. There is no coming back.*

"I am Nico," Nico said simply. "And I am my own master."

She lies! the Weaver cried. *Demons always lie. Don't listen. Don't fall for her tricks!*

Nico's yellow eyes narrowed to glowing slits. "No one knows that demons lie better than I do," she said. "But I am not one of those." She raised her arm, laying her thin white hand across her chest. "I fought and won. I was not eaten, and I never will be. I am the master of myself, I and no other. I am king of my own country. My power is my own to give, and I choose to use it to aid those who have stood by me."

She tilted her head, and her yellow eyes grew soft as she looked up at Josef. "I will fight the others for you," she whispered. "As you fought for me."

Josef nodded, and Nico turned back to the Weaver. Silently, she raised her arm, finger pointing straight up. "They're coming," she said. "I can feel them eating the edges as we speak. Soon there will be nothing left. The sky will split, and they will devour everything. So choose now. Accept my help and maybe live, or fight me and seal all our deaths."

She crossed her arms and stood, waiting. Behind her, Josef was beaming with pride. Eli was also smiling, standing beside his partners in crime with a smug satisfaction that made Miranda want to scream.

But she didn't. Miranda had seen this before, the three of them lined up in a united front. Every time she'd tried to stand against them, she'd lost. When the decision came, Miranda didn't know if it was good sense or simply the weariness of always being the odd one out. Whatever the reason, she didn't have time to worry about it.

Bending her stiff legs, Miranda started across the room. Gin followed her a second later, whining in confusion. Her boots slapped against the smooth white stone, the sound offensively loud in her ears. She ignored it, focusing only on keeping her breaths even and her head high as she closed the distance to Eli's group. And then, feeling a little sheepish, she turned and stepped into line beside the thief.

"Finally decided to join the winning team?" Eli's voice was almost purring in her ear. When Miranda glanced at him, his smile was so smug she wanted to punch it off his face.

"There's only one team now, thief."

This observation only widened his smile, and Miranda decided to ignore him, turning instead to face the Shapers and the Weaver. "I've seen Monpress and his lackeys perform miracles too many times to doubt them now," she said, raising her voice until her words echoed through the white cavern. "The Spirit Court stands with Eliton Banage."

She caught Eli's wince out of the corner of her eye, and then it was her turn to smirk.

Across the room, Slorn shook his head. "So be it," he muttered, turning to the Weaver. "We must try. The Creator gave everything to protect the world he'd made. If we do not give everything trying to save it, we are unworthy of the life he gave us."

The Weaver closed his white eyes, his chin slumping into the snowfall of his beard. He looked ancient then, Miranda thought. Older than the Shaper Mountain, older than anything she'd ever seen.

Very well, he whispered, opening his eyes again to glare at Nico. *Do as you wish. I will support you however I can.*

"Fantastic," Eli said, slapping his hands together. The sound was loud enough to make Miranda jump, but Eli was already moving. He grabbed Nico's hand and led her to the glowing white wall that was still hanging in the air, the barrier Benehime had raised between herself and the world she'd abandoned.

"There you go," Eli said. "If a demonseed with the right leverage could kill a Power, then a fully fledged demon should surely be enough to break through one little wall."

Nico stared at the glowing surface, her face scrunched in thought. She reached out to touch the glowing surface and then snatched her fingers back with a hiss. Black smoke rose from her skin where she had touched the barrier.

"I can't break this," she said, yellow eyes going to Eli.

"Oh *come on!*" he cried. "Your kind are chewing through the shell of the *world*, and you're telling me you can't make one little hole—"

"There are a lot of demons breaking down the shell," Nico said, jerking her head toward the wall. "I'm just one, and that thing is held up by two Powers. Well..." She paused, leaning toward the barrier and wrinkling her nose, almost like she was sniffing it. "One and a half."

Eli groaned. "So what do we do now?" he said. "Get another demon to make things..."

His voice trailed off as his eyes lit up, a smile breaking over his face. The moment they saw it, Slorn, Miranda, the Shaper Mountain, and the Weaver all spoke at once.

"No!"

"I can't believe you talked us into this," Miranda muttered, holding the white hole in the air open as Eli, Josef, Gin, and Nico stepped through. "I mean, I really, really, *really* cannot believe it. This is a horrible, horrible idea."

"Yes, thank you," Eli said drily. "You've made your opinion very clear."

"Horrible," Miranda said again, stepping through before letting the hole in the world fall closed. "Just horrible."

It was a pretty horrible idea, Eli had to admit. But as old Monpress used to say, a bad out is still an out. Still, as the icy, high mountain wind hit his face, he wasn't so sure this *was* an out and not just another way to end the world.

Now that they were outside the Shaper Mountain, he could hear the panic loud and clear. The winds screamed around them and the ice whimpered under their boots. Even the mountain pass beneath their feet was rocking back and forth, moaning in terror. Snow blew in panicked bursts, and the clouds had pulled themselves into tight balls as they bounced against the scrambling winds.

Eli winced. He'd been hoping Miranda was exaggerating before, but the Spiritualist had told the truth. The world really was going insane, the whole of reality twisting itself into knots in its terror, with one large exception.

The Dead Mountain loomed in front of them. The enormous black shape rose like a thorn from the snow-filled valley, its bare slopes the sole point of stillness in the whole, trembling world. Just looking at it filled Eli with dread. He remembered his last trip here very clearly. It was an experience he had no desire to repeat, but as he'd said over and over again just minutes before, it was the only choice they had left.

If the world was to survive, a new Hunter must be born,

and that could only happen if they got his seed out of Benehime's world. But neither Nico nor the Weaver could break through the Shepherdess's barrier alone, and since they were opposites, the demon and the Power couldn't work together without canceling each other out. That being so, their remaining options were to get another Power or get another demon. Since getting another Power was completely impossible, the choice was irrefutably clear, even to the Weaver, which was why they were here.

Miranda began using her League-granted calming power as soon as she dropped the portal, laying down what Eli could only call the bleeding-heart-Spiritualist's version of the League's *Don't Move* command on their frantic surroundings. It worked wonders, though, and while the Spiritualist worked on quieting the area enough for them to pass through without being mauled, Eli strolled over to stand beside Josef.

The swordsman's face was drawn and pale. Nico's was no better as she took her place at Josef's right. They all recognized the mountain pass. It was the place where they had faced the Lord of Storms the first time, where Nico had snapped and Josef would have died had Eli not thrown himself in front of the Lord of Storms' blade, gambling that Benehime's constant watch would save them both. The memory brought a grimace to Eli's face. This wasn't a happy place for any of them, but here they were, and he had questions to ask before they moved forward.

"Josef," he said, his voice low. "Are you going to be able to go to the mountain with me this time?"

Josef's eyes didn't budge from the black slope, but his fingers tightened on the Heart's hilt. "I've always been able to go," he said. "But you're not asking about me. You're asking about the Heart."

"Same difference," Eli said.

Josef chuckled. "You're more right than you know." He turned then and fixed Eli with a look that stabbed right through him. "This isn't like before. The Heart and I are one now. It goes where I go, and we will see this thing to the end."

Eli nodded and leaned over, glancing around him at Nico. "Will—"

"Of course I'm going," Nico said, glaring at Eli with those intense yellow eyes. "The thing under that mountain has no power over me anymore."

Eli smiled at her. "Good," he said. "Because I don't think I can do this without you."

To his surprise, Nico smiled back. It was the largest smile he'd ever seen on her face, and it was astonishing how pretty she was when she did it. Eli smiled even wider before starting down the steep slope to the valley.

Even with Miranda there to calm things, it was hard going. The snow squirmed beneath their feet, and the wind seemed to be blowing every direction at once. Only Gin and Miranda, who was seated on his back, avoided falling on the way down.

The ghosthound trotted down the slope with the inborn self-assurance of a creature born to ice and snow, sliding through the blowing gusts like a graceful ghost. The dog knew it, too, and every time Eli slipped, Gin gave him the ghosthound equivalent of a superior smirk. He was loving this, Eli thought with a bitter scowl. Well, good thing *someone* could be happy in this mess.

The snow was so thick that they didn't see the man until they were almost on top of him. It was Josef who stopped first, grabbing Eli's arm and jerking the thief to a stop. Eli gasped in pain and surprise, but before he could ask what had gotten into the swordsman, Gin's growl fired up full force. The sound drained Eli's anger away to nothing, and he looked up to see a looming shadow standing directly in front of them.

The Lord of Storms stood at the edge where the valley snows met the Dead Mountain's bare slope. His sword was naked in his hands, and his face was set in a look of murderous determination. His long hair flew madly behind him, the strands fading in and out between solid black and swirling clouds, the same swirling clouds that churned at the edges of the enormous hole that ran from his shoulder to his hip, cutting his chest almost in half.

Josef pushed Nico behind him, but the Lord of Storms wasn't looking at her. His eyes were on Eli, and the hatred in them made him cringe.

"You will not pass, thief," the Lord of Storms said, his voice rumbling. He raised his sword, the glowing blade sliding through the wind with a screaming whistle. "Go back to your Shepherdess or die with the rest of us, your choice, but none of you will set foot on the demon's prison while I can lift a sword."

Eli wasn't a violent man, but it took every ounce of self-control he had right then not to punch the Lord of Storms in the face. There couldn't be more than twenty minutes remaining in the hour before the shell broke. He did *not* need this. But even when he was nearly cut in half, attacking the Lord of Storms was suicidally stupid, and so, optimistic fool that he was, Eli decided to take a long shot and try reason.

"Listen. You. Idiot," he said, spitting out each word. "Have you *looked* at the sky with those eyes of yours? Do you know what's happening?"

The Lord of Storms' look grew black as his storm clouds. "Better than you do, human."

"Then *why* are you *here*?" Eli shouted. "And why are you still injured? You should be off laughing it up with Benehime in paradise. Oh, let me guess, you told her you'd rather die making our lives difficult than spend eternity blowing around her little fishbowl with nothing to do."

The Lord of Storms didn't answer. He just stood there, sword raised, his body shifting between cloud and solid like he was barely holding himself together. The icy wind howled around them, tugging the clouds away from the Lord of Storms' wound. It was a strange, unsettling sight, and Eli couldn't shake the feeling he was watching the storm bleed out right in front of them. As the icy silence stretched on, a creeping realization formed in Eli's mind, and suddenly he was looking at the Lord of Storms in an entirely different light.

"She didn't offer to heal you, did she?" Eli said quietly, the

863

words barely audible over the wind and the distant screams of the spirits.

The Lord of Storms' glare didn't waver, and his voice was as sharp as the sword in his hand when he answered. "There's no need for storms in paradise."

"You've got to be *kidding*," Eli shouted. "After five thousand years of absolute loyalty, after you brought her the demonseed she used to kill the Hunter, she abandons you now?"

"And this surprises you?" The Lord of Storms' face fell into a disgusted sneer. "I was never more than a sword to her. A sword has no use in a world of peace."

"She cut you loose!" Eli cried. "After all those years, all you did for her." He clutched his head with his hands, amazed that he could hate the Shepherdess more than he already did. "But—" He almost couldn't get the words out. "Why are you here, then? Why are you still working as her guard? You should be—"

"*This is my purpose!*" the Lord of Storms roared. "I was bound together for one reason, to guard the world against the demon that lies beneath that mountain. For that I lost my names, my autonomy, lost everything but the purpose that binds me. And though the Shepherdess breaks all oaths and turns her back on the world, *I* will not be forsworn." He lifted his sword higher, training the point on Eli's heart. "So long as a spark of lightning flashes within me, I will serve my purpose!"

Eli cursed loudly. He was scrambling his brain for an argument powerful enough to make the man-shaped ball of thunderclouds see reason when he felt a hand grip his arm hard. Josef pulled him close, nearly taking him off his feet in the process.

"We don't have time for this," Josef whispered low. "I'll handle him. You need to go. Now."

Eli scrambled against the swordsman's grip. "But—"

"Nico!" Josef barked. "Take him up."

"Hold on now!" Eli shouted, but Nico's arms were already

around his waist. The last thing he saw was Josef lifting the Heart of War, and then the world vanished as Nico pulled him into the dark.

Josef set his feet in the snow, watching the Lord of Storms warily. The Heart was roaring through him, heightening his senses to a level he'd never felt before. He could feel each snowflake as it flew by, each icy stone holding up the snowdrift under his boots. He could taste the storm on the wind, smell the ozone smell of the Lord of Storms' fury. He dropped into a crouch, legs ready to jump after the League Commander the second he moved, but the Lord of Storms stayed put at the valley's edge, his sword waiting in his hands.

"Aren't you going after them?" Josef said.

The Lord of Storms shook his head. "I no longer have the strength to step onto the Dead Mountain."

Josef clenched his jaw. All that posturing, and they could have just gone around.

"But I do have the strength to stop you," the Lord of Storms said, his face breaking into a deadly smile. "Your demon is gone and the veil does not open this close to the Mountain, so even though I don't have the energy left to rip my gift from her, the Spiritualist behind you will be of no use. You have no way forward save through me, and I will not let you turn back." He held out his free arm, beckoning Josef forward. "Come, Josef Liechten, Master of the Heart of War. Let's finish our duel before the demons finish it for us."

Josef raised his eyes to the black slope of the Dead Mountain. Nico and Eli were on it somewhere, but he couldn't see them. He let his eyes drift up farther still to the sharp peak at the very top. It stood bold and dark against the late-afternoon sky, free of haze or cloud. That made sense, he supposed. Even mad, spirits knew better than to approach the demon's den.

Though he'd never been close enough to see it clearly before, Josef smiled at the peak like an old friend. He knew the folds of its crags better than he knew his own face. It was the peak that had filled his mind when he'd cut the Lord of Storms, the peak that had been the beacon to lure him back from death. Though the stone above him was black now instead of the white he saw in the Heart of War's memory, the sight of it stilled his mind and sharpened his purpose. He would end things here, in the shadow of his sword's former self.

Clutching the Heart in his hands, Josef stepped into first position, his boots sinking into the deep snow. But as he readied his body for the blow, he felt the Spiritualist dismounting behind him, whispering to her rings like she was getting ready to fight as well.

"Back off," he said, his voice harsh.

The Spiritualist froze behind him, and through his heightened senses he felt her take a breath to argue. "Shut up, back away, and don't interfere," he snapped. "This is my fight."

The commands only made her bristle, but the announcement that this was his battle seemed to stop her cold. All at once, her presence vanished, and he glanced over his shoulder to see she had moved back to the center of the valley, taking her dog with her.

Good, he thought. Pushy, annoying, and overbearing as she was, Miranda was a brave soldier of her order. Josef would hate to see her die.

"Come," the Lord of Storms said, his voice booming over the raging winds.

Clutching his sword, Josef obeyed. He launched himself at the Lord of Storms, and as his feet slammed into the snow, the image of the Heart's peak filled his mind. With the real thing hanging against the gray sky above him, it was easier than ever. He swung with a roar, meeting the Lord of Storms' sword with such force that the ground trembled under their feet.

The blades met with a crash. Met and held, the Lord of Storms bracing with both hands against the Heart's onslaught. Josef braced as well and shoved back, pitting his strength against the League Commander's. The seconds ticked by as the blades edged back and forth, grinding against each other in a stalemate. Sweat began to pour down Josef's face, but he refused to let up the pressure. This time he was going to make the Lord of Storms break the lock and step back. This time the League man would be on defense while Josef attacked, slicing away his clouds until nothing was left but clear air.

The Lord of Storms' face was only inches away from his own. Josef snarled over the crossed blades, trying to bait him, but the man's silver eyes were unnaturally calm. His hair was entirely storm now, a black mass of rolling clouds streaked with lightning. The cut in his chest was widening as well, the black coat unraveling into vapor. The smell of ozone was stronger than ever, but the lightning bolts flashing inside the wound were not as numerous as they once had been.

The longer the stalemate dragged on, the larger the hole in the Lord of Storms' chest grew until his entire lower torso was nothing but cloud. The storm was creeping up his neck beneath the high collar of his black coat now, but the Lord of Storms didn't seem to notice. He just kept staring at Josef over their crossed swords with those uncharacteristically calm eyes. And then, with an ear-splitting crack, the Lord of Storms' blue-white blade snapped.

The Heart surged forward, carrying Josef through the fading arc of the Lord of Storms' broken blade. Weaponless, the commander held out his arms, welcoming the Heart of War as it plunged toward the rolling clouds of his open chest. Josef's eyes widened, and then, with a move that made his head ache, he threw away the vision of the mountain and spun hard, breaking his momentum with a snap.

He felt his will lurch, and his body lurched with it, slamming to a stop. Josef skid to a stop inside the Lord of Storms' guard with the Heart of War's edge just touching the swirling clouds of the Lord of Storms' wound. He stood panting for a moment, centering himself before he dared look up. Above him, the Lord of Storms' face was open and betrayed.

"Go on!" he growled, the words fading into thunder. "Finish it!"

Josef stepped back, lowering the Heart to his side. "No."

The Lord of Storms lurched, grabbing Josef by the shoulders. His grip felt more like rain than flesh now, but it was still strong enough to make Josef wince as the League Commander dragged him close.

"You deny me a warrior's death," the Lord of Storms whispered. "I thought we understood one another, human. All my life I have served one purpose, and yet I longed for an opponent. Not a demon, but a true equal. Someone who could push me beyond the dog the Shepherdess created me to be." He looked down, silver eyes bitter as he searched Josef's face. "I'd thought it could be you."

"I am your opponent," Josef said, stepping out of the commander's weakening grasp. "But I am not your enemy. Not any longer."

"If you are my opponent, then finish what you started," the Lord of Storms growled. "My life is at an end one way or another, swordsman. The Shepherdess saw to that. All I ask is that you pay me the same kindness I showed you in our first battle. I offered you a clean death then. An honorable death, facing the sword of a worthy foe. Will you deny me the same?"

Josef's eyes flicked down. The Lord of Storms' body was falling apart. His legs were dissolving, as were his arms. Rolling black clouds licked at his face and neck, but no more lightning surged through the thunderheads, and no more thunder rolled through his voice. The Lord of Storms had told the truth. He was dying, fading away.

With a deep breath, Josef closed his eyes and nodded. "So be it."

The Lord of Storms stepped back, dropping his hands to his sides. He raised his chin as Josef stepped into position, his face calm, his body relaxed even as bits of him blew away. The Heart of War was heavier than Josef could ever remember it being as he raised it to his shoulder, readying the swing.

But then, just as his foot slid forward to begin the strike, a loud cry cut the air.

"*Stop!*"

Josef and the Lord of Storms both jumped as Miranda ran forward, her hands shooting out to grab the Heart of War's blade.

"Did I not tell you to stay away?" Josef shouted, but Miranda didn't seem to hear him at all. She was shoving herself between the men with seemingly no care at all that the Heart of War was hanging right over her head.

"How can you do this?" she cried.

Josef opened his mouth to explain that the League man had demanded it, but then he realized the Spiritualist wasn't yelling at him. She was yelling at the Lord of Storms.

"Why are you throwing your life away?" she shouted. "You were the one who was betrayed! Why should you die here obeying the Shepherdess's command?"

The Lord of Storms bared his teeth. "Don't lecture me, woman!" he snarled. "I have the right to choose my own death, and I chose to fall in the line of duty as a warrior should!"

"Don't talk to me about duty!" Miranda snarled back. "Duty means giving your life freely to a good that's greater than yourself. It means never compromising your principals, and never letting those who rely on you down. But you said yourself that you were made to be a sword. That you served thousands of years as a sword, and now that the Shepherdess has no use for you, you've been cast aside. That's not duty; that's abuse! You aren't forsworn. She *abandoned* you. What are you doing, giving your life in service of a horrible woman who cares nothing for the world she's supposed to protect?"

The Lord of Storms closed his eyes in frustration. "Listen, human, and try to understand. It's done. The Shepherdess is done with all of us. She's already pulled me apart. You can sit there and judge all you like, but until I dissolve it is my life, and if I wish to end it with dignity, that is none of your concern."

"That might be true if you were any other spirit," Miranda said. "But you are the *Lord of Storms*, and you *do* have a duty. Not to the Shepherdess or whatever purpose she made you for, but to the League you founded. Those men swore themselves to your service. My Spiritualists swore to use your powers to protect the Spirit World. Every one of those oaths binds you to this world and everything in it, and if you truly are a man of honor, a man of duty, you would understand that your job is to *live*, not to die here to assuage some sort of wounded warrior's pride!"

"You think I don't want to live?" the Lord of Storms roared, looming over her. "You think I *want* to blow away here, like this? Stabbed in the back by that traitorous woman? I want vengeance, Spiritualist! But I cannot have it." He held up his hands, now little more than vague shapes outlined by thinning clouds. "I am dead already. A walking corpse with too much power to lie still just yet. What would you have me do? Lead the League to battle while I fade away? If I die here as a warrior, my League and your Spiritualists will at least keep the power I've given them, but if I try and linger on I'll only sap that away and make everything worse."

Miranda blinked at him in confusion, but then he reached out and grabbed her, his cloud hands swirling uselessly around her arm before gathering enough strength to thrust her away.

"Go," he said as he pushed her. "Leave me in peace." When she fell sprawling in the snow, the Lord of Storms' cold silver eyes flashed back to Josef. "Finish it," he growled.

"No!" Miranda shouted again, slamming her fist down.

All at once, Josef felt something grab his legs and he looked down to see he was encased in stone up to his waist. A second pillar of stone shot up behind him, grabbing his arms at the wrists and biceps. He started struggling at once, but though he was strong enough to break any of the thin bands of rock, the angle was such that he could get no leverage at all. He could only stand there and thrash uselessly against the bindings.

The Lord of Storms was faring no better. The moment the rock shot up, a great pressure filled the air, and the Lord of Storms froze in place. His eyes were rolling, but he couldn't move more than an inch in any direction.

Panting, Miranda pushed herself to her feet. Her face was pale and wild, her hair flying behind her, but the pressure didn't let up and the Lord of Storms didn't move. He could only stand and stare as she walked forward and thrust out her hand.

"You want to live?" she asked, her voice hoarse. "Then live. I offer you power for service, strength for obedience, and part of my life for yours."

The Lord of Storms didn't answer. He just stood there, clouds swirling. The wind howled in the silence, blowing around Miranda who stood still as stone with her hand out, palm up.

"Why?" he said at last. "Why would you do that?"

"Because you deserve to live," Miranda answered. "Because you are still a great and powerful spirit, something we have precious little of, because you are the sworn enemy of that which is coming to devour us all, and because it is my duty. You are a spirit who has been done great wrong. It is my sworn obligation to help you, and I mean to do so."

Her hand reached out farther, fingers straining. "If the Shepherdess tore you apart, I will hold you together. If you need to draw power, I will give it to you, but you *will not die.* Now accept the oath. Let me be the strength she took from you, and together we will stop what is about to happen or die facing it, like warriors."

The Lord of Storms bared his teeth. "This bargain may well kill you, girl. You have a lot of spirits drawing on your life already, and even sundered as I am, I'm a lot bigger than your pet sea was."

Miranda lifted her chin. "I don't care. If you are large, than I shall be larger. I am human. Spirits tell me over and over again that my power is not limited to my physical size but to the breadth of my will, and it is my will that you should live." She stepped forward again, shoving her hand through the swirl of clouds that was all that remained of the Lord of Storms' chest. *"Accept the oath."*

The League Commander glared hard at her, and then bowed his head just slightly. The pressure vanished immediately, and Josef was suddenly glad of the stone around his legs. If the rock hadn't been holding him up, he would have fallen flat in shock at the sight of what happened next.

As soon as the pressure vanished, the Lord of Storms dissolved into a swirling mass of cloud, and then the whole valley went stark white as a bolt of lightning the size of a tree trunk crashed down from the clear sky and struck Miranda, lighting her up from the inside. The bolt lasted less than a second, and then Miranda fell forward, collapsing face-first into the trampled snow.

The moment she hit, the stone holding Josef fell away, and he collapsed beside her, staring at her unmoving body until Gin's body blocked his view. The ghosthound circled his mistress, snapping at Josef's legs until he moved them. The hound nudged the girl with his nose and began to whine. When the Spiritualist didn't move, the whining grew louder until Gin raised his head with a howl so full of fear and loss that even Josef's spirit-deaf ears caught its meaning. Instinctively, he turned away from the mourning ghosthound and looked instead at the place where, only seconds earlier, the Lord of Storms had stood with his arms open, waiting for death.

The spot was now empty, and though he sniffed the air, he caught no hint of ozone. Suddenly exhausted, he leaned back and gazed up at the Dead Mountain, silently begging for Eli to hurry.

Overhead, unseen, the sky shuddered and began to bulge inward.

CHAPTER
21

Nico and Eli were running, lungs pumping as they charged up the slope of the Dead Mountain. The jump had taken them to the first ledge. After that, Nico had said something about the demon's influence being too large to risk another trip through the shadows, and they'd decided to go the rest of the way on foot.

Eli was beginning to wish they'd taken their chances in the dark. He thought he'd remembered the feel of the Dead Mountain, but now that he was back, his memory felt like a rosy portrait. The cold, the stillness, the unrelenting *emptiness* of the air around him pressed like a lead weight on his mind, making him want to curl into a ball and never get up again, but that was nothing compared to the fear.

The panic had hit him as soon as they'd left the shadows, forcing him to take a few of their precious minutes to collect himself before going on. The fear leached his strength and gnawed on his bones, weighing him down until he was sure he couldn't take another step. He would have stopped several times over if not for Nico. She floated ahead of him, an inky spot blacker than the mountain's stone, her white hands tugging him whenever he fell too far behind.

Eventually, the prolonged exposure dulled the panic's edge, and Eli began to notice his surroundings. Or, rather, his lack of surroundings. On his first visit there'd been a meager town of cultists, those foolish humans who actually wanted demonseeds inside them. Now that was all gone. Buildings, people, everything had vanished without a trace. Only the flat stretch of ground and the cave leading into the mountain's side remained to show that Eli and Nico were in the right place. Eli wondered briefly what had happened to it all before shoving the thought out of his mind. He didn't actually want to know.

873

They ran across the flat stretch of stone where the town had stood and entered the cave, picking up speed as they began to climb. The farther they went, the thicker the dark became. Thanks to her flawless darksight, Nico moved the same as always, but Eli was forced to slow down, feeling the ground with his feet. Finally, Nico gave up and went back, shoving her hands into his and pulling him behind her like a wagon as she ran up the sloping tunnel.

For all the changes, some parts of the journey were the same. The return to the light, for example, was just as abrupt as Eli remembered. One moment he was stumbling like a blind man through the tunnel behind Nico; the next he was shielding his eyes and gripping the ledge to keep from plummeting down the steep cliffs.

They had emerged from the tunnel high up the mountain at the narrow path that led up to the demon's prison at the peak. Below them, the Sleeping Mountains stretched off in all directions, their enormous peaks small and almost delicate from this great height. Though they were almost at their destination, the way forward made Eli's head spin. The path from the cave wound along the back of a ridge with plunging cliffs on either side. There was nothing to guard against a fall, and in some places the stony path was little more than a foot wide. If any wind had dared to blow across the Dead Mountain, the way would have been completely impassable. But there were no winds here, not even the distant sound of them. Only the Dead Mountain's heavy silence, the view, and the long, long drop.

Mindful of their time limit, Eli gritted his teeth and forced himself to go on, dragging his feet in tiny, cautious steps along the narrow ridge. He kept his eyes on the path, never daring to look down, and eventually his pace picked up. He was really starting to think they'd make it when he realized he was alone.

Eli looked around the empty path in alarm, hoping frantically that Nico hadn't fallen before he spotted her all the way back at the tunnel's exit. She was pressed against the mountain, her hands clapped over her mouth, yellow eyes wide with horror. For a moment Eli wondered dumbly if she was scared of heights, but then he saw where her terrified eyes were staring.

She was looking down, all the way down the cliffs to the enormous valley that cut through the Sleeping Mountains like a scar. The valley ran north in an unnaturally straight line from the Dead Mountain's base. Its flat floor was riddled with craters and rubble, all that remained of the mountains that had once stood in its path. And though he couldn't see it from this distance, Eli knew that straight road of a valley ended at the slopes of the Shaper Mountain itself. A lasting reminder of the Demon's last and most successful attempt to take out the only spirit that could imprison the horror he'd unleashed on the world.

With a silent curse, Eli turned on his heel and picked his way as fast as possible back to her across the ridge. "Nico," he whispered, taking her hand. "Come on. We have to go."

He might have been talking to the mountain itself for all the good it did. Nico didn't budge, even when he touched her. She stood as still as the stone under her feet, staring at the scar like she'd seen a ghost.

"Nico," Eli said again, more firmly this time. He tugged her hand.

"I did this," she whispered, her voice so quiet he almost didn't hear it.

Eli closed his eyes and took a deep breath. "That was a long time ago, Nico, and it wasn't your fault."

"I did this," she said again, louder. "There were mountains there, and I ate them." Her voice raised to a wail. "I killed them!"

"Nico!" Eli shouted, grabbing her shoulders. "That wasn't you. That was the Daughter of the Dead Mountain. That was a slave, Nico. A slave with no choice and no mind of her own. You're *free*, remember? You won your freedom when you beat the demon. Remember what happened up by the bandit camp.

You won. You have no master but yourself. Now come on, we need you." He dropped his grip on her shoulders and reached down to gently touch her fingers instead, pressing them between his own. "Please?"

Nico shivered as though he'd dunked her in ice water, and the spell was broken. "I'm sorry," she whispered, pulling away. She began to stride forward only to stop a few steps later. "Thank you," she said, looking over her shoulder.

"You're welcome," Eli said, hurrying after her. "Now let's go. If we're not back by the time Josef is done thrashing the Lord of Storms, I'm going to have to listen to him *and* Miranda whining about waiting on us. Frankly, I'd rather be eaten by a demon."

Nico smiled at that. She waited until he reached her, and then they jogged together up the ridge path toward the steep switchback trail to the peak. When they reached it, they began to run full out, climbing the steep path as fast as they could until, at last, they stood before the entrance to the cave at the very top.

Eli stopped and bent over, clutching his knees as he panted. Nico wasn't winded at all, but she stopped as well, staring at the wall of darkness that waited beyond the cave's mouth. No light penetrated the shadows beyond the stone lip. Instead, the blackness seemed to press outward, lapping at the edges of the door like overflowing water.

"You sure you can do this?" Eli said, glancing at her as he straightened up.

"I already have," Nico answered, striding forward. "Come on."

Eli took a deep, final breath and followed her into the dark.

The shadows swallowed them the second their feet crossed the threshold. Eli remembered the seal at the last second, and he caught Nico's arm just before she stepped into it. She stopped at once, her bare foot hovering just above the circle carved deep into the stone, the physical edge of the demon's prison. Nico jerked back at once, and her eyes locked on the figure sitting at the center of the Lady's seal.

As before, the darkness here had a strange quality. Though there was no light, Eli could see clearly, and what he saw made him frown. The man sitting in the middle of the seal wasn't the one he'd spoken with weeks before when he'd come here searching for hints of how to find Slorn. That time, the demon had been a young man, little more than a boy. The person smiling up at them now was middle aged, a man who would have been handsome if not for his caved-in cheeks and the deep circles below his eyes. The voice, however, was exactly the same.

"Well, well," the man said, drawing each word out in that terrifying double harmonic that still haunted Eli's dreams. "Look who's come home. It is good to see you, daughter. You're looking well."

Nico stiffened. "I'm no child of yours, demon," she said. "And this was never my home."

The man shook his head with a *tsk*ing sound. "You wound me," he said. "How cruel. Cruel and stupid. Is that any way to talk when you're here to beg a favor?"

Nico's eyes widened, and the man's face split into a grin far too wide for normal human muscles. "Oh yes, I know what's happened," he said. "Not being of this world, I couldn't feel the Hunter's death, but I didn't need to. I can taste their joy, just as you can."

Nico looked away.

"Come now," the demon said. "You're one of us now. Surely you can feel them." He raised his hand, pointing up with one thin, dirty finger. "They're getting close. I'd say we're down to minutes before the first cracks appear." He dropped his arm, and his horrible smile grew wider still. "If you have an offer, dearest, you'd best speak it quickly."

Nico began to shiver, and Eli grabbed her arm. "I'm the one making the deal, demon," he said, holding her steady.

The demon's grin fell, and he gave Eli a skeptical look. "A deal from the swindler?" he said. "Eli Monpress, the great con man? This I have to hear."

"Even I can't pull a con on a deal this simple," Eli said. "We need you to help us break down the wall the Shepherdess has placed over the Between. In return, we will break the seal on your prison."

The demon leaned back on his bony haunches. "That's it?"

"That's it," Eli said. "Tit for tat."

"And what happens after I break this wall?"

"I don't know," Eli answered, his voice deep and sincere. "But if we don't break it, we all die. Given those odds, I'm willing to take a chance."

"And what if I betray you?" the demon drawled. "After all, you have to free me first. How do you know I won't just eat you whole and rush to help my long-lost brothers tear your world apart?"

Now it was Eli's turn to smile. "Because you don't want them here any more than we do. Demons are predators, and I never met a predator who willingly shared his territory. You may be a prisoner here, but you're locked in with the food while they're outside starving. If the shell breaks, the demons will charge in and eat everything, and then you'd all be out of luck, starving and alone in the infinite dark. You don't want that, do you?"

The demon stared at him for a long second, and then he stood up with a jerk. The man walked forward, his legs moving like a puppet's as it stepped to the edge of the seal, stopping just before his bare toes touched the line. This close, Eli could smell the decay of the human body the demon wore like a skin. The man's empty eyes were inches from his own, close enough that Eli could see the shadows twisting and boiling behind them.

"You see more than a blind human should," the demon whispered.

"But I'm right, aren't I?" Eli said, smirking in the demon's face. "Now, are you going to help us or not?"

Slowly, the demon's mouth turned up again into that too-wide grin. "I am your loyal servant," he said, his dual-tone

878

voice purring in his throat. "Set me free and I promise I will do whatever is necessary to preserve the shell. And that's a promise you can trust, just ask my little girl. She knows how seriously I take my obligations."

Eli didn't give him the pleasure of looking at Nico. Instead, he glanced pointedly at the seal's edge, right beside the demon's foot. "You'd better stand back."

The demon shrugged. "Wouldn't matter if I did. My true self is below the mountain, and I was tired of this skin anyway." The horrible grin grew wider still. "Besides, it shouldn't take much. This seal was always barely enough to hold me. A little more pressure and the mark will crumble, but be quick." The shadowed eyes flicked up to the ceiling. "Not much time."

Eli smiled back with his best professional smile before turning to Nico. She was huddled beside him, staring hard at the seal at their feet.

"Can you do it?"

Nico nodded. "Move against the wall and cover your ears."

Eli obeyed, pressing his back against the stone and plugging his ears with his fingers.

Nico watched until he was in position, and then she stepped up to stand where he had been, face-to-face with the grinning monster in the human skin. She glared at the demon for a second, nostrils flaring, and then, without warning, she dropped, her fist flying toward the edge of the seal.

When her knuckles struck it, the whole mountain rang like a gong. The sound rattled Eli's bones and knocked his teeth. Forgetting his ears, Eli clutched his chest. He could feel the vibrations in his lungs, turning his chest into a solid, quivering mass. Just when he thought it couldn't get any worse, Nico punched her fist down again.

This time, her hand landed with a sickening crack. At first, Eli thought she'd broken her fingers, but then he saw that it was the floor that had cracked. All at once, the great circular seal began to glow. Both demons hissed at the light, and the smell of burning skin filled Eli's nostrils. But it lasted only a moment. As soon as the light flared, the Lady's seal began to splinter.

Cracks ran fast as falling water between the intricate lines, splintering the Shepherdess's beautiful pattern into chaos. Each crack was as loud as a breaking bone, and the combined effect drowned out even the gong-like ring of the mountain below. The sound was so enormous Eli stopped trying to keep it out after the first seconds. Instead, he lay against the wall and let it flow through him, gritting his teeth as he waited for the end.

Fortunately, he didn't have to wait long. Fast as it had started, the cracking stopped, and the room plunged back into darkness. Shaking his head, Eli looked down. After the flash of light, the dark was impenetrable, but he didn't need to see. He could *feel* the truth. The oppressive air of the mountain had vanished. The Shepherdess's seal was broken. The demon was free.

As his eyes adjusted, the first thing Eli saw was the demon's human body falling to the ground. It crumbled like ash when it hit, bones and flesh falling away to dust. As the body disintegrated, the shadows above it twisted and took a step over the edge of the shattered seal, and as they crossed the barrier, they became a man.

Eli jerked back. The demon looked nothing like he'd expected. The man was as tall as Josef, but his face reminded Eli of his adopted father and mentor, Giuseppe Monpress. He couldn't quite place the resemblance, the nose, maybe, or the thin mouth turned up in a smug smile, but it was enough to make him suddenly homesick, which was a very odd feeling for him. Eli had never been homesick before.

But before he could fall any further into nostalgia, Eli caught sight of the man's eyes, and all feelings of warmth vanished. The demon's eyes were as yellow as Nico's, but where hers were determined, his were so cruel Eli took a step back, wincing as he bumped into the wall. The demon just smirked and stepped out of the cave and into the sunlight.

"What are we waiting for?" he said, and Eli winced again.

The demon's voice had never fit his form before. It had always been too deep, and that double harmonic had never matched a human throat. But the demon's voice matched this body perfectly, and Eli had to clench his teeth to keep from cowering.

"Nothing," Eli answered, proud that his voice wasn't as wobbly as his insides. "Let's go."

The demon looked back over his shoulder, pinning Eli with those cruel yellow eyes for a single breath before vanishing into his own shadow. Eli jumped with a curse and turned to Nico. She was still kneeling on the floor, cradling the fist she'd used to crack the seal in her lap.

"You okay?" Eli asked, moving to help her.

Nico nodded and held out her arms. "We need to hurry."

Eli didn't wait to be told twice. He stepped into Nico's arms. The moment he made contact, they slid into the dark.

Miranda woke with a start, sitting bolt upright. She regretted it immediately, slumping back to the ground with a sob. Powers, she felt like she'd been struck by lightning while getting run over by a cart. Her body was twitchy and everything ached, especially her skin, which felt far too small all of a sudden.

As her brain began to process the sensations, she slowly became aware of other things. She was cold, for one, but only on her back. Her shoulders were actually quite warm, and there was something hot and wet against her face.

She cracked her eyes. Gin's muzzle filled her vision, his red tongue sliding back between his teeth the second he saw her eyes.

"How are you feeling?" he growled.

"Like I always feel when I wake up like this," Miranda grumbled. "Horrible."

The ghosthound snorted, blowing a blast of hot air across her face. "Looks like your brain didn't get fried at least."

"Fried?" Miranda said. She tried to think back to what had happened, but her body cringed from the memory. Groaning, she reached up to rub her neck, but as her fingers landed, she realized her skin was covered in something slick and warm.

She snatched her hand away and held it up, eyes widening when she saw the slick, red liquid on her fingertips. Blood. She touched her neck again, running her fingers over her jawline. Blood covered her cheeks and neck in a red torrent running from her ears, which, now that she thought about it, hurt a great deal. Miranda touched them tenderly, wincing as the contact sent an echo of pain through her head. "What happened to me?"

"I did."

The low voice was a buzz in her body as well as a rumble in her ears, and her head snapped up to see the Lord of Storms sitting in the snow less than a foot away. He was solid again, his chest whole. His black hair fell across his shoulders just as it had back in the Spirit Court, and his sword lay across his knees, whole and safe in its blue sheath. She stared at him in wonder, and then it all came back. The fight, the oath, the lightning strike.

Suddenly, Miranda felt like she was going to throw up. She leaned over and retched. When nothing came up, she fell back against Gin's paws with a groan.

"You probably shouldn't move," the Lord of Storms said. "I had to take quite a bit of you to keep from coming apart."

Miranda's body shook as Gin started to growl deep in his chest, his muzzle sliding up to bear his long, sharp teeth at the Lord of Storms.

"Don't start, puppy," the Lord of Storms said. "We're on the same side now." His eyes flicked to Miranda. "And I'm not calling you master."

Gin's growling got louder, but Miranda didn't have the strength to care. She lay back and pressed her hands on the heavy golden chain at her neck. Distance strained the connection, but she could still feel the Tower like a strong, steady pulse through the metal.

After that, she checked her other spirits one by one. They

were all shaken by the new addition, especially Skarest, her lightning bolt, but their connections to her were still strong. That was good, because she felt as weak as a newborn kitten. Hopefully this was just a temporary faintness, like the one after she'd taken Mellinor.

"Don't count on it," the Lord of Storms said.

Her eyes snapped open. "You can read my mind?"

"A bit," he said, tapping his sword against his knees. "I'm part of you now. And don't look at me like that. You volunteered for this, remember? As I was saying, the weakness is only going to get worse. I was letting you rest a bit before I took more."

Gin snarled, but the Lord of Storms just shrugged. "Can't be helped. You want me in shape to fight, right?"

"Let him be, Gin," Miranda said, pressing her hands over her eyes. Powers, she was exhausted. She took a deep breath, trying to will her strength back. There would be time for rest later, she promised her aching body. That, or she'd be dead and resting forever. Either way, it would be over soon.

As if in reply, her stomach rumbled. "I don't suppose we have any food," she muttered.

"No," Gin growled. "I'd offer to hunt, but it'd take too long to catch anything, and I think we're out of time."

"Why do you say that?"

Gin's growling fell to a whimper. "Look up."

She did, leaning sideways to see around the dog's head.

The moment she saw the sky, she wished she hadn't. The blue dome was caving inward. The clouds were gone, scattered in fear. So were the winds and the snow they blew, which left nothing to hide the horror. The clear blue arch of the sky reminded Miranda of stretched silk, and behind it, she could see the outlines of clawed hands digging down toward them.

A blast of fear gripped her chest. Suddenly, Miranda couldn't breathe. Her hunger vanished, so did the pain. Everything vanished except the dread that turned her blood to water.

"Powers," she whispered.

"Better find someone else to call to," the Lord of Storms said bitterly. "The Powers can do nothing for you now."

Miranda had no answer to that. She just stared at things digging into the sky, unable to look away. She would have laid there watching forever, or what was left of forever, but a shout broke her out of the trance.

She tore her eyes away just in time to see Josef stand, and Miranda jerked in surprise. Apparently, he'd been sitting on the other side of Gin, staying so quiet she hadn't even known he was there. But he was up now with the Heart in his hand, standing between them and a tall man Miranda had never seen before.

The man was dressed in black, but other than that it was hard to pin his clothes down. The long drape that hid his torso and legs could have been a coat or a well-cut robe, but the high collar reminded her of the League. His pale face was handsome and strangely trustworthy. It actually looked a lot like she'd always imagined Master Banage's had when he was younger, and she wondered a moment who he was. A Spiritualist, perhaps, though she was sure she'd have remembered a face like that. Maybe he was one of the Shapers? Miranda was still trying to puzzle it out when she caught sight of his eyes.

Her breath stopped. The man's eyes were golden yellow, just like Nico's. The demon. She was looking at the Demon of the Dead Mountain.

The Lord of Storms went stiff beside her, and the air filled with the smell of ozone. But before he could do anything with the gathering power, Nico and Eli stepped out of the shadows behind the demon. Nico looked the same as ever, but the thief looked positively rattled. Somehow, that terrified Miranda even more than the two demons. Eli being anything less than perfectly self-assured felt like a betrayal of the world's order.

Fortunately, the moment was fleeting. As soon as Eli's feet were firmly in the snow, he started talking. "We need to break in now," he said, looking at the Lord of Storms. "Since you're being so quiet, I presume someone's talked you over?"

"More or less," the Lord of Storms said.

Eli shrugged. "Can you open the veil to the Between?"

"I used to have that power," the Lord of Storms said, pushing himself up. "Let's see if she's cut me off."

Miranda was about to say she'd never do such a thing when she realized he wasn't talking about her.

The Lord of Storms raised his hand, and the air in front of him ripped open. All at once, the snowy valley was filled with blinding white light as Benehime's wall was revealed again. "That's the best I can do," he said, dropping his arm.

"It's a bit small," the Demon of the Dead Mountain said, his handsome face falling into a sneer. "After all this time, I expected so much more of you, my dear Lord of Storms."

The League Commander's eyes flashed, and Miranda felt his killing instinct like a blade of hot steel in her gut. She yanked on their connection, and the Lord of Storms grunted.

"Not yet," she whispered, panting from the effort of holding him back. "We need him to do this."

The Lord of Storms shot her a look of pure poison, but he did not move as the demon walked up to the white wall floating in the air.

"Well, my daughter," the demon said, smiling at Nico. "Shall we play our part?"

Nico snarled at the endearment, but she stepped up beside him, her little body tense beside his large form. "Let's just get this over with."

The demon laughed and held out his hand. All at once, his fingers flickered and vanished, revealing an enormous, black claw. A second later, Nico's did the same. Her claw was slightly smaller, but the curved edges were just as wicked as they hovered above the white barrier.

"When you're ready, love," the demon said, his double-harmonic voice cloying as poisoned honey.

Nico's hand clenched, and then she brought her claws down. The second they hit the white wall, the air began to scream. The veil squealed beneath her attack and began to pitch wildly.

Smoke rose from Nico's black talons, and her face distorted in pain and rage.

Just before her hand dissolved in the white light, the demon's claw joined hers. They pressed together, and shadows began to gather despite the blinding light, the darkness clinging to their bodies like syrup. For several moments the white wall did nothing but scream and burn their claws, and then, with an ear-splitting crack, the barrier shattered.

The demons' claws sliced through the white wall like knives through flesh. The blinding light faded, and Nico and the demon dropped their arms, the claws flickering back to their human shapes.

Josef ran over to Nico, and they exchanged a few words Miranda couldn't hear. Eli joined them a second later, and the three began to whisper rapidly. On the sidelines, the demon stood back with a sardonic smile, his eyes fixed on the sky overhead. "Settle it quickly, children," he called. "They're almost through."

Miranda's eyes shot up. The bulging sky was lower than ever. Now that she'd seen demon claws firsthand, she could make out the traces of the same shapes straining against the sky's surface.

The thought drained the blood from her face. Watching them digging into the shell, Miranda could already see what would happen in her mind's eye. The dark claws would rip through the blue sky as they had ripped through the wall of light seconds earlier, and the creatures would fall on them, enormous mouths open to devour the world. With that, the fear came roaring back, and she began to shake uncontrollably.

"Who's going in?"

The Lord of Storms' voice cut through her panic, and she looked up to see him striding over to Eli's group.

"I am," Eli said, pushing Josef aside. "And I'm going alone."

The Lord of Storms sneered. "Change your mind about paradise, thief?"

Eli's expression flipped in an instant, and the pure fury

886

Miranda saw there took her breath away. "Never suggest that again," he said, his voice as cold as the snow underfoot.

The Lord of Storms crossed his arms. "Just checking."

Eli shot him a final glare before turning back to his group, his face returning to its usual earnest charm.

"I'm the only one who can do this," he said. "Benehime is the most powerful thing in the world right now. We can't fight her, so it has to be me. Meanwhile, I need the rest of you to make sure the world doesn't fall to pieces while I'm in there."

"Easy for you to say," the Lord of Storms growled.

"I'll be quick," Eli promised, and then he turned to face the Lord of Storms. "Do you still live for a good fight?"

"Of course," the Lord of Storms answered. "Why do you ask this now?"

"No reason," Eli said, smiling in the way that usually meant there were a lot of reasons. "Just hold tight, I'll be back as soon as I can."

He grinned at them one last time and turned around. Lifting his leg high, he stepped up through the ripped hole and into the white world beyond. The light ate him at once, and the portal in the veil snapped closed without a sound, the glowing line fading instantly into the air.

"He's not coming back," the Lord of Storms announced.

No one else said a word.

CHAPTER
22

Eli took a deep breath as the veil closed behind him. He was locked in now, no turning back. That thought actually made him feel better. First rule of thievery: You can do absolutely anything when there's a wall at your back.

He was standing alone in the Between. The white nothing stretched out forever in all directions, endless and blinding. But, though Benehime's world looked the same as ever, something was different. There was a pressure in the air strong enough to make Eli's ears pop, like the whole place was being squeezed.

With a muffled curse, Eli started to run. There was no time to stand around gawking. He ran straight forward, his boots slapping soundlessly against the white floor. He didn't have a destination in mind, didn't need one. All directions here led to only one place.

He'd been running for less than a minute before he spotted her. Benehime was sitting beside her sphere, her white hair swept back over her shoulders, leaving her perfect body naked. Her white eyes were narrowed, watching him run, and at her throat hung a shining white pearl on a strand of light.

He slowed as he reached her, coming to a stop a few feet from her white form. For several moments they just stared at each other, and then Benehime looked away, hand going to the glowing pearl at her neck. *I knew you would come.*

Eli winced at her voice. He'd never heard it so cold.

She turned away from him, reaching out to cradle the small orb floating beside her. The paradise lit up as she touched it, glistening like a jewel garden inside its tiny, perfect shell. It had changed from the last time Eli had seen it. The flat blank she'd left in preparation for the Shaper Mountain was gone. In its place, a high mountain meadow full of flowers shone in the white light of her touch. When she saw him looking, Benehime turned her hand, hiding the beautiful world from his view.

No, no, she whispered. *You threw that away, remember? You chose to stay here.*

She stepped aside to reveal the larger sphere floating behind her, neglected, and Eli's skin went cold. The world's sphere was no longer perfect and round, but dented as though it were being squeezed in a vise. Inside, the seas were shaking, sending great waves surging miles into the coast. Rivers writhed in their beds, and the mountains quaked in fear as the sky bent down like it was folding under enormous pressure. There were depressions in the bedrock base, but worst by far was the dome's top. The arch of the sky was crumpling as Eli watched, the blue wall warping as though under enormous pressure.

Won't be long now, Benehime said, her white eyes hateful. *But that's why you're here, isn't it?*

"Yes," Eli said. "It is."

Benehime's lip curled in a sneer. *You always were such a selfish creature, Eliton. But then, all humans are. I should know; I made you so. And do you know why?*

Eli's eyes flicked back to the sphere. The sky was starting to discolor as it bent, turning from blue to a stretched gray-white. He had to speed this up. "Benehime, please—"

My brother the Weaver thought I was cruel, Benehime said, completely ignoring him as she fondled the glowing pearl at her neck. *Of the three of us, I alone had our father's gift of creation. Why, he asked, would I use it to make a race of blind, deaf creatures whose lives ended in the blink of an eye? Why give them a fraction of my own power?*

She glanced up, waiting, and though time was running out, Eli played along. "Why?"

Benehime smiled, a cruel curving of her white lips. *Because I was always the cleverest. After our father trapped us in here, the spirits were in panic. Why not? Diligent as the Weaver was, they could still see the demon's claws on the shell's edge, especially against the sky. Every time they looked up, they were reminded of the doom that was never more than an hour from breaking through. This knowledge proved impossible for the spirits to handle, and we had constant problems.*

Problems, she called them, Eli thought with a mental eye roll, but the Shepherdess wasn't finished.

The Weaver wanted to talk them through their fear, she said, her voice disgusted. *He wanted to give them knowledge, to make them feel safe by imparting understanding.* She shook her head.

My brother never understood spirits. That's why he was sent to mind the veil while I was given dominion over creation. I understood, as my brother did not, that all spirits, great or small, are fundamentally the same: panicky, stupid, prey animals.

She turned back toward the crumpling world. *Look at them,* she said. *Even now, when there's no hope at all, the whole world has launched itself into a pointless fit, burning their last minutes in terror and agony. Stupid, like I said. It was always like this before. No matter how my brother tried to explain that they were safe, the world never listened. Every time one of those idiot sheep glanced at the sky or the Dead Mountain, we'd have a panic. It went on and on, even after I strictly forbade them to look or speak of what they saw. That's when I decided I needed a distraction.*

She looked at Eli, waiting for him to say something. When he didn't, she answered for him. *Humans. I made humans in the image of the Powers, complete with a fraction of my own will, giving you dominion over all the spirits of the world. And then, to keep you from panicking too, I made you blind and forbade my spirits from telling you anything of importance.*

"Why would you do that?" Eli snapped. It was a stupid thing to do, but he couldn't help himself. "To put so much power in the hands of blind, ignorant—"

It was your ignorance that made it work. Benehime laughed. *My humans burst into the world like a plague, and, since they could not see the spirits under their feet, they assumed it was all theirs. It was glorious. Where my brother had been working for years to stop the panics with knowledge and reason, blind human hubris stopped them in a day. The spirits were so busy trying to deal with the wizards who suddenly had mastery over them, they no longer had time to worry about the demons. And since I cut your lives so short, even the really awful Enslavements never lasted too long. Never as long as the earlier panics had, anyway.*

Benehime's face lit up with smug satisfaction. *With humans there to occupy all their fears, even those spirits who broke my edict and looked at the sky never looked long enough to remember what they should really be afraid of.* She spread her hands wide. *Blind, ignorant, and all-powerful. You were my perfect distraction and, in your own way, helped save the last of a greater world than you could ever know. It was a brilliant solution, and no one, not even Durain, ever realized the truth of it. Truly, you blind fools are my greatest creations.* Then her face fell. *Too bad it was all for nothing.*

As she finished, Eli just stared at her, speechless, and Benehime, knowing how rare this state was for him, reveled in it. When his voice finally returned, he was so furious the words came out in a stammer. *"That's it?"* he shouted. "That's why you made us? A dog-and-pony show to distract the spirits from remembering they were in a lifeboat surrounded by sharks? *That's* why we have wizards?"

Yes, Benehime said, smiling again. *Genius, isn't it?*

Eli closed his eyes. His first thought was that Miranda was going to blow her top. But the more he tried to make sense of the Lady's claim, the more he felt something was wrong. The story didn't sit right. Eli opened his eyes again, fixing Benehime with an even stare. "Why are you telling me this now?"

Benehime's cruel smile grew sharper. *Because, darling, you seem to be laboring under the false assumption that the spirits are your friends. That they should be coddled and protected. But I made humans to be the spirits' enemies, not their allies. You were created to be the lesser but immediate threat. You are the feint, the ploy that kept the spirits from dwelling on the real danger. You are a tool, my tool to keep my spirits in line, and as such, you owe them nothing. Not your love, not your friendship, certainly not your life. I, on the other hand, am your entire world.*

She closed the distance between them, her white hair rustling behind her. This close, Eli could feel the heatless burn radiating from her skin, but he forced himself to remain still, staring up at her cold, white eyes.

I am your creator, she whispered. *Everything you have, every power, every breath, every clever thought in your head, I gave you. I gave you everything, Eliton, and you threw it back in my face. Now the world is collapsing, and you've come running back like nothing happened. But you've abused my generosity too many times for me to be lenient now, Eliton. If you want to leave this place alive, you must prove your sincerity.*

She held out her hand and closed her fingers, leaving the first pointing down. *Kneel*, she commanded. *And beg. Beg your creator for forgiveness, and we shall see if I am feeling merciful.*

Eli took a deep breath, filling his lungs with the cold, stale air of the Between, and then, slowly, he fell to knees. Benehime's eyes lit up as he leaned forward, lowering his head to the floor.

"I am begging," he said against the white ground. "But I'm not begging for myself."

Benehime tensed. *What?*

"I thought you loved me," Eli said, sitting back up with a glare. "Forever and always, that's what you promised."

Why are you saying this now? Benehime cried, stepping back. *You had your chance, Eliton. I gave you everything and you turned your back on me.*

"You gave me nothing!" Eli said. "You promised me everything, but it was all empty. You only loved me on your terms."

That's not true, Benehime said. *I loved you more than you can comprehend.*

"You're right. I don't comprehend it," Eli said. "I don't understand how you can say you love me and yet stomp on every happiness I find. You've threatened me, threatened my friends, taken my lava spirit, and your excuse for all of it was that you loved me. Is it any wonder I rejected your sort of love?"

You understand nothing about love! Benehime screamed. *What is your suffering compared to mine? Do you know what I sacrificed for you? What I gave up to have you with me?*

892

Eli leaned back, looking up at the White Lady. "And do you still want me with you? Do you still love me?"

Benehime's face softened. *You know I do, darling.*

Eli spread his arms. "Then prove it. Don't do this, Benehime. You cared for this world once, so go to your brother and help him repair it. Make a new Hunter who can guard the shell before it cracks completely. Go out into the world and show yourself for what you are: our Shepherdess, our guide. Make *this* world a paradise. Give me a reason to love you rather than a reason to hate you, and I will be yours forever. I will love you, cherish you, and I will never leave your side again."

His words echoed in the whiteness. Above him, Benehime stood frozen, her eyes so wide he could see the full circle of the silver shadow that rimmed her irises. At last, she fell to her knees, her white hair spreading around her with a whisper.

Eliton, she murmured, reaching out to pull him to her. For the first time in many years, Eli leaned into her embrace, wrapping his arms around her waist.

"Please, Benehime," he whispered against her burning skin. "You were everything to me once. You were my beautiful Shepherdess, the guardian and guide for the spirits. We could go back to that, you and me. It's not too late. Please, if you love me at all, help me now. Open the veil, go to the Weaver, and help save the world you were created to love."

He felt her arms tighten around him, and for a moment, Eli thought it had worked. But then her fingertips dug into his skin, and that hope shattered.

No, she whispered. *I can't keep on like this. Not even for you. I'm done with this world, Eliton. Done playing nursemaid to its stupid, sleeping spirits. Done holding out hope for a creator who's never coming back.* She turned her head and kissed him on the lips. *Come away with me,* she pleaded. *I'll be anything you want, darling, but not here. Not anymore.*

Eli sighed deeply. "Then I'm sorry."

You don't have to be, the Shepherdess said, her eyes tearing up. *I love you. Forget this world. Come with me and we'll start over. I promise. All will be forgiven.*

"No," Eli said. "Not this."

And then his hands shot up and yanked the glowing pearl from her throat.

The second he touched it, several things happened. Benehime's scream filled his ears, a surprised gasp that turned to an enraged shriek, but Eli was too overwhelmed to pay much attention. As soon as his fingers had wrapped around the Hunter's seed, blinding white light filled him. At first he felt nothing but shock, and then shock turned to anger as a surge of power ripped through him, nearly tearing him apart.

The Hunter's rage exploded into his mind. The raw fury at his sister's betrayal mixed with the bitter anger of regret. It pounded through Eli's veins, filling him to bursting, pulsing so strongly he couldn't move even as Benehime's hands shot forward to snatch the prize back.

Just before she reached him, another burning hand locked on Eli's shoulder and tore him away. He flew through the white nothing, landing on his back with such force that even the Hunter's fury fell silent. In the stunned calm, he looked up to see the Weaver. The old Power stood face-to-face with his sister, his gnarled fists clenched as his long, white hair writhed over his body like a nest of snakes.

Go! he shouted.

Eli tried to ask where, but before he could even open his lips, he saw Benehime draw something from the fall of hair at her back. It was long and so black it ate even the Between's whiteness as she wrapped her hand around it, brandishing it like a dagger at her unarmed brother.

Go! the Weaver shouted again, raising his hand to catch the demonseed as it fell. *Now!*

Eli didn't wait to be told again. He scrambled to his feet, hands clenched tight around the Hunter's burning seed, and ran. As he plunged into the blank whiteness of the Between, he heard a sound so loud it drowned out even the

Shepherdess's enraged scream. It was a great crack, like a thousand panes of glass had all broken at the same time, and the second Eli heard it, he knew. Knew without looking that the sky of the crumpled sphere floating forgotten behind Benehime had cracked at last.

The white Between bucked under his feet, and suddenly Eli could see the walls of Benehime's endless world at last. They were ripping, the whiteness tearing like rotted cloth as the black shapes so horrible Eli's mind couldn't comprehend them began to claw their way through.

As the Between ripped, fear hit Eli like a punch in the gut, mixing with the Hunter's rage and his own exhilaration until he felt he would fly apart. But he didn't. He ran. He ran like he had never run before, dodging the black, grasping hands as they reached blindly for him. He ran straight for the place where he had come in, trusting his feet to remember the way back in this world without markers. When he found it, he gripped the Hunter's white seed and, raising his leg with a furious roar, kicked a hole in the white world.

The veil shattered like glass as he struck it, and Eli began to fall.

Miranda wrapped her arms around herself and burrowed deeper against Gin's chest. Now that Eli was gone and the white gate had closed, things in the snowy valley were growing...tense. No, tense wasn't the right word. Tense was how she felt when she had to report bad news to Master Banage. This was a massacre waiting for an excuse.

They'd formed a rough triangle—Josef and Nico stood at the place where Eli had vanished, dividing their glares between the Lord of Storms, who was standing beside Miranda with his arms crossed over his healed chest, and the demon. For his part, the Lord of Storms was locked on the Demon of the Dead Mountain, and it was only Miranda's death grip on their connection that kept him from attacking. The demon was standing with his hands on his hips and looking far, far too pleased with himself for Miranda's taste. As his grin widened, Josef's hand drifted to the hilt of his sword, and Miranda felt she'd better say something before the four of them tore each other to bits.

She was still trying to decide what that something was when a loud sound made everything else insignificant. It was a crack. A sharp squeal like glass breaking, but infinitely larger. As it faded, Miranda could only wonder what in the world was large enough to make a sound that enormous when it broke. And then, with a horrible sinking feeling, her eyes turned up.

The breath fled from her lungs. There, running along the warped and crumpling sky, was a crack. It ran up from the eastern horizon, weaving back and forth in wide jags before finally thinning to nothing just beyond what had been the sky's zenith. The crack sparkled in the sunlight, its edges gleaming white.

For several seconds the world was silent. The wind didn't blow, the snow didn't stir, even the spirit panic seemed to have stopped. Everything was staring at the crack in the sky. And then, with another booming crack, a second fracture split off from the first.

This one grew as Miranda watched, running across the distended sky like lightning toward the western horizon. It stopped just at the edge of the afternoon sun, the tail end of the crack splitting the top of the yellow orb. As the sun cracked, its light skewed, and that was when Miranda began to panic in earnest.

Even though the Weaver and the Shaper Mountain had warned her, even though she *knew* this was coming, there was something about seeing the world lit from that new, unnatural angle that her mind simply could not wrap itself around. All she could do was raise her shaking hand, catching the broken sunlight with her rings, and wonder if there was a sun at all. Was anything real, or was the world she'd taken for granted her whole life little more than a painted backdrop?

She didn't realize she was screaming until the Lord of Storms' hand wrapped around her neck. She heard Gin's snarl far in the distance, but the ghosthound was drowned out by the thunder that was suddenly pounding through her head. The Lord of Storms lifted her by the throat and leaned in until his pale face and waving black hair were all she could see. The rage behind his flashing eyes overwhelmed her, but when he spoke, the words were low and controlled.

"If you fall apart on me now, Spiritualist, I will take everything you have to give until you die," he whispered. "Do you understand?"

There was no hatred in the threat, no malice. It was simply a promise to do what must be done, and the calm reality of it snapped Miranda's jarred mind back into place. She swallowed against his grip and nodded. The Lord of Storms nodded as well and dropped her onto Gin's back. She scrambled, nearly falling, but Gin's nose nudged her into place.

"Never do that again," he snarled once she was seated.

"I do what I need to, pup," the Lord of Storms said, looking back at the sky. "See you don't get in my way."

Gin snapped at the Lord of Storms' leg before Miranda could stop him. But the hound's teeth slid harmlessly through his body as his leg dissolved into storms. The dog growled and went for another snap, but Miranda grabbed his ear.

"Let it be," she commanded. "Now's not the time."

Gin bared his teeth one last time, and then turned back to the sky. They were all looking up now, the demons, the humans, everyone. Josef had drawn the Heart, Miranda noticed out of the corner of her eye. What he meant to do with it, she had no idea. Compared to the crack in the sky, even the Heart's enormous blade looked small and useless. They all did. She bit her lip as the sky began to whine under the pressure. Even if Eli was successful, even if a new Hunter was born, how were they ever to stop this?

"Stand firm," the Lord of Storms commanded. "Here they come."

Miranda tangled her fingers in Gin's shifting fur as the crack splintered and then splintered again, shooting across the sky like branches from a tree. The new cracks spread in long lines, carving the bulging sky into a network of shards until the blue was almost gray from the strain. With each crack, the groaning, glass-on-glass sound of the sky grinding against itself grew worse. And then, just when Miranda was sure she could bear the creaking no longer, the sky shattered.

After the cracks, the actual break was startlingly quiet. At the place where the three largest cracks met, the sky simply fell apart. The blue shards rained down, dissolving to nothing before they hit the ground with a soft sigh. The sound that came next, however, Miranda knew she would never be able to forget no matter how desperately she tried.

As the sky broke, a scream burst into the world. It wasn't a spirit's scream, or a human sound, or even the cry of an animal in pain. It wasn't like anything Miranda had ever heard. The sound was strangely empty, like a chord missing its key note. It was almost like the dissonance of Nico's voice, but a million times more. And then the fear hit Miranda like a punch in the gut.

Even though she was expecting it, she nearly fell over. Fear rolled over the world like a sticky fog, and the spirits, already worn to breaking by the earlier panics, began to howl anew. Miranda wanted to howl with them, but she forced the fear away, clamping down on her own terror as well as her spirits', and though every instinct she had was screaming at her to run and hide, she held her ground and raised her eyes.

Where the sky had broken was a hole filled with the deepest black she had ever seen. It was like looking into the opposite of light, and Miranda had the feeling that even if she were to take the sun itself and shine it through, it still wouldn't be enough light to show her what was on the other side. That would actually be fine with her. Miranda didn't want to know what lived in such darkness. Unfortunately, her ignorance was short lived. For one long second, the black hole hung empty in the sky, its edges vibrating with the strange screaming, and then, a clawed hand shot through the opening and plunged toward the mountains.

It was enormous. Truly enormous and utterly black, its great fingers opening to grasp as it plummeted. On and on and on it reached until the arm was as long as a mountain range, its claws each as large as a city. But long as it was, the arm was so thin compared to its length that it turned Miranda's stomach. Thin and sickly, the arm fell down through the air until, at last, the enormous clawed fingers dug into one of the distant mountain peaks. A new scream drowned out all the others when it connected. A scream of triumph and endless, mad hunger as the hand tore the mountain from its roots and began lifting it back toward the broken sky.

Even this far away, even with all the other sounds, Miranda felt the mountain's scream in her bones. The stone sobbed with impotent fury, gripping the ground even as the claws tore it away. It kept screaming even as the claws dragged it into the air, crying and begging for help. The cries shot through her like arrows, but Miranda could do nothing except watch, horrified and helpless, as the hand pulled the mountain up toward the dark.

And then, in a flash, everything changed again.

Miranda felt the blow before she saw it, a great iron wave of power that knocked her into the snow. It swelled and vanished in the space of a second, and the enormous hand split in two.

The demon's scream doubled, the alien sound twisting from triumph to enraged pain as the arm jerked back. But it was too late. The cut was razor straight across the back of the monstrous black palm. The beetle-shiny flesh peeled away in a line as three claws fell free and began to plummet, taking the mountain with them. The severed demon flesh dissolved like smoke as it fell, and by the time the mountain crashed back into the ground, there was no trace of the severed claws at all save for the long, burned imprints of the demon's hand on the mountain's slope.

Miranda stared a second longer and then turned her wide eyes to Josef as he lowered the Heart of War. She could still feel the enormous power rolling out of him like heat off a bonfire, but the swordsman's stance was even and calm as he watched the enormous arm writhe and slither back up toward the splintered sky.

"You always did have a flair for the barbaric," the Demon of the Dead Mountain said, his handsome face broken by a sharp-toothed smile.

Nico snarled at the comment, but Josef just set the Heart point first into the snow at his feet. "Any time you feel like holding up your end, feel free."

The Demon of the Dead Mountain began to laugh, a two-toned cackle with that missing harmonic that made Miranda's skin crawl, and the more he laughed, the less human his face became. His cheeks split as his teeth lengthened, the white crowns fading to jagged, black points. His clothes stretched and changed as his body grew. He doubled in size, and then doubled again, and with every inch he grew, the fear that crawled over the world thickened.

It took forever, and yet it was finished sooner than Miranda would have thought. One minute the demon had stood before her looking too much like a young Banage to trust; the next all she saw was the monster. It towered over them, so large and so terrifying she couldn't see the whole of it at once.

Unlike the thing outside of Izo's, this demon was no mad, stumbling horror. Nor was it like the hand in the sky, all thin desperation and hunger. This was a monster in its prime, cold and compact and radiating predatory menace. Its arms were triple-jointed as Den's had been after the change, and the creature balanced delicately on them as it rocked back on sturdy legs braced by nine-foot claws that dug into the screaming ground. Its head was a long, hard muzzle covered in a glossy black shell and filled with row after row of jagged black teeth. On top, three enormous, golden eyes narrowed in anticipation as its six-clawed fingers tapped against its snout.

When the demon had finished growing, its yellow eyes roved down and focused on Josef. The swordsman glared back without flinching. The demon smiled at his bravado, showing its thousands of teeth, and moved its gaze to Nico. Unlike Josef, she shrank under the unblinking stare, and the demon's smile grew wider.

"Well, then, daughter." The horrible mouth didn't even move as it hissed the words. "Show the good people what you've made of yourself."

Josef started to raise his sword but stopped when Nico's hand landed on his arm. She shook her head and said something Miranda couldn't hear over the screaming. Josef's face tightened, but in the end he nodded. Only then did Nico begin to change.

Her change wasn't like the other demon's. There was no stretching, no horrible bending of her human form. She simply vanished into a column of shadow, her body washed away beneath a torrent of liquid black.

Pain shot through Miranda's chest, and she looked to see the Lord of Storms straining against their bond, his teeth clenched as the shadows around Nico grew solid. Like the Demon of the Dead Mountain, her skin was glossy and black. Unlike him, however, her form was almost human.

She stood on clawed feet that reminded Miranda of a raven's. Unlike the other demon with his four legs and curled, stout body, Nico's two-legged form was straight and tall, her long torso hidden beneath a cloud of swirling shadows that shifted and spun in the memory of her coat. Her shoulders were sharp and narrow beneath the flowing shadow, and her arms, while still proportionally too long and clawed, had only one joint at the elbow.

Her head, however, was totally different. It sat on her

shoulders like a mask, a great, horned carapace with two narrow, angled eyes glowing like golden lanterns above a narrow, jackal-like snout filled with even, razor-sharp black teeth.

"My, how fancy," the Demon of the Dead Mountain said, his horrible voice thick with laughter. "You can't do anything normally, can you?"

Nico didn't answer. She simply looked up as the darkness around her began to spread. It rose and solidified, forming four enormous, swirling wings that blacked out the sky. The Lord of Storms sucked in a breath as she rose with one, slow flap and began to climb toward the hole in the sky. "Daughter of the Dead Mountain."

He spoke the name with such fury that Miranda didn't dare ask him how he knew the thing that Nico had become. Instead, she focused on the cracked sky where the wounded arm was still thrashing. By this point, other clawed fingers were working their way in, worming past the squirming arm of the injured demon to pry at the sky in an attempt to break the hole wider.

Josef gave a shout and swung his sword again. The blow shot past Nico and sliced the end off one of the newcomer's claws. The creature's scream was lost in the roar, and the new hand vanished only to be instantly replaced by another. Josef frowned and glared at the Demon of the Dead Mountain. The demon smiled back wide enough to show every one of his uncountable black teeth and then, almost lazily, stretched his long, stocky body and jumped after Nico.

Miranda was trying to decide if she should cheer or cry at that when a loud snap cut through the screams. Her head shot up so fast she almost broke her neck, and she cried out in alarm. A second crack was sprouting from a small branch of the first one, spidering across the crumpled dome of the sky directly over their heads. Almost as soon as the crack formed, the sky broke, and two more hands just as large as the first burst through.

They shot screaming toward the ground, one of them coming

902

straight for Miranda's head. It happened so fast, she didn't even think to move out of the way. She just stood there staring as the hand came down to squash her like a bug. She was imagining how the black claws would rip through her when something strong and painful clamped on to her arm and jerked her around.

Despite that she was on Gin's back and he was standing on the ground, the Lord of Storms towered over her, his hand like a vise on her arm. "Time to honor your part of our bargain, woman," he said, his voice fading into thunder as the wind began to pick up.

Miranda didn't have to ask what he meant. She could already feel her link with him tightening as he began to pull, draining her through their bond. His hand vanished from her arm, turning into cloud as she watched. The rest of him followed, and the sky filled with enormous thunderheads lit up with bolt after bolt of branching, tree-thick lightning.

Gin went stiff beneath her, and Miranda was glad. It made him easier to cling to as the storm rolled through her, taking everything it could. She gave herself gladly, pouring her will into the storm as she had poured into Mellinor back on the beach at Osera. That time, she had been one with her beloved sea. Now she was nothing but the ground the storm rose from, the wind that lifted the heavy clouds.

The Lord of Storms took and took, drinking everything she was without apology. She let him, clinging to Gin's fur with her soul roaring open and her spirits cowering in their rings. Around her neck, she felt the Spirit Court's Tower distancing itself, probably to avoid being sucked in by the Lord of Storms' ravenous thirst for strength.

She let the stone spirit go, pushing him away so she would have more to give the storm. As her eyes closed, she promised herself that if she survived this she was never letting another Great Spirit other than Mellinor into her body ever again. That was her last thought before the air flashed white and something heavy and kicking landed right on top of her.

CHAPTER
23

Eli groaned and lay back on the lumpy ground, thankful for whatever it was that had broken his fall, even though that kind cushion was now elbowing him in the ribs and cursing at him in a very familiar voice. Obligingly, he rolled off, landing on his knees in the snow with the Hunter's seed clutched against his chest. He steadied himself and looked up just in time to see a furious Miranda kick to her feet in front of him.

"Good positioning," he said, rubbing his bruised ribs. "You might have just saved me a broken neck."

"I'll give you a broken neck!" Miranda roared, but then the fury seemed to drift out of her as her eyes latched on to the glowing pearl in Eli's hand. "You did it!"

"'Course I did it," Eli said, sticking out his free arm for her to pull him up. "How much time do we have left?"

Miranda's hand was icy as it grabbed his, and her voice was no less bleak. "See for yourself," she said, nodding at the sky as she yanked him up.

Bracing himself for the worst, Eli looked up...

...and realized that there is no amount of bracing that can prepare you to see the sky ripped open.

There were three holes in total, and each one was filled with monstrous black hands the size of mountains straining like starving animals as they reached for whatever they could grab. For a long, confused moment, Eli couldn't understand how the cracked shell was still holding. Then, as his mind worked its way around the crack and the giant hands, he saw the defenders.

Josef stood on the lowest ridge of the Dead Mountain, the Heart of War flying in his grip like the blade was part of him. Every time he swung, one of the grasping hands lost a chunk,

904

even though they were miles away. But even as one demon squealed in rage and yanked its hand back, another would surge forward to take its place, the new hand just as desperate as the last as it fought to reach the screaming spirits below.

But Josef wasn't the only one holding the invaders back. Flitting between the enormous black hands were two other shadows that, though smaller, were equally unsettling. Just looking at them made Eli's stomach heave, but he forced himself to study them long enough to see that the two were different.

One was all teeth and predatory malice. It snarled and bit the invading hands, driving them back with territorial fury. The other was softer, quieter, but no less deadly. Her body was shrouded in a shadow, and her back was dominated by four wings that rippled like black water. Her long claws dragged over each demon she passed, and every place she touched crumpled under enormous pressure, making the demons scream in pain. Eli almost smiled then. Leave it to Nico to stay quiet even when she was the monster in the night.

But the demons weren't the only monsters fighting the things from the other side of the sky. Down below, where the hands would have broken through to dig into the mountains, a wall of black cloud prevented them, driving them back with arcing silver lightning.

The Lord of Storms carpeted the land in all directions, a barrier against whatever Josef, Nico, and the Demon of the Dead Mountain missed. Every time a claw came near, the lightning would rise up in a great thunderhead that opened like the mouth of a wolf, biting the grasping claws with crackling teeth that flashed out before the demon could eat them in retaliation. Each time one vanished, another took its place in an endless series of lightning strikes that drove the ravenous demons back.

The four defenders were such an impressive sight, Eli almost felt hopeful. The worst had come, and they were still holding. But then his eyes went to the sky again, to the network of shining cracks, the split sun, the black claws fighting for purchase on the rims of the broken holes, picking away at the shell's edge, and his fledgling hope vanished as quickly as it had come.

He looked down at the seed in his hand. Wherever the pearl touched his fingers, his skin was pure white. White as Benehime's. Power flowed through him, hot with rage, tingling with promise. For a moment, Eli let it fill him, burning away his fear and exhaustion until he was strong enough to make the decision that shouldn't have been his to make.

He turned to Miranda. "Call the Lord of Storms."

"What?" she cried over the screaming.

"You're connected to him, right?" Eli shouted back. "Call him down."

"Are you paying attention?" Miranda roared. "He's the only thing keeping—"

"Now," Eli snapped.

Miranda glared furiously at him, but then she lifted her head. The storm thundered in answer, and then the Lord of Storms appeared in a flash of lightning.

"What do you mean by yanking me—"

Eli didn't wait for the spirit to finish his tirade. He lunged straight at the Lord of Storms' chest. The storm was so furious at Miranda's infraction, he didn't even notice as Eli's shoved the Hunter's glowing seed deep into his stomach.

The second it was inside, the Lord of Storms froze. Overhead, the clouds stopped swirling and the lightning hung midflash. On the ground, the Lord of Storms' body was still as a statue, his silver eyes wide and unreadable as they watched Eli remove his now-empty hand and step back, drawing Miranda back with him.

She tried to protest, but he forced her down behind Gin with the last of the Hunter's fading strength. Good thing, too, because not a second after he'd gotten her to shelter, the Lord of Storms' face broke into an enormous grin and the Hunter's rage filled the valley with a white flash.

The light was blinding, filling not just the Lord of Storms' body but the thunderclouds as well, washing out even the lightning flashes in a flood of pale brilliance. It was so bright Eli didn't even try to watch. Instead, he kept his head down, crouching behind Gin with Miranda huddled against him, her eyes closed tight against the light and her hands clutching her chest like she was trying to staunch a wound.

On and on and on it went until, finally, the light began to fade. Eli was about to peek over Gin's back to see if his plan had worked when Miranda grabbed his shoulders and whirled him around. "*What did you do?*" she screamed in his ear.

"I made him the Hunter," Eli said, wincing.

Miranda's furious face grew horrified. "That's it? You just *made* him the Hunter? Don't you think you should have *asked* first?"

"I did!" Eli shouted, prying her fingers off him. "Sort of. Anyway, we had no time and it's not like he would have said no." He pushed up and glanced over Gin's back. "There, see for yourself."

Miranda shot up, and then nearly fell back again in surprise.

The Lord of Storms was standing exactly as he had before, sword in his hand, his face suffused in an enormous grin, but he was now pure white. His coat, his sword, his skin, his long hair, even his silver eyes were now whiter than moonlit chalk, so white that the snow around him looked ashy by comparison. The light of him filled the valley with harsh, cold radiance, and though the fear was still thick in the air, the spirits around him had stopped screaming. One by one, they bowed down, trembling before the presence of a newborn Power.

The Lord of Storms ignored them completely. He sheathed his sword and strode forward, white eyes locked on Eli. "Where is she?"

The hatred in his voice was like a knife against Eli's ear, and he didn't have to ask who the Lord of Storms meant. "She's fighting the Weaver," he answered. "And you'd better hurry."

The Lord of Storms nodded and lifted his arm to make a portal through the veil. This time, though, instead of forming the usual neat, white line, the Lord of Storms took a handful of air and ripped it sideways. The veil tore open with a sound that made Eli wince, but the Lord of Storms paid it no mind. He kept tearing, splitting the veil until he'd made a hole large enough for him to step through.

"Wait!" Miranda cried.

The Lord of Storms froze and turned on the Spiritualist with a look that would have killed anyone else. Miranda just glared back. "What about them?" she snapped, pointing up at the remaining three defenders. "They need you."

The Lord of Storms' white lips split into a blinding grin. *When I'm done, there won't be anything left for them to fight.*

Eli closed his eyes. The voice was still the Lord of Storms', but it filled his mind with that strange echo he now recognized as the hallmark of a Power. Miranda must have recognized it, too, because her face went almost gray. The Lord of Storms only smiled wider.

Come on, both of you, he said, marching through the hole in the veil. *We have unfinished business.*

Eli and Miranda exchanged a look and silently followed the Lord of Storms into the Between. Gin tried to go, too, but Miranda shook her head, motioning for the dog to stay as they walked into the blank nothing. The ghosthound watched them until an unseen curve of the Between hid him from view. It was only then that Eli realized with a cold, creeping dread that the veil had not closed behind them.

Nico closed her claws around the demon's enormous wrist and twisted. The creature screamed as she sliced through the hard tendons, and she smiled beneath her mask as the black hand retreated. She followed it, twisting again, cutting again, until the hand pulled back through the hole completely.

A new one took its place immediately, shooting past Nico toward the ground. She fell after it, but Josef got there first, severing two of the six fingers with one strike. Nico smiled at him, but Josef didn't see. How could he? Her face was hidden beneath the mask of glowing eyes and sharp teeth.

At that thought, Nico felt the hunger rising in her again, the black water bubbling from her depths. She snarled and crushed it back down. She'd won that battle already, and she had no intention of fighting two fronts at once. The grasping hands from the sky were almost too much to handle as it was. She closed her eyes and fought the black water of her demon nature back down until her mind was once again a calm, dry field. Only when the absolute control filled her body did she resume her attack.

The most recent black hand was still flailing from the Heart's attack. Nico folded her wings and dove toward the lashing claws. She'd take it out at the elbow this time, she decided. That was, if the second of the three hinge joints could even be called an elbow.

Honestly, she wasn't sure if the long limbs were arms or legs. The demons looked nothing like anything she'd ever seen, even herself. They were huge, true, far larger than she, but so thin they made her form look healthy by comparison. Next to their dull, wasted blackness, the Demon of the Dead Mountain positively shone as he took down the limb to her left, breaking the thin appendage with a snap of his enormous jaw.

Even if the Weaver hadn't told her these demons were starving, Nico would have known. They tore at the sky without intelligence or guile. Any cunning they might have possessed had been eaten long ago, along with everything else. Now they cared only for getting in, and as each scrambled to be first, they inadvertently blocked their only entrance. Had they not been so hungry, they would already be inside.

Of course, it was only a matter of time.

Nico looked up. She had no human eyes now. Spirit sight was her only sight, and through it she could see why the world below shook with panic. The sky, usually full of the enormous, weaving trails of the winds, was now empty, its blue arch a sickening, bruised purple where the pressure of the demons' hunger had crushed it in. But worse still were the cracks. They were everywhere now, white, jagged lines running from horizon to horizon. They creaked and groaned under the demons' assault, sending cascades of dust down with each new impact.

The sight of them filled Nico with hopelessness. With the shell so broken, it was only a matter of minutes before another hole opened and more hands thrust out of the impenetrable dark on the other side. They could barely keep the three they had under control as it was. One more, one tip of the balance, and everything would fall.

"Daydreaming, my daughter?"

She bared her teeth at the hateful voice and turned to see the Demon of the Dead Mountain hovering nearly on top of her, his enormous fanged mouth open in a wide grin.

"Go back to your work," she hissed, digging her lower claws into the demon hand below her. The monster screamed and yanked back, but the Demon of the Dead Mountain didn't move.

"Is it not natural for a father to show concern for his child's well-being?" he said, that deep, smooth voice as sweet as honey, just like always.

Nico ignored him, kicking off the now-writhing arm to finish the one the demon had been working on before he'd decided to come and chat. The cold at her back told her he was following, but she kept her eyes ahead, forcing her body down until she was as calm and cold as one of Josef's blades, even when she felt the demon's teeth brush her wings.

Horrible as he looked, Nico actually preferred the Demon of the Dead Mountain in this form. Anything was better than the face he'd worn when he walked off the broken seal. It was similar to the one he'd worn before when he'd met her in the dark of her mind, during the fight at Izo's. Just like then, his features were a handsome melding of Josef and Eli; only now Tesset's firmness was in there, too.

Looking at that combination, she couldn't help wanting to

910

trust him, even though she knew better. That face was dangerous. It messed with her control. Every time she thought she knew it, the demon's face would shift, now looking like Josef that first morning she met him, now looking closer to Eli when she'd woken up on the beach at Osera.

The changes came so fast, so effortlessly that Nico was beginning to suspect the demon didn't have a true face at all. His human form was nothing but a reflection of the desires of those who saw him. A shifting trap that used remembered trust as its bait. Nico bared her teeth, grabbing hold of the enormous grasping arm and pulling the black skin apart. Nivel was right. The demon could never, ever be trusted.

"You're thinking awful things about me, aren't you?"

Nico didn't dignify that with a response. Instead, she fixed her yellow eyes on Josef as she pulled the demon arm straight, giving him a clean shot.

"Of course you are," the Demon of the Dead Mountain purred, closing in. "I can see it on your face."

"You can't see my face," Nico said, stretching the arm farther.

"I don't need to," he answered. "I'm part of you, Nico. I always will be. You're far more demon than human now, and that's why I'm going to ask you one last time—"

"No," Nico snapped, bracing as the Heart of War's blow sliced the arm she held in half.

"You didn't even hear my offer." The demon sounded hurt.

"I don't have to," Nico said, tossing the disintegrating arm to the ground. "Unless you're offering me your life, I want nothing of yours. We are done, demon."

She turned and glared at him then, baring her black teeth instinctively to drive the point home, but the Demon of the Dead Mountain didn't return the threat. Still grinning, he jumped backward, putting a hundred feet of empty air between them, and began to plummet toward the storm-shrouded ground.

Nico was about to abandon him to the Lord of Storms when

a flash of white blinded her. She froze, yellow eyes rolling as she fought to get her vision back. Slowly, the white faded and the world came back into focus, and as it did, she realized that the lightning-dense clouds that had protected the ground were gone. There was nothing to stand in the demon's way as the Master of the Dead Mountain landed on a foothill of the now-unprotected Sleeping Mountains and, slamming his enormous claws into the stone slope, began to devour the stone whole.

"No!" she screamed, shooting toward him. But before she'd gone more than fifty feet, a writhing black arm struck her across the back. The blow knocked her off course, slamming her into a valley several mountains away. Hissing in pain, Nico pushed herself out of the crater she'd made and launched back into the air, grabbing the demon hand's grasping claws as they came down on top of her, desperate for the ground below.

"Josef!" she bellowed, using all her strength to keep the enormous hand from slamming into the ground and crushing her in the process.

All at once, the hand went slack, the dull black carapace crumbling to nothing under her claws, severed in one blow from the Heart of War. Tossing the ruined limb aside, Nico shot into the air and looked frantically for the demon she'd once called Master.

She found him immediately. He was still on the ground where he'd landed, shoveling small mountains into his enormous gaping mouth. Behind him, a long trail of black, dead stone showed where he'd gorged himself already.

Nico's heart fell in her chest. Already, he was noticeably larger, his great, black body towering over the mountain's foothills. Another few minutes at this pace and he would be larger than the limbs that shot down through the holes.

With a snarl that grew into a howl, Nico charged.

He kept eating until the moment her claws touched his neck, and then he vanished into the shadows. She felt him move behind her and turned just in time to see him surface again. The size of him was intimidating. He towered over her, a great menace of teeth and powerful muscle even as he sank into a crouch. Fear began to curdle in her stomach, but Nico pushed it aside in favor of raw fury.

"Eating wasn't part of the deal!" she roared. "What are you doing?"

"Betraying you," the Demon of the Dead Mountain said, shoving another handful of stone down his throat. "I should think that was obvious."

His honesty stopped Nico like a wall, and the demon began to laugh, a terrible, dry sound, like wind in dead grass. "Now, now, my dear," he said. "You knew this was coming."

This was true, but Nico still couldn't quite believe he'd do it before the shell was sealed.

The demon sighed. "Don't be an idiot, darling. Did you honestly think I'd wait politely until you all were free to gang up on me?" The topmost of his three yellow eyes rolled back toward the Dead Mountain. "When I saw the thief return, I waited to see if you'd notice. You didn't, of course, but then you never were any good at keeping your eyes on more than one target at a time. Still, I thought I'd better take one last shot at bringing you over to the winning side. Waste of time, really, but I've always been the sentimental sort."

Nico started to growl, but the demon shook his head. "Moot point now, dear. Didn't you see the flash? The Hunter's been reborn. He'll undoubtedly be along shortly to take care of this." The demon swept a clawed hand across the sundered sky and the clawing black arms. "But I didn't let you free me just so I could go back to my prison. I intend to eat everything I can, and after your Powers reseal the shell, I mean to make myself king of this little feed bowl."

He paused, his golden eyes roving over her. "This is your last chance, you know. There's more than enough food here to share. We could rule together. I'd even let you keep your swordsman." His triple-jointed arm reached out, claw turned up. "Last chance, daughter. I suggest you take it, or I'll have to end you just like all the rest."

Nico didn't answer. Instead, fast as a flash, she slashed the Demon of the Dead Mountain straight across his claw, severing it at the wrist. She paused, waiting for the scream, but the demon didn't even blink. He just grinned at her, his enormous mouth opening in a wall of sharp, black teeth.

"Remember," he said, "you brought this on yourself."

And then he was gone.

Nico blinked, focusing on the slimy, cold feel of him as he slipped through the shadows. He moved faster than she'd ever thought possible, popping up north of her. With a roar, she took off after him, slipping in and out of the shadows as she picked up speed.

In the sky, things were quickly getting out of control. Josef was holding all three cracks alone now, and without the Lord of Storms to block them, the hands were starting to reach the ground again, the clawed fingers eating the land wherever they touched. Nico cursed and moved faster. She had to put the demon down and get back to Josef before they were overwhelmed.

But as she closed in on the spot where the demon should have been, his presence vanished. Nico jerked to a stop, confused. She was at the foot of the Dead Mountain's north slope. She'd felt the Demon of the Dead Mountain sliding up from the shadows here a second earlier, but now he was gone completely. She turned her head in a full circle, roaring a challenge. As her cry echoed through the sky, she suddenly felt him again, coming out of the shadows a few hundred feet away.

Even as she felt him surface, she knew she was too late. She'd been fooled. The black stone beneath her was the Dead Mountain, the demon's prison for thousands of years. Of course he would know his way around it, know how to slide deep into its roots to avoid her before popping up in another location.

Nico shot into the air anyway, but it was far, far too late. A second after she left the ground, Josef's scream ripped through her. She cleared the mountain's ledge just in time to see Josef, her Josef, drop to his knees, the Heart of War falling from his limp hands. Below him, the demon's claws poked up through the swordsman's shadow, the enormous, curved tips stabbing through his blood-soaked chest.

The demon emerged fully as she watched, lifting Josef with him. He grinned at the swordsman before he flicked his claw. Josef hit the stone with an echoing crash. He didn't cry out as he landed, just collapsed like a doll, motionless and limp even as the demon reached down to grasp his head delicately between his talons. He was seconds from twisting the swordsman's head clean off when Nico barreled into him. The shock of her impact knocked Josef from his claws, and the demon went flying off the mountain.

Nico didn't follow him. Instead, she crouched over Josef. Gathering his broken body delicately, she lifted him and gently moved him so that he was lying beside his sword. Using the tips of her claws, she wrapped his bloody fingers around the Heart of War's hilt. She did not allow herself to notice how still he was, did not think about how his chest wasn't moving. She allowed no thought into her head save two, that Josef would live, and that she was going to make the demon pay.

When her swordsman was with his sword, Nico turned on the demon. He was crouched at the edge of the snowy valley where she had thrown him, his claws spanning the entire swath of mountain that formed one half of the pass where she and Josef had once sheltered. It was only then that Nico realized just how enormous he'd become. He was easily twice her size now, his mouth big enough to swallow her head whole.

Sensing her fear, the Demon of the Dead Mountain grinned, baring his thousands of ragged teeth as his three yellow eyes shone with amusement. "If you want to beg, it's not too late," he said, his deep voice almost crooning.

Nico's answer was to sink into the shadows. She moved like water through the dark, exploding out of the shadow cast by his enormous bulk on the cliff face behind him. Her momentum knocked them both off the mountain, and they fell in a black tangle, crashing into the snowy valley with enough force to rock the foundations of the world.

The demon pushed her off, using his superior strength to peel her claws back. Nico just snarled as she sank her teeth into the black flesh below his jaw. They both roared then, the demon in pain, Nico in furious vengeance as they tumbled in the snow.

Overhead, forgotten and uninhibited, the enormous hands shot down from the sky to dig into the defenseless mountains, lifting them up one by one as the holes in the sky grew larger. As the first mountain left the shell, a chorus of screeches echoed down through the cracks, a great call of victory that drowned out even the panicked screaming of the spirits below.

CHAPTER

24

Miranda rubbed her eyes as they ran, not quite believing that a place could be so *white*. She'd thought the Shaper Mountain's heart was blinding, but it was dingy compared to the landscape they were now running through. The Lord of Storms led the way, though he was now so white himself that she kept losing him. So, instead, she followed Eli.

The thief's posture was grim as he jogged just ahead of her, his dirty, torn shirt sitting tight across his tense shoulders. Miranda understood. Her own body felt like a spring pulled to breaking. Her spirits cowered in their rings, utterly silent. Even the Tower was still, hovering at the very edge of their connection. The only thing that felt truly alive was the Lord of Storms.

From the moment Eli had thrust the Hunter's seed into his

chest, the Lord of Storms' presence in her body had grown from enormous to overwhelming. Even though he was no longer pulling strength from her, Miranda felt utterly drained just from being attached to so much power. She kept waiting for him to sever the connection. After all, what did the Hunter need with a wizard? But he didn't. He just surged forward, a white fury in a white world, while she bobbed in his wake, drawn inexorably toward the Power at the center of everything.

As they ran, the world grew less white. Cracks were starting to appear, bits and pieces of the Between falling away to reveal glimpses of the world below. Miranda saw forests, mountains, even a snatch of Zarin's skyline. The longer they ran, the more holes they passed and the more alarmed Miranda became. She had no idea what counted as normal in this place, but she was fairly certain this wasn't it. Worse still, every time they ran by a gap, she could feel her spirits cringe.

"Are these more cracks in the shell?" she asked, wincing at the loudness of her own voice.

The shell is the wall between creation and the nothing outside, the Lord of Storms said, like this was the most obvious thing in the world. *So unless you're seeing black, the answer is no.*

Miranda was going to drop it there, but her next step changed things completely. She put her foot down as always, but instead of hitting the strange white floor, her foot hit nothing. She fell with a cry, her boot going straight through the white world as the floor crumbled.

She caught a glimpse of ocean below before Eli grabbed her hand. For a moment, she dangled between the white world and the endless sea, and then the Lord of Storms' hand joined the thief's and she was yanked up. The Lord of Storms tossed her down on mercifully stable ground, and Miranda clung to it, staring in horror at the now-gaping hole. "What is going on?"

"The veil is crumbling," Eli said, pulling her to her feet. "Come on, we need to move."

"What do you mean?" Miranda said, letting him yank her up. "I thought the Weaver maintained the veil."

"He does," Eli said, pulling her after him. "But I left him fighting the Shepherdess. Now the veil is crumbling, so what do *you* think is happening?"

Miranda swallowed and dropped his hand, moving into a jog beside him. Fortunately, the floor didn't give out again before the Lord of Storms stopped them a minute later, his hand raised in warning. When Miranda peeked around his enormous shoulders, what she saw made her want to shrink to nothing.

Directly ahead, two blindingly white figures stood in tableaux. One was a woman, pure white and impossibly beautiful. She was as tall as the Lord of Storms, her glorious naked body clad only in her shining hair. She held a sharp, black object in her hand like a dagger, and her white eyes looked down with scorn at the man on the floor.

The Weaver lay before her, his breathing loud in the white silence. His hair lay spread out around him like a robe, but his chest was bare and slick with a glowing substance that was so beautiful it took Miranda several moments to realize the Weaver was bleeding from a stab wound in his stomach. He'd covered the wound with both hands, and she could see the skin knitting together under his touch, healing before her eyes, but even the miraculous speed was far too slow.

Above him, the White Lady wasn't even panting. She watched the Weaver like a hawk, her white eyes clear and sharp with rage. Behind her, a crumpled sphere lay smashed on the floor like a discarded toy. Above that, another sphere floated. This one was little bigger than the white pearl of the Hunter's seed, but unlike the seed or the dull, shattered orb on the ground, this sphere was filled with glorious color. It hung in round perfection, the only color in the whole, white world, and the White Lady stood before it like a guardian.

The Powers were wholly focused on the other, and neither seemed to have noticed the three strangers intruding on their private fight. Miranda glanced at the Lord of Storms, waiting for him to say something arrogant, or at least tell the Shepherdess to back away, but he did neither. Instead, he drew his sword with a whisper of steel and lunged straight for the White Lady's throat.

Miranda covered her mouth, stifling the surprised yelp with her hands. The Lord of Storms moved faster than anything she'd ever seen, and for a split second she was sure it was already over. But then a great crash filled the silence, and she saw the Lord of Storms' white sword grinding against the Lady's long, black dagger inches from her face.

The Shepherdess stared at her former servant, her eyes round with shock. *You.*

The word was spoken like a curse. And though Miranda couldn't see the Lord of Storms' face, she could feel his grin in her gut. *Me*, he growled.

As he spoke, his white sword flashed down, flying toward the Lady's thigh. But the black dagger moved just as fast, blocking him again. No longer caught off guard, the Shepherdess stepped back, keeping her dagger up. The weapon was hideous to look at, two feet long and grossly uneven, tapering to jagged points at both ends. As the Lady caught the Lord of Storms' next blow, Miranda wondered briefly why the Shepherdess, the queen of all spirits, would use anything so ugly.

The Shepherdess flicked the black dagger, carelessly throwing off the Lord of Storms' blow. The Lord of Storms growled and raised his sword again, but the Lady only laughed, holding her arms wide.

What? she cried, her beautiful voice mocking. *You think that now that you have my brother's seed you can cut me? Go on.* She waved at her bare stomach. *Try.*

The Lord of Storms struck before she'd finished speaking, his white sword stabbing into her unguarded belly. The Lady didn't even wince as the blow landed, her lovely face turned up in that hateful smile.

Though she knew what she would see, Miranda forced

herself to look anyway. The Lord of Storms' sword lay against the Shepherdess's stomach, its cutting edge pressed into the unmarked white flesh. The Lord of Storms stared at the stopped blow, and Miranda could feel his rage burning under her skin, but before either of them could master it, the Shepherdess backhanded the new Hunter across the face.

He flew backward, landing on his back to Miranda's left. The Lady was on him in a flash, straddling him as she brought the demonseed up. The Lord of Storms scrambled, barely raising his sword up in time to stop the black point from stabbing into his chest. The Lady was about to try again when, with a thundering roar, the Lord of Storms threw her off. She landed and rolled, her hair flying as she pulled herself into a crouch, panting as she clutched the demonseed in her hands.

Why won't you just die? she screamed, lunging at him again.

The Lord of Storms roared his answer, white sword flying up to meet her.

Left on her own, Miranda would never have been able to tear her eyes away from the Powers' fight. It wasn't until she heard the groan that she remembered there were other things to do. She looked down to see Eli already on his knees by the injured Weaver. Wincing with guilt at her own thoughtlessness, she dropped down to join him.

"What can I do?" she said, reaching for his wound.

The old man batted her hands away. *Leave it be, human*, he whispered. *Mending things is my purpose.* He stared at her as she jerked back, his white eyes looking through her. *You have bound the Hunter*, he said, his voice incredulous.

"He wasn't the Hunter at the time," Miranda started, but the Weaver interrupted her, grabbing her hands.

Listen, he said, his voice low and urgent. *He's not a full Power yet. It's too soon after the transition. The seed hasn't taken full root yet. That's why he can't cut the Shepherdess. Their battle is grossly uneven, and if he continues to fight, he will surely die. We cannot lose him again. You have to help.*

"Help how?" Miranda said. "If he can't cut her, surely there's nothing I—"

You are his Spiritualist, the Weaver said, his hands gripping hers with a strange, painless burning. *Strength for service, power for obedience, that is your oath, is it not? Honor it. He's fighting for you, for all of us, so feed him your power.*

Miranda turned to stare at the White Lady. She was so beautiful as she stalked after the Lord of Storms. The idea of going against her felt so wrong that Miranda could barely think of it. She tried to imagine hitting the woman from behind and was almost sick where she sat as her body violently rejected the concept. "I can't!" Miranda cried, not even knowing where the words came from. "She's my Shepherdess!"

She betrayed us all! the Weaver said.

Miranda gritted her teeth and tried, but her body refused to obey. Something fundamental was blocking her, some deep rule of nature she'd never known before this moment. She didn't even think she could open her spirit right now if she tried. Hot, shameful tears began to well up behind her eyes, and she knew she'd failed. She'd come this far only to fail.

"Miranda."

Eli's voice made her jump. She looked up to see the thief kneeling beside her, his hands on her shoulders as he gently turned her away from the Shepherdess, away from the Weaver, straight toward himself.

"Don't think about the Shepherdess," he said softly. "The Lord of Storms is your oath-bound spirit, just as Mellinor was. Don't think about what he's doing. Don't think about why. Just relax and let the power flow."

Miranda shook her head. "But—"

Eli's hand covered her mouth, cutting off her words as he leaned closer, his voice little more than a whisper. "He's going to die if you don't help him. If he dies, the world dies, and your oath to protect the spirits is broken forever." He stared at her, blue eyes boring into hers with an intensity that reminded her more of Banage than anything else she'd seen in him.

921

"You've never once failed in your resolve. Don't let her break you now. Close your eyes, forget the fight, and honor your oath. Feed him the power he needs to win."

Miranda stared at Eli for three long heartbeats, and then she obeyed. She closed her eyes and shut it all out, the Powers and the whiteness, the demon fear and the crumbling veil. She thrust every thought from her head save the oath that made her what she was and sank into the well of her soul.

She could feel her spirits clinging to her as she fell deeper, their connections strong as steel. She could feel the Tower drawing nearer as the gems at her neck began to grow warm, but most of all she could feel the enormous presence of the Lord of Storms, a great swirling vortex of rage and power tied like a cable around her center.

Her connection to him was larger than any of the others, larger even than her link to Mellinor had been, though not as close. Still, she could feel him like he was a part of her own body. He was straining, fighting with everything he had, and yet there was no pull on the connection, no request for help. Nor would there be, she was sure. The Lord of Storms would fight on his own until he fell, and it was up to her to make sure he didn't. With that certainty hanging in her mind, Miranda set herself against the wall of her instinct and, pushing with everything she had, pried her spirit open.

Power filled her to bursting. It boiled up until she felt she would pop, but she did not let it go. Instead, she took that power, the power that sustained her spirits, the power that linked her to the Tower, the power that had served as Mellinor's shore, *her* power, and fed it through her link to the Lord of Storms.

She encountered resistance immediately. The Lord of Storms rejected her offer, his disgust at being helped filtering up their connection like backwash. Gritting her teeth, Miranda thrust the rejection aside. *Power for service*, she snarled, filling each word with enough strength to stop a Great Spirit cold in its tracks. *Strength for obedience.* Her soul was roaring now, the power building to the breaking point, but she did not let

922

it out. She would not. Her mind was set beneath the full weight of her will. The Lord of Storms would take this power or she would die making him, but she would not let him fight alone.

Accept the offer!

With a roar that shook her bones, the Lord of Storms' barriers went down and her strength flooded into him. Once he accepted, he took it all, draining her dry in an instant, but Miranda refused to close their connection. She sank deeper and deeper into herself, deeper than when she'd bound Mellinor, deeper even than she'd gone in Osera. She fell into depths she hadn't even known she possessed, reaching for more power, more strength. And the further she reached, the stranger things became.

The more Miranda gave, the more aware she became that the power she was sending the Lord of Storms was no longer solely her own. Her rings were humming on her fingers, feeding their own strength into the flow. She nearly closed the connection then, terrified that she'd somehow broken her oath and begun draining her rings.

No sooner had the thought crossed her mind than the rejection of it overwhelmed her senses. Her spirits were screaming at her to keep going, to use what they freely gave, and it wasn't just her rings. The Tower was there as well, the enormous strength of the bedrock flowing through her to become the foundation of something larger. There was even an echo of Mellinor, a freezing rush of power that vanished a second after it came. One by one, every spirit she'd ever bound gave itself to the Lord of Storms, braiding their power through hers until she was sure she would be crushed under the weight.

But she was not crushed. She stood firm, holding her oath in her mind. Today, she would save the spirits or die trying. Today, they would win. That was the only truth she allowed as the flow of power finally settled into a steady stream.

When she opened her eyes again, everything had changed.

The Shepherdess was now crouching several feet from the Lord of Storms, the ugly black dagger clutched in front of her. Her earlier confidence was gone, and there was a thin, glittering slash along her cheek. Across from her, the Lord of Storms stood with his sword at his side. His chest was bright with blood, but his face held no pain. Though he was the bloodier one, he stood straight and proud, his body so taut with power he nearly glowed from it. Next to him, the Shepherdess looked gray and dirty, her face screwed up in an expression very close to panic.

How? she demanded, her lips curling back to reveal her sharp, white teeth. *Where are you getting all this strength?* Her white eyes flicked to Miranda. *It can't be the human. No human can stand against me. I created them. They cannot—*

You created them, the Lord of Storms said, raising his blade. *And in your arrogance you gave them a fraction of your will. It's not just me you're fighting, Benehime. It's everything. Everything you've betrayed, everything you've cast aside in your selfishness.*

You are still a Power! Benehime screamed. *You cannot touch me! That is the law!*

If you hadn't killed your brother, that might still be true, the Lord of Storms sneered. *But you upset the system. I may bear the Hunter's essence and power, but I'm still a storm and a sworn spirit. I'm no essence of the Creator, no part of his balance. I am my own will now, and you cannot stop me anymore.*

The Shepherdess's eyes went wide at that, and she screamed, charging forward. The Lord of Storms brought his sword down, biting into her arm, but she did not stop. She ran into him, and though she was smaller, it was the Lord of Storms who went down with her on top, the demonseed clutched in her hands as she raised it over his head.

Miranda watched, helpless. Everything she had was already flowing into the Lord of Storms, but as good as he was, the Shepherdess was still older, still stronger, and fueled with such mad hatred Miranda couldn't bare to look at her eyes. She could only stand there as the Shepherdess brought the crude

924

dagger down, the tapered point flying down to stab the Lord of Storms' throat.

And then, just before the point pierced the new Power's skin, the Shepherdess stopped.

It happened so suddenly that Miranda thought it must be a trick. Or maybe the world had ended at that moment and she hadn't noticed. But her heart was still beating. Time was still flowing, and the Shepherdess still did not move. No one did. At last, the Lady's head turned. The movement was painfully slow, but her expression was pure horrified fury as her eyes slid past Miranda, past the Weaver, to land somewhere behind the crumpled sphere.

And that was when Miranda realized she hadn't seen Eli in a while.

Swallowing against the sudden dryness in her throat, Miranda forced herself to turn as well.

Eli was standing beside the broken sphere. His posture was casual, like he just happened to be there. One hand was in his pocket; the other was tossing something small, round, and beautiful up and down, up and down.

"What?" he said, catching the tiny, beautiful sphere up between his fingers. "Lose something?"

For a long second the air seemed to turn solid, and then the Shepherdess lurched off the Lord of Storms.

She moved faster than light, appearing on top of Eli instantly, but it still wasn't fast enough. The moment she lunged, Eli slammed his foot down, cracking the veil like rotten wood. He was already raising his arm when the hole appeared, and the second the veil was breached, Eli threw the tiny, perfect world down as hard as he could.

Benehime's hand flew out, her long, white fingers brushing the sphere as it passed, but it wasn't enough. The tiny world tumbled through the hole in the veil, and the moment it touched the real world, the fragile sphere cracked.

All at once, the air was filled with ringing, glorious shouts as the stars burst into freedom. They flew from the crumbling sphere in a shower of color so beautiful, so brilliant, Miranda couldn't bear to watch. Instead, she focused on the reflection the colors cast against the white world, each one sparking and vanishing until, in a heartbeat, it was over.

As the Between faded back to white, Benehime lay frozen on the ground at Eli's feet, her hand still flung out after her lost paradise. Her face was a mask of loss more bitter than anything Miranda had ever seen, but the look was gone in an instant, replaced with absolute fury.

Without a word, without a warning, without even a sound, the Shepherdess shot up. Miranda caught a glimpse of black in the white rush before the Power wrapped herself around Eli. She saw him tense, his smug expression falling away to one of shock, then resignation.

For several seconds, Miranda wasn't actually sure what had happened. But then she saw the Shepherdess's hand pull back with deliberate slowness, the black dagger dripping crimson before she slammed it again into Eli's chest. He grunted as the blade entered, and then Benehime stepped back, letting Eli fall face-first onto the white floor at her feet.

"Eli!"

Miranda didn't recognize her own voice as the scream echoed across the crumbling white nothing. She scrambled toward the thief's crumpled body, so desperate to get to him that she didn't even feel the Shepherdess's foot in her ribs until she was flung backward. Miranda landed hard on her side and lay stunned for a moment, watching helplessly as the Shepherdess threw the black dagger down.

It landed with an echoing, metallic clang that went on and on as the dagger's uneven surface rocked back and forth against the veil. The Shepherdess fell to her knees beside the thief, her white eyes empty as she took him in her arms.

Why, she whispered. *Why? Why?* Her voice grew louder with each question until her scream filled the Between. *Why did you make me do this?*

The scream faded to a choked sob as she wrapped herself

926

around Eli's bloody body. *You didn't have to break it*, she whispered, turning his face toward hers. *There was no paradise without you.*

And then she kissed him, her lips pressed hard against his even as the Lord of Storms' hand wrapped around her neck.

She did not struggle as he lifted her, not even to pry his fingers off her throat. She merely hung from his hand like a limp doll as he carried her to the edge of the white world. When he reached the wall of the shell, a black portal opened in front of him, and Miranda gasped as the air of the Between began to pour out in a great gale.

Beyond, grasping hands shot out, grabbing the Lord of Storms and the Shepherdess, struggling to pull them both into the blackness. The Lord of Storms ignored them. He walked into the dark, carrying the Lady at arm's length until the darkness swallowed them both. The wind died as the door closed behind them, and Miranda felt her connection to the Lord of Storms snap like a cut thread.

The backlash nearly made her black out, but she forced herself to stay conscious, dragging her body across the floor toward Eli. Wincing with effort, she yanked her hand up and held her fingers under his nose. For several long seconds, nothing happened, and then she felt his faint breath on her skin. Relief flooded through her, and she turned back to the Weaver to see him sitting up, his eyes closed, his hand out toward Eli.

I caught him, the old man said, his voice impossibly tired. *He won't get any worse, though whether or not he gets better is up to him.*

Miranda looked back to Eli, her face as pale as the white world around them. "What do we do now?"

The Weaver opened his eyes with an incredulous look as he pulled himself to his feet. *We fix the world*, he said, spreading his hands out in front of him. *What else?*

Miranda had no answer to that, so she sat back, watching in wonder as the Weaver flexed his fingers and began to weave.

CHAPTER
25

The Demon of the Dead Mountain's roar echoed off the cliffs. His claws tore long rents across Nico's wings, lacerating her shadow-wrapped body and breaking her teeth. Nico ignored the pain, even as one of her wings tore free. Though the demon was much larger than her now, Tesset's training gave her the edge. Her front teeth were still locked around the demon's throat, still chewing on the tender black flesh, and though he slammed her against the mountains over and over, she would not let go. She was the master now.

The demon's struggles grew more frantic, and Nico bit down harder, her claws digging into the joint where the monster's arm met its body. Out of the corner of her eye she could see the sky breaking apart as more hands thrust down toward the screaming spirits. The world was crumbling, collapsing under the weight of the demon's hunger. Fragments of the sky fell like snow over mountains that rolled like waves in their fear. The only still peak was the one under their feet. The Dead Mountain stood as solid and black as ever, its empty husk a reminder of what was to come. Never loosening her grip, Nico's yellow eyes flicked up to the ledge where Josef had fallen. There, too, all was still. All was lost, and yet she would not let go.

The demon was flailing now, his claws scrambling to pry between her teeth from his jaw. Nico snarled and bit down harder, feeling the demon's furious scream through her grip. The scream grew louder as the demon surged up, his long, hideous arms wrapping around Nico's torso. She panicked as his grip tightened, thinking he was about to crush her, but the demon did no such thing. Instead, he yanked her away with all his might.

Nico's hold never faltered, but the demon's own flesh was

not so strong. He tore her off him, taking off a large chunk of his neck and one arm in the process. The demon barely seemed to notice the loss in his fury as he flung her away, his enraged roar shaking the Dead Mountain to its roots.

She landed hard, her claws grabbing the mountain's peak to keep herself from falling into the sharp rocks below. Down the slope, the Demon of the Dead Mountain was growling at her, his black claws folded around the gaping hole she'd left in his throat. "You always were a dirty fighter," he rumbled, his three yellow eyes narrowing.

Nico's answer was to spit out the piece of him she'd torn away. The demon's flesh was already turning to dust in her mouth. It dissolved completely as it struck the Dead Mountain's bare slope, and the demon growled deep in what was left of its throat. "Why are you doing this?"

"To stop you," Nico answered.

"Stop me?" The demon burst out laughing. "Look around, girl. I'm hardly the greatest threat."

"I don't care," Nico snarled. "You killed Josef. I couldn't stop them all on my own anyway, but I can kill you."

"No, you can't," the demon said. "That was the same mistake your king made, the one called the Creator. He thought he could starve us by locking us away. Make us turn on each other. And I'm sure they did, those mad skeletons, but it didn't work. Think, child. If demons could kill other demons, there'd be nothing left outside the shell. The Creator's plan would have worked and the Powers would have led you out to recolonize the emptiness ages ago. But nothing created has ever understood us. Nothing that is born can know the truth of our kind, which is really tragic, because the truth is so simple. We cannot die because we do not live. We are nothingness, the reverse of creation. We are consumption, destruction, the darkness that persists with or without light. You can no more kill us than kill death itself."

"I don't care," Nico said, digging her claws into the stone. "I will fight you."

"I'm sure you will," the demon sneered. "You always were a bit stupid that way." He shook his head, torn neck sliding grotesquely. "What I don't understand is why you give all that endless, idiot energy fighting for a world that will turn on you the first chance it gets. Even you can't be foolish enough to still believe you're human."

"I am myself," Nico snapped.

"Well, good for you," the demon snapped back. "But let's play a game, shall we? Let's say you win. Let's say I vanish, the shell is mended, the demons are pushed back, and everything comes up daffodils for you and your swordsman. What happens then?"

Before Nico could answer, the demon's mouth opened in an enormous grin. "I'll tell you," he crooned, reaching down to caress the Dead Mountain's slope. "You'll end up here, right where I was. Because no matter how well you may think you control yourself, you're not a spirit of creation anymore. You're like me, like all of us. You'll never die, even if you long to. You'll never be able to rest, never be able to drop your guard. I'm impressed you've been able to keep your hunger at bay this long, but how much longer can you do it, Nico? A century? A millennia?"

The demon shook its head. "No one's will holds forever, my child. The hunger will win in the end, and then you'll be everything they already think you are—a monster, a predator, a devourer of spirits. Something to be stomped on and pinned at all costs."

As he finished, Nico realized with horror that his throat was nearly mended. Her eyes widened. How? They were on the Dead Mountain. There should be nothing to eat. Then she saw that one of his long legs was arched backward, his biggest claw just touching the valley beyond the Dead Mountain's border. Where it touched, the once-snowy valley was now as black and dry as the Dead Mountain's own slopes.

The sight of it made her snarl, and she pulled herself to her full height, her broken wing hanging painfully from her shoulder. Nico ignored it. She stood on the mountain's peak, glaring down at the demon. In her mind, Nivel's warning was playing over and over. *Don't listen. He always lies, don't listen.* But he wasn't lying, not this time, though Nico wished he were. A lie would be nicer than this ugly truth. But ugly as it was, hateful as it was, the truth was there, hanging between them, and she could not ignore it. Though she no longer needed air, Nico took a deep breath and raised her eyes to the sky, steeling herself to see the world break.

The breath caught in her throat. Above them, three of the six hands had vanished. For a second, she felt nothing but panic. If they were gone, what more would come through? But even as the thought slid through her like an icy spike, a flash of white blazed in the sky. For a moment, the whole, battered arc was illuminated, and then, with a demon's jagged scream, one of the three remaining hands began to fall, dissolving to dust before it could hit the ground.

The second flash came a moment later, slicing the next arm through. She saw it better this time—a curved white blade biting through the darkness beyond the sphere, singing with pure, bloody joy as it sliced the demon flesh. By the time the final arm was cut, the shell itself was shaking, and the dome of the sky began to groan. Overhead, the cracks flashed and ground against one another, the shattered sections popping back into place like puzzle pieces.

As the edges came together, they began to melt into one another, the cracks fraying before weaving back together as though they'd never broken. It was beautiful to watch, more beautiful than anything she'd ever seen. So beautiful that Nico couldn't tear her eyes away from the world as it put itself back together, and that was her fatal mistake.

She felt the Demon of the Dead Mountain right before his claws closed on her throat. She roared and began to fight his grip, but he loomed over her, his strength infinite.

"You never could learn to pay attention to your surroundings, darling daughter," the demon purred in her ear, his jagged teeth tearing the flesh on the side of her head. "Looks like your thief won his gambit. They're repairing the shell as we speak. So it's time for you to go."

Nico's feet kicked in the air as he lifted her. Holding her at arm's length, the demon turned and raised his other arm, the one she had injured, and dragged his curved, black claws across the air. For a second, nothing happened, and then, with a horrible, unnatural ripping, the veil began to tear.

"The Weaver is too busy to stop a little hole like this," the demon told her, his jagged teeth blacker than midnight in the pure white light that spilled through the hole in the air. "It pains me to treat you this way, my child, but if you won't stand with me, then you leave me no choice. After all"—the black grin widened—"I can't kill you."

Nico lashed at him with her claws, but his long arms held her well out of reach. With a sickening lurch, the demon hopped up through the sundered veil, taking her into a world of blinding white. The moment they were inside, the demon raised her up and slammed her against a wall she hadn't even seen.

The impact sent an explosion of pain through her body, and Nico screamed as the wall cracked behind her, bowing out with the force of the demon's blow. When he pulled her back, her body was too limp to fight him, too stunned even to struggle as he dug his claws into the white floor and slammed her a second time. This time, the wall shattered.

Nico's body shrank as freezing cold, colder even than the world inside the shadows, surrounded her. The demon had broken the shell with her body. Even as Nico realized what had happened, she felt the demon's claws leave her throat, and then she began to fall.

She couldn't even flap her wings anymore. The hole in the shell shrank above her, the light growing farther and dimmer, leaving only endless, hungry blackness. For one long breath, Nico fell into the dark, and then, with a deafening cry, the hands grabbed her.

They wrapped around her body, large and small, clawed and spindly, all pulling her into the dark. Black mouths bit down on her flesh only to roar in impotent fury when they realized she was not food. She was like them.

After that, they thrust her aside, trampling her as they scrambled madly for the hole the demon had punched in the shell of the world with her body. Far, far overhead, Nico could still see the outline of the demon against the light, his grotesque face split in an enormous smile. And with that, rage took over where strength could not.

With a roar that made the hands on her snatch away, Nico surged forward. She could not let it end like this, could not let him win. She tore through the other demons, ripping them to shreds as she clawed her way up. Starving and mad, they barely noticed, moving their limbs out of her way only when she took a piece off. Ahead of her, the hole in the shell was closing, cutting off the light. Nico screamed and climbed faster, clawing her way up the endless demons until, at last, her hand closed on the hole's jagged edge.

The Demon of the Dead Mountain's claws were on her at once, prying her grip free. Nico slammed her other hand up in answer, her claws biting deep into the Demon of the Dead Mountain's arm. As he screamed in pain, Nico yanked herself forward, tearing her other hand off the shell's edge only to plant it in the demon's chest. Her claws cut through the shiny, protective carapace and dug into his core, locking in place. At the same time, she brought her head forward, jaws flung wide as she latched herself onto his shoulder.

"You're right," she hissed against his flesh while he flailed beneath her, screaming in pain. "There's no place for our kind here." And with that, she pushed off the shell, using her weight as an anchor to drag them both into the dark.

The demon's roar rattled her teeth, but Nico didn't let go. As he locked his limbs against the closing shell, she clung to him like a lead weight. If they had been inside the shell, it never would have worked. He was too large now, and she too

933

small. But here, on the edge, things were different. Nico's body buffeted as the demon hands shot past her, scrambling for purchase on the shell's broken edge. They grabbed the Demon of the Dead Mountain as well, pulling him down in their rush to clear the hole and get inside, using his bulk as leverage to pull themselves up.

The demon screamed again, and this time there was real fear in his roar. He tore at Nico with his claws, digging into the shell with his feet as he tried to free himself. But the broken shell was too fragile to hold him, the thousands of hands too much even for his strength. Even so, he might have worked himself free had Nico not been latched to him, her weight an anchor on his own, dragging him inch by painful inch into the dark. When he finally toppled, Nico went with him, her claws and teeth buried in his flesh as the hands dragged them both into the dark.

It was a good end, she thought as they started to fall. Even if she lived forever out here in the dark, she was still herself, and she had used the last of her strength to take the Demon of the Dead Mountain with her. For a creature who could no longer die, she'd earned herself a death to be proud of. A warrior's death. She smiled against the Demon of the Dead Mountain's flesh, still straining under her teeth. She only wished Josef could have seen it.

But even as she thought his name, a shadow appeared against the white light of the closing hole. It was a small shadow, man-sized, and Nico slumped in relief. Good, the Weaver was here to seal the breach. But the figure didn't try to close the hole. Instead, he leaned out, one arm holding onto something behind him, the other reaching into the dark. And as he reached, he screamed.

"Nico!"

Josef cursed and slammed his sword into the strange white floor. It cracked under the Heart's blunt point like an eggshell, but the blade held. Grabbing the hilt as his anchor, Josef leaned out beyond the edge of the world. Hands clawed at him, but he beat them away, slamming them against the sharp cracks of the shell without looking. Even as he fought, his eyes never left the spot where he had seen Nico vanish.

His chest burned as he reached out. He'd barely let the gash close before going after Nico, barely made it through the hole the demon had ripped in the veil. He'd pulled himself on his elbows the last few feet even after he saw both demons tumble out of the shell into the dark, even when he *knew* it was too late.

It didn't matter. Josef couldn't stop. The idea of losing her now, after everything they'd gone through, after all they'd fought, was simply unacceptable. He wouldn't give up, and he wouldn't let her go. He would stand here reaching into the freezing dark until the healing shell took his arm off if there was so much as a chance that her fingers would close on his.

Josef leaned out farther still, looking frantically through the dark for a pair of golden eyes, but there was nothing outside except blackness and hungry hands. *"Nico!"* he screamed again, cringing in pain as his wounded lungs expanded.

As the name left him, Josef couldn't shake the horrid, creeping feeling that, even if she could hear him, Nico wouldn't answer. He'd seen her shoving her claws into the demon when he'd climbed in. She'd dragged the creature into the dark with her on purpose, and now he may have lost her forever.

Josef swore loudly. Whatever form she took, Nico was Nico. Demon, human, or anything in between, she would sacrifice anything to keep him and Eli safe. It drove him crazy. She didn't seem to understand that she had value, too, that she was worth saving.

"Dammit, Nico!" he roared into the dark. "I will not let you go like this! I will chase you out of this hole if you don't come back!"

His words vanished into the blackness, eaten like everything else. Josef didn't care. "You told me you wanted to live!" he screamed. "The demon ate your childhood. He ate everything

935

you had. Don't give him this, too! Don't let him take you from me!"

He threw himself forward until his fingertips on the Heart's pommel were the only things anchoring him to the world. His legs were braced on the closing edge of the shell, his hand thrust out so far his joints were screaming. Josef didn't care. He pushed out farther, the scream wrenching out of him. "*Take my hand!*"

The demons screamed back at him, black claws scrambling to eat him. Josef thrust them away with his will and stayed perfectly still, an iron statue, waiting. The light was fading quickly now as the shell closed behind him. Soon, the healing wound would be too small for him to retreat, but Josef didn't look back. He stood, hand grasping, aching lungs bellowing in his chest.

"Nico!"

And then, without warning, he saw something. It was tiny in the infinite dark, little more than a pale flash, but it caught his eyes like a spark. He locked onto it, bashing the mad demons out of his way until he saw it flash again. It was a finger. One white finger, reaching out.

Josef lurched into the dark, and his straining hand brushed soft, human flesh. The moment the white finger touched his, he hooked the joint with his own and yanked back. The white finger jerked forward, revealing a white hand.

Josef reached out again, grabbing the tiny palm with his larger grip. Holding his sword with his anchoring hand, he pulled with every ounce of the Heart's monstrous strength, and together, inch by inch, they dragged her out of the dark.

The hand was followed by a white arm, and then the crown of her head came into view, her short, black hair falling over her face. Next came her shoulders, her thin white chest, her hips, her legs.

Nico emerged with painful slowness, as though they were pulling her out of tar, but as Josef braced his legs and leaned back, pulling with all his weight, Nico's head lifted and her yellow eyes locked onto his. She was crying, screaming, and though the demons ate her words, he could see them on her lips. She wanted to live. She wanted to live with him.

With a final roar, Josef yanked her free, dragging her against his chest and falling backward just as the shell closed. The wound slammed shut, slicing through the grasping hands that had tried to follow them. As the severed limbs crumbled to ash, Josef slammed onto his back, holding Nico against him with one hand and the Heart with the other as his chest thundered. He almost didn't believe they'd made it until he felt Nico grab him and bury her head in his side.

"I'm sorry." She sobbed. "I shouldn't have come back. I don't belong here. I'm a—"

"I don't care," Josef said, cutting her off before she could finish. He slid his hand up her back to grab her head, forcing her to look at him. "You. Are. Nico," he said, grinding each word between his teeth. "That's the only thing that matters."

Nico's golden eyes widened. "But I—"

"If there's a problem, we'll figure it out," Josef said. "Or make Eli figure it out. That's what we keep him around for."

Nico laughed at that, a tearful snort as she ducked her head against him. Satisfied, Josef lay back and focused on overcoming the enormous pain that he'd been putting off. As he blacked out, he felt Nico's hands on his face.

"Thank you for saving me," she whispered.

"We save each other," he said. "That's why we're here."

He felt a soft brush on his forehead. Her lips, he realized. That thought made him grin wide as he slid into blissful unconsciousness, his fingers tangled in Nico's short, soft hair.

Eli woke to the most horrible pain he'd ever experienced, which was a joy in and of itself. He hadn't expected to wake up at all. After all, the Shepherdess had stabbed him, twice. He should be dead, expected to be. Death was the reward you got for playing the hero, and he'd been frightfully heroic there toward the end. That's why the good thieves were never heroes. Hard to spend your ill-gotten gains when you were dead.

"I think he's waking up."

He went still. It was Miranda's voice, and it was close, as though she were sitting beside him. A great feeling of relief crushed into his chest, and Eli realized he'd half believed that the only reason he was alive was because Benehime had won and somehow saved him for worse punishment. But Benehime would never let Miranda near him.

Slowly, hopefully, Eli cracked his eyes. Miranda's face filled his vision. She was hovering over him, and he felt a pressure on his chest as she shook him gently. "I knew it," she said, her pretty face pulling into the sneer he recognized as well as his own reflection. "Stop faking and get up, you degenerate."

"Well hello to you, too," Eli croaked, opening his eyes all the way.

He was lying on his back in the white nothing of the Between. Miranda was sitting beside him, fiddling with the gems in the Rector's mantle as she glared in his direction. That much wasn't surprising. What was, was that they weren't alone. The Weaver sat on his other side, his old face pulled in a kindly smile as he peered down at Eli.

Welcome back to the living, Eliton.

"Don't call me that," Eli muttered, sitting up.

As the wave of nausea hit him, Eli realized this was a terrible idea and promptly lay back down.

You should take it easy, the Weaver said. *I've repaired most of the damage, but you were on the edge of death for almost an hour while I repaired the shell. Some trauma was sadly unavoidable. Best to stay still.*

"Right," Eli said, swallowing. "Good plan."

Rather than risk lifting his head again, Eli slid his fingers up his chest to assess the damage. After the way Benehime had stabbed him, he expected to find gaping holes, or at least a bloody mess, but his shirt was cleaner than it had been in days, and his skin was smooth and painless to the touch. He smiled. Having a Power to play surgeon certainly had its benefits.

938

As he moved his fingers down to prod the place where the second stab had hit his abdomen, Eli brushed a rough spot on his skin and jumped off the floor.

"Eli!" Miranda shouted, slapping him back down. "What part of 'lie still' don't you understand?"

Eli didn't answer; he was too busy undoing the buttons of his shirt. As he tore it open, he nearly cried in relief. There, spanning the center of his chest, was Karon's burn. The moment he saw it, he felt Karon turn deep in his mind, settling himself sleepily below Eli's conscious.

He was released when you smashed the paradise, the Weaver said. *He was deathly exhausted. Apparently he'd been fighting the stars, trying to get back to you. After he was free, he refused to leave until I let him return to your body. I hope you don't mind.*

"How could I mind?" Eli said, laughing as he ran his fingers over the burn's circular pattern. Everything really was coming back together, the loose ends tying themselves off. All but one.

He glanced at Miranda, buttoning his shirt again. "Where's..." He trailed off. Somehow, it was hard to say her name. Fortunately, Miranda caught his meaning.

"The Shepherdess is gone," she said. "After losing both her paradise and her favorite, she stopped fighting. The Lord of... I mean the Hunter took her with him outside the shell. I don't know what happened next, but the demons were driven back and the Weaver was able to repair the shell."

Not fully, the Weaver said, his voice despairing. *I am not the Creator. I have patched the cracks, but the shell will never be truly whole again. And though the new Hunter bears the seed of the old, he will never be as strong as that which the Creator wrought with his own hands.* He closed his white eyes and rubbed his forehead with tired hands. *So many spirits lost who can never be replaced. The trust of the world is shaken, and our Shepherdess is gone. We are diminished forever, I fear.*

"Surely not forever," Miranda said.

Forever, the Weaver said again. *We avoided destruction*

today, Spiritualist, but the problems that drove my sister mad still remain. The spirits will continue to grow smaller, sleepier, and stupider in their confinement, perhaps even faster now that we've lost so many. I can weave the shell stronger, but I can't make new spirits. Even the Shepherdess had only one act of creation, and she spent that long ago.

"Making us," Eli said.

The Weaver nodded and sat back with a deep sigh. *This sphere is too small to support a true spirit ecosystem. It was meant as a lifeboat, not a home. Unless the Creator returns to breathe new energy into this world, the best we can hope for is a slow, peaceful decline.*

He shook his head, white eyes locking sadly on Miranda. *It may be soon enough that you humans find yourselves alone in this prison. And though wizards will continue to be born, there won't be anything awake enough left to talk with. The Hunter will hunt and the Weaver will weave, but our jobs only keep back the tide. This is the spirits' world, not ours, and in the end even the Shepherdess couldn't make them thrive.*

Miranda flushed, and Eli knew she was about to argue. The thought made him grin. Trust a Spiritualist to argue with a Power of creation. But before she could open her big mouth, a noise made them all jump, even the Weaver.

It was a demon scream, a sound Eli could now recognize instantly, much to his dismay. But not just one. Thousands. Hundreds of thousands, all screaming in the distance. Beside him, the Weaver closed his eyes, his fingers twitching frantically as he searched for the hole in the shell. But the white world was flawless again, as though the last few hours had never occurred.

Just when Eli was growing well and truly stumped, he spotted it. There, a dozen feet away, a black line was falling through the air. It fell quickly, forming a door in less than a second, and a blast of cold hit Eli like a blow to the face. He jerked back, lifting his arm to shield against whatever might be coming. He'd barely gotten it over his nose when the Lord of Storms stomped into the shell.

940

It was strange to see him so white, Eli thought idly as the black door closed behind him, cutting off the screams like a knife. Everything else was the same, the sword, the coat, the long hair, the insufferable expression. Only the color was missing, and with it, any trace of kindness, though Eli wasn't sure the old thunderhead had possessed any of *that* to begin with.

The Weaver stood as the Hunter approached. *Welcome back, brother.*

The Hunter didn't answer, just thrust out his fist. As he opened his hand, a soft, white radiance shone from his palm. Eli blinked in surprise. He hadn't thought the Between or its Powers could get any whiter, and yet the light kept shining from the Lord of Storms' hand. He held it there until the Weaver offered his own hands, and then he dumped the light unceremoniously into the old man's cupped palms.

Eli sucked in a breath as it came into view. The thing that fell from the Lord of Storms' hand was a perfect pearl, its smooth surface glowing whiter than the moon through alabaster. It rolled as it landed in the Weaver's hands, filling his palms with light.

The moment the white pearl was transferred, the Hunter turned and marched away. The black line appeared with a jerk of his hand, and even though Eli expected it this time, the cold mixed with the screams made him cringe anyway. The Hunter didn't even flinch as he strode into the dark, but he did pause at the threshold.

I can see your fear, old man, he said, his low voice rumbling like thunder. *Make no mistake. I am not your brother, but, like him, I was also born to fight the demons.* He smiled, his white eyes glittering with pure, bloody joy. *I will not fall.*

I know you shall not, the Weaver said. *And I will still name you brother, if you will have it.*

The Hunter turned back and strode through the door. *As you like. See you in a hundred years.*

The Weaver nodded. *Good hunting, brother.*

The Hunter was gone before he finished, the black line vanishing behind him without a trace. The Weaver sighed and looked down at the light in his cupped hands. *All is not lost, it seems.*

Eli leaned forward, arching his neck to see, despite the pain. "That's the Shepherdess's seed, isn't it?" When the Weaver nodded, he added, "What are you going to do with it?"

There's no choice but to make a new Shepherdess, the Weaver said. *We must be three, else we are incomplete.*

"This from the man who was going to lock her away," Eli said with a snort.

The Weaver's eyes narrowed. *The Shepherdess would still have existed then,* he said. *A dead Power does us no good. She must be reborn.*

"Fine, fine." Eli groaned. "Who's the lucky girl?"

Actually, the Weaver said. *I mean it to be you.*

Eli jerked up so fast he was staring the Weaver in the face before he remembered sitting was bad. He fell back again, fighting the nausea all the way down. When he had himself under control, he glared at the Weaver and said, in what he considered a very measured tone given the circumstances, "Are you out of your muddled white mind?"

It's the logical choice, the Weaver said. *As a star, you're already familiar with the spirit's power structure and politics. Of all her favorites, you were certainly the most popular, and since you're a powerful human wizard who bore her mark for years, you carry a large fraction of her will with you already. That should help ensure that as much power as possible survives the transfer. Really, I can't think of anyone better suited for the task.*

Eli closed his eyes. "Listen, old man, I can't believe I'm having to explain this, but the Shepherdess or Shepherd or whatever is the Power responsible for every spirit in existence. Obviously you're not a fan of my work, or you'd have realized by now that, overlooking today's extremely uncharacteristic heroics, I'm probably the least responsible man in this

942

oversized spirit preserve. Ask Miranda, she'll vouch for me."
Eli glanced at the Spiritualist, who dutifully nodded her head.
"See?"

The Weaver sighed. *I'm sure you would be—*

"No, I wouldn't," Eli said. "Even if I would make a fine
Shepherd, I don't want the job."

The Weaver stared at him. *Didn't you hear me? There* must
be a—

"I don't care," Eli said, jerking his thumb at his chest.
"Irresponsible, remember? And anyway, I've done my time.
I've spent the last decade trying to get away from this boring
white whatever. If you think I'm coming back of my own free
will now that Benehime can't make me, you're crazier than
the Shepherdess. I don't care how much power is in that glow
rock, count me *out.*"

The Weaver stared down at the glowing pearl in his hands.
If you won't take it, I don't know who else could.

"I do," Eli said. "And I cast my vote for Miranda."

Eli bit back a grin as the Spiritualist jumped. Actually, the
more he thought about this new solution, the better he
liked it.

"It's an inspired choice," he went on. "I mean, she works
all the time, she's stubborn as a mountain, and she always has
the spirits' best interests at heart. I can't even count how many
times she's nearly killed herself for some ungrateful ball of
water or hunk of rock. Illir the West Wind is half in love with
her already, so that's the Wind Courts right there, and they're
always the worst. Even the Shaper Mountain respects her, and
let's not forget that you have her to thank for the fact that we
have such a hardworking new Hunter. If she hadn't bound the
Lord of Storms, we might have ended up with Josef in the
job, and then the world would *really* have been doomed."

The Weaver tilted his head, staring at Miranda with new
interest. For her part, the Spiritualist looked like someone had
just dunked her in freezing water. Her mouth kept opening
and closing, and she was staring bug-eyed at Eli like she was

trying to choose between being flattered or punching him in the face. Since his face was one of the few parts of his body that didn't hurt, Eli hurried to clinch the deal.

"She's a wizard strong enough to power the Lord of Storms, who's also utterly, almost pathologically dedicated to serving the spirits," he said solemnly. "And I guarantee you she's a much better choice than I am. In fact, I don't think you could create a better candidate for Shepherdess if you tried."

If that is true, then I would be glad to offer you the task, the Weaver said to Miranda, his face breaking into a warm smile. *Considering all you have done for us already, Spiritualist, I would be honored to call you sister.*

Miranda just sat there, her eyes flicking between the Weaver, Eli, and the white seed in the Weaver's hands. Eli could almost see the wheels turning in her head, and he kept his face earnest, willing her to accept. He hadn't been exaggerating when he said she would be a good choice, but he'd left out the part where such a choice would benefit him doubly. If Miranda became Shepherdess, the world would get a competent minder for the first time in centuries, and the Spirit Court would lose the only person they had who could possibly catch him. He'd miss their rivalry, true, but it was a small price to pay for the good of the world, and he *was* in a heroic mood today.

Finally, after almost two minutes of silence, Miranda took a deep breath, and Eli burst into a wide grin. She was going to do it. He could see it by the way her mouth was set in that responsible frown of hers. But as he was celebrating in his mind, planning all the work he was going to do in Zarin now that the Spiritualist was out of the way, Miranda opened her mouth and ruined everything.

"No."

No? the Weaver said.

"No?!" Eli shouted at the same time.

Miranda glared at them both. "I won't be Shepherdess, but not because I don't want the job. All my life I've had to face the knowledge that I can't help every spirit, that I can't fix

944

every bad thing. As Shepherdess, I could, and that's very tempting, but it's also wrong." She lifted her head, chin set at that stubborn angle that made Eli's heart sink. "I can't accept because I don't think there should be a Shepherdess at all."

Eli buried his face in his hands, but the Weaver said what he'd meant to anyway.

What in creation are you going on about?

"Actually, I've been thinking about it for a while now," Miranda said. "When the Shaper Mountain showed Slorn and me his memories, he showed us the world as it was before the Shepherdess. A world of change under a sky full of stars. A world without Powers."

We needed none, the Weaver said. *The Creator was with us then.*

"The Creator didn't manage the day-to-day life of the spirits," Miranda said. "He was too busy creating what the demons destroyed. But the spirits, the winds and mountains, the seas, they lived free. As I understand it, the lessening wasn't a problem then. Everything was awake and aware. Spirits grew instead of shrinking, and even though they lived under the constant threat of demon attack, they thrived. It was only after we entered the sphere that things started falling asleep, right?"

True, the Weaver said.

"How could they not?" Miranda said, holding out her hands. "There was nothing to fight, nothing to do, and nowhere to go. Even the demons weren't a problem anymore, and the Shepherdess took care of everything. You said yourself that this was a lifeboat, not a home. Everything was under emergency rule, and as the emergency became the new normality, the spirits fell into complacency. With nothing to do, no power of their own, and no escape from the Shepherdess who demanded their loyalty rather than earning it, what other choice was there but to bury themselves deep and fall asleep?"

The Weaver started to speak, but Miranda looked down, clenching her fists in her lap. "I love the spirits," she said. "I love serving them. I love protecting them. Ever since I first heard their voices as a little girl, I knew they were my calling. A Spiritualist was the only thing I've ever wanted to be, and I will not accept that slowly falling into a stupor is the only possible future for the spirits I've sworn to protect.

"But the Shepherdess got one thing right," Miranda continued, lifting her hands to her chest. "Us. I've heard my whole life that she made us blind, but that's not all she made us. We each have a bit of her will. That's how we're able to command the spirits, because we each carry an echo of her power."

And that's why one of you must become the Shepherdess, the Weaver said.

"No," Miranda said again, shaking her head. "I've always noticed that spirits who live around humans are more awake than spirits who live in solitude. If the world really was lessening like you say, then all the spirits should be falling asleep at the same rate, but they're not. A Shaper's work stays awake for years in the hand of a good wizard, and in Zarin even the cobblestones wake easily. Do you see what I'm saying?"

No. The Weaver sighed.

"I do," Eli said. He pushed himself up on his elbows, biting back the nausea so he could look Miranda in the eye. "You're saying spirits are falling asleep because there's nothing to do. They've been locked up in this tiny box with a Shepherdess who spent her whole life trying to keep them calm. She told them what to think and what to say and gave them no challenges and no real threats other than humans, and then never for more than our short life spans." He felt himself starting to smile. "Horrible as Gaol was, everything there was awake. The threat of the duke kept them that way."

"Right," Miranda said, her face lighting up. "Of course, I'm not saying we should terrify the world, but I am saying that if we want spirits to stop sliding into sleep, if we want the world to grow again rather than settle, we're going to have to change the way we do things. Now is not the time to thrust another Power back on top of the heap. We have to give the spirits power over their own lives again, like it was always meant to be."

That would be a disaster, the Weaver said. *Spirits are panicky in the best of times. They'll tear each other apart without a Shepherdess.*

"Only because they've been told for so long that they can't live without her," Miranda said heatedly. "Of course spirits are panicky. They have no power. But I have seen spirits stand against demonseeds even when they can't do anything. Spirits as a whole may be prone to panic, but that's true for humans, too. Individually, any of us can be brave if we have cause to stand firm. I've worked as a Spiritualist all my adult life, and the one thing I've learned over and over is that the spirits are all different. Some are clever, some are helpful, some are stupid, and some are cruel, but they're all individuals, and they don't deserve to have their choices made for them without their say, even by someone who has their best interests at heart."

What would you have us do, then? the Weaver said. *Let the Shepherdess's power rot?*

"No," Miranda said, shaking her head. "Give it to the spirits. You said it yourself. This is their world. For five thousand years they've had an all-powerful mother telling them how to live. Their complaints were ignored and their voices silenced whenever they questioned her rule. Under such a system, how could the world do anything but stagnate? Well, I say enough. This world may have been created as a temporary shelter, but it's our home now. If we want to keep living in it, we need to accept the truth that things change, and so must the Powers if they are to keep serving the world they were created to nourish and sustain."

Change how? the Weaver said. *This world stands on our work.*

"On you and the Hunter's work," Miranda said. "But the world doesn't need a Shepherdess any longer. If you want

947

to avoid spirits sinking into sleep, then you shouldn't use that seed to create a new Shepherdess. You should use it to give all spirits a fraction of the Shepherdess's will, just as humans have. That way, just as one human's will cannot dominate another's, so will all spirits be free of human control."

Impossible, the Weaver said. *They will crush you because you cannot see or hear enough to understand.*

"So take away our blindness," Miranda said. "Let humans see and hear as the spirits do so that we can all understand the world we live in. With will, the spirits will no longer be helpless victims of humans or demons. They'll be able to stand against whatever comes, just as we do. Share the Shepherdess's power, give the world a reason to wake up, and we will make this lifeboat into a world we can all thrive in. A world where no one has power over another simply by virtue of being human. *Our* world, spirits, humans, and Powers, all working together to make a place worth saving, a world that can grow."

The Weaver closed his eyes. *You ask a great thing, girl.*

"The world is fading," Miranda said. "I could ask nothing less."

The Weaver bowed his head, sinking deep into thought. Eli glanced at Miranda, but her eyes were locked on the Weaver and the glowing pearl in his hands. Finally, the old Power nodded.

So be it, he said. *But such a thing can be done only by the Shepherdess. Someone will have to take on the power in order to give it away.*

Without a word, Miranda reached for the collar around her neck. She lifted the heavy gold chain over her head and carefully laid it aside. Next, she plucked her rings off one by one, piling them beside the chain. The pendant under her robes went last, and she lined it up beside the others, careful not to tangle the chain.

Once all her spirits were lying on the floor, Miranda

948

solemnly held out her hand. The Weaver reached out and gently placed the Shepherdess's seed in her palm. The moment the white pearl touched her skin, Miranda changed.

She made no sound, only shivered as the whiteness flooded over her body, washing away her color and her humanity in a great bleaching tide. Her skin was now as white as the floor she knelt on, as white as the robe across her shoulders. Her curly hair was like a snowdrift around her face, and her sharp green eyes were as pale as frost when they opened again, a silver rim the only thing separating her iris from the white of her eye.

Eli shuddered when he saw her. He couldn't help it. The face was still Miranda's, with its tilted nose and stern mouth, so was the unruly hair. But though he told himself color was the only thing missing, he couldn't help seeing the resemblance. The Shepherdess's presence clung to her like a shadow. The stillness of her chest, the fall of her white hair across her face, everything about her screamed of Benehime until Eli could barely look at her without bile rising in his throat.

As the white woman raised her head, Eli could almost hear the hated endearments on her lips. But then the woman spoke, and it was Miranda's voice cut through with that strange resonance all the Powers shared. The words weren't even directed at Eli, and there were only three.

Use it well.

She whispered the command, and then Eli heard something shatter. All at once, the power left Miranda as quickly as it had come, the whiteness draining away. Her eyes closed in pain, and she fell backward, nearly landing on her head.

Eli's arm shot forward, grabbing her just before she hit. He winced as he touched her. Her skin was freezing, and though the faintest touch of the Shepherdess's burn lingered, it faded quickly, leaving only a shell behind.

Eli cursed and sat up, ignoring his churning stomach as he pressed his hands against Miranda's neck. She was breathing and her pulse was strong, but she was out cold. Just as he was about to pry her eyes open to test her pupils, Miranda seized up and launched into a coughing fit. Eli laughed with relief, pounding her back.

As the coughing faded, she pushed him off and started replacing her rings. "Did it work?" she whispered, her voice raw.

The Weaver smiled. *See for yourself.*

All at once, the Shepherdess's sphere spun into view. The crumples and cracks were gone, and it hung perfect in the air once again, its gentle curve filled with glittering seas, green forests, and golden deserts. But the colors weren't as clear as Eli remembered.

Worried, he leaned in for a closer look and saw that it wasn't the colors that were fading. The air itself was tinged with white.

All across the world, a fine white rain was falling. The shimmering drops fell not from the clouds but from the dome of the sky itself, falling on every rock, every wind, every tree. They sparkled like diamonds in the light of the restored sun, falling thick as a blizzard over the whole of the world. Wherever they landed, the white drops sunk in with a faint flash, and whatever they sank into changed.

All across the sphere, the damage done by the loss of the stars and the demon invasion began to right itself. Toppled forests pushed themselves up. Rivers returned to their beds, taking their silt back with them. The churning sea retreated, drawing back its water and salt to leave the coast bone dry and fertile again. One by one, every spirit in the world seemed to tremble to life, and as they woke, the sphere began to vibrate with the sound of their voices.

When the change was finished, only the mountains remained silent. They had been hit worst of all by the demons, especially the Master of the Dead Mountain, and they were slow to change by nature. But at their heart, the Shaper Mountain stood taller than ever before, its white slopes shining like a

950

great beacon to all the rest, its deep, rumbling voice calling them forward until, with slow, grinding effort, the mountains began the long, tedious work of filling in that which had been sundered.

When the flurry of motion finally finished, the Weaver leaned back and ran a tired hand across his face. *I hope you're prepared for what you've unleashed*, he said. *It's all different now. You're no longer wizards. Nothing is. Even those rings of yours don't have to obey you anymore.*

Miranda gave him a superior glare and started carefully sliding her rings back onto her fingers. "If you think a Spiritualist needs magical dominance to keep her spirits, Weaver, you obviously don't know much about our order."

The Weaver's eyes widened, and Eli started to laugh. Everything might have changed, but Miranda would always be prickly about her spirits.

"Cut the poor man some slack," he said, grinning wide. "You've just given him a world of headaches. Imagine, rocks with will, trees who can scream in terror when the lumberjack comes to chop them down. Spirit sight and hearing for all! It's going to be a madhouse."

"Then the Spirit Court will do its job, as always," Miranda said. "I mean to put every Spiritualist I have into helping the world adjust to the changes. It won't be easy, but at least there won't be any more Enslavers to worry about." She glanced at Eli out of the corner of her eye. "Or wizard thieves abusing their power."

Eli leaned back, folding his hands under his head with a broad grin. "Lady," he said, "you have no idea."

Miranda's look of alarm made him burst into laughter, and Eli let it go, laughing in utter freedom for the first time he could ever remember.

EPILOGUE

A lber Whitefall sat in the tent that served as his temporary office and stared glumly at his ruined Citadel. He'd been told he should be happy, that Zarin had suffered far less than most places since Etmon Banage had been on hand to protect it, but the relative luck of his lot wasn't much comfort right now. His eyes slid over the gaping hole in his entry hall roof, the broken tower that was still scattered across his courtyard, its hammered gold roof crumpled beyond recognition. Even ignoring the destruction of Sara's levels, which he considered her fault and would be taking out of her budget, this was going to cost a fortune.

He reached for his tea, mentally adding up the cost of stone and timber. But as his fingers closed around the delicate porcelain teacup, the thing jerked away. "What did we talk about?" it said. "Gently, please."

And then there were the other changes to deal with.

Alber gritted his teeth. "My apologies."

"Just mind your fingers," the cup said with a sniff, which was impressive since it didn't have a nose. "I'm over a hundred years old, you know."

Alber knew this very well. The cup had been reminding him of it every time he so much as tipped it the wrong way. He took a careful sip and set the cup on its saucer as gently as a mother with her new baby. When he managed to get his fingers back without further comment, Alber added *find less-talkative teacup* to his mental checklist. This led to a fit of nostalgia for happier days when his citadel was still in one piece and he didn't have to worry about talkative teacups.

"Sir?"

Alber looked up to see a page standing at his tent flap. "The Rector is here."

952

Whitefall nodded and the boy hurried off, leaving little swirling eddies of wind behind him. Alber shuddered despite himself. That was another thing he was never going to get used to, seeing things like wind. When the change had first come, he'd been sure he'd gone mad. A few minutes later it had become clear that, if he was going mad, he wasn't going alone. Everyone, young and old, wizard or not, could suddenly see and hear an entire new world.

The initial panic had lasted about a day, after which people finally seemed to realize their talking doors weren't going to eat them alive. Once that was out of the way, the shift to the new normal was almost terrifyingly swift. After all, there were still goods to sell and farms to mind, even if the goods were demanding a say in their handling now. Still, life rolled on, and the Spirit Court had played an invaluable part in making sure it rolled smoothly. Which was, of course, the entire reason he'd asked the Rector for this meeting.

The tent flap whispered again, politely this time, he noticed, and Alber turned to smile as the new Rector of the Spirit Court entered his tent. She was quite young for a Rector, not yet out of her twenties and a bit too pretty for most of the Council to take seriously, which was always their mistake. Even his limited experience had taught him that Miranda Lyonette never took anything less than absolutely seriously.

She was dressed for official business today in her crimson robes with the heavy chain of her office around her neck, the rings gleaming on her fingers with an unnatural light he no longer dismissed. "Rector Lyonette," he said, taking her hand. "Thank you for the pleasure of your company."

"Merchant Prince," the Rector said, inclining her head.

He escorted her to the velvet folding chair at the end of his makeshift desk. As she sat, he couldn't help but notice there was something else in her, something large and blue. Alber walked around his desk and sat down, watching her covertly. He'd gotten used to the way humans looked now, but no one he'd encountered had the large presence in their chests that the Rector did. He was trying to puzzle out what the strange, fluctuating light behind her eyes meant when he realized the Rector had caught him staring.

He bit his tongue at being caught like a gawking schoolboy, but to his surprise, the Rector looked amused. "You can look if you like," she said. "Mellinor's a bit of a shock to most people, but I promise he's not dangerous unless you give him cause to be."

"I don't mean to pry," Whitefall said.

"Prying is fine," the Rector said, laughing. "Curiosity's a good thing in a new world. And he's a sea, in case you were wondering."

Whitefall nodded politely, wondering how in the world anyone got a sea in their body. Maybe such things were common for Spiritualists? "Does he always..."

"Live in me?" the Rector finished. "Yes. Well, we had a bit of a gap for a while, but everything shook out in the end."

She beamed like this was the best possible news. Whitefall smiled back weakly and decided it was time to retake control of the conversation. After all, he hadn't put off his meeting with the Council Trade Board so he could talk about seas.

"I'm sorry Sara couldn't join us," he said, getting down to business. "Prior obligations, I believe, what with things being how they are."

That wasn't a total lie. Sara had actually gone missing. This in itself wasn't terribly unusual. The woman would often vanish without a trace for days on end if something caught her curiosity, and the new changes to the world were certainly curious. He'd been a bit surprised by her going this time, though, considering how she'd been mortally wounded not three days before. Then again, Sara never was one to let a little thing like a punctured lung stand between her and her work. Fortunately, the Rector took the news of Sara's absence in stride.

"I understand," Miranda said with a strange scowl. "Better for both of us, actually. I don't much care to see Sara, either."

That suited Whitefall just fine. Sara's absence made this next bit easier.

"Rector Lyonette," he said, leaning forward. "I asked you here rather than calling the full Council because I'd like to offer you a bit of a personal apology. Our two organizations haven't exactly been on the best of terms in recent times, and I feel that, as Merchant Prince, I demanded things I should not have."

That *was* a total lie. He had been completely reasonable right up to the cliff Banage had pushed him off. But swallowing your pride was as much a part of being Merchant Prince as the parades, and Alber had been a politician long enough to know the power of a little applied groveling.

"I was overzealous in the pursuit of what I thought would make my lands safer," he continued. "And in the process, I fear I may have injured one of the oldest and most mutually beneficial relationships in my Council's history."

"You did," Miranda said, though there was no anger in her voice. She was just stating a point. "But that doesn't mean we can't rebuild that trust."

She looked at him and smiled. "I told you, it's a new world, Whitefall. Everything's different now. If you asked me here to reforge the ties between my Court and the Council of Thrones, then you don't have to apologize. We are glad to offer our hands in friendship to anyone, provided they agree to the standards we have always set."

"The right treatment of spirits," Whitefall said, nodding.

"The *fair* and *open* treatment of spirits," Miranda corrected. "The right treatment is expected of everyone. Anything less makes the Court your enemy."

Whitefall sighed. "I find I grow tired of secrets, Rector Lyonette. From this day forward, I give you my word that my Council and its member countries will abide by your rules to the letter. In return, however, I would ask your assistance regarding the recent—"

"Of course," Miranda said. "You just went from a Council

of human kingdoms to a Council whose lands are now shared by Great Spirit dominions and the Wind Courts. Of course you need our help, and we give it gladly. My Court is at your disposal, Merchant Prince. We're a little undercapacity at the moment, but we've had a surge of new applicants now that being a wizard isn't a necessity of membership. I'll assign a liaison to you first thing when I return. Bring all problems to him and we will do our best to help teach your people how to ease any difficulties you encounter. After all"—her smile grew into a grin—"we *do* have a little experience mediating between humans and spirits."

"Yes, well, glad we could come to an understanding," Whitefall said, rising again to see her out. "It's been a bit of a shake-up for all of us. I'm still not quite sure how to move forward, actually. Tell me, do I need to negotiate with the stone masons for what it will cost to rebuild my citadel, or do I talk to the stones themselves and see if I can't get a better rate?"

He'd meant this as a joke, but the Rector pursed her lips and peered over his shoulder at the fallen tower. "The stones look mostly fine to me," she said. "Have you tried just asking them to repair themselves?"

Whitefall froze midstep. "No, actually."

"Can't hurt to ask," she said. "Most natural things righted themselves when they woke up, but human-made structures often need human input to get themselves together again. I don't think you'll have much of a problem here, though. This place was very well built, and bright white stones fine enough to go into a citadel often like being fancy. They may jump back up on their own if you promise to keep your towers spotless. And if all else fails, you can always try a little charm. It's worked before."

That last bit was accompanied by a small eye roll that Whitefall wasn't quite sure how to interpret, but he had the distinct feeling he'd missed out on a joke. "I'll try your suggestion," he said mildly, holding the flap for her. "And thank you again."

She nodded and glanced up, staring at the sky. Frowning, Alber leaned out as well, stomach clenching. Ever since that awful day, he'd tried not to look at the sky for fear of spotting another crack, or worse, one of the horrible, unthinkable black hands. But the sky was clear and empty, its vault so blue he couldn't even see the edges of the ever-present winds. He glanced back at the Rector to see if he'd missed anything only to find her smiling with rapt wonder.

When she didn't move for several second, he asked, "What are you looking at?"

"The spirits," she answered, grinning wide as her eyes dropped to his again. "After so many years of wondering, I don't think I will ever tire of seeing as they see."

Whitefall was deathly tired of it, but he kept that thought to himself as he watched the Rector climb up onto the monster of a dog she rode. As soon as she was settled on its back, the creature bolted, clearing the Council's miraculously unruined gate in a single leap. Whitefall watched them until they vanished around the corner, and then he went back inside to deal with the serious business of picking his empire up out of the dirt.

When Miranda returned to the Tower, Banage was waiting for her. He was dressed in traveling clothes, rubbing his hand absently across the high back of his jade horse. He smiled as she and Gin trotted to a stop in front of him and moved to help Miranda down. "Well?"

"Nothing," Miranda said, taking his offered hand. "Sara wasn't there, and though Whitefall gave the expected excuses, I don't think he knows where she is, either. I worry Mellinor might be right."

"Of course I'm right," Mellinor's deep voice said in Miranda's ear. "When all that water came pouring out of her thrice-cursed tanks, it went straight to the river. Rellenor was a little pre-occupied at the time, but once things calmed down she was furious. Ollor was a river spirit before he made the mistake of trusting Sara, and most of the other water came from Rellenor."

Miranda winced. "She's not taking it well, then?"

"She's taking it as a personal attack," Mellinor replied. "And she's got the other rivers on her side. That wouldn't have mattered before, but now that they don't have to worry about Sara's power as a wizard, well, you don't have to be an expert on spirit politics to know how that meeting is going to end."

Banage gave a long, tired sigh. "Then I suppose I'd better get going while there's still hope left."

"I don't see why you bother," Miranda said, crossing her arms. "Sara did horrible things. She deserves everything she gets from those rivers."

"That she does," Banage said, climbing onto his stone horse. "But for good or ill, she's still my wife, and I honor my oaths."

"Even when the other person doesn't?" Miranda said.

"Our oaths are our own, Miranda," Banage said solemnly. "You know that."

Miranda glowered. "She doesn't deserve such loyalty."

Banage just gave her a long, sad smile. "I'll never give up on her," he said. "The game's not over yet." And with that, he started down the tree-lined boulevard, his jade horse picking up speed as its green stone hooves clattered on the paving stones, raising a chorus of complaints.

"Remind me to schedule that formal inquiry to determine which stones actually want to be paving stones," Miranda said wearily, pinching the bridge of her nose.

Gin nudged her back with his muzzle. "He'll be back, you know. Maybe even with Sara, assuming he can convince the rivers not to drown her for her crimes."

"I hope so, for his sake," Miranda said. "Personally, I don't understand what he ever saw in her."

"Humans are strange," Gin said, flicking his ears.

Miranda sighed and turned back to the Tower. "Come on, we have work to do."

Gin swished his tail and followed his mistress up the stairs.

Krigel was waiting just inside the Tower door, his arms full of papers containing thousands of details that awaited the Rector's attention. Miranda looked at the pile and sighed again. Then, pulling herself straight, she held out her arms to accept her duty.

Alric, Deputy Commander of the League of Storms, or what was left of it, crouched silent and unseen on a ridge surrounded by delicate, yellow-leafed trees, watching the house on chicken legs. Beside him, the other League agent crouched just as silently, but his eyes were on Alric, and he did not look happy.

"How long do you mean to let this continue, sir?" he said in a low voice as the bear-headed man and his daughter went back inside the house. "The Lord of Storms' orders were very clear."

"The Lord of Storms isn't here anymore, Chejo," Alric said, just as low. "Or if he is, he isn't worried about us. The demon is gone, the Dead Mountain empty and abandoned, the demon-seeds cold and sleeping safely in the vault."

"Even more reason," Chejo countered. "She's the last."

"That she is," Alric said. "But let me frame it like this: Even at its peak with the Lord of Storms beside us, the League was defeated by the Daughter of the Dead Mountain. That was three years ago. Part of being a commander is understanding what the men under your command can and cannot do, and I know we cannot take her down. Not with all our men, maybe not even if the Lord of Storms returned. Our gifts may remain, but without our Commander we can't replenish our numbers with new recruits. Any attempt to fight the demon would cost us men we cannot replace, and anyway, it's not like she's running rampant through the countryside, is it?"

They both turned to glance at the knot of three people lying on the rocks beside the crouching house. The thief was talking as always, waving his arms in great circles. The swordsman was sprawled like a lizard in the sun and didn't seem to be listening, but the girl was. She sat on the edge of the stone,

959

her head tilted in a way that reminded Alric of an entranced cat.

It certainly wasn't how you expected to find a demonseed, but the Daughter of the Dead Mountain had never been a normal seed. He wasn't even sure she was a seed anymore now that the world had nearly collapsed, but she was surely a demon. She hid it well, but Alric could see the signs if he looked close enough—the way her black clothes seemed to eat the light, the faint waver of her shadow on the rock though the sun had not moved at all, and of course, the face he knew so well.

"My orders stand," Alric said, settling down on the ridge. "We watch. If she panics so much as a pebble, we move in. I don't think we can kill her, but there's always the Shaper's box. Still, seeing as she can afford a confrontation better than we can, we move only if she forces us. If she plays nice, we'll play nice."

"And just how long do you mean to play, sir?" Chejo said, gripping the hilt of his blood-red sword.

"Until the game ends," Alric answered. "Now, report back to the citadel. I expect my relief to find me in three hours."

Chejo saluted and vanished through a slit in the air. When he was sure he was alone, Alric released the breath he'd been holding. The League was a dangerous tangle of aggressive personalities without the Lord of Storms to keep them all in check. He would have to tread carefully, but then he'd been treading carefully for centuries. After almost a thousand years as the de facto organizational leader of the League, handling the sort of brute fighters the Lord of Storms preferred came to Alric as naturally as breathing.

He glanced down at the girl, still smiling in the sunshine. It was probably all a trick, of course, but Alric saw no reason a demon couldn't be happy every once in a while. Especially when that happiness seemed to involve no eating of spirits for once.

Alric smiled, leaning back to catch a shaft of the warm

sunshine the rest of them were enjoying. Watching a happy demon might not be exciting, but it was far better than martyring yourself fighting one. The demon lounged on the rock, feet swinging in the breeze like any normal, happy girl enjoying a nice day, and Alric's smile widened before he could stop it. Good for her, he thought. For all he cared, she could stay like this forever. And so, for that matter, could he.

Basking in the sunlight that was so rare for a man who'd spent his immortality in a fortress of storms, Alric relaxed into the grass and set about enjoying the next three hours of his watch.

"And that's the plan," Eli said, finishing with a flourish. "What do you think?"

"I don't know," Josef said, scratching at the bandages that swaddled his chest. "Seems needlessly risky to me. And we've never pulled a job in Zarin before."

"That was to avoid my father," Eli pointed out. "But I've put the past behind me and come to embrace the target-rich environment Zarin provides."

Josef made a noncommittal noise, and Eli turned his eyes to Nico, pleading. The girl just shrugged and smiled, legs swinging back and forth in the air beneath her.

Seeing her like this still threw Eli for a loop. He was used to Nico being a ball of coat, not kicking limbs. But now she sat in the sunlight in a pair of trousers, boots, and a loose shirt that dropped to her wrists despite the heat. All black, of course, but everything she made for herself was. There didn't seem to be much option for color when you formed your clothes out of shadow.

Still, it all looked normal enough except for the long, ragged scarf she wore around her neck. The scrap of black cloth was all that remained of the coat Slorn had made for her so long ago. They'd come here hoping to get it patched, but even Slorn couldn't work a miracle that large. Still, even torn to bits and changed by Miranda's gift of will, the scrap of coat had never lost its loyalty to Slorn, Nico, and its duty, and Nico absolutely refused to give it up. It clung to her neck like a snake, twitching occasionally whenever Eli looked at it sideways.

"Maybe we should keep lying low," Josef suggested, his voice warped by a wide yawn. "Give things a chance to shake out. I know I haven't gotten used to doors yelling at me when I slam them yet."

"That's *exactly* why we shouldn't wait," Eli said, exasperated. "The unrest is what creates the sort of wide-open opportunities we'll need for a job like this. It's perfect. We'll hit the opera first and then Whitefall's private manor house, netting five priceless treasures in a little under two hours. This is the sort of heist people will be talking about for *years*. Think of my bounty!"

"What is your bounty now, anyway?" Josef said, yawning again.

"Two hundred and eighty-five thousand," Eli recited. "Which is still seven hundred and fifteen thousand from where it needs to be."

Josef shrugged and lay back in the sunshine, completely oblivious to the seriousness of the matter. Folding his arms over his chest, Eli decided to raise the stakes. "Josef," he said calmly. "If you don't get off that rock so we can get going, I'm going to write your ministers and tell them I found their king."

Josef's body went stiff, and Eli broke into a cruel smile. "I'm sure they'd be willing to fork over some of Den's bounty to drag you home," he continued. "One way or another, my number is going up. So which will it be, your majesty?"

Josef sat up with a long sigh. "When do we leave?"

"That's more like it," Eli said, starting off toward the edge of the clearing where Slorn and Pele were talking with the trees of the Awakened Wood. "And we leave as soon as I thank our hosts."

"Wait a moment, Eli," Josef said, standing up.

Eli stopped and looked over his shoulder to see his swordsman lift the Heart of War and look at it for a long moment before slinging it over his shoulder, well away from his injured chest. "I've been thinking," he said at last. "Can we even pull the heists anymore?"

Eli frowned. "What do you mean?"

"I mean now that you're not a wizard," Josef said. "Is that going to change the way we do things?"

Eli stared at him a moment, and then stepped over to the side of Slorn's house where a small tool chest had been fastened onto the wooden exterior. Its door was locked with a latch and fastened tight with three ornate hinges, all wrought from the same smooth, black iron. After a glance to make sure Josef was watching, Eli fixed his face in his best smile and leaned down, tapping the door with his long fingers.

"Excuse me," he said. "I was just walking by when I happened to notice the extraordinary grain of your wood."

The shed door rattled slightly. "*My* wood?"

"Who else's?" Eli said.

The door waggled happily a moment, and then froze. "Wait," it said. "You're the thief, aren't you? Slorn said I wasn't supposed to listen to you, Eli Monpress."

"Slorn's a tinkerer," Eli said, waving dismissively. "He doesn't like anyone messing with his toys. But I'm not going to *do* anything. I just want a closer look."

"Well, I guess that's all right," the door said, angling its wood so Eli could see the grain clearly.

"Absolutely stunning," Eli said, stroking the door with his fingers as he pored over the completely normal wood grain like it was a list of lock combinations for the Council of Thrones' tax vault. "Can I see the other side?"

"Of course," the door said, its voice swelling with pride. "Let me have a word with the lock."

The spirits chattered among themselves for a moment, and then the lock popped with a grudging click. The door sprang open, revealing Slorn's neat and near-priceless collection of custom awakened saws. Eli nodded appreciatively and turned to Josef with a smug smile. "Any more questions?"

963

Josef shook his head.

Eli thanked the door and stepped away. As he started toward Slorn to make his farewells, he glanced again at Josef and Nico only to see them both waiting by the rocks, fully armed and ready to go. Grinning wide, he hurried toward the bear-headed Shaper while visions of his new bounty danced through his head with all the little zeros trailing behind.

ACKNOWLEDGMENTS

Five books and seven years after he sauntered into my life and told me I was going to write a novel about him, Eli's story is now finished. It's been a far more enjoyable journey than I could ever have anticipated, and I could never have done it without Matt Bialer, my tireless agent, and Lindsay Ribar, whose wonderful suggestions created most of the really good parts of this series. I am also deeply grateful to Devi Pillai and the fantastic team at Orbit, whose love and enthusiasm for my books never ceases to amaze me into sputtering befuddledness. Also, thank you to my wonderful fans. Eli loves each and every one of you personally.

But most of all, these books could not have happened without the original Slorn, my husband, Travis. Thank you for always being there for me, love, and thank you for letting me put a bear on your head.

ABOUT THE AUTHOR

Rachel Aaron was born in Atlanta, GA. After a lovely, geeky childhood full of books and public television, and then an adolescence spent feeling awkward about it, she went to the University of Georgia to pursue English literature with an eye toward getting her PhD. Upper-division coursework cured her of this delusion, and she graduated in 2004 with a BA and a job, which was enough to make her mother happy. She currently lives in a '70s house of the future in Athens, GA, with her loving husband, overgrown library, and small, brown dog. Find out more about the author at www.rachelaaron.net

Find out more about Rachel Aaron and other Orbit authors by registering for the free monthly newsletter at www.orbitbooks.net